COMMUNICATION

Principles for a Lifetime

Seventh Edition

Steven A. Beebe
Texas State University

Susan J. Beebe
Texas State University

Diana K. Ivy
Texas A&M University–Corpus Christi

 Pearson

Director, Portfolio Management: Karon Bowers
Content Producer: Barbara Cappuccio
Content Developer: Ellen Keohane
Portfolio Manager Assistant: Dea Barbieri
Product Marketer: Christopher Brown
Field Marketer: Kelly Ross
Content Producer Manager: Melissa Feimer
Managing Editor: Maggie Barbieri
Content Development Manager: Sharon Geary
Content Developer, Learning Tools: Amy Wetzel
Art/Designer: Kathryn Foot
Digital Studio Course Producer: Amanda Smith
Full-Service Project Manager: SPi Global
Compositor: SPi Global
Printer/Binder: LSC Communications, Inc.
Cover Printer: Phoenix Color/Hagerstown
Cover Designer: Lumina Datamatics, Inc
Cover Illustration: pjjones/GettyImages

Credits and acknowledgments borrowed from other sources and reproduced, with permission, in this textbook appear on the appropriate page of appearance or in the Credits on pages 429–432.

Library of Congress Cataloging-in-Publication Data

Names: Beebe, Steven A., author. | Beebe, Susan J., author. | Ivy, Diana K., author.
Title: Communication : principles for a lifetime / Steven A. Beebe, Texas State University, Susan J. Beebe, Texas State University, Diana K. Ivy, Texas A&M University, Corpus Christi.
Description: Seventh edition. | Boston : Pearson Education, [2019]
Identifiers: LCCN 2017035713 | ISBN 9780134553528 | ISBN 0134553527
Subjects: LCSH: Communication.
Classification: LCC HM1206 .B44 2019 | DDC 302.2—dc23 LC record available at https://lccn.loc.gov/2017035713

Instructor's Review Copy:
ISBN 10:   0-13-455385-3
ISBN 13: 978-0-13-455385-6

Access Code Card:
ISBN 10:   0-13-456730-7
ISBN 13: 978-0-13-456730-3

à la carte Edition:
ISBN 10:   0-13-455381-0
ISBN 13: 978-0-13-455381-8

Student Rental Edition:
ISBN 10:   0-13-455352-7
ISBN 13: 978-0-13-455352-8

1   18

 Pearson

For our teachers … and our students

Brief Contents

Contents

UNIT II INTERPERSONAL COMMUNICATION

Preface

Communication is essential for life. The purpose of this book is to document this claim by presenting fundamental principles of human communication that enhance the quality of our communication with others as well as the quality of our own lives. Most students who read this book will take only one course in communication during their entire college career. We want students to view this course on communication as a vital, life-enriching one that will help them enhance their communication with others—not just as another course in a string of curricular requirements. Because communication is an essential element of living, we want students to remember essential communication principles and skills for the rest of their lives. To remember and apply these essential communication principles, we believe students need a digest of classic and contemporary research and practice that will help them with both the mundane and the magnificent, the everyday and the ever-important communication experiences that constitute the fabric of their lives.

In this edition, as in the six that preceded it, we strive to create a highly appealing, easy-to-use text that is more effective than ever in helping students understand and use the five vital principles of communication.

Revel™

Revel is an interactive learning environment that deeply engages students and prepares them for class. Media and assessment integrated directly within the authors' narrative lets students read, explore interactive content, and practice in one continuous learning path. Thanks to the dynamic reading experience in Revel, students come to class prepared to discuss, apply, and learn from instructors and from each other.

Learn more about Revel

www.pearson.com/revel

Special Features for Communication Students

Revel is a dynamic learning experience that offers students a way to study the content and topics relevant to communication in a whole new way. Rather than simply offering opportunities to read about and study public speaking, Revel facilitates deep, engaging interactions with the concepts that matter most. For example, as they are introduced to the concept of communication competence in Chapter 1, students are prompted to complete a self-assessment of their own self-perceived communication competence. Also in Chapter 1, students are first presented with our pentagon model, which illustrates the relationships among the five communication principles that are the overarching structure of the book. In Revel, students can interact with this figure to learn more about

Video Self-Check: Listening

1. According to the video, what component of communication do we *study* the most?

- Gesturing
- Writing
- Listening
- Speaking

these five principles. By providing opportunities to read about and practice communication concepts and techniques in tandem, Revel engages students directly and immediately, which leads to a better understanding of course material. A wealth of student and instructor resources and interactive materials can be found within Revel. Some of our favorites include:

- **Audio Excerpts and Speech Annotations**

  Students can listen to audio recordings of interpersonal conversations, typical and useful phrases for group discussions, and public speech excerpts while they read. These audio clips bring examples and communication tips to life.

- **Videos and Video Self-Checks**

  Students are presented with video examples throughout the book on topics such as ethical communication, diversity and understanding, perception and self, active listening, listening barriers, effective group roles, and leadership styles, among other topics. Many videos have correlating self-checks, enabling students to test their knowledge.

- **Interactive Figures**

  Interactive figures show processes in action and provide active visualizations for most of the figures in the text.

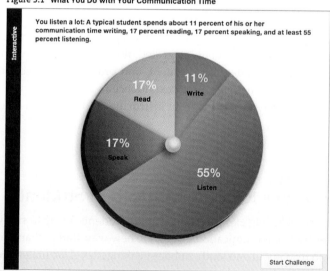

Figure 5.1 **What You Do with Your Communication Time**

You listen a lot: A typical student spends about 11 percent of his or her communication time writing, 17 percent reading, 17 percent speaking, and at least 55 percent listening.

17% Read

11% Write

17% Speak

55% Listen

- **Integrated Writing Opportunities**

  To help students connect chapter content with personal meaning, each chapter offers two varieties of writing prompts: Journal prompts elicit free-form, topic-specific responses (one per module) and an end-of-chapter Shared Writing prompt encourages students to share and reply to each other's brief responses to high-interest topics.

  For more information about all of the tools and resources in Revel and access to your own Revel account for the *Communication: Principles for a Lifetime*, Seventh Edition, go to www.pearson.com/revel.

What's New to the Seventh Edition?

You should pause and think twice before firing off an angry message on social media. Chris Rout / Alamy Stock Photo

Reviewers, instructors, and our students have given us feedback about the six previous editions. This feedback has helped us make this new edition the best possible teaching and learning resource. We listened and responded (Principle Four) to their suggestions. Our commitment to providing a digest of essentials that does not overwhelm students has also led us to make some changes. One immediate change you'll see in this edition is a fresh new design with many new photos to help draw today's visually oriented learners into the text.

We have also included the following new features in every chapter:

- New **Communication & Social Media** features explore ways to effectively use social media as an important communication tool.
- The chapter-end **Study Guide** has been significantly revised and reorganized for this edition. Learning objectives, review summaries, key terms, and apply and assess questions are now organized by section. These features have been designed to help students master chapter content, prepare for exams, and apply chapter concepts to their own lives.

STUDY GUIDE: CHAPTER **5**

> **REVIEW, APPLY, AND ASSESS**

The Importance of Listening and Responding Skills

5.1 Explain the principle of listening and responding thoughtfully to others.

REVIEW: You spend more time listening than doing any other communication activity. Being a good listener and responding thoughtfully to others will help you

- Enhance the quality of your interpersonal relationships.
- Develop good collaboration skills.
- Forge a stronger link between speaker and audience.

APPLY: Identify specific instances from your own experience in which poor listening skills resulted in a sig-

Listening Styles

5.3 Describe four listening styles.

REVIEW: Each person develops a preferred listening style based on his or her personality, the listening situation, and the listening goal. The four listening styles are relational, analytical, critical, and task oriented. Knowing your typical listening style can help you adapt your listening approach for maximum listening effectiveness.

KEY TERMS:
listening style
relational listeners
analytical listeners
critical listeners
second guessing
task-oriented listeners

- Significantly updated and expanded research incorporates the latest research findings about the principles and skills of human communication.
- Fresh, contemporary examples and illustrations are ones to which students can relate.
- New photos and illustrations amplify the content of our message.

We've also updated popular continuing features that appear throughout the book, including the following:

- Revised **learning objectives** appear at the beginning of each chapter to provide students with advance organizers and reading goals for approaching the chapter.
- Revised **Communication & Diversity** features complement and expand discussions of new applications of research about diversity throughout the book.
- Revised **Communication & Ethics** features reinforce the importance of being an ethical communicator and may spark discussion of ethical questions.

LEARNING OBJECTIVES

After studying this chapter, you should be able to

5.1 Explain the principle of listening and responding thoughtfully to others.

5.2 Identify the elements of the listening process.

5.3 Describe four listening styles.

DEVELOPING YOUR SPEECH STEP BY STEP

Delivering Your Speech

The long-awaited day of Dezerae's speech has arrived at last. She got a full night's sleep last night and ate a light breakfast before setting out for class.

As she waits to speak, Dezerae visualizes herself delivering her speech calmly and confidently. When her name is called, she rises, walks to the front of the room, and establishes eye contact with her audience before she begins to speak. Dezerae focuses on adapting her message to her listeners. She looks at individual members of her audience, uses purposeful and well-timed gestures, and speaks loudly and clearly.

Even before she hears her classmates' applause, Dezerae knows that her speech has gone well.

- Revised **Developing Your Speech Step by Step** features in the public speaking chapters walk students through the process of designing and delivering a speech.
- Two new speeches in **Appendix B** model best practices in public speaking.

We've made many other specific changes to chapter content throughout the book. Here's a brief list of selected major revisions, changes, and additions that we've made to specific chapters:

Chapter 1: Identifying Foundations of Human Communication More examples of social media use and information about online relationship development are provided in this chapter. Additional research on frequent communication and excessive multitasking has also been included. Data on the top factors for obtaining employment immediately after college have been updated. The Revel version includes interactive figures showing models of communication as action, interaction, and transaction. There are also videos with accompanying Video Self-Checks, enabling students to test their knowledge of topics, such as miscommunication and ethical communication.

Chapter 2: Self-Awareness and Communication A revised chapter introduction focuses on privacy and social media use. New data on self-esteem fluctuation resulting from social media usage have also been added to the chapter. A new Communication & Social Media feature focuses on selfies as a unique form of communication and identity expression. Revel also provides an interactive activity on self-concept components. Videos in Revel help students better understand chapter content, such as the self-concept, understanding diversity, and enhancing one's powers of perception.

Chapter 3: Understanding Verbal Messages The discussion of polarizing language has been updated with a new example. Additional content on gender-fair language has been included. A new Communication & Social Media feature explores how people use language on Twitter. Figure 3.1, which illustrates the five Communication Principles for a Lifetime, is interactive in Revel. Students can test their knowledge after reviewing the material in the figure.

Chapter 4: Understanding Nonverbal Messages A new section on how people use nonverbal cues to detect deception has been added to the end of the chapter. A new Communication & Diversity feature shares a lesson about nonverbal communication and cultural sensitivity, and a new Communication & Social Media feature focuses on social media fitness posts. Additional coverage of the visual dominance ratio has also been included. Numerous videos are available in Revel, including Martin Luther King, Jr.'s "I Have a Dream" speech and John F. Kennedy's Inaugural Address.

Chapter 5: Listening and Responding The chapter now begins with a discussion of how the visible presence of a phone can distract from the quality of a conversation. Research has been updated on listening styles, receiver apprehension, and active listening. A discussion of how social media plays an important role in our relationships with others is highlighted in a new Communication & Social Media feature. Revel content includes two interactive tables covering social support topics.

Chapter 6: Adapting to Others: Diversity and Communication The section on cultural values has been updated to include the most recent cultural dimensions that intercultural researcher Geert Hofstede has added to his discussion of human cultural values. The new material focuses on expectations about happiness. The coverage of sex and gender has been updated, and the definition of race has also been revised. A discussion of communication accommodation theory has also been added to the chapter. A list of suggestions on how to ethically adapt to others in various situations has been updated. In Revel, numerous videos highlight topics related to intercultural communication.

Chapter 7: Understanding Interpersonal Communication This chapter now includes new content on sexual attraction and online dating apps and services, as well as new research on online interpersonal relationships. The impact of technological innovations has also been added to the discussion of long-distance relationships. Two new Communication & Social Media features have been added to the chapter. The first explores trends related to social media, such as the flirtmoji, and the second discusses couples' decisions to become "FBO" (Facebook official). Content on self-absorption now includes more social media examples. In Revel, several videos in this chapter are accompanied by Video Self-Checks, allowing students to test their knowledge of interpersonal communication topics. The Revel version also includes an interactive figure of the Johari Window.

Chapter 8: Enhancing Relationships The discussion of relational de-escalation has been revised to reflect five stages instead of six. Figure 8.1 on relationship stages has been updated. New apply and assess questions have been added to the end of the chapter. Several Recap boxes in this chapter are interactive in Revel, allowing students to test their knowledge of relationship topics.

Chapter 9: Understanding Group and Team Performance Section 9.1 includes a new discussion about the advantages and disadvantages of working in virtual groups and teams. A new Communication & Social media box highlights research on the differences in the way men and women react to someone using his or her phone during a meeting or conversation. The Revel version offers a multimedia gallery highlighting different communication networks.

Chapter 10: Enhancing Group and Team Performance The discussion of better brainstorming has been revised. Figure 10.1, which illustrates the needed balance of structure and interaction in groups, has been updated. Additional content on transformational leadership has been added. Video and audio excerpts and examples, as well as interactive tables on topics, such as leadership styles and solving meeting agenda problems, are available in Revel.

Chapter 11: Developing Your Speech The Developing Your Speech Step by Step feature boxes have been updated with a new speech example about the health reasons for not drinking soda. A new Communication & Social Media feature explores the impact of Facebook on the 2016 U.S. Presidential Election. A number of new figures illustrate public speaking anxiety, building confidence, brainstorming topics, web directory searches, narrowing a broad topic, and the appropriateness of the central idea. Revel offers a host of interactive figures that illuminate such topics as speaking anxiety, brainstorming, narrowing a broad topic, and developing a central idea. The chapter also includes numerous audio clips of sample speeches.

Chapter 12: Organizing and Outlining Your Speech The sample preparation outline feature has been updated with a new example on the health risks of drinking soda. A new Communication & Social Media feature discusses how to make a "content sandwich." New examples have been added throughout the chapter for the following topics: cause and effect organization, specificity, soft-to-hard evidence, initial and internal previews, personal anecdotes, rhetorical questions, hypothetical illustrations, and memorable lines. Revel provides an interactive, annotated outline with accompanying audio clips and a video.

Chapter 13: Delivering Your Speech The section on effective presentation aids has been revised and reorganized. A discussion on how to communicate social media statistics with computer-generated presentation aids is highlighted in a new Communication & Social Media feature. Four new figures illustrate tips for effective manuscript, memorized, impromptu, and extemporaneous speaking. New figures on figurative language and effectively using various presentation aids have also been added. Examples of bar, pie, and line graphs have been updated. The Revel version includes videos of two presidential speeches: Barack Obama's Farewell Address and Bill Clinton's address to Congress on healthcare.

Chapter 14: Speaking to Inform New figures illustrating word pictures and attention-getting supporting material have been added to the chapter. A new Communication & Social Media feature on best practices for social media presentations has also been included. The sample informative speech on Elvis Presley has accompanying video and audio annotations in Revel.

Chapter 15: Speaking to Persuade This chapter features a new sample student persuasive speech on private ambulance companies. Additional content on social media has been added to a discussion of how to narrow a speech topic. Figure 15.4, which illustrates targeting attitudes, beliefs, and values in specific purpose statements, has been updated. In Revel, students can listen to excerpts and examples of sample speeches.

Appendix A: Interviewing Material on preparing a résumé and networking has been updated and revised. A new Communication & Social Media feature highlights how employers routinely review social media sites, such as Facebook and Twitter, to learn more about job applicants. In Revel, a number of Recap boxes and bulleted lists are interactive.

Appendix B: Sample Speeches for Discussion and Evaluation Appendix B includes a new informative speech on audism, and a new persuasive speech on doctors and sex abuse. Students can view videos of both speeches in Revel.

What Stays the Same in This Edition?

In our seventh edition of *Communication: Principles for a Lifetime*, our goal remains the same as in the first edition: to provide a cogent presentation of what is essential about human communication by organizing the study of communication around five fundamental communication principles that are inherent in the process of communicating with others.

Our Integrated Approach Remains Unchanged

To help students remember and integrate essential communication principles, we've organized the study of human communication around five fundamental communication principles:

Principle One: Be aware of your communication with yourself and others.
Principle Two: Effectively use and interpret verbal messages.
Principle Three: Effectively use and interpret nonverbal messages.
Principle Four: Listen and respond thoughtfully to others.
Principle Five: Appropriately adapt messages to others.

We don't claim that everything you need to know about communication is embedded in our five communication principles. These principles do, however, synthesize essential research and wisdom about communication. They are designed to help students in an introductory communication course see the "big picture" of the role and importance of communication, both as they sit in the classroom and as they live their lives.

The problem with many introduction to communication courses is that there is often too much of a good thing. An introductory course covers a vast terrain of communication concepts, principles, and skills. Besides learning about several theories of communication, students are also presented with what may appear to them to be miniature courses in interpersonal communication, group communication, and public speaking.

At the end of a typical hybrid or introductory communication fundamentals course, both students and instructors have made a breathless dash through an astounding amount of information and number of skills. The barrage of ideas, contexts, and theories can leave students and instructors feeling overwhelmed by a seemingly unrelated hodgepodge of information. Students may end up viewing communication as a fragmented area of study that includes a bushel basket full of concepts and applications, but they have little understanding of what is truly fundamental about how we make sense out of the world and share that sense with others. Rather than seeing communication as a crazy quilt of unrelated ideas and skills, we want students to see a unified fabric of common principles that they will remember long after the course is over. The five fundamental principles provide a framework for understanding the importance of communication in our lives.

Our pentagon model illustrates the relationships among the five communication principles that provide the overarching structure of the book. As a principle is being introduced or discussed, the appropriate part of the model is highlighted. In most texts, communication principles are typically presented in the first third of the book and then abandoned, as material about interpersonal, group, and public communication is presented. We don't use a "hit-and-run" approach. Instead, using examples and illustrations to which students can relate, we carefully discuss each principle early in the book. Throughout the latter two-thirds of the book we gently remind students of how these principles relate to interpersonal relationships, group and team discussions, and public presentations.

We link the five communication principles with specific content by using a margin icon to indicate that a discussion in the text of a skill, concept, or idea is related to one or more of the five communication principles. The icons, described in Chapter 1 and illustrated here, first appear in the margin in Chapter 7, "Understanding Interpersonal Communication," which is the first context chapter of the book. The icons help students see the many applications our five communication principles have to their lives as they read about interpersonal communication, group and team communication, and public speaking.

A subtext for these five principles is the importance of communicating ethically with others. Throughout the book we invite students to consider the ethical implications of how they communicate with others, through the use of probes and questions. As we discuss in Chapter 1, we believe that in order to be effective, a communication message must achieve three goals: (1) it must be understood; (2) it must achieve its intended effect; and (3) it must be ethical. Our five Communication Principles for a Lifetime are designed to help students achieve these three goals.

The Successful Structure of the Book Stays the Same

This seventh edition retains the overall structure of the six previous editions and is organized into four units.

Unit I introduces the five principles (Chapter 1), and then each principle is explained in a separate chapter (Chapters 2 through 6). Each communication principle is discussed and illustrated to help students see its value and centrality in their lives. Chapter 2 discusses the principle of being self-aware. Chapter 3 focuses on using and interpreting verbal messages, and Chapter 4 focuses on using and interpreting nonverbal messages. Chapter 5 includes a discussion of the interrelated processes of listening and responding, giving special attention to the importance of being other-oriented and empathic. The final principle, appropriately adapting to others, is presented in Chapter 6; we use this principle to illustrate the importance of adapting one's behavior to culture and gender differences among people.

Unit II applies the five communication principles to interpersonal relationships. Unlike many treatments of interpersonal communication, our discussion links the concepts and strategies for understanding interpersonal communication with our five Communication Principles for a Lifetime. Chapter 7 presents information to help students better understand the nature and function of communication in relationships. Chapter 8 identifies communication strategies that can enhance the quality of interpersonal relationships.

Unit III discusses how the five communication principles can help students understand and enhance communication in small groups and teams. Chapter 9 explains how groups and teams work. We offer practical strategies for collaboratively solving problems, leading groups and teams, and running and participating in meetings in Chapter 10.

Finally, Unit IV presents classic content to help students design and deliver a speech, referring to contemporary research and using the latest tools of technology. Based on our popular audience-centered approach to developing a speech, we emphasize the importance of adapting to listeners while also being an ethically vigilant communicator. Chapters 11 through 15 offer information and tips for developing speech ideas, organizing and outlining speeches, delivering a speech (including using presentational and multimedia aids), crafting effective informative speeches, and developing ethical persuasive messages.

We conclude the book with two appendices designed to supplement our instruction about communication fundamentals. Appendix A includes practical strategies for being interviewed and for interviewing others. We relate our discussion of interviewing to the five Communication Principles for a Lifetime. Appendix B includes examples of recent presentations to illustrate what effective, well-planned speeches look like.

Our Partnership with Students to Help Them Learn Stays the Same

A textbook is essentially a "distance learning" tool. As we write each chapter, we are separated from the learner by both time and space. To help lessen the distance between author and reader, we've incorporated a variety of learning resources and pedagogical features to engage students in the learning process. This engagement is heightened significantly in Revel, but you'll also find many features designed to engage students in the traditional print text as well. As we note in the text, information alone is not communication. Communication occurs when the receiver of information responds to it. Our special features help turn information into a responsive communication message that has an effect on students' lives.

Principles Model and Icons   Our pentagon model and margin icons help students see connections between the various communication concepts and skills we present. Throughout the text we provide an integrated framework to reinforce what is fundamental about human communication. Long after students may have forgotten the lists they memorized for an exam, we want them to remember the five fundamental principles we highlighted throughout the book. Remembering these principles can also help them remember strategies and concepts to enhance their interpersonal relationships, improve group and team meetings, and design and deliver effective presentations.

Chapter-End Summary of Communication Principles for a Lifetime   In addition to using the margin icons to highlight material in the text related to one or more communication principles, we conclude each chapter with a summary of the chapter content organized around the communication principles. Our chapter summaries at the ends of the first six chapters distill essential information about the specific communication principle presented in the chapter. Starting in Chapter 7, we review and summarize the chapter content using all five Communication Principles for a Lifetime as a framework.

Miniature versions of our principles icons appear with headings to highlight the five fundamental principles. The purpose of this chapter-end feature is to help students synthesize the material related to the context discussed (e.g., interpersonal communication) and the five principles that undergird the descriptive and prescriptive information presented in the chapter. This feature will help students connect the variety of ideas and skills with the five communication principles.

Communication & Ethics   To help students consider the ethical dimensions of human communication, in each chapter we provide a special boxed feature called "Communication & Ethics." Students are asked to consider a case study or to ponder their responses to ethical questions. The cases and questions we pose are designed to be thought-provoking, to spark insightful class discussion, or to be used in combination with a journal assignment or other learning method to help students see connections between ethics and communication.

Communication & Social Media   Because of the importance of social media in our lives, in each chapter we include special material about social media and communication to help students become sensitive to the sometimes mindboggling impact that social media platforms like Facebook, Twitter, Snapchat, and Instagram have on our communication with others. We also discuss the importance and role of social media in several chapters throughout the book. The prevalence of social media in students' lives offers powerful teachable moments to help students learn and apply communication principles.

Communication & Diversity   Each chapter includes a "Communication & Diversity" feature designed to help students see the importance of diversity in their lives. Yet we don't relegate discussions of diversity only to a boxed feature. Because we believe diversity is such an important communication topic in contemporary society, we discuss diversity in the text, not only in relation to our fifth principle of communication (appropriately adapt messages to others) in Chapter 6, but throughout the book.

Comprehensive Pedagogical Learning Tools   To help students master the material, we've built in a wealth of study aids:

- Learning objectives provide a compass to help students know where they are headed, which they can check at key points throughout each chapter.
- Chapter outlines preview key concepts.
- Concise and highly praised Recap boxes distill essential content.
- Key terms in boldface with marginal glossary help students master essential terms.
- Chapter-end Study Guides offer narrative summaries and key terms lists.
- The Principle Points, chapter-end summaries of the five Communication Principles, recap applications of the principles to students' real-life communication.
- Chapter-end apply questions guide students to think critically about how they can apply chapter concepts to their lives and relationships.
- Many chapter-end skills assessment and collaborative learning activities have been revised and updated for this edition.

Our Partnership with Instructors Stays Strong

As authors, we view our job as providing resources that instructors can use to bring communication principles and skills to life. A textbook is only one tool to help teachers teach and learners learn. As part of our partnership with instructors to facilitate learning, we offer an array of print and electronic resources to help teachers do what they do best: teach. In addition to the vast array of learning resources we've built into the text, we offer a dazzling package of additional resources to help instructors generate both intellectual and emotional connections with their students.

Key instructor resources include an Instructor's Manual (ISBN 0-13-455386-1), TestBank, (ISBN 0-13-455378-0), and PowerPoint Presentation Package (ISBN 0-13-455373-X). These supplements are available on the catalog page for this text on Pearson.com/us (instructor login required). MyTest online test-generating software (ISBN 0-13-455383-7) is available at www.pearsonmytest.com (instructor login required).

For a complete list of the instructor and student resources available with the text, please visit the Pearson Communication catalog, at www.pearson.com/communication.

Pearson MediaShare

Pearson's comprehensive media upload tool allows students to post videos, images, audio, or documents for instructor and peer viewing, time-stamped commenting, and assessment. MediaShare is an easy, mobile way for students and professors to interact and engage with speeches, presentation aids, and other files. MediaShare gives professors the tools to provide contextual feedback to demonstrate how students can improve their skills.

The best of MediaShare's functionality, including student video submissions with grading and video quizzes, is now available to use and assign *within Revel*, making Revel an even more complete solution for Communication courses. By placing these key components of MediaShare within Revel, students have one all-inclusive space to practice and have their performance assessed while actively learning through interactive course content. Revel with MediaShare is an unparalleled immersive learning experience for the Communication curriculum.

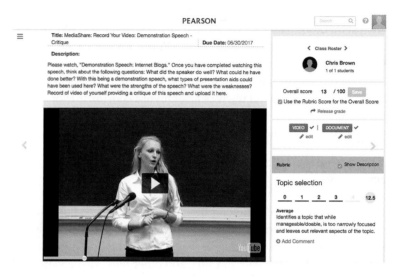

- Use MediaShare to assign or view speeches, video-based assignments, role plays, and more in a variety of formats including video, Word, PowerPoint, and Excel.
- Assess students using customizable, Pearson-provided rubrics or create your own around classroom goals, learning outcomes, or department initiatives.

- Set up assignments for students with options for full-class viewing and commenting or private comments between you and the student.
- Record video directly from a tablet, phone, or other webcam.
- Embed video from YouTube via assignments to incorporate current events into the classroom experience.

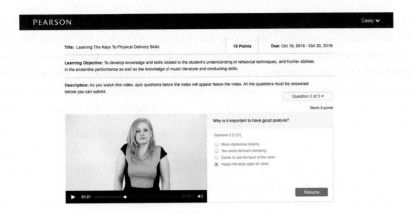

- Set up quiz questions on video assignments to ensure students master concepts, and interact and engage with the media.
- Import grades into most learning management systems.
- Ensure a secure learning environment for instructors and students through robust privacy settings.

Acknowledgments

Although our three names appear on the cover as authors of the book you are holding in your hands, in reality hundreds of people have been instrumental in making this book possible.

Communication scholars who have dedicated their lives to researching the importance of communication principles, theories, and skills provide the fuel for this book. We thank each author we reference in our voluminous endnotes for the research conclusions that have brought us to our contemporary understanding of communication principles. We thank our students who have trusted us to be their guides in their study of human communication. They continue to enrich our lives with their enthusiasm and curiosity. They have inspired us to be more creative by their honest, quizzical looks and challenged us to go beyond "textbook" answers with their thought-provoking questions.

We are most appreciative of the outstanding editorial support we continue to receive from our colleagues and friends at Pearson. We thank Joe Opiela for helping us keep this project moving forward when we wondered if the world needed another communication book. Karon Bowers, Pearson Publisher, has continued to provide valued support and encouragement. Our exceptionally thoughtful and talented development editor, Ellen Keohane, helped us polish and prune our words and gave us a wealth of ideas and suggestions. We acknowledge and appreciate the ideas and suggestions from Mark Redmond, a valued friend, gifted teacher, and skilled writer at Iowa State University. His coauthorship with us on *Interpersonal Communication: Relating to Others* significantly influenced our ideas about communication, especially interpersonal communication.

We are grateful to the many educators who read the manuscript and both encouraged and challenged us. We thank the following people for drawing on their teaching skill, expertise, and vast experience to make this a much better book:

Reviewers of the First Edition: Michael Bruner, University of North Texas; Diana O. Cassagrande, West Chester University; Dan B. Curtis, Central Missouri State University; Terrence A. Doyle, Northern Virginia Community College; Julia F. Fennell, Community College of Allegheny County, South Campus; Phil Hoke, The University of Texas at San Antonio; Stephen Hunt, Illinois State University; Carol L. Hunter, Brookdale Community College; Dorothy W. Ige, Indiana University Northwest; A. Elizabeth

Lindsey, The New Mexico State University; Robert E. Mild, Jr., Fairmont State College; Timothy P. Mottet, Texas State University–San Marcos; Alfred G. Mueller II, Pennsylvania State University, Mont Alto Campus; Kay Neal, University of Wisconsin–Oshkosh; Kathleen Perri, Valencia Community College; Beth M. Waggenspack, Virginia Tech University; Gretchen Aggert Weber, Horry-Georgetown Technical College; Kathy Werking, Eastern Kentucky University; Andrew F. Wood, San Jose State University.

Reviewers of the Second Edition: Lawrence Albert, Morehead State University; Leonard Assante, Volunteer State Community College; Dennis Dufer, St. Louis Community College; Annette Folwell, University of Idaho; Mike Hemphill, University of Arkansas at Little Rock; Teri Higginbotham, University of Central Arkansas; Lawrence Hugenberg, Youngstown State University; Timothy P. Mottet, Texas State University–San Marcos; Penny O'Connor, University of Northern Iowa; Evelyn Plummer, Seton Hall University; Charlotte C. Toguchi, Kapi'olani Community College; Debra Sue Wyatt, South Texas Community College.

Reviewers of the Third Edition: Dom Bongiorni, Kingwood College; Jo Anne Bryant, Troy University; Cherie Cannon, Miami–Dade College; Thomas Green, Cape Fear Community College; Gretchen Harries, Austin Community College; Xin-An Lu, Shippensburg University of Pennsylvania; Sara L. Nalley, Columbia College; Kristi Schaller, University of Hawaii; David Shuhy, Salisbury University; John Tapia, Missouri Western State College.

Reviewers of the Fourth Edition: Ellen B. Bremen, Highline Community College; Patricia A. Cutspec, East Tennessee State University; Edgar D. Johnson III, Augusta State University; Peter S. Lee, California State University, Fullerton; Kelly Aikin Petcus, Austin Community College; Natalia Rybas, Bowling Green State University; Sarah Stout, Kellogg Community College.

Reviewers of the Fifth Edition: Leonard Assante, Volunteer State Community College; Sandra Bein, South Suburban College; Robert Dixon, St. Louis Community College; Glynis Holm Strause, Coastal Bend College; Linda Kalfayan, Westchester Community College; Barbara Maxwell, Linn State Technical College; Kay Neal, University of Wisconsin Oshkosh; Jeff Pomeroy, Southwest Texas Junior College.

Reviewers of the Sixth Edition: Kevin Clark, Austin Community College; Cynthia Brown El, Macomb Community College; Diane Ferrero-Paluzzi, Iona College; Gary Kuhn, Chemeketa Community College; Travice Obas, Georgia Highlands College; John Parrish, Tarrant County College; Daniel Paulnock, Saint Paul College; Shannon Proctor, Highline Community College; Kimberly Schaefer, Baker University; Katie Stevens, Austin Community College; Jayne Violette, Eastern Kentucky University.

Reviewers of the Seventh Edition: Tasha Davis, Austin Community College; Thomas Damp, Central New Mexico Community College; Kevin Clark, Austin Community College; Tila Maceira-Klever, Chemeketa Community College; Narissra Punyanunt-Carter, Texas Tech University; John Parrish, Tarrant County College; James Lohrey, Mercyhurst College.

We have each been influenced by colleagues, friends, and teachers who have offered support and inspiration for this project. Happily, colleagues, friends, and teachers are virtually indistinguishable for us. We are each blessed with people with whom we work who offer strong support. Steve and Sue thank their colleagues at Texas State University for their insights and ideas that helped shape key concepts in this book. Cathy Fleuriet and Tom Burkholder, who served as basic course directors at Texas State, influenced our work. Tim Mottet, also a former basic course director at Texas State and now President of Colorado State University-Pueblo, is a valued, inspirational friend, coauthor, and colleague who is always there to listen and freely share his ideas and experience. Marian Houser, a former basic course director at Texas State, is a wonderful friend and provides important insight and support. Kristen LeBlanc Farris, Director of Texas State's award-winning basic communication course, is a valued friend and continues to offer generous support. Long-time friend Kosta Tovstiadi, University of Colorado, provided skilled research assistance to help us draw upon the most contemporary interpersonal communication research. Michael Hennessy, Patricia Margerison, and Daniel Lochman are Texas State English faculty who have been especially supportive of Sue's work. Finally, Steve thanks his skilled and dedicated administrative support team at Texas State: administrative assistant Sue Hall, a cherished friend and colleague, and Bob Hanna provided exceptional support and assistance for this project and many others.

Ivy is grateful to her students, colleagues, and friends at Texas A&M University–Corpus Christi, for their patience and unwavering support for her continued involvement in this book project. In particular, President Kelly Quintanilla, Associate Provost Amy Aldridge Sanford, Dean Mark Hartlaub, and Chair David Gurney constantly reaffirm the value of a well-written, carefully crafted book—one that speaks to students' lives. Their support of Ivy's research efforts, along with constant fueling from her wonderful students, always make this project a joy. Ivy's deepest thanks also go to Steve and Sue Beebe for their generosity in bringing her into this project, and for their extraordinary friendship.

Finally, we express our appreciation to our families. Ivy thanks her ever-supportive sister Karen Black, and nephew, niece, and grandnieces Brian, Sumitra, Mackenzie, and Sidney Black. They have been constant and generous with their praise for her writing accomplishments. Ivy will always be especially grateful to her late parents, Carol and Herschel Ivy, for lovingly offering many lessons about living the highly ethical life.

Sue and Steve especially thank their parents, Herb and Jane Dye, and Russell and Muriel Beebe, who taught them much about communication and ethics that truly are principles for a lifetime. They also thank their sons, Mark and Matthew Beebe, and their daughter-in-law, Amanda Beebe, for teaching them life lessons about giving and receiving love that will remain with them forever.

Steven A. Beebe
Susan J. Beebe
Diana K. Ivy

CHAPTER **1**

IDENTIFYING FOUNDATIONS OF HUMAN COMMUNICATION

There is no pleasure to me without communication. —MICHELE DE MONTAIGNE

Monkey Business Images/Shutterstock

CHAPTER OUTLINE

LEARNING OBJECTIVES

After studying this chapter, you should be able to

1.1 Explain why it is important to study communication.

1.2 Define communication and describe five characteristics of the communication process.

1.3 Explain three communication models.

1.4 Describe three criteria that can be used to determine whether communication is competent.

1.5 Describe the nature of communication in the 21st century.

1.6 Identify and explain three communication contexts.

1.7 List and explain five fundamental principles of communication.

Like life-sustaining breath, communication is ever-present in our lives. That makes understanding and improving how we communicate with others a basic life skill.

Communication is an inescapable and fundamental aspect of being human. Consider the number of times you have purposefully communicated with someone today as you worked, ate, studied, shopped, or went about your daily duties. With the constant presence of social media in our lives, you are likely to be connected to others day and night. Most people spend between 80 and 90 percent of their waking hours communicating with others.[1] Even if you live in isolation, you talk to yourself through your thoughts. It is through the process of communication that we convey who we are, both to ourselves and to others; it is our primary tool for making our way in the world.

In the course of our study of human communication, we will discuss myriad skills, ideas, concepts, and contexts. To help you stitch together the barrage of ideas and information, we will organize our study around five fundamental communication principles:

Principle One: Be aware of your communication with yourself and others.
Principle Two: Effectively use and interpret verbal messages.
Principle Three: Effectively use and interpret nonverbal messages.
Principle Four: Listen and respond thoughtfully to others.
Principle Five: Appropriately adapt messages to others.

We don't claim that everything you need to know about communication is covered by these five principles. They do, however, summarize decades of research, as well as the wisdom of those who have taught communication over the years, about what constitutes effective and ethical communication.

Before we elaborate on the five fundamental communication principles, it is helpful in this first chapter to provide some background for our study of communication. We will discuss why it is important to study communication, define communication, examine various models of, or perspectives on, communication, and identify characteristics of human communication. Having offered this prelude, we will then discuss the five foundational principles of human communication that we will use throughout the book to help you organize the concepts, skills, and ideas we present in our discussion of interpersonal, group, and presentational speaking situations.

Why Study Communication?

1.1 Explain why it is important to study communication.

Why are you here? No, we don't mean "Why do you exist?" or "Why do you live where you do?" What we mean is "Why are you taking a college course about communication?" Perhaps the short answer is "It's required." Or maybe your advisor, parent, or friend encouraged you to take the course. But required or not, what can a systematic study of human communication do for you?

Communication touches every aspect of our lives. To be able to express yourself to other people is a basic requirement for living in a modern society. From a practical standpoint, it's very likely that you will make your living with your mind rather than your hands.[2] Even if you do physical labor, you will need communication skills to work with others. When you study communication, you are also developing leadership skills. "The art of communication," says author James Humes, "is the language of leadership."[3]

Although the value of being a competent communicator is virtually undisputed, there is evidence that many people struggle to express themselves clearly or to accurately understand messages from others. One study estimated that one-fifth of the students in the United States were not successful with even elementary communication tasks; in addition, more than 60 percent of the students could not give clear oral directions for someone else to follow.[4] When leaders in major corporations were asked to specify the most important skills for workers to have, 80 percent said listening was the most important work skill; 78 percent identified interpersonal communication skill as the next most important. However, the same leaders said only 28 percent of their employees had good listening skills and only 27 percent possessed effective interpersonal communication skills.[5] In support of these leaders' observations, another national study found that adults listen with 25 percent accuracy.[6] There is also evidence that the majority of adults are fearful of speaking in public and that about 20 percent of the population is highly apprehensive of presentational speaking.[7]

Aren't some people just born to be better communicators than others? If so, why should you work to develop your communication skill? Just as some people have more innate musical talent than others, there is evidence that some people may have an inborn biological ability to communicate with others.[8] This does not mean you should not work to develop your communication ability. Throughout the book, we will offer ample evidence that if you work to improve your skill, you will be rewarded by enjoying the benefits of enhanced communication competence. What are these benefits? Read on.

To Improve Your Employability

Regardless of your specific title or job description, the essence of what you do when working at any job is to communicate; you talk, listen, relate, read, and write. People who can communicate effectively with others are in high demand. As noted by John H. McConnell, CEO of Worthington Industries, "Take all the speech and communication courses you can because the world turns on communication."[9] McConnell's advice is supported by research as well as by personal observations.

Based on a survey of employers, here's a ranking of the top factors in obtaining employment immediately after college:[11]

1. Oral communication
2. Teamwork skills in diverse groups
3. Written communication
4. Critical thinking and analytic reasoning
5. Complex problem solving
6. Information literacy
7. Innovation and creativity
8. Technological skills
9. Quantitative reasoning

We're sure you know why we cited this survey. Communication skills were the number one valued skill. And this survey isn't the

▼ Warren Buffett, whose savvy investing has made him one of the richest people on the planet, agrees with many other leaders about the importance of communication skills at work. In one televised interview, Buffet declared, "If you improve your communication skills, I guarantee you that you will earn 50 percent more money over your lifetime!"[10] Kent Sievers/Shutterstock only one that reached the same conclusion; several other research studies have shown that communication skills are the most sought-after skills in the workplace.[12] Whether you are communicating face to face or online, communication skills are highly valued. Increasingly, you will communicate with others on the job via text, video chat, and social media. If you are searching for a job, perhaps you have a LinkedIn account to showcase your skills and talents.[13] Being able to effectively communicate with others, either in person or via an electronic means, enhances your employability.[14] Research has consistently found that communication skills, including interpersonal and teamwork skills, continue to be the most valued skills on the planet.[15]

To Improve Your Relationships

We don't choose our biological families, but we do choose our friends. For unmarried people, developing friendships and falling in love are the top-rated sources of satisfaction and happiness in life.[16] Conversely, losing a relationship is among life's most stressful events. Most people between the ages of 19 and 24 report that they have had five to six romantic relationships and have been "in love" once or twice.[17] Understanding the role and function of communication can help unravel some of the mysteries of human relationships. At the heart of a good relationship is good communication.[18]

Virginia Satir, a pioneer in family enrichment, described family communication as "the largest single factor determining the kinds of relationships [we make] with others."[19] Learning principles and skills of communication can give us insight into why we relate to other family members as we do. Our early communication with our parents had a profound effect on our self-concept and self-worth. According to Satir, people are "made" in families. Our communication with family members has shaped how we interact with others today.

Many of us will spend as much or more time interacting with people in our places of work as we do at home. And although we choose our friends and lovers, we don't always have the same flexibility in choosing those with whom, or for whom, we work. Increasing our understanding of the role and importance of human communication with our colleagues can help us better manage stress on the job as well as enhance our work success.

To Improve Your Health

Life is stressful. Research has clearly documented that the lack or loss of close relationships can lead to ill health and even death. Having a social support system—good friends and supportive family members—seems to make a difference in our overall health and quality of life. Good friends and intimate relationships with others help us manage stress and contribute to both physical and emotional health. For example, physicians have noted that patients who are widowed or divorced experience more medical problems, such as heart disease, cancer, pneumonia, and diabetes, than do married people.[20] Grief-stricken spouses are more likely than others to die prematurely, especially around the time of the departed spouse's birthday or near their wedding anniversary.[21] Terminally ill patients with a limited number of friends or social support die sooner than those with stronger ties.[22] Without companions and close friends, our opportunities for intimacy and stress-managing communication are diminished. Studying how to enrich the quality of our communication with others can make life more enjoyable and enhance our overall well-being. Because of Snapchat, Instagram, and other social networks, we are increasingly involved in relationships with others even when we are not interacting face to face. Relating to others, whether online or in person, occurs through communication.[23]

So again, we ask the question: Why are you here? We think the evidence is clear: People who are effective communicators are more likely to get the jobs they want; have better-quality relationships with friends, family, and colleagues; and even enjoy a healthier quality of life.

The Communication Process

1.2 **Define communication and describe five characteristics of the communication process.**

Communication is one of those words that seem so basic you may wonder why they need to be formally defined. Yet scholars who devote their lives to studying communication don't always agree on the definition of the term. One research team counted more than 126 published definitions.[24] In this section, we'll examine our definition of communication, the characteristics shared by all communication, major models that researchers and theorists have used to explain and study communication, and the three general contexts in which communication happens.

Communication Defined

In its broadest sense, **communication** is the process of acting on information.[25] Someone does or says something, and others think or do something in response to the action or the words as they understand them. Communication is not unique to humans; researchers study communication in other species, as well as between species. For example, you communicate with your pet dog if the dog sits in response to your spoken command, or if you respond to your dog's begging gaze by giving him a treat.

The focus of this text is **human communication**, *the process of making sense out of the world and sharing that sense with others by creating meaning through the use of verbal and nonverbal messages.*[26] Let's look at the key components of this definition.

Making Sense *Communication is about making sense.* We make sense out of what we experience when we begin to interpret what we see, hear, touch, smell, and taste with sensations, feelings, thoughts, and words. Identifying patterns and structure in what we experience is key to making sense out of what happens to us. Although we often think that "making sense out of something" means rationally and logically interpreting what we experience, we also make sense through intuition, feelings, and emotions.[27]

Sharing Sense *Communication is about sharing sense.* We share what we experience by expressing to others and to ourselves what we experience. We typically use words to express our thoughts, but we also use music, art, clothing, and a host of other means to convey what we are thinking and feeling to others.

communication
The process of acting on information.

human communication
The process of making sense out of the world and sharing that sense with others by creating meaning through verbal and nonverbal messages.

▲ Signs are usually carefully crafted examples of symbolic communication. What are the creators of this sign trying to communicate?

Patrick Strattner/Shutterstock

symbol

A word, sound, gesture, or visual image that represents a thought, concept, object, or experience.

Creating Meaning *Communication is about creating meaning.* As we will discuss later in this chapter, it's more appropriate to say that meaning is *created* through communication rather than sent or transmitted. To say that we send or transmit messages is to imply that what we send is what is received. However, presenting information to others does not mean communication has occurred: "But I told you what to do!" "It's there in the memo. Why didn't you do what I asked?" "It's in the syllabus." These exasperated communicators assumed that if they sent a message, someone would receive it. However, communication does not operate in a simple, linear, what-you-send-is-what-is-received process. *Information is not communication.* In fact, what is expressed by one person is rarely interpreted by another person precisely as intended.

Messages *Communication is about verbal and nonverbal messages.* We communicate by using **symbols**, words, sounds, gestures, or visual images that represent thoughts, concepts, objects, or experiences. The words on this page are symbols you use to derive meaning that makes sense to you. Not all symbols are verbal; some are nonverbal. You use gestures, posture, facial expression, tone of voice, clothing, and jewelry to express ideas, attitudes, and feelings. Nonverbal messages primarily communicate emotions, such as our likes and dislikes, whether we're interested or uninterested, and our feelings of power or lack of power.

Some scholars assert that *all* human behavior is really communication. When you cross your arms while listening to your friend describe her day, she may conclude that you're not interested in what she's talking about. But it could just be that you're chilly. While all human expression has the potential to communicate a message (someone may act or respond to the information they receive from you), it does not mean that you are *intentionally* expressing an idea or emotion. People don't always accurately interpret the messages we express—and this unprofound observation has profound implications.

Because of the ever-present potential for misunderstanding, communication should be *other-oriented*—it should acknowledge the perspective of others, not just that of the creator of the message. Communication that does not consider the needs, background, and culture of the receiver is more likely to be misunderstood than other-oriented communication. We'll emphasize the importance of considering others or considering your audience throughout the book. Knowing something about the experiences of the person or persons you're speaking to can help you communicate more effectively and appropriately.

Communication Characteristics

The following characteristics are evident any time communication occurs: Communication is inescapable, irreversible, and complicated; it emphasizes content and relationships; and it is governed by rules.

Communication is Inescapable Opportunities to communicate are everywhere. We spend most of our waking hours sending messages to others or interpreting messages from others.[28] Many of our messages are not verbalized. As you silently stand in a supermarket checkout line, for example, your lack of eye contact with others waiting in line suggests you're not interested in striking up a conversation. Your unspoken messages may provide cues to which others respond. As was noted earlier, some communication scholars question whether it is possible to communicate with someone unintentionally. However, even when you don't intend to express a particular idea or feeling, others may try to make sense out of what you are doing—or not doing. Remember: People judge you by your behavior, not your intent.

Communication is Irreversible "Disregard that last statement made by the witness," instructs the judge. Yet the clever lawyer knows that, once the witness has said something, he or she cannot really "take back" the message. In conversation, we may try to modify the meaning of a spoken message by saying something like "Oh, I really didn't mean it." But in most cases, the damage has been done. Once created, communication has the physical property of matter; it can't be uncreated. As the spiral shown in Figure 1.1 suggests, once communication begins, it never loops back on itself. Instead, it continues to be shaped by the events, experiences, and thoughts of the communication partners. A Russian proverb nicely summarizes this point: "Once a word goes out of your mouth, you can never swallow it again."

Communication is Complicated Communicating with others is not simple. If it were, we would know how to dramatically reduce the number of misunderstandings and conflicts in our world. In addition, this book would be able to offer you a list of simple techniques and strategies for blissful management of communication hassles in your relationships. But you won't find that list in this book or any other credible book, because human communication is complicated by the number of variables and unknown factors involved when people interact.

To illustrate the complexity of the process, communication scholar Dean Barnlund has suggested that whenever we communicate with another person, at least six "people" are really involved:

1. Who you think you are
2. Who you think the other person is
3. Who you think the other person thinks you are
4. Who the other person thinks he or she is
5. Who the other person thinks you are
6. Who the other person thinks you think he or she is.[29]

Whew! And when you add more people to the conversation, it becomes even more complicated.

Life is not only complicated but also uncertain. There are many things we do not know. We seek information about such everyday things as the weather or about such questions as what others think about us. Several communication theorists suggest that we attempt to manage our uncertainty through communication.[30] In times of high uncertainty (when there are many things we do not know), we will communicate more actively and purposefully so as to manage our uncertainty. For example, we are likely to ask more questions, seek information, and listen intently when we are uncertain.

Adding to the complexity of communication and the problem of our own uncertainty is that messages are not always interpreted as we intend them. Osmo Wiio, a Scandinavian communication scholar, points out the challenges of communicating with others when he suggests the following maxims:

1. If communication can fail, it will.
2. If a message can be understood in different ways, it will be understood in just the way that does the most harm.
3. There is always somebody who knows better than you what you meant by your message.
4. The more communication there is, the more difficult it is for communication to succeed.[31]

FIGURE 1.1 Helical Model of Communication

Interpersonal communication is irreversible. Like the spiral shown here, communication never loops back on itself. Once it begins, it expands infinitely as the communication partners contribute their thoughts and experiences to the exchange.

Nishi 55/Fotolia

Although we are not as pessimistic as Wiio, we do suggest that the task of understanding each other is challenging.

Communication Emphasizes Content and Relationships   What you say—your words—and how you say it—your tone of voice, amount of eye contact, facial expression, and posture—can reveal much about the true meaning of your message. The **content dimension** of communication messages refers to the new information, ideas, or suggested actions the speaker wishes to express. When you tell your roommate you want the room cleaned, you convey an intentional message that you want a tidier room.

content dimension

The new information, ideas, or suggested actions that a communicator wishes to express; *what* is said.

The **relationship dimension** of a communication message is usually less explicit; it offers cues about the emotions, attitudes, and amount of power and control the speaker directs toward others.[32] If one of your roommates loudly and abruptly bellows, "HEY, DORK! CLEAN THIS ROOM!" and another roommate uses the same verbal message but more gently and playfully suggests, with a smile, "Hey, dork. Clean this room," both are communicating the same message content, aimed at achieving the same outcome. But the two messages have very different relationship cues. Your use of emoticons in text messages is another way of expressing relational meaning. One study found that emoticons were especially helpful in communicating sarcasm in a message.[33]

relationship dimension

The aspect of a communication message that offers cues about the emotions, attitudes, and amount of power and control the speaker directs toward others; *how* something is said.

Another way to distinguish between the content and relationship dimensions of communication is to consider that the content of a message refers to *what* is said. The relationship cues are provided in *how* the message is communicated. For example, when you read a transcript of what someone says, you can get a different meaning than you would if you actually heard the person's words.

Communication is Governed by Rules   When you play Monopoly, you know there are rules about how to get out of jail, buy Boardwalk, or pass "Go" and collect $200. According to communication researcher Susan Shimanoff, a **rule** is a "followable prescription that indicates what behavior is obligated, preferred, or prohibited in certain contexts."[34] The rules that help define appropriate and inappropriate communication in any given situation may be explicit or implicit. The rules of Monopoly are explicit; they are even written down. For a class, explicit rules are probably spelled out in your syllabus.

rule

A followable prescription that indicates what behavior is required or preferred and what behavior is prohibited in a specific situation.

▼ What are the implicit rules for waiting in a medical waiting room?

Robert Kneschke/Shutterstock

However, your instructor has other rules that are more implicit. They are not written or verbalized because you learned them long ago: Only one person speaks at a time; you raise your hand to be called on; you do not send text messages during class. Similarly, you may follow implicit rules when you play Monopoly with certain friends or family members, such as "always let Grandpa buy Boardwalk." Communication rules are developed by those involved in the interaction and by the culture in which the individuals are communicating. Most people learn communication rules from experience, by observing and interacting with others.

Communication Models

1.3 Explain three communication models.

Communication researchers have spent considerable time trying to understand precisely how communication takes place. In the course of their study, they have developed visual models that graphically illustrate the communication process. By reviewing the development of communication models, you can see how our understanding of communication has evolved over the past century.

Communication as Action: Message Transfer

"Did you get my message?" This simple question summarizes the earliest, communication-as-action approach to human communication. These early models viewed communication as a transfer or exchange of information; communication takes place when a message is sent and received. Period. Communication is a way of transferring meaning from sender to receiver. In 1948, Harold Lasswell described the process as follows:

> Who (sender)
> Says what (message)
> In what channel
> To whom (receiver)
> With what effect[35]

Figure 1.2 shows a simplified representation of the communication process developed by communication pioneers Claude Shannon and Warren Weaver, who viewed communication as a linear input/output process. Today, although researchers view the process as more complex, they still define most of the key components in this model in basically the same way that Shannon and Weaver did.

Source The **source** of communication is the originator of a thought or an emotion. As the developer of that thought or emotion, the source puts a message into a code that can be understood by a receiver.

- **Encoding** is the process of translating ideas, feelings, and thoughts into a code. Vocalizing a word, gesturing, and establishing eye contact are means of encoding our thoughts into a message that can be decoded by someone.
- **Decoding**, the process that is the opposite of encoding, occurs when the words or unspoken signals are interpreted by the receiver.

Receiver The **receiver** is the person who decodes the signal and attempts to make sense of what the source encoded. Think of a TV station as a source broadcasting to a receiver (your TV) that picks up the station's signal. In human communication,

source
The originator of a thought or emotion who puts it into a code that can be understood by a receiver.

encoding
The process of translating ideas, feelings, and thoughts into a code.

decoding
The process of interpreting ideas, feelings, and thoughts that have been translated into a code.

receiver
The person who decodes a message and attempts to make sense of what the source has encoded.

FIGURE 1.2 A Model of Communication as Action

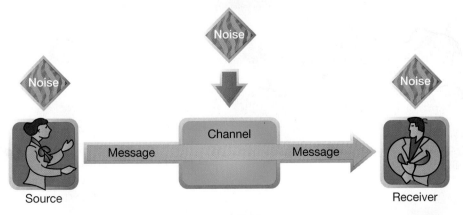

however, there is something between the source and the receiver: We filter messages through past experiences, attitudes, beliefs, values, prejudices, and biases.

message
Written, spoken, and unspoken elements of communication to which people assign meaning.

channel
The pathway through which messages are sent.

noise
Interference, either literal or psychological, that hinders the accurate encoding or decoding of a message.

Message   **Messages** are the written, spoken, and unspoken elements of communication to which we assign meaning. As we have noted, you can send a message intentionally (talking to a friend before class) or unintentionally (falling asleep during class); verbally ("Hi. What's up?"), nonverbally (a smile and a handshake), or in written form (this book); or through any number of electronic channels.

Channel   A message is communicated from sender to receiver via some pathway called a **channel**. With today's technological advances, we receive messages through a variety of channels, including print, airwave, and wireless. Ultimately, however, communication channels correspond to your senses. When you call your mother, the message is conveyed via an electronic channel that activates auditory cues. When you talk with your mother face to face, the channels are many. You see her: the visual channel. You hear her: the auditory channel. You may smell her perfume: the olfactory channel. You may hug her: the tactile channel.

Noise   **Noise** is interference. Noise keeps a message from being understood and achieving its intended effect. Without noise, all our messages would be communicated with considerable accuracy. But noise is always present. It can be literal—the obnoxious roar of a lawn mower—or it can be psychological, such as competing thoughts, worries, and feelings that capture our attention. Instead of concentrating on your teacher's lecture, you may start thinking about the chores you need to finish before the end of the day. Whichever kind it is, noise gets in the way of the message and may even distort it. Communicating accurate messages involves minimizing both literal and psychological noise.

The communication-as-action approach was simple and straightforward, but human communication rarely, if ever, is as simple a matter as "what we put in is what we get out." Other people cannot automatically know what you mean, even if your meaning seems very clear to *you*.

Communication as Interaction: Message Exchange

To take into account some of the complexities of actual communication, the early view evolved to include a more interactive, give-and-take approach. The communication-as-interaction model, shown in Figure 1.3, uses the same elements as the action model but adds two new ones: feedback and context.

FIGURE 1.3 A Model of Communication as Interaction

Interaction models of communication include feedback as a response to a message sent by a communication source and place the process in a context.

Feedback is the response to a message. Without feedback, communication is less likely to be effective. When you order your pepperoni pizza and the server asks in response, "That's a pepperoni pizza, right?" he has provided feedback to ensure that he decoded the message correctly.

Feedback can be intentional (applause at the conclusion of a symphony) or unintentional (a yawn as you listen to your uncle tell his story about bears again); or it can be verbal ("That's two burgers and fries, right?") or nonverbal (blushing after being asked out on a date).

As the cliché goes, "Everyone has to be somewhere." All communication takes place in some **context**, the physical, historical, and psychological communication environment. A conversation with your good friend on the beach would likely differ from one the two of you might have in a funeral home. Context encompasses not only the physical environment but also the number of people present, their past relationship with the communicators, the communication goal, and the culture in which the communicators are steeped. The psychological context includes the effect of what is going on in the minds of the communicators; the speaker's and listener's personalities and styles of interacting with others influence how messages are understood.

RECAP
Components of the Human Communication Process

Term	Definition
Source	Originator of an idea or emotion
Receiver	Person or group toward whom a source directs messages and who decodes the message
Message	Written, spoken, and unspoken elements of communication to which we assign meaning
Channel	Pathway through which messages pass between source and receiver
Noise	Any literal or psychological interference with the clear encoding or decoding of a message
Encoding	Translation of ideas, feelings, and thoughts into a code
Decoding	Interpretation of ideas, feelings, and thoughts that have been translated into a code
Context	Physical, historical, and psychological communication environment
Feedback	Verbal and nonverbal responses to a message

feedback
The response to a message.

context
The physical, historical, and psychological communication environment.

Communication as Transaction: Message Creation

Although it emphasizes feedback and context, the interaction model of communication still views communication as a linear, step-by-step process. But in many communication situations, both the source and the receiver send and receive messages *at the same time*. The communication-as-transaction perspective, which evolved in the 1960s, acknowledges that when we communicate with another, we are constantly reacting to what our partner is saying and expressing. Most scholars today view this perspective as the most realistic model of communication. Although this model uses such concepts as action and interaction to describe communication, as Figure 1.4 indicates, all the interaction is simultaneous. Even as we talk, we are also interpreting our partner's nonverbal and verbal responses. Transactive communication also

FIGURE 1.4 A Model of Communication as Transaction
The source and the receiver of a message experience communication simultaneously.

An Evolving Model of Human Communication

Human Communication as Action

Human communication is linear, with meaning sent or transferred from source to receiver.

Human Communication as Action

Human Communication as Interaction

Human communication occurs as the receiver of the message responds to the source through feedback. This interactive model views communication as a linear sequence of actions and reactions.

Human Communication as Interaction

Human Communication as Transaction

Human communication is simultaneously interactive. Meaning is created on the basis of mutual, concurrent sharing of ideas and feelings. This transactive model most accurately describes human communication.

Human Communication as Transaction

occurs within a context, and noise can interfere with the quality and accuracy of our encoding and decoding of messages.

For example, if you ask your friend out for coffee but you're not sure she'd like to go with you, even as you're talking to her, you carefully observe her reactions to determine whether she's really interested in your invitation. If you'd really like her company and you sense she'd rather not go with you, you may try harder, using your best persuasive pitch to get your friend to join you. During each communication transaction you have with another person, you look for information about how your message is being received even before you finish talking.

In a communication transaction, the meaning of a message is *co-created* by the individuals who are involved in the communication process. Meaning is created in the hearts and minds of both the message source and the message receiver, based on such things as the characteristics of the message, the situation, and the perceptions and background of the communicators. By drawing on our own experiences while attempting to make sense of a message, we actually shape the meaning of that message. As one research team puts it, communication is "the coordinated management of meaning" through episodes during which the message of one person influences the message of another.[36] Technically, only the sender and receiver of those messages can determine where one episode ends and another begins. We make sense out of our world in ways that are unique to each of us.

Communication Competence

1.4 Describe three criteria that can be used to determine whether communication is competent.

What does it mean to communicate competently? Does it mean that you are able to present a well-delivered speech? Or does it mean that you are able to carry on a brilliant conversation with someone? Is it evidence of communication competence if you often are asked to chair committee meetings because you are so organized? Being a competent communicator is more than just being well liked, glib, able to give polished presentations, or able to interact smoothly with individual people or in groups and teams. Although it is difficult to identify core criteria that define competent communication in all situations, we believe that certain goals of communication serve as measures of **communication competence**, or the ability to communicate appropriately and successfully, regardless of the setting. We suggest the following three criteria:[37]

communication competence
The ability to communicate appropriately and successfully.

- The message should be understood as the communicator intended it to be understood.
- The message should achieve the communicator's intended effect.
- The message should be ethical.

The Message Should Be Understood

A primary goal of any effective communication transaction is to develop a common understanding of the message from both the sender's and the receiver's perspectives. You'll note how the words *common* and *communication* resemble each other. One of the aims of the principles we discuss in this book is to create clarity of expression and a common understanding.

Message clarity is missing in the following headlines, which have appeared in local U.S. newspapers:

Panda Mating Fails: Veterinarian Takes Over

Drunks Get Nine Months in Violin Case

Include Your Children When Baking Cookies

Police Begin Campaign to Run Down Jaywalkers

Local High School Dropouts Cut in Half

We acknowledge the challenge of communicating with others; differences in culture, language, experience, gender, education, and background all are sources of misunderstanding. Meanings are fragile, and messages can be misunderstood. An effective message is one that the receiver understands.

The Message Should Achieve Its Intended Effect

Another criterion for judging the effectiveness of communication is whether the intent of the message is achieved. When you communicate intentionally with others, you do so for a specific purpose: to achieve a goal or to accomplish something. Because different purposes require different strategies for success, being aware of your purpose can enhance your probability of achieving it.

We often use specific types of communication to achieve typical goals:

- The goal of *public speaking* may be to inform, to persuade, or to entertain.
- In *small groups,* our goals are often to solve problems and make decisions.
- In our *interpersonal relationships*, our goals may be to build trust, develop intimacy, or just enjoy someone's company.

The Message Should Be Ethical

A message that is understood and achieves its intended effect but that manipulates listeners, unfairly restricts their choices, or uses false information may be effective, but it is not appropriate or ethical. **Ethics** are the beliefs, values, and moral principles by which we determine what is right or wrong. Ethics and ethical behavior have long been considered critical components of human behavior in a given culture.

ethics
The beliefs, values, and moral principles by which we determine what is right or wrong.

Philosophers have debated for centuries whether there is such a thing as a universal moral and ethical code.[38] British author and scholar C. S. Lewis argued that the teachings of cultures throughout the world and through time support the existence of a shared ethical code that serves as the basis for interpreting the "goodness" or "badness" of human behavior.[39] In their book *Communication Ethics and Universal Values,* communication scholars Clifford Christians and Michael Traber claim that, "Every culture depends for its existence on norms that order human relationships and social institutions."[40] They suggest there are three universal cultural norms: (1) the value of truth, (2) respect for another person's dignity, and (3) the expectation that innocent people should not suffer harm.[41] As represented in the Communication & Ethics box, there appears to be a moral code for how people should treat others that can be seen across most of the world's major religions.[42]

Our purpose is not to prescribe a specific religious or philosophical ethical code, but rather to suggest that humans from a variety of cultures and traditions have sought to develop ethical principles that guide their interactions with others. Having an ethical code does not always mean that people follow the code, however. Scholars and

COMMUNICATION & ETHICS

Is There a Universal Ethical Code?

Most religions of the world emphasize a common spiritual theme, which is known in Christianity as the Golden Rule: Do unto others what you would have others do unto you.[43] This "rule" is also perceived as the basis for most ethical codes throughout the world.

Hinduism	Do nothing to others which would cause pain if done to you.
Buddhism	One should seek for others the happiness one desires for oneself.
Taoism	Regard your neighbor's gain as your own gain, and your neighbor's loss as your loss.
Confucianism	Is there one principle which ought to be acted upon throughout one's whole life? Surely it is the principle of loving-kindness: do not unto others what you would not have them do unto you.
Zoroastrianism	The nature alone is good which refrains from doing unto another whatsoever is not good for itself.
Judaism	What is hateful to you, do not do to others. That is the entire law: all the rest is but commentary.
Islam	No one of you is a believer until he desires for his brother that which he desires for himself.
Christianity	Do unto others what you would have others do unto you.

Does the fact that virtually all religions appear to have a common theme of valuing others as yourself provide evidence that there are universal human ethical standards?

philosophers who suggest that a universal code of ethics exists do not claim that people always behave in ways that are true to these universal standards.

Philosophy and religion are not the only realms that focus on ethical behavior. Most professions, such as medicine, law, and journalism, have explicit codes of ethics that identify appropriate and inappropriate behavior. The National Communication Association has developed a Credo for Communication Ethics to emphasize the importance of being an ethical communicator:

> Ethical communication is fundamental to responsible thinking, decision making, and the development of relationships and communities within and across contexts, cultures, channels, and media. Moreover, ethical communication enhances human worth and dignity by fostering truthfulness, fairness, responsibility, personal integrity, and respect for self and others.[44]

For most people, being ethical means being sensitive to others' needs, giving people choices rather than forcing them to behave in a certain way, respecting others' privacy, not intentionally decreasing others' feelings of self-worth, and being honest in presenting information. Unethical communication does just the opposite: It forces views on others and demeans their integrity. Echoing the wisdom offered by others, we suggest that competent communication is grounded in an ethical perspective that is respectful to others.

Communication in the 21st Century

1.5 Describe the nature of communication in the 21st century.

We live in a technological age. Reportedly 26 million "swipe right" matches are made each day on the popular dating app Tinder. (You swipe right if you like the person; swipe left if you don't.) And since Tinder launched in 2012, more than 6 billion matches have been made.[45] Collectively, Tinder users swipe at the rate of a million times a minute.[46] Whether you're seeking to meet new people or connecting with friends and family, it is increasingly important to use technology competently when communicating in the 21st century. When you use a medium such as a smartphone or the Internet to carry your message, you are using **mediated communication**, which is any communication expressed via some channel other than those used when we communicate in person. Some physical media, such as a wire, a cable, a phone line, smartphone, a TV set, a computer, or some other technology, carry the messages between sender and receiver. The channel of communication is not only physical but also electronic, in the form of the signal coming into your TV set, your phone, or your computer.

Mass communication occurs when a mediated message is sent to many people at the same time. A TV or radio broadcast is an example of mass communication. Although mass communication is important, our focus in this book is primarily on unmediated and mediated interpersonal, group, and presentational communication.

mediated communication
Any communication that is carried out using some channel other than those used in face-to-face communication.

mass communication
Communication accomplished through a mediated message that is sent to many people at the same time.

Immediate Communication

What's new today is that there are so many different ways of *immediately* connecting with someone.[47] Facebook, Snapchat, Instagram, and other contemporary methods of communicating with others are relatively recent inventions when we consider the entire spectrum of human history, but people have been communicating with others without being face to face for centuries; sending letters and other written messages to others is a long-standing human practice. In fact, a printed textbook provides a form of mediated "distance learning." And even in an electronic textbook, the words were written some time before students read them.

Today's technology makes it as easy to communicate with someone either across the street or across the globe. And we can time shift when we communicate. Face to face, we communicate with *synchronous* communication, in real time when we receive immediate feedback. But using e-mail or text messages, we interact with *asynchronous* communication, or out of sync; that is, there may be a time delay between when you send a message and when it is received.

Frequent Communication

In 2011, approximately a third of all Americans owned a smartphone. By 2016, almost two-thirds had one.[48] And according to a recent research survey, almost half of all smartphone owners in the United States said their phones were something "they couldn't live without."[49] Another study found that young adults thought they were using their phones less than three hours a day when in reality they were using their phones about five hours a day on 85 separate occasions.[50] Clearly, we are not always conscious of how frequently we glance at our phone. Most interactions with a phone, according to the study, were 30 seconds or less. But those seconds add up.[51]

In addition to using our phones more frequently than in the past, there is evidence that we increasingly multitask as we connect with others, such as when we check messages on our phones while visiting with a friend or sitting through a meeting. Or we may be participating in multiple text or Snapchat conversations at once. One research team suggests that excessive multitasking may be a reflection of our personality. For example, frequent multitasking may be a symptom of attention-deficit/hyperactivity disorder (ADHD)—we may simply have difficulty focusing on one thing at a time for a sustained period of time. Or, multitasking may suggest a desire to always be "on" and connected due to a high need for social assurance, especially prominent among females according to one research study.[52]

Switching between face-to-face and mediated communication is a normal, seamless way of communicating with others, especially if you are using computers or mobile devices, technological tools that have probably always seemed to be part of your life. If you're under age 25, you are much more likely to text friends than to phone them, for example.[53] But, can you really communicate *interpersonally* with someone on the Internet? Yes, of course. You probably do so every day.

If you are attending a college or university away from family, friends, and loved ones, you may have found that sending text messages, Skyping, or connecting on

Facebook or Instagram can help you stay in touch with others who are important to you. The evidence summarized in the Communication & Social Media box suggests that Facebook is especially helpful in maintaining relationships.[54] College freshmen and their parents also report that Skype, e-mail, and text connections reduce students' homesickness and the sadness parents often feel when their son or daughter leaves home.

ZITS ©2007 Zits Partnership, King Features Syndicate

COMMUNICATION & SOCIAL MEDIA

Got Facebook? How We Connect on Social Media

Facebook is the predominant social networking site of the second decade of the 21st century. It is now more popular than Google in the United States. Although evidence suggests that Facebook use among teens between the ages of 13 and 17 has dropped, the number of people age 55 and older using the site continues to grow.[55] In contrast, Instagram and Snapchat have dramatically increased in popularity among younger social media users. Instagram has grown from 40 million users in 2012 to more than half a billion in 2016.[56] And Snapchat has grown from 50 to 200 million users during the same time period. But Facebook still has more users than WhatsApp, Twitter, and Instagram combined.[57] We connect not only with words but also with video; 400 hours of video are uploaded to YouTube each minute.[58] Overall, Facebook use continues to grow. But what precisely are we using Facebook to do? Researchers have identified several patterns that provide clues to the way we communicate today.

- *You check Facebook often.* Almost 80 percent of students surveyed log on to Facebook every day, and more than 60 percent said they sign in several times a day.[59] Half of all 18- to 24-year-olds in the United States check Facebook when they first wake up.[60] And 44 percent of Facebook users "like" their friends' content or comment on their friends' posts at least once a day.[61]
- *You have a lot of friends.* Teens have an average number of 300 friends (and 70 percent of teens are Facebook friends with their parents); millennials, those born between 1982 and 2002, have an average of 250 friends (and 62 percent of millennials post what they are doing, where they are, and who they are with);

members of Generation X have an average of 200 friends; baby boomers (born between 1943 and 1960) have fewer friends—between 50 and about 100.[62]

- *You're an active communicator.* There are more than 1.7 billion Facebook users with more than 1.66 billion mobile connections.[63] Five new profiles are created every second.[64] Forty percent of users check Facebook more than once a day.[65] About two-thirds of users post status updates to their profile and add comments and likes to their own and others' statuses.[66] The highest traffic occurs in the middle of the week between 1 and 3 p.m.[67]
- *You're most likely to share pictures.* More than 85 percent of students surveyed share photos. Eighty percent share their relationship status, and 70 percent share their favorite media, such as movies or TV shows. Fewer share their religious views (46 percent) or political views (40 percent), although college graduates are more likely to share their political and religious views than are current college students.[68]
- *Women and men use Facebook differently.* Men are more likely to share their political and religious views on Facebook than are women. Men are also more likely to post current events and news-related topics. Women are more likely to post comments and likes.[69] Women share and see photos and videos more than men.[70]
- What you like least about Facebook is people who share too much information about themselves or post your information or photos of you without your permission.[71]

Got Facebook? Apparently you do. Although not everyone finds Facebook a vital method of communication, for many it's an important means of communicating with others.

Although some research has found that mediated communication can be as satisfying as face-to-face conversation,[72] some observers still express concerns about overreliance on mediated communication. The title of communication researcher Sherry Turkle's book, *Alone Together*, suggests that even though we may be "connected" electronically, we are nonetheless literally alone, separated from others. As Turkle notes, "Our networked life allows us to hide from each other, even as we are tethered to each other. We'd rather text than talk."[73]

Communication That Meets Our Needs

Some researchers have wondered whether spending a lot of time online reduces people's need for face-to-face interactions. A team of researchers led by Robert Kraut and Sara Kiesler made headlines when they published the results of their study, which concluded that the more people use the Internet, the less they interact with people in person.[74] These researchers also found a relationship between people who said they were lonely and those who used the Internet. Yet three follow-up studies found that people who use the Internet are *more* likely to have a large number of friends; they are more involved with community activities and overall have greater levels of trust in other people.[75]

▲ Can an overreliance on mediated communication lead to increased loneliness and social isolation? Yulia Grogoryeva/123rf.com

The follow-up research suggests that for some people—those who are already prone to being shy or introverted—there may be a link between Internet use and loneliness or feelings of social isolation. This link might exist, however, because shy and introverted people are simply less likely to make contact with others in any way, not because they use the Internet a lot. For people who are generally outgoing and who like to interact with others, in contrast, the Internet is another tool with which to reach out to others. Whether communicating face-to-face or using social media, we express ourselves to meet our need for human interaction.

Comfortable Communication

Cyberspace can be a more comfortable place to communicate with others if you are apprehensive about talking in face-to-face situations or even on the phone. People who spend a lot of time online may not be more lonely; rather, they may just feel more comfortable having the ability to control the timing of how they interact with others. An ever-increasing number of people are meeting via social media and eventually developing in-person relationships, for example. One study suggests that many of us may prefer to use a less immediate communication channel when we are feeling some apprehension or relationship uncertainty. The researchers found that you are more likely to call a romantic partner on your cell phone when the relationship is going well than when the relationship isn't as positive.[76]

Another concern is dishonest communication. In a digital world, it is easy to send messages and provide feedback anonymously. Because of anonymity, it's easier to be deceitful. For example, in 2017, there were reported to be up to 83 million fake Facebook profiles.[77] Personal appearance plays less of a role in shaping initial impressions when using only text messages, unless we add photos or video. Even then, especially with photos, we can more easily manipulate our image (for example, by sharing a photo of us when we were younger or thinner).

Our recommendation? Your method of communication should fit well with your communication goal. Although connecting to others via the Internet seems to be a normal way to communicate for a significant and growing percentage of the world's population, at times relating to someone live and in person is best—especially for expressing feelings and emotions. In other situations, the ease and speed of mediated communication make it preferable to face-to-face communication.

Communication Contexts

1.6 Identify and explain three communication contexts.

Communication takes place in a variety of situations. As we've discussed, a great deal of the communication in our lives today is mediated. In this section, we'll describe the three classic, face-to-face contexts to which communication researchers study human communication: interpersonal communication, group communication, and presentational communication. All three contexts are part of communication in organizational and health settings.

Interpersonal Communication

Interpersonal communication is a special form of human communication that occurs when we interact simultaneously with another person and attempt to mutually influence each other, usually for the purpose of managing relationships. At the heart of this definition is the role of communication in developing unique relationships with other people.[78]

When we treat people as objects, or when we respond to their roles rather than to who they are as unique people, we are engaging in **impersonal communication**. Based on this definition, asking a server for a glass of water at a restaurant is impersonal rather than interpersonal communication. If you strike up a conversation with the server—say you discover that it's her birthday or that you both know the same people—your conversation moves from impersonal to interpersonal. We're not suggesting that impersonal communication is unimportant or necessarily inferior or bad. Competent communicators are able to interact with others in a variety of situations.

Interpersonal communication reflects the characteristics of the transactional model of communication discussed earlier. It is a dialogue in the sense that all communicators are influenced and meaning is created simultaneously.[79]

Interpersonal communication is the fundamental means we use to manage our relationships, the ongoing connections we make with others. To relate to someone is to give and take, listen and respond, act and react. When we talk about a good or positive relationship with someone, we often mean that we are "together" or "in sync." We will discuss interpersonal communication in more detail in Chapters 7 and 8.

Group Communication

Human beings are social, collaborative creatures. We do most of our work and play in groups. One focus of this book is the communication that occurs in groups—how we make sense of our participation in groups and share that sense with others. We define **small group communication** as the verbal and nonverbal message transactions that occur among three to about fifteen people who share a common goal, who feel a sense of belonging to the group, and who exert influence on one another.[80] Today's globe-shrinking technology makes it possible for people to be linked with others in *virtual groups* even when they are in different physical locations.[81] In Chapters 9 and 10, we will discuss groups and teams, both in-person and virtual, more thoroughly.

Presentational Communication

For many people, speaking in public is a major source of anxiety. **Presentational communication** occurs when a speaker addresses a gathering of people to inform, persuade, or entertain. In this book, we will focus on applying the principles of communication

---

interpersonal communication
Communication that occurs simultaneously between two people who attempt to mutually influence each other, usually for the purpose of managing relationships.

impersonal communication
Communication that treats people as objects or that responds only to their roles rather than to who they are as unique people.

small group communication
The transactive process of creating meaning among three to about fifteen people who share a common purpose, feel a sense of belonging to the group, and exert influence on one another.

presentational communication
Communication that occurs when a speaker addresses a gathering of people to inform, persuade, or entertain them.

▼ We engage in interpersonal communication when we interact with another person.
Golden Pixels LLC/Shutterstock

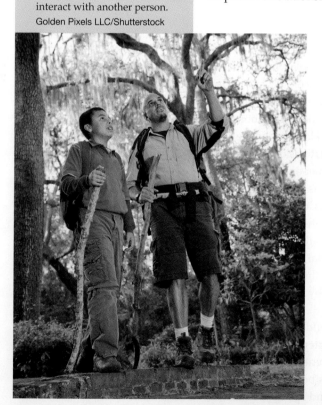

when informing and persuading listeners. In Chapters 11 through 15, we present basic strategies for designing and delivering a speech to others. Effective public speakers are aware of their communication and how they interact with their audience. They also effectively use, interpret, and understand verbal and nonverbal messages; listen and respond to their audience; and adapt their message to their listeners.

Of the three contexts in which the principles we present in this book are applied, public speaking has the distinction of being the one that has been formally studied the longest. In 333 BCE, Aristotle wrote his famous *Rhetoric*, the first fully developed treatment of the study of speech to convince an audience. He defined **rhetoric** as the process of discovering the available means of persuasion in a given situation. In essence, persuasion is the process of using symbols to persuade others. Although we have certainly advanced in our understanding of informing and persuading others in the past two millennia, much of what Aristotle taught has withstood the tests of both time and scholarly research.

rhetoric
The process of using symbols to influence or persuade others.

Applying Communication in Organizational and Health Contexts

Many researchers study the communication that occurs in organizations such as businesses, government agencies, and nonprofits such as the American Cancer Society and other charities. **Organizational communication** is the study of human communication as it occurs within organizations. Although organizational communication includes applications of interpersonal, group, and presentational communication, there are unique ways in which communication functions in contemporary organizations.

organizational communication
The study of human communication as it occurs within organizations.

Health communication, a growing area of communication study, examines the role and importance of communication that has an effect on our health. Health communication researchers study the interaction between health care workers (such as physicians, physician's assistants, and nurses) and patients. One study found that doctors who take the time to talk and listen to their patients had a profound and positive effect on their patients' health.[82] Health communication scholars also study how to best design campaigns to encourage healthy habits, such as messages about getting fit, losing weight, avoiding sexually transmitted diseases, or quitting smoking.

health communication
The study of communication that has an effect on human health.

Communication Principles for a Lifetime

1.7   List and explain five fundamental principles of communication.

As you saw at the beginning of this chapter, underlying our description of human communication are five principles that provide the foundation for all effective communication, whether we are communicating with others one on one, in groups or teams, or by presenting a public speech to an audience. Throughout this book, we will emphasize how these principles are woven into the fabric of each communication context. We provide a brief introduction to these five Communication Principles for a Lifetime here. Then, in the next five chapters, we will present a more comprehensive discussion of their scope and power.

Principle One: Be aware of your communication with yourself and others.
Principle Two: Effectively use and interpret verbal messages.
Principle Three: Effectively use and interpret nonverbal messages.
Principle Four: Listen and respond thoughtfully to others.
Principle Five: Appropriately adapt messages to others.

These five principles operate together rather than independently to form the basis of the fundamental processes that enhance communication effectiveness. The model in Figure 1.5 illustrates how the principles interrelate. Moving around the model clockwise, the first principle, being aware of your communication with yourself and others, is followed

FIGURE 1.5 Communication Principles for a Lifetime

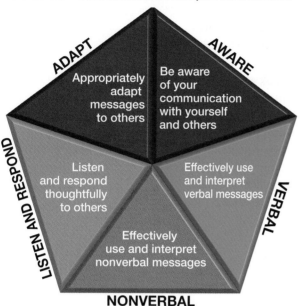

by the two principles that focus on communication messages, verbal messages (Principle Two) and nonverbal messages (Principle Three). The fourth principle, listening and responding, is followed by appropriately adapting messages to others (Principle Five). Together, these five principles can help explain why communication can be either effective or ineffective. A violation of any one principle can result in inappropriate or poor communication.

Throughout this book, we will remind you of how these principles can be used to organize the theory, concepts, and skills we offer as fundamental to human communication. Chapters 2 through 6 will each be devoted to a single principle. Chapters 7 through 15 will apply these principles to the most prevalent communication situations we experience each day: communicating with others interpersonally, in groups and teams, and when giving a talk or presentation.

To help you see relationships among the five communication principles and the various skills and content we will present in Chapters 7 through 15, we will place in the margin a small version of the model presented in Figure 1.5, like the one that appears in the margin here. We will also label which principle or principles we are discussing. Refer to Figure 1.5 as we introduce each of these principles.

Principle One: Be Aware of Your Communication with Yourself and Others

The first foundation principle is to be aware of your communication with yourself and others. Effective communicators are conscious, or "present," when communicating. Ineffective communicators mindlessly or thoughtlessly say and do things that they may later regret. Being aware of your communication includes being conscious not

COMMUNICATION & DIVERSITY

Communication Principles for a Lifetime: Principles for All Cultures?

Are the five Principles for a Lifetime applicable to all human communication, across a variety of cultures? Culture is the learned system of knowledge, behavior, attitudes, beliefs, values, and norms that is shared by a group of people. Is it true that people of all cultures should be aware of their communication, use and interpret verbal and nonverbal messages, listen and respond thoughtfully, and appropriately adapt their messages to others?

We suggest that these five fundamental principles may provide a common framework for talking about communication in a variety of cultures. We're not suggesting that all cultures use each principle the same way. There are obvious differences from one culture to another in language and use of nonverbal cues (Principles Two and Three), for example. But in all cultures, the use and interpretation of verbal and nonverbal messages are important in determining whether communication is effective. There are

also clear cultural differences in the way people choose to adapt messages to others (Principle Five), but people in all cultures may adapt messages to others in some way, even though adaptations vary from culture to culture.

Do you agree or disagree with our position? In your communication class, there are undoubtedly people from a variety of cultural backgrounds. Respond to the following questions, and then compare your answers with those of your fellow students.

1. How applicable are the five communication principles to your cultural experience?

2. Do any of the communication principles *not* apply in your culture?

3. Can you think of another fundamental communication principle that you believe should be added to our list of five? If so, what is it?

4. Do you agree that these communication principles apply to all people?

only of the present moment but also of who you are, your self-concept, your self-worth, and your perceptions of yourself and others. Being aware of your typical communication style is also part of this foundation principle. For example, some people realize that their communication style is to be emotional when interacting with others. Others may be shy.

As has been noted, self-awareness includes being conscious of your intrapersonal communication messages. By **intrapersonal communication**, we mean the communication that occurs within yourself, including your thoughts, your emotions, and your perceptions of yourself and others. Talking to yourself is an example of intrapersonal communication. Although our intrapersonal communication is often the focus of psychologists, our intrapersonal messages also form the basis of our communication with others.[83]

intrapersonal communication
Communication that occurs within yourself, including your thoughts and emotions.

Competent communicators are aware of the choices they make when they communicate both intrapersonally and with others; incompetent communicators react to others' messages with thoughtless, quick, knee-jerk responses. Because they do not mindfully censor themselves, they may blurt out obscene, offensive, or profane words. Ineffective communicators operate in an unthinking "default" mode. Being aware of our communication is a foundation principle because all the choices we make when communicating rest on our ability to make conscious choices when we respond to others.

Earlier in this chapter, we noted that human communication is the process of making sense out of the world and sharing that sense with others. Being aware of who we are and how we perceive, or "make sense of," what we observe is a fundamental principle that helps explain both effective and ineffective communication.

Principle One also involves being aware of not just your own communication, but also of what others do and say. We are more effective communicators if we are aware of how other people communicate. In the next chapter, we develop the principle of being aware of self and others. We also describe how this principle relates to a variety of communication situations.

Principle Two: Effectively Use and Interpret Verbal Messages

The second principle we introduce here and elaborate on in Chapter 3 is to use and interpret verbal messages effectively. Verbal messages are created with language. A **language** consists of symbols and a system of rules (grammar) that make it possible for people to understand one another.

language
The system of symbols (words or vocabulary) structured by rules (grammar) that makes it possible for people to understand one another.

As we noted earlier, a symbol is a word, sound, gesture, or visual image that represents a thought, concept, object, or experience. When you read the words on this page, you are looking at symbols that trigger meaning. The word is not the thing it represents; it simply symbolizes the thing or idea.

Your reading skill permits you to make sense out of symbols. The word *tree*, for example, may trigger a thought of the tree you may be reading under now, a tree in your own yard or a nearby park, or a great sequoia you saw on your family vacation in Yosemite National Park. Effective communicators use appropriate symbols to create accurate meaning. Author Daniel Quinn once commented, "No story is devoid of meaning, if you know how to look for it. This is as true of nursery rhymes and daydreams as it is of epic poems."[84] Meaning is created when people have a common or shared understanding.

The effective communicator both encodes and decodes messages accurately; he or she selects appropriate symbols to form a message and carefully interprets the messages of others. The process of using and interpreting symbols is the essence of how we make sense out of the world and share that sense with others. Some people feared that greater use of texting would lead to lower skills in language use and overall literacy. Research doesn't support that supposition, however: People who send and receive numerous text messages show no deterioration of language and literacy skills.[85]

Words have power. The words we use to describe ourselves and our world have considerable influence on how we perceive what we experience. Any good advertising copywriter knows how to use words to create a need or desire for a product. Political consultants tell politicians how to craft sound bites that will create just the right audience response. And words can hurt us. As Robert Fulghum wisely noted, "Sticks and stones may break our bones, but words break our hearts."[86] Words have the ability to offend and create stress. For example, derogatory words about someone's gender or ethnicity can do considerable harm. Throughout this book, we will present strategies and suggestions for selecting the best word or symbol to enhance your listeners' understanding.

Principle Three: Effectively Use and Interpret Nonverbal Messages

Messages are also nonverbal. **Nonverbal communication** is communication by means other than written or spoken language that creates meaning for someone. Nonverbal messages can communicate powerful ideas or express emotions with greater impact than mere words alone. An optimistic hitchhiker's extended thumb and an irate driver's extended finger are nonverbal symbols with clear and intentional meanings. But not all nonverbal symbols are clearly interpreted or even consciously expressed. You may not be aware of your frown when someone asks whether he or she may sit next to you in a vacant seat in a restaurant. Or your son may excitedly be telling you about his field trip to the fire station while you stare at the screen of your smartphone. You have no intention of telling your son he is not important, but your lack of nonverbal responsiveness speaks volumes. Our nonverbal messages communicate how we feel toward others.

When there is a contradiction between what you say and what you do, your nonverbal message is more believable than your verbal message. When asked how your meal is, you may tell your server that the meal is "great," but your nonverbal message—facial expression and flat tone of voice—clearly communicates your unhappiness with the cuisine. As was noted earlier, when we discussed the concept of content and relationship messages, our nonverbal cues often tell people how to interpret what we are saying.

Effective communicators develop skill in interpreting the nonverbal messages of others. They also monitor their own messages to avoid unintentionally sending contradictory verbal and nonverbal messages. It's sometimes hard to interpret nonverbal messages because they don't have a neat beginning and ending point—the flow of information is continuous. It might not be clear where one gesture stops and another begins. Cultural differences, combined with the fact that so many different nonverbal channels (such as eye contact, facial expression, gestures, posture) can be used at the same time, make it tricky to "read" someone's nonverbal message accurately. We provide an expanded discussion of the power of nonverbal messages in Chapter 4.

nonverbal communication
Communication by means other than written or spoken language that creates meaning for someone.

▼ Your gestures, facial expressions, and other nonverbal cues communicate your emotions, often more honestly than your words do. Is this person telling the truth?
Karelnoppe/Shutterstock

Principle Four: Listen and Respond Thoughtfully to Others

So far, our list of principles may appear to place much of the burden of achieving communication success on the person sending the message. But effective communication with others also places considerable responsibility on the listener. As we explained earlier, because communication is a transactional process—both senders and receivers are mutually and usually simultaneously expressing and responding to symbols—listening to words with sensitivity and "listening between the lines" to nonverbal messages join our list of fundamental principles.

Listening can be hard because it looks easy. You spend more time listening than you do performing any other communication activity—probably more than any other thing you do except sleep.[87] But research suggests that many, if not most, of us do not always listen effectively. Both psychological, or internal, noise (our own thoughts, needs, and emotions) and external distractions (noise in the surroundings in which we listen) can create barriers to effective listening.

A widespread perception that listening is a passive rather than an active task also makes listening and accurately interpreting information a challenge. Effective listening is *not* a passive task at all; the effective and sensitive listener works hard to stay on task and focus mindfully on a sender's message. Effective listening requires you to develop an orientation or sensitivity to others when you listen and respond. When you are **other-oriented**, you consider the needs, motives, desires, and goals of your communication partners while still maintaining your own integrity. The choices you make in both forming the message and selecting when to share it should take into consideration your partner's thoughts and feelings. People who are skilled communicators both listen and respond with sensitivity; they are other-oriented, rather than self-focused.

other-oriented

Being focused on the needs and concerns of others while maintaining one's personal integrity.

Principle Five: Appropriately Adapt Messages to Others

It is not enough to be sensitive and to accurately understand others; you must use the information you gather to modify the messages you construct. It is important to **adapt** your response appropriately to your listener. When you adapt a message, you make choices about how best to formulate both your message content and delivery, and how to respond to someone, in order to ethically achieve your communication goals. Regardless of whether you are giving a speech, talking with a friend, or participating in a small group meeting, as an effective communicator you consider who the listeners are when deciding what to say and how best to say it. Adapting to a listener does *not* mean that you tell a listener only what he or she wants to hear. That would be unethical. Adapting involves appropriately editing and shaping your responses so that others accurately understand your messages and so that you achieve your goal without coercing or using false information or other unethical methods.

One of the elements of a message that you adapt when communicating with others is the structure or organization of what you say. Informal interpersonal conversations typically do not follow a rigid, outlined structure. Our conversation freely bounces from one topic to another. Formal speeches delivered in North America, however, are usually expected to have a more explicit structure—an introduction, a body, and a conclusion—with clearly identified major ideas. Other cultures, such as those in the Middle East, expect a greater use of stories, examples, and illustrations, rather than a clearly structured, outlined presentation. Knowing your audience's expectations can help you adapt your message so that it will be listened to and understood. In Chapter 6, we will discuss this principle in greater detail by discussing the diverse nature of potential listeners and how to adapt to them. Adapting to differences in culture and gender, for example, may mean the difference between a message that is well received and one that creates hostility. Effective communicators not only listen and respond with sensitivity; they use the information they gather to shape the message and delivery of their responses to others.

adapt

To adjust both what is communicated and how a message is communicated; to make choices about how best to formulate a message and respond to others to achieve your communication goals.

STUDY GUIDE:

〉 REVIEW, APPLY, AND ASSESS

Why Study Communication?

1.1 Explain why it is important to study communication.

REVIEW: Communication is essential for life. It is important to learn about communication because being a skilled communicator can help you obtain a good job, enhance the quality of your relationships, and improve your physical and emotional health.

APPLY: Why are you here? What benefits do you hope to gain or what questions do you hope to answer by studying human communication?

ASSESS: Keep a communication log for one day. Note the amount of time you read, write, speak, and listen. How does your log compare with the statistics presented in this chapter?

The Communication Process

1.2 Define communication and describe five characteristics of the communication process.

REVIEW: At its most basic level, communication is the process of acting on information. Human communication is the process of making sense out of the world and sharing that sense with others by creating meaning through verbal and nonverbal messages. Communication is inescapable, irreversible, complicated, and governed by rules. It also emphasizes content and relationships.

KEY TERMS:
communication	content dimension
human communication	relationship dimension
symbol	rule

APPLY: List the communication rules for a situation you are in regularly, such as a particular class, a regular group or team meeting, or a line at a deli or coffee shop on campus.

ASSESS: How effectively can you identify the content and relational messages when interacting with others? After you conclude a conversation with a friend or acquaintance today, take a moment to write down the content of the message (the essence of what was said) and the relational message (how positive or negative, pleasant or unpleasant the interaction was). Were you aware of which specific behaviors led you to perceive the conversation as pleasant or unpleasant?

Communication Models

1.3 Explain three communication models.

REVIEW: Early models viewed human communication as a simple message-transfer process. Later models evolved to view communication as interaction and then as simultaneous transaction. Key components of communication include source, receiver, message, channel, noise, context, and feedback.

KEY TERMS:
source	channel
encoding	noise
decoding	feedback
receiver	context
message	

APPLY: Describe in your own words an example of a communication transaction in which all parties are sending and receiving information at the same time.

ASSESS: Reflect on a recent conflict you had with another person. Analyze the exchange by identifying the components in the communication (such as source, receiver, message, channel, etc.). What could or should have been changed to enhance the quality of communication?

Communication Competence

1.4 Describe three criteria that can be used to determine whether communication is competent.

REVIEW: To be both effective and appropriate, a communication message should be understood as the communicator intended it to be understood, achieve the communicator's intended effect, and be ethical.

KEY TERMS:
communication competence   ethics

APPLY: Identify recent communication situations in which you felt competent and those in which you felt incompetent. What factors helped you determine whether your communication was competent or incompetent?

ASSESS: Based on the description of communication competence in this chapter, think about the communication you typically have with your instructor in this course. How would you assess your communication competence with him or her?

Communication in the 21st Century

1.5   Describe the nature of communication in the 21st century.

REVIEW: Today, we commonly use various forms of media to communicate, either asynchronously or synchronously. Mediated communication is usually more anonymous than in-person communication and places less emphasis on a person's physical appearance. Shy or introverted people may prefer online to in-person communication, as do people who are feeling temporary uncertainty about their relationships.

KEY TERMS:
mediated communication   mass communication

APPLY: How much time do you spend using technology to communicate with others? Keep a log for a specific period of time (such as six hours, twelve hours, or a day) noting how much you use your phone, computer, and other devices to read, write, speak, and listen.

ASSESS: Overall, consider how effectively you use technology to communicate with others. Do you, for example, glance at your phone when talking with others? Do you multitask and perhaps miss some messages because you are trying to do several things at once?

Communication Contexts

1.6   Identify and explain three communication contexts.

REVIEW: Three classic contexts of unmediated communication that researchers have studied are (1) interpersonal communication, in which two people interact simultaneously and mutually influence each other, usually for the purpose of managing relationships; (2) small group communication, interaction among a small group of people who share a common purpose or goal, who feel a sense of belonging to the group, and who exert influence on the others in the group; and (3) presentational communication, in which a speaker addresses an audience for the purpose of informing, persuading, or entertaining. Communication in organizational and healthcare settings involves all three contexts.

KEY TERMS:
interpersonal communication	impersonal communication
	small group communication
presentational communication	organizational communication
rhetoric	health communication

APPLY: Which contexts of communication have you experienced so far today? Have you communicated interpersonally or in small groups? Have you listened to or given a presentation?

ASSESS: In which of the three contexts of in-person communication do you have the strongest skills? Which area(s) do you want to improve and what skills would you like to develop?

Communication Principles for a Lifetime

1.7   List and explain five fundamental principles of communication.

REVIEW: The following five principles are fundamental to good communication.

1. Be aware of your communication with yourself and others. Being mindful of your communication is important to help you improve your communication.
2. Effectively use and interpret verbal messages. Words are powerful and influence our thoughts, actions, and relationships with others.
3. Effectively use and interpret nonverbal messages. Unspoken cues provide important information about our emotions, feelings, and attitudes.
4. Listen and respond thoughtfully to others. Being able to interpret the messages of others accurately enhances comprehension and relational empathy.
5. Appropriately adapt messages to others. It is important to adapt messages to others to enhance both understanding and empathy.

KEY TERMS:
intrapersonal communication	nonverbal communication
	other-oriented
language	adapt

APPLY: As we noted at the beginning of this chapter, the five principles described in Figure 1.5 and throughout this text may not tell you everything you need to know about communication. What additional communication principle(s) would you suggest adding to the list?

ASSESS: Which communication principle or principles do you perform well? Which principles do you need to improve?

⟩ THE PRINCIPLE POINTS

Principle One:

Be aware of your communication with yourself and others.

- Be aware of your intrapersonal communication.
- Be conscious of how your intrapersonal communication or self-talk has an effect on your communication with others and your overall communication behavior.
- Be aware of the communication behavior of others.

Principle Two:

Effectively use and interpret verbal messages.

- Use clear and precise words to explain ideas and concepts to others.
- Make a concerted effort to accurately interpret the words of others.

Principle Three:

Effectively use and interpret nonverbal messages.

- Use nonverbal, unspoken cues to express feelings and emotions to others or to modify the explicit verbal message you are communicating to others.
- Make a conscious effort to accurately decode the nonverbal messages of others.

Principle Four:

Listen and respond thoughtfully to others.

- Be other-oriented by taking special care to listen to both the verbal and the nonverbal messages of others.
- Be deliberate in how you provide feedback to those to whom you are listening.

Principle Five:

Appropriately adapt messages to others.

- Use your listening and nonverbal communication skills to help you appropriately adjust both your message and how you communicate it to others.
- Make ethical choices about how to best formulate a message and respond to others to achieve your communication goals.

CHAPTER 2

EXPLORING SELF-AWARENESS AND COMMUNICATION

A person who buries his head in the sand offers an engaging target. —MABEL A. KEENAN

saltodemata/Shutterstock

→ CHAPTER OUTLINE

- Self-Awareness: How Well Do You Know Yourself?

- Self-Concept: Who Are You?

- Self-Esteem: What's Your Value?

- Communication and the Enhancement of Self-Esteem

- The Perception Process

- Communicate to Enhance Your Powers of Perception

- Study Guide: Review, Apply, and Assess

LEARNING OBJECTIVES

After studying this chapter, you should be able to

2.1 Discuss the importance of self-awareness in the process of improving one's communication skills.

2.2 Describe the components of the self-concept and major influences on self-concept development.

2.3 Describe how gender, social comparisons, self-expectations, and self-fulfilling prophecies affect one's self-esteem.

2.4 Practice six communication strategies for enhancing one's self-esteem.

2.5 Explain the three stages of perception and why people differ in their perceptions of people and events.

2.6 Summarize three communication strategies that can improve one's powers of perception.

These days, most college students have some sort of online presence, usually on multiple social media sites. A 2016 survey of college students' preferred social media sites lists the top three as Instagram, Snapchat, and Facebook, primarily because they allow users to post, view, and comment on photos and videos.[1] The sites used least by subjects in the study included LinkedIn because of students' lesser interest in developing a professional network and Pinterest because of the limitations of posting in set categories. The survey revealed that college students use social networking sites from 1 to 10 hours per day, with heavier use on weekends.

Do you think much about your choices when you use social media? Do you pause to consider who will see your post, photo, or video? Do you wonder who might comment on it and how you'll deal with people's responses? Some people regularly change their Facebook profile photo, while others leave the same one up for years. Does your photo depict you as you currently are, or is it a photo of you at a younger age, when you may have been thinner and had more hair? What about your privacy settings—what information do you share and what do you keep private? Developing an engaging and appropriate social media presence relies on a central, important element: self-awareness.

Stephen Covey, author of *The Seven Habits of Highly Effective People*, describes self-awareness as a characteristic that "enables us to stand apart and examine even the way we 'see' ourselves."[2] Interpersonal communication scholar David Johnson points out the importance of self-awareness: "Self-awareness is the key to self-knowledge, self-understanding, and self-disclosure. Being open with another person begins with being aware of who you are and what you are like. To disclose your feelings and reactions, you must be aware of them.[3]

Figure 2.1 presents the Communication Principles for a Lifetime model introduced in Chapter 1. The five principles provide the foundation for effective communication in various contexts you may encounter throughout your life. In this chapter, we explore the first principle: *Be aware of your communication with yourself and others*. Developing self-awareness involves being conscious not only of the present moment, but also of who you are, your values, and your perception of yourself and others.

FIGURE 2.1 Communication Principles for a Lifetime

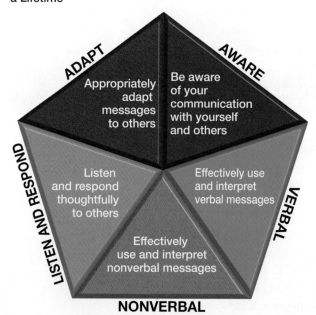

Self-Awareness: How Well Do You Know Yourself?

2.1   Discuss the importance of self-awareness in the process of improving one's communication skills.

Benjamin Franklin once said, "There are three things extremely hard: steel, a diamond, and to know oneself."[4] Knowing oneself is a lifelong process; we never reach a point at which we have maxed out our self-awareness. But it's also true that many of us experience phases of heightened self-awareness in life, perhaps in moments or periods when we're acutely aware that we're learning something important—something that will change us in some profound way. (College years can be full of these moments.) While a great deal of self-awareness comes gradually and simply, some is thrust upon us in dramatic fashion, causing us to take leaps in our maturity and understanding of ourselves. In this chapter, we deal with all forms of awareness—the simple and the profound, the casual and the dramatic—because any kind of awareness influences how we communicate and respond to communication from others.

By one definition, **self-awareness** is "the capacity to observe and reflect upon one's own mental states."[5] A related view holds that self-awareness, sometimes referred to as **symbolic self-awareness**, is the unique human ability to develop a representation of oneself and communicate that representation to others through language.[6]

The better we understand the complex, multilayered nature of the self, the more aware we will become of our own being; this awareness is critical to effective communication. Research shows that people who are highly self-aware are more able to anticipate others' opinions of themselves, take others' perspectives, and communicate empathy.[7] A framework attributed to Abraham Maslow helps explain the process of becoming self-aware. The same framework has also been used to explain our attainment of communication skill. It suggests that people operate at one of four levels:

1. *Unconscious incompetence.* We are unaware of our own incompetence. We don't know what we don't know.

2. *Conscious incompetence.* At this level, we become aware or conscious that we are not competent; we know what we don't know.

3. *Conscious competence.* We are aware that we know or can do something, but it has not yet become an integrated skill or habit.

4. *Unconscious competence.* At this level, skills become second nature. We know or can do something but don't have to concentrate to be able to act on that knowledge or draw on that skill.

To illustrate this framework, let's look at an example. Your coworker, Stella, sometimes says inappropriate things; she just doesn't seem to know how to talk to people in a way that doesn't make her come across like she was raised by wolves. Stella is at Maslow's level 1 when it comes to communication: She doesn't know that she communicates poorly. Eventually, customers and coworkers complain to Stella's supervisor. The supervisor calls Stella into the office, reprimands her for her poor communication skills, and requires her to enroll in communication training so that she can improve. Now Stella is at level 2 because she has become conscious of her own incompetence as a communicator. Stella embraces her communication training and, once back on the job, actively works to improve how she relates to coworkers, bosses, and customers. Her hard work pays off when her colleagues notice the changes she's making and provide positive feedback. Stella achieves level 3, in which she is conscious of her own

self-awareness

The capacity to observe and reflect on one's own mental states.

symbolic self-awareness

A unique human ability to develop and communicate a representation of oneself to others through language.

competence as a communicator. If Stella continues to progress over time, at some point she may reach level 4. At that level, communication effectiveness would be incorporated into her style and self-concept and would no longer be something she would need to make a conscious effort to achieve.

Almost any communication skill can be described in terms of these four levels. It's also possible to be at one level with one skill and at a different level with another skill. For instance, you may skillfully meet new people but poorly manage conflict with a close personal friend. Someone may be very engaging when conversing with friends, but she or he would rather have a spinal tap than give a presentation.

Reading a book like this one and taking a communication course like the one you're enrolled in can spark periods of heightened self-awareness. You'll no doubt be challenged to think long and hard about who you are, inventorying what you believe about yourself and how such aspects of identity as gender, ethnicity, nationality, sexual orientation, and social class contribute to your view of self. You'll be encouraged to go a step further to consider how you communicate that view of self to others. But the key beginning point is awareness. As Phil McGraw (a.k.a. Dr. Phil) says, "Can't fix what you don't acknowledge."

Self-Concept: Who Are You?

2.2 Describe the components of the self-concept and major influences on self-concept development.

If someone asked you, "Who are you?" would you respond with basic demographic information such as your age and where you're from? Or would you describe yourself in relation to groups and organizations to which you belong? Or might you talk about the various roles you assume, such as "I'm a student at State" or "I'm so-and-so's daughter (or son)"? Whatever answer you give will be incomplete because you can't really convey the totality of who you are to others.

Psychologist Karen Horney defines **self** as "that central inner force, common to all human beings and yet unique in each which is the deep source of growth."[8] Your "Who are you?" responses are part of your **self-concept**—your interior identity or subjective description of who you think you are, which remains relatively stable despite the changing world in which you live.[9] The self-concept is the way you consistently describe yourself to others; it is deeply rooted and slow to change.[10]

Self-Concept Components

The self-concept contains many components, but three critical ones are your **attitudes**, **beliefs**, and **values**. Table 2.1 describes each of these components in more detail. Of these three aspects, attitudes are the most superficial and likely to change, whereas values are more fundamental to a person and least likely to change.

self
The sum of who you are as a person; your central inner force.

self-concept
Your interior identity or subjective description of who you think you are.

attitudes
Learned predispositions to respond to a person, object, or idea in a favorable or unfavorable way.

beliefs
Ways in which you structure your understanding of reality—what is true and what is false.

values
Enduring concepts of good and bad or right and wrong.

TABLE 2.1 Self-Concept Components

Component	Definition	Dimensions	Example
Attitudes	Learned predispositions to respond favorably or unfavorably toward something	Likes–Dislikes	You like ice cream, video games, and posting photos on social media.
Beliefs	Ways in which you structure reality	True–False	You believe your parents love you.
Values	Enduring concepts of right and wrong	Good–Bad	You value honesty and truth.

COMMUNICATION & DIVERSITY

Self-Concept from East and West

The view of a relatively stable self-concept is culturally rooted in a Western perspective. Communication scholar Gabriel Bukobza has found that people from Eastern cultures tend to view the self-concept as "malleable, contextual, inconsistent, relational, interdependent, and oriented to group hierarchy."[11] According to this view, your self-concept could be quite open to change.

Different cultures have different views of the *sources* of the self-concept. In Asian countries, the self-concept tends to be constructed around significant social groups—one's immediate family, extended family, or community—with each member wanting to fit in and feeling a strong commitment to group identity. In contrast, Westerners tend to use personal reflection and investigation to form the self-concept and then pursue feedback from others to validate it.[12] We like it when others' views correspond with our own view of self, and we tend to reject messages (and people) who negate our self-concept.

In a world where access to members of other cultural groups is only a mouse click away, remember that even the most basic element—the self-concept—can vary interculturally. People in the United States tend to hold independence and individuality as core elements of our self-concepts, but it's important to refrain from judging someone from another culture whose self-concept stems from strong ties to others and an emphasis on community over individual.[13]

The self-concept that we develop through communication with our family stays with us throughout our life. Wong Yu Liang/Fotolia

One or Many Selves?

"I'm just not myself this morning," sighs Sandy, as she drags herself out the door to head to class. If she isn't herself, *who is she?* Does each of us have just one self? Is there a more "real" self buried somewhere within?

One of the most enduring and widely accepted frameworks for understanding the self was developed by philosopher William James. He identified three components of the self: the material self, the social self, and the spiritual self.[14]

The Material Self　Perhaps you've heard the statement "You are what you eat." The material self goes a step further than that by suggesting "You are what you have." The **material self** is a total of all the tangible things you feel ownership over: your body, your possessions, your home.

material self
The element of the self reflected in all the tangible things you own.

One element of the material self receives considerable attention in our culture: the body. Do you like the way you look? Most of us would like to change something about our appearance. Studies have determined that in the United States, women and girls tend to experience more negative feelings about their bodies than men and boys, which affects how women and girls view themselves.[15] Women also feel more intense pressure to be physically attractive than men, according to research.[16] However, research also shows that men and boys increasingly experience weight problems and body dissatisfaction from comparing themselves with the ideal muscular male bodies displayed in the media (including male characters in video games). Increasingly, men and boys are concerned about what others want and expect them to look like.[17] When there is a discrepancy between our desired material self and our self-concept, we may respond to eliminate the discrepancy. We may try to lose weight, have a nose job, get another tattoo, or buy new clothes.

social self

Your concept of self as developed through your personal, social interactions with others.

The Social Self Your **social self** is the part of you that interacts with others. William James believed that you have as many social selves as you have people who recognize you, and that you change who you are depending on the people with whom you interact. For example, when you talk to your best friend, you're willing to "let your hair down" and reveal more thoughts and feelings than you might with your professor, parents, or boss. Each relationship you have with another person is unique because you bring to it a unique social self. This doesn't mean that you're false with people. Rather, you're multifaceted because you have different selves in relation to different people.

Have you ever been in an important relationship that changed your self-concept? As we said, the self-concept remains fairly stable over time, however, research has explored the topic of "when 'we' changes 'me.'"[18] When people are in relationships (particularly romantic or intimate ones) that are supportive, accommodating, and forgiving (when the need for forgiveness arises), their self-concepts tend to improve and expand. Conversely, when people are in relationships that are not supportive and involve such attributes as jealousy, revenge seeking, and threats of breakups, their self-concepts tend to degrade.

spiritual self

Your concept of self based on your beliefs and your sense of who you are in relation to other forces in the universe; also includes your thoughts and introspections about your values and moral standards.

The Spiritual Self Your **spiritual self** is a mixture of your beliefs and your sense of who you are in relationship to other forces in the universe. Notice that this aspect of the self is termed "spiritual," not "religious." The term *religious* implies adherence to a specific religion or faith, typically accompanied by a belief in a supreme being or creator. However, people who see themselves as spiritual often don't subscribe to any one religion, preferring to develop their views from an array of philosophies and belief systems. From William James's perspective, the spiritual self contains all your internal thoughts and introspections about your values and moral standards. It's not dependent on what you own or with whom you talk; it's the essence of who you *think* you are and how you *feel* about yourself. It's your attempt to understand your inner essence, whether you view that essence as consciousness, spirit, or soul. Your spiritual self is the part of you that attempts to answer the question "Why am I here?"

RECAP

William James's Dimensions of Self

Dimension	Definition	Examples
Material Self	The component of self derived from physical elements that reflect who you are	The self you reveal through your body, clothes, car, phone
Social Self	The variety of selves that appear in different situations and roles, reflected in interactions with others	Your informal self interacting with friends; your formal self interacting with your professors
Spiritual Self	The component of self based on introspection about values, morals, and beliefs	Belief or disbelief in a supreme being or force; regard for life in all its forms

How the Self-Concept Develops

Research suggests we address the question "Who am I?" through four basic means: (1) our communication with other people, (2) our association with groups, (3) the roles we assume, and (4) our self-labels.

Communication With Others   A valued colleague of ours often says, when he teaches communication courses, that every time you lose a relationship you lose an opportunity to see yourself. What he means is that we don't come to know and understand ourselves in a vacuum. We learn who we are by communicating with others, receiving their feedback, making sense out of it, and internalizing or rejecting all or part of it, such that we are altered by the experience. For example, let's say you like to think of yourself as a comedian. Now think about it for a moment: How would you know you were funny if not for the people who laugh at the humorous things you say or do?

In 1902, scholar Charles Horton Cooley first advanced the notion that we form our self-concepts by seeing ourselves in a figurative looking glass: We learn who we are by interacting with others, much as we look into a mirror and see our reflection.[19] Like Cooley, theorist George Herbert Mead also believed that our sense of self develops as a consequence of our past and present relationships with others.[20] Contemporary research confirms this idea. Results from a study of self-concept development in adolescents reinforced the important role parents play in developing a strong sense of self in their children. When parents, both generally and through daily conversations, affirmed their adolescents' sense of self and challenged them to realize their greater potential, this form of communication had a powerful effect on their children's self-concept development.[21]

We each have two components to our identity. Your **avowed identity** is one you personally assign to yourself and portray, such as student, athlete, or friend. Your **ascribed identity** involves characteristics others attribute or assign to you, which you may or may not agree with. For example, you may think you're a shy person (avowed identity), but others perceive your shyness as being aloof or conceited (ascribed identity). When contradictions emerge, you could simply dismiss others' views, but you'll enhance your self-awareness if you instead process the ascribed identity. Take it in, contemplate why people see you the way they do, and consider whether any changes are necessary in the way you relate to others. Avowed and ascribed identities aren't static; they shift and are negotiated through interactions with others.[22]

avowed identity

An identity you assign to yourself and portray.

ascribed identity

An identity assigned to you by others.

Association With Groups   I'm a native New Yorker. I'm a soccer player. I'm a rabbi. I'm a real estate agent. Politically, I'm an independent. Each of these self-descriptive statements answers the "Who am I?" question by citing identification with a group or organization. Our awareness of who we are is often linked to those with whom we associate. Some groups we're born into; others we choose on our own. Either way, group associations are significant parts of our identities.[23]

Assumed Roles   A large part of most people's answers to the "Who am I?" question reflects roles they assume in their lives. Mother, aunt, brother, manager, salesperson, teacher, partner, and student are labels that imply certain expectations for behavior, and they are important in shaping the self-concept.

Sex (biological) and gender (psychological and cultural) assert a powerful influence on the self-concept from birth on. As soon as many parents learn the sex of their child, they begin socializing their child according to cultural roles. They give their children sex-stereotypical toys, such as baseball mitts, train sets, and guns for boys, and dolls, tea sets, and

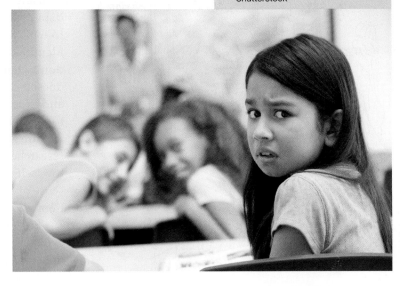

▼ Although identities change along with our circumstances and relationships, messages we receive early in life can have a long-lasting influence on our identities. How might an experience like this one shape these girls' later views of themselves?
Monkey Business Images/ Shutterstock

RECAP

How the Self-Concept Develops

Communication with Others	The self-concept develops as we communicate with others, receive their feedback, make sense out of it, and internalize or reject all or part of it.
Association with Groups	We develop our self-concept partly because of, and through, our identification with groups or organizations.
Assumed Roles	The self-concept is affected by roles we assume, such as son or daughter, employee, parent, spouse, or student.
Self-Labels	The terms we use to describe our attitudes, beliefs, values, and actions play a role in shaping the self-concept.

self-reflexiveness

The human ability to think about what you are doing while you are doing it.

dress-up kits for girls. These practices, which are based on cultural expectations and traditions, play a major role in shaping our self-concept and our behavior.[24] By the time we reach adulthood, our self-concepts are quite distinguishable by sex, with men describing themselves more in terms of giftedness, power, and invulnerability, and women viewing themselves in terms of likability and morality.[25]

Self-Labels   Although our self-concept is deeply affected by others, we aren't blank slates they can write on. The labels we use to describe our own attitudes, beliefs, values, and actions also play a role in shaping our self-concept.[26] Where do our labels come from? We interpret what we experience; we are self-reflexive. **Self-reflexiveness** is the human ability to think about what we're doing while we're doing it. We talk to ourselves about ourselves. We are both participants and observers in all that we do.[27] This dual role encourages us to use labels to describe who we are.

Self-Esteem: What's Your Value?

self-esteem

Your assessment of your worth or value as reflected in your perception of such things as your skills, abilities, talents, and appearance.

self-concept clarity

The extent to which beliefs about oneself are clearly and confidently identified and stable over time.

2.3 **Describe how gender, social comparisons, self-expectations, and self-fulfilling prophecies affect one's self-esteem.**

It may sound crass to consider your *value*, but you do this every day. Your assessment of your value is termed **self-esteem**. This *evaluation* of who you are is closely related to your self-concept, or your *description* of who you are.[28] Feminist author Gloria Steinem explains that, "It's a feeling of 'clicking in' when that self is recognized, valued, discovered, *esteemed*—as if we literally plug into an inner energy that is ours alone, yet connects us to everything else."[29] While self-concept focuses on who you are, self-esteem centers on how you *feel* about who you are.

While the self-concept pertains to your enduring identity, self-esteem pertains more to your current state of mind or view of self. But are the two aspects of the self related? Researchers continue to explore that very question, focusing on the notion of **self-concept clarity**, which Canadian psychologist Jennifer Campbell defines as the extent to which beliefs about oneself are clearly and confidently identified and stable over time.[30] It doesn't mean that you don't change as a person or that your view of yourself doesn't change; we know that people evolve as they mature and experience new things. But self-concept clarity relates to the stability associated with having a clear sense of who you are and feeling confident about that. One of the things researchers have determined is that people who suffer from low self-esteem also tend to have a less clearly defined sense of self; in other words, they tend to have more questions about who they are.[31]

Self-esteem can fluctuate because of relatively minor events, such as getting a high grade on a paper, or major upheavals, such as the breakup of an important relationship.[32]

Theresa McCracken/CartoonStock

College graduates who struggle to land a job related to their field of study may suffer a downturn in self-esteem.[33] Self-esteem can rise or fall within the course of a day; sometimes just a look from someone (or being ignored) can send you into a tailspin and make you feel devalued. A certain level of self-esteem can also last for a while—you may have a series of months or even years that you look back on and think, "I felt pretty lousy about myself in those days. Glad that period is over." Four factors provide clues about the nature of self-esteem: gender, social comparisons, self-expectations, and the self-fulfilling prophecy.

Gender

Your **gender** is a complex cultural construction that includes your biological sex; psychological and emotional characteristics that cause you to be masculine, feminine, or androgynous (a combination of feminine and masculine traits); your attitudes about appropriate roles and behavior for the sexes in society; and your sexual orientation (to whom you are sexually attracted).[34] All of these elements affect your self-esteem.

Research documents ways that boys' self-esteem develops differently from girls' during childhood and adolescence. Even though women have made great strides in recent decades, the United States is still considered a patriarchal (male-dominated) culture. In such a culture, women and girls suffer loss of self-esteem to a greater degree than men and boys. This trend continues into adulthood.[35] Several prominent women have written books addressing the problem of American women's general lack of self-esteem and confidence. Katty Kay and Claire Shipman's *The Confidence Code*, Sheryl Sandberg's *Lean In*, and Mika Brzezinski's *Knowing Your Value* all speak to women's general lack of belief in their own worth and how such a deficit impedes their progress, both professionally and personally.[36]

gender

A cultural construction that includes one's biological sex, psychological and emotional characteristics, attitudes about the sexes, and sexual orientation.

Social Comparisons

One way we become more aware of ourselves and derive our sense of self-worth is by measuring ourselves against others, a process called **social comparison**.[37] I'm good at basketball (because I'm part of a winning team); I can't cook (others cook better than I do); I'm good at meeting people (whereas many people are uncomfortable interacting with people they've just met); I'm not handy (but my dad can fix anything). Each of these statements implies a judgment about how you perform certain tasks in comparison to others.

One powerful social comparison that contributes to self-esteem fluctuation is the use of social media. Surveys of U.S. adults reveal that Facebook is the most popular social networking platform, primarily because of a significant increase in older adults joining the site in recent years.[38] Given that 68% of all American adults are now Facebook users, the majority of whom report checking in on the site daily, it's no wonder that researchers are concerned with how people socially compare themselves to others online.

Some researchers find that Facebook usage enhances self-esteem, especially when users interact primarily with online close friends.[39] However, other studies suggest that comparing oneself to other Facebook users can be a self-esteem downer. We generally want to hear positive or good news from online close friends, but we can be deeply affected if we receive criticism or negative information from them, causing our self-esteem to suffer. We may also experience self-esteem loss when we read about what others have achieved, as revealed in their posts and profiles. We may also feel loneliness and envy (even depression) when we see

social comparison

Process of comparing oneself to others to measure one's worth.

▲ High-school student Galia Slayen built this life-size Barbie doll to show how unrealistic standards for physical attractiveness can damage the self-esteem of girls and women. According to Slayen, if Barbie were a real woman, she would stand six feet tall and have an 18-inch waist.
CB2/ZOB/WENN.com/Newscom

self-expectations
Goals you set for yourself; how you believe you ought to behave and what you ought to accomplish.

others' posts, photos, or videos, suggesting that they are more beautiful or healthier than we are, they have more fun, or they have more impressive friends or a larger social network. In general, online social comparison can be a risky business for your self-esteem.[40]

It can be self-defeating to take social comparisons too far, to cause your self-esteem to suffer because you compare yourself unfairly or unrealistically to others. If you're going to do any comparing at all, compare yourself to friends and acquaintances, people you know and who are similar to you in many ways, rather than to people who are obviously not like you.

Self-Expectations

Another factor that affects your self-esteem is your estimation of how well you accomplish your goals. **Self-expectations** are goals we set for ourselves, such as losing weight, developing a "buff" body, earning better grades, being elected to an important office in an organization, graduating by a certain time, or acquiring wealth by a certain age. Self-esteem is affected when you evaluate how well you measure up to your own expectations.

Have you set a goal for yourself this semester to make all As? Or perhaps your goal is to focus more on your studies in order to raise your grade point as much as you can? Do such expectations motivate you or put extra stress on you as a student? What if you fall short of these goals? Will you value yourself less, figure out a way to justify not meeting your own expectations, or just blow it off and say "better luck next time?" Some people place enormous expectations on themselves, perhaps because their parents had enormous expectations for them when they were growing up. Being goal-oriented is a good thing, but placing unrealistic, high demands on yourself can backfire, causing your self-esteem to plummet and stress to rise.

COMMUNICATION & SOCIAL MEDIA

The "Selfie"

Be honest: How often do you take a "selfie" on your mobile phone? Selfie-taking is quite the fad these days; it can be entertaining to snap a pic of yourself (with or without others) doing something fun as a way of preserving the moment, documenting your accomplishments, or adding to the camaraderie you feel with your friends, family members, or coworkers. Selfies are cheap, easy, and fun to share, but as with many things, it's interesting to take a longer or broader view of selfie-taking within one's culture.

While posting or sharing selfies can be considered a form of communication and identity expression, some scholars view selfies as objects, as well as forms of media, examples of self-portraiture, and reflections of our culture.[41] Perhaps one day fine art portraits that now hang in museums and galleries will be replaced with selfies of today's famous or important people. Or perhaps the selfie fad will fade away like many other fads.

Research has begun to examine the communicative properties of selfie-taking as a popular activity. Most subjects in studies report that impression management is a prime motivation for taking, sharing, and posting selfies. As this research indicates (which should be no surprise to anyone with a social media account), selfies are clearly a powerful tool we can use to shape how others perceive us. Subjects also revealed that sharing selfies enhanced their self-esteem.[42] But as with most things, overkill is a concern when it comes to taking and sharing selfies; some people may over-selfie and over-share, perhaps out of insecurity or a constant need to self express.

Self-Fulfilling Prophecy

A concept related to the creation of self-expectations is the **self-fulfilling prophecy**, the idea that what you believe about yourself often comes true because you expect it to come true.[43] If you think you'll fail a math quiz because you have labeled yourself inept at math, then you must overcome not only your math deficiency but also your low expectations of yourself when it comes to math. If you hold the self-perception that you're pretty good at conversation, then you're likely to act on that assumption when you talk with someone. Your conversations, true to form, will go well, thus reinforcing your belief in yourself as a good conversationalist.

RECAP

Factors Affecting Self-Esteem

Gender	In male-dominated cultures, girls and women suffer self-esteem loss to a much greater degree than boys and men, primarily as a result of males' feeling better able to do things than females.
Social Comparisons	Judgments about how well or poorly you can perform certain tasks as compared to others can be self-defeating and can cause self-esteem to suffer.
Self-Expectations	Your estimation of how well you perform in comparison to your own goals or self-expectations has a profound effect on self-esteem.
Self-Fulfilling Prophecies	What you believe about yourself often comes true because you expect it to come true.

Communication and the Enhancement of Self-Esteem

2.4   Practice six communication strategies for enhancing one's self-esteem.

We know the damage low self-esteem can do: It can limit our ability to develop and maintain satisfying relationships, to experience career successes and advancement, and to create a generally happy and contented life. Experts suggest that many societal problems stem from our collective feelings of low self-esteem. Our feelings of low self-worth may contribute to our choosing the wrong partners; becoming addicted to drugs, alcohol, sex, online activities, or gambling; experiencing problems with eating and other vital activities; and opting, in too many cases, for death over life. So we owe it to society, as well as ourselves, to develop and work to maintain a healthy sense of self-esteem, as an integral part of the process of becoming more self-aware.

Now is the *prime time* to develop a healthy self-esteem! Although there is no simple list of tricks that can easily make someone with low self-esteem feel valued and appreciated, it is possible to improve how you think about yourself. One thing is clear from research about the process of building and maintaining self-esteem: Communication is essential.[44]

self-fulfilling prophecy
The notion that predictions about one's future are likely to come true because one believes that they will come true.

Engage in Positive Self-Talk

Intrapersonal communication refers to how you take in information or stimuli in your environment and make sense of them.[45] It also involves communication within yourself—**self-talk**, or what some scholars term "inner speech."[46] Your self-concept and level of self-esteem influence the way you talk to yourself about your abilities and skills. The reverse is also true, in that your inner dialogue has an effect on both your self-concept and your level of self-esteem. Athletes use positive self-talk to motivate themselves to play better, especially if they're struggling on the court or field of play. Some also talk to themselves negatively when they perform poorly. Research shows, however, that athletes who engage in negative inner dialogue usually do nothing to improve their performance.[47]

intrapersonal communication
How you take in stimuli in the environment or information and make sense of it; also, thoughts and ideas that you say to yourself.

self-talk
Inner speech; communication with the self.

COMMUNICATION & ETHICS

Can You Have TOO Much Self-Esteem?

For decades, U.S. scholars, teachers, counselors, and others in helping roles have agreed that many people suffer from debilitatingly low levels of self-esteem. However, growing evidence suggests that the efforts of self-help gurus, psychologists, and parents to build children's self-confidence may have paid off in a big way, perhaps too big of a way. Some children in the United States and around the globe have now grown into adults whose self-esteem is so healthy that, in some instances, it has led to self-centeredness.[48] The question now may be, "How much self-esteem is too much?"

Jean Twenge, author of *Generation Me: Why Today's Young Americans Are More Confident, Assertive, Entitled—and More Miserable Than Ever Before*, is a leading researcher of **narcissism**, a personality attribute that carries as its primary characteristic a positive but inflated view of self, especially regarding areas of one's own power, importance, and physical attractiveness.[49] In a study of more than 16,000 college students, Twenge and colleagues found that student narcissism had sharply risen since the 1980s.[50]

People who score high on narcissism scales tend to check Facebook multiple times a day and spend more time on the site than those who are low or moderate in narcissism.[51] Narcissists are also drawn to social networking sites that allow them to self-select information for their profiles (possibly inflating their positive qualities), post photos that reveal their lives to the public, update their status to show others what they're doing or thinking about, and provide positive self-descriptions.[52]

While some positive outcomes are related to narcissism, such as enhanced self-esteem and levels of life satisfaction, the downsides include distorted judgment of one's abilities, risky decision making, and potential addictive disorders and compulsions (e.g., alcohol abuse, compulsive shopping, and gambling).[53]

---

narcissism

An inflated view of self, especially about one's own power and importance.

visualization

The technique of imagining that you are performing a particular task in a certain way; a method of enhancing self-esteem.

▼ Positive self-talk can motivate us to do our best in challenging situations. Are there situations in which you could make your own self-talk more encouraging?
Anna Jurkovska/Shutterstock

Visualize

Visualization—imagining oneself behaving in a certain way—takes the notion of self-talk one step further. Besides just telling yourself that you can achieve your goal, you can actually try to "see" yourself conversing effectively with others, performing well on a project, or exhibiting some other desirable behavior.[54] Because the United States is such a visual culture, most of us have no trouble visualizing elaborate scenarios in our heads.

Research suggests that an apprehensive public speaker can manage her or his fears by visualizing positive results.[55] In fact, visualization reduces anxiety as well as negative self-talk or the number of debilitating thoughts that enter a speaker's consciousness.[56] If you're one of the many people who fear making presentations, try visualizing yourself walking to the front of the room, taking out your well-prepared notes, delivering a well-rehearsed and interesting presentation, and returning to your seat to the sound of applause from your audience. This visualization of positive results enhances confidence and speaking skill. The same technique can be used to boost your sense of self-worth about other tasks or skills.

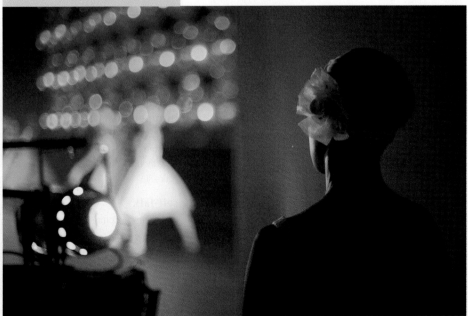

Reframe

The process of redefining events and experiences, of looking at something from a different point of view, is termed **reframing**. When a movie director gets different "takes" or shots of the same scene, she or he is striving to get the best work possible. A director may alter small details, like camera angles or actor movements, to get yet another look or vision for a scene. Just like a movie director, you can reframe your "take" on events or circumstances that cause you to lose self-esteem.[57]

reframing
The process of redefining events and experiences from a different point of view.

For example, your supervisor says you should improve an area of your performance, but instead of engaging in self-talk about how you're terrible at your job, you reframe the event within a larger context. You tell yourself that one negative comment doesn't mean you're a bad employee.

Develop Honest Relationships

The suggestion that you develop honest relationships may sound like the latest advice from some self-help website, but it's actually harder to accomplish than it sounds. Think about it: How many people in your life really give you the straight scoop about yourself? Most of us can count the number of those people on one hand.

Having at least one relationship with someone who will give you honest feedback and help you objectively reflect on your virtues and vices can be extremely beneficial in fostering healthy, positive self-esteem. As we noted earlier, other people play a major role in shaping our self-concept and self-esteem. You don't want to find yourself at a point where you're oblivious to the feedback of others. That kind of attitude can make you narcissistic, unrealistic, and rigid, unable to adjust to life's changing circumstances. Most people who reject or overlook others' honest and objective feedback end up isolated and with low self-esteem.

Another benefit of having a trusting, honest relationship is that you will feel more comfortable telling the other person about feelings of low self-esteem. Conversations in which people can divulge their weaknesses can be very affirming. Yet some people have learned bravado, an ability to communicate a strong, confident air and work their way through challenges or situations in which their self-esteem may suffer.[58] But *everyone*, at some time or another, suffers a lack of self-esteem about *something*. Whether you reveal that fact and to whom you reveal it are important decisions.

Surround Yourself with Positive People

Related to the development of honest relationships is a suggestion about the people you choose to associate with the most in your life. If you want to improve your self-esteem and develop a more positive outlook, it's better to surround yourself with people who tend to have higher levels of self-esteem than people who are "Debbie Downers."

Granted, sometimes you don't have a choice; you get assigned a roommate in college, your instructor pairs you with a lab or study partner, and you rarely get to choose the people

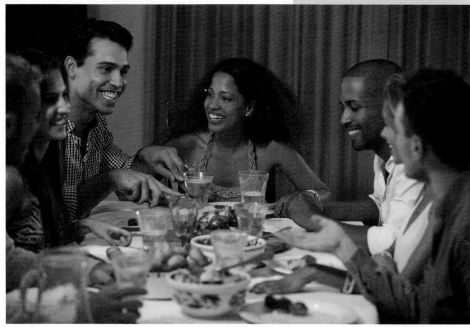

▼ One way to improve your self-esteem is to surround yourself with uplifting people.　Monkey Business Images/Shutterstock

RECAP

Strategies for Enhancing Self-Esteem

Engage in Positive Self-Talk	If you want positive results, talk positively to yourself. If you are self-critical and negative, you may set yourself up for failure. Rephrase doubts and negative thoughts into positive, uplifting encouragement.
Visualize	In anticipation of a significant event, picture how you want the event to go, as a mental rehearsal. If you feel anxious or nervous, visualize success instead of failure.
Reframe	Try to look at experiences and events, especially those that can cause you to lose self-esteem, from a different point of view. Keep the larger picture in mind rather than focusing on one isolated negative incident.
Develop Honest Relationships	Cultivate friends whom you can confide in and who will give you honest feedback for improving your skills and abilities. Accept that feedback in the spirit of enhancing your self-esteem and making yourself a wiser, better person.
Surround Yourself with Positive People	Associating with people with high self-esteem can help you enhance your own self-esteem and develop a more positive outlook.
Lose Your Baggage	Dump your psychological and experiential baggage: Work to move beyond the negatives of your past so that you focus on the present and relieve your self-esteem of the burden of things you cannot change.

you work with. So we're not suggesting that you disassociate yourself from people who have low self-esteem, because that's unrealistic. What we *are* saying is that people with low self-esteem need to be around uplifting people—those whose positive self-regard will rub off on them.

For example, we know an elderly woman, Hazel, who was in good enough health to be able to help the Meals on Wheels organization deliver food to shut-ins in her town. Hazel often talked about how sour many of the people on her route were, how their attitudes had "gone south" because of poor health, limited options, and fading hope. She believed that her main purpose wasn't to deliver a hot meal but to extend the gift of her positive outlook. One time Hazel described what she viewed as a personal triumph: The most sour person on her route—a woman with very low self-esteem and a cranky disposition—began to "thaw." One day when Hazel delivered her meal, the woman greeted her at the front door and seemed genuinely glad to see Hazel. She complained less often as she slowly began to enjoy the warm glow of Hazel's sunny disposition and empathic responses. Hazel felt that the woman's self-esteem had begun to improve and that her outlook on life had begun to change.

Lose Your Baggage

Not making the team. Getting passed over for a key promotion at work. Seeing a long-term relationship end. Feeling like a failure. We've all had experiences we would like to undo or get a second chance at, so we could do them differently or so we could *be* different. We all carry around experiential or psychological baggage, but the key question is, how much space does that baggage take up within your self-concept? To phrase this another way, how negatively is your self-esteem affected by your baggage?

People with low self-esteem tend to lock onto events and experiences that happened years ago and refuse to let go of, or move past, them. Looking back at what we can't change only reinforces a sense of helplessness. Constantly replaying negative experiences only serves to make our sense of self-worth more difficult to repair. A traumatic or defining experience in the past has a serious effect on your self-concept; it will probably always remain a part of you. But it doesn't have to affect your current level of self-esteem. It's important to take mental inventory of experiences in your past and then decide to let go of your baggage and move past those experiences that cause your present-day self-esteem to suffer.[59]

The Perception Process

2.5   Explain the three stages of perception and why people differ in their perceptions of people and events.

This chapter focuses on Principle One of our Communication Principles for a Lifetime: Be aware of your communication with yourself and others. Awareness involves developing greater understanding and skill by becoming more cognizant of yourself, others, and communication. Awareness includes exploring how we perceive ourselves and our communication with others, as well as the many ways in which we perceive other people and their communication. But just what is perception?

On the most basic level, **perception** is the arousal of any of our senses. A sound travels through the air, vibrates in the eardrum, activates the nerves, and sends a signal to the brain. A similar sequence of events takes place when we see, smell, feel, or taste something. So perception begins with the process of attending to stimuli in the environment. The process of perception also includes structuring and making sense of information provided by the senses. You come out of a building and see wet pavement and puddles of water, hear thunder, smell a fresh odor in the air, and feel a few drops of water on your head. You integrate all those bits of information and conclude that it's raining and has been for a while.

Perceiving people, however, goes beyond the simple processing of sensory information. We try to decide what people are like by making judgments about their personalities and giving meaning to their actions by drawing inferences from what we observe.[60] When you meet someone new, you notice basic things like her or his physical appearance, the sound of the person's voice, whether or not he or she smiles, and so forth. You also attend to specific details that the person verbally and nonverbally communicates. Once you've chosen these stimuli to pay attention to, you then categorize the information into some sort of structure that works for you. Finally, you attempt to make sense of your structured perceptions; you assign meaning to what you have perceived. Let's more closely examine each of these three stages in the perception process.

Stage One: Attention and Selection

You're watching a group of parents at a playground with their children. The kids are playing, running around, laughing, and squealing, as children will do. You view the activity, hear the noise, feel the heat of the day on your skin, and smell hot dogs cooking on a grill. They smell so good you can almost taste them. After a moment, a parent jumps up and runs over to comfort a child who has fallen down and is crying. You were watching the action but didn't see the particular incident and didn't register the child's cry amidst all the noise. But the child's parent did. How did this happen?

The ability of parents to discern their own child's voice from a chorus of voices is a mystery of human nature, but it also exemplifies the first stage of perception. Our human senses simply cannot process all the stimuli that are available at any given moment, so we select which sensations make it through to the level of awareness and ignore or filter out the rest. The activities of **attention** and **selection** constitute the first stage of the perception process.

Selectivity can also cause us to fail to perceive information that's important.[61] A professor may be so focused on lecture material that she or he fails to realize that students are lost and not tracking the information. By selecting certain stimuli, we sometimes miss other important clues that might help us better understand what's happening and determine how to respond.

Stage Two: Organization

After we select stimuli to attend to and process, we start to convert the information into convenient, understandable, and efficient patterns that allow us to make sense of what we've observed. This activity, termed **organization**, makes it easier for us to process complex information because it

perception
The arousal of any of your senses.

attention
The act of perceiving stimuli in your environment.

selection
The act of choosing specific stimuli in your environment on which to focus.

organization
Converting information into convenient, understandable, and efficient patterns that allow us to make sense of what we have observed.

▼ Because we cannot process every stimulus in our environment, we need to select which ones will get our attention. When you communicate in a noisy, distracting setting, how can you focus your attention to improve your powers of perception?
People Images/Getty Images

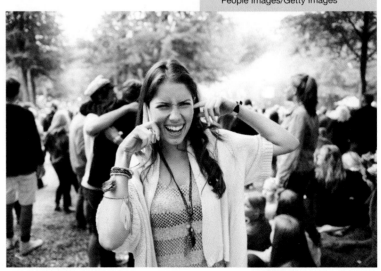

FIGURE 2.2 What Do You See?

Item A   Item B   Item C

OMMUNICATION

allows us to impose the familiar onto the unfamiliar and because we can easily store and recall simple patterns.

Look at the three items in Figure 2.2. What does each of them mean to you? If you're like most people, you'll perceive item A as a horseshoe, item B as the word *communication*, and item C as a circle. Strictly speaking, none of those perceptions is correct. For item A, you see a pattern of dots that you label a horseshoe because a horseshoe is a concept you know and to which you attach various meanings. Rather than processing a set of dots, it's much easier to organize the dots in a way that refers to something familiar. For some people, a more familiar pattern than a horseshoe might be an inverted U. For similar reasons, we organize patterns of stars in the sky into various constellations like the Big and Little Dippers.

In Figure 2.2, items B and C also reveal our inclination to superimpose structure and consistency on what we observe. This tendency leads us to create a familiar word from the meaningless assemblage of letters in item B and to label the figure in item C a circle, even though a circle is a continuous line without any gaps. The process of filling in missing information is called **closure**, and it applies to our perceptions of people as well. When we have an incomplete picture of another human being, we impose a pattern or structure, classify the person on the basis of the information we do have, and fill in the gaps.

Have you ever shown up early to class or to a public gathering, watched other people arriving, and tried to guess what they did for a living, what their personalities were like, or what their backgrounds were? As you looked at people's clothing and saw how they walked or behaved, you made inferences about them. You superimposed some structure by using a general label and filling in the gaps in your information.

closure
The perceptual process of filling in missing information.

interpretation
Attaching meaning to what is attended to, selected, and organized.

RECAP

The Perception Process

Term	Explanation	Example
Perception	The arousal of any of our senses	Hearing the sound of laughter
Attention and Selection	The first stage in the perception process, in which we perceive stimuli and choose which ones to focus our awareness on	Watching TV in your room while hearing giggling and laughter and ignoring the TV show to eavesdrop on the giggler
Organization	The second stage in the perception process, in which we structure stimuli into convenient and efficient patterns	Realizing that the laughter is coming from your younger sister, who's on the phone
Interpretation	The final stage in the perception process, in which we assign meaning to what we have perceived	Deciding that your sister is talking on the phone to her boyfriend because she only laughs like that when she talks to him

Stage Three: Interpretation

Once we've organized stimuli, we're ready to assign meaning, a process termed **interpretation**. We attach meaning to all that we observe. In some cases, the meanings are fairly standardized, as they are for language, for example. But others are much more personalized. If you meet someone whose cologne is too heavy and has a scent you don't like, what's your impression of that person? What if the person also has a great handshake and warm smile? Does that change your interpretation of events and your impression of the person? This example illustrates how we impose meaning on what we observe to complete the perceptual process.

Our interpretations can be off-base; we may perceive a situation one way when in fact something entirely different is occurring.[62] Maybe you've been in a club or at a party and thought someone was flirting with you, only to discover the person was focused on someone behind or near you. Embarrassing? Yes, but inaccurate interpretations of our perceptions are commonplace.

When Perceptions Vary

George and Martha have been married for, well, forever. They know each other very well, and each knows how the other thinks. So you'd think their perceptions of things, events, and people would line up, right? Wrong. George and Martha are driving home from a party, chatting about the evening. George believes that everyone had a good time; that the house was filled with interesting, pleasant, relatively good-looking people; and that he received positive responses from everyone he talked to. Martha saw the party differently. She tells George that the reason people looked good was that most of them either had had plastic surgery to "hold back Father Time"; were Botoxed beyond all recognition; or were younger, "replacement" partners for all the divorced people there. Many people at the party disliked each other so intensely that they stayed on opposite sides of the room all night. Martha's interpretation of events is based not on prior or external knowledge, but on her perceptions from observing and interacting with people at the party. And what about George's perception that everyone at the party liked him? Martha says, "Think again." She tells George that as soon as he walked away after having a conversation with one group of men, they nonverbally signaled to one another indicating that they thought George was a doofus. What's going on here? Who's right, George or Martha?

Neither is right and both are right. This example illustrates two differing perceptions of the same reality. There's no "truth" to be found, only different "takes" on the same people and set of events. Both sets of perceptions are valid even though they differ, because varying perceptions are the norm in life. You know this to be true in your own life experience—even people you're very similar to and know quite well can differ from you dramatically in their perceptions of people and events. Your life experiences, how you were raised, and how you developed contribute a great deal to how you perceive things, events, and people in your life. These elements create a filter through which you observe and process the world around you.

Communicate to Enhance Your Powers of Perception

2.6 Summarize three communication strategies that can improve one's powers of perception.

Has anyone ever told you that they formed a perception about you when they first met you, but you changed that perception over time? On occasion, people who are shy, serious, or simply more quiet in their communication style than others are perceived as being conceited, aloof, or cocky. Outgoing, extroverted people may be viewed as overbearing when really they just enjoy the company of others.

Sometimes our powers of perception are sharp, but other times we miss the mark.[63] Because our communication is affected by our perceptions of others, it's important to work toward forming the most accurate perceptions you can, because then you have better, more reliable information on which to act. How can you improve your ability to form accurate perceptions? Here are three suggestions: increase your awareness, avoid stereotypes, and check your perceptions against others' perceptions.

Increase Your Awareness

We've made this topic—awareness—our first of five Communication Principles for a Lifetime for a reason. Exercise your senses, especially your sense of hearing. Work at really listening to people—*fully* listening, without interrupting them to put in your two cents' worth. Try to be more verbally and nonverbally aware; monitor how you communicate with others and how people respond to you. If you don't like the responses you're getting from people, it may be time for a change in *your* behavior, not theirs. You also want to monitor the verbal and nonverbal cues others exhibit. Pay attention to contextual cues, such as where an interaction is taking place, the time of day, the perceived moods of those interacting, and any physical or psychological barriers that impede the communication exchange. Learn from your mistakes, rather than repeating them.

Avoid Stereotypes

stereotype

A generalization applied to persons perceived to have attributes common to a particular group.

"She's a snob." "He's a nerd." "They're a bunch of dumb jocks." These statements reflect **stereotypes**, or generalizations we apply to individuals because we perceive them to have attributes common to a particular group.[64]

What comes to mind when you hear the term *homeless*? Do you associate the word with someone begging on the street, people living in shelters or their cars, or "bums" or "bag ladies" in parks, alleys, or subway stations? If these images came to mind, you've just invoked a stereotype. What may not have come to mind are the many families who are homeless because of an economic downturn, home foreclosure, or other societal factors. Research shows that many of us hold unfortunate stereotypes about homeless people and homelessness in general.[65]

Some positive or functional aspects of stereotypes emerge from our human nature to simplify and categorize stimuli in our environment, which we described earlier as components of the perception process. Stereotypes serve as a baseline of information. If you know nothing else about a person other than she or he is a "northerner," for instance, then you can think about commonly held characteristics of other people you've met from the northern part of the country and go from there. Social psychologist Douglas Kenrick and his colleagues point out that, "Stereotyping is a cognitively inexpensive way of understanding others: By presuming that people are like other members of their groups, we avoid the effortful process of learning about them as individuals."[66] But obviously, there's a serious downside.

Have you ever taken a class and, from day one, felt that the teacher pegged you a certain way? The instructor may have perceived you to be a slacker or uninterested in the course topic (on the negative side) or a straight-A student or future PhD candidate (on the positive side). The bottom line is that no one likes to be treated as a stereotype because it's limiting and impersonal. You can also feel pressure to try to live up to a stereotype, such as "all Asian students are exceptionally bright." Stereotypes are often degrading, as in age-old references to dumb blondes, bad women drivers, and dirty old men. Many of the worst stereotypes are related to gender, race/ethnicity, age, and physical appearance.[67]

Often we try to inhibit or suppress stereotypical thoughts before they have a chance to affect our behavior.[68] For example, if you grew up hearing family members invoke stereotypes about different ethnic groups, you may decide as an adult that you will not follow suit—that assigning ethnic stereotypes is inappropriate. However, because it's part of your upbringing and ingrained in you, your first thoughts may be stereotypical when you encounter someone from an ethnic group other than your own. You have to assert mental control to suppress the stereotypical thoughts and adjust your communication. Remember that there's nothing inherently wrong with a stereotype as a baseline of information. But the rigid way we enforce a stereotype, the expectations we form on the basis of the stereotype, and our ensuing communication with the stereotyped person are problematic.

Check Your Perceptions

You can check the accuracy of your perceptions and attributions indirectly and directly so that you increase your ability to perceive things and people and respond to them effectively. **Indirect perception checking** involves an intensification of your own perceptual powers. You seek additional information to confirm, refute, or expand your interpretations of someone's behavior. If you suspect that your romantic partner wants to end your relationship, for instance, you're likely to look for cues in his or her tone of voice, eye contact, and body movements to confirm your suspicion. You'll probably also listen more intently and pay closer attention to the language your partner chooses to use. The information you gain is "checked" against your original perceptions.

indirect perception checking
Using your own perceptual abilities to seek additional information to confirm or refute your interpretations of someone's behavior.

Direct perception checking involves asking straight out whether your interpretations of a perception are correct. You can accomplish this in two ways: asking people directly for their interpretations of their own actions or asking other observers for their take on a situation (going to a third or outside party). Asking people directly is often more difficult than asking a third party for an interpretation. For one thing, we don't like to admit uncertainty or suspicions to others; we might not trust that they'll respond honestly. And if our interpretations are wrong, we might suffer embarrassment or anger. But asking someone to confirm a perception shows that you're committed to gaining a better understanding.

direct perception checking
Asking someone else whether your interpretations of what you perceive are correct.

Perception checking with colleagues, as well as with family members and trusted friends, is an invaluable tool, particularly when emotions are involved. It can be very helpful to discuss situations with other people and get their input as to what happened, why it happened, how they would feel about it if it happened to them, and what you might do about it. This is especially advisable in work settings, when the wisdom of someone else's perceptions can save you professional embarrassment or prevent you from losing your job. The "Can I run something by you?" strategy gives you a broader perspective and a basis of comparison.[69]

STUDY GUIDE:

〉 REVIEW, APPLY, AND ASSESS

Self-Awareness: How Well Do You Know Yourself?

2.1   Discuss the importance of self-awareness in the process of improving one's communication skills.

REVIEW: Self-awareness is the ability to develop and communicate a representation of yourself to others.

KEY TERMS:

self-awareness   symbolic self-awareness

APPLY: Describe an example of how you or someone you know progressed through Maslow's levels of competence. What skill did you or the other person develop, and how was each level demonstrated in behavior?

ASSESS: How well do you know yourself? If you have a Facebook, Instagram, or other social media account, look at it with a critical eye. Does it reflect who you think you are?

Self-Concept: Who Are You?

2.2   Describe components of the self-concept and major influences on self-concept development.

REVIEW: Your self-concept is your interior identity or subjective description of who you think you are. Your self-image is your view of yourself in a particular situation. The self-concept contains three components: attitudes, beliefs, and values. Philosopher William James believed that three "selves" exist in each of us: the material self, the social self, and the spiritual self. Our self-concept develops through our communication with others, our association with various groups, the roles we assume in our lives, and the labels we use to describe ourselves. Our avowed identity is assigned by ourselves, whereas our ascribed identity involves characteristics other people assign or attribute to us.

KEY TERMS:

self	beliefs
self-concept	values
attitudes	material self

social self   ascribed identity
spiritual self   self-reflexiveness
avowed identity

APPLY: How has communication with family, friends, teachers, or others influenced your self-concept, either in the past or now?

ASSESS: Write down five words or phrases that best describe you, at this point in time. Analyze your list. How many of the five entries are nouns? How many are adjectives? How many entries imply or reflect your relationships with others? Why did you put the first entry first? If you had to remove one entry, which one would it be and why?

Self-Esteem: What's Your Value?

2.3   Describe how gender, social comparisons, self-expectations, and self-fulfilling prophecies affect one's self-esteem.

REVIEW: Your assessment of your worth as a person in terms of skills, abilities, talents, and appearance constitutes your level of self-esteem. Self-esteem is affected by many factors, but primary among them are your gender, your comparisons of yourself to others, the expectations you hold for yourself, and your self-fulfilling prophecies.

KEY TERMS:

self-esteem	social comparison
self-concept clarity	self-expectations
gender	self-fulfilling prophecy

APPLY: In addition to self-comparisons sparked by social media, what situations or stimuli tend to make people engage in more self-comparisons?

ASSESS:

1. Rosenberg Self-Esteem Scale
One of the most widely used scales to measure a person's self-esteem is the Rosenberg Self-Esteem Scale, developed in the 1960s by Dr. Morris Rosenberg, a sociologist.

Respond to items on the scale using the following system: SA = Strongly Agree, A = Agree, D = Disagree, and SD = Strongly Disagree. Scoring information follows the scale.

1. I feel that I'm a person of worth, at least on an equal plane with others. SA A D SD

2. I feel that I have a number of good qualities. SA A D SD

3. All in all, I am inclined to feel that I am a failure. SA A D SD

4. I am able to do things as well as most other people. SA A D SD

5. I feel I do not have much to be proud of. SA A D SD

6. I take a positive attitude toward myself. SA A D SD

7. On the whole, I am satisfied with myself. SA A D SD

8. I wish I could have more respect for myself. SA A D SD

9. I certainly feel useless at times. SA A D SD

10. At times, I think I am no good at all. SA A D SD

Scoring Instructions

To score the scale, assign a value to each of the ten items as follows and total the values:

For items 1, 2, 4, 6, and 7: Strongly Agree = 3, Agree = 2, Disagree = 1, Strongly Disagree = 0.

For items 3, 5, 8, 9, and 10: Strongly Agree = 0, Agree = 1, Disagree = 2, Strongly Disagree = 3.

Scores on the scale range from 0 to 30, with 30 indicating the highest score possible, or the highest level of self-esteem the scale can measure. If you score on the low end of the scale, we suggest that you reread and perhaps try the suggestions in the section of this chapter on self-esteem enhancement.

Source: M. Rosenberg, *Society and the Adolescent Self-Image* rev. ed. (Middletown, CT: Wesleyan University Press, 1989). Reprinted with permission; retrieved from www.bsos.umd.edu.

2. Inventory Your Self-Esteem

One way to begin to improve your self-esteem is to take an honest measure of how you feel about yourself *right at this very point in time*. Take some time to think about yourself—who you used to be, who you were only a short time ago, and who you have developed into at this moment in time. Ponder the relationships that had the greatest effect on your development and maturation, and think about the events that caused you to change in some profound way. Then use the columns below to inventory where you stand and to reveal where you may need to put some energy into making change happen for yourself.

Things I Like About Myself	Things I Don't Like About Myself	How to Make Some Changes

Communication and the Enhancement of Self-Esteem

2.4 **Practice six communication strategies for enhancing one's self-esteem.**

REVIEW: Because enhanced self-esteem is a goal for most of us, we recommend the following six means of improving the way you feel about yourself.

- Engage in positive self-talk.
- Visualize the behavior you want to enact or the attributes you wish to acquire.
- Reframe, meaning redefine events and experiences from a different point of view.
- Develop honest relationships, ones in which people tell you the truth about yourself so you can get some growth from the feedback.
- Surround yourself with positive people, not "Debbie Downers."
- Lose your baggage, meaning let go of the past and those experiences that can cause your self-esteem to suffer.

KEY TERMS:
intrapersonal communication   visualization
self-talk   reframing
narcissism

APPLY: Describe a situation or event in your life for which it would be—or already has been—helpful to use positive self-talk or visualization to enhance your self-esteem.

ASSESS: Read or reread the Communication & Ethics feature box in this chapter. Do your own experiences correspond to the research conclusions? Have you noticed high or increasing narcissism in yourself or people you know? What are the consequences of the narcissism you see for the individuals, for people they know, and for society?

The Perception Process

2.5 **Explain the three stages of perception and why people differ in their perceptions of people and events.**

REVIEW: Perception, the process of receiving information from your senses, involves three stages:

1. Attention and selection, when you notice and choose stimuli in your environment on which to focus

2. Organization, when you convert stimuli into understandable information

3. Interpretation, when you attach meaning to what you have attended to, selected, and organized

People often differ in their perceptions of things, events, and other people. Your life experiences, how you were raised, and how you developed contribute a great deal to how you perceive the world around you.

KEY TERMS:

perception   organization
attention   closure
selection   interpretation

APPLY: In addition to the example given in this chapter of mistakenly thinking a person was flirting with you, what experiences have you had with inaccurately perceiving other people's communication?

ASSESS: Rate yourself in terms of your powers of perception. Are you a 10, meaning you think of yourself as highly perceptive about people, communication, and events? Or are you closer to a 1 or 2, meaning that your perception often doesn't match the reality of a situation?

Communicate to Enhance Your Powers of Perception

2.6   Summarize three communication strategies that can improve one's powers of perception.

REVIEW: If you want to enhance your perceptual accuracy, we recommend you first increase your awareness by fully listening, observing, and paying attention to your surroundings and other people. Secondly, avoid stereotypes or generalizations about people. And finally, check your perceptions—indirectly and directly—to confirm or refute your interpretations of events or someone's behavior.

KEY TERMS:

stereotype   direct perception checking
indirect perception checking

APPLY: What are some stereotypes held by people you know? Have you had a stereotype negatively inflicted on you? How did it affect your relationship with the person who used the stereotype? How did it affect your communication?

ASSESS: Generate statements that reveal common stereotypes about people in the following groups. Try to think of stereotypes that reflect positive as well as negative perceptions. We've provided a couple of examples to get you started. Then focus on the damage that stereotypes can do to someone's self-esteem. How might your communication with someone from each group be affected by these stereotypes?

Group	Positive Stereotype	Negative Stereotype
elderly	Old people are wise.	Old people can't fend for themselves.
women	Women are naturally loving and nurturing.	Women are terrible drivers.
men		
straight-A students		
blondes		
fundamentalist Christians		
bodybuilders		
southerners		
overweight people		
athletes		
rednecks		
video gamers		

⟩ THE PRINCIPLE POINTS

Principle One:

Be aware of your communication with yourself and others.

- Becoming aware of yourself as you develop your self-concept involves communicating with others, associating with groups with whom you identify, assuming social roles, and selecting self-labels that describe who you are.

- Inventory yourself for any negative self-fulfilling prophecies that can be detrimental to your self-esteem.

- Engage in positive intrapersonal communication, or self-talk, because a heightened awareness of how you talk to yourself can help enhance self-esteem.

- Develop your perceptual abilities by becoming more aware of yourself and others.

- Use direct and indirect perception checks to sharpen your perceptual accuracy.

UNDERSTANDING VERBAL MESSAGES

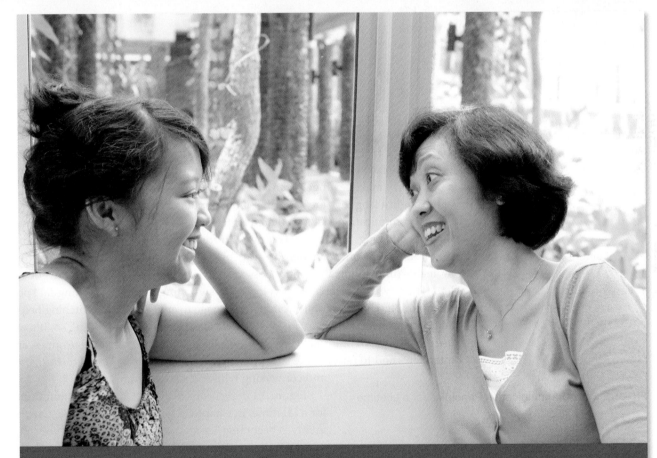

Words—so innocent and powerless as they are, as standing in a dictionary, how potent for good and evil they become in the hands of one who knows how to combine them. —NATHANIEL HAWTHORNE

Ampyang/Shutterstock

→ CHAPTER OUTLINE

- Why Focus on Language?
- The Nature of Language
- The Power of Words
- Confronting Bias in Language
- Using Words to Establish Supportive Relationships
- Study Guide: Review, Apply, and Assess

LEARNING OBJECTIVES

After studying this chapter, you should be able to

3.1 List two reasons why it is important to study verbal communication.

3.2 Summarize how words are used as symbols that have denotative, connotative, concrete, and abstract meanings and are bound by culture and context.

3.3 Identify five primary ways in which words have power.

3.4 Describe the major ways in which language reveals bias about race, ethnicity, nationality, religion, gender, sexual orientation, age, class, and ability.

3.5 Explain how language helps create supportive or defensive communication climates.

"cul8tr"

"j/k"

"fomo"

"by4now"

Many students are familiar with and comfortable using abbreviated messages, known as *textisms,* in their texts and e-mails. You probably deciphered the above textisms as shorthand for "see you later," "just kidding," "fear of missing out," and "bye for now." But don't assume everyone decodes textisms with equal skill. One comic joked about how her mother thought "btw" was short for Booker T. Washington. Textisms and acronyms (using the first letters of words to form a new word) make texting, instant messaging, and e-mailing faster. These adaptations of the English language are becoming more popular in everyday communication, especially communication that's mediated by technology.[1] A persistent use of slang may be fine when texting, posting, or talking with friends, but when it becomes such a habit that it slips into other written or oral communication—especially at inappropriate moments (like calling a potential boss at a job interview "dude")—you've got a problem. The key is to be able to develop **code-switching** abilities, as bilingual speakers often exhibit when they shift from one language to another. Code switching helps you adapt to listeners. However, make sure you use discretion when doing so. It's wise to use more standard or formal language for college papers, professional résumés, and job interviews and to relegate the shortcuts and "slanguage" to informal texting, posting, and conversing with friends who translate.[2]

code switching

Changing seamlessly from one form of language use to another form.

Figure 3.1 depicts our five core Communication Principles for a Lifetime. In Chapter 2 we explored Principle One, which involves becoming more aware of yourself and your perceptions of things and people. An important step in this process of coming to know and understand yourself better is an honest, insightful examination of how you talk.

Consider this: *What you say is who you are.* That may sound like a strong statement, but it's true that the words you use reveal who you are. Granted, you communicate with more than your words. Your background, culture, values, experiences, and the way you express yourself nonverbally reveal who you are as well. But it's a provocative notion that every time we use language, we reveal our thoughts, our very selves to others—no matter how inane, superficial, or emotion-laden the conversation. In addition to their tremendous potential to reveal the self, our words also carry the power to make and break relationships and careers and to shape cultures. Because of the immense power of words, we've chosen to make verbal communication the second of our five key Communication

FIGURE 3.1 **Communication Principles for a Lifetime**

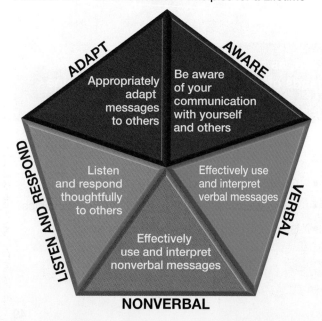

Principles for a Lifetime. As we explore the power of words, we challenge you to think about the incredible tool you have at your disposal: verbal communication.

Why Focus on Language?

3.1 List two reasons why it is important to study verbal communication.

Take an inventory of your use of language as you read this chapter. Do you use language that accurately and effectively represents who you are to other people? Do some areas need improvement? How do you come across when meeting someone new? When talking with your best friends? What kind of communicator do your closest friends and family members think you are?

On occasion, we do stop to consider the effects of our language on others—usually when we're attempting to persuade or when we've said something that has injured or angered someone else. We've all been in situations that made us wish we could get a conversational second chance. The first reason we study verbal communication relates to one of our main messages in this chapter: *Words are powerful.* They affect your emotions, thoughts, actions, and relationships. They affect how you're perceived by others. As we stated in Chapter 1, communication is irreversible. Once your words are "out there," they can't be reversed or unspoken, as much as we might like to try to take them back.

Interviews with employers reveal their concern about college graduates' lack of language skills, attributed to growing up in a culture that is more visual than oral, stressing nonverbal cues over language. In recent surveys by both the Association of American Colleges and Universities and the Society for Human Resource Management, employers expressed significant concerns about college graduates' writing and speaking skills.[3] This is clearly a negative trend, in light of other research that has determined that an ability to use words to effectively participate in conversation is a key component in judgments about a person's competence as a communicator. In that study, people who talked less in conversation were perceived as being less interpersonally skilled than those who comfortably and actively engaged in conversation.[4] By gaining a better understanding of the nature and power of language, attending to your use of language, and working to use words with forethought and skill, you can exert great influence and enhance your relationships.

The second reason we study verbal communication relates to this reality: *We choose language.* We don't use language as an involuntary reflex to a stimulus, in the way our knee might jerk when rapped with a doctor's mallet. We choose the language we use—even if we make that choice in the split second it takes our brain to select a symbol (word) to communicate our thoughts or impulses. At times we go into "default mode," choosing language we've used before. We're prone to patterns in our language because, as humans, we prefer regularity. We also choose particular words because we like them, they've worked well for us in the past, or we grew up with those words and have used them for many years. But pattern and history can breed too much comfort, preventing us from asking ourselves, "Is this the best way to say this? Should I say this another way?" We have an incredible wealth of words from which to choose and the power to make choices that allow us to communicate who we are to others in the most effective way possible.

Leo Cullum/The New Yorker Collection/The Cartoon Bank

The Nature of Language

3.2 Summarize how words are used as symbols that have denotative, connotative, concrete, and abstract meanings and are bound by culture and context.

language
A system of symbols (words or vocabulary) structured by rules (grammar) and patterns (syntax) common to a community of people.

A **language** is a system of symbols (words or vocabulary) structured by grammar (rules and standards) and syntax (patterns in the arrangement of words) common to a community of people. Two language researchers, Edward Sapir and Benjamin Lee Whorf, developed what has come to be known as the Sapir–Whorf Hypothesis.[5] This hypothesis suggests that human language and thought are so interrelated that thought is actually rooted in and controlled by language. One implication of this supposition is that you cannot conceive of something for which you have no word. As a quick illustration of what we mean by this, think about colors. A woman describes her new dress to her friend using the term *puce,* but if the friend does not have the term *puce* in her frame of reference, she will be unable to conceive of the color her friend mentions. (For those of you with a possibly underdeveloped color-term repertoire, puce is a brilliant purplish-red color.)

The Sapir-Whorf Hypothesis provides further evidence of the *power* of language. When you choose words, you reveal how you think and what you think about. In essence, the quality of your language reflects the quality of your thought. The more extensive your vocabulary, the more options you have to communicate your ideas to others and to understand theirs. The connection between language and thought strengthens the argument in favor of learning more than one language; some ideas, emotions, or impulses may be better captured by words in a different language than your native one. Learning other languages, in turn, expands your thinking.

People Use Words as Symbols

symbol
A word, sound, gesture, or visual image that represents a thought, concept, object, or experience.

As we noted in Chapter 1, words are **symbols** that represent something else. Just as a flag is a symbol of a country, words are symbols that trigger thoughts, concepts, or feelings. For instance, what comes to mind when you see or hear the word *freedom*? Perhaps you think historically, remembering what you studied in grade school about Abraham Lincoln freeing the slaves, or perhaps you picture U.S. armed forces defending our national freedom. Or maybe you envision something a bit closer to home, like the feeling you get during a break between semesters at college.

People Attach Meanings to Words

meaning
A person's interpretation of a symbol.

Now imagine using the word *freedom* in a conversation, in an effort to convey to the other person the concept or image in your mind. You know what you're thinking when you say the word; the challenge is for the other person to understand your thoughts behind your word choice. In communication terms, this is the process of creating **meaning**. The meaning of a word is a person's interpretation of that symbol—it's how the person makes sense of the symbol. Meanings don't reside in the words themselves but in the ways in which communicators use the words. You attach a meaning to the word *freedom*, the symbol you choose in conversation; your listener creates meaning for the word when he or she attempts to interpret what you've said. Words aren't the culprits in communication problems; the meanings people create for words lead to successful or problematic communication.

bypassing
A communication problem that arises when the same words mean different things to different people.

Sometimes speakers' and receivers' meanings don't correspond because the same words mean different things to different people; the term for this communication problem is **bypassing**. Using the *freedom* example, think about a couple in a long-term romantic relationship. If one partner said to the other, "I need more freedom in this relationship," what might that mean? It might mean that the relationship is over because one partner wants out completely, to be *free* to explore other relationships. But it might also mean that the partner is suffocating or feeling a lack of *freedom* to do as she or he pleases in the relationship. If the partner is using *freedom* in this latter sense, the relationship might stay intact. The couple might only need to make some changes in the amount of time they spend together. Some conflicts in relationships can be boiled down to a simple difference in the meaning of the words that get exchanged.

People Create Denotative and Connotative Meanings for Words

Symbol sharing through language isn't just a simple process of uttering a word and having its meaning clearly understood by another. People create meanings for language on two levels: the denotative and the connotative.[6]

The **denotative meaning** of a word conveys content. Denotation is the restrictive, or literal, meaning of a word. For example, one dictionary defines *apartment* as "a room or suite of rooms used as a residence."[7] This definition is a literal, or denotative, definition of the word *apartment*; it describes what the word means in American culture.

By contrast, the **connotative meaning** of a word conveys feelings; people create personal and subjective meanings for words.[8] To you, the word *apartment* might mean a comfortable place where you can relax at the end of the day or a setting in which to entertain friends. To others, though, the word *apartment* might engender feelings of guilt (if the apartment hasn't been cleaned in a while) or feelings of dread (if rent is draining the wallet or relationships with roommates leave something to be desired). Clearly, the connotative level of language is more individual. While the denotative or objective meaning of the word *apartment* can be found in any dictionary, your subjective response to the word is probably not contained there.

People Convey Concrete and Abstract Meanings through Words

Meanings for words can be placed along a continuum from concrete to abstract.[9] A word's meaning is **concrete** if we can experience what the word refers to (the referent) with one of our senses; if we can see it, touch it, smell it, taste it, or hear it, it's concrete. If we cannot do these things, the word's meaning is **abstract**. In general, the more concrete the language, the easier it is for others to understand and retain. For example, the word *patriotism* is abstract because we cannot hear or taste patriotism. But a word that suggests a demonstration of patriotism, such as *voting*, is more concrete, because we can physically perform the act of voting. Minimize the use of abstract words when you're trying to clarify a message. Concrete terms help make a message clearer and more memorable.[10]

denotative meaning
The restrictive, or literal, meaning of a word.

connotative meaning
The personal and subjective meaning of a word.

concrete meaning
Meaning that refers to something that can be perceived with one of the senses.

abstract meaning
Meaning that refers to something that cannot be perceived or experienced with one of the senses.

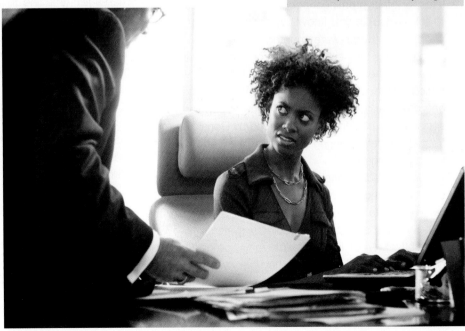

▼ Because different people can attach different meanings to the same word, it's easy to get confused. What can you do to help clarify your own meaning so that others understand you?
Christopher Robbins/Getty Images

Meanings Are Culture Bound

culture

A learned system of knowledge, behavior, attitudes, beliefs, values, rules, and norms that is shared by a group of people and shaped from one generation to the next.

co-culture

A culture that exists within a larger cultural context (e.g., LGBTQ cultures, Amish culture).

neologism

A new term introduced into a language.

Culture is a learned system of knowledge, behavior, attitudes, beliefs, values, rules, and norms that is shared by a group of people and shaped from one generation to the next.[11] The meaning of a word, just like the meaning of any symbol, can change from culture to culture and across **co-cultures** (cultural groups that exist within a larger culture). To a European, for example, a *Yankee* is someone from the United States; to a player on the Boston Red Sox baseball team, a *Yankee* is an opponent; and to an American from the South, a *Yankee* is someone from the North. Some years ago, General Motors sold a car called a *Nova*. In English, *nova* means "bright star," and in Latin, *nova* means "new"—both appropriate connotations for a car. In Spanish, however, the spoken word *nova* sounds like the words *no va*, which translate to "It does not go." As you can imagine, this name was not a great sales tool for the Spanish-speaking market.

Sometimes a cultural group will have a need for a completely new word or combination of words because some phenomenon emerges without language to capture or communicate it. New terms introduced into a language are called **neologisms**. Examples include *sexual harassment*, a term introduced into the English language by feminists in the 1960s who wished to describe sexist treatment experienced primarily by women in the American workforce. Nowadays, it's hard to imagine not having the term *sexual harassment* exist in the English language, but the term is only about five decades old. Other attempts at adding new language haven't been as successful, such as efforts in the 1970s to persuade English speakers to use "tay" or "gen" as non-sex-specific pronouns, as in "If a student wants to be successful, *tay* should not get behind in assigned reading."[12]

COMMUNICATION & SOCIAL MEDIA

To Tweet or Not to Tweet: 140 Characters or Less

Do you tweet? Do you follow others' Twitter feeds? If so, do you follow mostly celebrities, political figures, athletes, or other prominent people? Or are you more likely to follow people you know? In early 2016, 310 million people worldwide were monthly active Twitter users, which means they either tweeted or followed the Twitter stream of others. By the end of 2016, that figure was 319 million; Twitter usage increased by 9 million people within one calendar year.[13] No doubt Twitter's popularity as a social media platform was enhanced by Donald Trump's frequent tweeting during his presidential campaign and into his presidency.[14]

Social media platforms continue to increase in number and change rapidly, so much so that it's hard for researchers to keep up with how people communicate using various platforms and delivery systems, and with what effect. Most people (particularly college students) now own mobile devices that they carry with them at all times. Which of the following are you most likely to do: post, text, tweet, or actually talk to someone on your smartphone? Do you prefer texting to tweeting because you're not limited to Twitter's 140 characters?[15] If you can only use 140 characters to get your message across, what effect does that have on how you communicate a message? (Imagine if face-to-face conversations were restricted to a certain word or character limit.) Researchers have studied how people use language to form their 140-character messages.[16] Results show that "in the moment" tweets tend to contain intensifiers (e.g., so, very, really), egocentric language (frequent references to self), and more negative than positive language (people tend to vent or rant on Twitter). Regardless of the sex or gender of the Twitter user, researchers also noted the use of more masculine than feminine language. They described masculine language as competitive, forceful, and aggressive, with message content more related to one's workplace or profession. In contrast, feminine language was described as gentle, warm, and tender, with a greater focus on relationships and connections to others. As of 2016, a fairly even balance of women and men worldwide were Twitter users, so findings about language usage in tweets are more interesting in light of this statistic.

Meanings Are Context Bound

Politicians often claim that the media "takes them out of context," causing the intended meanings of their words to be lost or distorted. Many times, the politicians are right. In an effort to deliver a speedy, pithy sound bite to an audience, reporters may edit politicians' comments, deleting context and sometimes changing the intended message.

Context plays a central role in how accurately our communication is interpreted by receivers. The context includes all of our words, plus ever-present nonverbal elements, like the setting in which the communication occurs as well as people's facial expressions, tone of voice, and other nonverbal cues that accompany a verbal message and help us decode it. Removing words from their context distorts their meaning.

RECAP

The Nature of Language

- People use words as *symbols:* Symbols represent something else.
- People create *meanings* for words: Meaning is a person's interpretation of a symbol.
- Words have both *denotative* and *connotative* meanings: The denotative meaning is a restrictive, or literal, meaning; the connotation is a personal and subjective meaning.
- People convey *concrete* and *abstract* meanings through words: A word's meaning is concrete if we can experience what the word refers to with one of our senses; if not, the meaning is abstract.
- Meanings are *culture bound:* The meaning of a word can change from culture to culture.
- Meanings are *context bound:* The situation or context for communication aids people as they attach meanings to symbols.

The Power of Words

3.3 Identify five primary ways in which words have power.

No doubt you've heard the old schoolyard chant, "Sticks and stones may break my bones, but words can never hurt me." We don't know who first came up with that statement, but we imagine it was someone who never experienced the sting of name calling, the harmful effects of being labeled a "slow reader," or the legacy of an unfortunate family nickname. Words *do* hurt. With all the national headlines about the tragic consequences of bullying, teasing, and harassment, it's important to consider the damage language can do.[17]

Words have the power to evoke a wide range of emotions in listeners. But words can also heal, inspire, and transform the human spirit, which is another reason why one of our five Communication Principles for a Lifetime is about the effective use and interpretation of verbal messages. Let's explore five powers of words.

- *The Power to Create and Label Experience.* Alzheimer's, Parkinson's, Tourette syndrome—each of these afflictions is named after the person who discovered the condition. The name of a phenomenon has the power to label the experience and make it more real.[18] One humorous addition to the English language is the term *broverwhelm*, which Eden Sher, the author of *The Emotionary*, describes as the activity of surrounding oneself with an "excess of bros or to overpower with a single bro's bro-ishness."[19]

▼ This woman's strong reaction to a text shows the power of words to convey our emotions and to affect other people's thoughts and feelings. What steps help you to consider others' feelings when choosing your words?
Zea Lenanet/Fotolia

RECAP

The Power of Words to . . .

- *Create and Label Experience.* New experiences may lead to new words.

- *Communicate Feelings.* Words help create and communicate our moods and emotional states.

- *Affect Thoughts and Actions.* Words influence how we think and behave.

- *Shape and Reflect Culture.* Cultures change; language both creates and reflects the changing nature of culture.

- *Make and Break Relationships.* Verbal communication creates opportunities for us to know others and be known by them. It also helps establish and deepen relationships; sometimes it causes them to end.

- *The Power to Communicate Feelings.* Words help communicate your moods and emotional states, giving labels to feelings that otherwise would be hard to convey.[20] Think of how many terms exist for sadness: *blue, down, depressed, in the depths, mopey, bummed, down in the dumps, out of sorts, feeling punk.* The emotional power of words is not limited to expressing your feelings; your words and corresponding outlook may also have the power to affect your emotional, mental, and physical health.

- *The Power to Affect Thoughts and Actions.* A few decades ago, a weight-loss product called Ayds came on the market. Ayds were small, brown, chewy squares that manufacturers claimed would help reduce appetite. You can guess why this product disappeared in the 1980s. Given what we now know about the disease AIDS, who today would buy a product called Ayds? Advertisers have long known that the way a product is labeled greatly affects the likelihood that consumers will buy it, because words affect the way we think about things and react to them.

- *The Power to Shape and Reflect Culture.* International students often puzzle over English slang and ask such questions as "What does it mean to 'cowboy up'?" (When things get tough, you have to get up and dust yourself off) or "What is a 'back burner relationship'?" (This metaphor for relationships refers to stoves and their various front and back burners. Communication scholars have begun to study the back burner relationship, which refers to keeping in contact with potential romantic partners in case one's current relationship ends.)[21] Cultures and co-cultural groups within them develop unique languages as a way to forge connections and enhance solidarity, so the language you use both shapes and reflects your culture.

- *The Power to Make and Break Relationships.* You have probably used words to draw people to you and to maintain all sorts of relationships. But you have probably also had the experience of saying something you regret, or being too blunt and offending someone. If you've ever said something so inappropriate that it cost you a romantic relationship or friendship, you know firsthand the power of words to make and break relationships.

Confronting Bias in Language

3.4 Describe the major ways in which language reveals bias about race, ethnicity, nationality, religion, gender, sexual orientation, age, class, and ability.

For all of us, our language could use a bit of reflection, and then some refreshing. Improving your linguistic choices isn't about conforming to some societal standard of how you should talk; it's about using the best language adapted for your listeners. It's also about using language that shows you're a highly educated person with excellent communication skills. Insensitive or stereotypical language use often arises out of ignorance or a lack of education. But even well-meaning, educated people can communicate bias through the language they choose to use. Words that reflect bias toward members of other cultures or groups can create barriers for listeners. In addition, such language ignores the fact that the world is constantly changing. In the following section, we explore a few categories of language that illustrate the constant evolution of verbal communication. As you read this information, think to yourself: Do I have some "refreshing" to do?

Biased Language: Race, Ethnicity, Nationality, and Religion

Think about whether you have ever said or overheard someone say the following:

"I made money on my garage sale, but people kept trying to jew down my prices."

"You can't have that back, you Indian giver!"

"She's a real Bible banger."

"He doesn't have a Chinaman's chance of making the team."

"That divorce settlement gypped me out of what's rightfully mine!"

The language used in each of these examples demonstrates an insensitivity to members of different cultural groups. (The last statement tends to puzzle people more than the others. It includes the term *gypped,* which is derived from the word for the nomadic cultural group known throughout the world as gypsies. The stereotype relates to being suckered or cheated out of what one is due.) Each of these statements contains a word barrier known as **allness**, which occurs when words reflect unqualified, often untrue generalizations that deny individual differences or variations.

allness

A word barrier created through the use of language that reflects unqualified, often untrue generalizations that deny individual differences or variations.

Terms pertaining to racial and ethnic groups continue to change over time. Refer to Table 3.1, which provides some racial categories that appeared as options in the U.S. censuses of 1970, 1980, 1990, 2000, and 2010. Not all cultural groups' terms are represented in the table, but you'll see how much more specific our language has become over time in an attempt to better communicate racial and ethnic identity in this country. These terms will likely change again with the 2020 census.

Sometimes it's a challenge to keep pace as language changes over time, but try not to get lazy with language. It's important to inventory and revolutionize your language with regard to the racial, ethnic, national, and religious affiliations of people. After all, the language you choose to use is your primary tool for creating the reality of your existence. It reveals how you think. It's also how you are known by others, and how you know others.[22]

Biased Language: Sex, Gender, and Sexual Orientation

Language that reveals bias in favor of one sex and against others, termed **sexist (exclusive) language**, is more prevalent than you'd think. Decades of effort, spurred by the women's liberation movement in the 1960s, have raised the consciousness of American culture regarding exclusive language. But even in this day and age of heightened awareness about sex and gender issues, many people still don't use gender-fair verbal communication.

sexist (exclusive) language

Language that reveals bias in favor of one sex and against others.

Language and the Sexes   Even though women now constitute 50 percent of the U.S. population, to listen to the language of some people, you'd think it was still a man's world. Sexist language can reflect stereotypical attitudes or describe roles in exclusive

TABLE 3.1   U.S. Census Racial Categories

1970	1980	1990	2000	2010
White	White	White	White	White
Negro or Black	Negro	Black	Black or African American	Black, African American, or Negro
Indian (American)	Indian (American)	Indian (American)	American Indian or Alaska Native (specify tribe)	American Indian or Alaska Native

SOURCES: Table based on information from M. Anderson and S. Feinberg, 2000, "Race and Ethnicity and the Controversy over the U.S. Census," *Current Sociology* 48.3: 87–110; National Research Council, *Measuring Racial Discrimination* (Washington, DC: National Academies Press, 2004); U.S. Census Bureau, 2001, "Population by Race and Hispanic or Latino Origin for All Ages and for 18 Years and Over for the United States: 2000," www.census.gov/PressRelease/www/2001/tables/st00_1.pdf; U.S. Census Bureau, 2010, *Questionnaire Reference Book* (Washington, DC: U.S. Department of Commerce, Bureau of the Census, Washington DC), retrieved from 2010census.gov.

▲ The gender-neutral term *firefighter* describes both of these people, whereas the sexist term *fireman* excludes the person on the left.
Monkey Business/Shutterstock

generic language
General terms that stand for all persons or things within a given category.

terms, ignoring others' experiences.[23] Research indicates that exclusive language usage does the following: (1) maintains sex-biased perceptions, (2) shapes people's attitudes about careers that are appropriate for one sex but not others, (3) causes some people to believe that certain jobs and roles aren't attainable, (4) contributes to the belief that men deserve more status in society than other people do, and (5) mutes the voices of many people, because the words and norms formed by the dominant group don't allow for the articulation of others' experiences.[24]

The most common form of sexism in language is the use of **generic language**, using a masculine term to describe all people. There are two primary ways in which masculine-as-generic language typically appears in written and oral communication: in pronoun usage and in man-linked terminology.[25]

Consistent evidence from research on sexist language shows that people—particularly in American culture—simply do not tend to think in neuter. When we hear the term "policeman," we don't think of some amorphous sex-less person. Instead, we tend to picture a male police officer. Likewise, we don't tend to think of living entities as *it*, and we rarely use that pronoun to refer to them. When most people read or hear the word *he*, they think of a masculine person, not a sexless person.[26] Using generic masculine language, in essence, turns all persons into male persons. For example, a student giving a speech on how to project a winning, confident style in a job interview said, "When you greet the boss for the first time, be sure to look him straight in the eye, give him a firm handshake, and let him know you're interested in the job." The student's exclusive language choice only allowed for the possibility of a male boss, not a female or transgender boss.

We don't know what you were taught in high school or in other college classes about generic language, but current publishing standards require the use of nonsexist language, which means that masculine terms cannot stand for all persons.[27] Note that we use inclusive language in this text—because it reflects our value system and because our publisher requires it.

The solution to the problem of sexist language is not to replace each *he* with *she* but to use terms that include all sexes and genders so that your language reflects the contemporary world. If you want to refer to a person of any sex or gender, the clearest, most grammatical, and nonsexist way to do that is to use *she or he, he/she,* or *s/he*.[28] Other options include (1) omitting a pronoun altogether, either by rewording a message or by substituting an article (*a, an,* or *the*) for the pronoun; (2) using *you* or variations of the indefinite pronoun *one;* or (3) using the plural pronoun *they*.[29] The third option is becoming much more popular and grammatically acceptable than in times past because of its common conversational usage and the changing times. In 2016, *The Washington Post* became one of the first newspapers to adopt a singular "they" into its style standards.[30] So it's less likely now that your English teacher will correct such a statement as this: "If a person wants to be successful in life, they must work hard."

What form of gender-fair language should be used with transgenders? It's much more likely now than in the past that you'll meet, befriend, or at least become aware of a transgender person. (We explore transgenderism and other forms of gender identity in more depth in Chapter 6.) It's also becoming more common for people of all sexes and genders to communicate their preferred pronouns so that others can comfortably use sensitive and accurate language.[31] Some people include their preferred pronouns in their signature file, which is information that can be automatically inserted at the end of every outgoing email message. Some people provide contact information in their signature file, while others include electronic signatures, inspirational quotes, or graphics, like a university logo. Providing your preferred pronoun is a form of metacommunication (communication about communication) that clues people what language you'd prefer they use. Some transgender students contact their professors if their legal names on class rosters reflect their biological sex, rather than their transgender identities, and clue the profs as to their preferred pronouns. Some transgender people prefer pronouns related to the sex they're transitioning to. For example, some transmen (those transitioning from biological female to a male or masculine transgender identity) prefer "he," "his," and "himself" as pronouns, while other transgenders prefer "they," "their," and "themselves" because no sex or gender is indicated. It's wise to be aware of these different options and take cues from others, so that our language keeps pace and reflects sensitivity.

Consciously remembering to use nonsexist, inclusive language brings the following benefits:[32]

- Gender-inclusive language reflects inclusive attitudes. Monitoring your verbal communication for sexist remarks will make you aware of any sexist attitudes or assumptions you may hold.

- Using inclusive language helps you become more other-oriented, which will have a positive effect on your relationships. Consciously ridding your language of sexist remarks reflects your awareness of others and their sensitivities.

- Inclusive language makes your communication more contemporary and unambiguous. If you say *he*, for example, how is a listener to know whether you're referring to a male person or to just any person?

- Nonsexist language strengthens your style and demonstrates sensitivity that can empower others. By eliminating sexist bias from your communication, you affirm the value of all individuals with whom you interact.[33]

COMMUNICATION & DIVERSITY

Sex/Gender Complexity: Facebook's Fifty-Six Terms for Gender Identity

In 2014, Facebook distributed a list of fifty-six options to describe your sex and gender. At the time, some people reacted with terminology fatigue: "What? I have to learn all this?" Some users thought Facebook was taking gender sensitivity to a ridiculous degree, creating "much ado about nothing." Others celebrated because the complexity of sex and gender was finally being placed front and center—on the world's most popularly used social media platform, no less.[34]

Several of the terms include the prefix *cis*, as in *cisgender*. *Cis* is Latin for "on this side of" and it refers to people who identify with the sex they were assigned to or born with, such as a person who was born female and identifies as a woman. *Cis* is a better, less value-laden term than "normal."[35] Multiple entries also appear in the Facebook list for *trans* status, depending on what people want to emphasize about their transition to another sex or gender.

Although the term *asexual* doesn't appear on the Facebook list, this word refers to people whose gender identity stems, in part, from the fact that they're not sexually attracted to anyone, ever.[36] They may have sexual relations (both heterosexually and homosexually) because their bodies have sexual needs, just like anyone else's, but they don't feel sexual attraction, and therefore they believe they are "a-sexed." (They may go by "Ace" or "Ase" for short.) This may be new information to you, but the Asexual Visibility and Education Network (AVEN) is an organization working to enhance our understanding of this form of gender identity.[37]

We're not the language police here, but throughout this book we stress the importance of taking an other-oriented approach to communication. This means that others' interpretations of your messages, not just your intentions, are central to communication effectiveness. We encourage you to keep an open mind about sex and gender language and to consider the possibility that someone you know and care about might request you to stretch your language usage to include that person's gender identity.

Language and Sexual Orientation   We realize that sexual orientation is one of the more difficult topics to discuss, mainly because people tend to hold strong opinions about it. But no matter your views about sexuality, it's vital to use sensitive, appropriate communication with whomever you encounter.

Insensitivity or intolerance toward persons who are gay, lesbian, bisexual, or queer (a term of liberation from labels about gender identity and sexual orientation) is often reflected in **homophobic language**.[38] Homophobic language denigrates people of non-heterosexual orientations and may arise out of a fear of being labeled gay, lesbian, or queer (homophobia). Sometimes homophobic language is obvious, such as calling someone a derogatory term that we've heard all too often. But homophobic language is often subtle and is sometimes cloaked in an attempt at humor. Examples include blithe references to a lesbian as "wearing the pants in the family" or a gay man as being "light in the loafers." Such language could be perceived as being more tolerable than something overtly homophobic, but both subtle and overt homophobic language reveals insensitive attitudes and a rigid communication style.

Transphobia is defined as a resistance to transgenderism or antagonism toward transgender people.[39] Thus it follows that **transphobic language** is verbal communication that conveys resistance and antagonism toward transgenders. The U.S. is currently in a political and cultural battle about appropriate bathroom use for people who identify as transgender; perhaps this conflict will be resolved by the time you're reading this book. Meanwhile, pay attention to the language used on different sides of this issue. No doubt some references to people who are "not normal" or other discriminatory uses of language will emerge, likely out of ignorance over what transgenderism actually is, what is a real threat, and what is steeped in fear and a lack of compassion.

Another way to communicate bias is through the use of **heterosexist language**, language that reflects an assumption that the world is (or should be) heterosexual, as if romantic and sexual attraction other than heterosexual isn't possible or acceptable. For example, we often hear students in public speaking classes start a speech something like this: "How many of you ladies have trouble getting your boyfriend to go shopping with you?" In a mixed-sex/gender audience, what are some possible

homophobic language
Language that overtly denigrates persons of non heterosexual orientations, usually arising out of a fear of being labeled gay, lesbian, or queer.

transphobia
A resistance to transgenderism or antagonism toward transgender people.

transphobic language
Language that conveys resistance and antagonism toward transgender people.

heterosexist language
Language that reveals an assumption that the world is heterosexual, as if other orientations did not exist.

COMMUNICATION & ETHICS

"That's So Gay!"
Although the primary definition of *homophobia* is a fear of being labeled or viewed as homosexual, research has found two other meanings for the term. A secondary meaning is a discriminatory attitude toward or hatred of people who are homosexual. Some forms of language certainly reflect this negativity. Yet a third meaning is used among homosexual persons, as either a form of self-hatred or as an aggressive, derogatory term that people who share this sexual orientation hurl at each other.[40]

Some years ago, saying, "That's so gay" in response to someone's communication, actions, or choice of clothing, accessories, or furnishings (typically things not expected to be owned or used by members of one's sex) was made popular by the characters Joey and Chandler on the TV sitcom *Friends*. College students picked up this language, using the term *gay* to refer to anything disagreeable and often justifying its use by saying that it was just a funny thing to say and not meant to refer to homosexuals or to be discriminatory or inappropriate. Many communication professors, as well as gay rights activists and educators, across the country took a stand to curb the use of this form of language, contending that it was indeed homophobic and discriminatory.[41] You may not hear the phrase "That's so gay" much anymore; if that's the case, we're glad it's on its well-deserved way out of the lexicon, because here's the problem: Substitute any word for the term *gay* and see if it sounds derogatory. Would someone say "That's so Jew" or "That's so black" and dare to think that these phrases weren't racial/ethnic slurs?

interpretations of this speech introduction? One take is that the speaker is addressing only those women in the audience that he or she believes to be straight and in possession of a boyfriend and is excluding all others. Another interpretation is that the use of the term "ladies" is derogatory and intended to include some of the men in the audience, particularly the gay men who might have boyfriends. Either way, such an introduction shows a speaker's biased assumptions as well as his or her poor choice of language.

Just as you have learned to avoid racially charged terms that degrade and draw attention to someone's ethnicity, it's important to learn to avoid language that denigrates a person's sexual orientation or gender identity and that draws undue attention to this element of cultural diversity. One of your authors was quite taken aback a few years ago when she received a paper from a first-year student in which the derogatory term *fag* frequently appeared. Such language is a clear signal of homophobia.

Heterosexist language is often more subtle than homophobic language. It may emerge through *omission*, meaning what *is not* said, rather than *commission*, or what *is* said. Earlier in this chapter we exemplified the offense of omission, when we mentioned the public speaker who opened a speech with the question, "How many of you ladies can't get your boyfriend to go shopping with you?" This language use assumes the women in the audience are all straight (and it may leave out others, like bisexuals, transgenders, and people who identify as queer). An interesting form of heterosexist language surrounds people's level of comfort with using "husband" and "wife" to refer to the married partners of gays and lesbians. Granted, some people hold religious views or notions from their upbringing that preclude them from acknowledging gay marriage and the language that goes with it, but since gay marriage has been the law of the land since 2015, our language should, at the very least, reflect the changing times.[42]

Biased Language: Age, Class, and Ability

"Just turn the car, grandpa!" Ever heard a driver say something like this in irritation or said it yourself? Ever call an elderly person a "geezer" or an "old-timer"? Just as some people contend that Americans are hung up on gender and racial diversity, many believe that Americans are hung up on age. We live in a culture that glorifies youth and tends to put its elders out to pasture.[43] Age discrimination is a very real problem in the workforce—so much so that laws have been enacted to guard against someone's being denied professional opportunities because of age. In contrast, people may also hold stereotypes about young people and speak to them as though their youth exempts them from intelligence or responsible action. We recommend that you inventory your language for any terms that either show disrespect for elders or are patronizing or condescending to younger people.

Another factor influencing language that has received research attention is socioeconomic class.[44] Class distinctions are typically revealed in derogatory references to "blue-collar workers," "manual laborers," "welfare recipients," or "one percenters" (a reference to the wealthiest one percent of Americans). Another class slur is "white trash." In the late 1990s, when Paula Jones filed a sexual harassment lawsuit

▼ People sometimes use the word *retarded* in casual conversation to refer to occasions when someone does something foolish or incorrectly. Recent publicity campaigns have helped to curb the use of this biased language, as has the increasing visibility of celebrities with Down syndrome, such as Jamie Brewer, a member of the cast of *American Horror Story*.
2013 HPA/Hutchins Photo/Newscom

Confronting Bias in Language

Inventory your language for subtle and not-so-subtle indications of bias in several areas:

- *Race, Ethnicity, and Nationality.* Avoid language that denigrates members of a racial or ethnic group; be careful not to overemphasize race or ethnicity or "mark" a person by using adjectives referring to national origin, as in "that Oriental student in my class."

- *Religion.* Watch stereotypical language pertaining to religious affiliation, such as derogatory references to Jews, Muslims, or fundamentalist Christians, for example.

- *Gender.* Include all sexes and genders in your language, especially in your use of pronouns; avoid masculine generic pronouns and male-linked terms that exclude others. Try to stay current in your use of language, even if terms for sex and gender identity change quickly.

- *Sexual Orientation.* Be alert to the potential for heterosexism in your language—the assumption that everyone is heterosexual or that heterosexuality is the only possible orientation. Eliminate homophobic and transphobic language that degrades and stereotypes gays, lesbians, bisexuals, queers, and transgender individuals.

- *Age.* Avoid calling too much attention to a person's age in your verbal communication. Be especially vigilant not to label or stereotype the elderly or to condescend to or glorify youth.

- *Class.* Monitor references to socioeconomic differences, such as distinctions between blue-collar and white-collar workers.

- *Ability.* Avoid verbal communication that draws attention to a person's physical, mental, or learning ability.

against then-president Bill Clinton, she was ridiculed and called "white trash" and "trailer trash" in the press and in living rooms across the country. Inventory your language so that you rid it of references that reveal a condescending or disrespectful attitude toward someone's education (or lack of it) and socioeconomic status. You don't want to come off as an entitled college student.

Finally, an area of bias in language that most people became conscious of by the turn of the 21st century relates to ability. Some years ago, Helen Keller was described as "deaf, dumb, and blind." Nowadays, the appropriate term for her inability to communicate vocally would be *mute*. Be careful that your language doesn't make fun of or draw attention to someone's physical, mental, or learning disability, such as calling someone a "gimp," "retard," or "slow reader" or describing someone as having an "ADD moment." Research has found that when people with disabilities are called demeaning names, they're perceived as less trustworthy, competent, persuasive, and sociable than when they're described in positive terms.[45] However, just as some people have reclaimed the word "queer" as a pride term, once-derogatory language like "crip communication" and "crip identity" have also been reclaimed to signal a point of pride and to emphasize solidarity among persons with disabilities.[46]

Using Words to Establish Supportive Relationships

3.5 Explain how language helps create supportive or defensive communication climates.

For more than five decades, communication scholar Jack Gibb's research has been used as a framework for both describing and prescribing verbal behaviors that contribute to feelings of either supportiveness or defensiveness.[47] Some scholars have elevated Gibb's work to "iconic status."[48] Gibb spent several years listening to and observing groups of individuals in meetings and conversations, noting that some exchanges seemed to create a supportive climate whereas others created a defensive one. Words and actions, he concluded, are tools we use to let someone know whether we support them or not. Thus, Gibb defined **supportive communication** as communication that uses language to create a climate of trust, caring, and acceptance. The language used in **defensive communication**, in contrast, creates a climate of hostility and mistrust. When someone gets defensive, communication is seriously impeded.

Two specific uses of language tend to engender negative reactions and defensiveness in most of us; thus, we view them as word barriers that can damage even the most secure of relationships.

supportive communication
Language that creates a climate of trust, caring, and acceptance.

defensive communication
Language that creates a climate of hostility and mistrust.

polarization
The tendency to describe things in extremes, as though no middle ground existed.

- **Polarization** occurs when we describe things in extremes or opposites without any middle ground. One romantic partner might say to the other, "You either love me or you don't." Pronouncements of this kind can be interpreted as ultimatums, as though there were only two options and no compromise position. It's wise to avoid language that creates a false or forced choice for people, making them feel controlled, hemmed in, or manipulated.[49]

In our current political climate, polarizing language isn't hard to find, as people with divergent views may resort to heated terms in defense of entrenched positions. Lynn H. Turner, the former president of the National Communication Association, recently warned readers against using polarizing speech in a column in the association's newsletter:

> Using inflammatory language and demonizing people who espouse a perspective other than your own encourages us to see things as opposites and obscures any search for common ground. We won't be heard if our language instantly puts others on the defensive. We don't have the luxury of indulging ourselves in invectives and pushing each other into opposing camps. Our knowlege of good communication practices should help us pull together now when we need it most. "You cut the cake, I choose the slice" might just be the type of technique we could really use right now.[50]

- **Trigger words** arouse our emotions. Travis, a former student, described in class a word his wife used during arguments that really irked him more than anything else. When Travis would make a point that would frustrate his wife—one for which she had no comeback—she would look at him, toss her hand in the air, and say, "Whatever." Perhaps this word triggers you too, because it punctuates a conversation; it dismisses the other person and her or his point. Do you know what words trigger your emotions, in both positive and negative ways? Certain uses of language can make us feel accepted and appreciated or disrespected and hostile.[51]

trigger words
Forms of language that arouse strong emotions in listeners.

Think about times when your words made someone defensive and how hard you had to work to get the person to let those defenses down. In the following section, we suggest six ways to use verbal communication to create a supportive rather than an antagonistic climate.

Describe Your Own Feelings Rather Than Evaluate Others

Most of us don't like to be judged. One way to avoid evaluating others is to use "I" statements instead of accusatory "you" statements. Statements like, "You always say you'll call, but you never do" or "You need to clean your apartment" attack a person's sense of self-worth and usually result in a defensive reaction. Instead, use the word *I* to describe your own feelings and thoughts about a situation or event: "I find it hard to believe you when you say you'll call" or "It's hard for me to feel comfortable spending time in an apartment that isn't clean." When you describe your own feelings instead of berating the receiver of the message, you take ownership of the problem. This approach leads to greater openness and trust because your listener is less likely to feel rejected or as if you are trying to control him or her.

Solve Problems Rather Than Control Others

When you were younger, your parents gave you rules to keep you safe. Even though you may have resented their control, you needed to know that the stovetop was hot, when not to cross the street, and how dangerous it was to stick your finger in a light socket. Now that you're an adult, when people treat you like a child, it often means they're trying to control your behavior, to take away your options.

Most of us don't like to be controlled. Someone who presumes to tell us what's good for us instead of helping us puzzle through issues and problems to arrive at our own solutions or higher understanding is likely to engender defensiveness. In truth, we have little or no control over others. Open-ended questions such as "What's going on?"

or "How can we deal with this issue?" create a more supportive climate than critical comments such as "Here's where you are wrong" or "You know what your problem is?" or commands like "Don't do that!"

Empathize Rather Than Remain Detached from Others

empathy
The ability to understand and feel what another person is feeling.

Empathy, one of the hallmarks of supportive relationships, is the ability to understand and actually feel or approximate the feelings of others, and to communicate accordingly.[52] We discuss empathy more in Chapters 5 and 6, but for now, we will focus on word choices that convey empathy. To be empathetic, you need to work to put yourself in another person's shoes, to experience as closely as you can what she or he is experiencing. It's also important to use language that reflects your own emotional response. The opposite of empathy is neutrality, which is indifference or apathy toward others. A statement that epitomizes this concept of neutrality is "I don't love you or hate you; I just *don't* you." Such language generates defensiveness in most people.

Let's say you're upset about an argument you just had with someone you're dating, so you seek the support and ear of a good friend. But that friend is in "party mode" or in such a good mood that he or she chooses not to concentrate and really listen to what's going on with you. Rather than engaging in your situation, your friend remains detached and blows off your concerns. In situations like this, most of us become defensive and frustrated, and the quality of our friendship may suffer. Empathy is a building block of a supportive relationship; it may come naturally to some people, but most of us have to work at it, just like many other skills we can develop with a bit of effort.[53]

Be Flexible Rather Than Rigid Toward Others

Some people are just *always* right, aren't they? (These people spend a lot of time alone, too.) Most people don't like people who always seem certain that they are right, because such a stance creates a defensive climate. This doesn't mean that you should have no opinions and go through life passively agreeing to everything. And it doesn't mean that there isn't a clear-cut right and wrong in many situations. But instead of making rigid pronouncements, at times you may want to qualify your language by using phrases such as "I may be wrong, but it seems to me . . ." or "Here's something you might want to consider." Conditional, provisional, and flexible language gives your opinions a softer edge that allows room for others to express a point of view; it opens the door for alternatives. Declarations tend to shut the door.

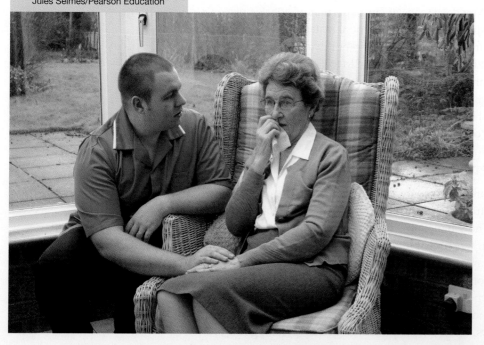

▼ Being genuine and showing empathy for others' feelings are two ways to help establish supportive relationships. What words can help convey your empathy when a friend is troubled?
Jules Selmes/Pearson Education

Present Yourself as Equal Rather Than Superior

You can antagonize others by letting them know that you view yourself as better than they are. You may be gifted and extraordinarily intelligent, but it's not necessary to announce or publicize it. Ever hear of the humblebrag? It's language that, at first glance, makes a person sound humble, but upon further inspection, it's a way to tell others about your achievements.[54] Examples include, "When I bought my Mercedes, no one told me I'd get pulled over all the time" and this one from comedian Dane Cook: "Being famous and having a fender bender is weird. You want to be upset, but the other driver's just thrilled and giddy that it's you." This subtle style of bragging doesn't typically engender supportiveness in conversations with others; even the humblebrag will eventually be interpreted as pompous and can create defensiveness in listeners.

Here's another use of language to watch out for: Although some people have the responsibility and authority to manage others, "pulling rank" doesn't usually produce a supportive climate. With phrases such as "Let's work on this together" or "We each have a valid perspective," you can avoid erecting walls of resentment and defensiveness. "We" language can be preferable to "you" language; it builds a sense of camaraderie and shared experience, and by using it, you avoid setting yourself apart from listeners.

Avoid using "high-falutin'" (unnecessarily complicated) words just to posture, impress others, or project some image. Sometimes referred to as "bafflegab," this kind of language can come in the form of words, phrases, or verbal shorthand that people use but no one understands. People with particular expertise may use abbreviated terms or acronyms. The military is notorious for its use of language that doesn't easily translate outside of military circles. It's better to use informal language appropriate to the situation and your listeners than to attempt to talk over the heads of everyone in the room.

You can also create defensiveness by using language that is too simplistic for your listeners. Granted, when you communicate with someone from another culture or even from another U.S. co-cultural group, you may need to alter your message to get your meaning across. But this means your verbal communication should be explicit, not condescending. For example, some people use oversimplified words when communicating with elderly people. This approach can be evidence of ageism, as we discussed earlier in this chapter. It's inappropriate to assume that aging diminishes one's capacity to understand. Try to use language to present yourself on equal ground with your listeners and establish a supportive, open climate for communication.

Avoid Gunny-Sacking

Gunny-sacking involves dredging up someone's past mistakes or problems and linking them to a current situation. Suppose your best friend has just been dumped by his "one true love," but you—being the good friend that you are—remind him that the last three people he dated were also his "one true love," at least at the time. Your friend wants empathy, but you respond by highlighting his tendency to turn "Ms. Right" into "Ms. Right Now." Such an approach will likely make him feel criticized and engender defensive reactions in him.

RECAP

Using Words to Create a Supportive Climate

- Describe your own feelings instead of evaluating the point of view or behavior of others.
- Keep the focus on problem solving rather than controlling others.
- Instead of ignoring someone's feelings, try to empathize.
- Use conditional language and demonstrate flexibility rather than rigidity in your communication.
- Present yourself as an equal rather than a superior. Speaking like a know-it-all, talking over the heads of listeners, or condescending to them usually breeds defensiveness.
- Avoid gunny-sacking, or reminding someone of past mistakes or issues.

STUDY GUIDE:

⟩ REVIEW, APPLY, AND ASSESS

Why Focus on Language?

3.1 List two reasons why it is important to study verbal communication.

REVIEW: Words are powerful; they affect your emotions, thoughts, actions, and relationships, as well as how you're perceived by others. The better your choices of language, the better your overall communication skill and your relationships.

KEY TERM:
code switching

APPLY: In taking a mental inventory of your use of language, what did you notice that you can change to improve the effectiveness of your communication?

ASSESS: How much of a challenge is it for you to change your language, in ways both large and small? Recall a time when you became acutely aware that you needed to "watch your language." How successful were you at making changes?

The Nature of Language

3.2 Summarize how words are used as symbols that have denotative, connotative, concrete, and abstract meanings and are bound by culture and context.

REVIEW: Language is a system of symbols (words or vocabulary) structured by grammar (rules and standards) and syntax (patterns in the arrangement of words) common to a community of people. The Sapir–Whorf Hypothesis suggests that language and thought are so interrelated that thought is rooted in and controlled by language. The limits of your language may be the limits of your thought. Six important aspects of language are: (1) people use words as symbols (something that represents something else); (2) people attach meanings to words, and sometimes meanings differ (bypassing); (3) people use denotative and connotative meanings for words; (4) people convey concrete and abstract meanings through words; (5) meanings are culture bound; and (6) meanings are context bound.

KEY TERMS:

language	concrete meaning
symbol	abstract meaning
meaning	culture
bypassing	co-culture
denotative meaning	neologism
connotative meaning	

APPLY: Do you find that people's verbal communication seems to accurately reflect the quality of their thoughts? Have you ever run across anybody whose verbal skills did not seem to match his or her thinking skills?

ASSESS:

Practicing Denotation and Connotation

Below we review the differences between denotative and connotative meanings of words and provide examples.

Level	Definition	Example
Denotative	Literal, restrictive definition of a word	*Teacher:* the person primarily responsible for providing your education
Connotative	Personal, subjective reaction to a word	*Teacher:* the warm, supportive person who fostered a climate in which you could learn or the cold taskmaster who drilled lessons into you and made you feel inferior

For each of the following terms, provide a denotative, or dictionary-type, definition; then generate connotative meanings of your own.

Term	Denotative Definition	Connotative Meanings
work		
parent		
infidelity		
professionalism		
loyalty		

The Power of Words

3.3 Identify five primary ways in which words have power.

REVIEW: Words are extremely powerful. They can create and label our experiences, communicate our feelings, affect our thoughts and actions, shape and reflect our culture, and make and break our relationships.

KEY TERM:
allness

APPLY: Give an example of a time when you became acutely aware of the power of words, because someone said something that either worked miracles or turned out badly for everyone involved.

ASSESS: Do your words have power, meaning do you use verbal language in a way that corresponds to any of the five primary ways words have power? Assess whether you tend to use words to create or label an experience, to communicate your attitudes and feelings, and so forth. Work through the five ways words have power.

Confronting Bias in Language

3.4 Describe the major ways in which language reveals bias about race, ethnicity, nationality, religion, gender, sexual orientation, age, class, and ability.

REVIEW: Our language often reveals our biases. Monitor your language to avoid bias in these categories: (1) race, ethnicity, nationality, and religion; (2) gender and sexual orientation; and (3) age, class, and ability.

KEY TERMS:
sexist (exclusive) language	transphobia
generic language	transphobic language
homophobic language	heterosexist language

APPLY: What do you do when someone makes a biased remark around you or to you? How can you effectively respond to show that you don't accept such language?

ASSESS:

Your Bias Is Showing

Here's an activity to illustrate how people reveal their biases through their use of language. Generate a list of stereotypical terms, both positive and negative, often associated with each word below. For example, if you think about the word *Democrat*, you might think of positive and negative terms like "liberal," "tax and spend,"

"big government," "antiwar," "environmentalist," and "populist."

Term	Positive Stereotypical Language	Negative Stereotypical Language
conservatives		
liberals		
international students		
homeless people		
churchgoers		
movie stars		
rappers		

Using Words to Establish Supportive Relationships

3.5 Explain how language helps create supportive or defensive communication climates.

REVIEW: Supportive communication creates a climate of trust, caring, and acceptance; defensive communication creates a climate of hostility and mistrust. Two uses of language that breed hostility and mistrust are polarization and trigger words. Here are six tips for developing a supportive communication climate: (1) describe your own feelings rather than evaluate others; (2) solve problems rather than control others; (3) empathize rather than remain detached from others; (4) be flexible rather than rigid toward others; (5) present yourself as equal rather than superior; and (6) stick to the present situation and avoid gunny-sacking (dredging up past mistakes, problems, and issues).

KEY TERMS:
supportive communication	trigger words
defensive communication	empathy
polarization	

APPLY: Think of language you have used or someone has used toward you that reflects polarization, as though there was no common ground. What effect did such language have on you or your listener? If you used polarizing language, what efforts can you make to not repeat this practice, as it often leads to defensiveness in listeners?

ASSESS: What are your trigger words? Think about experiences related to these words and ponder how they came to trigger your emotions and attitudes. How might you react more effectively when these forms of language are directed at you in the future?

〉 THE PRINCIPLE POINTS

Principle Two:

Effectively use and interpret verbal messages.

- Realize that communication problems may not have to do with the words used, but rather with the meanings people attach to the words.
- Recognize the difference between denotative and connotative language.
- Use concrete terms whenever appropriate, because abstract language is harder to understand and remember than concrete language.
- Understand that words are affected by the culture within which the language is used.
- Pay attention to the words communicators choose to use, and attempt to interpret those words in the spirit and context in which they were intended.
- Avoid biased language when speaking about race, ethnicity, nationality, religion, sex, gender identity, sexual orientation, age, class, and ability.
- Use words to engender supportiveness rather than defensiveness.

UNDERSTANDING NONVERBAL MESSAGES

We respond to gestures with an extreme alertness and, one might say, in accordance with an elaborate and secret code that is written nowhere, known by none, and understood by all. —EDWARD SAPIR

Anna Karwowska/Shutterstock

→ CHAPTER OUTLINE

- Why Focus on Nonverbal Communication?
- The Nature of Nonverbal Communication
- Codes of Nonverbal Communication
- How to Interpret Nonverbal Cues More Accurately

- An Application of Nonverbal Communication Research: Detecting Deception
- Study Guide: Review, Apply, and Assess

LEARNING OBJECTIVES

After studying this chapter, you should be able to

4.1 Provide four reasons for studying nonverbal communication.

4.2 Discuss six elements that reveal the nature of nonverbal communication.

4.3 Identify and explain the seven nonverbal communication codes.

4.4 Explain Mehrabian's three-part framework for interpreting nonverbal cues.

4.5 Describe the primary nonverbal cues associated with deception.

PROFESSOR: "You okay? You looked a bit tense during the exam."

STUDENT: "Yeah, I have test anxiety. What was I doing that made you notice me?"

PROFESSOR: "Nothing strange or out of the norm—just fidgeting with your hair, shifting in your seat, and staring off into space, like you were trying to recall material you studied or something. This kind of thing is quite common when students take exams."

STUDENT: "Hmmm, that's interesting. I'm aware of how I twirl my hair when I'm tense, but I didn't realize others would notice."

PROFESSOR: "It's no big deal. Just do what you need to do, because test anxiety is a real thing that happens to a lot of students."

The comments in the above example all center on *nonverbal communication*, a form of human communication that occurs without words. In this conversation, comments about eye gaze, body shifts, and habitual movement all relate to nonverbal elements that have a profound effect on how we interact with one another. As we explained in Chapter 1, **nonverbal communication** is communication other than written or spoken language that creates meaning for someone. An exception to this definition is sign language. For people who have no hearing impediments, sign language appears to be nonverbal communication. However, to people who are deaf, sign language is verbal communication; certain movements, signs, and facial expressions convey words, phrases, and emphasis.[1]

We know you're becoming familiar with our five-sided model of Communication Principles for a Lifetime, shown in Figure 4.1, but let's do a quick recap. In Chapter 2, we explored ways to become more aware of yourself and your perceptions of things and people with whom you come into contact. An important step in this process of coming to know and understand yourself better is an honest, insightful examination of how you talk. In Chapter 3, we challenged you to consider the power of words, to take inventory of your use of language, and to think about ways to improve your verbal communication so that you extend yourself to others and respond to them in an appropriate, effective manner.

Now we get to what most people consider an even greater challenge: understanding and evaluating your own nonverbal communication and improving your ability to interpret the nonverbal behavior of others. Nonverbal communication is of great importance; a person who can read others' nonverbal communication with sensitivity and skill makes a memorable impression on other people. Because of the power of nonverbal communication to complement verbal communication, to further reveal the self—particularly in situations when talking is inappropriate, impossible, or inadequate—and to affect how

nonverbal communication
Communication other than written or spoken language that creates meaning for someone.

FIGURE 4.1   Communication Principles for a Lifetime

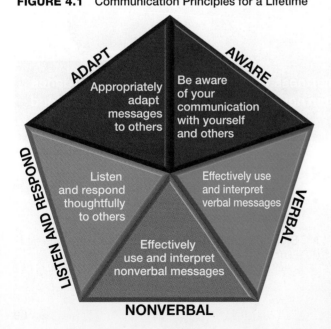

you connect with others as you initiate and build relationships, we've chosen to make this the third of our five key Communication Principles for a Lifetime.

We have two primary goals in this chapter:

- To help you become more aware of your own nonverbal communication and
- To enhance your nonverbal receiving skills, or your ability to detect and interpret the nonverbal cues of others more accurately.

Why Focus on Nonverbal Communication?

4.1 Provide four reasons for studying nonverbal communication.

Have you ever watched a person interact with someone else and thought, "That person just doesn't have a clue"? We've all seen or met people who appear not to pick up on the communication clues of others. For example, have you ever tried to end a conversation because you were late or needed to be somewhere else, and the person you were talking to just wouldn't let you out of the conversation? The person didn't seem to notice you looking at your watch, angling your body away, taking a few steps back, and making minimal vocal responses to what was being said. We all have times when we can't "catch a clue," even if we consider ourselves to be fairly perceptive people. Certain people, places, moods, or topics of conversation may impede our ability to give and receive nonverbal communication effectively. But we don't want to be clueless. We want to be able to exhibit effective nonverbal communication and to read and interpret the clues others give us more sensitively and accurately.

No one can become a perfect interpreter of the nonverbal communication of others, because human beings are unique, complicated, and ever-changing creatures. Although we encourage you to deepen your understanding of nonverbal communication, sharpen your powers of observation, and develop greater skill in interpreting the meanings behind others' nonverbal actions, we also suggest that you remain keenly aware of the idiosyncratic and complex nature of nonverbal communication. To begin to explore this topic, let's look at four reasons for studying nonverbal communication.

Nonverbal Messages Communicate Feelings and Attitudes

Nonverbal communication is a primary tool for conveying our feelings and attitudes and for detecting the emotional states of others.[2] Nonverbal communication scholar Albert Mehrabian suggests that the most significant source of emotional information is the face, which can channel as much as 55 percent of our meaning. Vocal cues such as volume, pitch, and intensity convey another 38 percent of our emotional meaning. In all, we communicate approximately 93 percent of our emotional meaning nonverbally; as little as 7 percent of the emotional meaning is communicated through explicit verbal channels.[3]

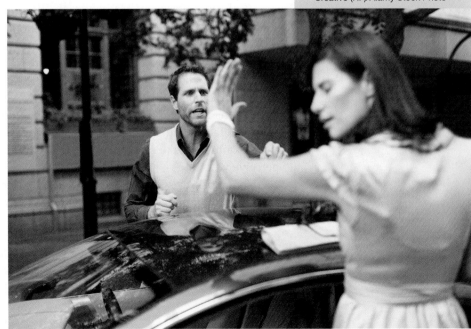

▼ How aware are you of the power of your nonverbal communication with others? Think about confrontations you've had in the past. In your opinion, which communicates emotions most effectively: the volume, pitch, and intensity of the voice; nonverbal gestures, facial expressions, and body positions; or the meaning of the actual words spoken? Cultura Creative (RF)/Alamy Stock Photo

Nonverbal Messages Are More Believable Than Verbal Ones

> JONAS: "Hey—are you mad or something?"
>
> DANITA: (Big sigh.) "Oh, no. I'm not mad." (Said in a subdued tone of voice and without making eye contact.)
>
> JONAS: "You sure? Because you're acting funny, like you're ticked off." (One more try and then Jonas will likely give up.)
>
> DANITA: "I SAID I'M NOT MAD, OKAY? WILL YOU LEAVE IT ALONE PLEASE?"

Despite Danita's claim to the contrary, the real story is—she's mad. The reason the phrase "Actions speak louder than words" is used so often that it's become a cliché is because nonverbal communication is more believable than verbal communication. Verbal communication is a conscious activity; it involves the translation of thoughts and impulses into symbols. Some nonverbal communication is conscious, but a great deal of it is generated subconsciously as we act and react to stimuli in our environment. It's easier to control your words than to control a quiver in your voice when you're angry, the heat and flush in your face when you talk to someone you're attracted to, or shaky knees when you're nervous.

When a person's verbal and nonverbal communication contradict, as in Danita's case, which should an astute observer believe? The nonverbal actions carry the truer message most of the time.

Nonverbal Messages Are Critical to Successful Relationships

One researcher suggests that as much as 65 percent of the way we convey messages is through nonverbal channels.[4] Of course, the message others receive from our behavior may not be the one we intended. But we begin making judgments about people just a fraction of a second after meeting them, based on nonverbal information.[5] We may decide whether a date is going to be pleasant or dull during the first thirty seconds of meeting the person, before he or she has had time to utter more than "Hello."[6]

Consider the handshake, a simple ritualistic greeting between two people used in many cultures. Have you ever considered the power of a handshake to communicate? If you get a half-handed, limp handshake (a.k.a., a "fingerella") from someone, what are you likely to conclude about that person? William Chaplin and his colleagues examined the judgments Americans make about someone's personality based on a handshake and determined that the most positive handshake was strong (but not so strong as to cut off the blood supply), vigorous, not too brief or too long, and complete (meaning that the people gripped each other's hands fully, with palms touching).[7] We form more favorable first impressions of people with good handshakes than of those with lousy ones, so even a simple nonverbal ritual such as a handshake can have a definite and long-lasting impact on how others perceive you.[8]

Nonverbal cues are important not only in the early stages of relationships, but also as we maintain, deepen, and sometimes terminate those relationships. In fact, the more intimate the relationship, the more we use and understand the nonverbal cues of our partners. We also use nonverbal cues to signal changes in the level of satisfaction with a relationship. When we want to cool things off, we may start using a less vibrant tone of voice and cut back on eye contact and physical contact with our partner.

COMMUNICATION & ETHICS

Do We Have a Rhythm or Are You Just Mimicking Me?

People often talk about being "out of synch" with others or having "timing problems" that cause some relationships to end. Sometimes you'll hear people say, "Our relationship went down in flames because we just couldn't get a rhythm." Many of us are very sensitive to the rhythm of relationships and communication with key people in our lives.

In research, this rhythm phenomenon (sometimes termed the "chameleon effect" or "mimicry") is called *interactive synchrony*; it's specifically defined as the coordination of speech and body movement between at least two speakers.[9] Often, people are so in synch that they mirror each other's movements unintentionally. It's a fascinating phenomenon to observe and experience.

However, we can also purposely mirror our conversational partners. Is intentionally mirroring someone ethical, or is it taking synchrony too far?

At times, such purposeful mirroring may be an example of adapting our communication. Adaptation is our fifth Principle for a Lifetime, and we discuss it fully in Chapter 6. A good deal of our ability to adapt our communication involves nonverbal awareness and sensitivity to how we and others nonverbally communicate.

At other times, our goal may be more self-serving than simply adapting to our conversational partners. People who study persuasion and marketing will tell you that one of the keys to successful selling is to develop camaraderie or rapport with the potential buyer so he or she feels a kinship with the seller and a relationship gets established. One technique marketing trainers often teach salespeople is mimicry, mirroring how a potential buyer dresses, stands, walks, gestures, and uses eye contact and facial expressions, and even the rate, volume, and other aspects of the buyer's speech. A customer who perceives the salesperson's matching behavior may feel a rapport and be more likely to buy. For example, wait staff at some restaurants are trained to squat to be at table level when talking to customers so that they're not hovering and can more easily adapt their behaviors in response to diners. Research has found that this simple adaptation increases wait staff tips by 3 percent.[10]

Is this form of nonverbal adaptation just smart business, an ethical use of what research reveals about interactive synchrony? Or is it unethical to pretend to be in synch with someone just to win a sale or persuade people to see things your way? Is it really synchrony or is it chicanery?

Nonverbal Messages Serve Multiple Functions

Nonverbal messages function in a variety of ways:

- Nonverbal cues can *substitute for* verbal messages. Raising your index and middle fingers in the air can mean "peace" or "V" for victory, or it can simply be someone's way of ordering two of something in a noisy, crowded environment where it's hard to be heard.

- Nonverbal cues delivered simultaneously with verbal messages *complement*, clarify, or extend the meaning of the verbal cues, conveying more information and allowing for a more accurate interpretation. When someone waves, makes eye contact, and says "Hello," the hand gesture and eye contact are nonverbal complements to the verbal greeting, providing context and revealing emotions and attitudes.

- Sometimes our nonverbal cues *contradict* our verbal cues. In our earlier example, Danita said she wasn't mad but her nonverbal cues revealed her true emotional state. In most instances when verbal and nonverbal cues contradict each other, the nonverbal message is the one we should believe.

- We use nonverbal messages to *repeat* our verbal messages. You and a friend head in different directions after class. You yell, "See you at the dorm at 4," but your friend can't hear you over the hall noise, so he makes a face as though he's confused.

RECAP

Why Focus on Nonverbal Communication?

- Nonverbal communication is our primary means of communicating feelings and attitudes toward others.
- Nonverbal messages are usually more believable than verbal messages.
- Nonverbal communication is critical in the initiation, development, and termination of relationships.
- Nonverbal messages function to substitute for, complement, contradict, repeat, regulate, and accent verbal messages.

You point in the direction of the dorm and then raise four fingers in the air, to which your friend nods his head up and down, signaling that he understands your message. In such a situation, the verbal message comes first, but the nonverbal cues repeat the message to create greater understanding.

- Nonverbal cues *regulate* our participation in conversation. When talking with people, we rely on such nonverbal cues as eye contact, facial expressions, audible intakes of breath, vocalizations such as "um," shifts in posture or seating position, and movements closer to or farther away from others.

- We may use nonverbal cues to *accent* or reinforce a verbal message. "We simply must do something about this problem or we will all bear the blame," bellows the mayor. When the mayor says the word *must,* she pounds the podium and increases her volume for emphasis. Such a vocalization and gesture serve to accent or add intensity to the verbal message.

The Nature of Nonverbal Communication

4.2   Discuss six elements that reveal the nature of nonverbal communication.

While the benefits of studying and improving one's facility with nonverbal communication are clear, deciphering unspoken messages can be tricky. Dictionaries help us interpret words, but no handy reference book exists to help decode nonverbal cues. Below are some of the challenges inherent in the interpretation of nonverbal communication.

The Culture-Bound Nature of Nonverbal Communication

Some evidence suggests that humans from every culture smile when they are happy and frown when they are unhappy.[11] They also all tend to raise or flash their eyebrows when meeting or greeting others, and young children in many cultures wave to signal that they want their parents, raise their arms to be picked up, and suck their thumbs for comfort. These trends indicate some underlying commonality in human emotion. Yet each culture tends to develop unique rules for displaying and interpreting the expression of emotion.[12]

Nonverbal behavior is culture bound. If you don't situate nonverbal actions within a cultural context, you'll make critical errors in communicating nonverbally and in attempting to interpret the nonverbal behavior of others. Intercultural communication scholars teach us that one culture's friendly or polite action may be another culture's obscene gesture.[13]

The Rule-Governed Nature of Nonverbal Communication

You operate according to many rules in your nonverbal communication. You may be unaware that you function according to these rules, but when your rules are violated, you definitely know it. For example, have you ever been in a conversation with someone who got too close, all up in your face? For some reason, the other person's rule about appropriate distance differed from yours.

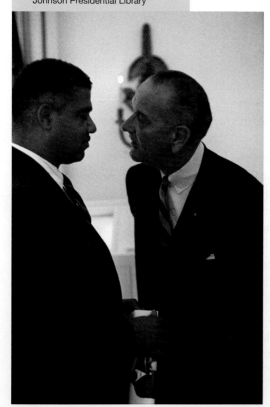

▼ We're usually uncomfortable when someone breaks our unwritten rules for nonverbal communication. President Lyndon Johnson, for example, was known for standing too close when he talked to people, giving listeners what came to be called "the Johnson treatment." In this 1966 conversation, civil rights leader Whitney Young seemed to be so uncomfortable with President Johnson's space invasion that he closed his eyes. How do you typically respond when someone violates your nonverbal communication expectations?
White House Photo Office/Lyndon B. Johnson Presidential Library

Communication scholar Judee Burgoon created a theory of how nonverbal communication functions, termed **expectancy violations theory**.[14] The theory suggests that we develop expectations for appropriate nonverbal behavior in ourselves and others, based on our cultural backgrounds, personal experiences, and knowledge of those with whom we interact. When those expectations (or rules) are violated, we experience heightened arousal (we become more interested or engaged in what's happening), and the nature of our interpersonal relationship with the other person becomes a critical factor as we attempt to interpret and respond to the situation.

When someone stands too close to you in conversation, expectancy violations theory claims that you'll react to the nonverbal rule infraction according to the credibility, status, and attractiveness of the person who's violating your space. If the person isn't attractive (physically or personally) or of respectable status and credibility, you'll likely compensate for the space invasion nonverbally, usually by stepping back or moving away from the person. Only rarely do most of us resort to a verbal response such as "Please back up; you're violating my personal space." We all violate nonverbal rules from time to time, and at those moments we become acutely aware that rules or expectations of appropriateness have a powerful influence on nonverbal communication.

expectancy violations theory
A theory that suggests that we develop rules or expectations for appropriate nonverbal behavior and react when those expectations are violated.

The Ambiguous Nature of Nonverbal Communication

Most words are given meaning by people within a culture who speak the same language. But the intended meaning of a nonverbal message is known only to the person displaying it. The person may not mean to convey the meaning that an observer sees in it. In fact, the person may not intend for the behavior to have any meaning at all.

Some people have difficulty expressing their emotions nonverbally. They may have frozen facial expressions or monotone voices. Often it's a challenge to draw meaningful

COMMUNICATION & DIVERSITY

Lessons from a Student in a Wheelchair

When many people think of cultural diversity, they may only think about nationalities and customs in other countries, like we just discussed in the previous section. But it's important to consider other forms of cultural diversity that may relate to physical or learning ability, sex and gender identity, racial and ethnic diversity, and so forth.[15]

The following is an important lesson about nonverbal communication and cultural sensitivity. With his permission, we tell our student Kurt's story: Kurt has been in a wheelchair for most of his life as a result of having a condition from birth called osteogenesis imperfecta (OI). This condition causes a person's bones to become brittle and break easily. Like diabetes, there are many levels or types of OI. Some people with OI are ambulatory on their own, without the support of a wheelchair or braces. But many others, like Kurt, cannot support their own weight, so they use wheelchairs to facilitate their lives. One day in our Introduction to Communication class we were discussing nonverbal cues and awareness, and Kurt recounted a situation he had experienced multiple times. Recently, in a crowded elevator on campus, another student rested his hand on one of Kurt's grips—the handles on the back of most wheelchairs that allow someone to push it. Kurt recognized the extra weight on his chair, so he gently reached over his shoulder and slid the person's hand off of the grip. Yet this person was so oblivious and engrossed in conversation that he put his hand back on the grip. Kurt said he realized that some people don't understand that "his wheelchair feels like part of his body," so the touch on the chair was a nonverbal violation. He didn't make a big deal out of it, but revealed that he has commented on these forms of intrusion in the past, when people have placed their hands on his chair—either the armrests or back grips. Kurt hopes to educate people that, for him, when people touch his wheelchair (usually out of ignorance or a lack of awareness), it's an uninvited touch on his body.

As you think about nonverbal communication and its link to culture, we encourage you to broaden your view of what constitutes "culture." It's important that we all continue to be enlightened about *many* forms of diversity, so that we can become more appropriate and sensitive communicators.

perception checking

The skill of asking other observers or the person being observed whether your interpretation of his or her nonverbal behavior is accurate.

conclusions about these people's behavior, even if we know them quite well. One strategy that helps us interpret others' nonverbal cues is called **perception checking**, as we mentioned in Chapter 2 in our discussion of self-awareness. Jonas, whom we read about earlier in this chapter, was trying to check Danita's perceptions when he asked whether she was mad. To check your own perceptions, observe in detail the nonverbal cues, make your own interpretation, and then do one (or both) of two things: (1) Ask the people you're observing how they feel or what's going on, and/or (2) run your interpretation by another observer to get a second opinion or more input before you draw a conclusion.

The Continuous Nature of Nonverbal Communication

Words have a beginning and an end. You can point to the first word in this sentence and underline the last one. Our nonverbal behaviors are not as easily dissected because they're continuous. Imagine you're standing in the hallway after class, talking to a classmate. You both make eye contact as you talk, and your facial expressions coordinate with what you're saying. You stand a certain distance apart, move and change your posture as the conversation flows, add a hand gesture or two to emphasize what you're saying, and change your pitch, volume, and rate of speaking to further make yourself understood. Your classmate's cell phone rings. Your classmate apologizes, answers the phone, and makes eye contact with you once again, along with a facial expression of apology. Your classmate then signals to you with a hand gesture that she or he has to go, and you understand that your conversation is over. You wave goodbye, break eye contact, and go your separate ways, and your nonverbal behaviors go with you. In this simple example, the nonverbal cues are flying faster than the verbal ones, but they're essential in getting the message across. The sheer volume and continuous flow of nonverbal cues—not to mention complications such as culture and emotion—make accurate interpretation a challenge.

The Nonlinguistic Nature of Nonverbal Communication

Even though some writers in the 1960s and 1970s tried to make readers think otherwise, there is no "language of the body." Julius Fast, author of the 1970 book *Body Language*, believed that nonverbal communication was a language with pattern and grammar, just like verbal communication.[16] He suggested that if you were savvy and observant enough, you could quickly and easily interpret certain nonverbal behaviors to mean certain things—in any case, at any time. For example, Fast contended that if a woman sat cross-legged and pumped her foot up and down while talking to a man, that was a clear-cut sign of her romantic interest in him. If someone didn't make eye contact, she or he was automatically dishonest and untrustworthy. If people crossed their arms in front of them, that indicated hostility.

The problem is that the body language approach didn't take into account the complexities of individual, contextual, and cultural differences. Pumping the foot might be an indication of nervousness or impatience, not attraction. Some people are shy; others come from a culture in which making direct eye contact is considered rude. It's important to remember that nonverbal communication doesn't conform to the patterns of a language.

"Of course I'm listening to your expression of spiritual suffering. Don't you see me making eye contact, striking an open posture, leaning towards you and nodding empathetically?"

Aaron Bacall/Cartoon Stock

The Multichanneled Nature of Nonverbal Communication

The "second screen" phenomenon is gaining popularity in the United States and globally. Research shows that a growing number of TV watchers view (or listen to) programming while also using their mobile phones, tablets, or laptop computers (a.k.a., a "second screen"). According to a recent survey, 87 percent of people surveyed indicated that they used other devices while watching TV, mainly for the purpose of searching for information related to the TV show they were watching. (This statistic was 41% in 2014.) Globally, the number one second screen device was the smartphone, compared to the U.S.-preferred laptop computer. Besides searching for information related to what was watched on TV, other survey respondents reported using social media, such as Twitter and Facebook, to comment about the TV programming. In addition, others said they used a second screen device to multitask, perhaps sending e-mail messages or texts while a TV

> **RECAP**
>
> **The Nature of Nonverbal Communication**
>
> - *Nonverbal communication is culture bound.* Nonverbal behaviors vary widely across cultural and co-cultural groups. Interpret nonverbal cues within a cultural context.
> - *Nonverbal communication is rule governed.* We develop rules or expectations for appropriate nonverbal behavior in ourselves and others.
> - *Nonverbal communication is ambiguous.* Nonverbal behavior is difficult to interpret accurately because the meanings for different actions vary from person to person.
> - *Nonverbal communication is continuous.* Unlike the stop-start nature of verbal communication, nonverbal messages flow from one situation to the next.
> - *Nonverbal communication is nonlinguistic.* Nonverbal communication does not have the regularities of vocabulary, grammar, and pattern that language has.
> - *Nonverbal communication is multichanneled.* Nonverbal cues register on our senses from a variety of sources simultaneously, but we can actually attend to only one nonverbal cue at a time.

was on in the background.[17] But even with your powers of multitasking and an ability to switch your attention rapidly, you can really focus on only one medium at a time.

Nonverbal communication works the same way; nonverbal cues are communicated in multiples or clusters, but we process the cues individually. Before you try to interpret the meaning of a single nonverbal behavior, look for clusters of corroborating nonverbal cues, in conjunction with verbal behavior, to get the most complete picture possible.

Codes of Nonverbal Communication

4.3 Identify and explain the seven nonverbal communication codes.

Many researchers and theorists have long been fascinated with nonverbal communication, but two who have made perhaps the greatest contributions to our understanding are Paul Ekman and Wallace Friesen, sometimes referred to as the "great classifiers" of nonverbal behavior.[18] Next, we introduce and explain each code and then provide a few research findings to illustrate how we can apply knowledge of nonverbal communication to further our understanding of human behavior.

Appearance

Many cultures around the world place a high value on appearance—body size and shape, skin color and texture, hairstyle, and clothing—but it seems like Americans *really* emphasize this one nonverbal cue. In 2015, Americans spent a record $13.5 billion on procedures to modify physical appearance. Over twelve million surgical and nonsurgical cosmetic procedures were performed in the United States, up from ten million in 2014. Ninety percent of these procedures were performed on women, with liposuction and breast augmentation being the top two most popular procedures.[19]

We put such pressure on ourselves and others to be physically attractive that our self-esteem may decline when we realize we cannot match up with some perceived ideal.[20] People tend to elevate highly physically attractive people onto a pedestal (whether or not they actually deserve this kind of accolade). We often attach all sorts of desirable qualities to them, a phenomenon known as the **halo effect**.[21] Research shows that we tend to think physically attractive people are more credible, happy, popular,

halo effect

Attaching positive qualities to people who we deem highly physically attractive.

socially skilled, prosperous, employable, persuasive, honest, poised, strong, kind, outgoing, and sexually warm than other people.[22] And studies have shown that college students perceive physically attractive teachers to be more approachable than other teachers and give them higher evaluation scores.[23]

Another aspect of physical appearance is clothing, which serves many functions. Chief among them are keeping the body warm and protected; preserving a person's modesty and a society's sense of decency; conveying one's personality, status, and culture; demonstrating one's sexuality; and communicating identification with a group, such as wearing your university's logo on a T-shirt.[24] **Artifacts** such as jewelry, tattoos, piercings, makeup, cologne, and eyeglasses are also displays of culture and personality. These nonverbal elements of appearance affect how we feel about ourselves and how we are perceived by others.[25]

artifact

Clothing or another element of appearance (e.g., jewelry, tattoos, piercings, makeup, cologne).

Body Movement, Gestures, and Posture

kinesics

Study of human body movements, gestures, and posture.

Kinesics is the study of human body movements, gestures, and posture, all of which are affected by your self-esteem and emotional state. For example, when you're feeling upbeat and good about yourself, you're likely to carry yourself more upright and possibly exhibit a "spring in your step." Conversely, if you're having a bad day, your posture might be more slumped over or stooped, because some days it's just hard to hold your head and shoulders up.

One component of kinesics is gestures, which are culture bound, context bound, and rule governed.[26] Most gestures are specific to a culture's history and traditions. However, some have cross-cultural, widely understood meanings, such as the pointing gesture and the "come here" and "stay away" gestures accomplished with the placement of the palms and motion of the hands and arms. But here's our repeated warning about nonverbal cues: *Don't assume.* Don't assume a universal interpretation applies to a gesture you've grown up using in your home culture. These forms of nonverbal communication are complicated; some take centuries to develop through a culture.

Another component of kinesics is how you carry yourself, and more specifically, how you walk. Have you ever thought about how you walk? Each person has a unique walk that can become easily recognizable with even a small amount of observation. But technology

COMMUNICATION & SOCIAL MEDIA

Fitness Posts on Social Media: Do Comparisons Have Consequences?

We've all seen them—photos and posts on social media by a friend or acquaintance who has run a marathon, accomplished some physical hurdle after a year of preparation, completed the roughest workout in history, met a weight loss goal, and so forth. People love to post their physical accomplishments online and who can blame them?

Using social media as an outlet of expression about physical appearance and body image is a common activity, one that researchers have explored for what such posts and photos do for the person publicizing the achievement. But even more interesting is recent research examining how other people *respond* to such posts and photos. Two communication scholars, Analisa Arroyo and Steven Brunner, explored online friends' responses to

others' fitness posts.[27] They found that such posts generate negative body talk, especially from individuals who have a high tendency to compare themselves to others. Examples of such responses include, "Wow, congrats on finishing the marathon; I sure couldn't do that. I'd keel over at the second mile" and "Glad you lost weight. Now I'm eating for both of us!"

It is understandable to want to communicate online achievements related to physicality, as well as other accomplishments. All we caution here is to think about the receivers of your online messages (just as we encourage you in this book to become more other-oriented in all of your communication). Might someone suffer self-esteem loss or body image issues because they see you and others managing your physical fitness, diet, and health more successfully? Do you have a responsibility here?

is affecting this phenomenon. Anyone on a college campus has seen this: people staring down into their smartphones, reading or responding to texts, but certainly not watching where they're walking. They meander and weave, almost running into you or inanimate objects. Eventually, they may suddenly look up and realize they weren't paying attention to their surroundings. We get it: Smartphones are mesmerizing. We've all gotten absorbed in our phones, focused on the task of checking our social media accounts, texting someone, or seeing if someone called us while we were in class. But here's something you may not know: Just like talking or texting on your phone makes you a dangerous driver, it also makes you a dangerous, inefficient *walker.*

▲ Texting or talking on your phone while walking slows you down and makes you a dangerous, inefficient walker.
Monkey Business/Fotolia

Eric Lamberg and Lisa Muratori, professors at Stony Brook University in New York, studied the effects of cell phone use on walking behavior.[28] Their results weren't surprising: Like drivers who slow down when using their phones, students who walked across campus while talking or texting walked more slowly than others who were not using their phones. In addition, cell phone walkers evidenced significant "lateral deviation," straying by as much as 61 percent from a straight path as they walked toward their destination. Although both talking and texting caused walking problems, texters were worse at walking than talkers.

We know students are going to use their smartphones on campus—that's not going to change. But we encourage you to try to have more awareness when using your phone. Notice your own nonverbal behavior, such as how you walk, how loudly you talk, how little eye contact you make (preferring your phone over a face-to-face conversation), and the amount of time you're engaged in activities related to your phone. You may be motivated to make some changes that can make your life more efficient and productive (or at least keep you from walking into a professor or a wall).

Eye Contact

Do you agree that the eyes are the "windows to the soul"? What can people tell about you by looking into your eyes? Are you comfortable making eye contact with most people or only with people you know well? Eye contact is extremely important in American culture and in many other cultures around the world. People make all kinds of judgments about others—particularly about their trustworthiness, truthfulness, and sincerity—on the basis of whether they make or avoid eye contact.[29] Table 4.1 summarizes circumstances under which we're more or less likely to make eye contact with a conversational partner.[30]

TABLE 4.1　When Do We Make Eye Contact?

You are more likely to look at your conversational partner when you . . .	You are less likely to look at your conversational partner when you . . .
• are physically distant from the person.	• are physically close to the person.
• are discussing impersonal topics.	• are discussing intimate topics.
• have nothing else to look at.	• have other objects, people, or backgrounds to look at.
• are interested in your partner's reactions.	
• are romantically interested in or like your partner.	• aren't romantically interested in or dislike your partner.
• wish to dominate or influence your partner.	• come from a culture that doesn't value visual contact in interaction.
• come from a culture that emphasizes visual contact in interaction.	• are an introvert.
• are an extrovert.	• are embarrassed, ashamed, sorrowful, sad, or submissive.
• are listening, rather than talking.	• are trying to hide something.
• are female.	• are male.

visual dominance ratio
Amount of eye contact made while speaking with others, versus listening to them.

How much eye contact do you make when you are speaking with others, versus when you are listening to them? In nonverbal communication research, this phenomenon is called the **visual dominance ratio**, defined as the amount of eye contact made while speaking with others, versus listening to them.[31] Romantic partners may feel agitated by an imbalance in this regard. For example, suppose you are the partner who maintains a lot of direct eye contact—no matter if you're speaking or listening—but your partner breaks eye contact when it comes time to listen. Once you start speaking, your partner may turn her or his attention to a phone, other people, a computer or TV screen, or other distractions, which may leave you feeling unimportant and unheard. Some people may be unaware that they exhibit poor eye contact while listening, but for others, it's an intentional power move or show of dominance. They want to "hold court" when they have something to say, but their nonverbal cues (lack of eye contact) when listening reveal their true attitude toward others.

Facial Expressions

Actor/comedian Steve Carell has a very expressive face. Researchers suggest that the human face is capable of producing 250,000 different facial expressions.[32] Steve Carell can probably make them all.

As early as 1872, when Charles Darwin systematically studied the expression of emotion in both humans and animals, scientists realized that nonverbal cues are the primary ways humans communicate emotion.[33] As we stated earlier in this chapter, facial and eye expressions, along with posture, gestures, and body movements (such as how we walk) reveal our feelings.[34] Your face tends to express which *kind* of emotion you're feeling, whereas your body reveals the intensity or how *much* emotion you're feeling.

You've downloaded a new app on your phone and show it to your romantic partner or a friend. Or as an interviewer reads your résumé, you sit in silence across the desk. In both of these situations, you scan the other person's face, eagerly awaiting some reaction. To interpret someone's facial expressions accurately, you need to focus on what the other person may be thinking or feeling. It helps if you know the person well, can see her or his whole face, have plenty of time to observe, and understand the situation that prompted the reaction.[35]

Even if you don't know people well, you can still learn a lot from their facial expressions. For example, Oxford scholar, psychologist, and nonverbal communication expert Peter Collett analyzed the facial expressions of U.S. President Donald Trump during his campaign and the early stages of assuming the presidency.[36] In an article written for the British newspaper *The Guardian,* Collett first noted the "sheer variety" of "dramatic and over-stated" facial expressions that the president displays. He then summarized these nonverbal cues into seven categories, including one called the "alpha face" (designed to communicate a macho personality by lowering the brows, narrowing the eyes, and firmly setting the mouth). Another category that Collett termed the "puckered chin" incorporated a "zipped smile." This facial expression is accomplished by pulling the chin in toward the chest and using a smile that doesn't reveal the teeth. According to Collett, this oft-used facial expression is in response to feeling threatened.

How accurately do we interpret emotions expressed on the face? Researchers who have attempted to measure subjects' skill in identifying the emotional expressions of others have found it a tricky business. Classic research by Ekman and Friesen determined that the human face universally exhibits six primary emotions: happiness, sadness, surprise, fear, anger, and disgust or contempt.[37] More recently, however, researchers at Ohio State University have documented people's abilities to consistently express

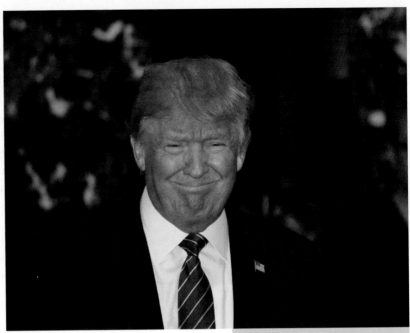

▲ You can learn a lot from people's facial expressions. On the left is what nonverbal communication expert Peter Collett calls U.S. President Donald Trump's "alpha face" and on the right is his "puckered chin" incorporating a "zipped smile." Mike Post/WireImage/Getty Images (left), PACIFIC PRESS/Alamy Stock Photo (right)

twenty-one recognizable facial expressions that reflect combined, even contradictory or conflicting, emotions, such as "happily disgusted" or "sadly angry."[38]

Even though our faces provide a great deal of information about emotions, we quickly learn to control our facial expressions. One fascinating study examined children's facial expressions when they received either wonderful, new toys or broken, disappointing toys.[39] When they received the disappointing toys, the children showed a flash of disappointment on their faces, but then very quickly they masked their disappointment and changed their facial expressions to reveal a more positive, socially appropriate reaction. Even very young children learn to control the way an emotion registers on their face.

Touch

Touch is the most powerful form of nonverbal communication; it's also the most misunderstood and carries the potential for the most problems if ill used. Consider some moments involving accidental touch. Standing elbow to elbow in an elevator or sitting next to someone in a crowded airplane, you may find yourself in physical contact with total strangers. As you stiffen your body and avert your eyes, a baffling sense of shame and discomfort may flood over you. Why do we sometimes react this way to accidental touching? Normally, we touch to express affection and intimacy. When affection or intimacy isn't our intended message, we instinctively react to modify the impression our touch has created.

Countless studies on touch, termed **haptics** in research, have shown that intimate human contact is vital to our personal development, well-being, and physical health.[40] Being deprived of affection tends to lead to psychological problems, but it also impacts how well we sleep and our ability to cope with physical pain.[41]

Think about your role models and the lessons you learned about touch while growing up. If you grew up in a two-parent family, did your parents show each other affection in your presence? If not, you may have grown up believing that affectionate touching should not be done in front of others. As an adult, you may be uncomfortable with public displays of affection. If you grew up with parents or family members who

haptics
The study of human touch.

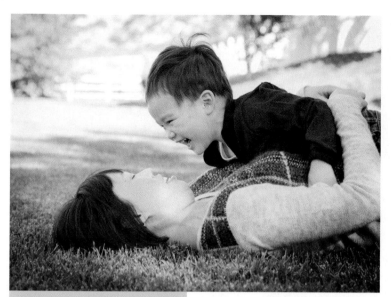

▲ Our views of appropriate touch, termed the *touch ethic*, are typically formed early in life, as we interact with family members.
Andy Dean/Fotolia

touch ethic
A person's own guidelines or standards as to appropriate and inappropriate touch.

paralanguage (vocalics)
Nonverbal aspects of voice (e.g., pitch, rate, volume, use of silence).

were affectionate with each other and their children, your **touch ethic**—what you consider appropriate touching—as an adult is influenced by that experience.[42] We don't mean to insinuate that a touch ethic that accepts public affection is somehow more psychologically healthy than one that reserves touching for private moments. But what if you date or partner with someone whose experiences while growing up led to a very different touch ethic than yours? You may be headed for some conflict but, ideally, some compromise as well.

The amount of touch we need, initiate, tolerate, and receive also depends on our cultural background.[43] Certain cultures are high contact—meaning that touching is quite commonplace—such as some European and Middle Eastern cultures in which men kiss each other on the cheek as a greeting and may even hold hands. Other cultures are low contact, such as some Asian cultures in which public demonstrations of affection are rare and considered inappropriate.[44]

The Voice

"We have nothing to fear but fear itself."

"Ask not what your country can do for you—ask what you can do for your country."

"I have a dream . . . I have a dream today."

"I am not a crook."

"Mr. Gorbachev, tear down this wall."

If you recognize these statements as having been made by American leaders and you have heard them live or in recordings, you're likely to read them aloud (or hear them in your mind) using the same pauses and changes in pitch, volume, and emphasis as did the famous speakers. John F. Kennedy greatly emphasized the word *not*, as in "Ask NOT what your country. . . ." Martin Luther King Jr. used rising pitch and increased volume as he uttered the word *dream* over and over again in his speech. These leaders learned to use the tremendous capacity and versatility of the voice to create memorable moments.

Like your face, your voice is a major vehicle for communicating your thoughts, your emotions, and the nature of your relationships with others. It also provides information about your self-confidence and influences how you're perceived.[45] The pitch, rate, and volume at which you speak and your use of silence—elements termed **paralanguage** or **vocalics**—all provide important clues. Most of us would conclude, as has research, that a speaker who mumbles, speaks very slowly and softly, continually mispronounces words, and uses "uh" and "um" is less credible and persuasive than one who speaks clearly, rapidly, fluently, and with appropriate volume.[46]

Sometimes it's jarring when a person's physical appearance doesn't seem to match her or his voice.[47] A famous example is former boxing champ Mike Tyson, whose high-pitched voice isn't what we tend to expect out of someone with such a muscular physique. You may have an opinion on the very public transition of Bruce Jenner (the former stepdad in the Kardashian clan) into Caitlyn Jenner, as documented in the TV series *I Am Cait*. But one interesting discussion among transgender people featured on the show surrounded the topic of voice, or as one person put it, the "betrayal" of having a deep, masculine sounding voice in contrast to an outer feminine appearance. One transwoman described how jarring it was for people to see her appearance and then hear her voice, which didn't seem to correspond to expectations. Hormone treatments help with the issue, as does speech therapy, but some transmen and transwomen do not want to alter their voices, believing that a transition can be complete enough without including vocal transformation.[48]

Physical Environment, Space, and Territory

Close your eyes and picture your bedroom as it is right now—whether it's a dorm room you share with one or more roommates, the room you've had since you were a child, your own room, or a bedroom shared with a spouse or partner. If one of your professors were to walk into your bedroom right now, what impressions would he or she form about you?

This question has to do with your interaction with the physical environment and the space around you. You may be unused to looking at the environment as a form of nonverbal communication, but the miniworld you create for yourself reveals a good deal about you. Also, your preferred amount of space, the level of ownership you attach to that space, and your behavior as you delineate and protect that space are fascinating nonverbal elements that researchers continue to study.[49]

The Physical Environment   What's so great about a corner office with wall-to-wall windows? It's one of many indications in American culture of high status. In a working world increasingly structured into cubicles, an employee's work location serves as a symbol of importance.[50] The physical environment is important to the study of nonverbal communication in two ways:

- The choices we make about the environments in which we live and operate reveal a good deal about who we are; physical environments are extensions of our personalities.[51] We tend to put our "signature" on our environments by adorning the settings in which we work, study, and reside to make them unique and personal.

- Nonverbal behavior is altered by the various environments in which we communicate.[52] Formal settings may make our movements more restrained, our body posture more rigid, and our speech limited and whispered. Informal settings tend to cause us to expand and relax our nonverbal behaviors.

One of the more cutting-edge and interesting lines of research into the environment as a form of nonverbal communication surrounds designing spaces for people with disabilities.[53] Although college students without physical disabilities might think this area pertains to building ramps and installing elevators in older campus buildings, design for disability means much more. Some examples include placing extensive Braille signage on campuses (not just in elevators), retrofitting computer labs to offer people with disabilities better access to technology, and providing furniture design in classrooms that assimilates into the environment and accommodates learners of all physical types.[54]

Space   Imagine that you're sitting alone at a long, rectangular table in your campus library. As you sit dutifully with your head in a textbook, you're startled when a complete stranger sits directly across from you at the table. Because there are several empty chairs at the other end of the table, you may feel uncomfortable that this unknown individual has invaded *your* area.

Every culture has well-established ways of regulating spatial relations. How physically close we are willing to get to others relates to how well we know them, to considerations of power and status, and to our cultural background.[55]

A pioneer in helping us understand personal space was Edward T. Hall, who studied **proxemics**, or the distances that people allow between themselves and objects or other people. Hall identified four spatial zones, which are diagrammed in Figure 4.2:[56]

proxemics
The study of how close or far away from people and objects we position ourselves.

FIGURE 4.2   Edward T. Hall's Four Zones of Space

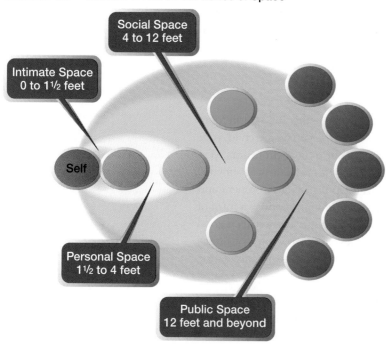

- *Intimate space.* The most personal communication occurs when people are from 0 to $1^1/_2$ feet apart. Unless we're forced to stand in a crowded space, intimate space is open only to those with whom we are well acquainted.

- *Personal space.* Most of our conversations with family and friends occur when we are $1^1/_2$ to 4 feet apart. We feel uncomfortable if someone we don't know well enters our personal space zone on purpose.

- *Social space.* The majority of formal group interactions and many of our professional relationships take place in the social space zone, which ranges from 4 to 12 feet.

- *Public space.* Many public speakers position themselves at least 12 feet away from their audiences, but interpersonal communication doesn't usually occur in the public space zone.

The specific space that you and others choose depends on several variables, most specifically your cultural background.[57] Generally, however, the more you like people, the closer you tend to stand to them. Higher-status and larger people are afforded more space than lower-status and smaller people.[58] We also tend to stand closer to others in a large room than we do in a small room. In general, women tend to stand closer to others than men do.[59]

territoriality

The study of how humans use space and objects to communicate occupancy or ownership of space.

territorial marker

A thing or action that signifies that an area has been claimed.

Territory   The study of how people use space and objects to communicate occupancy or ownership of space is termed **territoriality**.[60] You assumed ownership of that part of the table in the library and the right to determine who sat with you. You may have reacted negatively not only because your sense of personal space was invaded, but also because the intrusive stranger broke a cultural rule governing territoriality.

You announce your ownership of space with **territorial markers**—things and actions that signify that an area has been claimed. If you arrive early to class, for example, you may put your book bag on a chair while you get up and go out into the hall to make a call on your cell phone. That book bag signifies temporary ownership of your seat. If you returned to find that someone had moved your stuff and was sitting in your seat, you would probably become indignant. The most common form of territorial marker is a lock. We lock our doors and windows, cars, offices, briefcases, TVs (using V-chips), and computers (using passwords) to keep out intruders.

While we traditionally think of space as a physical dimension, with increased accessibility and use of technology, we have begun to think of space differently.[61] With the ease of hacking into personal computers and smartphones these days, we all have to

RECAP

Codes of Nonverbal Communication

Appearance	Influences perceptions of credibility and attractiveness.
Body Movement, Gestures, and Posture	Communicate information, status, warmth, credibility, interest in others, attitudes, and liking.
Eye Contact	Conveys trustworthiness, sincerity, honesty, and interest.
Facial Expressions	Reveal thoughts and express emotions and attitudes.
Touch	Communicates intimacy, affection, and rejection.
Voice	Communicates emotion and clarifies the meaning of messages through pitch, rate, and volume.
Environment	Communicates information about the person who functions in that environment; provides context that alters behavior.
Space	Provides information about status, power, and intimacy.
Territory	Provides cues as to use, ownership, and occupancy of space.

face the reality of someone violating our territory and gaining access to our personal information and communication with others. As hacking increases, more innovative methods of protecting private information continue to be developed, such as anti-skimming wallets and two-step authentication systems. It seems we are in a tug-of-war with regard to who wins the privacy-territory battle at any given point in time.

How to Interpret Nonverbal Cues More Accurately

4.4 Explain Mehrabian's three-part framework for interpreting nonverbal cues.

How do we make sense of all the nonverbal cues we receive from others? If you earnestly want to accurately interpret and sensitively respond to someone's nonverbal communication, you must be willing to spend time and effort to develop this skill. Enhancing your interpretive skills requires, first, an awareness of the importance of nonverbal elements in the communication process. A second requirement is the willingness and emotional maturity to make your own behavior secondary to that of someone else. In other words, if you're so wrapped up in yourself that you can think about and deal only with how *you're* feeling, what *you're* thinking, and what *you* want at a given moment, your ability to take in others' nonverbal cues, interpret them accurately, and respond appropriately will be hampered.

Here is a three-part framework developed by Albert Mehrabian that can help you improve your nonverbal interpretive skills. Mehrabian found that we synthesize and interpret nonverbal cues along three primary dimensions: immediacy, arousal, and dominance.[62]

- *Immediacy.* Mehrabian contends that **immediacy**—nonverbal cues that communicate liking and engender feelings of pleasure and closeness—explains why we're drawn to some people but not others.[63] In U.S. social contexts, we watch for eye contact, smiling and other pleasant facial expressions, head nods, an open and relaxed posture, a body orientation toward us rather than away from us, close proximity, a rising intonation in the voice, and culture- and context-appropriate touch to find out whether someone likes us or views us favorably.[64]

- *Arousal.* Nonverbal cues of **arousal** communicate feelings of interest and excitement. As nonverbal scholar Peter Andersen puts it, arousal is "the degree to which a person is stimulated or activated."[65] Primary arousal cues include increased eye contact; closer conversational distances; increased touch; animated vocal expressions (such as laughing); more direct body orientation, smiling, and active facial expressions; and interactive synchrony (or mimicry, as discussed earlier in this chapter).[66]

immediacy
Nonverbal behaviors that communicate feelings of liking, pleasure, and closeness.

arousal
Nonverbal behaviors that communicate feelings of interest and excitement.

▼ Who is the most powerful person in this room? What nonverbal cues indicate that person's dominance?
Picture Factory/Fotolia

dominance

Nonverbal behaviors that communicate power, status, and control.

- *Dominance.* The third dimension of Mehrabian's framework communicates the balance of power in a relationship. **Dominance** cues indicate status, position, and importance. People who are high in status tend to have a relaxed body posture, less direct body orientation toward lower-status people, a downward head tilt, and less direct eye contact, smiling, head nodding, and facial animation than lower-status people.[67] As we alluded to earlier, "power people" usually have more space around them; they have bigger offices and more barriers (human and nonhuman) protecting them. They may communicate their sense of power through clothing, possessions, and their use of time.

An Application of Nonverbal Communication Research: Detecting Deception

4.5 Describe the primary nonverbal cues associated with deception.

Communication research is incredibly practical and useful, especially because we can apply it to our daily lives and see real results. However, one area of nonverbal communication research that is especially helpful is deception detection.[68] What nonverbal cues are reliable indicators of deceit? What do you need to look and listen for? What behaviors do you enact when you are being less than truthful? Granted, nonverbal cues can change depending on whether you're telling a "little white lie" ("No, that outfit does not make you look fat") versus a "big whopper" ("No, I did not cheat on you"). Cues can also change if someone has had time to prepare a lie, versus lying spontaneously, on the spur of the moment.

Research has found that people intent on lying (or who lie easily because they are unconcerned with ethics or the impact of their actions) can learn commonly held beliefs about deception cues and can *change* these cues.[69] For instance, it used to be a commonly held belief that people could not look others in the eye and lie, straight to their faces. A lack of, or break in, eye contact was seen as a reliable deception cue. However, this is no longer the case! Once word got out about eye contact and lying, liars changed their behavior so they wouldn't get caught. The "best" liars now believe that successful deception is associated with keeping a steady, normal gaze when lying.

In addition, research now indicates that the most reliable, accurate nonverbal deception cues aren't visual, but auditory. Scholars contend that we should pay attention to people's voices, rather than trying to read their eyes, facial expressions, body positioning, and so forth.[70] Here's why: Vocal cues are the hardest to control because they are so connected to the body's physical state at the time of deception. Just like it's hard to control a shaking or cracking voice when you're nervous or a change in pitch when you're surprised, fearful, or excited, it's hard to regulate your voice (and the breathing that produces sound) when your body is activated by an act of deception.

response latency

How long it takes someone to respond to another person's communication.

A change in **response latency**, which is the amount of time it takes someone to respond to a question, can also be a sign of deception. For example, if someone responds more quickly to a question than normal (either for the person specifically, or in general, meaning how most people tend to respond), such a vocal cue might indicate deception. Alternatively, if someone who usually responds quickly takes a longer than usual time to respond, that might also indicate deception.

message duration

How short or long someone's message is, typically in response to another person's communication.

A change in **message duration** can also be a sign of deception. If someone typically gives brief responses to another person's communication, an exceptionally long response from that person might indicate deception. Alternatively, if a typically "chatty" and long-winded person starts answering questions with short, abrupt comments or one-word answers, this behavior might also imply deception. Other reliable vocal deception cues include disfluency (struggling for words, not having a normal rhythm to speech); speech errors (lapses in word pronunciation or using incorrect words or word substitutions); filled pauses (filling short silences with utterances like "um," "er," or "ah"); and an unusual shift in volume, pitch, or rate of speaking.[71]

Most of us tend to have extra energy or activation in our bodies when we choose to be deceptive, mainly because we were taught or we believe that deceiving others is wrong. This extra body activation has to go somewhere and for many of us, that energy is released through our extremities.[72] So if you observe someone making unusual foot movements or perhaps clutching their hands together or wringing them, those cues might also indicate deception.

Note that we keep saying "*might* be a cue of deception," because you can never know for certain. We have provided you with research findings on a number of nonverbal deception cues, but caution you not to apply these findings too liberally. You don't want to declare to the entire world that someone is lying to you when they aren't. Many factors must be taken into account when interpreting nonverbal cues as indications of deception.[73] It's better to look for a cluster of nonverbal cues, rather than only one. The safest approach is to have a baseline of information about a person. If you know how a person normally behaves, then you can look, listen, and evaluate cues more accurately.

When you attempt to interpret someone's nonverbal communication, realize that there's a good deal of room for error. Humans are complex, and they don't always send clear signals. But the more you learn about nonverbal communication and the more you become aware of your own nonverbal communication and the nonverbal cues of others, the greater your chances of accurately perceiving and interpreting someone's message.

STUDY GUIDE:

〉 REVIEW, APPLY, AND ASSESS ────────────

Why Focus on Nonverbal Communication?

4.1 Provide four reasons for studying nonverbal communication.

REVIEW: Nonverbal communication is communication other than written or spoken language that occurs without words. It's important to become more aware of your own nonverbal communication and to enhance your ability to detect and interpret others' nonverbal cues more accurately. Nonverbal messages communicate our feelings and attitudes and are critical to successful relationships. They can substitute for, complement, contradict, repeat, regulate, and accent verbal messages. Nonverbal messages are also more believable than verbal messages.

KEY TERM:
nonverbal communication

APPLY: Give an example of how you or someone you know has used nonverbal communication to substitute for, complement, contradict, repeat, regulate, or accent a verbal message.

ASSESS: Conduct an honest assessment of your skill level, as a nonverbal communicator. Do others have a hard time accurately interpreting your nonverbal cues? In other words, are you easy or hard to read? Do you wish to change any of your nonverbal cues? If you want to successfully incorporate new behaviors into your repertoire and rid yourself of unwanted past behaviors, how will you go about this?

The Nature of Nonverbal Communication

4.2 Discuss six elements that reveal the nature of nonverbal communication.

REVIEW: Nonverbal communication is culture bound, rule governed, ambiguous, continuous, nonlinguistic, and multichanneled.

KEY TERMS:
expectancy violations theory
perception checking

APPLY: In addition to the personal space rules described in the chapter, give an example of another nonverbal communication rule you hold and what happens when people violate it.

ASSESS: Think about how much you have traveled in your life, even within your own state or territory. Did you have any trouble understanding people's nonverbal communication in any area or place you visited? Did you feel that your own nonverbal cues were correctly interpreted?

Codes of Nonverbal Communication

4.3 Identify and explain the seven nonverbal communication codes.

REVIEW: Ekman and Friesen provided the primary codes or categories of nonverbal behavior, which are enacted differently by people depending on their cultural background. Each code has been researched extensively and applied to different contexts and relationships. The primary codes include appearance, kinesics (body movement), eye contact, facial expressions, touch (haptics), the voice (paralanguage or vocalics), the physical environment, and how we interact with space (proxemics).

KEY TERMS:

halo effect	touch ethic
artifact	paralanguage (vocalics)
kinesics	proxemics
visual dominance ratio	territoriality
haptics	territorial marker

APPLY: Think about the research findings regarding the various codes or categories of nonverbal communication presented in this chapter. Does your experience with nonverbal communication correspond to these findings?

ASSESS: 1. Inventory your nonverbal communication according to the codes or categories provided in this section of the text. What nonverbal codes represent your strengths? Which areas are weaker for you and need improvement? How will you work to change those behaviors?

2. Body Movement and Emotion

Provide examples of body movements or expressions that reveal each of the six primary emotions listed below. Then generate possible alternative meanings for the same movement. For example, having your arms crossed across your chest might reveal anger or that you're closed off and not open to conversation. It might also mean that you're just chilly. We've provided an example to get you started.

Emotion	Body Movements	Alternative Meaning of Movement
Embarrassment	Covering your face with your hands	Could also indicate deception
Happiness		
Anger		
Surprise		
Fear		
Disgust		
Sadness		

How to Interpret Nonverbal Cues More Accurately

4.4   Explain Mehrabian's three-part framework for interpreting nonverbal cues.

REVIEW: It takes time and effort to develop our skills in detecting and accurately interpreting others' nonverbal communication. Albert Mehrabian's work suggests that nonverbal cues can communicate *immediacy* (liking and pleasure); *arousal* (excitement and interest); and *dominance* (status, position, and importance).

KEY TERMS:
immediacy   dominance
arousal

APPLY: Find a quiet (and unobtrusive) place to sit and observe people in casual conversation. Can you detect who likes who and who dislikes who (and by how much)? Who holds more status and power in the conversation, based on the nonverbal cues you observed?

ASSESS: Consider how you behave nonverbally when interacting with someone you are attracted to, someone you like (as a friend, acquaintance, or coworker), and someone you don't like. Would an observer be able to detect, from your nonverbal cues, how you feel about these people?

An Application of Nonverbal Communication Research: Detecting Deception

4.5   Describe the primary nonverbal cues associated with deception.

REVIEW: While we cannot be certain someone is deceiving us based on their nonverbal communication, researchers have found some nonverbal cues that are reliably associated with deception. Vocal cues tend to be more reliable cues of deception than eye contact, facial expressions, and body movements, because the voice is affected by emotions and hard to control. It is preferable to get a baseline of information about how a person behaves nonverbally, then compare "normal" behavior to behavior that is out of the norm, to help you form a judgment about truthfulness.

KEY TERMS:
response latency   message duration

APPLY: Which nonverbal cues do you believe are the most reliable when attempting to detect deception in others?

ASSESS: What nonverbal signals do you make when you are less than truthful in your communication with someone? Do your nonverbal cues align with research findings?

⟩ THE PRINCIPLE POINTS

Principle Three:

Effectively use and interpret nonverbal messages.

- Realize the importance of physical appearance and attractiveness in American culture.
- Use culturally appropriate body movement, including posture and gestures, to convey messages.
- Work on making appropriate eye contact with others, given that eye contact is the key nonverbal behavior North Americans link with credibility and trustworthiness.
- Become more aware of your and others' facial expressions, because this nonverbal channel is a primary one for conveying emotions.
- Use touch appropriately, given the cultural context within which you communicate.
- Become more aware of the potential you have for vocal expression and how others use their vocal capacities to communicate emotions and ideas.
- Become more aware of your rules regarding space and territoriality so that you may better understand and enact appropriate, effective proxemic nonverbal behaviors when interacting with others.
- Recognize that body movement, eye contact, facial expressions, touch, vocal behaviors, and use of space and territory communicate liking, interest, and dominance.

5

LISTENING AND RESPONDING

Listening, not imitation, may be the sincerest form of flattery. —DR. JOYCE BROTHERS

Ilya Andriyanov/Shutterstock

→ CHAPTER OUTLINE

- The Importance of Listening and Responding Skills
- How We Listen
- Listening Styles
- Listening Barriers

- Improving Your Listening Skills
- Improving Your Responding Skills
- Study Guide: Review, Apply, and Assess

LEARNING OBJECTIVES

After studying this chapter, you should be able to

5.1 Explain the principle of listening and responding thoughtfully to others.

5.2 Identify the elements of the listening process.

5.3 Describe four listening styles.

5.4 Identify and describe barriers that keep people from listening well.

5.5 Identify and use strategies that can improve your listening skills.

5.6 Identify and use appropriate responding skills.

You have heard about distracted driving—driving while texting, talking on your phone, or looking at your GPS instead of the road. But have you heard about distracted listening? Researchers have found that even the visible presence of a phone when you are face-to-face with someone distracts from the quality of the conversation.[1] Your tendency to periodically glance at the phone to see if someone has sent you a message results in distracted listening.

You spend more time listening to others than almost anything else you do. Americans spend up to 90 percent of a typical day communicating with people, and they spend 55 percent of that communication time listening to others.[2] As Figure 5.1 shows, if you're like most people, you spend the *least* amount of your communication time writing, yet you receive more training in writing than in any other communication skill.[3] Most people have not had any formal training at all in listening or responding.[4] Reading this chapter will provide you with the information and skills many people lack.

In this chapter, we focus on the principle of increasing your sensitivity to others—your awareness of and concern for them—by listening. Becoming sensitive to others includes more than just understanding and interpreting their words, thoughts, and ideas—sensitivity. It also involves understanding the emotions underlying the words and unspoken messages of others.[5] Increasing your skill in listening to others is one of the most productive ways to increase all these aspects of your communication sensitivity.

As shown in our familiar model of the Communication Principles for a Lifetime (Figure 5.2), effective communicators do more than absorb a message; they also provide an appropriate response to the speaker. We'll address both listening and responding to others in this chapter.

The Importance of Listening and Responding Skills

5.1 **Explain the principle of listening and responding thoughtfully to others.**

Some researchers suggest that because listening is the first communication skill we learn (we respond to sounds even while in our mother's womb), it's also the most important skill.[6] Listening and responding skills are vital as we develop relationships with others, collaborate, and listen to lectures and speeches.

Listening Enhances Our Relationships with Others

Your skill as a listener has important implications for the relationships you establish with others.[7] In interpersonal communication situations, the essence of being a good conversationalist is being a good listener. Listening

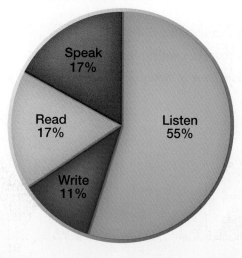

FIGURE 5.1 **What You Do with Your Communication Time**

Speak 17%

Read 17%

Write 11%

Listen 55%

to others is a way to express your interest in, compassion for, and even your love for another.[8] Listening also influences how others respond to us; when people are in the presence of someone whom they perceive to be a good listener, they are likely to respond with greater empathy and interest.[9] One research study found that a key difference between couples who remain married and those who divorce is the ability to listen to each other.[10] Partners in marriages that endure report that being a good listener is key to a satisfying marital relationship.

People who are perceived to be good listeners also enjoy greater success in their jobs than those who are perceived to be poor listeners.[11] For example, physicians, nurses, and other healthcare professionals who are good listeners are perceived to be more competent and skilled than those who listen poorly.[12]

Listening Helps Us Collaborate with Others

One study found that being a good listener was the most important skill to have when working with others in groups and teams.[13] In addition, one of the hallmarks of an effective leader is being a good listener.[14]

Your ability to listen and connect to others will affect your value to other group members whether you are the appointed or emerging leader of a group or a member.[15] Group members who verbally dominate meetings are not usually held in high esteem. Groups need people who can listen and connect conversational threads that often become tangled or dropped during group dialogue.

Listening Links Speaker and Audience

Without effective listening skills, you'll likely miss some messages in public speaking situations. Listening skills are especially important when you need to understand and retain spoken information. There is evidence, for example, that listening skills correlate with academic ability. One study found that almost half of college students who had low scores on a listening test were on academic probation at the end of their first year in college. In comparison, just over 4 percent of the students who had high scores on the same listening test were on academic probation.[16] Improving your listening skills can improve your grade-point average.[17]

Listening is not just for audience members; it is also important for speakers. Good speakers are audience-centered. They consider the needs of their listeners first. They

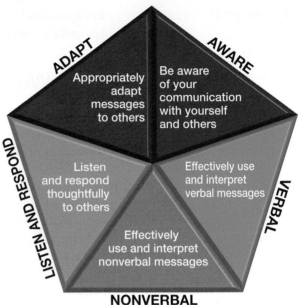

FIGURE 5.2 Communication Principles for a Lifetime

understand what will hold listeners' attention. Many effective speakers acquire this knowledge by listening to audience members one on one before a talk or lecture. Effective speakers also listen to the feedback from their audiences and use that feedback to adjust their speeches while giving them.[18]

How We Listen

5.2 Identify the elements of the listening process.

Do you know someone who is interpersonally inert? Interpersonally inert people are those who just don't "get it." You can drop hints that it's late and you'd rather they head home instead of playing another hand of cards, but they don't pick up on your verbal and nonverbal cues. The physiological processes that let their ears translate sound waves into information in the brain may be working so they can *hear* you, but they certainly aren't listening; they are not making sense out of your symbols.

Hearing is the physiological process of decoding sounds. You hear when the sound waves reach your eardrum. Hearing and listening are two different processes.

Defined succinctly, **listening** is the process we use to make sense out of what we hear; it is a complex process of receiving, constructing meaning from, and responding to verbal and nonverbal messages.[19] Listening involves five activities: (1) selecting, (2) attending, (3) understanding, (4) remembering, and—to confirm that listening has occurred—(5) responding. Understanding these five elements in the listening process can help you diagnose where you sometimes get off track when listening and figure out how to get back on track to increase your listening skill.[20]

Selecting

To listen, you must first **select**, or focus on, one sound among the myriad noises always competing for your attention. Even now, as you are reading this book, there are probably countless sounds within earshot. Stop reading for a moment. What sounds surround you? Do you hear music? Is a TV on? Can you hear traffic noises or birds? Maybe there is the tick of a clock, a whir of a computer, a whoosh of a furnace or an air conditioner. A listener who is sensitive to others selects the sound or nonverbal behavior that symbolizes meaning. The interpersonally inert person does not pick up on the same clues, because he or she is oblivious to the information.

Attending

After selecting a sound, you attend to it. To **attend** is to maintain a *sustained* focus on a particular message. When you change channels on your TV, you first select the channel and then attend to the program you've selected. Just as you tune in to TV programs that reflect your taste in information while you channel surf, you attend to messages of others that satisfy your needs or whims. Attending to a message is vital to being a good listener. There is clear evidence that a person who is skilled in maintaining sustained attention to a message (just listening without interrupting) is perceived as a better listener than someone with a "restless mind."[21]

Understanding

It has been estimated that we hear more than one billion words each year but understand a mere fraction of that number. To **understand** is to assign meaning to messages—to interpret a message by making sense out of what you hear. You can select and attend to sounds and nonverbal cues but not interpret what you see and hear. Understanding occurs when you relate what you hear and see to your experiences or knowledge.[22] Perhaps you have heard the Montessori school philosophy: "I hear and I forget, I see

---

hearing
The physiological process of decoding sounds.

listening
A complex process of receiving, constructing meaning from, and responding to verbal and nonverbal messages, which involves selecting, attending, understanding, remembering, and responding.

select
To focus on one sound as you sort through various sounds competing for your attention.

attend
To maintain a sustained focus on a particular message.

understand
To assign meaning to messages.

and I remember, I do and I understand." It is when we can relate our experiences to what we hear and see that we achieve understanding.

Remembering

Remembering information is considered part of the listening process because it is the primary way we determine whether a message was understood. To **remember** is to recall information. But you can't consciously retrieve or remember all the bits of information you experience; your eye is not a camera; your ear is not a microphone; your mind is not a hard drive. Sometimes, even though you were present, you have no recollection of what occurred in a particular situation. When we are not aware of our actions, our thoughts, or what we perceive—when we are mindless—our ability to remember what occurs plummets. We increase our ability to remember what we hear by being not only physically present, but also mentally present.

remember
To recall information.

You tend to remember what is important to you (such as the time of a meeting mentioned in a voice message) or something you try to remember (like the information in this book for your next communication test). You tend to remember dramatic information (such as where you were when you heard extremely good news or bad news) or vital information (such as your phone number or your mom's birthday).

Responding

As you learned in Chapter 1, communication is a transactive process, not a one-way, linear one. Communication involves responding to others as well as simply articulating messages. You **respond** to let people know that you understand their message. Your lack of response may signal that you didn't understand the message. Your predominant response is often unspoken; direct eye contact and head nods let your partner know you're tuned in. An unmoving, glassy-eyed, frozen stupor may tell your communication partner that you are physically present yet mentally a thousand miles away.[23] There is some evidence that there are cultural differences in our perception of how effectively we respond to others. Students from the United States, for example, perceived themselves to be more responsive listeners than students from Iran.[24] As you'll discover in the next section, you likely have a certain style of listening and responding to others.

respond
To confirm your understanding of a message.

Listening Styles

5.3. **Describe four listening styles.**

Your **listening style** is your preferred way of making sense out of the messages you hear and see. Listening researchers have found that you tend to listen using one or more of four listening styles: relational, analytic, critical, and task oriented.[25] The specific style you use depends on your personality, the specific listening situation, and your listening goal.[26]

listening style
A person's preferred way of making sense out of messages based on that person's personality, listening situation, and listening goal.

Relational Listening Style

Relational listeners tend to prefer listening to people's emotions and feelings. They are quite interested in hearing personal information from others. Perhaps for that reason, evidence suggests that relational-oriented listeners are less apprehensive than people with other listening styles when communicating in small groups and interpersonal situations, and especially when listening to just one other person.[27]

A person with a relational listening style searches for common interests and seeks to empathize with the feelings of others—she or he connects emotionally with the sentiments and passions others express.[28] Relational listeners seem to have greater

relational listeners
Those who prefer to focus on the emotions and feelings communicated by others verbally and nonverbally.

skill than other listeners in empathizing with and understanding the thoughts and feelings of others.[29] One study found that jurors who are relational listeners (originally described as people oriented) are less likely to find a defendant at fault in a civil court trial, perhaps because of their tendency to empathize with others.[30]

Research also shows that relational listeners have a greater tendency than those with other listening styles to be sympathetic to the person to whom they are listening.[31] A sympathetic listener is more likely to voice concern about the other person's welfare when that person is sharing personal information or news about a stressful situation. A sympathetic listener says, for instance, "Oh, Pat, I'm so sorry to hear about your loss." They are also more likely to use a relational listening style when listening to others share personal information about themselves.[32]

Analytical Listening Style

analytical listeners

Those who withhold judgment, listen to all sides of an issue, and wait until they hear the facts before reaching a conclusion.

Analytical listeners listen for facts and tend to withhold judgment before reaching a specific conclusion. Analytical listeners would make good judges; they generally consider all sides of an issue before making a decision or reaching a conclusion. They tend to listen to an entire message before assessing the validity of the information they hear. To help them analyze information, they take the perspective of the person to whom they are listening, which helps them suspend judgment. Analytical listeners also like the information they hear to be well organized so that they can clearly and easily analyze it. While listening to a rambling personal story, the analytic listener focuses on the facts and details of the story rather than on the emotions being expressed. Analytical listeners prefer listening to rich message content and then finding ways of organizing or making sense of the information.

Critical Listening Style

critical listeners

Those who prefer to listen for the facts and evidence to support key ideas and an underlying logic; they also listen for errors, inconsistencies, and discrepancies.

second guessing

Questioning the assumptions underlying a message.

task-oriented listeners

Those who look at the overall structure of the message to see what action needs to be taken; they also like efficient, clear, and briefer messages.

Critical listeners are good at evaluating the information they hear. They are able to identify inconsistencies in what someone says. They are comfortable listening to detailed, complex information and focusing on the facts, yet they are especially adept at noting contradictions in the facts presented. Critical listeners are also likely to catch errors in the overall logic and reasoning being used to reach a conclusion.

Critical listeners tend to be a bit more skeptical and demanding than relational listeners of the information they hear. Researchers call this skepticism **second guessing**—questioning the assumptions underlying a message.[33] It's called second guessing because critical listeners don't always assume that what they hear is accurate or relevant; they make a second guess about the accuracy of the information they are hearing. Accuracy of information is especially important to critical listeners because if they are going to use the information in some way, they want it to be valid.

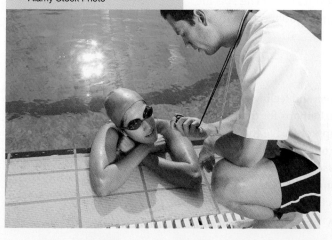

▼ A task-oriented listener is interested in achieving a specific outcome. Image Source Plus/ Alamy Stock Photo

Task-Oriented Listening Style

Task-oriented listeners are more interested in focusing on a specific outcome or task than on the communication relationship when listening to others. They emphasize completing a specific transaction such as solving a problem, taking action, or making a purchase. Task-oriented listeners focus on verbs—what needs to be done. Consequently, they don't like to listen to rambling, descriptive messages that don't seem to have a point. They appreciate efficient communicators who organize messages so that their listeners can focus on the outcomes—the "bottom line."

The Benefits of Understanding Your Listening Style

There are at least three reasons to think about your listening style and those of others: (1) to enhance your self-awareness, (2) to adapt your own listening style to different situations, and (3) to communicate more effectively.

Enhance Your Self-Awareness Understanding your preferred listening style can help you become more aware of how you behave in communication situations. Some research suggests that women are more likely to be relational listeners, whereas men have a tendency to assume one of the other listening styles.[34] Your listening style, however, may be less influenced by your gender than by the overall approach you take to interpreting and remembering the information you hear. Your cultural traditions, one research team suggests, may have a major influence on your particular listening style. People from a more individualistic, self-focused cultural perspective (such as the United States) tend to be more action-oriented listeners than people from other places. Relational listeners, according to research, are more likely to have collectivistic values, are group oriented, or were raised in a collaborative cultural tradition (such as some Asian cultures).[35]

You may wonder, "Do I have just one listening style, or do I have more than one?" According to listening researchers Larry Barker and Kitty Watson, who have done extensive research into listening styles (using different labels than the styles we've described), about 40 percent of all listeners have one primary listening style that they use, especially if they are under stress. Another 40 percent of listeners use more than one style—for example, they may prefer to listen to evaluate (critical listening style), but they also want the information delivered in a short amount of time and they want it focused on the task to be accomplished (task-oriented listening style).

About 20 percent of people do not have a specific listening style preference. These individuals may want to avoid listening altogether because they are shy and don't like to be around others in social situations, they may have receiver apprehension, or they may just have listener burnout—they are weary of listening to other people.[36] Or they may not have a predominant style because they are good at adapting to others.

Adapt to Different Listening Situations Knowing your preferred listening style can help you adapt and adjust your listening style to fit the specific listening situation you are experiencing. Evidence suggests that the occasion, time, and place all have an effect on the listening style or styles you adopt.[37] For example, if you tend to be a relational listener and you are listening to a message that has little information about people but lots of technical details, you will have to work harder than other types of listeners to stay tuned in to the message. Research has found that you sometimes adjust your listening style to fit your listening goal.[38] If you are listening to your communication professor tell you what will be covered on the next exam, you may shift to a task-oriented or critical listening style because you want to do well on the test. But when your roommate tells you about his frustrating day, you may adopt a more relational listening style.

Communicate Effectively Your awareness of others' listening styles can help you communicate messages that they are more likely to listen to. If you know that your spouse is an analytical listener, you should communicate a message that is rich in information because that's what your spouse prefers. Tell the analytical listener, "Here are three things I have to tell you," and then say those three things. The information preview tells your analytical listener that you are about to convey three pieces of information. It may be difficult to determine someone's

RECAP

Listening Styles

Relational Listening Style	Listeners prefer to attend to feelings and emotions and to search for common areas of interest when listening to others.
Analytical Listening Style	Listeners prefer to withhold judgment, listen to all sides of an issue, and wait until they hear the facts before reaching a conclusion.
Critical Listening Style	Listeners are likely to listen for the facts and evidence to support key ideas and an underlying logic; they also listen for errors, inconsistencies, and discrepancies.
Task-Oriented Listening Style	Listeners are focused on accomplishing something and look at the overall structure of the message to see what action needs to be taken; they also like efficient, clear, and brief messages.

listening style, especially if you don't know the person very well. But it is worth the time to try and determine what it is. Keep in mind that it is easier to consider the listening styles of people you do know well (your family members, your coworkers, your instructors, your boss).

Listening Barriers

5.4 **Identify and describe barriers that keep people from listening well.**

Although we spend almost half of our communication time listening, some say that we don't use that time well. One day after hearing something, most people remember only about half of what was said. Two days later, our retention drops by another 50 percent. The result: Two days after hearing a lecture or speech, most of us remember only about 25 percent of what we heard.

Our listening deteriorates not only when we listen to speeches or lectures, but also when we interact interpersonally. Even in the most intimate relationships (or perhaps we should say *especially* in the most intimate relationships), we tune out what others are saying. One study reported that we sometimes pay more attention to strangers than to our close friends or spouses. Married couples tend to interrupt each other more often than unmarried couples and are usually less polite to each other than are strangers involved in a simple decision-making task.[39]

What keeps us from listening well? The most critical elements are: (1) self barriers—personal habits that work against listening well, (2) information-processing barriers—the way we mentally manage information, and (3) context barriers—the surroundings in which we listen.

Self Barriers

"We have met the enemy and he is us" is an oft-quoted line from the vintage comic strip *Pogo*. Evidence suggests that we are our own worst enemy when it comes to listening to others. We often attend to our own internal dialogues and diatribes instead of to others' messages, and when we do, our listening effectiveness plummets.

Self-Focus Most of us are egocentric—self-focused—although we may develop a consciousness of others' needs as we grow and mature. Scholars of evolution might argue that it is good that we are self-focused; looking out for number one is what perpetuates the human race. Yet an *exclusive* focus on ourselves inhibits effective communication. While trying to listen, we may be carrying on an internal narration, one that is typically about us. "How long will I have to be here for this lecture?" "Wonder what's for dinner tonight?" "I've got to get that report finished." "She's still talking—will we be out of here in ten minutes?" "Do I have a school meeting tonight, or is that tomorrow night?" Focusing on such internal messages often keeps us from selecting and attending to the other person's message.

What can you do to regain your listening focus if you are focused on yourself rather than on the other person's message? Consider these suggestions:

- *Become aware of the problem.* Become consciously competent. Notice when you find yourself drifting off rather than concentrating on the speaker.
- *Concentrate.* Yes, some messages are boring, useless, and stupid. But even if you think you're listening to such a message, avoid mindlessly tuning it out. The habit of quickly dismissing ideas and messages without making an effort to stay focused on them will keep you from being nominated for the Listening Hall of Fame.
- *Be active rather than passive.* The key to concentration is finding ways to be actively involved in the communication process. Taking notes when appropriate and providing nonverbal and even sometimes verbal feedback to the speaker can help keep your focus on the speaker rather than on you. If you don't understand

something the speaker says, ask for clarification. Don't just sit there and "take it;" if you find your concentration waning, you'll more than likely "leave it."

Emotional Noise   Emotions are powerful. What we see and hear affects our emotions. **Emotional noise** occurs when our emotional arousal interferes with communication effectiveness. Certain words or phrases can arouse emotions very quickly, and, of course, the same word may arouse different emotions in different people. You respond emotionally because of your personal experiences, cultural background, religious convictions, or political philosophy. Words that reflect negatively on your nationality, ethnic origin, or religion can trigger strong emotional reactions. Cursing and obscene language may also reduce your listening efficiency. If you grew up in a home in which R-rated language was never used, four-letter words may distract you.

Sometimes it's not just a word but a concept or idea that causes an emotional eruption. Late-term abortion and public school prayer, for example, are topics guaranteed to get talk radio hosts' audiences involved in lively discussion.

The emotional state of the speaker may also affect your ability to understand and evaluate what you hear. Research has shown that if you are listening to someone who is emotionally distraught, you will be more likely to focus on his or her emotions than on the content of the message.[40] Another researcher advises that when you are communicating with someone who is emotionally excited, you should remain calm and focused and try simply to communicate your interest in the other person.[41]

What are other strategies to keep your emotions from getting the best of you? Psychologist Daniel Goleman offers several research-based strategies in his best-selling book *Emotional Intelligence*.[42] To be emotionally intelligent is to have the ability to understand, manage, and appropriately express emotions. There is evidence that people who are emotionally intelligent—because of their skill in recognizing, expressing, and managing their emotions—are better listeners than others.[43] Being attuned to the emotions of your listening partner helps you discern the underlying, sometimes not explicitly expressed, meaning of a message.[44] For example, one simple yet powerful strategy to manage emotions when you find you may be about to lose control is to take a deep breath. Yes, just breathe. Taking a deep, slow breath is a way of regaining control by calming down. It helps make you more conscious of your anger or frustration, much like the old technique of counting to ten.

Another strategy for managing emotions is to use the power of self-talk, a concept we discussed in Chapter 2. Tell yourself you won't get angry. Early detection of the emotions bubbling up inside you can help you assess and then manage them before your irrational, emotional impulses take control. And sometimes, of course, expressing your frustration is appropriate.

Awareness of the effect that emotions have on your listening ability (such as how you feel after reading this section) is a constructive first step to avoid being ruled by unchecked emotions. Becoming consciously aware of our emotions and then talking to ourselves about our feelings is a way to avoid emotional sidetracks and keep your attention focused on the message. When emotionally charged words or actions kick your internal dialogue into high gear, make an effort to quiet it down and steer back to the subject at hand. The principle of self-awareness gives you choice *and* control.

Criticism   We usually associate the word *criticism* with negative judgments and attitudes. Although critiquing a message can provide positive as well as negative insights, most of us don't like to be criticized. The well-known advocate for the poor, the late Mother Teresa, once said, "If you judge people, you have no time to love them."[45] Being inappropriately critical of the speaker may distract us from focusing on the message.

A person's appearance and speech characteristics can affect your ability to listen to him or her. Many a speaker's droning monotone, lack of eye contact, and distracting mannerisms have contributed to his or her ideas not being well received. The goal of a sensitive communicator is to be conscious of when the delivery or other distracting features of the message or messenger are interfering with the ability to listen.

emotional noise
A form of communication noise caused by emotional arousal.

It would be unrealistic to suggest that you refrain from criticizing speakers and their messages. It is realistic, however, to monitor your internal critiques of speakers to make sure you are aware of your biases. Good listeners say to themselves, "Although this speaker may be distracting, I am simply not going to let appearance or mannerisms keep my attention from the message." For example, Stephen Hawking is a prize-winning physicist at Cambridge University in England; because of a disability, he is able to speak only through computer-synthesized sounds. He is unquestionably brilliant, and if you let his speaking delivery overpower you, you'd miss his marvelous message. Avoid using your mental energy to criticize a speaker unnecessarily; the longer your mental critique, the less you'll remember.

Information-Processing Barriers

In addition to self barriers that contribute to our loss of focus on messages, the way we process the information we hear may keep us from being good listeners. Four information-processing listening barriers are: (1) processing rate, (2) information overload, (3) receiver apprehension, and (4) shifting attention.

Processing Rate   You can think faster than people speak. Most people speak 125 words per minute, give or take a few words. You have the tremendous ability, however, to process four to ten times that amount of information. Some people can listen to 600 to 800 words per minute and still make sense out of what the speaker is saying; another estimate puts the processing rate up to 1,200 words per minute. Yet another estimate claims that we think not just in words but also in images and sounds: We can process 2,000 bits of information per minute for short periods of time. This difference between the average speaking rate and your capacity to make sense out of words as they register in your cortical centers can cause trouble. You have extra time on your hands to tune in to your own thoughts rather than focusing on the speaker.[46]

You can use your information-processing rate to your advantage if you use the extra time to mentally summarize what a speaker is saying. By periodically sprinkling in mental summaries during a conversation, you can dramatically improve your listening ability and make the speech-rate/thought-rate difference work to your advantage.

Information Overload   One word to describe many beleaguered listeners is "weary." We spend 55 percent of our communication time listening, and the pace at which the information zips toward us exhausts us. The billion words we hear each year contribute to our fatigue. The pace has only increased now that much of that information is electronic. Incoming e-mail, texts, voice messages, or social media updates can interrupt conversations and distract us from listening to others.

Again we recommend self-awareness. Be on the alert for drifting attention because of information overload. And when the encroaching information dulls your attentiveness, either take a break or consider conducting some *communication triage*—determining what's urgent and what's not urgent—so that you can focus on the information that is most important.

Receiver Apprehension   Just as some people are fearful of presenting a speech or speaking up during a meeting, research suggests that some people are fearful of receiving information. **Receiver apprehension** is fear of misunderstanding or misinterpreting the messages spoken by others or of not being able to adjust psychologically to messages expressed by others.[47] Some people may be fearful of receiving

receiver apprehension

The fear of misunderstanding or misinterpreting the messages spoken by others or of not being able to adjust psychologically to messages expressed by others.

▼ Remaining aware of the dangers of information overload can help you keep electronic messages from distracting you from conversations. It is much harder to give your full attention to another person while continually glancing at your phone for incoming messages. Olena Yakobchuk/Shutterstock new information because they worry about being able to understand it. Or apprehension may be a characteristic of the way some people respond psychologically to information; they may not be able to make sense out of some of what they hear, which causes them to be anxious or fearful of listening to others.[48] There is evidence that if English is not your native language, you are likely to experience receiver apprehension when listening to someone speak English.[49] If you are fearful of receiving information, you'll remember less information.

If you know that you are fearful of listening to new information, you'll have to work harder than others to understand the information presented. Recording video or audio of a lecture may help you feel more comfortable and less anxious about trying to remember every point. Becoming actively involved in the listening experience by taking notes or mentally repeating information to yourself may also help.[50]

COMMUNICATION & DIVERSITY

Does Gender Influence Listening Skill?

There is evidence that men and women can be equally good listeners, but research suggests that they sometimes (although not always) have different approaches to listening. They also have different approaches to interrupting others when listening. According to one study that reviewed a number of research investigations, men tended to interrupt others more than women. Specifically, men were sometimes perceived as interrupting to control the conversation. When women interrupted, they were more likely either to express agreement or to add something to the conversation.[51]

Listening differences can be characterized as a feminine style (a more relational approach) or a masculine style (more task oriented). These characterizations may vary based on a person's socially-constructed gender and are not necessarily based on one's biological sex as male or female. The following chart summarizes research conclusions from several studies about feminine and masculine listening styles.[52]

	Feminine Listening Style	Masculine Listening Style
Different Listening Focus	• Tends to search for existing relationships among separate pieces of information	• Tends to look for a new structure or organizational pattern when listening
	• Tends to identify individual facts and other isolated pieces of information	• Tends to listen for the big picture and seek the major points being communicated
	• Tends to shift from one idea to another or to shift listening focus among people who may be speaking at the same time	• Tends to lock on to a specific message without shifting between two or more conversations
Different Listening Goals	• More likely to listen to new information to gain greater understanding and new insights	• More likely to listen to new information to solve a problem
	• Tends to use information to develop relationships with listening partners	• Tends to listen to reach a conclusion; shows less concern about relationship cues and more concern about using the information gained
	• Tends to have a greater ability and motivation to listen when providing supportive and positive feedback[53]	• Tends to have less ability and motivation to listen in situations that call for providing supportive feedback

Not all researchers agree that there are style differences between men and women. Listening experts Stephanie Sargent and James Weaver suggest that studies of listening style differences between men and women may simply be measuring listening stereotypes[54] or a self-fulfilling prophecy: Men and women assume that they *are* listening the way they think that they *should* listen.[55] Although there are some discernible patterns in masculine and feminine listening styles, the differences may not be as consistently pronounced as was once thought.

By noting some perceived differences in listening style, we don't want to be guilty of promoting gender- or sex-based stereotypes. So we repeat our caution: *Don't assume that all men or all women have typical masculine or feminine listening styles.*

Shifting Attention   Can you multitask? A few people can easily do two things at once, but our performance on at least one of the tasks suffers when most of us try it. Emerging research evidence suggests that men are more likely to have difficulty attending to multiple messages: When they are focused on a message, they may have more difficulty than women in carrying on a conversation with another person.[56] Men have a tendency to lock onto a message, whereas women seem more adept at shifting between two or more simultaneous messages. When many men watch a TV program, they seem lost in thought—oblivious to other voices around them. Women, by contrast, are more likely to be carrying on a conversation with one person and also focusing on a message they hear nearby. This difference doesn't mean that women are more likely to eavesdrop intentionally, but it does mean that some women have greater ability to listen to two things at once. What are the implications? It may be especially important for women to stop and focus on the messages of others rather than on either internal or external competing messages. And men may need to be sensitive to others who may want to speak to them rather than becoming fixated on their own internal message or on a single external message such as a TV program.

Cultural Differences   Different cultures place different emphases on the importance of listening. Some cultures are more source or speaker oriented, whereas others are more receiver or listener oriented. North American communication, for example, often centers on the sender. Much emphasis is placed on how senders can formulate better messages, improve credibility, and polish their delivery skills. Recently, there has been increased interest in listening in the United States. Communication scholars and practitioners recognize that listening is necessary not only to aid comprehension but also, and more importantly, to provide the speaker with the satisfaction of being listened to.[57] However, far more U.S. colleges and universities offer courses in speaking than provide courses in listening.

In contrast, the emphasis in East Asia has typically been on listening and interpretation. The Chinese culture, for example, places considerable emphasis on the listener. It's understood by both speaker and listener that the listener can make infinite interpretations of what has been said. A strategy called **anticipatory communication** is common in Japan. Instead of having the speaker explicitly say or ask for what he or she wants, listeners guess and accommodate the speaker's needs, sparing him or her the embarrassment that could arise if the verbally expressed request could not be met.[58] Thus, foreign students from East Asia may be puzzled about why they are constantly being asked what they want when visiting American homes. In their home countries, a good communicator should anticipate what others want and act accordingly, so the host or hostess should not have to ask what is needed.

Context Barriers

In addition to the barriers that relate to how you process information and those that occur when your emotions and thoughts crowd out a message, listening barriers can arise from the communication context or situation. **Noise** is anything that interferes with your ability to listen to a message. Although you may think of it as sounds you hear, noise can be processed by any one of your five senses. Not only sounds, but also sights, the feeling of something touching you, and even tastes and smells can affect your listening ability. Two factors that can increase interfering noise are *when* you listen and *where* you listen.[59]

Barriers of Time   Are you a morning person or an evening person? Morning people are cheerfully and chirpily at their

---

anticipatory communication
A listening process in which the listener guesses the speaker's needs and accommodates them so that the speaker does not have to say what he or she wants.

noise
Anything that interferes with your ability to listen to a message.

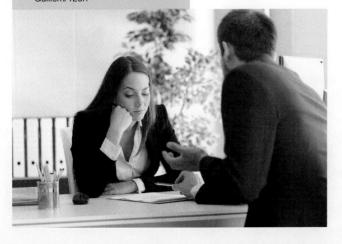

▼ Be sensitive to the timing of your message. Just because you're ready to talk, it doesn't mean your communication partner is ready to listen. Antonio Guillem/123rf mental peak before lunch. Evening people find it easier to tackle major projects after dark; they are at their worst when they arise in the morning.

The time of day can affect your listening acuity. If you know you are sharper in the morning, schedule your key listening times then whenever possible. Evening listeners should try to shift heavy listening to the evening hours. Of course, that's not always practical. If you can't change the time of listening, you can increase your awareness of when you will need to listen with greater concentration.

Daily activities, such as work, can also cause timing issues. When a person wants to converse with you at a time when you're busy with other things, for example, it may be tempting to try to do two things at once. We have all tried to get away with a few "uh-huhs" and "mm-hmms" to indicate that we're listening to everything that's being said while, in fact, our attention was divided.

Respect the effect of timing on other people, too. Don't assume that because you are ready to talk, the other person is ready to listen. If your message is particularly sensitive or important, you may want to ask your listening partner, "Is this a good time to talk?" Even if he or she says yes, look for eye contact and a responsive facial expression to make sure the positive response is genuine.

Barriers of Place Listening takes all the powers of concentration you can muster. A good listener seeks a quiet time and place to maximize listening comprehension. For most people, the best listening environment is one that offers as few distractions as possible.

When *you* want to talk to someone, pick a quiet time and place, especially if you know that you will be discussing a complex or potentially difficult topic. Even in your own home, it may be a challenge to find a quiet time to talk. Closing a door or window, turning off music or the TV, asking noisy or offensive talkers to converse more quietly or not at all, and simply moving to a less distracting location are steps you may need to take to manage the noise barrier.

RECAP

Managing Listening Barriers

Listening Barriers	What to Do
Self Barriers	
Self-Focus	• Shift attention back to the speaker.
	• Become actively involved in the message.
	• Take meaningful notes.
Emotional Noise	• Act calm to remain calm.
	• Use self-talk to stay focused on the message.
	• Take a deep breath if you start to lose control.
Criticism	• Focus on the message, not on the messenger.
Information-Processing Barriers	
Processing Rate	• Use the difference between speech rate and thought rate to mentally summarize the message.
Information Overload	• Realize when you or your partner is tired or distracted and not ready to listen.
	• Assess what is urgent and not urgent when listening.
Receiver Apprehension	• Record the message to be sure you capture it; review the audio later.
	• Take notes.
	• Make mental summaries of the information you hear.
Shifting Attention	• Make a conscious effort to remain focused on one message.
Cultural Differences	• Acknowledge that some cultures place greater emphasis on the listener than on the speaker.
Context Barriers	
Barriers of Time	• If possible, schedule difficult listening situations for when you're at your best.
Barriers of Place	• Eliminate distracting noise.

Improving Your Listening Skills

5.5   Identify and use strategies that can improve your listening skills.

At the heart of listening is developing sensitivity to focus on the messages of others rather than on your own thoughts. A skilled listener is attentive, friendly, and responsive to others. Good listeners also maintain the flow of the conversation and provide feedback indicating that the message was understood.[60] In this section, we discuss several specific underlying skills that will increase your sensitivity so you can be a good listener.

At first glance, the skills we present may look deceptively simple—as simple as the advice given to most elementary students about crossing the street: (1) stop, (2) look, and (3) listen. Despite the appearance of simplicity, these three words summarize decades of research and insight about how to avoid being interpersonally inert. Those steps may seem like common sense, but they are not common practice.[61] Let's consider each one separately.

Stop: Turn Off Competing Messages

As we noted earlier, while you are listening, you may also be talking to yourself, providing a commentary about the messages you hear. These internal, self-generated messages may distract you from giving your undivided attention to what others are saying. To stop and focus on a message, you need to: (1) be aware of the competing messages, (2) stop the internal competing chatter and attend to the message, and (3) socially decenter to focus on the thoughts of others.

Be Aware of Competing Messages   Becoming aware of your internal dialogue is the first step toward stopping your own running commentary about issues and ideas that are self-focused rather than other-focused.[62] To be aware of what you are doing is to be consciously mindful of what you are attending to. If you aren't aware that you are talking to yourself, you will likely continue your internal monologue and miss a portion of the message from your listening and speaking partner.[63] How can you increase your awareness of competing messages? At any given moment, you are either on task or off task when listening. Periodically ask yourself, "Am I on task? Am I focused on the speaker or my own internal conversation? Am I aware of what I'm doing?"

Stop Internal Noise   Two listening researchers conducted a study to identify the specific behaviors that good listeners perform when listening.[64] What they discovered supports our admonition that after being aware of whether you're on task, the next step is to stop focusing on your own mental messages. Specifically, you should be other oriented by taking the following actions during what the researchers called the *preinteraction phase* of listening:

- Put your own thoughts aside.
- Be there mentally, not just physically.
- Make a conscious, mindful effort to listen.
- Take adequate time to listen; don't rush the speaker; be patient.
- Be open-minded.

It may also help if you simply speak less. Members of some religious groups take a vow to be silent and not talk to anyone else. They literally stop talking. Does that make them better listeners than those who do not talk? One research team studied this question by comparing groups of research participants.[65] One group heard a lecture about how to be better listeners—probably like the lectures you hear in this course—and then took a test to assess their overall listening skill. A second group promised not to talk to anyone for twelve hours—they literally gave others the "silent treatment." Then they, too, took a test to assess their listening ability. A third group both heard a listening lecture and were silent for twelve hours; then they also took the listening test. The results: There were no differences in listening test scores among the groups. All groups seemed to listen equally well, according to test results—but those who kept silent for twelve hours reported *thinking* that they were more attentive to others and more conscious of being good listeners. The researchers concluded that literally ceasing to speak can increase our awareness of listening. Their research supports the maxim, "You have been given two ears and one mouth so that you will listen more and

▼ Some people find that yoga or quiet meditation helps dissolve the internal barriers that prevent effective listening. What strategies have you used to become more aware of your intrapersonal communication and any internal barriers to listening you may have experienced? What methods have you found helpful for making you conscious of the way your own self-talk affects your ability to listen to and communicate with others?

Chris Collins/Shutterstock

talk less." No, we're not suggesting that you stop talking entirely; rather, you should increase your awareness of how your own thoughts and talk can interfere with being a good listener. Stop—do your best to eliminate mental messages that keep you from listening well.

Socially Decenter   After becoming aware of competing messages and stopping your internal chatter, try a process called social decentering. **Social decentering** is a cognitive process that involves stepping away from your own thoughts and attempting to experience the thoughts of another. Instead of making yourself the center of your focus, you *decenter*—you are not the center of the conversation. Instead, you place your focus on the other person. In essence, you ask yourself, "If I were the other person, what would I be thinking?" Although the goal is to focus on someone else, decentering first requires you to practice the first principle of communication—self-awareness. You need to become aware that your own thoughts are keeping you from focusing on another's message. Then you can focus on the other person.[66] Of course, we are not suggesting that your own ideas and internal dialogue should be forever repressed; that would be both impossible and inappropriate. We are suggesting that to connect to another, you must focus on the other person rather than on yourself and, while doing so, consider what the other person may be thinking as he or she is communicating with you.

social decentering

Stepping away from your own thoughts and attempting to experience the thoughts of another.

Look: Listen with Your Eyes

Sensitive listeners are aware of nonverbal as well as verbal messages; they listen with their eyes as well as their ears. As we discussed in Chapter 4, nonverbal messages are powerful, especially in communicating feelings, attitudes, and emotions.[67] A person's body movement and posture, for example, communicate the intensity of his or her feelings, whereas facial expression and the vocal cues that accompany spoken words provide clues about the specific emotion being expressed. A competent listener notices these cues; an incompetent listener attempts to decode a message based only on what is said rather than "listening between the lines." When there is a contradiction between the verbal message and the nonverbal message, we will almost always believe the unspoken one; nonverbal cues are more difficult to fake. How do you focus on nonverbal messages? We suggest two strategies: (1) attend to the meta-message, and (2) nonverbally communicate *your* interest in the other person.

Attend to the Meta-Message   *Meta-communication* is communication about communication. By attending to your interpersonal partner's unspoken message, you are looking for the **meta-message**—the message about the message. The nonverbal meta-message provides information about the emotional and relational effect of what a speaker is expressing with the verbal message. Accurately decoding unspoken meta-messages helps you understand what people really mean.

meta-message

The message about the message.

Often, a person will express a positive feeling with a nonverbal message, such as smiling, that matches a verbal message, such as "I'm happy to be here." Sometimes, though, the nonverbal communication contradicts the verbal message. Your friend may say, "Oh, that's just great," but may use an exaggerated, sarcastic tone of voice and a facial expression that communicates just the opposite of the verbal message. The sarcasm expressed by your friend's tone of voice and facial expression (relationship cues) modifies the meaning of the verbal message (the actual content of the message).[68] The tone of voice and facial expression are a meta-message about what your friend really means. Your friend may not explicitly say that he or she is angry, upset, or irritated, but the nonverbal cues let you know that your friend is not happy.

How can you clarify the meaning of a nonverbal meta-message? Ask. For example, when you detect a smirk or a grimace from your listening partner, you can seek information about the communication by asking, "Is what I'm saying bothering you?"

A key aspect of the "look" step of good listening is to actually look at the person you are listening to—establish eye contact, which signals that you are focusing your attention on your partner. Even though mutual eye contact typically lasts only one to seven seconds, when you carry on an interpersonal conversation, your eye contact reveals how attentive and responsive you are to your listening partner.[69] If you look as if you are listening, you will also be more likely to listen. We usually have more eye contact with someone when we are listening than when we are talking.[70]

In addition to eye contact, other nonverbal cues signal whether you are on task and responsive to others' messages. Remaining focused, keeping your hands and feet still, and even leaning forward slightly communicate to someone that you are listening. Appropriate head nods and verbal responses also signal that you are attending to the other person's message.[71]

Listen: Understand Both Details and Major Ideas

How do you improve your listening skill? Now that you've stopped your own internal dialogue and looked for nonverbal cues, it's time to listen. Here are six additional strategies for improving your listening skill.[72]

Identify your Listening Goal   You listen to other people for a variety of reasons. Knowing your listening goal can increase your self-awareness of the listening process and increase your skill. As we discussed earlier in this chapter, adapting your listening style to your listening goal can enhance your listening skill.[73] If you're listening to Aunt Deonna talk about her recent trip to northern Minnesota for the annual bear hunt, you need not worry about taking extensive notes or trying to remember all the details of her expedition. But when your Sociology professor tells a story to illustrate a sociological theory, you should be more attuned to the point he or she is making; the theory may be on a test. At other times, you need to be on your guard to evaluate the message of a politician or salesperson. Having a strong motivation to listen for specific kinds of information can enhance your listening effectiveness.[74] There are four primary listening goals: to enjoy, to learn, to evaluate, and to empathize.

- *Listening to enjoy*. Sometimes we listen just because it's fun. You might listen to music, watch TV, go to a movie, or visit with a friend. Because you know you won't be tested on Jimmy Fallon's monologue, you can relax and just enjoy the humor.

- *Listening to learn*. Nothing snaps a class to attention more quickly than a professor's proclamation, "This next point will be covered on the test." Another key reason we listen is to learn. But you don't have to be a college student to listen to learn. Phone calls and conversations with family and friends also often contain information that you will want to remember.

- *Listening to evaluate*. When you listen to evaluate, you try to determine whether the information you hear is valid, reliable, believable, or useful. One problem you may have when you listen to evaluate is that you may become so preoccupied with your criticism that you may not completely understand the message.

- *Listening to empathize*. The word *empathy*, which we introduced in Chapter 3 and will discuss in more detail later in this chapter, comes from a Greek word for "passion" and the German word *Einfühlung*, meaning "to feel with." To empathize with someone is to try to feel what he or she is feeling rather than just to think about or acknowledge the feelings.[75] Empathic listening serves an important therapeutic function; just having an empathic listener may help someone out. No, we are not empowering you to be a therapist, but we are suggesting that sometimes simply listening and acknowledging someone's feelings can help that person sort things out.

Mentally Summarize the Details of the Message   You can process words more quickly than a person speaks, so you can use the extra time to your advantage by periodically summarizing the names, dates, and facts embedded in a message. If a speaker is disorganized and rambling, use your tremendous mental ability to reorganize the speaker's information into categories or try to place events in chronological order. It is important to have a grasp of the details your communication partner presents. But remember that to listen is to do more than focus on facts. Research suggests that poor listeners are more likely than good listeners to focus *only* on facts and data, rather than on the overall point of the message.[76] If you listen too much for the details, you may miss the main point.

Link Message Details with the Major Idea of the Message   As we just pointed out, facts and data make the most sense when we can use them to support an idea or point. Mentally weave your summaries of the details into a focused major point or series of major ideas. Use facts to enhance your critical thinking as you analyze, synthesize, evaluate, and finally summarize the key points or ideas your partner makes.

Practice by Listening to Difficult or Challenging Material   Learning any skill takes practice. Listening experts suggest that our listening skills deteriorate if we listen only to easy and entertaining material. Make an effort to listen to news or documentary programs. As you listen to a lecture that seems full of content, make a conscious effort to stay focused, concentrate, and summarize facts and major ideas.[77]

Work to Overcome Listening Barriers   If you can avoid the listening barriers discussed earlier, you will be well on your way to improving your listening skill. Avoid being self-focused, letting emotional noise distract you, or criticizing a message before you've understood it. Watch out for information overload. And, when possible, take steps to minimize external noise and provide an environment more conducive to listening.

Don't Interrupt   One of the best things you can do to be perceived as a good listener is to not interrupt a speaker when he or she is talking. When we interrupt someone, we are saying, "What I have to say is more important than what you have to say." This translates to the other person as, "I'm more important than you are." Interrupting others when listening is more than just rude; it decreases your credibility and lowers your ability to understand the other person. Do you want to make sure you *don't* get hired because of the impression you make during a job interview? Interrupt your interviewer and you're less likely to get the job, according to one research study.[78] To listen without interrupting seems simple, but because thoughts are bouncing around in our heads, we sometimes blurt them out,[79] or we think that we know what the other person is going to say, so we talk over her or him. Resist these temptations.

Listen Actively   Our suggestion that you listen actively is a distillation of the other recommendations we've offered. Active listeners are engaged listeners who listen with both their minds and their hearts. They are engaged physically and mentally in the listening process.[80] Active listeners are aware of what they are doing; they stop thinking about things that might take them off track.[81] They also maintain good eye contact with the speaker and communicate their interest with an intent facial expression and a slight forward lean. By contrast, passive listeners are not involved listeners; they are detached and may fake attention with a frozen, blank facial expression or a single, unchanging expression that mimics interest.

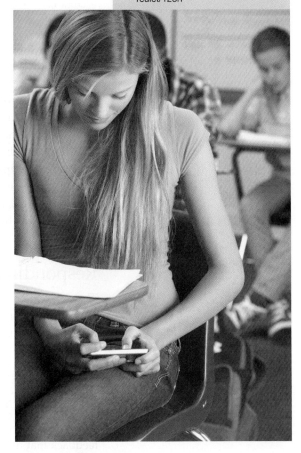

▼ Personal concerns and distractions such as texts are challenges to effective listening for many students. You can, however, make yourself a better listener by learning to overcome these and other barriers. Cathy Yeulet/123rf

RECAP

How to Listen Well

What to Do	How to Do It
Identify your listening goal.	Decide whether you are listening to enjoy, learn, evaluate, or empathize. Your listening goal should determine the strategies you use to achieve it.
Mentally summarize the details of the message.	Every few minutes, take time to create your own mental recap of the key information presented. In just a few seconds, you can summarize much information.
Link message details with the major ideas of the message.	Consciously relate the bits of information you hear to the key points the speaker is developing rather than focusing only on facts and details or only on major points.
Practice by listening to difficult or challenging material.	Periodically make an effort to listen to material that is complex and richer in detail and information than what you typically listen to; while listening to this more complex material, make a conscious effort to stop, look, and listen.
Work to overcome listening barriers.	Identify the key obstacles that keep you from listening at peak effectiveness (self barriers, information-processing barriers, or context barriers); make conscious efforts to overcome the underlying causes of these barriers.
Don't interrupt.	Increase your awareness of whether you interrupt others. Wait until the other person has finished speaking before you speak.
Listen actively.	Be engaged in the listening process by maintaining good eye contact with the speaker and an alert posture (slight forward lean, sitting up rather than slouching).

One listening research team noted that a passive listener receives information by being talked *to* rather than as an equal partner in a speaking-listening exchange.[82]

This same team described active listeners as people who do the following:

- Give full attention to others.
- Focus on what is being said.
- Expend considerable energy participating in the listening process.
- Have an alert posture.
- Maintain much direct eye contact.

Another research study found that listeners who offered person-centered comments (comments that acknowledge the feelings of others) and provided immediate nonverbal responses (eye contact, natural forward lean, appropriate head nods) were judged to be better listeners than those who did not use those skills.[83]

It seems that the best listeners are mentally alert, physically focused on the other person, and actively involved in seeking understanding. In short, they stop, they look, and they listen.

Improving Your Responding Skills

5.6 **Identify and use appropriate responding skills.**

To respond is to provide feedback to another about his or her behavior or communication. Your response can be verbal or nonverbal, intentional or unintentional.

Your thoughtful response serves several purposes. First, it tells a speaker how well you have understood his or her message. Second, your response lets a speaker know how the message affects you. It indicates whether you agree or disagree. Third, it provides feedback about statements or assumptions that you find vague, confusing, or wrong. It helps an individual keep the communication on target and purposeful. Finally, your response signals to the speaker that you are still "with" him or her—that you are still ready to receive messages. We respond to let others know that we understand what we have heard, to empathize with the feelings of others, and to provide support.

Responding to Clarify and Confirm Understanding

The skill of thoughtfully responding to others lets them know that you have understood their message and that they communicated clearly. There are several ways to ensure that your confirming responses are helpful.

Be Descriptive Although one listening goal is to evaluate and make critical judgments about messages, don't start your evaluation until you're sure you understand the speaker. Effective feedback describes rather than evaluates what you hear. We're not suggesting that it's easy to listen from a nonevaluative perspective or that you should refrain from ever evaluating messages and providing praise or negative comments. But feedback that first acts like a mirror to help the speaker understand what he or she has said is more useful than a barrage of critical comments. Describing your own reactions to what your partner has said rather than pronouncing a quick judgment on his or her message is also more likely to keep communication flowing. "I see that from a different point of view" often evokes more thoughtful responses than "You're wrong, I'm right."

If your partner thinks that your prime purpose in listening is to take potshots at the message or the messenger, the communication climate will cool quickly. Not surprisingly, listening researcher Eve-Anne Doohan found that when wives expressed negative emotions and critical evaluative comments to their listening husbands, the husbands were less satisfied with the overall quality of their relationships with their wives.[84]

Be Timely   Feedback is usually most effective at the earliest opportunity after the behavior or message is presented, especially if the purpose is to teach. Waiting to provide a response after much time has elapsed invites confusion.

Now let us contradict our advice. Sometimes, especially if a person is already sensitive and upset about something, delaying feedback can be wise. Use your critical-thinking skills to analyze when feedback will do the most good. Rather than automatically offering an immediate correction, use the just-in-time approach. Provide feedback just before the person might make another mistake, just in time for the feedback to have the largest benefit.

Be Brief   Less information can be more. Cutting down on the amount of your feedback can highlight the importance of what you do share. Don't overwhelm your listener with details that obscure the key point of your feedback. Brief is usually best.

Be Useful   Perhaps you've heard this advice: "Never try to teach a pig to sing. It wastes your time, it doesn't sound pretty, and it annoys the pig." When you provide feedback to someone, be certain it is useful and relevant. Ask yourself, "If I were this person, how would I respond to this information? Is it information I can act on?" Immersing your partner in information that is irrelevant or that may be damaging to the relationship may make you feel better, but it may not enhance the quality of your relationship or improve understanding.

Ask Appropriate Questions   As you listen for information and attempt to understand how another person is feeling, you may need to ask questions to help clarify your conclusions. Most of your questions will serve one of four purposes: (1) to obtain additional information ("How long have you been living in Buckner?"), (2) to check how the person feels ("Are you frustrated because you didn't get your project finished?"), (3) to ask for clarification ("What do you mean when you say you want to telecommute?"), or (4) to verify that you have reached an accurate conclusion about your partner's intent or feeling ("So are you saying you'd rather work at home than at the office?").

Another way to sort out details and get to the emotional heart of a dialogue is to ask questions to help you (and your communication partner) identify the sequence of events. Asking questions like "What happened first?" and "Then what did he do?" can help both you and your partner clarify a confusing event.

Your ability to ask appropriate questions will demonstrate your supportiveness of your partner and signal that you are interested in what he or she is sharing. Of course, if you are trying to understand another's feelings, you can just ask how he or she is feeling in a straightforward way—don't ask questions just for the sake of asking questions. Also, monitor how you ask your questions. Your own verbal and nonverbal responses will contribute to the emotional climate of your interaction.

Paraphrase Message Content   After you have listened and asked questions, check whether your interpretations are accurate by paraphrasing the content you have heard. **Paraphrasing** is restating in your own words what you think a person is saying. Paraphrasing is different from repeating something exactly as it was spoken; that would be parroting, not paraphrasing. Paraphrase when you need to confirm your understanding of a murky message or to help the speaker sort out a jumbled or confusing situation.

paraphrasing

Checking the accuracy of your understanding by restating your partner's message in your own words.

Your paraphrase can summarize the essential events, uncover a detail that was quickly glossed over, or highlight a key point. Typical lead-ins to a paraphrase include statements such as the following:

> "So here is what seems to have happened. . . ."
> "Here's what I understand you to mean. . . ."
> "So let me see if I get what you are saying. . . ."
> "Are you saying . . . ?"

Does paraphrasing a speaker's message really enhance the overall quality and accuracy of communication? Yes. Several researchers have found considerable support for the value of paraphrasing the messages of others in enhancing communication.[85]

Listening researcher Harry Weger and his colleagues found that listeners perceived people who skillfully used paraphrasing as more socially attractive than other people. That is, the listener liked the person who paraphrased more than a person who didn't. The researchers found that people liked skillful paraphrasers better even when listeners didn't feel well understood or satisfied with the conversation.[86]

Imagine the Conversation you Anticipate Having with Someone   Are there times when you know that you are going to have a conversation with someone that may call upon your empathic responding skills? For example, perhaps a friend has lost a loved one or had a difficult day and needs someone to listen to him or her. Before approaching that person, imagine what the conversation will be like. One research team found that you can increase your empathic listening and responding skills if, prior to having a difficult or challenging conversation with someone, you imagine what that conversation

COMMUNICATION & SOCIAL MEDIA

Keep Social Media Social

Does it happen often to you? You read a tweet or Facebook post from a "friend" that you strongly disagree with. Whether an emotionally-charged statement about politics, religion, or human rights, or a negative personal comment directed at someone you know, the message raises your blood pressure and you consider firing back an angry response. Social media plays an important role in our relationships with others. How we "listen" and whether we thoughtfully respond can have serious consequences for our relationships.[88]

Before quickly reacting with a negative, emotionally-escalating response just stop, take a breath, and consider the implications of what you may post. In all probability, the sender is not thinking about you but is merely expressing his or her opinion—you just happen to strongly disagree. Will hurling a reciprocal post or angry tweet change the other person's mind? Probably not. Make a conscious choice not to make someone's post personal.

Although it may seem personal because messages are often directed to a closed group of Facebook "friends" or Twitter followers, social media is actually more like a media broadcast, even though in actuality it is "narrowcast." Stop, think, and seek to deescalate emotions before you impulsively post or tweet a negative message you might regret. Keep social media social.

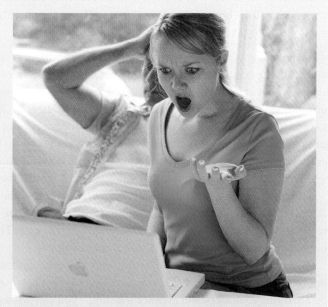

You should pause and think twice before firing off an angry message on social media. Chris Rout / Alamy Stock Photo

might be like. Just thinking about how someone may respond can help you anticipate that person's emotions and enable you to be more supportive and empathic.[87]

Responding to Empathize with Others

Empathy, as was noted earlier in this chapter, is the process of feeling what another person is feeling. Empathizing is more than just acknowledging that another person feels a particular emotion. Being empathic involves making an effort to feel the same emotion yourself.[89]

Central to being empathic is being emotionally intelligent, which, as we discussed earlier in this chapter, includes being able to understand and express emotion, interpret emotions in yourself and others, and regulate or manage emotions.[90] Emotional intelligence theorist Daniel Goleman summarizes the importance of emotions in developing empathy by quoting Antoine de Saint-Exupéry: "It is with the heart that one sees rightly; what is essential is invisible to the eye."[91] Researchers have found evidence supporting Goleman's ideas. Studies suggest that empathic listeners make better salespeople, teachers, counselors, and therapists and develop better relationships with others overall than nonempathic listeners.[92]

At the heart of empathic listening is the ability not only to know when to speak, but also to know when to be silent. Henri Nouwen eloquently expressed both the challenge and the rewards of empathic listening:

> To listen is very hard, because it asks of us so much interior stability that we no longer need to prove ourselves by speeches, arguments, statements, or declarations. True listeners no longer have an inner need to make their presence known. They are free to receive, to welcome, to accept. . . . Listening is a form of spiritual hospitality by which you invite strangers to become friends, to get to know their inner selves more fully, and even to dare to be silent with you.[93]

Psychologist Carl Rogers suggests that empathic listening is more than a technique; it's a "way of being."[94] Effective empathic listeners make empathy a natural and normal way of interacting with others. Some people are simply better at being empathic than others. Just as you inherit physical qualities from your parents, there is evidence that you inherit communication traits as well.[95] Some people may have a personality and communication traits that result in being a skilled empathic listener.[96] This does not mean that if you are not naturally empathic, you can never develop empathic skills, but it does mean that you may have to work a bit harder than others to enhance these skills. Can people be taught to be more empathic? Research suggests that the answer is a clear "yes." One goal of this book is to enhance your skill in appropriately adapting to others; empathy is at the heart of focusing on the needs and emotions of others.[97]

Being empathic is not a single skill but several related skills that help you predict how others will respond.[98] Two strategies to help you respond empathically are to understand your partner's feelings and to paraphrase his or her emotions.

Understand your Partner's Feelings   If your goal is to empathize, or "feel with," your communication partner, you might begin by imagining how you would feel under the same circumstances. If your roommate comes home from a hassle-filled day at work or school, try to imagine what you might be thinking or feeling if you had had a stressful day. If a friend calls to tell you his mother died, consider how you would feel if the situation were reversed. Even if you have not yet experienced the loss of your mother, you can imagine what it would be like to suffer such a loss. Of course, your reaction to life events is unlikely to be exactly like someone else's response. Empathy is not telepathically trying to become your communication partner.[99] But you do attempt to decenter—to consider what someone may be thinking—by first projecting how you might feel and then asking appropriate questions and offering paraphrases to confirm the accuracy of your assumptions. Considering how others might feel has been called

COMMUNICATION & ETHICS

Paraphrase Properly

If used with wisdom, paraphrasing can help both you and your partner clarify message accuracy. The most essential guideline is to use your paraphrasing skills *only* if you are able to be open and accepting. If you try to color your paraphrased comments to achieve your own agenda, you aren't being ethical.

Also avoid the overuse of paraphrasing. Too much of it can slow down a conversation and make the other person uncomfortable or irritated. A sensitive communicator tries not to let his or her technique show.

Other guidelines to keep in mind when you ask questions and paraphrase content and feelings are the following:

- Use your own words—don't just repeat exactly what the other person says.
- Don't add to the information presented when paraphrasing.
- Be brief.
- Be specific.
- Be accurate.

the Platinum Rule—even more valuable than the Golden Rule ("Do unto others as you would have others do unto you."). The Platinum Rule invites you to treat others as *they* would like to be treated—not just as *you* would like to be treated.

Paraphrase Emotions The bottom line in empathic responding is to make certain that you understand your communication partner's emotional state. You can paraphrase his or her feelings using common lead-in phrases, such as "So you feel . . .," "So now you feel . . .," and "Emotionally, you are feeling. . . ." Although active listening may not always solve a person's problem, there is evidence that listening and paraphrasing the emotions of someone can provide needed emotional and social support to those who need a friendly, supportive listening ear.[100]

Using these or other ways of paraphrasing feeling (as well as content) can be especially useful in situations in which messages could escalate emotions or produce conflict, such as the following:

Before you take an important action
Before you argue or criticize
When your partner has strong feelings
When your partner just wants to talk
When your partner is speaking "in code"—using unclear jargon or abbreviations you don't understand
When your partner wants to understand your feelings and thoughts
When you are talking to yourself (you can question and check your own emotional temperature)
When you encounter new ideas[101]

As a final word on responding with empathy, realize that although we have discussed empathic responses and the active listening process using a tidy, step-by-step textbook approach, in practice the process won't be as neat and tidy. You may have to back up and clarify content, ask more questions, and rethink how you would feel before you summarize how your partner feels. Or you may be able to summarize feelings without asking questions or summarizing the content of the message. Be sure to adapt the skills appropriately, and ethically, to each specific communication situation. The Communication & Ethics box offers more advice for when and how to paraphrase.

social support
Sensitive and empathic listening, followed by messages of comfort or confirmation, that lets a person know that he or she is understood and valued.

Responding to Provide Social Support

Responding with empathy is especially important if you are listening to provide social support or encouragement to someone. You provide **social support** to someone when

TABLE 5.1 Suggestions for Providing Social Support

What to Do	What to Say
Clearly express that you want to provide support.	"I would really like to help you."
Appropriately communicate that you have positive feelings for the other person; explicitly tell the other person that you are her or his friend, that you care about her or him, or that you love her or him.	"You mean a lot to me." "I really care about you."
Express your concern about the situation the other person is in right now.	"I'm worried about you right now, because I know you're feeling ___ [stressed, overwhelmed, sad, etc.]."
Indicate that you are available to help, that you have time to support the person.	"I can be here for you when you need me."
Let the other person know how much you support him or her.	"I'm completely with you on this." "I'm here for you, and I'll always be here for you because I care about you."
Acknowledge that the other person is in a difficult situation.	"This must be very difficult for you."
Paraphrase what the other person has told you about the issue or problem that is causing stress.	"So you became upset when she told you that she didn't want to see you again."
Consider asking open-ended questions to find out whether the other person wants to talk.	"How are you doing now?"
Let the other person know that you are listening and supportive by providing conversational continuers.	"Yes—then what happened?" "Oh, I see." "Uh-huh."
After expressing your compassion, empathy, and concern, just listen.	Say nothing; just establish gentle eye contact and listen.

you sensitively and empathically listen to him or her and then offer messages of comfort or confirmation that let the person know that he or she is both understood and valued. Providing social support does *not* mean trying to solve the issue or problem your communication partner has. Instead, it means communicating genuine concern rather than just going through the motions of pretending to listen.[102]

Provide Appropriate Social Support   What's the best way to express your support? Tables 5.1 and 5.2 summarize research-based suggestions that can help you say the right thing and avoid saying the wrong thing when you are providing social support

TABLE 5.2 What to Avoid When Providing Social Support

What Not to Do	What Not to Say
Don't criticize or negatively evaluate the other person. She or he needs support and validation, not judgmental comments.[104]	"Well, you never were the best judge of people. You should expect this kind of stress if you hang around with him."
Don't tell the other person to stop feeling what he or she is feeling.	"Oh, snap out of it!" "Don't be sad."
Don't immediately offer advice.	"So here's what you should do: Cut off all communication with her."
Don't tell the other person that all will necessarily be well.	"It's going to get better from here." "The worst is over."
Don't tell the other person that she or he really has nothing to worry about.	"Oh, it's no big deal." "Just think happy thoughts."
Don't tell the other person that the problem can be solved easily.	"You can always find another girlfriend."
Don't blame the other person for his or her problems.	"Well, if you didn't always drive so fast, you wouldn't have had the accident."
Don't tell the other person that her or his expression of feelings and emotion is wrong.	"You're just making yourself sick. Stop crying."

to others. Research suggests that following these guidelines as appropriate to the other person's situation can help you develop positive, empathic, comforting messages that are likely to be appreciated by your listener.[103] Remember, however, that there are no magic words or phrases that will always ease someone's stress or anxiety.

Don't be discouraged if your initial attempts to use these skills seem awkward and uncomfortable. Learning to use any new set of skills well takes time. The instructions and samples you have seen in this chapter should serve as a guide rather than as hard-and-fast prescriptions to follow every time. Being an empathic listener can be rewarding in both your personal and your professional life.[105] And here's some encouraging news about listening and responding skills: These skills can be improved. People who have received listening training show overall improvement in their ability to listen to others.[106] Reading this chapter, listening to your instructor give you tips on enhancing your skills, and participating in skill-building activities are well worth your time.

Provide an Appropriate Level of Social Support   What level or intensity of social support should you offer? One research study suggests that when we experience sadness, disappointment, or trauma, most of us prefer a "midlevel" intensity of social support. An intense, overly-dramatic response or a tepid, mild response may create additional "noise" for the person you are trying to support. When providing social support, consider offering a moderate level of positive, genuine, and authentic supportive communication.[107] Although the women in the study preferred a slightly higher level of comforting than the men, most of the people studied didn't want over-the-top, melodramatic expressions of support. Neither did they like weak or timid expressions of support. A thoughtful, personal, empathic, and yet not-too-dramatic response to someone's stress and anxiety seems to be a good place to begin when supporting others.

The following poem, "Listen," by an unknown author, summarizes the essential ideas of how to listen and respond with empathy.

> *Listen*
> When I ask you to listen to me and you start giving advice, you have not done what I asked.
> When I ask you to listen to me and you begin to tell me why I shouldn't feel that way, you are trampling on my feelings.
> When I ask you to listen to me and you feel you have to do something to solve my problems, you have failed me, strange as that may seem.
> Listen! All I asked was that you listen. Not talk or do—just hear me.
> Advice is cheap: 50 cents will get you both Dear Abby and Billy Graham in the same newspaper.
> And I can do for myself; I'm not helpless. Maybe discouraged and faltering, but not helpless.
> When you do something for me that I can and need to do for myself, you contribute to my fear and weakness.
> But when you accept as a simple fact that I do feel what I feel, no matter how irrational, then I quit trying to convince you and can get about the business of understanding what's behind this irrational feeling.
> And when that's clear, the answers are obvious and I don't need advice.
> Irrational feelings make sense when we understand what's behind them.
> Perhaps that's why prayer works, sometimes, for some people, because God is mute, and doesn't give advice or try to fix things,
> God just listens and lets you work it out for yourself.
> So, please listen and just hear me, and, if you want to talk, wait a minute for your turn; and I'll listen to you.
>
> *— Anonymous*

> REVIEW, APPLY, AND ASSESS

The Importance of Listening and Responding Skills

5.1 Explain the principle of listening and responding thoughtfully to others.

REVIEW: You spend more time listening than doing any other communication activity. Being a good listener and responding thoughtfully to others will help you

- Enhance the quality of your interpersonal relationships.
- Develop good collaboration skills.
- Forge a stronger link between speaker and audience.

APPLY: Identify specific instances from your own experience in which poor listening skills resulted in a significant communication problem. How would using effective listening skills have diminished or eliminated the problem?

ASSESS: Keep a listening journal for one day. Keep track of your listening goals and how long you have listened. Review your journal and note when you were an effective listener and when you were less effective.

How We Listen

5.2 Identify the elements of the listening process.

REVIEW: Listening is a complex process of receiving, constructing meaning from, and responding to verbal and nonverbal messages. The five activities of listening are (1) selecting, (2) attending, (3) understanding, (4) remembering, and (5) responding.

KEY TERMS:

hearing	understand
listening	remember
select	respond
attend	

APPLY: What captures or holds your attention when you are listening?

ASSESS: Which of the activities of listening do you do well? Which of the five activities need to be improved?

Listening Styles

5.3 Describe four listening styles.

REVIEW: Each person develops a preferred listening style based on his or her personality, the listening situation, and the listening goal. The four listening styles are relational, analytical, critical, and task oriented. Knowing your typical listening style can help you adapt your listening approach for maximum listening effectiveness.

KEY TERMS:

listening style	critical listeners
relational listeners	second guessing
analytical listeners	task-oriented listeners

APPLY: What is your usual listening style? How do you adapt your style depending upon your listening goal?

ASSESS: What listening situations are the most challenging for you? What are strategies you could use to help you become a more flexible listener?

Listening Barriers

5.4 Identify and describe barriers that keep people from listening well.

REVIEW: Many people struggle with the skill of listening. Barriers to effective listening include (1) self barriers: self-focus, emotional noise, and criticism; (2) information-processing barriers: processing rate, information overload, receiver apprehension, shifting attention, and cultural differences; and (3) context barriers: time barriers and place barriers.

KEY TERMS:

emotional noise	anticipatory communication
receiver apprehension	noise

APPLY: What are the most challenging listening barriers for you?

ASSESS: What are strategies you could use to overcome the most difficult listening barriers you experience?

Improving Your Listening Skills

5.5   Identify and use strategies that can improve your listening skills.

REVIEW: To become a better listener, consider three simple steps that may sound easy to do but are challenging to put into practice: stop, look, and listen. To stop means to be mindful of the message and to avoid focusing on your own distracting inner talk. To look is to listen with your eyes—to focus on nonverbal information. To listen involves the skill of capturing the details of a message while also connecting those details to a major idea.

KEY TERMS:
social decentering   meta-message

APPLY: Do you find yourself interrupting or getting interrupted often? What can you do—as a listener or a speaker—to avoid interruptions and deal with them if they happen?

ASSESS: Which of the skill steps (stop, look, listen) do you need to improve the most? What are specific strategies that can help you improve your listening skills?

Improving Your Responding Skills

5.6   Identify and use appropriate responding skills.

REVIEW: The other half of listening is responding to others accurately and appropriately. To respond thoughtfully means to consider the needs of the other person. Check the accuracy of your listening skills by reflecting on your understanding of what your partner has said. To respond effectively, be descriptive, timely, brief, and useful. To listen with empathy is to understand your partner's feelings, ask appropriate questions, paraphrase message content, and paraphrase emotions. When you provide social support, offer messages of comfort and concern so your partner feels understood and valued.

KEY TERMS:
paraphrasing   social support

APPLY: Do you usually paraphrase when listening to others in everyday life? If so, how do you summarize messages in a helpful and natural-sounding way? If you don't paraphrase much, what kinds of phrases do you think would help you?

ASSESS: How would you assess your ability to empathize with others? What are specific strategies that you could use to enhance your ability to empathize?

〉 THE PRINCIPLE POINTS

Principle Four:

Listen and respond thoughtfully to others.

- Stop: Work to turn off competing mental messages that distract your listening focus.
- To overcome self barriers to listening effectively, consciously become aware of your drifting attention. Then, to get back in synch, use self-talk and emotion management skills (such as deep breathing) to remain calm and focused on the message, not the messenger.
- To overcome information-processing listening barriers, make mental summaries of the message you hear, recognize when you are tired and not at your listening best, take effective notes, and remain focused.
- To overcome context listening barriers, become aware of your best and worst times of the day for listening; consciously intensify your concentration if you know you're not at your listening best; and assertively take action, such as closing a door or a window, to reduce external noise when listening.
- Look: Listen with your eyes to discern nonverbal information that provides important information about emotions, attitudes, and relationship cues.
- Listen: Work to link facts and details with major ideas you hear.
- Respond: Use effective responding skills by providing feedback that is descriptive, timely, brief, and useful while remaining an active listener.
- Be empathic: Try to imagine how you would feel in a situation like the one your communication partner is in. To confirm your interpretation of his or her message, ask appropriate clarifying questions and then paraphrase both the content and the emotions expressed.
- Paraphrase by briefly summarizing the message in your own words while trying to accurately capture the essence of what your listening partner said; don't add to the information presented when paraphrasing.

ADAPTING TO OTHERS: DIVERSITY AND COMMUNICATION

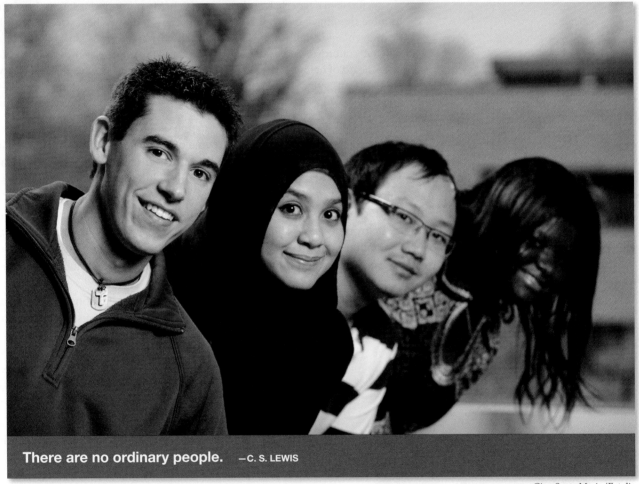

There are no ordinary people. —C. S. LEWIS

Gino Santa Maria/Fotolia

CHAPTER OUTLINE

- Understanding Diversity

- Culture and Communication

- Barriers to Bridging Differences and Adapting to Others

- Adapting to Others Who Are Different from You

- Study Guide: Review, Apply, and Assess

117

LEARNING OBJECTIVES

After studying this chapter, you should be able to

6.1 Describe how differences of gender, sexual orientation, ethnicity, and age influence communication.

6.2 Define *culture,* and compare and contrast cultural contexts and cultural values.

6.3 Illustrate four barriers that inhibit communication between individuals.

6.4 Describe seven strategies that will help bridge differences between people and help them adapt to differences.

O verheard from a student before class:

> I've had it with all this cultural diversity and gender crap. It seems like every textbook in every class is obsessed with it. My music appreciation class is trying to force the music of other cultures down my throat. What's wrong with Bach, Beethoven, and Brahms? In English lit, all we're reading is stuff by people from different countries. And it seems my history prof talks only about obscure people I've never heard of before. I'm tired of all this politically correct nonsense. I mean, we're all Americans, aren't we? We're not going off to live in Africa, China, or India. Why don't they just teach us what we need to know and cut all this diversity garbage?

Have you heard this kind of sentiment expressed before? Perhaps you've encountered such a "diversity backlash" among some of your classmates, or you may harbor this attitude yourself. Some people may find it unsettling that school curricula and textbooks have increased their focus on issues of culture and gender differences. But these changes are not motivated by an irrational desire to be politically correct. We'll see in this chapter that they are taking place because diversity is increasing in the United States and many other parts of the world. School textbooks and courses are *reflecting* the change, not initiating it. To live comfortably in the 21st century, we must learn ways to appreciate and understand human differences rather than ignore them, suffer because of them, or wish they would disappear.

One of life's unprofound principles with profound implications for human communication is this: *We each have different backgrounds and experiences.*[1] Your employers, teachers, religious leaders, best friends, or romantic partners may have grown up with cultural traditions different from your own. And the not-so-startling fact that people *are* different from one another provides the context for discussion of our final Communication Principle for a Lifetime: *Effective communicators appropriately adapt their messages to others.* Figure 6.1 presents our now-familiar model, which includes this final principle of appropriately adapting messages to others.

We introduce this principle last because often people learn how to adapt only after they have learned the other communication principles. Being able to adapt to others requires a relatively sophisticated understanding of the communication process. The ability to adapt suggests that you already have a sense of who you are and a consciousness of the presence of others—self-awareness and other-awareness, the components of the first principle we presented.[2] Studies in developmental communication suggest that the ability to appropriately adapt our behavior to others evolves after we have become aware that there is a "me," after we have learned to use verbal and nonverbal symbols to communicate, and after we have developed an ability to hear and listen to others. We begin to develop all of these skills as infants and refine them throughout our lives.

FIGURE 6.1 Communication Principles for a Lifetime

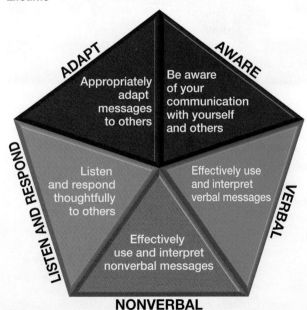

The goals of this chapter are to identify human differences that may inhibit communication with others and to suggest adaptive strategies that can improve the quality and effectiveness of our communication with others. To frame our discussion of diversity and communication, we'll note differences in gender, sexual orientation, ethnicity, and age, and the implications these differences have for communication. As you read in Chapter 2, each of us perceives the world differently. To some degree, we are each estranged from others. Following our discussion of some of the classic ways we are diverse, we'll turn our attention to cultural differences and then note how human differences create communication barriers.

But simply understanding that there are differences is not enough to improve communication; it is important to learn how to use effective communication skills to adapt to those differences. In his book *Thank You for Being Late,* journalist Thomas Friedman suggests that the pace of our lives is accelerating at an astounding rate due to dramatic changes in technology, globalization, and climate.[3] Friedman suggests that the best way to address the dizzying changes happening to us is to be able to skillfully adapt to those changes. Those who survive in the 21st century may not be the fittest (as evolution theory suggests) but the most adaptable. The ability to adapt is a quintessential communication principle that will serve you well for a lifetime.[4]

The goal of being able to appropriately adapt your communication to other people does not mean you have to abandon your own traditions and preferences. It does suggest that appropriately using communication strategies to understand and bridge differences that exist among people can enhance human understanding. So we'll conclude the chapter by identifying strategies to enhance the quality of communication with others by appropriately adapting to our differences.

Understanding Diversity

6.1 Describe how differences of gender, sexual orientation, ethnicity, and age influence communication.

Communication researchers have found that differences in our gender, sexual orientation, ethnicity, and age affect the way we interact with one another. Some of these differences among groups of people are learned, and some are based on biology—or, in the case of age differences, simply how long someone has lived—but they all have an effect on how we perceive and interact with others. As we study these group differences, however, keep in mind that groups are made up of individual people, and every single person has different experiences. As C. S. Lewis observed in the quotation that opens this chapter, there are no ordinary people—which implies that each of us is unique. Although you may have some things (such as your gender, age, skin color, where you grew up, or your language) in common with a larger group of people, you nonetheless are a unique individual. And so is everybody else.

Sex and Gender

Perhaps the most obvious form of human diversity is biological sex. As we discussed in Chapter 2, a person's sex is determined by biology. In contrast, gender is a complex, culturally-constructed and psychologically-based perception of oneself as feminine, masculine, or **androgynous** (a blend of feminine and masculine traits). Some people reject the sex assigned to them at birth; instead, they choose to transcend the boundaries of conventional sex and gender and become **transgender**. Being transgender is a unique gender identity that is not confined by traditional notions of masculinity or femininity. It is independent of one's sexual orientation.[5]

At one time or another, you have probably thought, "Why doesn't that person act like people of *my* sex?" You may not think of yourself as stereotyping others on

androgynous
Exhibiting both masculine and feminine characteristics.

transgender
Choosing to transcend the boundaries of conventional sex and gender by rejecting one's sex assigned at birth. A unique identity not confined by traditional notions of masculinity or femininity and independent of one's sexual orientation.

▲ Have you ever been in a social situation like the one pictured here, in which friends, relatives, or loved ones seem to self-segregate according to gender? What does this common social phenomenon reveal about the nature of gender and communication? How can you appropriately adapt messages to others across gender lines?
SuperStock

the basis of their sex or gender, but there is evidence that many of us do make snap judgments about someone's behavior on the basis of his or her sex. You may also have heard (or said), "Vive la différence"—a French expression that celebrates that men and women are different. Why celebrate? Because that difference makes us fascinating and mysterious, and it keeps the world from being awfully dull. Whatever your view of the relationship between the sexes or among different genders, your day-to-day interaction with members of both sexes—or different genders—is a fact of life (unless you're a hermit). Women, men, and those who identify with feminine or masculine genders work, live, and play together, so it's important to explore the effects of sex and gender on communication to improve our ability to relate to one another.

John Gray, author of the book *Men Are from Mars, Women Are from Venus,* would have us believe that the sexes are so different that we approach life from two distinct "planets," or spheres of perspective.[6] Although communication scholars have challenged several of Gray's conclusions because they are not supported by research, there are some research-documented differences in the ways men and women communicate.[7] Deborah Tannen, author of several books on the behavior of the sexes, views men and women as distinctly different cultural groups.[8] She suggests that female–male communication is cross-cultural communication, with all the challenges inherent in exchanging messages with persons of very different backgrounds and value systems.

Perhaps these viewpoints are a bit extreme and the sexes are actually more alike than different. Research using multiple methods and originating in various disciplines consistently shows that differences in men's and women's communication have more to do with *why* we communicate than with *how* we communicate. Research reveals that men tend to approach communication from a content orientation. They view the purpose of communication as primarily goal oriented and tend to talk to accomplish something or complete a task. In other words, you talk when you have something to say. This is consistent with the tendency for men to base their relationships, especially their male friendships, on sharing activities rather than talking.

Women, research suggests, tend to use communication for the purpose of relating or connecting to others, of extending themselves to other people to know them and be known by them. What you talk about is less important than the act of talking, because talking implies a relationship. One study found that when interrupted, women are sometimes more likely to simply smile, agree, politely nod, and laugh. According to researchers, these actions suggest a greater effort, even when interrupted, to maintain a positive relationship and facilitate the flow of conversation.[9]

To summarize this difference: *Men often communicate to report; women often communicate to establish rapport.*[10] So the point of difference isn't in the way the sexes actually communicate but in the motivations or reasons for communicating.[11] Our instrumental and expressive orientations to the world translate into our communication behavior.

To bridge the gap, here's what we suggest you do:

- First, work to understand the differences that may exist.

- Second, make an insightful examination of your own behavior in light of the differences discussed and then determine how you conform to and differ from the description of members of your sex.

- Third, be a gender researcher yourself. Note differences as well as similarities between you and those whose gender is different from yours. Be careful not to ascribe differences in communication only to a person's sex or gender. Consider other reasons for communication differences such as age, personality, ethnicity, or culture, too.

- Finally, make a conscious effort to adapt your behavior appropriately; be mindful of how you interact with others to enhance the quality of your relationships with them.

When in conversation with someone of a different sex or gender, try to assess the person's communication motivation: What does the other person view as the purpose for the conversation? Sometimes it's wise simply to ask the person what he or she wants. Then adapt your response accordingly. Just because you're female or identify more closely with the feminine gender doesn't mean that you have to or will take an expressive approach to every interaction; just because you're male or view yourself as masculine doesn't mean that conversations are always about exchanging information. By developing the ability to accomplish both content and relational approaches to communication, you broaden how you adapt to others. Your communication skill increases.

> ## RECAP
>
> ### Gender-Based Approaches to Communication
>
> **Masculine Approach**
>
> - More instrumental; often characterized by assertiveness and getting things done
> - Usually more emphasis on the content of messages and the information being exchanged (the *what*) rather than on relational elements (the *how*) in the message
> - More attention given to verbal than nonverbal messages
>
> **Feminine Approach**
>
> - More expressive; often characterized by an emphasis on connecting with others and fostering harmonious relationships
> - Usually more emphasis on the relational elements of messages
> - More attention given to nonverbal elements, such as *how* something is said rather than *what* is said

Gender Identity and Sexual Orientation

The lesbian, gay, bisexual, transgender, and queer (LGBTQ) communities are important groups within the larger U.S. culture. Although we are using the terms *lesbian, gay, bisexual, transgender,* and *queer* (a term that communicates a liberation from labels about sexual orientation), there are many more ways of describing one's gender identity and sexual orientation. In fact, as we discussed in Chapter 3, on Facebook you can select from fifty-six terms.[12] So rather than thinking about a person's gender identity and sexual orientation in terms of just a few rigid categories, it's more accurate to consider a wide range of gender and sexual orientation identities.

Perspectives on Sexual Orientation   Regardless of the label, sexual orientation has become a source of pride for some people but remains socially stigmatized for others. Although 92 percent of LGBTQ individuals in a recent survey said that society is becoming more accepting of them, there is evidence that LGBTQ individuals continue to be judged negatively solely on the basis of their sexual orientation.[13] Research has found that a heterosexual person who knows someone who is gay or a lesbian is more inclined to be accepting of gays or lesbians and more likely to support same-sex marriage. Still, about 40 percent of LGBTQ individuals report that at some point in their lives a family member or close friend rejected them because of their sexual orientation.[14] In addition, people who hold negative attitudes toward gays and lesbians are less likely to communicate with them than are those with more accepting views. Research further suggests that heterosexuals who have negative perceptions of gay and lesbian people are more likely to have rigid views about gender roles and will assume that their peers also

homophobia

Fear of, aversion to, or discrimination against gays or lesbians.

hold such rigid views and negative impressions of gays and lesbians.[15] Perhaps related to such perceptions, **homophobia**, which is a fear or aversion toward gay and lesbian people often accompanied by the fear of being labeled or perceived as LGBTQ, continues to exist among many people.

It is because of the persistence of these negative attitudes toward gays and lesbians, as well as antigay violence and harassment, that some gays and lesbians continue to live "in the closet," concealing their sexual orientations.[16] For example, research has found that LGBTQ individuals are frequent communicators via social media; 80 percent report that they have used Facebook or Twitter, compared to 58 percent of the general public. Yet only 16 percent of LGBTQ people indicate that they regularly discuss LGBTQ issues online.[17]

Enhancing Awareness   An effective and appropriate communicator draws upon our first Principle of Communication for a Lifetime; he or she is aware of, and sensitive to, issues and attitudes about sexual orientation in contemporary society. Just as you have been taught to avoid biased expressions that degrade someone's race or ethnicity, it is equally important to avoid using language that demeans a person's sexual orientation or gender identity. Telling stories and jokes whose point or punch line relies on ridiculing a person because of his or her gender identity or sexual orientation lowers perceptions of your credibility not only among LGBTQ people, but also among people who dislike bias against gays and lesbians.

It's important to create a communication climate in which LGBTQ individuals can be themselves and comfortably talk about who they are without fearing rejection or discrimination. Creating a climate of openness and acceptance is important for any human relationship. Family members who have a gay, lesbian, bisexual, transgender, or queer member report more overall relational satisfaction if their family doesn't avoid a discussion of gender identity and sexual orientation. In addition, there is less anxiety and negativity if issues of sexuality and gender identity are discussed openly and appropriately. Many universities offer training courses, known as ally training, to help faculty and staff members create safe, accepting relationships. Participants are informed about LGBTQ culture and taught how to provide appropriate support. A faculty or staff member who has completed ally training may post a sign on his or her door to indicate that it's safe to be yourself in that person's office or classroom.[18]

Sometimes we unintentionally offend someone through subtle use or misuse of language. For example, gays and lesbians typically prefer to be referred to as *gay* or *lesbian,* rather than as *homosexual,*[19] and the term *sexual orientation* is preferred over *sexual preference* in describing a person's sexual orientation. The key point is this: It is important to be aware of the range of human sexual expression and to be sensitively other oriented as you interact with those whose sexual orientation and gender identity is different from your own.

Age

Because different generations have experienced different cultural and historical events, they often view life differently. If your grandparents or great-grandparents experienced the Great Depression of the 1930s, they may have different attitudes about bank savings accounts than you or even your parents do. Today's explicit song lyrics may shock older Americans who grew up with such racy lyrics as "makin' whoopee." The generation gap is real and has implications for how we communicate with others.

There is considerable evidence that people hold stereotypical views of others based on others' perceived age.[20] You may see someone with graying or thinning hair and wrinkles and make assumptions about that person's preferences in music, food, or even politics. Similarly, older people who see someone with tattoos, piercings, and wildly colored hair may make stereotypical assumptions about a host of preferences of the younger person. (Even our example of old and young draws on stereotypes and runs the risk of reinforcing those stereotypical images.)

Regardless of the accuracy of the assumptions we make about others on the basis of perceived age, a person's age has an influence on his or her communication with others, including how messages are processed. For example, one study found that older adults have greater difficulty in accurately interpreting the nonverbal messages of others than do younger people.[21] Older adults don't like to be patronized or talked down to (who does?).[22] And younger people seem to value social support, empathic listening, and being mentored more than older people do.[23]

Generation Characteristics   Authors Neil Howe and William Strauss, researchers who have investigated the role of age and generation in society, define a generation as "a society-wide peer group, born over a period roughly the same length as the passage from youth to adulthood, who collectively possess a common persona."[24] Table 6.1 summarizes the labels and common characteristics and values of several generational types.

Baby boomers is the label for the generation of people born between 1943 and 1960. Perhaps your parents or grandparents are "boomers." If you are not a boomer, you may experience some communication differences and conflicts with those who are because of differing values and perspectives.

Generation X is the term used for people born between 1961 and 1981. Of course, not all Generation Xers share all of the characteristics listed in Table 6.1, such as living with uncertainty, valuing a balanced life, or saving for the future. While these attributes provide a general overview, they vary from person to person.

Millennials are those born between 1982 and 2002—the age of many of today's traditional college students. Researchers Howe and Strauss suggest that, as a group, "millennials are unlike any other youth generation in living memory. They are more numerous, more affluent, better educated, and more ethnically diverse. More importantly, they are beginning to manifest a wide array of positive social habits that older Americans no longer associate with youth, including a focus on teamwork, achievement, modesty, and

TABLE 6.1   Summary of Generation Characteristics[25]

Generation Name	Birth Years	Typical Characteristics
Matures	1925–1942	• Work hard • Have a sense of duty • Are willing to sacrifice • Have a sense of what is right • Work quickly
Baby boomers	1943–1960	• Value personal fulfillment and optimism • Crusade for causes • Buy now/pay later • Support equal rights for all • Work efficiently
Generation X	1961–1981	• Live with uncertainty • Consider balance important • Live for today • Save • Consider every job as a contract
Millennials	1982–2002	• Are close to their parents • Feel "special" • Are goal and team oriented • Frequently use social media • Focus on achievement

good conduct."[26] Not surprisingly, millennials are more comfortable with technology than people in other age groups because the Internet, cell phones, and personal computers have always been part of their lives.[27] According to research by the Pew Research Center, millennials are also less likely to be tied to a specific religious institution and more likely to build their own personal networks using social media. Although recent economic trends have left many millennials financially stressed, as a group, they still feel optimistic about the future.[28]

Postmillennials are people born since 2002. Because postmillennials are just emerging, there is less research that identifies the specific attributes of this generation. One clear observation is that postmillennials view technology as an even more seamless method of interacting with others than do millennials. For postmillennials, technological tools to connect socially have always been a way of relating to others.

Implications for Communication   Your generation of origin has important implications for communication, especially as you relate to others in both family and work situations. Each generation has developed its own set of values, anchored in social, economic, and cultural factors stemming from the times in which the generation has lived.

Our values—core conceptualizations of what is fundamentally good or bad and right or wrong—color our way of thinking about and responding to what we experience. Generational and age differences may create barriers and increase the potential for conflict and misunderstanding. For example, after investigating the role of generations in the workforce, one team of researchers suggests that Generation X workers are paradoxically both more individualistic (self-reliant) and more team oriented than boomers.[29] In contrast, boomers are more likely to have a sense of loyalty to their employers, expect long-term employment, value a pension plan, and experience job burnout from overwork. Generation Xers, by contrast, seek a more balanced approach between work and personal life, expect to have more than one job or career, value working conditions over other job factors, and have a greater need to feel appreciated.[30] This research suggests that if you have a boomer boss and you are a Generation Xer, your boss may not understand why you want to take extra vacation time just to "clear your head" when there is a lot of work that needs to be done. Of course, these broad generalizations do not apply to all people in these categories.

Ethnicity

ethnicity

A social classification based on factors, such as nationality, religion, and language, as well as biological ancestral heritage, that are shared by a group of people with a common geographic origin.

Ethnicity is a *social classification* based on a variety of factors, such as nationality, religion, and language, as well as biological ancestral heritage, shared by a group of people with a common geographic origin. Simply stated, an ethnic group is a group of people who have identified themselves as such, based on a variety of factors that may or may not include ancestral heritage or biological characteristics such as skin color.

Ethnicity fosters common bonds that affect communication patterns. Although ethnic groups bring vitality and variety to American society, members of these groups may experience persecution or rejection by members of other groups in our society.

race

A group of people with a common cultural history, nationality, or geographical location who may share some genetically transmitted physical attributes.

A concept closely related to ethnicity is **race**, a term that has evolved over time. In the past, race focused more on genetically transmitted physical attributes. However, today it refers to a group of people with a common cultural history, nationality, or geographical location.[31] A person's racial classification was originally based on phenotypes, which are such visible physiological attributes as skin color and other physical features, including body type, hair color and texture, and facial attributes. Skin color and other physical characteristics continue to affect our responses to others and influence the way people of different races interact.

Although it may seem easy to classify individuals genetically as belonging to one race or another, it's not quite that simple. One geneticist has concluded that there is much more genetic variation *within* a given racial category than *between* one race and another.[32] There really aren't vast genetic differences between people assigned to two racial categories.[33] However, some scholars point out that, in practice, many of us think of race as a category that includes not only biological or genetic characteristics, but also such factors as cultural, economic, social, geographic, and historical elements.[34] Communication scholar Brenda Allen emphasizes that ethnicity refers in large part to the common culture shared by people who identify with an ethnic group. Ethnicity may include race, but race is a category that historically has been based on more genetic or biological factors that are not clear-cut.[35] The term *race* is therefore a fuzzy, somewhat controversial way of classifying people.

One of the most significant problems stemming from attempts to classify people by racial or ethnic type is the tendency to discriminate and unfairly, inaccurately, or inappropriately ascribe stereotypes to racial or ethnic groups. **Discrimination** is the unfair or inappropriate treatment of people based on their group membership. One of the goals of learning about diversity and becoming aware of both differences and similarities among groups is to eliminate discrimination and stereotypes that cause people to rigidly and inappropriately prejudge others.

discrimination

The unfair or inappropriate treatment of people based on their group membership.

Culture and Communication

6.2 Define *culture*, and compare and contrast cultural contexts and cultural values.

You need not travel the world to encounter people who are different from you; the world is traveling to you. The following Communication & Diversity feature documents how diverse the United States is already and also provides evidence that the trend toward greater diversity will continue.[36]

Globalization, the integration of economics and technology that is contributing to a worldwide, interconnected business environment, is changing the way we work and relate to people around the world.[37] For example, when you call to get technical assistance with your computer or advice on fixing your TV, you may talk to someone in India rather than in Indiana. One statistician notes that if the world were a village of 1,000 people, the village would have 590 Asians, 122 Africans, 96 Europeans, 84 Latin Americans, 55 members of the former Soviet Union, and 53 North Americans.[38] Clearly, globalization has increased the probability that you will communicate with someone today who has a cultural background different from your own.[39] To ignore the range of human cultural differences is to ignore a significant factor, which can mean the difference between effective and ineffective communication.

globalization

The integration of economics and technology that is contributing to a worldwide, interconnected business environment.

Defining Culture

Culture is a learned system of knowledge, behavior, attitudes, beliefs, values, and norms that is shared by a group of people and shaped from one generation to the next.[40]

culture

A learned system of knowledge, behavior, attitudes, beliefs, values, and norms that is shared by a group of people and shaped from one generation to the next.

COMMUNICATION & DIVERSITY

Diversity Almanac

1. Two-thirds of the immigrants on this planet come to the United States.[41] For example, 60 percent of the residents of Miami, Florida, are foreign-born.[42]

2. "About one in three U.S. residents is a minority," said U.S. Census Bureau Director Louis Kincannon. "To put this into perspective, there are more minorities in this country today than there were people in the United States in 1910. In fact, the minority population in the U.S. is larger than the total population of all but eleven countries."[43]

3. By 2050, more than 50 percent of the U.S. population will be nonwhite; whites will no longer be a majority.[44] Even earlier, by the year 2023, nearly half of all young adults in this country will come from minority groups, according to the U.S. Census Bureau.[45]

4. One in seven U.S. marriages occurs between spouses of different races or ethnicities.[46]

5. It is estimated that more than 40 million U.S. residents learned something other than English as their first language, including 18 million people whose first language is Spanish.[47] One of every eight U.S. residents speaks a language other than English at home, and one-third of children in urban U.S. public schools speak a first language other than English.[48]

6. By 2050, two of every five children under age 5 in the United States will be Hispanic. Today, more than 50 percent of all children under age 5 are part of an ethnic minority.[49]

7. In 2010, over half of U.S. doctoral degrees granted were earned by women.[50]

8. Estimates of gay and lesbian populations in the United States vary from 1 to 9 percent of the general male population and from 1 to 5 percent of the general female population.[51]

9. Millennials, or Americans born between 1982 and 2002, represented more than a quarter of the U.S. population in 2014, outnumbering their parents' generation, the baby boomers.[52]

10. Millennials are more diverse than previous generations, with 44 percent of their ranks belonging to a minority race or ethnic group.[53]

Communication and culture, says anthropologist Edward T. Hall, are inseparable—you can't talk about one without the other.[54] There is ample evidence documenting the influence of culture on how we work and live.[55] In the broadest sense, culture includes how people think, what they do, and how they use things to sustain their lives. Researcher Geert Hofstede says culture is the "mental software" that helps us understand our world.[56] Like the software and operating system in a computer, our culture provides the framework within which we interpret the data and information that enter our lives.

Cultures are not static; they change as new information and new technologies modify them.[57] We no longer believe that bathing is unhealthy or that we should use leeches as the primary medical procedure to make us healthy. Through research, we have changed our cultural assumptions and values about personal hygiene and medical care.

Some groups of individuals can best be described as a **co-culture**—a cultural group within a larger culture. Examples of co-cultures include people with physical disabilities, different age groups, and various religious groups. Different Christian denominations, such as the Amish or members of the Church of Jesus Christ of Latter-day Saints (Mormons), have distinct traditions and cultural norms. A person's gender also places her or him in one of the co-cultures that researchers have used to analyze and investigate the influence of communication on our relationships with others. Gay, lesbian, bisexual, and transgender people constitute another example of an important co-culture in our society.

Intercultural communication occurs when individuals or groups from different cultures communicate. The transactional process of listening and responding to people from different cultural backgrounds can be challenging; the greater the difference in culture between two people, the greater the potential for misunderstanding and mistrust. There is evidence that studying the role of culture in our lives can help us adapt when we encounter cultural differences—whether those differences occur in our

co-culture

A culture that exists within a larger cultural context (e.g., LGBTQ cultures, Amish culture).

intercultural communication

Communication between people who have different cultural traditions.

hometown or when we are living in a culture different from our own.[58] Understanding the nature of culture and cultural differences helps us develop strategies to make connections and adapt to others with different "mental software."[59]

When you encounter a culture that has little in common with your own, you may experience **culture shock**, a sense of confusion, anxiety, stress, and loss.[60] If you are visiting or actually living in the new culture, your uncertainty and stress may take time to subside as you learn the values and message systems that characterize the culture. Research has found that one of the ways we seek to adapt to a new culture is by using social media. International exchange students, for example, often use Skype or Facebook to make them feel closer to their friends and family back home and less stressed when in a new culture. Research has found that students were more likely to Skype with family and close friends.[61]

Our culture and life experiences determine our **worldview**—the general cultural perspective that shapes how we perceive and respond to what happens to us. A culture's worldview, according to intercultural communication scholar Carley Dodd, encompasses "how the culture perceives the role of various forces in explaining why events occur as they do in a social setting."[62] These beliefs shape our thoughts, language, and actions. Your worldview permeates all aspects of how you interact with society; it's like a lens through which you observe the world. Since, as we noted in Chapter 1, communication is how we make sense of the world and share that sense with others, our worldview is one of the primary filters that influence how we communicate. Two frameworks for describing how culture influences our worldview are cultural contexts and cultural values.

culture shock

Feelings of confusion, loss, stress, and anxiety that a person may experience when encountering a culture different from his or her own.

worldview

A perspective shared by a culture or group of people about key beliefs and issues, such as death, God, and the meaning of life, that influences interaction with others; the lens through which people in a given culture perceive the world around them.

COMMUNICATION & SOCIAL MEDIA

Adapting to Differences When Making E-Connections

As we have noted, it is increasingly likely that you communicate with people who are far from where you work and live. It's not unusual to use Facebook, instant messages, e-mail, or texts to contact people from other cultures. With the advent of Facebook and other social media, as well as Skype and other easy-to-use videoconference methods, it's also not surprising to see and hear the person you're talking with. According to a *Business Week* survey, most people working in an organization today believe that they will be interacting with someone in an international location.[63]

A team of communication researchers points out that when we communicate via e-mail, phone, or social media it takes a bit longer to interpret information about relationships, because often there are fewer nonverbal cues available.[64] Evidence also shows that, because of these limited cues, we are more likely to inaccurately stereotype others, especially on the basis of gender, when interacting via electronic channels than we are when communicating face to face.[65] One study found that different cultures use different emojis to express nonverbal messages on social media. For example, people from more individualistic cultures are more likely to use :-) to communicate happiness while those from a collectivistic culture are more likely to use ^-^.[66] Research has also confirmed that we are more

interculturally sensitive when someone is standing in front of us than when we communicate via social media.[67]

With the growing importance and prevalence of social media and e-communication, there comes an increased potential for misunderstanding. So how can you enhance the quality of your relationships online? Consider these suggestions:

- If you are using a "lean" communication channel, such as e-mail or texting, to interact with a person who is from a high-context culture, you may need to provide more explicit references to your feelings and emotions by telling your partner how you feel or by using emoticons.
- When appropriate, consider asking more questions to clarify meanings.
- Consciously make more small talk about the weather or other topics that may not directly be related to the task at hand. Such interaction helps connect you to others, makes the interaction less task oriented, and provides a balance of relational information that humanizes the communication.
- Use paraphrasing to confirm that you understand what others are saying.
- Finally, you may simply need to be more patient with others; relationships may take longer to develop because of the diminished nonverbal cues. Be mindful of the differences and consciously develop other-oriented skills.

Cultural Contexts

cultural context

Additional information about a message that is communicated through nonverbal and environmental cues rather than through language.

The **cultural context** of any communication consists of the nonverbal cues that surround and give added meaning to the message. In this sense, *all* nonverbal cues are part of a cultural context. When interpreting the overall meaning of a message, some cultures give more weight to the surrounding nonverbal context than to the explicit verbal message. In contrast, other cultures place less emphasis on the nonverbal context and greater emphasis on what someone says.

For example, when you interview for a job, you may be scanning the face of your interviewer and looking for nonverbal messages to provide cues about the impression you are making on the interviewer. These contextual cues (in this case, the nonverbal messages) provide meaning to help you interpret your interviewer's message. Edward T. Hall helped us understand the importance of cultural context when he categorized cultures as either high- or low-context.[68]

high-context culture

A culture in which people derive much information from nonverbal and environmental cues and less information from the words of a message.

High-Context Cultures   In **high-context cultures**, nonverbal cues are extremely important in interpreting messages. Communicators rely heavily on the context of subtle information such as facial expression, vocal cues, and even silence in interpreting messages—hence the term *high-context cultures,* to indicate the emphasis placed on the context. Asian, Arab, and southern European peoples are more likely to draw on context for message interpretation.

low-context culture

A culture in which people derive much information from the words of a message and less information from nonverbal and environmental cues.

Low-Context Cultures   People in **low-context cultures** rely more explicitly on language and the meaning of words and use fewer contextual cues to send and interpret information. Individuals from low-context cultures, such as North Americans, Germans, and Scandinavians, may perceive people from high-context cultures as less attractive, knowledgeable, and trustworthy because they violate unspoken low-context cultural rules of conduct and communication. Individuals from low-context cultures often are less skilled in interpreting unspoken contextual messages.[69] Figure 6.2 describes differences in communication style between high-context and low-context cultures.

Cultural Values

Ancient Egyptians worshiped cats. The Druids of England believed they could tap into spiritual powers in the shadow of the mysterious rock circle of Stonehenge at the summer solstice. Some would say contemporary Americans place a high value on accumulating material possessions and making pilgrimages to sports arenas on weekends. By paying attention to what a culture values, we can get important clues about how to respond to communication messages, establish relationships, and avoid making embarrassing errors when interacting with people from a given culture. Identifying what a particular group of people values or appreciates can give us insight into the behavior of an individual raised within that culture. Although there are considerable differences among the world's **cultural values**—clearly, not all cultures value the same things—Geert Hofstede has identified six categories for measuring values that are important in almost every culture.[70] These generalizations are based on several surveys that he developed and administered to more than 100,000 people. Even though his data were collected more than thirty-five years ago and sampled only employees (predominantly males) who worked at IBM—a large international company with branch offices in many countries—Hofstede's research remains one of the most comprehensive studies to help us describe what people from a culture may value.[71]

cultural values

Whatever a given group of people values or appreciates.

According to Hofstede's research, every culture establishes values relating to (1) individualism versus collectivism, (2) distribution of power (either centralized or shared), (3) avoidance of uncertainty versus tolerance for uncertainty, (4) masculine

FIGURE 6.2   A Scale of High-Context and Low-Context Cultures

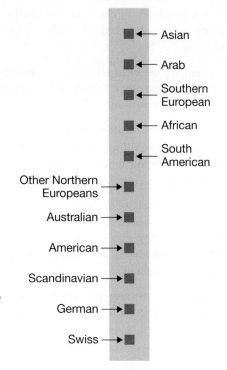

High-Context Cultures
Place emphasis on nonverbal expressions and surrounding context

- Consider nonverbal cues important
- Take into account the environment and situation
- Observe a communication partner's gestures, facial expressions, tone of voice, and overall mood
- Maintain extensive information networks

Asian

Arab

Southern European

African

South American

Other Northern Europeans

Australian

American

Scandinavian

German

Swiss

Low-Context Cultures
Place emphasis on words

- Are less aware of nonverbal environment and situation
- Need detailed background information
- Tend to segment and compartmentalize information
- Control information and share it on a "need to know" basis
- Prefer explicit and careful directions from someone who "knows"
- Consider knowledge an important commodity

or feminine cultural perspectives, (5) long-term and short-term orientation to time, and (6) expectations about happiness in terms of indulgence or restraint. An overview of Hofstede's research conclusions for several countries is included in Table 6.2 at the end of this section, but first we'll consider each of these six categories of values in more detail.

As we discuss these six cultural values, keep in mind that we are applying generalizations to a cultural group. There are vast differences *within* a culture as well as between cultural groups; certainly not all the people within a cultural group will hold the cultural values we will discuss. Think of these values as explaining cultural *group* differences viewed from an anthropological perspective rather than *individual* differences viewed from a psychological perspective.[72] Using Hofstede's six cultural values to describe a given culture or geographic region is a bit like flying over a country at 35,000 feet; at that height, you can't see the details and notice nuances of difference, but you can gain a broad overview of the landscape.

Individualistic and Collectivistic Cultural Values   Which of the following two sayings better characterizes your culture: "All for one and one for all" or "I did it my way"? If you chose the first one, your culture is more likely to value group or team collaboration—it is what researchers call a **collectivistic culture**. Collectivistic cultures champion what people do together and reward group achievement. In contrast, the "I did it my way" phrase emphasizes the importance of the individual over the group.[73] A culture that celebrates individual achievement and in which individual recognition is important is an **individualistic culture**.

Traditionally, North Americans place a high value on individual achievements. The United States—with its Academy Awards; its reality TV shows in which contestants vie for the title of "American Ninja Warrior" or try to be the lone "Survivor"; its countless

collectivistic culture

A culture that places a high value on collaboration, teamwork, and group achievement.

individualistic culture

A culture that values individual achievement and personal accomplishments.

sports contests; and its community awards to firefighters for dedicated service, to winners of spelling bees, to chefs for their barbecue recipes—perhaps epitomizes the individualistic culture. Psychologist Alan Waterman summed up the American value system this way:

> Chief among the virtues claimed . . . is self-realization. Each person is viewed as having a unique set of talents and potentials. The translation of these potentials into actuality is considered the highest purpose to which one can devote one's life.[74]

People from Asian cultures are more likely to value collective or group achievement. In a collectivistic culture, people strive to accomplish goals for the benefit of the group rather than the individual. As one communication author describes, Kenya is another country with a culture that emphasizes group or team collaboration:

> Nobody is an isolated individual. Rather, his [or her] uniqueness is a secondary fact. . . . In this new system, group activities are dominant, responsibility is shared and accountability is collective. . . . Because of the emphasis on collectivity, harmony and cooperation among the group tend to be emphasized more than individual function and responsibility.[75]

Some researchers believe that the values of individualism and collectivism are the most important values of any culture—they determine the essential nature of every other facet of how people behave.[76] Other researchers, however, caution that cultures are complex and that it is dangerous to label an entire culture as individualistic or collectivistic.[77] We agree—as we've pointed out, not everyone in a given culture fits a single label. But in trying to understand the role of culture and its effect on human communication, we believe that Hofstede's concept of cultural values, with special emphasis on individualism and collectivism, can help to explain and predict how people may send and interpret communication.[78]

▼ Awards for individual achievements are one indicator of how much North American cultures tend to value individualism.
FOX/Getty Images

SO YOU THINK YOU CAN
DANCE

Decentralized and Centralized Approaches to Power and Cultural Values   Some cultures are more comfortable with a broad distribution of power than other cultures. People from such cultures prefer a decentralized approach to power. Leadership is not vested in just one person. Decisions in a culture that values decentralized power distribution, as found in countries such as Australia and Ireland, are more likely to be made by consensus in a parliament or congress rather than by decree from a monarch or dictator.

Cultures that place a high value on centralized power, such as those found in Indonesia, India, and the Philippines, are more comfortable with a more structured form of government and with managerial styles that feature clear lines of authority. Hierarchical bureaucracies are common, and the general assumption is that some people will have more power, control, and influence than others.

Uncertainty and Certainty and Cultural Values   "Why don't they tell me what's going on?" exclaims an exasperated student. "I don't know what my grades are. I don't know what my SAT score is. I'm in a complete fog." Many people like to know "what's going on." They like to avoid uncertainty and to have a general sense of what's going to happen. Too much uncertainty makes them uncomfortable. Others tolerate more ambiguity and uncertainty.

Cultures in which people need certainty to feel secure are likely to develop and enforce more rigid rules for behavior and establish more elaborate codes of conduct. People from cultures with a greater tolerance for uncertainty have more relaxed, informal expectations for others. "It will sort itself out" and "Go with the flow" are phrases that characterize their attitudes.[79]

Again, we remind you that although there is evidence for the existence of the general cultural value of uncertainty avoidance, not all people in a given culture or country find this cultural value equally important. There is considerable variation within a culture as to how people respond to uncertainty.

Masculine and Feminine Cultural Values   Some cultures emphasize traditional "male" values such as getting things done and being assertive; other cultures place greater emphasis on traditional "female" values such as building relationships and seeking peace and harmony with others. These values are not really about biological sex differences but about general assumptions that underlie the values of interacting with others. People from **masculine cultures** also tend to value more traditional roles for men and women. People (both men and women) from masculine cultures value achievement, heroism, material wealth, and making things happen. Men and women from **feminine cultures** tend to value such things as caring for the less fortunate, being sensitive toward others, and enhancing the overall quality of life.[80] Later in this chapter, we will discuss how gender contributes to the development of a culture, but for now it is enough to realize that whole cultures can be typified by whether they identify with or emphasize masculine or feminine values.

We caution you once more to avoid making sweeping generalizations about every person in any cultural group. Just as there are differences between and among cultures, there are differences within a cultural group. For centuries, most countries have had masculine cultures. Men and their conquests are featured in history books and all aspects of society more than women are. But today's cultural anthropologists see some shift in these values. There is some movement toward the middle, with greater equality between masculine and feminine roles.

Long-Term and Short-Term Time Orientation and Cultural Values   A culture's orientation to time falls on a continuum between long-term and short-term.[81] People from a culture with a long-term orientation to time place an emphasis on the future and tend to value perseverance and thrift because these are virtues that pay off over a long period of time. A long-term time orientation also implies a greater willingness to subordinate oneself for a larger purpose, such as the good of society or the group.

In contrast, a culture that tends to have a short-term time orientation values spending rather than saving (because of a focus on the immediate time rather than the future), tradition (because of the value placed on the past), and preserving face of both self and others (making sure that an individual is respected and that his or her dignity is upheld). A short-term time oriented culture also has an expectation that results will soon follow the actions and effort expended on a task. In addition, short-term cultures place a high value on social and status obligations.

masculine culture
A culture that values achievement, assertiveness, heroism, material wealth, and traditional male and female roles.

feminine culture
A culture that values being sensitive toward others and fostering harmonious personal relationships with others.

TABLE 6.2 Six Categories of Cultural Values

Cultural Value	Countries Where People Scored Higher on This Cultural Value	Countries Where People Scored Lower on This Cultural Value
Individualism: Societies with higher individualism scores generally value individual accomplishment rather than the collective or collaborative achievement valued by societies with lower scores.	United States, Australia, Great Britain, Canada, Netherlands, New Zealand, Italy, Belgium, Denmark, Sweden, France	Guatemala, Ecuador, Panama, Venezuela, Colombia, Indonesia, Pakistan, Costa Rica, Peru, Taiwan, South Korea
Power Distribution: Societies with higher power distribution scores generally value greater power differences between people; they are generally more accepting of fewer people having authority and power than are those with lower scores on this cultural dimension.	Malaysia, Guatemala, Panama, Philippines, Mexico, Venezuela, Arab countries, Ecuador, Indonesia, India	Australia, Israel, Denmark, New Zealand, Ireland, Sweden, Norway, Finland, Switzerland, Great Britain
Uncertainty Avoidance: Societies with higher uncertainty avoidance scores generally prefer to avoid uncertainty; they like to know what will happen next. Societies with lower scores are more comfortable with uncertainty.	Greece, Portugal, Guatemala, Uruguay, Belgium, Japan, Peru, France	Singapore, Jamaica, Denmark, Sweden, Hong Kong, Ireland, Great Britain, Malaysia, India, Philippines, United States
Masculinity: Societies with higher masculinity scores value high achievement, men in more assertive roles, and more clearly differentiated sex roles than people with lower scores on this cultural dimension.	Japan, Australia, Venezuela, Italy, Switzerland, Mexico, Ireland, Jamaica, Great Britain	Sweden, Norway, Netherlands, Denmark, Costa Rica, Finland, Chile, Portugal, Thailand
Orientation to Time: Societies with higher scores have a longer-term orientation to time; they tend to value perseverance and thrift. Societies with lower scores have a shorter-term orientation to time; they value the past and present, respect for tradition, saving face, and spending rather than saving.	China, Hong Kong, Taiwan, Japan, Vietnam, South Korea, Brazil, India, Thailand, Hungary, Singapore, Denmark, Netherlands	Pakistan, Czech Republic, Nigeria, Spain, Philippines, Canada, Zimbabwe, Great Britain, United States, Portugal, New Zealand
Happiness: Societies with higher scores have a greater expectation of happiness as a right; they tend to value freedom of speech, leisure activities, and sports. Societies with lower scores are more restrained; they do not necessarily expect to have all of their needs met to achieve happiness.	United States, Canada, Mexico, Brazil, Australia	Russia, China, much of Eastern Europe

SOURCE: Adapted with permission from Geert Hofstede, Gert Jan Hofstede, and Michael Minkov, *Cultures and Organizations, Software of the Mind*, Third Revised Edition (New York: McGraw Hill, 2010). ISBN 0-07-166418-1 © Geert Hofstede BV.

As shown in Table 6.2, cultures or societies with a long-term time orientation include many Asian cultures, such as China, Hong Kong, Taiwan, and Japan. Cultures with a short-term time orientation include Pakistan, the Czech Republic, Nigeria, Spain, and the Philippines. Both Canada and the United States are closer to the short-term time orientation than the long-term time orientation, which suggests an emphasis on valuing quick results from projects and greater pressure toward spending rather than saving, as well as a respect for tradition.[82]

Indulgent and Restrained Expectations About Happiness Do you expect to be happy? Embedded in the U.S. Constitution is the explicit quest for "life, liberty and the pursuit of happiness."[83] The newest cultural dimension added by Hofstede focuses on expectations about happiness.[84] According to Hofstede, some cultural values include the expectation that people should and will be happy.

What Hofstede called an **indulgent culture** includes the desire and expectation for freedom and happiness. People from indulgent cultures tend to place a high value on freedom of speech, leisure activities, and sports. The United States, Canada, Mexico, Brazil, and Australia are examples of more indulgent cultures.

In contrast, a **restrained culture** is one in which people do not necessarily expect to achieve happiness by having all of their needs met. People from more restrained cultures are less likely to remember positive emotions of the past and have fewer expectations about being happy in the future. In general, they also participate less frequently in leisure activities, including sports.[85] More restrained cultures include

indulgent culture
A cultural value that tends to place a high value on happiness and also values freedom of speech, leisure activities, and sports.

restrained culture
A cultural value that does not assume happiness is a right and that happiness should not be expected as evidenced by a more limited focus on leisure activities and sports.

Russia, China, and much of Eastern Europe. Although there is less data to support this newest cultural dimension, Hofstede has been including it in his latest research results as yet another dimension of our mental software.[86]

Barriers to Bridging Differences and Adapting to Others

6.3 Illustrate four barriers that inhibit communication between individuals.

Now that we've paid attention to some of the ways people are different from one another, let's identify barriers that *increase* the differences that exist between people. Differences, whether based in culture, age, ethnicity, sexual orientation, or gender, often breed misunderstanding, which can lead to feelings of distrust, suspicion, and even hostility. News headlines continue to chronicle the prevalence of terrorism, war, and conflict around the globe, which are due, in part, to different cultural perspectives.

Is it possible to develop effective relationships with people who are different from ourselves? The answer is "of course." Although almost every relationship experiences some degree of conflict, most of the world's people do not witness annihilating destruction each day. Bridging culture and gender differences is possible. To develop effective strategies to adapt to others who are different from ourselves, we'll examine some of the barriers that often separate us from one another.

RECAP	
Cultural Values	
Individualistic vs. Collectivistic	• Individualistic cultures value individual accomplishments and achievement.
	• Collectivistic cultures value group and team collaboration.
Decentralized vs. Centralized Power	• Centralized power cultures value having power in the hands of a smaller number of people.
	• Decentralized power cultures favor more equality and a more even distribution of power in government and organizations.
Uncertainty vs. Certainty	• Cultures that value certainty do not like ambiguity and value feeling secure.
	• Cultures with a greater tolerance for uncertainty are comfortable with ambiguity and less information.
Masculine vs. Feminine	• Masculine cultures value achievement, assertiveness, heroism, material wealth, and more traditional sex roles.
	• Feminine cultures value relationships, caring for the less fortunate, overall quality of life, and less traditional distinctions between sex roles.
Long-Term vs. Short-Term Orientation to Time	• Cultures with a long-term orientation to time tend to be future oriented and value perseverance and thrift.
	• Cultures with a short-term orientation to time tend to value the past and present, respecting tradition, preserving face, and fulfilling social obligations.
Indulgent vs. Restrained Expectations About Happiness	• People from indulgent cultures tend to have a greater expectation of happiness as a right.
	• People from restrained cultures do not necessarily expect to achieve happiness by having all of their needs met.

Assuming Superiority

One of the most powerful barriers to adapting to others is the belief that one's own culture or gender is better than that of others. **Ethnocentrism** is the attitude that our own cultural approaches are superior to those of other cultures.[87] Extreme ethnocentrism is the opposite of being other oriented. When fans from two rival high schools at a Friday night football game scream, "We're number one!" they are hardly establishing high-quality communication. Competition is, of course, expected in sports; but when the mind-set of unquestioned superiority is created through cultural or religious identification, the resulting mistrust and suspicion are breeding grounds for conflict. Ethnocentrism and cultural snobbery create a barrier that inhibits rather than enhances communication.

It would probably be impossible to avoid feeling most comfortable with our own culture and people who are like us. In fact, some degree of ethnocentrism can play a useful role in perpetuating our own cultural traditions; we form communities and groups based on common traditions, beliefs, and values. A problem occurs, however, if we become so extremely biased in favor of our own cultural traditions that we fail to recognize that people from other cultural traditions are just as comfortable with their

ethnocentrism

The belief that one's own cultural traditions and assumptions are superior to those of others.

approach to life as we are with ours. And when we mindlessly attack someone else's cultural traditions (which may be a prelude to physical aggression), we erect communication barriers.

A person who assumes superiority may also assume greater power and control over others. Conflicts are often about power—who has it and who wants more of it. Differences in power are, therefore, breeding grounds for mistrust and conflict. Nineteenth-century British scholar Lord Acton said that absolute power corrupts absolutely; although this may not always be the case, an ethnocentric mind-set that assumes superiority may add to the perception of assumed power over others. It's true that there are cultural differences in attitudes toward power (whether power is centralized or decentralized), but world history has taught us that people who are consistently pushed and pulled and pummeled eventually revolt and seek greater equity of power.

Assuming Similarity

We've all done it. On meeting a new acquaintance, early in the conversation we usually explore what we may have in common. "Do you watch 'Game of Thrones'?" "Oh, you're from Buckner. Do you know Mamie Smith?" The search for similarities helps us develop a common framework for communication. But even when we discover a few similarities, it's a mistake to make too many assumptions about our new friend's attitudes and perceptions. Because of our human tendency to develop categories and use words to label our experiences, we may lump people into a common category and assume similarity where no similarity exists. Even if they appear to be like you, people do not all behave the same way.[88] As an ancient Greek proverb tells us, "Every tale can be told in a different way."

Anthropologists Clyde Kluckhohn and Henry Murray have suggested that every person is, in some respects, (1) like all other people, (2) like some other people, and (3) like no other people.[89] Our challenge when meeting another person is to sort out how we are alike and how we are unique. Focusing on superficial factors such as appearance, clothing, and even a person's occupation can lead to false impressions. Instead, we must take time to explore the person's background and cultural values before we can determine what we really have in common.

Our cultural worldview has a profound effect on how we describe ourselves and people in other cultures. Each of us perceives the world through our own frame of reference. We not only see the world differently, but also express those differences in the way we talk, think, and interact with others. For example, research has found that English-speaking people describe themselves and others by identifying individual personality traits ("Matt is friendly") rather than merely describing behavior ("Matt brings snacks to the meeting").[90] If we fail to be mindful of others' cultural values and individual worldviews, we may take communication shortcuts, use unfamiliar words, and assume that our communication will be more effective than it is.

Assuming Differences

Although it may seem contradictory to say so, given what we just noted about assuming similarities, another barrier that may keep you from bridging differences between yourself and someone else is to automatically assume that the other person will be different from you. It can be just as detrimental to communication to assume that someone is essentially different from you as it is to assume that someone is just like you. The fact is, human beings *do* share common experiences and characteristics despite their differences. Although you don't want to assume that everyone is just like you, it also hinders communication to assume that you have nothing in common with others.

We are all members of the human family. If we don't seek to connect with those factors that make us all human, we may miss opportunities for bridging the real differences that exist. The words *communication* and *common* resemble each other. We communicate effectively and appropriately when we can connect to others based on discovering what we hold in common. Identifying common cultural issues and similarities can also help you establish common ground with your listeners when speaking before an audience.

How are we all alike? Cultural anthropologist Donald Brown has compiled a list of hundreds of "surface" universals of behavior.[91] According to Brown, people in all cultures:

- Have beliefs about death.
- Have a childhood fear of strangers.
- Have a division of labor by sex.
- Experience certain emotions and feelings, such as envy, pain, jealousy, shame, and pride.
- Use facial expressions to express emotions.
- Experience empathy.
- Value some degree of collaboration or cooperation.
- Experience conflict and seek to manage or mediate conflict.

Of course, not all cultures have the same beliefs about death or the same way of dividing labor according to sex, but all cultures address these issues.

Communication researcher David Kale believes that protecting the dignity and worth of the human spirit is another universal value. Therefore, he suggests that all people can identify with the struggle to enhance their own dignity and worth, although different cultures express it in different ways.[92] Another common value that Kale notes is world peace.

Intercultural communication scholars Larry Samovar and Richard Porter assert that there are other elements that cultures share.[93] They note that people from all cultures seek physical, emotional, and psychological pleasure while avoiding personal harm. It's true that each culture and each person decides what is pleasurable or painful; nonetheless, Samovar and Porter argue, all people operate somewhere on this pleasure-pain continuum.

Another advocate for common human values was Oxford and Cambridge professor and widely read author C. S. Lewis. In his book *The Abolition of Man*, Lewis argued for the

▼ People from many different cultures similarly value close, happy families, but they may have different ideas about what makes a family close and happy. How can you discover the similarities and differences in your values when you communicate with someone from another culture?

Jane September/Shutterstock

existence of universal, natural laws, which he called the Tao, that serve as benchmarks for all human values.[94] Lewis identified such common values as do not murder; be honest; hold parents, elders, and ancestors with special honor; be compassionate to those who are less fortunate; keep your promises; and honor the basic human rights of others.

What are the practical implications of trying to identify common human values or characteristics? If you find yourself disagreeing with another person about a particular issue, identifying a larger common value such as the importance of family or of peace and prosperity can help you find common ground so that the other person will at least listen to your ideas. Discovering how we are alike can provide a starting point for human understanding.

Communication effectiveness is diminished when we assume that we're all different from one another in every aspect, just as communication is hindered if we assume that we're all alike. We're more complicated than that.

Stereotyping and Prejudice

Similar to ethnocentrism and feelings of cultural and gender superiority, making a rigid judgment against a class or type of people can also be a barrier to effective communication.

> All Russians like vodka.
>
> All men like to watch wrestling.
>
> All Asians are good at math.
>
> All women like to go shopping.

stereotype

To place a person or group of persons into an inflexible, all-encompassing category.

These statements are stereotypes. They are all inaccurate. To **stereotype** someone is to place him or her in an inflexible, all-encompassing category. The term *stereotype* started out as a printing term to describe a process in which a typesetter uses the same type to print text again and again. When we stereotype, we "print" the same judgment over and over again, failing to consider the uniqueness of individuals, groups, or events. Such a "hardening of the categories" becomes a barrier to effective communication and inhibits our ability to adapt to others. There is evidence that we are even more likely to stereotype others when viewing bits and pieces of someone's life on social media or via email.[95] Being aware of our tendency to stereotype other people, whether online or offline, is a first step to ensuring that stereotypes won't dominate the way we perceive others.

COMMUNICATION & ETHICS

Can Stereotyping Others Ever Be a Good Idea?

Reaching conclusions about someone before you get to know him or her can hinder communication and result in a dishonest relationship. Most people are taught not to be prejudiced toward others. Yet might stereotypes sometimes serve a useful purpose, especially when a quick decision is needed and you have only partial information?

Imagine, for example, that you are driving your car late at night and have a flat tire in a neighborhood that's known to have a high crime rate. While wondering what to do, you see two people who have observed your plight and are moving toward you. Do you hop out of your car and seek their help? Or do you lock your doors and be thankful that you have your cell phone to call for assistance? Could a case be made that the ability to respond stereotypically may be useful in times of stress when quick thinking is needed?

We never know all the facts about a situation, and we sometimes (maybe even often) have to respond with only the partial information we have at hand. Malcolm Gladwell, author of *Blink: The Power of Thinking without Thinking*, describes how people often make snap judgments and argues that sometimes these "thin-sliced," momentary decisions can be quite accurate.[96] Of course, snap judgments can also sometimes be way off base.

What do you think? Is it ever appropriate to hold stereotypical views of others and to make judgments about them without knowing all the facts? Why or why not? When do stereotypical evaluations hinder communication? When is it preferable to avoid stereotypical decisions?

A related barrier, **prejudice**, is a judgment based on the assumption that we already have all the information we need to know about a person. To prejudge someone as inept, inferior, or incompetent on the basis of that person's ethnicity, race, sexual orientation, gender, or some other factor is a corrosive practice that can raise significant barriers to effective communication. Some prejudices are widespread. Although there are more women than men in the world, one study found that even when a man and a woman held the same type of job, the man's job was considered more prestigious than the woman's.[97] Even though it is illegal in the United States to negatively discriminate because of a person's gender, race, or age in offering employment or promotions, women and

RECAP	
Barriers to Bridging Differences and Adapting to Others	
Assuming Superiority	Becoming ethnocentric—assuming that one's own culture and cultural traditions are superior to those of others
Assuming Similarity	Assuming that other people respond to situations as we respond; failing to acknowledge and consider differences in culture and background
Assuming Differences	Assuming that other people are always different from ourselves; failing to explore common values and experiences that can serve as bridges to better understanding
Stereotyping and Prejudice	Rigidly categorizing others and prejudging others on the basis of limited information

members of minority groups may still be discriminated against. Stereotyping and prejudice are still formidable barriers to communicating effectively with others.

Mark Twain once said, "It is discouraging to try and penetrate a mind such as yours. You ought to get out and dance on it. That would take some of the rigidity out of it." Learning how to break rigid stereotypes and overcome prejudice is an important part of the process of learning how to adapt to others.

prejudice

A judgment of someone based on an assumption that you already know relevant facts or background information about the person.

Adapting to Others Who Are Different from You

6.4 Describe seven strategies that will help bridge differences between people and help them adapt to differences.

Eleanor Roosevelt once said, "We have to face the fact that either we, all of us, are going to die together or we are going to live together, and if we are to live together we have to talk."[98] In essence, she was saying that we need effective communication skills to overcome our differences. It is not enough just to point to the barriers we have identified and say, "Don't do that." Identifying the causes of misunderstanding is a good first step, but most people need more concrete advice with specific strategies to help them overcome these barriers.[99]

Aim for Intercultural Communication Competence

To have **intercultural communication competence** is to be able to adapt your behavior toward another person in ways that are appropriate to the other person's culture. As we've stressed, intercultural competence involves more than merely being aware of what is appropriate or being sensitive to cultural differences.[100] The interculturally competent person *behaves* appropriately toward others. Research has found that people who are interculturally competent do the following three things: (1) They prepare by doing things such as learning the language and studying others' cultural traditions, (2) they thoughtfully engage in conversations with others, and (3) they evaluate and periodically reflect on their interactions with others.[101]

One team of intercultural communication researchers has developed a framework for describing the stages of interpersonal communication competence. Before we are able to behave appropriately toward others, we need to have knowledge about other cultures and the motivation to adapt or modify our behavior.[102] This framework has six stages, progressing from least to most competent behavior.[103]

intercultural communication competence

The ability to adapt one's behavior toward another person in ways that are appropriate to the other person's culture.

Stage One: Denial	In this stage, a person believes that there is only one real, authentic culture: his or her own. The interculturally incompetent person, characterized by extreme ethnocentrism, denies that there are other ways of doing things or other ways of behaving.
Stage Two: Defense	In this stage, a person acknowledges the presence of other cultures but still believes that his or her culture has the best way of doing things and that other culturally based views are wrong. So the person defends his or her own culture as the best culture.
Stage Three: Minimization	In this stage, a person recognizes that there are other cultural perspectives but minimizes them, suggesting that there are no real differences in the way people behave and interact. He or she simply doesn't see the nuances or the major differences reflected in culture.
Stage Four: Acceptance	In this stage, a person's ethnocentrism (perception of cultural superiority) is diminished, and he or she recognizes and accepts cultural differences.
Stage Five: Adaptation	In this stage, intercultural competence emerges in full blossom. A person consciously seeks to adapt his or her behavior appropriately in response to cultural differences.
Stage Six: Integration	At this highest stage of intercultural competence, a person moves freely in and out of his or her own cultural mind-set while adapting to others. The person skillfully modifies his or her behavior to appropriately adapt to other cultures because the person's focus on his or her own cultural identity is minimized; instead, the focus is on others.

ethnocentric cultural perspective
The view that one's own culture is superior to all other cultures.

ethnorelative cultural perspective
An appreciation for and sensitivity to cultural differences.

The first three stages of this six-stage framework reflect an **ethnocentric cultural perspective**, in which a person assumes that her or his own culture is superior to all other cultures. Ethnocentric people believe that their appearance (for example, whether or not they have tattoos and piercings), the style of music they listen to, or the specific holidays they celebrate are superior to (rather than just different from) those of other cultures.

The last three stages of cultural competence reflect a more **ethnorelative cultural perspective**. This perspective requires an appreciation for and sensitivity to cultural differences; one's own cultural perspective is not viewed as always superior to other cultural perspectives.[104] An ethnorelative person understands that there are wide ranges of perceptions about what is stylish or beautiful, that other people listen to a variety of musical genres, and that holidays other people celebrate may be different from theirs. You need not abandon your own preferences, tastes, and cultural traditions; but it is important to acknowledge that other people act, speak, and think in ways that are different from—and just as good as—your own ways.

To become competent at any task, you need three things: knowledge, motivation, and skill. The remaining portion of this chapter presents the following specific strategies to help you develop your intercultural communication competence:[105]

To increase your knowledge about others,

- Seek information about a culture.
- Ask questions and listen to the responses.

To motivate yourself to adapt when communicating with others who are different from you,

- Be patient.
- Strive to tolerate ambiguity and uncertainty.
- Become mindful of differences.

To develop your communication skill set,

- Become other oriented.
- Learn appropriate ways to adapt your communication.

Seek Information

Philosopher André Gide said, "Understanding is the beginning of approving." Prejudice often is the result of ignorance. Learning about another person's values, beliefs, and culture can help you understand that person's messages and their meaning. Researchers have found, not surprisingly, that if you have increased contact and experience interacting with someone from another culture, you will be more sensitive, mindful, and other oriented when communicating with that person.[106] The more you know about someone and can comfortably anticipate how he or she will respond, the more interculturally competent you are likely to be. As you speak to a person from another culture, think of yourself as a detective, watching for implied, often unspoken messages that provide information about the values, norms, roles, and rules of that person's culture.

You can also prepare yourself by studying other cultures. If you are going to another country, start by reading a travel guide or another general overview of the culture. You may then want to learn more detailed information by studying the history, art, or geography of the culture. The Internet offers a wealth of information about the cultures and traditions of others. In addition, talk to people from other cultures. If you are trying to communicate with someone closer to home who is from a different background, you can learn about the music, food, and other aspects of his or her culture. Given the inextricable link between language and culture, the more skilled you become at speaking another language, the better you will understand the traditions and customs of the culture where it is spoken.[107]

▲ A good way to understand people from other cultures is to learn all you can about their culture. If you were planning a visit to another country, how would you find out about its culture and people?
Image Source/Getty Images

Ask Questions and Listen

Communication, through the give-and-take process of listening, talking, and asking questions, helps reduce the uncertainty present in any relationship. When you meet people for the first time, you are typically not certain about their likes and dislikes, including whether they like or dislike you. When you communicate with a person from another culture or co-culture, the uncertainty level escalates. When you talk with people who are different from you, you may feel some discomfort and uncertainty. This is normal. We are more comfortable talking with people we know and who are like us. However, as you begin to talk with this person, you exchange information that helps you develop greater understanding. If you continue to ask questions, eventually you will feel less anxiety and uncertainty. You will be better able to predict how the person will behave.

When you meet a person who is different from you, ask thoughtful questions and then pause to listen.[108] This is a simple technique for gathering information and confirming the accuracy of your expectations and assumptions. Just asking questions and sharing information about yourself is not sufficient to remove communication barriers and bridge differences in culture and background, but it is a good beginning. The skills of stopping (focusing on the message of the other person), looking (observing non-verbal cues), and listening (noting both details and major ideas) that we presented in Chapter 5 will serve you well in enhancing communication with people from cultural traditions different from your own.

Tolerate Ambiguity

Many people become uncomfortable when faced with uncertainty and ambiguity—especially if they are from a low-context culture such as those in North America. As we discussed earlier in the chapter, people from low-context cultures prefer a more direct approach to getting information. North Americans, for example, often say things like "Tell it to me straight," "Don't beat around the bush," or "Just tell me what you want."

Communicating with someone from a culture that does not value such directness produces uncertainty. It may take time and several exchanges to clarify a message. If you are from a cultural tradition that values certainty and you are uncomfortable with uncertainty, you may have to acknowledge this cultural difference. Be patient and work at tolerating more ambiguity. Don't be in a hurry to have all the details nailed down. Remind yourself that the other person does not have the same attitudes about knowing the future or appreciating details.

Develop Mindfulness

mindful
Aware of what you are doing and how you are communicating with others.

To be **mindful** is to be aware of how you communicate with others. A mindful communicator puts into practice the first communication principle presented in this book: *Be aware of your communication with yourself and others.* To be a mindful communicator, you should constantly remind yourself that other people are not like you. Also, you should be aware that other people do not use different communication strategies to offend or to be rude; they just have different culturally based strategies of interacting with others. Intercultural communication scholars William Gudykunst and Young Kim suggest that being mindful is one of the best ways to approach any new cultural encounter.[109] Mindfulness is a conscious state of mind, a realization of what is happening to you at a given moment. If you are not mindful, you are oblivious to the world around you. You are on mental cruise control.[110]

self-talk
Inner speech; communication with the self; the process of mentally verbalizing messages that help a person become more aware or mindful of how he or she is processing information and reacting to life situations.

How can you cultivate the skill of being mindful? You can become more mindful through **self-talk**, something discussed earlier in the book. Self-talk consists of messages you tell yourself to help you manage your discomfort, emotions, or negative thoughts about situations. For example, acknowledging cultural differences through self-talk, rather than emotionally and mindlessly becoming offended, can help you maintain your composure and communicate in a manner appropriate to the circumstances. There is also evidence that mindfully reflecting on different cultural experiences that you have can also improve your intercultural competence.[111] Consider keeping a journal of your thoughts and reactions to cultural differences you experience as a tool to help you reflect.

Become Other Oriented

other-oriented communication
Communication in which we focus on the needs and concerns of others while maintaining our personal integrity; achieved through the processes of socially decentering and being empathic.

Other-oriented communication is communication in which we take into account the needs, motives, desires, and goals of our communication partners while still maintaining our own integrity. Most of us are **egocentric**—focused on ourselves.[112] Our first inclination is to focus on meeting our own needs before addressing the needs of others.[113] Scholars of evolution might argue that our tendency to look out for number one is what ensures the continuation of the human race. But as we noted earlier, assuming superiority is a major barrier to communicating with others. If we focus exclusively on ourselves, it is very unlikely that we will be effective communicators.

egocentric
Focused on oneself and one's importance.

We should consider the thoughts and feelings of others when forming messages and selecting the time and place to deliver them. If we fail to adapt our message to listeners, especially listeners who are different from us (and isn't everyone different from you?), it is less likely that we will achieve our communication goal. As we noted earlier, adapting messages to others doesn't mean that we tell others only what they want to hear. That would be unethical, manipulative, and ineffective. Nor does being considerate of others mean we abandon all concern for our own interests.

How do you become other oriented? We suggest a two-stage process, using skills discussed previously. The first stage, which we previewed in Chapter 5, is called social decentering—consciously *thinking* about another's thoughts and feelings. The second stage is developing empathy, a set of skills we also discussed in Chapter 5. To empathize is to respond *emotionally* to another's feelings and actions. We'll discuss each of these two stages in more detail.

Social Decentering   **Social decentering** is a *cognitive process* through which we take into consideration another person's thoughts, values, background, and perspectives. It is seeing the world from the other person's point of view. To socially decenter is not to be a mind reader but to use past experiences and the ability to interpret the clues of others to understand what they may be thinking or how they may be perceiving issues or situations. According to Mark Redmond, a scholar who has extensively studied the process of social decentering, there are three ways to socially decenter.[114]

social decentering

A cognitive process through which we take into account another person's thoughts, values, background, and perspectives.

1. *Consider how you have responded in the past.* Develop an understanding of the other person based on how you have responded when something similar has happened to you.[115] For example, when someone you know says that he or she feels frazzled because he or she was late for a major meeting, you can think about what would be going through your mind if the same thing happened to you.

2. *Consider how the other person has responded in the past.* Base your understanding of what another person might be thinking on your knowledge of how that person has responded in similar situations. When communicating with someone who is different from you, the more direct experience you have interacting with that person, the better able you usually are to make predictions about how that person will react and respond. For example, suppose that you have never known a particular friend to be late for a meeting; you know that this friend is generally punctual. You can, therefore, guess that your friend would be quite frustrated by being late for a meeting.

3. *Consider how most people respond to similar situations.* The more you can learn about others' cultural or gender perspectives, the more accurate you can become in socially decentering. If your friend is from Germany and you have some general idea of the high value many Germans place on punctuality, your ideas about how most German people would react to being late for a meeting might help you understand how your friend feels. It is important, however, not to develop inaccurate, inflexible stereotypes and labels for others or to base your perceptions of others only on generalizations.

Developing Empathy   Socially decentering involves attempting to understand what another person may be thinking. Developing **empathy**, a second strategy for becoming other oriented, is feeling the *emotional* reaction that the other person may be experiencing. When we feel empathy, we feel what another person feels.

Empathy is different from **sympathy**. When you sympathize, you acknowledge someone's feelings or let the person know that you recognize the way he or she feels. When you empathize, however, you experience an emotional reaction that is similar to the other person's; as much as possible, you strive to feel what he or she feels. Emotional intelligence, which includes accurately assessing the emotions of others, is essential to both sympathy and empathy, which in turn help us establish high-quality relationships with others, especially when there are cultural differences.[116]

empathy

An emotional reaction that is similar to the reaction being experienced by another person.

sympathy

An acknowledgment that someone is feeling a certain emotion, often grief; compassion.

RECAP

How to Become Other Oriented

Socially Decenter	View the world from another person's point of view.

- Develop an understanding of someone based on your own past experiences.
- Consider what someone may be thinking, based on your previous association with the person.
- Consider how most people respond to the situation at hand.

Develop Empathy	Consider what another person may be feeling.

- Stop: Avoid focusing only on your own ideas or emotions.
- Look: Determine the emotional meaning of messages by observing nonverbal cues.
- Listen: Focus on what the other person says.
- Imagine: Consider how you would feel in a similar situation.
- Paraphrase: Summarize your understanding of the other person's thoughts and feelings.

adapt

To adjust behavior in response to someone else.

communication accommodation theory

A theory that suggests people adapt their style and approach to communicating with others in order to enhance the quality of the relationship and understanding.

▼ Today's technology can help you adapt your communication. For example, your phone can translate your words or show a map when you don't speak the local language. But you must still be aware of what adaptations are appropriate and ethical.
Image Source/Getty Images

As we discussed in Chapter 5, you develop the ability to empathize by being sensitive to your own feelings, assessing how you feel during certain situations, and then projecting those feelings onto others.[117]

The late author and theologian Henri J. M. Nouwen suggested that empathy lies at the heart of enhancing the quality of our relationships with others. As Nouwen phrased it, to bridge our differences, we need to "cross the road for one another":

> We become neighbors when we are willing to cross the road for one another. There is so much separation and segregation: between black people and white people, between gay people and straight people, between young people and old people, between sick people and healthy people, between prisoners and free people, between Jews and Gentiles, Muslims and Christians, Protestants and Catholics, Greek Catholics and Latin Catholics.
>
> There is a lot of road crossing to do. We are all very busy in our own circles. We have our own people to go to and our own affairs to take care of. But if we could cross the road once in a while and pay attention to what is happening on the other side, we might indeed become neighbors.[118]

Ethically Adapt to Others

After you have thought about how you may be different from others and have identified your own potential barriers to communication, you reach this question: So now what do you *do?* What you do is appropriately and ethically adapt.

To **adapt** is to adjust your behavior in response to the other person or people you are communicating with. Adapting to others gets to the bottom line of this chapter. You don't just keep communicating in the same way you always did. Instead, make an effort to change how you communicate, to enhance the quality of communication. Whether you are in an interpersonal interaction, a group, or a presentational speaking situation, adapting your message to others makes common sense. Even so, being sensitive to others and wisely adapting behaviors to others is often not common practice.

Communication accommodation theory suggests that effective communication occurs when we adapt to the communication style of our communication partner.[119] To maximize our understanding and to build a positive relationship with others, we accommodate—or adapt—the way we communicate. Adapting to others or accommodating our communication message does not mean that you do or say only what others expect or that your primary goal in life is always to please others. You don't have to abandon your own ethical principles and positions. In fact, it would be unethical to change your opinions and point of view just to avoid conflict and keep the peace—like a politician who tells audiences only what they want to hear.[120] As President Harry Truman said, "I wonder how far Moses would have gone if he'd taken a poll in Egypt?"[121] When we encourage you to adapt your messages to others, we are not recommending that you become a spineless jellyfish. We are suggesting that you be sensitive and mindful of how your comments may be received by others.

We do not advocate adapting communication in any way that is false or manipulative. You have a responsibility to *ethically* adapt your messages to others. To be ethical is to be truthful and honest while also observing the rights of others. Ethical communication is responsible, honest, and fair; enhances human dignity; and maintains listener options rather than coerces or forces someone to behave against his or her will. Ideally, both (or all) parties' goals are met.

We adapt messages to others for several reasons: to enhance their understanding of the message, to help us achieve the goal or intended effect of our communication, to ensure that we are ethical in our communication with others, and to establish and develop satisfying relationships. Your goal can help you choose from among the following adaptation strategies.

To . . .	You may need to . . .
Enhance understanding	• Slow down or speed up your normal rate of speech.
	• Use more examples.
	• Use appropriate examples or illustrations that your communication partner can easily identify.
	• Use simple, concrete words.
	• Speak in a very structured, organized way.
	• Stop to ask if your partner has any questions.
	• Make your message more redundant; preview and summarize key ideas.
	• Use pictures or other images to support your verbal message.
	• Be cautious when telling jokes because humor may not translate well from one culture to another.
Meet your own communication goals	• Present evidence that is most valuable to your listener; statistics may prove your point to some listeners, but others may be more moved by a story that poignantly illustrates your point.
	• Think about your specific communication goal and then clarify that goal with your communication partner.
	• Make sure you understand your partner's goal.
	• Identify areas in which your goal is similar to your partner's goal.
Ensure ethical communication	• Give your partner choices and identify options rather than coercing or making demands.
	• Tell the truth, without withholding information.
	• Give your partner a chance to respond. Use good listening skills. Rather than providing long stories or lengthy details, pause to see if your partner has questions or concerns about what you are sharing.
	• Treat your partner how you believe your partner would like to be treated.
Establish and develop relationships	• Use communication that generates positive feelings.
	• Clearly express your positive regard for others.
	• Find areas of common interest.
	• Develop empathy: Stop, look, listen, and imagine how you would feel in similar situations. Ask questions. When appropriate, paraphrase content and emotions.
	• Be aware of your own bias, stereotypes, and prejudices; set them aside and listen to the other person nonjudgmentally.

It is not possible to prescribe how to adapt to others in all situations, but you can draw on the other four Communication Principles for a Lifetime presented in this book:

1. *Be aware of your communication with yourself and others.* You will be more effective in adapting to others if you are aware of your own cultural traditions and gender-related behavior and how they are different from those of other people.

2. *Effectively use and interpret verbal messages.* To be able to interpret spoken information accurately is a linchpin of competence in adapting to others.

3. *Effectively use and interpret nonverbal messages.* Being able to "listen with your eyes" to unspoken messages will increase your ability to adapt and respond to others.

4. *Listen and respond to others thoughtfully.* The essential skills of listening and responding to others are key competencies in being able to adapt to others—to be oriented toward others.

RECAP

Adapting to Others

Develop Knowledge

Seek Information	Learn about a culture's worldview.
Ask Questions and Listen	Reduce uncertainty by asking for clarification and listening to the answer.

Develop Motivation

Tolerate Ambiguity	Take your time and expect some uncertainty.
Develop Mindfulness	Be consciously aware of cultural differences rather than ignoring them.

Develop Skill

Become Other Oriented	Put yourself in the other person's mental and emotional frame of mind; socially decenter and develop empathy.
Adapt to Others	Listen and respond appropriately.

Can the skills and principles we have suggested here make a difference in your ability to communicate with others? The answer is a resounding "yes."[122] Several research studies document the importance and value of skillfully being able to adapt your communication behavior.[123] Communication researcher Lori Carrell found, for example, that students who had been exposed to lessons in empathy as part of their study of interpersonal and intercultural communication improved their ability to empathize with others.[124] There is also evidence that if you master these principles and skills, you will be rewarded with greater ability to communicate with others who are different from you—which means everyone.[125]

STUDY GUIDE:

❯ REVIEW, APPLY, AND ASSESS

Understanding Diversity

6.1 Describe how differences of gender, sexual orientation, ethnicity, and age influence communication.

REVIEW: Human differences result in the potential for misunderstanding and miscommunication. Differences in gender, sexual orientation, age, and ethnicity contribute to the challenges of communicating with others. To overcome these challenges, you must employ Communication Principle Five: Effective communicators appropriately adapt their messages to others.

KEY TERMS:

androgynous	ethnicity
transgender	race
homophobia	discrimination

APPLY: In addition to the differences described in this chapter—gender, sexual orientation, age, ethnicity, and culture—what are other differences among people that might affect the way we communicate with each other?

ASSESS: How would you assess your ability to adapt to those who are different from your gender, sexual orientation, age, and ethnicity?

Culture and Communication

6.2 Define *culture*, and compare and contrast cultural contexts and cultural values.

REVIEW: Culture is a system of knowledge that is shared by a group of people. Because of the powerful role culture plays in influencing our values, culture and communication are clearly linked. Cultural values reflect how individuals regard stereotypically masculine perspectives (such as achieving results and being productive) and stereotypically feminine perspectives (such as consideration for relationships), their tolerance of uncertainty or preference for certainty, their preference for centralized or decentralized power structures, the value they place on individual or collective accomplishment, their long-term or short-term orientation to time, and their expectation of happiness.

KEY TERMS:

globalization	intercultural communication
culture	culture shock
co-culture	worldview

cultural context	individualistic culture
high-context culture	masculine culture
low-context culture	feminine culture
cultural values	indulgent culture
collectivistic culture	restrained culture

APPLY: Provide an example of a recent intercultural interaction you had with a person from a different culture than yourself. Identify cultural similarities and differences between you and your intercultural communication partner.

ASSESS: Based on the descriptions of cultural values described in this chapter, use the scales below to evaluate your own cultural values. Place an X or other mark to indicate where your culture falls on each scale.

Individualistic _ _ _ _ _ _ _ Collectivistic

Decentralized _ _ _ _ _ _ _ Centralized

Uncertainty _ _ _ _ _ _ _ Certainty

Masculine _ _ _ _ _ _ _ Feminine

Long Term _ _ _ _ _ _ _ Short Term

Indulgent _ _ _ _ _ _ _ Restrained

After assessing your cultural values, think of a friend, teacher, classmate, family member, or colleague who may have a different cultural value profile than yourself. Based on the discussion of ways to enhance intercultural competence that you studied in this chapter, what specific strategies could you use to adapt to someone whose cultural values are different from your own?

Barriers to Bridging Differences and Adapting to Others

6.3 Illustrate four barriers that inhibit communication between individuals.

REVIEW: By doing the following, we create barriers that inhibit our communication with others:

- *Assuming superiority.* When one culture or gender assumes superiority or is ethnocentric, communication problems often occur.

- *Assuming similarity.* It is not productive when individuals or groups from different backgrounds or cultures assume that others should behave with responses similar to their own.

- *Assuming differences.* Don't automatically assume that other people are different from you.

- *Stereotyping and being prejudice.* We stereotype by placing a group or person into an inflexible, all-encompassing category. Stereotyping and prejudice can keep us from acknowledging others as unique individuals and therefore can hamper effective, open, and honest communication.

KEY TERMS:

ethnocentrism   prejudice

stereotype

APPLY: Describe an example of a time when you experienced one of the barriers mentioned in this chapter. For example, have you tried to communicate with someone who assumed that you were more like them than you actually are? Or did you ever find yourself assuming that people were much more different from you than they turned out to actually be?

ASSESS: Consider the four barriers discussed in this chapter that inhibit effective communication. Now rank them in order from your "biggest barrier" to your "smallest barrier." How do these barriers impact your communication with others? What could you do to reduce or remove your biggest barriers?

Adapting to Others Who Are Different from You

6.4   Describe seven strategies that will help bridge differences between people and help them adapt to differences.

REVIEW: You develop intercultural communication competence when you are able to adapt your behavior toward another person in ways that are appropriate to the other person's culture. Specific strategies for becoming interculturally competent include the following:

- Seek information.
- Ask questions and listen.

- Tolerate ambiguity.
- Be mindful.
- Become other oriented by socially decentering and empathizing with others.
- Appropriately and ethically adapt your communication to others.

KEY TERMS:

intercultural communication competence	other-oriented communication
ethnocentric cultural perspective	egocentric social decentering
ethnorelative cultural perspective	empathy sympathy
mindful	adapt
self-talk	communication accommodation theory

APPLY: You've been assigned to work on a semester-long research project with a partner who has told you that his or her sexual orientation is different from your own. How could you use the skills in this section of the chapter to appropriately adapt your communication with your research partner?

ASSESS: Assessing Your Intercultural Skill

This chapter presented six specific strategies to help bridge differences between people. Rank these strategies in the order of what you need to improve the most to what you need to improve the least in your interactions with people from different backgrounds. For example, assign a rank of 1 to the skill that you need to develop the most, then assign a rank of 2 to the next area you feel you need to work on, and so on. Rank yourself on all six strategies.

Seek information	___
Ask questions and listen	___
Tolerate ambiguity	___
Be mindful	___
Become other oriented (socially decenter and empathize)	___
Appropriately and ethically adapt to others	___

⟩ THE PRINCIPLE POINTS

Principle Five:

Appropriately adapt messages to others.

- Appropriately adapt messages based on gender differences in communication by doing the following: (1) Seek to understand differences between genders as well as acknowledge similarities; (2) consider your own preferences, needs, and communication goals; (3) avoid assuming that differences you observe are solely the result of gender; and (4) consider both your needs and goals and those of the other person.

- Appropriately adapt your messages, paying particular attention to your verbal messages, to reflect differences in sexual orientation.

- Appropriately adapt your messages to respond to differences in age and ethnicity.

- Appropriately adapt messages to others on the basis of whether an individual is from a high-context culture, in which emphasis is placed on nonverbal messages and the surroundings, or a low-context culture, in which emphasis is placed on words and explicitly communicated messages.

- Appropriately adapt messages to others on the basis of the cultural value of individualism versus collectivism, preference for certainty versus tolerance of uncertainty, tendency to emphasize stereotypically masculine versus stereotypically feminine values, preference for centralized or decentralized power, preference for a long-term or short-term orientation to time, and an expectation of happiness.

- Acknowledge differences. Don't assume that everyone does things the same way you do or holds the same attitudes, beliefs, or values that you hold.

- Seek to explore and establish common ground with others. Don't assume that because someone is from another culture or geographic area, you don't have anything in common with the person.

- Seek to bridge differences between yourself and others who speak a different language or have different interpretations for nonverbal expressions; learn the language of others.

- Bridge cultural differences by learning as much as you can about another culture.

- Listen and ask questions to enhance your understanding of others.

- Be patient and tolerate some ambiguity and uncertainty when you communicate with people who are different from you.

- Become mindful, or aware that differences will exist, to help yourself better tolerate differences.

- Develop your skills at being other oriented. Focus on the needs and concerns of others while maintaining your personal integrity.

- Socially decenter. Think about how your communication partner would respond to information and situations; take into account people's thoughts, values, background, and perspectives.

- Empathize. Try to imagine how you would feel if you were in the other person's position.

CHAPTER **7**

UNDERSTANDING INTERPERSONAL COMMUNICATION

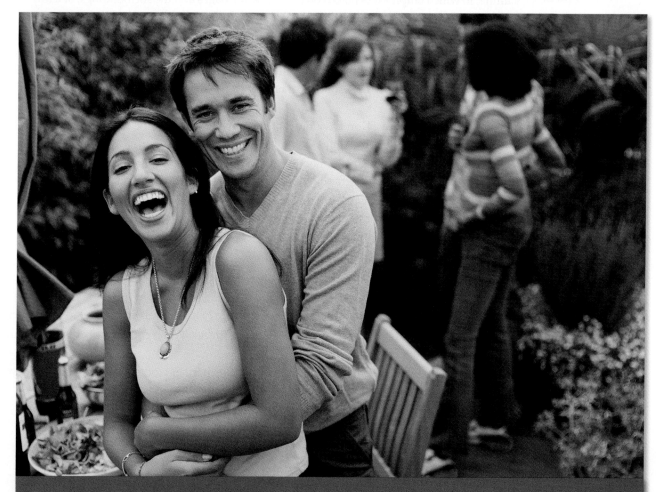

The best of life is conversation, and the greatest success is confidence, or perfect understanding between sincere people. —RALPH WALDO EMERSON

Digital Vision/Getty Images

CHAPTER OUTLINE

- What Is Interpersonal Communication?
- Initiating Relationships

- Maintaining Relationships
- Study Guide: Review, Apply, and Assess

LEARNING OBJECTIVES

After studying this chapter, you should be able to

7.1 Define interpersonal communication and discuss its three unique attributes.

7.2 Describe the roles of communication in revealing interpersonal attraction and initiating relationships.

7.3 Explain the roles of self-disclosure and emotional expression in maintaining face-to-face and online relationships.

"Hi. I'm ___. Nice to meet you." This simple statement can strike fear in the heart of even the most outgoing person. Yet we know that meeting and getting to know people, as well as becoming known by them, are some of the most rewarding experiences in life. If we cannot break out of our comfort zones to communicate with others, we likely won't survive.

Interpersonal communication is the form of communication we experience most often in our lives, and it involves all five of our Communication Principles for a Lifetime, shown in Figure 7.1. *In the remaining chapters of the book, you'll see a small version of the communication principles model in the margin to highlight our reference to one or more of the communication principles.*

Effective interpersonal communication begins with an *awareness* of oneself. As you interact with people, you make mental notes of what works well and what doesn't. You learn from these experiences and develop a personal style of communication. We continue this process by reshaping our communication styles throughout our lives with the goal of becoming better communicators. The second and third principles involve the *effective use of verbal and nonverbal messages.* We experiment with verbal and nonverbal communication as we interact with people, form and develop relationships, and, in some cases, let go of those relationships. A major element that enhances relationships is the ability to *listen and respond thoughtfully* to others, our Principle Four. Finally, few interpersonal relationships last without *adaptation*. We live in an extremely diverse and complex world. If we want to be effective communicators, it is imperative to learn to adapt our communication to others' cultural backgrounds and values, personalities, communication styles, needs, and goals.

interpersonal communication
Communication that occurs between two people who simultaneously attempt to mutually influence each other, usually for the purpose of managing relationships.

mediated communication
Communication that is carried out using some channel other than those used in face-to-face encounters.

What Is Interpersonal Communication?

7.1 Define interpersonal communication and discuss its three unique attributes.

Interpersonal communication is a special form of human communication that occurs when two people interact simultaneously and attempt to mutually influence each other, usually for the purpose of managing relationships. Traditionally, interpersonal communication research has focused primarily on the face-to-face (FtF) encounter. However, given greater accessibility, affordability, and the ease of using technology, it is important to also study how interpersonal communication occurs through mediated channels such as cell phones and computers.[1]

In Chapter 1, we defined **mediated communication** as communication carried out using some channel other than those used in face-to-face (FtF) encounters. It then follows that

FIGURE 7.1 Communication Principles for a Lifetime

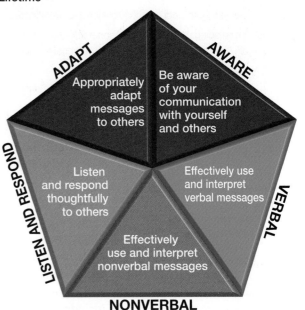

mediated interpersonal communication

Communication that occurs when two people attempt to mutually influence each other through the use of a mediated channel, usually for the purpose of managing relationships.

mediated interpersonal communication is communication that occurs when two people attempt to mutually influence each other through the use of a mediated channel, usually for the purpose of managing relationships. In this chapter, we explore some similarities and differences between mediated interpersonal communication and FtF interpersonal communication.

Let's begin by considering three attributes that help us better understand the nature of interpersonal communication:

- *Interpersonal communication involves quality.* If you're having dinner with a friend, let's hope that your communication with your friend is different from communication with your waitperson. The quality of the communication makes the difference. Interpersonal communication occurs not just when we interact with someone, but when we treat a person as a unique human being. Conversely, **impersonal communication** occurs when we treat people as objects or respond to their roles rather than to who they are as unique people.[2] In terms of mediated interpersonal communication, e-mailing or texting a friend is interpersonal communication; by contrast, responding to a mass text or e-mail message is impersonal communication because you likely don't know all the receivers of your message.

impersonal communication

Communication that treats people as objects or that responds only to their roles rather than to who they are as unique people.

- *Interpersonal communication involves mutual influence.* We don't mean to imply that interpersonal communication exclusively involves persuasion—changing someone's mind or swaying someone's opinion. We simply mean that people who interact *affect* each other in some way. During that dinner with a friend, you might ask where your friend grew up. You've both been affected by this question—there's something you want to know and it is information your friend can provide. But what if your friend doesn't hear you because of a distracting noise in the restaurant? In this case, interpersonal communication hasn't really occurred because there's no mutual interaction; you have been affected by your attempt at communication, but your friend has not.

relationship

An ongoing connection made with another person.

- *Interpersonal communication helps manage relationships.* **Relationships** are ongoing connections we make with others through interpersonal communication. For some people, the term *relationship* signals something serious and usually romantic, but we use the word in a much broader sense in this text. You probably have a wide variety of relationships, such as those with family members, coworkers, classmates, friends, and romantic interests. Some relationships are formed and maintained solely through mediated channels; others involve a combination of FtF and mediated interaction.

RECAP

What Is Interpersonal Communication?

- High quality: Interpersonal communication is superior to impersonal communication.
- Mutually influential: Both people in the relationship are affected.
- Relationship managing: We use interpersonal communication to help start, maintain, and sometimes end our interpersonal relationships.

Initiating Relationships

7.2 Describe the roles of communication in revealing interpersonal attraction and initiating relationships.

relationship of circumstance

A relationship that forms situationally, simply because one life overlaps with another in some way.

relationship of choice

A relationship that is sought out and intentionally developed.

Relationships form for different reasons. **Relationships of circumstance** form situationally, simply because our lives overlap with others' in some way or because a situation brings us into contact. Relationships with family members, teachers, classmates, and coworkers typically fall into this category. An online relationship of circumstance might be formed between members of a group, such as students enrolled in an online class. In contrast, relationships that we seek out and intentionally develop are termed **relationships of choice**. These relationships typically include those with friends, lovers, and spouses or relational partners. These categories of relationships are not mutually exclusive. Relationships of circumstance can change into relationships of choice; your sister or brother can turn out to be your best friend. Most of your online relationships are probably relationships of choice.

Some people make relationships look easy; they just seem to meet people and make positive impressions effortlessly. For others, meeting and getting to know people is a huge challenge. We'll let you in on a little secret: Initiating relationships really isn't all that easy for anyone. Let's explore the nature of attraction—what draws us into a conversation in the first place.

▲ Attraction is fascinating to observe, as well as to feel for another person. How do you typically communicate the attraction you feel for someone? Do your nonverbal cues reveal your attraction, or do you use language to convey your feelings?
Monkey Business/Fotolia

Interpersonal Attraction: Why We Like Whom We Like

What does it mean to say that you're attracted to another person? Most of the time, we tend to think of physical or sexual attraction. But there are many forms of attraction besides physical and sexual, including intellectual, spiritual, and personality attraction. **Attraction**, in general, is a motivational state that causes someone to think, feel, and behave in a positive manner toward another person.[3] More specifically, **interpersonal attraction** is the degree to which you desire to form and possibly maintain an interpersonal relationship with another person. Several factors come into play when you decide to act on your attraction and establish a relationship.

Physical and Sexual Attraction   Volumes have been written about the role that physical and sexual attraction play in the formation of relationships.[4] While these forms of

attraction

A motivational state that causes someone to think, feel, and behave in a positive manner toward another person.

interpersonal attraction

The degree to which one desires to form or maintain an interpersonal relationship with another person.

COMMUNICATION & DIVERSITY

Besties: Straight Women and Gay Men

Many straight women seem to have a special and interesting affinity for gay men and vice versa. What's the draw? Is it just that they're both attracted to men, so that commonality links them as friends? Is it that, because gay men and straight men have maleness in common, straight women seek advice on things "man"-kind from their gay male friends, viewing them as relationship advisors who have some sort of special insight? Another confusing observation is that you rarely see straight men having lots of lesbian friends. Why doesn't the trend seem to work in reverse?

Researchers have studied the increasingly common connection between straight women and gay men.[5] One study found that straight women were drawn to friendships with gay men because, with their gay male friends, they didn't experience self-esteem loss and that sense of being judged on attractiveness and sex appeal that they often felt with straight men (and other straight women). The straight female/gay male friendship was just easier, some

women in the study reported.[6] Another element seems to be the fact that, since gay male friends are sexually off limits for straight women, the lack of sexual tension takes the heat off the relationship, leaving the friends to just *be*.

Gay men sometimes describe a feeling of tension in their friendships with some straight men. The level of tension seems to depend on the straight men's self-awareness and self-confidence. Friendships seem to work if the straight men are comfortable with their own sexuality and their gay friends' sexuality and aren't concerned about speculation, gossip, or being labeled as gay. Those restrictions on the kind of straight man who can feel comfortable in a friendship with a gay man tend to make this profile of friendship the exception rather than the rule. So it's common for many gay men to feel more comfortable being friends with straight women.

How do these research findings compare with your own observations and experiences?

physical attraction
The degree to which one finds another person's physical self appealing.

attraction are often lumped together or viewed as the same thing, actually they're different. In FtF situations, the degree to which we find another person's physical self appealing represents our **physical attraction** to that person, which is a powerful nonverbal cue. That appeal might be based on height, size, skin tone and texture, clothing, hairstyle, makeup, or vocal qualities. By this definition, even if you're heterosexual, you can still be attracted to a person of your own sex because you admire her or his physical attributes.

Is physical attraction a factor in establishing online relationships? Research reveals that many online communicators find the *lack* of emphasis on physical appearance and attractiveness in online relationships to be one of the most positive features of this approach to relationship development.[7] One set of researchers described the Internet as "a world where what you write, not how you look or sound, is who you are."[8]

However, because most online dating sites and apps now require that you post a photo before using their services, physical attractiveness plays a greater role in online relationship formation than in the past.[9] Even if an online dating site or app doesn't require a photo, many people are suspicious about or turned off by someone who won't post a picture of themselves to their online profile. The popular dating app Tinder relies exclusively on physical attraction—users swipe right or left on their mobile phones to indicate interest.[10]

sexual attraction
The desire to have sexual contact with a certain person.

matching hypothesis
A tendency to seek out individuals who represent the same level of physical attractiveness as oneself.

Sexual attraction has been defined as "the desire to engage in sexual activity with someone," a desire that "typically is accompanied by feelings of sexual arousal in the presence of the person."[11] You may be physically attracted to someone but not sexually attracted, as we stated before. But can you be sexually attracted but not physically attracted? We're not sure about the answer to that one because it may be a uniquely individual judgment. You may find another person's online communication sexually arousing even if you've never seen the person in the flesh. Suffice it to say that these two forms of attraction usually operate in tandem, even though they represent different kinds of appeal.

Our perceptions about others' physical attractiveness affect relationship possibilities. In general, although we may be attracted to a range of people, we tend to seek out individuals who represent the same level of physical attractiveness we do.[12] In research, this tendency is termed the **matching hypothesis**.[13] Perhaps you perceive yourself to be average looking, not model-beautiful but not unattractive. You may be physically or sexually attracted to extremely good-looking people; but if you're average looking, you're more likely to seek someone who is also average looking to date and even marry.

▼ Video chats, Facebook usage, texts, and other technological innovations have redefined the meaning of proximity in attraction. How do your face-to-face relationships compare to your mediated ones in terms of proximity?
Art Family/Fotolia

Similarity Opposites certainly do attract, and differences between people can be interesting. But we like to add another phrase to the "opposites attract" cliché: "Opposites attract, but dramatic opposites seldom last." People who are significantly different from each other in dispositions and preferences may intrigue and teach each other something in the short run, but similarity appears to be a more important factor in highly committed, long-term relationships than in short-term, noncommitted relationships.[14]

In general, you're attracted to people with whom you have **similarity**—those whose personality, values, upbringing, experiences, attitudes, or interests are similar to yours.[15] You may also be more attracted to people who are similar to you in age, intelligence, and life goals. The Internet allows people with similar interests to find one another much more easily than in the past and form online relationships.[16] In the initial stages of an online or FtF relationship, we try to emphasize positive information about ourselves to create a good first impression and an attractive image. We reveal those aspects of ourselves that we believe we have in common with the other person, and the other person does the same.[17]

similarity
The degree to which one's characteristics, values, attitudes, interests, or personality traits are like those of another person.

Proximity   In a traditional sense, the principle of **proximity** in interpersonal relationships refers to the fact that we're more likely to be attracted to people who are nearer to us physically and geographically than to those who are farther away.[18] You're more likely to form relationships with classmates sitting on either side of you than those at the opposite end of the room. Physical proximity increases our communication opportunities, and these opportunities to interact are likely to increase attraction.

proximity
The likelihood of being attracted to people who are physically close rather than to those who are farther away.

People in long-distance romantic relationships know firsthand that proximity plays an important role in whether a relationship will last or not.[19] Technological innovations (e.g., social media outlets, video chat applications like Skype and Facetime) are inexpensive and more readily accessible than ever before, and they do help keep geographically-separated partners in virtual proximity. But people in these kinds of relationships still reveal that having the money and the time to travel to be physically with each other on weekends or vacations is extremely important when trying to keep a long-distance relationship going.[20]

Technology has turned the notion of proximity on its head, however, by giving us virtual access to people around the globe in an instant. Those of you who are "digital natives" grew up in a world of computers where online information was always easily found at your fingertips. You have a different sense of boundaries, geographic limitations, and globalism than previous generations— those known as "digital immigrants," who discovered and adopted technology along the way.[21] People who have never met (and may never meet) in the physical world can come to feel a sense of proximity and develop relationships with people in the virtual world. In fact, some scholars contend that the instantaneous and pervasive nature of online communication bridges physical distance, creating a virtual closeness that FtF relationships might not achieve.[22]

RECAP

Elements of Interpersonal Attraction

Physical Attraction	This form of attraction is based on a person's physical self.
Sexual Attraction	This form of attraction is based on the desire to have sexual contact with another person.
Similarity	Attraction increases if our characteristics, values, attitudes, interests, and personality traits are similar to those of another person.
Proximity	We are more likely to be interpersonally attracted to people who are physically close to us.
Complementarity	We may be attracted to someone whose abilities, interests, and needs differ from but balance or round out our own.

Complementarity   Although we tend to like people with whom we have much in common, most of us wouldn't find it very exciting to spend the rest of our lives with someone who had identical attitudes, needs, and interests. We tend to be attracted to friends and romantic partners who are similar to us in important ways, such as our values, but when we consider less essential characteristics, we may be more interested in people with whom we share a **complementarity** of abilities and needs.[23] For example, if you're highly disorganized by nature (and that's fine by you), you might be attracted to someone who's very organized because you appreciate that person's sense of structure. Research has applied the concept of complementarity to other kinds of relationships where communication and rapport are extremely important, such as between therapists and clients.[24]

complementarity
The degree to which a person's different abilities, interests, and needs balance or round out one's own.

Communicating Our Attraction

According to research, we can size up a potential romantic partner or good future friend within the first three minutes of meeting the person.[25] That's impressive, but daunting. What kind of impression do you make in the first three minutes of meeting someone? What kind of vibe do you get from someone in the first three minutes that lets you know whether you'd like to talk with the person further or whether there's a chance of something more meaningful developing?

When we're attracted to people, we use both verbal and nonverbal strategies to communicate our liking. Verbally, we ask questions to show interest, listen responsively, probe for details when others share information, and refer to information shared in past interactions in an attempt to build a history with people. But we most often communicate our attraction nonverbally, through indirect cues referred to as **immediacy**. As described in Chapter 4, immediacy behaviors reduce the physical and psychological distance between people.[26] Research findings have shed light on the connection between immediacy and perceptions of closeness and supportive listening in relationships, as well as the effects of immediacy on such contexts as the workplace and speed dating.[27] Some examples of nonverbal immediacy cues include the following:

immediacy

Nonverbal cues, such as eye contact, a forward lean, touch, and open body orientation, that communicate feelings of liking, pleasure, and closeness.

- Sitting in closer proximity,
- Increasing our eye contact,
- Increasing our use of touch,
- Leaning forward,
- Keeping an open body orientation rather than a closed-off position,
- Using more vocal variety or animation,
- Smiling more often than we do normally, and
- Preening (adjusting clothing, playing with our hair) as a means of attracting attention.[28]

Immediacy, as a means of showing people that you like them, applies to all sorts of connections and relationships. Yet, when thinking about physical or sexual attraction associated with romantic interests, most people don't think of immediacy—they think of flirtation.[29] Common nonverbal flirtation cues include surveying a room with our eyes; making prolonged, mutual eye contact; giving sidelong and darting glances at a person of interest; using more facial animation; and changing our tone of voice to reveal excitement.[30]

Given the rising popularity of online dating and dating apps in recent years, a question emerges as to how people convey attraction in an online or mediated context.[31] One study asked approximately 6,000 people how they flirt in person as well as online.[32] The majority of people in the study reported that flirting

▼ What nonverbal immediacy cues are these two people using to communicate their liking to each other? What immediacy cues do you exhibit when you find yourself attracted to someone?
Siri Stafford/Getty Images

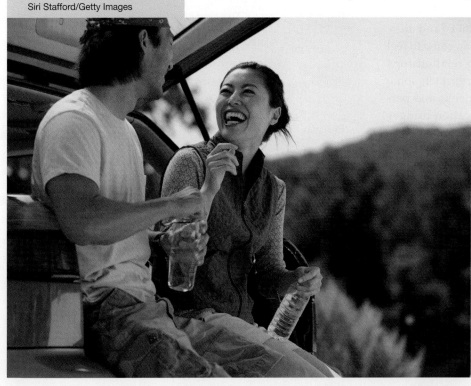

COMMUNICATION & SOCIAL MEDIA

Consider the Flirtmoji

College students are great sources of information, especially about trends related to social media. A student recently educated her professor on the meaning behind "Netflix and chill." The professor thought that texting such a message or posting it privately to a Facebook friend meant, "Want to come over, watch something on Netflix, and relax?" Actually, the phrase is code for "Want to have sex?" Wikipedia describes the phrase as a "euphemism for sex, either between partners or casually, as a booty call."[33]

People's inclusion of certain emojis like the eggplant and the pizza slice, used alone or with other images or words, can also indicate sexual interest. But now you can take it to another level: The flirtmoji can turn a text into a "sext." While we won't go into graphic detail describing these sexualized emojis, some of the tamer ones include a banana wearing a condom and the back hatch of an SUV opened to reveal two sets of bare legs.[34]

was accomplished online similarly to how it's done in person, meaning that people translate physical actions into text for mediated communication such as typing an acronym like LOL or inserting emojis into texts, e-mail messages, or posts. With the rise in webcam use and video chatting, the more traditional nonverbal cues associated with flirtation can be effective, except, of course, cues that involve actual physical contact (though people often touch the screen of their computers or tablets during video chats to try to create the sensation of a touch).

Initiating Relationships

How do we get a new relationship off the ground? Are you more comfortable initiating a relationship through online or mediated channels versus a face-to-face conversation?

In some ways, online interpersonal relationships have an advantage over FtF relationships in that they often develop out of conversation, meaning that online communication may be what launched the relationship in the first place.[35] Initial online interactions are critical in that they can make or break future exchanges. With repeated virtual contact, online topics of discussion often become very personal and intimacy can develop at a more rapid pace than it typically does in FtF relationships. If rapport develops, it may lead to more personal texting, telephone conversations, and FtF meetings.[36]

We realize that in FtF situations, the various steps of noticing someone interesting, realizing that you're interested (physically, sexually, or interpersonally), finding a way to meet the person, and starting up a first conversation can all be nerve-racking.[37] Even though many people find communicating online easier than face-to-face interactions, we don't want to get rusty at having in-person conversations. Like any other skill, from playing a sport to improving our writing, conversation skills can diminish if unused. Sherry Turkle, author of *Reclaiming the Conversation: The Power of Talk in a Digital Age*, suggests that flight from face-to-face conversation in our digital age can hamper our relationships, as well as our creativity and productivity.[38]

In FtF settings, once you realize you're attracted to someone, what do you do next? Research indicates that people who meet and have that all-important first conversation feel enduring effects of the encounter even months later, no matter what direction the relationship took (if it took any direction at all).[39] We have some practical suggestions for how to approach those first conversations so that you feel confident and keep your self-esteem intact while communicating effectively.

Reducing Uncertainty   Even though most of us like surprises from time to time, human beings are much more comfortable with certainty than with uncertainty. We prefer the known to the unknown, the predictable to the chaotic. Communicating in a new FtF or online relationship can involve *uncertainty*, or a fear of not knowing what

uncertainty-reduction theory
A driving human motivation to increase predictability by reducing the unknown in one's circumstances.

passive strategy
A noncommunicative strategy for reducing uncertainty by observing others and situations.

active strategy
A communicative strategy for reducing uncertainty by getting information from a third party.

interactive strategy
A strategy of communicating directly with the source who has the greatest potential to reduce one's uncertainty.

to expect in a potential relationship. One communication research team developed an explanation, which they call the **uncertainty-reduction theory**, of how we use information as we endeavor to reduce our uncertainty, especially as it relates to communicating with people we don't know (or know well). Communication researchers Charles Berger, Richard Calabrese, and James Bradac contend that this driving motivation among humans to reduce our uncertainty prompts us to communicate.[40]

We typically respond to uncertainty in three ways:

- **Passive strategy:** We seek information by observing people and scoping out situations before more actively working to reduce uncertainty. Suppose you just started a new job, a transition that creates a level of uncertainty in most of us. One way to begin to reduce your uncertainty is to simply observe how your coworkers, supervisors, and clients interact. In an online context, you may read a person's tweets or Facebook posts to get a sense of the person before communicating with her or him directly.

- **Active strategy:** After making passive observations, we might decide to check our perceptions of things with a third party. We might ask a coworker about something associated with our new job or colleagues, for example. Finding out others' perceptions increases our knowledge, reduces our uncertainty, and helps us decide how to behave. People often network online in an attempt to learn more information from a third-party source before making a decision about contacting a person online directly. Online daters often conduct background checks on their online partners before even thinking about arranging for more contact, such as one-on-one video chats or FtF meetings.

- **Interactive strategy:** The final strategy is going "straight to the horse's mouth," communicating directly with the person who has the most potential to reduce our uncertainty. At a new job, this person might be our boss, a coworker who's been on the job for a while, or perhaps someone in personnel or human relations. Online, many people reduce their uncertainty by directly asking a person for more information about himself or herself, an interaction that may have less risk than a FtF meeting.

These strategies don't necessarily have to be used in order. You might bypass the active strategy and head to interactive, deeming it better to get the "straight scoop" from a direct source. We also don't always need to use all three strategies. In some cases, uncertainty can be reduced enough through passive and active strategies; there may be no cause for an interactive approach.[41]

Interactive strategies are frequently used in online relationships because starting up an online conversation or exchanging e-mails with someone tends to evoke less uncertainty than FtF first conversations. Online exchanges usually happen in private, with less potential for embarrassment than in FtF situations, when such factors as physical appearance and nervousness are in play. But one element can inject uncertainty into an online situation: the potential for deception. Because you stare at a computer monitor rather than into someone's eyes when you "meet" online, you really don't know whom you're talking to. Research has shown people's tendencies to give false information or to omit pertinent facts in their online communication.[42] Subjects in studies reported lying about age, weight, details of physical appearance, marital status, and even their sex/gender, meaning that some gender-bending experimentation certainly occurs.

What Do You Say First?   In some contexts, the first words you exchange with someone may be fairly scripted or expected. For example, in a job interview, introductions and ritualistic greetings typically take up the first few minutes. (See Appendix A for helpful information on communicating in interviews.) But what about situations in which there are no prescribed, explicit rules or expectations for behavior? Our students tell us that the official "date" is a dying institution—they just don't date much anymore. More common than dating is "hanging out," in which two people meet somewhere or a group of people gather together, many of whom are "talking," "seeing each other," or have a special connection that goes beyond what they have with other people.

This first-conversation business used to be easier in the past, though perhaps not particularly satisfying. Men were taught by their fathers or older brothers how to use opening or pickup lines to attract women; women were schooled by their mothers or older sisters about how to respond (or ignore).[43] You might think such opening lines as "Come here often?" "Haven't I met you before?" and (the post-1960s all-time favorite) "What's your sign?" are relics of the past, but according to research, many opening lines are surprisingly still effective at getting a conversation going.[44] Researchers tested the effectiveness of three categories of opening lines said by men to women: (1) flippant and flirtatious, such as "You must be tired, because you've been running through my mind all day"; (2) direct and complimentary, such as "It took a lot of courage to approach you, so can I at least ask your name?"; and (3) innocuous, meaning that the line masked the man's interest, as in "What do you think of the band?" The women in the study liked the direct complimentary line the most, believing that it conveyed more trustworthiness and intelligence than other forms.

We don't recommend a one-size-fits-all approach to initiating first conversations with the use of a stereotypical pickup line. Instead, rely on our fifth Communication Principle for a Lifetime, which encourages communicators to appropriately adapt their messages to others. Each situation and the unique qualities of each person you meet should dictate how you communicate.

The Art and Skill of Asking Great Questions   When students ask us, as they frequently do, "What makes someone a good conversationalist?" a variety of things come to mind. All five of our Communication Principles for a Lifetime could be reflected in our answer, but one important element is the ability to ask another person a great question designed to initiate a meaningful exchange. This skill doesn't just magically appear. It takes time, maturity, and experience with a variety of people and relationships to develop fully.[45]

Social media doesn't exactly encourage people to develop their question-asking skills, because we tend to post more declarative statements than questions on sites like Twitter and Facebook. But just because people on social media interact more through statements than questions, try not to let your question-asking skills go to waste.[46]

What do we mean by "asking great questions"? We don't mean tossing rapid-fire, superficial questions at someone as though you were in the first five minutes of a job interview or gathering data for the census. Asking a great question means, first, tailoring the question to the person as much as possible. Use what you've observed and what you've learned from other sources to formulate your questions. Online, it's typical to ask basic information just to break the ice, but the use of too many "yes/no" questions or questions requiring one-word responses is not likely to advance a conversation. Avoid questions that might be too personal or probing in the early stages of developing FtF and online relationships.

A second, very critical skill to develop is really listening to the person's answers to your questions. Then pose a follow-up question based on the person's response to your question. You can offer your opinion on something, but opinions work best when followed up with "Do you agree?" or "That's what I think, but what do you think?" Great conversationalists are great because they listen and then form responses that show they're listening—responses that are designed to draw other people out and let them shine.

Avoiding Self-Absorption   Too many people think the best way to be conversationally impressive is by talking glibly, smoothly, confidently, and virtually nonstop *about themselves*. In an online context, when one person's messages or posts are consistently five times as long as another's and the content rambles on and on, it can be a turnoff. Some people interact on social media more frequently than others, constantly posting new profile pictures and sharing photos and information about where they are, what fun things they're doing, who they're with, what they're eating and drinking, what new thing they just bought, what cute thing their dog just did, and so forth. Might these folks have narcissistic personalities and self-absorbed communication styles, or are they just avid users of social media? Some people worry that increased use of social media is contributing to a growing narcissism in our culture, given that most posts are about oneself—one's attitudes, opinions, and experiences.[47]

conversational narcissism (self-absorbed communicator style)
A dominating communication style in which one focuses attention on oneself.

trait conversational narcissism
Habitual use of a narcissistic or self-absorbed communicator style in which one focuses attention on oneself.

state conversational narcissism
Occasional use of a narcissistic or self-absorbed communicator style in which one focuses attention on oneself.

Researchers describe people who communicate like they are the center of the universe as having **conversational narcissism** or a **self-absorbed communicator style**. Some people who always (or predominantly) communicate this way have **trait conversational narcissism**; this type of narcissism may be an outgrowth of a personality trait in which oneself is the constant focus.[48] Other times, this kind of self-absorbed behavior reflects **state conversational narcissism** (not trait), which is a temporary style of interacting rather than a more pervasive personal characteristic. We're all likely to be self-absorbed from time to time, but if this kind of communication continues and becomes a more permanent state, it is less likely that the person will be positively perceived.

Some verbal indications of self-absorption include the number of times a person uses the pronoun *I* instead of *you* or *we*. Narcissistic communicators converse mostly about themselves and typically provide more detail in their narratives than necessary (perhaps because they enjoy the sound of their own voice).[49] They talk more in statements than questions and constantly try to top someone's story or to draw the topic of conversation toward themselves, as in "Oh, you think *you're* tired—let me tell you about the kind of day *I* had." No one's day is as bad, no one's opinion as valuable or information as correct as the self-absorbed communicator's. The person may feign empathy in a conversation: "Oh, I know exactly how you feel." This usually leads to "The same thing happened to me," followed by a long story that takes attention away from the original communicator. Another indication of self-absorption is talking ad nauseam on topics about which one has some particular knowledge or expertise but that may bore the socks off listeners. Many times, these types of communicators are driven by insecurity and uncertainty rather than a belief that they truly are the center of the universe.

As for nonverbal cues, self-absorbed communicators tend to increase their vocal volume and assume dominant body postures in order to hold the floor and stave off interruptions from others. They may move closer to people to keep them in conversation, even to the extent of physically blocking a person from attempting to exit the scene. They are generally oblivious to others' nonverbal cues. People with self-absorbed personalities soon find themselves with a dwindling number of friends because few of us can tolerate such an out-of-balance relationship.

In sum, the best conversationalists aren't great talkers—they're great listeners and responders (as articulated in Principle Four). In other words, it's not what *you* say, but how you respond to what *others* say that makes you a good conversationalist.

The Art and Skill of Giving and Receiving Compliments   Sometimes it seems as though people don't comment about one another unless it's to criticize. That's unfortunate because positive reinforcement and support from others are central to our self-esteem. British linguistic scholar Janet Holmes calls compliments "social lubricants."[50] She explains that the most common purpose of a compliment is to make someone feel good by offering praise and encouragement, but an important by-product is a sense of increased goodwill and solidarity between the complimenter and the receiver. Research shows that compliments between romantic partners can enhance self-esteem and are viewed as a form of intimate talk. The sharing of positive feelings is also linked to how satisfied partners are with the relationship.[51]

However, giving compliments is a tricky business because some attempts at flattery can be interpreted in ways you didn't intend. For example, many female professionals tire of receiving workplace compliments on their looks while their male coworkers are more often complimented on their work. Some compliments are too personal and can make people feel uncomfortable. A pattern of personal compliments may be grounds for a claim of sexual harassment. But these are extreme examples. We encourage you to think about complimenting as a communication skill and a strategy that's particularly useful in first conversations, whether online or face to face. You don't want to come across as a phony or a predator, but a well-thought-out compliment can open the door to further conversation.

It's also important to know how to *receive* a compliment graciously—not by agreeing with the complimenter (and sounding cocky) or by disagreeing or attempting to talk the person out of his or her compliment, as in "You like this old outfit? I've had it for years—I just threw it on today." The best response is a simple "thank you" that acknowledges that something nice was said about you.[52]

Maintaining Relationships

7.3   Explain the roles of self-disclosure and emotional expression in maintaining face-to-face and online relationships.

Not only do relationships bring us life's greatest joy, but they also dramatically improve our physical health. Research examining data from more than 300,000 people found that a lack of strong relationships increased one's risk of premature death by 50 percent. This statistic represents a health risk comparable to smoking up to fifteen cigarettes a day and a greater risk than obesity or physical inactivity.[53]

Once a relationship has been initiated, we rely on many forms of interpersonal communication (whether conveyed face to face, online, or both) to maintain the connection.[54] Relationship experts John Harvey and Ann Weber describe relationship maintenance as "minding." By "minding," they mean "thought and behavior patterns that interact to create stability and feelings of closeness in a relationship."[55] In this section, we explore two forms of communication that are most central to relationship maintenance: self-disclosure and emotional expression. These topics are among the most heavily researched in the communication discipline.

Self-Disclosure: Revealing Yourself to Others

Imagine you're hanging out with someone you just met at a party or club, you both feel some attraction, and the conversation is going fairly well. But as you continue talking, the person starts describing sexual details about his or her last date or romantic partner—information that is just too intimate and private for a first encounter or, by some people's standards, for *any* encounter. How would you react?

Self-disclosure, originally studied by psychologist Sidney Jourard, occurs when we voluntarily provide information to others that they would not learn unless we told them.[56] Communication scholar David Johnson provides eight reasons why people self-disclose:

- We begin and deepen a relationship by sharing reactions, feelings, personal information, and confidences.
- Self-disclosure improves the quality of relationships.

self-disclosure
Voluntarily providing information to others that they would not learn if one did not tell them.

- Self-disclosure allows us to validate our perceptions of reality.
- Self-disclosure clarifies our understanding of ourselves.
- The expression of feelings and reactions is a freeing experience.
- Disclosing or withholding information about ourselves can be a means of social control.
- Self-disclosing is an important part of managing stress and adversity.
- Self-disclosure fulfills a human need to be known intimately and accepted.[57]

Properties of Self-Disclosure

Self-disclosure is a building block of intimacy, and greater intimacy generally leads to enhanced relationships, whether those relationships are developed face to face or online.[58] Because of the importance of self-disclosure, we first need to understand three properties of this unique form of interpersonal communication.

- *Reciprocity.* When we share information about ourselves with others, we expect them to share information similar in risk or depth about themselves, that is, to provide **reciprocity**. Sharing information about yourself gives others a certain amount of power over you. If the other person reciprocates by disclosing similar information, it helps maintain a balance of power. Over time, unreciprocated self-disclosure may cause someone to end a relationship. The reciprocity aspect applies online as well. If someone doesn't respond to our social media posts or e-mail messages with as much depth of disclosure as we'd like, we may reduce or end our online communication with that nonreciprocating person.[59]

- *Appropriateness.* It is sometimes hard to gauge what is appropriate to talk about and what is not while you're in the process of getting to know someone.[60] Some information isn't right for the early stages of a relationship but is appropriate to disclose at a later stage. People vary a good deal on this judgment. Unwanted disclosures may emerge because one person misjudges the nature of the relationship, assuming or wanting a greater level of intimacy than his or her partner assumes or wants. Be sensitive when you choose what and when to disclose; consider how the recipient of your disclosure will react. Conversely, when someone reveals information to you, try to determine whether it's highly personal to her or him and respond appropriately.

- *Risk.* Self-disclosure can be extremely rewarding because of its potential to deepen a relationship and enhance trust. But self-disclosure, whether performed face to face or via social media, is not without its risks. Some people find it de-stressing to vent about their relationships or to post something negative or judgmental about a friend or romantic partner on social media. However, it's wise to avoid venting online because social media outlets are *public* sites.[61] It's sometimes hard to remember that the Internet has made the world smaller. In our increasingly open culture, protecting our privacy is a challenge.[62] For example, even in a society that is becoming more accepting of homosexuality, bisexuality, and transgenderism, "coming out of the closet" as a form of self-disclosure is still a risky prospect. Relationships with family members and friends can be hurt by the revelation, and the potential for rejection of, and hostility toward, the discloser is very real.[63] When we disclose, we make ourselves vulnerable and forfeit control of information. We might offend, hurt, or insult another

reciprocity

Sharing information about oneself with another person, with the expectation that the other person will share information that is similar in risk or depth.

RECAP

Self-Disclosure

. . . is providing someone with information about yourself that she or he couldn't learn about you unless you revealed it.

. . . is highly rewarding in that it is a building block of relational intimacy.

. . . should be reciprocal, meaning that the person you reveal something to should respond with information about himself or herself that is similar in depth. The frequency with which partners self-disclose should be reciprocal as well.

. . . should be appropriate, meaning that it can be a mistake to reveal information that is too personal too soon in the development of a relationship.

. . . involves some risk, because knowledge is power. By revealing information to another person, you give that person a degree of power over you.

COMMUNICATION & SOCIAL MEDIA

Becoming Facebook Official: A Current Incarnation of "Going Steady," "Wearing a Letter Jacket," or "Getting Pinned"

Public statements (verbal and nonverbal) about relationships have been around a long time. You probably know what "going steady" means, but you might not be familiar with the other status language in the title of this box. A few decades ago, if a heterosexual guy (typically in middle school or high school) had a varsity letter jacket that identified him as an athlete, a significant moment in a romantic relationship would be giving his girlfriend his jacket to wear to school (and everywhere else). We suspect this practice doesn't happen much anymore (but we can always be surprised). Less well known is the "getting pinned" reference, which happened at the collegiate level as recently as the 1970s, when a heterosexual man would give his girlfriend his fraternity pin to wear. Such a statement was more serious than "going steady," which to college students was something done when younger. Wearing a man's pin was viewed as a midway step between dating and getting engaged. Ah, the joy of nostalgia.

It's still the case that a key relationship maintenance decision surrounds the outing and defining of a relationship, but nowadays it's more about if and when to publicize the connection on social media. Given that most Facebook users have between 200 and 250 people in their social network, for many couples—no matter gay, straight, bi, or trans—a decision to become "FBO" (Facebook official) is a critical relationship maintenance moment.

Communication scholars Brianna Lane and Cameron Piercy studied the reasons behind couples' decisions to become FBO, as well as decisions to *not* declare their relationship status.[64] Facebook has now expanded its relationship descriptions to include "in a relationship," "engaged," "married," "civil union," "domestic partnership," "open relationship," and "'complicated'." There are significant ramifications for a decision to go "social media public." Since people can link their profiles to their partners' by "tagging" each other on Facebook, such actions significantly increase the size of a couple's social network. With just a few clicks, a much wider audience of people on Facebook can know your relationship status and can share that information on their networks (and so forth). Some people may feel positively about such a chain reaction, but others may not like it, nor realize the extent of the social media reach.

One might assume that both partners in a relationship will talk about the decision to become FBO, the pros and cons, and which status term to select that defines and explains the relationship to others. But in Lane and Piercy's study, more subjects (college students) who went FBO with their relationships reported that *their partners did not do the same.* Granted, some partners may not have been Facebook users, so that accounts in part for the findings. But consider the potential for a one-sided definition and publicity process to lead to conflict in a relationship.

Subjects in this study primarily cited privacy concerns behind their decision not to become FBO with their relationship. Others worried that publicizing and labeling the relationship might lead to higher expectations from other people, which could translate into pressure for the couple. What's your view and experience with the FBO phenomenon? Do you view becoming FBO as a celebratory moment for a couple, or is the practice ego-driven and yet another indication of self-absorption fueled by social media?

person by our disclosure, thus damaging the relationship. In relationships, we typically seek a balance between the potential risks and rewards of disclosing personal information.

Two Models of Self-Disclosure

Research has explored the way in which self-disclosure works to move a relationship toward intimacy. Here we examine two of the more prominent models that illustrate the process by which this happens.

The Social Penetration Model Irwin Altman and Dalmas Taylor developed the **social penetration model**, which illustrates how much and what kind of information we reveal in various stages of a relationship.[65] According to their theory, interpersonal communication in relationships moves gradually from the superficial to the more intimate. Two aspects of this communication increase: the breadth of the information (the variety of topics discussed) and the depth (the personal significance of what is discussed).

social penetration model

A model of self-disclosure that asserts that both the breadth and the depth of information shared with another person increase as the relationship develops.

FIGURE 7.2 Altman and Taylor's Model of Social Penetration

As shown in Figure 7.2, the Altman and Taylor model is a configuration of rings, or concentric circles. The outermost circle represents breadth, or all the potential information about yourself that you could disclose to someone—information about athletic activities, spirituality, family, school, recreational preferences, political attitudes and values, and fears. Then there are a series of inner circles, which represent the depth of information you could reveal about yourself. The innermost circle represents your most personal information.

As an online or FtF relational partner interacts with you, that interaction can be seen as a wedge that's at first narrow (few topics are discussed) and shallow (topics are fairly superficial). People who have just started hanging out might talk about commonalities (such as being students at the same college), hobbies, interests, and favorite activities. As the relationship progresses, the wedge becomes broader (as more topics are discussed) and deeper (as more personal topics are discussed). Over time and with more conversations about hobbies and interests, topics might turn more to values, such as the importance of family and friendships or attitudes about politics or social issues. Self-disclosure causes your layers to be penetrated as you penetrate the layers of the other person.

Each of your relationships exhibits a certain degree of social penetration, determined by the extent to which the other person has entered your concentric circles. Some relationships reflect a narrow, shallow wedge because they don't involve a great deal of personal disclosure. A few relationships represent almost complete social penetration, the kind you achieve in an intimate, well-developed relationship in which a large amount of in-depth self-disclosure has occurred. This model is a helpful way to assess your relationships in terms of whom you allow or encourage to get close to you and why.

The Johari Window   The **Johari Window** in Figure 7.3 is another model of how self-disclosure varies from relationship to relationship. It reflects various stages of relational development, degrees of self-awareness, and others' perceptions of us. The Johari Window is named for the two men who developed it (Joe Luft and Harry Ingham) and for its window-like appearance.[66] The large square window represents the self, which encompasses everything about you, including things you don't see or realize. A vertical line divides the square into what you have come to know about yourself and what you don't yet know about yourself. A horizontal line divides the square into what another person knows about you and doesn't know about you. The intersection of these lines divides the Johari Window into the following four quadrants:

Johari Window
A model that explains how self-disclosure varies from relationship to relationship; the model reflects various stages of relational development, degrees of self-awareness, and others' perceptions.

- *The Open quadrant.* The part of yourself that you know and have revealed to another person is the Open quadrant. As a relationship becomes more intimate, the Open quadrant grows larger.

- *The Blind quadrant.* Information that another person knows about you but that you fail to recognize is in your Blind quadrant. For example, your closest friends may be able to tell when you're attracted to someone even before you are aware of the attraction yourself. Before someone knows you well, the Blind quadrant is usually small; it grows larger as that person observes more information that's in your Unknown quadrant.

- *The Hidden quadrant.* Information that you know about yourself but haven't shared with another person makes up the Hidden quadrant. Initially fairly large, the Hidden quadrant shrinks and the Open quadrant grows as you disclose more and more.

- *The Unknown quadrant.* Information about yourself that you—as well as other people—have yet to discover or realize makes up the Unknown quadrant. People who aren't very introspective and don't have a very well-developed sense of self have larger Unknown areas than do those who've made a concerted effort to get to know themselves. This quadrant shrinks as you learn more about yourself or as others learn more about you.

FIGURE 7.3 Johari Window

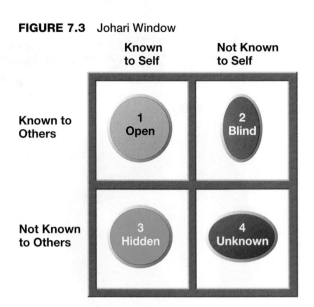

Expressing Emotions

"Emotion is the fuel of human communication," says scholar Paul Bolls.[67] Expressing emotions is another powerful way we reveal ourselves to others and maintain our relationships. Such expression comes more easily to some people than others, but it's a skill that can be improved in both your online and FtF relationships.[68] However, keep in mind that culture affects the expression of emotions; many cultures designate particular emotions as appropriate for only some people to display in certain situations.[69] If you placed emotional expression on a continuum according to cultural groups, with an open approach to emotional display at one end and the suppression of emotional display at the other end, the United States would fall somewhere in the middle.[70]

COMMUNICATION & ETHICS

Are You a Blurter?

Is honesty always the best policy in communication? People often say, "I'm just being honest" as a way to soften or excuse something they just said that shocked or offended others. As a judge on *American Idol* and other TV talent competitions, Simon Cowell was notorious for this behavior, frequently delivering brutal put-downs of well-intentioned young contestants. When people booed him or looked at him as though he was the cruelest person on Earth, he shrugged off the criticism with a glib "I'm just being honest." Cowell may have played up his tactlessness to improve ratings, but we all know someone in real life who also seems to lack a social filter on their honesty.

We've probably all, at some time or another, blurted out something we were thinking, without stopping to consider the consequences. Many times, we regret our unfiltered remarks, and think or say, "It just came out. I don't know what came over me." One team of communication researchers has studied blurting, which they define for research purposes as the "production of speech that is spontaneous, unedited, and negative in its repercussions."[71] As Hample, Richards, and Skubisz explain,

"Blurters say the first (only) thing that occurs to them."[72] As instructors, we've seen our share of students forget something or have an "oops" moment while making speeches in class. Occasionally, a from-the-gut "sh_t" flies out of the student's mouth before the student realizes that she or he just cursed in front of an audience (for a grade). Such blurting, it turns out, is *very* human. It's often connected to our emotional and attitudinal states. People giving speeches often have heightened emotions, for example.

Sometimes, however, blurting is habitual and can be an indication of a lack of self-awareness or self-control in one's communication. Not surprisingly, in Hample et al.'s study, subjects who were self-described blurters were high in verbal aggression and low in their ability to take the perspective of others.

Honesty is a prized value for most people, often more valued than tact, which some perceive as potentially deceptive. What's your opinion? Where's the line between politeness and honesty? If you blurt out your uncensored thoughts, are you "just being honest"? If you apply a filter to what you say, so as to not hurt someone's feelings, are you being dishonest?

Families teach children very specific rules about the appropriateness of emotional display, rules that often perpetuate sex and gender distinctions.[73] In the United States, many men are taught to contain their emotions for fear that emotional expression may make them appear weak.[74] In fact, the male tendency to suppress emotion is so pronounced that it led Sidney Jourard (who first studied self-disclosure) to entitle one of his book chapters, "The Lethal Aspects of the Male Role."[75] Jourard found that men who had difficulty expressing their feelings had high levels of stress-related disease.

In American culture, it is socially acceptable for women to cry in most settings, whether prompted by sadness, fear, or joy. But many women receive negative reactions when they display anger. While these trends and expectations have changed somewhat with recent generations, there is still a significant tendency for men (as well as many women) to believe that emotional expression of any kind is more appropriate in women than in men.[76]

As relationships become more intimate, we have a greater expectation that our partner will disclose emotions openly. The amount of risk associated with such emotional disclosure varies from person to person.[77] Most of us are comfortable sharing the emotions of happiness and joy but are more reserved or hesitant about sharing fear or disappointment.

▲ Many American men learn at an early age to mute most of their emotional expressions, whereas American women often learn to express a wide range of feelings. What were you taught about emotional expression that affects the way you communicate in relationships today?

IKO/Shutterstock

While emotional expression can sometimes be difficult to handle, we generally want to know how our partners in intimate relationships are feeling, even if those feelings are negative. As we first mentioned in Chapter 5, it's critical to successful relationship maintenance that we learn how to accurately identify and effectively respond to someone's expression of emotions and offer needed emotional support.[78] Research on emotional support has shown that this skill is important in relationships that rely mostly on face-to-face communication, but also for relationships that are maintained primarily through social media. Social media outlets are tremendous vehicles for offering emotional support. For example, health challenges are often the subject of Facebook posts and Twitter comments. People who have experienced health problems themselves or have loved ones who are ill, often communicate support for a range of emotions associated with health concerns.[79]

In this chapter, we've explored several aspects of interpersonal communication, yet we've only scratched the surface of the complexities of relationships—those connections that give us life's greatest joys, as well as challenges. In the next chapter, we examine key aspects of communication that are critical to ongoing relationships with regard to our five Communication Principles for a Lifetime.

STUDY GUIDE:

> REVIEW, APPLY, AND ASSESS

What Is Interpersonal Communication?

7.1 Define interpersonal communication and discuss its three unique attributes.

REVIEW: Interpersonal communication occurs when two people interact simultaneously and attempt to mutually influence each other, usually for the purpose of managing relationships. Interpersonal communication research has traditionally focused on the face-to-face relationship, but more recently, studies have investigated how online relationships are initiated and maintained through mediated interpersonal communication.

Interpersonal communication has three attributes:

- Interpersonal communication involves quality, which can be contrasted with impersonal communication, in which people are treated as objects or are communicated with based on the roles they hold.

- Interpersonal communication involves mutual influence.

- Interpersonal communication helps manage relationships of choice and circumstance.

KEY TERMS:

interpersonal communication	mediated interpersonal communication
mediated communication	impersonal communication relationship

APPLY: In your own life, have you experienced the mutual influence of interpersonal communication within the past 24 hours? Describe your experience.

ASSESS: Learning to Ask Great Questions

Because we think that learning to ask great questions is so important, we want to provide you with an opportunity to practice this art and skill. For each of the situations and snippets of conversation that follow, generate follow-up questions that would deepen and extend the conversation. We've provided an example to get you started.

Sample Situation and Conversation: The situation is a first conversation between two classmates who have never met before. They are seated in a classroom before class begins.

Bob: Hi. My name's Bob. What's yours?

Sue: Hi. I'm Sue.

Bob: I've never taken a philosophy course before, have you? What do you think this course will be like?

Sue: Well, I've never taken one either, but I expect lots of reading. And I've heard the professor's tests are tough.

Bob: Oh, great! Is it too late to drop? When you say the tests are tough, tough in what way? Do you mean they cover lots of material, the professor's a hard grader, or what?

1. *Practice Situation:* At a fraternity/sorority mixer, a woman and a man are introduced to each other for the first time by other members of their organizations.

2. *Practice Situation:* After a staff meeting, two new coworkers who will be working on the same important project introduce themselves to each other.

Initiating Relationships

7.2 Describe the roles of communication in revealing interpersonal attraction and initiating relationships.

REVIEW: We are drawn to other people because of physical, sexual, and interpersonal attraction; similarity; proximity; and complementarity. We use nonverbal immediacy cues to convey our attraction and communicate to reduce uncertainty as we initiate and develop relationships. Besides listening, adapting, and being sensitive to nonverbal cues, good interpersonal communicators ask great questions, avoid self-absorbed communication, and give and receive compliments graciously.

KEY TERMS:

relationship of circumstance	uncertainty-reduction theory
relationship of choice	passive strategy
attraction	active strategy
interpersonal attraction	interactive strategy
physical attraction	conversational narcissism (self-absorbed communicator style)
sexual attraction	
matching hypothesis	trait conversational narcissism
similarity	
proximity	state conversational narcissism
complementarity	
immediacy	

APPLY: Provide examples of when you have used passive, active, and interactive strategies to reduce your uncertainty in a new situation or before meeting a new person.

ASSESS: Imagine you see an attractive person at a club. He or she doesn't appear to be with a date and you aren't with anyone either. You're intrigued and want to know more about him or her. Using the three types of strategies to reduce uncertainty, describe how you would go about getting more information about the person who has caught your eye.

Passive strategy:

Active strategy:

Interactive strategy:

Maintaining Relationships

7.3 Explain the roles of self-disclosure and emotional expression in maintaining face-to-face and online relationships.

REVIEW: An important communication skill is self-disclosure, or voluntarily providing information to others that they wouldn't learn if you didn't tell them. Self-disclosure is characterized by three aspects: (1) reciprocity, (2) appropriateness, and (3) risk. The social penetration model suggests that interpersonal communication in relationships moves gradually from the superficial to the more intimate. The breadth and depth of communication increase as intimacy increases in relationships. The Johari Window depicts various stages of relational development, degrees of self-awareness, and others' perceptions. Emotional expression is another powerful mechanism for revealing ourselves to others and deepening our relationships.

KEY TERMS:

self-disclosure	social penetration model
reciprocity	Johari Window

APPLY: Consider how open a person you are. How comfortably and readily do you communicate information about yourself—such as your background, history, beliefs, views, and opinions? Do you have circles of friends who you are comfortable with and, thus, share more information with? How open are you with family members?

ASSESS: Too Private to Talk About—Unless It's Online?

For the following topics, check the column to indicate in which situation you would freely disclose the information to another person you were trying to get to know. Then analyze your answers. What information would you share anytime in any format? What information are you unlikely to reveal to anyone in either context?

Topic	Would Disclose FtF	Would Disclose Online
Weight		
Racial/ethnic background		
Sexual history		
Family details		
Relationship status		
Weaknesses/strengths		
Religious/spiritual beliefs		
Political views		

⟩ THE PRINCIPLE POINTS

Principle One:

Be aware of your communication with yourself and others.

- Attraction emerges in several different forms; it is important to discover what traits in other people are attractive to you.
- Early in an online or FtF relationship, be aware of aspects of your personality that you want to emphasize to another person to create a positive and attractive image.
- One strategy to reduce uncertainty in interpersonal contexts is to be aware of your surroundings and situation as you passively observe others' interactions.
- The social penetration model and the Johari Window can help you become more aware of your relationships and your interpersonal communication.

Principle Two:

Effectively use and interpret verbal messages.

- In initial interactions, honest and direct approaches are preferable to canned opening lines.
- When initiating online or FtF relationships, use questions that will engage and draw out the other person.

- You may verbally reveal your liking for another person by using informal, personal, and inclusive language.
- You may verbally reveal your liking for another person by asking questions, probing for further information, and directly expressing your feelings.
- An active strategy to reduce uncertainty in interpersonal contexts is to ask third parties for their perceptions and knowledge.
- An interactive information-seeking strategy involves direct communication with the source who has the greatest potential for reducing your uncertainty.
- Asking great questions in a conversation draws a person out and helps a communicator avoid creating a perception of being self-absorbed.
- Practice giving sincere compliments generously and receiving others' compliments graciously.
- One of the key variables in relationship development is self-disclosure.
- As relationships grow more intimate, the expectation of deeper, more personal self-disclosure increases.
- As online and FtF relationships grow more intimate, the expectation of emotional expression and support for such expression increases.

Principle Three:

Effectively use and interpret nonverbal messages.

- Physical attraction is the degree to which you find another person's physical self appealing, whereas sexual attraction is the desire to have sexual contact with a certain person.
- In an FtF relationship, you may nonverbally reveal your liking for another person through the display of immediacy cues.
- Certain nonverbal behaviors such as increasing speech volume to ward off interruptions, shifting the body to block someone from exiting a conversation, or sending lengthy, self-involved text messages may signal a self-absorbed communication style.

Principle Four:

Listen and respond thoughtfully to others.

- Early in online and FtF relationships, it's important to concentrate on and listen to your partner's responses to your questions so that you can offer appropriate follow-up responses.
- You may verbally reveal your attraction and liking for other people by listening, asking questions to elicit more detail, and then responding appropriately and sensitively to the added information.
- The best conversationalists aren't great talkers; they're great listeners and responders.
- The formulation of great questions in conversation requires listening carefully and responding appropriately to someone's communication.
- It's important to attend carefully to someone's self-disclosure because it comes with an expectation of reciprocity, meaning that the receiver is expected to disclose in response to the sender's self-disclosure.

Principle Five:

Appropriately adapt messages to others.

- Adapt to others' communication, especially in first conversations, by attending to what is said and following up with great questions.
- Self-absorbed communication involves little adaptation.
- Adapt your self-disclosure to the other person and the context so that your revelations are appropriate.
- In face-to-face encounters and on social media, adapt thoughtfully when people reveal their emotions so that they receive your support.

CHAPTER 8

ENHANCING RELATIONSHIPS

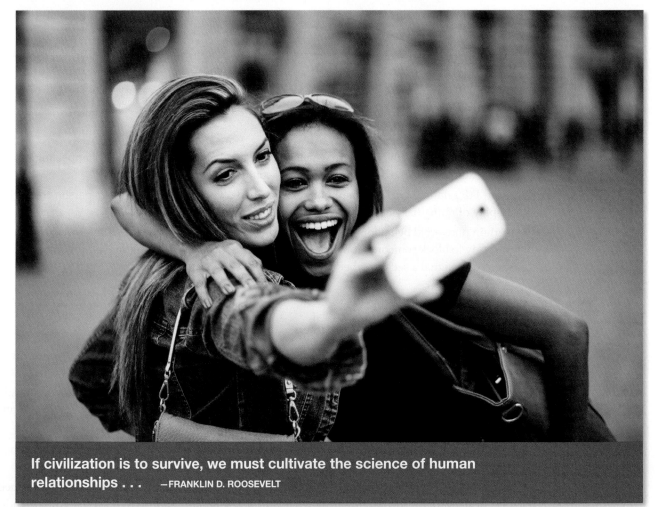

If civilization is to survive, we must cultivate the science of human relationships . . . —FRANKLIN D. ROOSEVELT

berc/Fotolia

→ **CHAPTER OUTLINE**

LEARNING OBJECTIVES

After studying this chapter, you should be able to

8.1 Explain how the five Communication Principles for a Lifetime apply to interpersonal communication among friends, family members, and colleagues.

8.2 Identify and describe the stages of relational escalation and de-escalation.

8.3 Summarize research findings on relationship dissolution, including communication in the on-again/off-again relationship and the postdissolutional relationship.

8.4 Discuss relational dialectics and three primary tensions in relationships.

8.5 Summarize the seven types of interpersonal conflict, the key characteristics of conflict management, and the ways in which people can cooperate in conflict situations.

W hat makes you happy? Staring at a computer screen? Working on a project for your job? Reading a great book? Playing a video game? Being by yourself, writing in your journal? Taking a long walk? Let us venture a guess: While any one of these things might bring some level of pleasure into your life, none of them could be considered *the* thing in life that gives you the most enjoyment. Probably most of us would answer that question with some response that involves other people or perhaps only one other person.

In Chapter 7, we examined some fundamental aspects of interpersonal communication that help us initiate and maintain online and face-to-face relationships. In this chapter, we move forward to discuss interpersonal communication as it occurs in ongoing, longer-term relationships, applying our five Communication Principles for a Lifetime.

The Importance of Relationships: Friends, Family, and Colleagues

8.1 Explain how the five Communication Principles for a Lifetime apply to interpersonal communication among friends, family members, and colleagues.

Our family members, friends, and coworkers are very important to us. We don't have to lecture students on the value of friendship. As for family, to some degree we all come from dysfunctional families—there's no such thing as a perfect family. No matter how imperfect our families are, how crazy our siblings still make us, or how far apart we've grown, almost all of us would agree that family relationships are extremely important. On the job front, when people discuss what they like best about their jobs, most often they talk about the people they work with. So, disregarding the few true hermits out there, most of us are "people who need people."

Friendship Matters

One of the best definitions of a friend, attributed to Aristotle, is "a soul that resides in two bodies." A friend is someone we like and who likes us. We trust our friends and share good and bad times with them. We expect a certain level of sacrifice from

▲ These two friends may have met just moments ago. Our earliest friendships are usually based on momentarily shared activities. How long does it take you now to decide someone is your friend? What influences that decision?

Thinkstock Images/Stockbyte/Getty Images

our friends. For example, you know you've got a good friend when he or she gives up something (like a hot date) to help you through a tough time.

Researchers have examined some differences among friendships at four stages in life: childhood, adolescence, adulthood, and old age.[1] When we start to talk (around age two) and interact with others, our first friendships are typically superficial, self-centered, and fleeting because they're based on momentarily shared activities.[2] As we grow and mature, we develop more of a give-and-take in friendships. During adolescence we move away emotionally from relationships with parents, and peer relationships have more influence on our behavior.[3]

Adult friendships are among our most valued relationships, even though they may be few in number. Research has found that, on average, adults have ten to twenty casual friends, four to six close friends, and only one to two best friends.[4] Rather than progressing through a series of stages in which intimacy deepens, which is typical of romantic relationships, friendships often alternate between periods of development and deterioration.[5] For many Americans, our jobs are our lives, so we increasingly find that our coworkers become some of our closest friends.

Friendships are extremely important in old age.[6] During retirement, when many individuals have more time for socializing, friendships become increasingly critical. Older adults tend to rely on enduring friendships and maintain a small, highly valued network of friends.

Our familiar five Communication Principles for a Lifetime can help you enhance your friendships.

- **Principle One: Be Aware of Your Communication with Yourself and Others** Knowing your own interests, likes, and dislikes is a first step if you're trying to expand your circle of friends.

- **Principle Two: Effectively Use and Interpret Verbal Messages** Our verbal communication tends to become more frequent and deepens as friendships develop.

- **Principle Three: Effectively Use and Interpret Nonverbal Messages** We also use nonverbal immediacy cues to establish friendships—behaviors that reveal our liking of other people, such as leaning forward, moving closer, making eye contact, smiling, and nodding.

- **Principle Four: Listen and Respond Thoughtfully to Others** Probably no other communication skill develops a friendship more than the ability to listen and respond appropriately. Most of us don't stay friends with people who don't seem to listen to us or who listen but respond inappropriately.

- **Principle Five: Appropriately Adapt Messages to Others** We extend different parts of ourselves and communicate differently with various friends. Having a wide range of friends taps into different parts of your personality, which, in turn, helps you develop your skills of adaptation.

Family Matters

To say that family life has changed is an understatement. Family units are dramatically different from what they were in the 20th century, when the predominant profile was a two-parent, father-as-breadwinner, mother-as-homemaker arrangement.[7] In the 1980s, the New York Supreme Court provided a very broad definition of a family, stating, "The best description of a family is a continuing relationship of love and care, and an assumption of responsibility for some other person."[8] The most common profile of the American family in the 21st century is the stepfamily, or blended family, with rising rates of extended family or multigenerational arrangements.[9] After same-sex marriage became legal in the United States in 2015, it's clear that we are now experiencing another paradigm shift in our basic views of what constitutes a family.[10]

Of all the relationships we experience in our lifetimes, none are more complicated than family relationships. All five Communication Principles for a Lifetime come into play when we interact with our families.

- **Principle One: Be Aware of Your Communication with Yourself and Others** Growing up in families, we begin to discover who we are and how we should communicate with others. Family members have more power to shape our self-concepts and affect self-esteem than other people do. Granted, at some point we can choose to lessen the effect family members can have on our lives. But for most of us, those early messages we received as children remain in our psyches and affect who we are today.

- **Principles Two and Three: Effectively Use and Interpret Verbal and Nonverbal Messages** Renowned family therapist Virginia Satir has conducted extensive research on family communication.[11] She suggests that the following elements are present in healthy families:

  - Self-worth of members is high.
  - Communication is direct and honest.
  - Rules are flexible.
  - People listen actively.
  - Family members look *at* one another, not *through* one another.
  - Family members treat children as people.
  - They touch one another affectionately regardless of age.
  - They openly discuss disappointments, fears, hurts, angers, and criticism, as well as joys and achievements.

- **Principle Four: Listen and Respond Thoughtfully to Others** One of the characteristics Satir recommends is active listening. Healthy family relationships are built on foundations of trust, which involves listening to one another and responding helpfully. Many conflicts arise because family members don't listen well to one another and respond on the basis of that faulty listening.[12]

- **Principle Five: Appropriately Adapt Messages to Others** Finally, family relationships involve a good deal of adaptation, particularly when, as adults, we visit our parents. Sometimes our parents and extended family members talk a certain way mainly because they've always talked that way.[13] But if you're the family member who has moved away, attended college, and adapted your communication to meet the changing times, relate to friends, and demonstrate professionalism at work, it can be quite awkward to be immersed once again in the family setting and realize how much you've changed. Reintegration into family patterns of communication can also be a challenge for military personnel who've served overseas and are returning to family life in the United States.[14]

COMMUNICATION & SOCIAL MEDIA

The Joys (and Woes) of the Video Chat

How cool was it when comic strip detective Dick Tracy used his "2-way wrist radio" and, later, his "2-way wrist TV" to talk to his police chief? How about the Jetsons, who had a videophone in their home? (Yes, we're old.) Several decades ago, having a video watch or phone was the stuff of futuristic cartoons. Now we just have to fire up our laptops, cell phones, or smart watches (like the Apple Watch) and we're video chatting. Stop and think for a moment how truly remarkable all of this technology is.

We know that video chat applications such as Skype, FaceTime, Google's Duo, and Facebook's Messenger service are increasingly helpful in the workplace, as our professional lives expand globally.[15] But video chatting has proven to be especially helpful for family members who are geographically separated because of work demands or relationship change, such as divorce.[16] Researchers have found that video chatting extends the reach of social media and can be therapeutic for children who are living apart from one or both parents.[17] Adult family members benefit, too. A bride-to-be can model wedding dresses for an ailing or far-away parent who can't be there to enjoy the shopping moment. Family members separated by work or military deployment might meet a new baby for the first time via video chat. And we can all enjoy being more "up close and personal" with people we care about who don't live where we live.

A good deal of research has focused on military families in which one member has been deployed to a war zone.[18] Findings from such research contribute to skills-training modules for service members and their families. Service members are trained in such topics as how to avoid the effects on spouses and children of having a video chat interrupted by gunfire or other noises that signal danger to a loved one.[19] Family members learn how and when to disclose a problem to a deployed family member.[20] One of the leading causes of suicides among members of the armed forces is a major crisis that occurs at home. It might be necessary, for example, to tell a soldier halfway around the world that his or her parent has been diagnosed with cancer. Training helps family members find the least distressing way possible to share such news.

Blend Images/Ariel Skelley/The Agency Collection/Getty Images

Colleagues Matter

For many of us, our work is our livelihood, our most time-consuming activity. Many things make a job worthwhile and rewarding, but most people say that relationships with people at work make the difference between job satisfaction and dissatisfaction.

What are the most important skills people need to be successful on the job? Year after year, among the top five skills employers look for in new hires is the ability to communicate effectively with others, both orally and in writing.[21] You land your job through an interview; you keep your job on the basis of your ability to do the work and get along with coworkers, bosses, and clients, which usually involves a large amount of interpersonal interaction. The higher you go in an organization, the more your job involves communicating with others, both online and in person. You'll likely apply all five Communication Principles for a Lifetime to help you succeed at your job.

Our familiar five Communication Principles for a Lifetime can help you enhance your work relationships.

- **Principle One: Be Aware of Your Communication with Yourself and Others** When we start a new job, we experience uncertainty. We need to learn the basics, like where to park and how the organization functions. We also need to figure out more important things, such as how to do your job well, who's who in the chain of command, and which colleagues have the potential to develop into friends.[22] We're most likely to observe our surroundings and how people interact on the job as a way of becoming more aware so that we'll know how to behave appropriately. Perception checking with our colleagues, supervisors, and trainers also increases awareness.

- **Principles Two and Three: Effectively Use and Interpret Verbal and Nonverbal Messages** As we begin to interact with people of varying status in the organization, we draw on our most effective verbal and nonverbal communication skills so that we make positive impressions on others.

- **Principle Four: Listen and Respond Thoughtfully to Others** It's important to listen patiently, fully, and nonjudgmentally at work and essential to exercise caution before responding so that you respond appropriately.

- **Principle Five: Appropriately Adapt Messages to Others** Finally, our Principle Five about adaptation is critical to successful coworker relationships. You won't be successful on the job if you communicate the same way to your boss as you do to your peers, subordinates, clients, and others in your life—including long-term friends, intimates, and family members.[23] This may seem obvious, but we find that people sometimes experience isolation on the job because they can't get along with coworkers. They don't adapt to the situation, and it often costs them their jobs.

Stages of Relationship Development

8.2　Identify and describe the stages of relational escalation and de-escalation.

In this chapter, we explore aspects of communication that are critical to the successful functioning of ongoing, longer-term relationships, but it's helpful to first understand that relationships tend to develop in discernible stages.[24] Although the research on relational stages is most often applied to dating or romantic relationships, the information can also apply to other types of relationships.

Understanding relationship stages is important for two main reasons:

- Interpersonal communication is affected by the stage of a relationship. For instance, people in advanced stages discuss topics and display nonverbal behaviors that rarely appear in the early stages of a relationship.

- Interpersonal communication (both face to face and mediated) facilitates movement between the various stages.[25] Ongoing relationships change and are constantly renegotiated by those involved. Interpersonal communication moves a relationship forward—possibly from friends to romantic partners to marital or committed partners. Communication can also move a relationship back to a previous stage, although regressing a relationship or changing a relationship's definition can be difficult to accomplish.[26]

FIGURE 8.1 Relationship Stages

SOURCE: From Steven A. Beebe, Susan J. Beebe, and Mark V. Redmond, *Interpersonal Communication: Relating to Others*, 8e. Reprinted and electronically reproduced by permission of Pearson Education, Inc., Hoboken, NJ. Copyright © 2017.

Types of Relationships	Escalation Stages	De-Escalation Stages
Best Friend/ Lover/ Spouse	Intimacy	Turmoil or Stagnation
Close Friend	Intensification	Deintensification
Friend	Exploration	Individualization
Acquaintance	Acquaintance	Separation
Stranger	Preinteraction Awareness	Post-Separation Effects

pre-interaction awareness stage
The first stage of becoming aware of one's attraction to another person and observing that person but not actually interacting.

initiation stage
The first contact with a person with whom one desires a relationship; usually characterized by asking and answering questions.

exploration stage
The stage that involves more in-depth interactions.

intensification stage
The stage in which partners begin to depend on each other for self-confirmation; characterized by more shared activities, more time spent together, more intimate physical distance and contact, and personalized language.

Think of relational stages as floors in a high-rise (see Figure 8.1). The bottom floor represents a first meeting; the penthouse is intimacy. Relational development is an elevator that stops at every floor. As you ascend, you might get off the elevator and wander around for a while before going to the next floor. Each time you get on the elevator, you don't know how many floors up it will take you or how long you'll stay at any given floor. If you fall head over heels in love, you might want to escalate quickly from floor to floor toward intimacy, possibly even skipping some floors. Other times, you stop at a particular floor and never get back on the elevator, electing instead to stay at a particular stage of relational development. This may represent stability or stagnation (which are not the same thing). Stagnation, which tends to have a negative connotation, is an indication that a relationship is flat and perhaps on the brink of de-escalation and termination. Stability may simply mean that a relationship has reached a comfortable point for both partners; it's not going up or down, but it's working. If one partner believes the relationship has stabilized and the other partner believes it has stagnated, dissatisfaction and conflict will often result.

The best approach to relationship development is to share this elevator with your partner or friend so that the two of you make decisions about how high to ride, how long to stay at each floor, and whether to take the elevator back down. But often partners don't share decisions about movement within the relationship. Sometimes one of the partners rides the elevator alone.

Relational Escalation

According to Mark Knapp and Anita Vangelisti, the two communication scholars who developed the model of developmental stages within relationships, relational escalation occurs in the following five stages:[27]

- **Pre-interaction awareness stage** is the first stage, one in which potential partners or friends observe each other and talk with other people about each other without having any direct interaction. If your impressions of a potential friend or relational partner aren't favorable or circumstances aren't right, you might not move beyond this first stage.

- In the **initiation stage,** first conversations occur between potential friends or romantic partners. Each person responds to the other's questions as both try to determine what they have in common. Nonverbal cues are important at this stage because they signal interest.

- The **exploration stage** occurs next as partners or friends begin to share more in-depth information. Minimal physical contact is typical, and the amount of time people spend together tends to be fairly limited as the relationship begins to build.

- If people proceed to the **intensification stage,** they start to depend on each other for self-confirmation, meaning that each partner's or friend's opinion of, or feeling about, the other weighs more heavily than the opinions of other people. Partners spend more time together in a wider variety of activities, adopt more intimate physical distance and contact, and personalize their language. The frequency and level of shared personal information increase, and the two people may decide to label their connection. Friends may move to "best friend" status; romantic partners may make a decision to publicize their relationship on social media, for example, deciding to become FBO ("Facebook official").[28]

- The top level of relationship escalation is the **intimacy stage**. At this stage, partners provide primary confirmation of each other's self-concept and communication is highly personalized and synchronized. Partners talk about anything and everything, and a commitment to maintaining a romantic relationship might even be formalized and socially recognized, such as with a decision to cohabitate or marry. Romantic partners share an understanding of each other's language and nonverbal cues and have a great deal of physical contact. Reaching this stage takes time—time to build trust, share highly personal information, observe each other in various situations, and create an emotional bond and commitment.

This is a nice and tidy model of what *may* happen as a relationship progresses, but we all know that relationships can be messier than this. Some people move through relational stages very quickly. We probably all know people whose relationships were extremely physical and perhaps sexual from the very start. Are those relationships doomed because they didn't follow set or prescribed paths for development? No; some relationships may just proceed through stages faster than others. Extremely physical or sexual relationships may burn out quickly, however, because they lack the emotional foundation necessary to survive. Partners may have difficulty developing an emotional connection or finding things in common once the physical spark wanes.

▲ At the intensification stage, a couple's relationship becomes the central focus of their lives.
Jupiterimages/Stockbyte/Getty Images

Relational De-Escalation

Sometimes relationships begin to unravel, some to the point of termination. But as you may already know, a relationship in decline doesn't simply go down the same way it went up; it's not a mere reversal of the escalation process.[29] Relational de-escalation contains the following five stages:

- The **turmoil or stagnation stage** comes first in a relationship's demise and is characterized by increased conflict as partners find faults in each other.[30] The definition of the relationship loses clarity and mutual acceptance declines. Conversations are tense, difficult, and forced. The relationship loses its vitality and

intimacy stage
The stage in which partners provide primary confirmation of each other's self-concept; characterized by highly personalized and synchronized verbal and nonverbal communication.

turmoil or stagnation stage
The stage characterized by increased conflict, less mutual acceptance, a tense communication climate, and an unclear relationship definition that causes the relationship to lose its vitality. Partners begin to take each other for granted, and communication and physical contact decline.

RECAP	
Relational Escalation	

Stage	Explanation
Pre-Interaction Awareness	You become aware of your attraction to someone and begin to observe that person.
Initiation	You initiate contact with the person with whom you want a relationship.
Exploration	Interactions deepen as questions and answers elicit more information from partners.
Intensification	Partners begin to depend on each other for confirmation of their self-concepts. They spend more time together, engage in more intimate touch, and personalize their language.
Intimacy	Partners provide primary confirmation of each other's self-concept. Verbally, language is highly personalized; nonverbal behaviors are synchronized.

partners take each other for granted, perhaps feeling bored.[31] Communication and physical contact decrease. Partners or friends spend less time together but don't necessarily engage in conflict. People in a stagnating relationship go through the motions of an intimate relationship without the commitment or joy. But a stagnating relationship can be salvaged. People can repair, redefine, and revitalize their relationship.

de-intensification stage

The stage involving significantly decreased interaction, closeness, and dependence on one's partner for self-confirmation.

- If turmoil or stagnation continues, friends or partners will likely experience the **de-intensification stage,** which involves decreased physical, emotional, and psychological closeness; significantly decreased interaction; and decreased dependence on each other for self-confirmation. Partners might discuss the definition of their relationship, question its future, and assess each other's level of dissatisfaction.

individualization stage

The stage in which partners define their lives more as individuals and less as a couple.

- After de-intensification, the **individualization stage** occurs, in which partners tend to define their lives more as individuals and less as a couple or unit. Interactions are limited; both partners tend to turn to others for self-concept confirmation. For romantic partners, physical intimacy is at an all-time low, if not nonexistent, and nonverbal distance is easily detected.

separation stage

The stage in which individuals make an intentional decision to minimize or eliminate further interpersonal interaction.

- In the **separation stage,** individuals make an intentional decision to minimize or eliminate further interaction. Friends may feel awkward if they are also roommates or classmates, and they may take action to distance themselves on campus. If a married or romantic couple share custody of children, attend mutual family gatherings, or work at the same place, the nature of their interaction noticeably changes. They divide property, resources, and friends. Interactions in this stage are increasingly tense and difficult, especially if the relationship has been sexually intimate.

cyber infidelity

Online sexual activity outside of one's monogamous relationship.

COMMUNICATION & ETHICS

Cyber Infidelity: Is It Cheating If You Don't Actually Touch?

What's your view of cyber infidelity? Should technologically-mediated liaisons outside of one's primary romantic relationship be viewed as breaches of ethics or morals, or simply as signs of the times?

We all know that technology and social media help us keep in touch with important people in our lives, including our romantic partners. But another use is to establish and maintain romantic connections with people *other* than our primary romantic partners.[32] As one source suggests, "Fueling our sexual freedom is our ability to pursue a fling without even opening the front door; we can simply open a laptop."[33] Such external liaisons may form through common interests and not begin as sexual relationships, but cyber relationships can quickly escalate. How many relationships have gone down in flames because one partner viewed another's browsing history, or checked text messages or voice mail on the other's phone and found evidence of infidelity?

Most people view in-person relational infidelity as a deal breaker.[34] Even people who haven't experienced it

say that they would respond negatively to a partner's infidelity.[35] But some people view **cyber infidelity** (online sexual activity outside of one's monogamous relationship) differently because no physical consummation actually occurs. In this view, if the connection is virtual, it's not real; therefore, it's not cheating.[36] Do you find this argument persuasive?

What if the cyber sex involves not just words (sexting) but also explicit photos? What about sexual activities via video chat? Does that now qualify as infidelity because people can see each other being sexual, whereas a text is just words that spark the imagination?

Researchers have asked people these questions.[37] One study found that 41 percent of respondents didn't believe online sexual activity was cheating on a partner under any circumstances. Some deemed it cheating only if a person engaged in cyber sex repeatedly with the same person, if webcams were used, or if the online sex led to phone sex. Thirty-three percent believed that any form of online sex was cheating and that it was just as much an act of infidelity as in-person sex with someone other than one's partner. Where do you stand on the issue?

- The final level in de-escalation is the **post-interaction stage**. It represents the lasting effects the relationship has on the self and others. Relationships—even failed ones—are powerful experiences in our lives, so the effects continue even after the relationship has ended. In this stage, partners engage in "grave dressing," meaning that they create a public statement for people who ask why they broke up or are no longer friends.[38] Often people will employ social media to inform their social networks of a change in relationship status.[39] Sometimes self-esteem gets battered during the final stages of a relationship, so partners work to regain a healthy sense of self.[40]

Have you ever experienced the turmoil or stagnation stage with a friend or romantic partner? Were you able to turn it around and repair the relationship? If so, how did you accomplish this?

RECAP

Relational De-Escalation

Stage	Explanation
Turmoil or Stagnation	Partners begin to take each other for granted and have more conflict. They exhibit less mutual acceptance, their communication climate is tense, and their relationship definition is unclear. The relationship loses its vitality; partners begin to take each other for granted and may experience boredom in the relationship. Communication and physical contact decline.
De-Intensification	Partners significantly decrease their interaction and their dependence on each other for self-confirmation; they increase their physical distance.
Individualization	Partners define their lives more as individuals and less as a couple.
Separation	Partners make an intentional decision to minimize or eliminate further interpersonal interaction.
Post-Interaction	This is the bottom or final level in relational de-escalation; it represents the lasting effects of a relationship on the individuals.

post-interaction stage
The bottom, or final, stage in relational de-escalation, which represents the lasting effects of a relationship on the self.

Relationship Dissolution (a.k.a. the Breakup)

8.3 Summarize research findings on relationship dissolution, including communication in the on-again/off-again relationship and the postdissolutional relationship.

Friendships can fade away, marriages can end in divorce, and romantic partners can break up—we all know this. **Relationship dissolution** is the research term for relational endings, possibly preferred because "relationship termination" has connotations of death.[41] Since ending relationships is an inescapable part of everybody's life, let's take a moment to think about communication and breakups, as well as what happens to a relationship after a breakup.

relationship dissolution
Ending a relationship.

Best Practices in Breaking Up

Friendships tend to end (or transition into a different level) more gradually than romantic relationships, sometimes just fading away because of distance or changed circumstances or priorities. But it's bewildering when romantic relationships just fade away (a phenomenon known as "ghosting"). People are usually left wondering what happened.[42] Without knowing, it's hard to gain some growth from the experience. So let's focus on what research can teach us about appropriate romantic relationship endings.

With the popularity of texting and social media, you may know someone who was broken up with via social media or with a text message; perhaps you have been on the short end of that stick. Let's be clear (and blunt) about this: *It's a coward's way to end a relationship*. We understand that it saves the "dumper" time and emotional angst, not having to witness in person the "dumpee's" reaction, but even in a superficial, short-term relationship, breaking up at a distance shows no respect for the other person. It also

▼ It's highly likely that you will have to break up with someone in your life, whether a friend or romantic partner. Stefano Lunardi/123RF

doesn't do your reputation any favors, because perpetrating a text or social media breakup reveals to others the kind of relational partner you are, even in short-term liaisons.

One study examined college students' methods of delivering a breakup message.[43] The researchers found that 43 percent of subjects' breakups were accomplished face to face; 32 percent were handled through a phone call; 10 percent were conveyed through instant messaging via computer; 8 percent were done in an e-mail message; 2 percent used a written letter; and another 2 percent used a third party, such as a friend, to be the bearer of the bad news. (Who would volunteer for *that* gig?) Some students used combinations of these methods. None said that they'd broken up with someone via text, explaining that they would be even angrier and more upset if someone broke up with them that way. The takeaway from this study is that the predominant breakup method reported by these students was the good old-fashioned face-to-face conversation, which is also how they would prefer someone break up with them.

So on the basis of what research tells us, here's some advice on communication and breaking up, should you find yourself needing to end a romantic relationship someday (or processing how someone broke up with you):

- *Don't be a ghost.* Avoid expanding distance by not calling someone back (ever), ignoring messages, unfriending or blocking him or her from your social networking sites, avoiding places and situations where you might run into the person, and hoping the person will get the hint. These methods generate confusion and ambiguity, causing undue hurt to the target of the breakup.[44] Relational fuzziness can also keep both parties from moving on.

- *Give the other person a chance to respond.* Using a mediated channel to end a relationship may make it easier on the dumper but is terrible for the dumpee (and, some would argue, unethical). Without even a short conversation, the person is cut off from a full explanation, a chance at negotiation, and the opportunity to express her or his feelings.[45]

- *Do it face to face.* A face-to-face interaction offers a chance to exercise your communication skills. Although the "dreaded conversation" is rarely pleasant, resist the instinct to duck out or postpone. Force yourself to have a conversation with the person.[46] Thinking, "If I see so-and-so, I might not be able to go through with it" is no excuse to avoid or put off the inevitable. Both parties will retain more dignity and self-respect through a breakup conversation than by being denied the opportunity to talk.

- *Avoid the trite "let's still be friends" line.* For most people in the position of being dumped, the last thing they want to do or can even conceive of is being friends with a former romantic partner.[47] It's understandable for a dumper to try to soften the blow or retain some kind of connection to the dumpee, but it's selfish to expect the other person to change the relationship definition easily or quickly. Maybe, with time, something can be salvaged that works for both parties.[48]

- *Also avoid the dreaded and trite "It's not you—it's me" bit.* People getting dumped don't tend to believe that anyway. When someone says to us, "It's not you, it's me," most of us will think, "It's me." Granted, there are times when we may agree with the person—it really *is* them. But this line is overused, hurtful, and simply not believable in most circumstances. It does more damage than it saves hurt.

- *Don't use the infamous "timing" explanation either.* You may be tempted to trot out the classic line, "It's just not a good time for me right now to be in a relationship." Most of us don't believe that. Instead, most dumpees would prefer that the dumper be honest enough to tell them that the relationship just isn't what the dumper wants.

After the Breakup: Communicating with an Ex

People may change the profile of their relationship, but that doesn't mean it can't change *again*. How many people do you know who "break up to make up"?

Research reveals a great deal about the **on-again/off-again relationship** (also called "cyclical" or "habitual"), which is quite common.[49] Communication scholar René Dailey conducts extensive research on this form of dating relationship, which occurs when people get back together with the same partner, sometimes over and over again. Some people return to a partner out of habit or because the relationship is comfortable or known, even if it's not great. Others experience turning points that cause breakups and reconciliations, such as key events like infidelity and the forgiveness that can come with a relational transgression.[50]

Studies also focus on the ways people create or reinvent a connection once they've broken up. Yes, some people actually want to have a relationship of some form with an ex, as challenging as that may be. The **postdissolutional relationship** has been defined as "the relationship formed between dating partners after their romance terminates."[51] (The term typically doesn't apply to divorced couples who negotiate a connection once their marriage has ended.) The factors that may determine whether this form of relationship can be successful include how much the partners like each other, how long the partners were together romantically (the longer the romantic relationship, the less successful the post-relationship), and how much the partners hope they will get back together romantically.[52]

on-again/off-again relationship
A relationship characterized by repeated breakups and reconciliations.

postdissolutional relationship
The relationship formed between dating partners after their romance terminates.

Tensions in Relationships: The Dialectical Perspective

8.4   Discuss relational dialectics and three primary tensions in relationships.

Relationships are living, breathing, evolving, dynamic entities; no two are the same. One way to view relationships is through **relational dialectics** or the dialectical perspective.[53] Developed by communication scholars Leslie Baxter and Barbara Montgomery, dialectics help us understand the messy, often illogical nature of interpersonal relationships. The theory describes tensions people in relationships commonly face, but by *tensions*, we don't mean to imply something negative. A dialectical perspective suggests that relationship issues are better understood in terms of push–pull dynamics.[54] Although tensions can occur in all sorts of relationships—among family members, between coworkers, within friendships—they're arguably most revealing in romantic relationships.

relational dialectics
A perspective that views interpersonal relationships as dynamic and constantly evolving, as they revolve around how relational partners manage tensions.

Researchers have identified multiple tensions. We focus on three primary issues that most relational partners face:

- **Integration–Separation: Autonomy Versus Connection.** Although people want to be connected to others and feel like they're part of a couple or group, they also want to be self-sufficient and independent. The amount of autonomy partners desire varies widely, making this tension one of the most difficult to confront. Early on, relational partners tend to spend as much time together as possible. However, when a time-consuming activity or work intrudes, friends or family members demand some time, or one partner wants a night out without the other, an autonomy-versus-connection conflict can arise.[55] Partners can benefit from honest, open, and nondefensive communication about this tension. It's also best if they can proactively negotiate how much time they expect (and want) to spend together and apart. Even the amount of desired phone calling or texting may need to be negotiated between partners, as research shows that overuse of mobile phones between partners can heighten this tension.[56]

▲ As the novelty wears off in relationships, we may find that we are bored with the predictability of our partner. How can you balance stability and change in your own relationships?
Rido/Shutterstock

- **Stability–Change: Predictability Versus Novelty.** Although people are drawn to stability and consistency in a relationship, we're also drawn to excitement and unpredictability. Becoming comfortable with a relationship's ebb and flow can be a challenge.[57] Typically, at the start of a relationship, people emphasize a partner's positive points and gloss over less-desirable personality traits or behaviors. Over time, however, people may have more difficulty accepting each other as they are; one partner may try to change the other. Being aware that this tension is likely to emerge at some point—or several points—within a relationship is key, because too many attempts to persuade or influence a partner often leads to less satisfaction with the relationship.

- **Expression–Privacy: Openness Versus Closedness.** We all differ in how open we wish to be (or are comfortable being) and our need for privacy. If relational partners are dramatically different in this area, they'll need to be proactive and work hard to manage this tension, or it might be a deal breaker. Couples, friends, even family members may feel a push–pull, with one person in the relationship wanting complete openness and equating openness with trust while the other wants to retain a degree of privacy and connects privacy with individual identity.[58] One topic in particular illustrates this tension: the discussion of past relationships, especially sexual ones, between romantic relational partners. One partner may want to reveal all and know all, whereas the other may not wish to bring the past into the present.[59] Both positions—and all points in between—are legitimate, but differences in partners' views about openness and privacy can create a tension that typically has to be addressed for a relationship of any kind to flourish.

Managing Interpersonal Conflict

8.5 **Summarize the seven types of interpersonal conflict, the key characteristics of conflict management, and the ways in which people can cooperate in conflict situations.**

We live in a world full of conflict. Whether it's a political coup in a foreign country or a disturbance generated by extremist groups right here at home, conflict seems inevitable. Although conflicts have always existed throughout the world, developing an understanding of conflict and effective communication skills to manage it begins one on one, in our day-to-day relationships. Conflict is rooted in interpersonal communication.

interpersonal conflict

A struggle that occurs when people cannot agree on a way to meet their needs.

Interpersonal conflict is a struggle that occurs when people cannot agree on a way to meet their needs. If needs or goals are incompatible, if there are too few resources to satisfy them, or if individuals opt to compete rather than to cooperate to satisfy them, conflict occurs. The bedrock of conflict is differences—different goals, experiences, expectations, and so forth.[60] Before we explore how to better manage and resolve conflict, let's first examine the nature of conflict and how it functions in interpersonal relationships.

Constructive Versus Destructive Conflict

constructive conflict

Conflict characterized by cooperation in dealing with differences; helps build new insights and patterns in a relationship.

Although we usually think of conflict in its most negative, destructive sense, conflict can be constructive in a relationship.[61] To construct something is to build or make something new. When you engage in **constructive conflict**, you cooperate to deal with differences. This process can help identify which elements of a relationship need to change or be improved so that new patterns are established. Here's an example:

Jake: You know, I'm getting tired of always going to your parents' house on Sundays. It's like we're in a rut or something. Just one weekend, I'd like to have a Sunday with no schedule or agenda.

Julie: Jake, I thought you liked going over there, because my mom's such a good cook and you and dad are working on that project together. Plus, it's one of the few times I get to spend time with my folks.

Jake: Well, I do like going over there, but not every weekend.

Julie: I didn't realize you were starting to resent it or feel like we were in a rut. Let's figure something out.

Notice that Julie transforms the issue of disagreement into a topic for discussion and relational adjustment. If Jake hadn't expressed his dissatisfaction, the issue might have taken on larger proportions. He might have expressed his feelings of being in a rut in a more hurtful way later on. A well-managed disagreement that includes expressing one's own needs or revising goals can lead people to examine and then revitalize their relationship. Constructive conflict enables both people to view a disagreement from different perspectives, even if the information shared seems negative at first.

A rapidly spiraling **destructive conflict** can do a great deal of damage. A conflict that starts over a seemingly small issue can increase in intensity as other issues and differences are brought into the discussion. Such destructive escalation blocks options for managing differences and makes a win–win solution more elusive. The primary characteristic of destructive conflict is a lack of flexibility in responding to others.[62] Combatants view their differences from a win–lose perspective rather than looking for solutions that allow each individual to benefit. This form of conflict dismantles relationships without restoring them. If both individuals are dissatisfied with the outcome of the conflict, it's been more destructive than constructive.

William Wilmot and Joyce Hocker are authorities on communication and conflict. Below are their six hallmarks of constructive conflict:[63]

destructive conflict
Conflict characterized by a lack of cooperation in dealing with differences; dismantles relationships without restoring them.

1. *People change.* In relationships, people are involved with each other. In conflict, people must work hard to *stay* involved with each other, because an interaction that escalates into conflict can pull people apart. Flexibility and a willingness to change are key.

2. *People interact with an intent to learn instead of an intent to protect themselves.* You can learn a great deal about yourself, your partner, and your relationship if you approach conflict as a learning experience—one that will take your relationship forward instead of allowing it to stagnate or regress. Protecting yourself against conflict doesn't help a relationship grow.

3. *People don't stay stuck in conflict when the conflict is constructive.* Destructive conflict can make you feel stuck in one place in a relationship. Constructive conflict is a dynamic process that emerges, plays out, and recedes.

4. *Constructive conflict enhances self-esteem in the participants.* You probably don't associate conflict with enhanced self-esteem. However, constructive conflict brings energy and productivity to a relationship and provides partners with a more honest, complete picture of themselves.

5. *Constructive conflicts are characterized by a relationship focus instead of a purely individualistic focus.* If parties in a conflict focus on the relationship instead of themselves, the conflict will more likely be constructive than destructive. Participants should emphasize the "we" over the "I" so that conflict is seen as an experience that builds the relationship.

6. *Constructive conflict is primarily cooperative.* Conflict built on competition, power struggles, and self-interest will destroy a relationship. Conversely, a cooperative, win–win approach to conflict will open the door for greater growth.

Types of Conflict

Communication scholars Gerald Miller and Mark Steinberg have identified three types of conflict:[64]

pseudoconflict

Conflict stemming from a lack of understanding.

simple conflict

Conflict over differences in ideas, definitions, perceptions, or goals.

ego conflict

Conflict based on personal issues in which people attack each other's self-esteem.

- **Pseudoconflict** reflects a basic lack of understanding; one person misunderstands the meaning in a message.
- **Simple conflict** stems from differences in ideas, definitions, perceptions, or goals.
- **Ego conflict** occurs when conflict gets personal, such that people attack each other's self-esteem.

Let's use an example to help distinguish these types. Two people start out with a simple misunderstanding about the time they were supposed to meet (pseudoconflict). If the misunderstanding escalates, they might argue over their varying perceptions of what being "on time" means (simple conflict), especially if they come from different cultural backgrounds. If the disagreement degenerates and becomes personal, such as one person accusing the other of something deeper than mere misunderstanding (as in "You did this on purpose" or "You're *always* late"), an ego conflict has erupted out of a simple conflict.

serial arguments

Argumentative episodes focused on the same issue that occur at least twice.

Two other types of conflict are worthy of note. First, people in ongoing relationships often have **serial arguments**, defined as "argumentative episodes focused on a given issue that occur at least twice."[65] How many times have you heard someone complain, "We have this same argument over and over"? Serial arguments typically involve repetitious, highly negative verbal communication (such as name calling) and negative nonverbal cues (yelling or aggressive movements). They usually spiral and are rarely productive. They engender mutual hostility in the partners and create a pattern that's very hard to break. Over time, unchecked serial arguments have an adverse effect on relationships and can erode self-esteem.

irresolvable (intractable) conflict

A conflict that one or both parties deem impossible to resolve.

Another form of conflict within interpersonal relationships is the **irresolvable or intractable conflict**, which occurs when one or both parties deem the conflict impossible to resolve.[66] A person who believes that an argument is irresolvable may not necessarily state that view out in the open, choosing simply to believe that compromise is impossible. She or he may adopt a "go along to get along" approach to appease the other person, or tolerate the situation rather than confronting the person and attempting to resolve it.

Properties of Conflict

interpersonal power

The ability to influence another in the direction one desires; getting another person to do what one wants.

It's surprising (and disconcerting) when people in relationships say, "We just get along so well. We belong together because we've never even had a fight." Conflict is a normal, inevitable element of relationships. Although we don't advocate staging or picking a fight with a partner as an experiment, we do believe that it's worrisome to commit to a person when you don't know how she or he handles conflict. If your partner or close friend is a screamer and you prefer to walk away from a conflict in silent protest, your relationship is headed for very rough waters. One of the best ways to improve a relationship is to understand conflict—how it functions; how each person in a relationship approaches, processes, and responds to conflict; and how we can better manage conflict when it inevitably arises.[67]

Conflict Involves Power One of the most significant elements in interpersonal relationships is power.[68] We might not realize it, but distributing power between partners requires a lot of subtle negotiation. Without this negotiation, conflict can become rampant. Power has been defined in a variety of ways, but for our purposes, **interpersonal power** means the ability to influence another in the direction we desire—to get another person to do what we want.[69] It also involves the ability to resist others'

Speed Bump

I DON'T FEEL LIKE HAVING THIS ARGUMENT AGAIN, TOM. STANDING IN FOR ME TONIGHT WILL BE SARA, MY UNDERSTUDY.

COMMUNICATION & DIVERSITY

Coping with Conflict across Cultures

Interpersonal conflict is difficult to manage, but cross-cultural conflict can be overwhelming. Some people are trained in negotiation and mediation techniques so that they can facilitate peaceful relations between nations and peoples. But what if you're not planning to become an international negotiator? What if you simply want to know a few things to keep from being tossed in jail in a foreign country?

Intercultural communication scholars have written extensively on this subject and have produced some insightful information that can help you anticipate and avoid intercultural conflict.[70] People from individualistic cultures, such as the United States, emphasize the importance of the individual over the group. Those in collectivistic cultures, such as the Japanese, emphasize group rather than individual achievement. These differing values contribute to intercultural conflict.

Below are seven assumptions about conflict that individualistic cultures hold and seven assumptions about conflict that collectivistic cultures hold. Compare the lists and assess the differences. Members of different cultural groups not only have different views of conflict, but also have different ways of dealing with or managing conflict. Research any countries you'll be visiting or moving to so that you understand how the basic cultural values differ from those of your home country.

Individualistic Cultures	Collectivistic Cultures
1. The purpose of conflict is to air major differences and problems.	1. Conflict is damaging to self-respect and relational harmony; it should be avoided as much as possible.
2. Conflict can be either functional or dysfunctional.	2. For the most part, conflict is dysfunctional.
3. Repressed, unconfronted problems can lead to dysfunctional conflict.	3. Conflict signals emotional immaturity and a lack of self-discipline.
4. Functional conflict provides an opportunity for solving problems.	4. Conflict provides a testing ground for skillful negotiation and face-saving.
5. Substantive or informational issues should be handled separately from relational issues.	5. Substantive and relational issues are always intertwined.
6. Conflict should be handled directly and openly.	6. Conflict should be handled discreetly and subtly.
7. Effective conflict management should be a problem-solving activity with a win–win outcome.	7. Effective conflict management should be a face-saving negotiation game with a win–win outcome.

influences on us.[71] Perhaps it's easier to think of it in terms of who has more *control* in a relationship rather than using the term *power*.

Most interactions, including conflicts, involve some level of power or control. If you ask a friend to go to a movie with you, you are attempting to influence him or her. If the answer is no, your friend is mustering resistance and demonstrating power over you. If you don't like the negative response, you might attempt to assert control once more, perhaps by offering to buy your friend's ticket or to drive.

Conflict May Involve Assertive or Aggressive Communication   Sometimes our emotions cause us to communicate aggressively when assertive communication would be preferable. You may think of assertive and aggressive communication as being the same thing, but they're actually different. **Assertive communication** takes the other person's feelings and rights into account; **aggressive communication** doesn't. Let's say you experience a mix-up with a close friend over plans for the weekend. You get your signals crossed and don't end up getting together. When you next see your friend, you have the choice of expressing your frustration over the situation in a passive, assertive, or aggressive manner. You could be passive and say nothing, which some people choose to do even when they've been wronged, a phenomenon known as self-silencing.[72] The passive approach tends merely to internalize frustration, which may build into rage that erupts later.

Another option is to take a self-oriented approach and blow up at your friend in an aggressive way that doesn't take into account your friend's rights. Unfortunately,

assertive communication
Communication that takes a listener's feelings and rights into account.

aggressive communication
Self-serving communication that does not take a listener's feelings and rights into account.

this is the tactic of choice for some people, especially if they have a great deal of anxiety and feel justified taking out their frustrations on others. An aggressive approach rarely achieves one's objectives.

Clearly, an assertive approach to conflict is best—for ourselves and for the people we interact with. It's important to assert yourself and express your perception of a problem to the person who can best correct or clear it up, rather than blowing off steam to an innocent bystander or third party. Communicating assertively means that you explain your concerns or cause for disagreement in a direct and firm manner, staying in control of your emotions but not allowing yourself to be bullied or discounted, while also taking your receiver's rights into account.[73]

An assertive response to the mix-up with your friend might be something like this: "Hey, we were supposed to get together last weekend, but you never called. What happened?" In this statement, you express your perception of the situation, but you ask the other person for her or his perception, rather than aggressively saying something in an angry tone that would make the other person defensive, such as "Why did you leave me hanging when we made plans?" If the person offers a weak excuse, an assertive follow-up might be "Well, I just want you to know that I don't like what happened. I hope it doesn't happen again." If you communicate in this manner, you're far more likely to reach a positive resolution to any conflicts than if you behave passively or aggressively.[74]

Styles of Managing Conflict

Scholars in communication and other academic disciplines like to talk about conflict in terms of *management*, meaning that interpersonal communication can help people work through and resolve conflict so that something positive results.[75] What's your approach to managing interpersonal conflict: fight or flight? Do you tackle conflict head-on or seek ways to remove yourself from it? Most of us don't have a single way of dealing with disagreements, but we do have a tendency to manage conflict by following patterns we learned early in life and have used before.[76]

Researchers have attempted to identify different styles of conflict management. One widely accepted approach organizes conflict styles into three types: (1) nonconfrontational, (2) confrontational or controlling, and (3) cooperative (also known as a *solution orientation*).[77]

Nonconfrontational Style   One conflict management style is to avoid conflict altogether, becoming aloof or giving in to the other person before or when a conflict emerges, which can have a chilling or silencing effect on a relationship.[78] Research shows that when conflict arises during problem-solving discussions, people who exhibit a **nonconfrontational style** are perceived as incompetent.[79] This dynamic often creates a lose–lose situation, where neither party feels the issue has been effectively addressed; instead, it has perhaps merely been postponed.

Confrontational Style   Each of us has some need to control others, but some people always want to dominate and make sure their objectives are achieved. In managing conflict, people with a **confrontational style** have a win–lose philosophy. They want to win at the expense of others, claim victory over their opponents, and control people and situations. They focus on themselves and usually ignore the needs of others. Confronters often resort to blaming or seeking a scapegoat rather than assuming responsibility for a conflict. For example, a confronter may claim, "I didn't do it," "Don't look at me," or "It's not my fault." If this strategy doesn't work, confronters may try hostile name calling, personal attacks, or threats.

nonconfrontational style

A conflict management style that involves backing off, avoiding conflict, or giving in to the other person.

confrontational style

A win–lose approach to conflict management in which one person wants control and to win at the expense of the other.

▼ People with a confrontational or win–lose approach to conflict may spend more effort trying to assign or avoid the blame for a problem than solving it.
Comstock/Stockbyte/Getty Images

Cooperative Style   Those who have a **cooperative style** of conflict management view conflict as a set of problems to be solved rather than as a competition in which one person wins and another loses. They work to foster a win–win climate by using the following techniques:[80]

- *Separate the people from the problem.* Leave personal grievances out of the discussion. Describe problems without making judgmental statements about personalities.

- *Focus on shared interests.* Emphasize common interests, values, and goals by asking such questions as, "What do we both want?" "What do we both value?" and "Where do we already agree?"

- *Generate many options to solve the problem.* Use brainstorming and other techniques to generate a range of solutions.

- *Base decisions on objective criteria.* Try to establish standards for an acceptable solution to a problem. These standards may involve costs, timing, effort, and other factors.

cooperative style

A conflict management style in which conflict is viewed as a set of problems to be solved rather than as a competition in which one person wins and another loses.

Conflict Management Skills

As we saw in the previous section, nonconfrontational and confrontational styles of conflict management don't solve problems effectively, nor do they foster healthy relationships. Managing conflict, especially emotionally charged conflict, isn't easy. Even with a fully developed set of skills, you shouldn't expect to melt tensions and resolve disagreements instantaneously. However, the following skills that we touched on in our discussion of the cooperative style can help you generate options that promote understanding and provide a framework for cooperation.[81]

RECAP

Conflict Management Styles

Nonconfrontational	A person avoids conflict and may become aloof or give in to another person just to stave off a conflict. This approach can be viewed as a lose–lose framework because issues aren't dealt with and conflict is likely to recur.
Confrontational	A person wants to manipulate others by blaming and making threats. This approach sets up a win–lose framework.
Cooperative	A person seeks mutually agreeable resolutions to manage differences and works within a win–win framework. This cooperative approach does the following: • Separates people from problems. • Focuses on shared interests. • Generates many options to solve problems. • Bases decisions on objective criteria.

Manage Emotions   Suppose you've been working for weeks on a group project for an important class. The project has a firm deadline that your professor will no doubt enforce. You submitted your portion of the project to your group members two weeks ago. Today you check in with the group and discover that very little has been done since you completed your portion. Your grade is on the line; you feel angry and frustrated. How should you respond? Maybe you're tempted to scream at your classmates. Maybe you decide to go to the professor and complain. Here's our best advice at a moment like this: Try to avoid taking action when you're in an emotional state.[82] You may regret what you say, and you'll probably escalate the situation into a heated conflict, making things worse.

The first sign that we're in a conflict situation may be a combination of anger, frustration, and fear that sweeps over us. In actuality, anger often isn't the predominant emotion generated by conflict. Many of us are unprepared for the aching, lonely, sad, and forlorn feelings that can emerge in conflict.[83] As tall an order as it is, it's important to try to understand the other person's feelings and take the emotion of the situation seriously.[84] Here are some specific strategies you can draw on when an intense emotional response to conflict clouds your judgment and decision-making skills:[85]

- *Select a mutually acceptable time and place to discuss a conflict.* If you're upset or tired (or really hungry), you're at risk for an emotion-charged confrontation. If you ambush someone with an angry attack, you can't expect that person to be in a productive frame of mind. Give yourself time to cool off, rest, or have a meal before you try to resolve a conflict. In the case of the group project, you could call a meeting for later in the week. Take the intervening time to gain control of your feelings and think things through.

- *Plan your message.* If you approach someone to discuss a disagreement, take care to organize your message, perhaps even on paper. Identify your goal and determine what outcome you would like; don't barge in unprepared and dump your emotions on others.

- *Monitor nonverbal messages.* Nonverbal communication plays a key role in managing an emotional climate. Monitor your own and others' nonverbal cues to defuse an emotionally charged situation. Speak evenly, use direct eye contact, and maintain a calm facial expression and body position to signal that you wish to collaborate rather than control. Try to interact on the same physical plane as others. For example, it's unwise to tower over people (standing when others are sitting) because such a power move can exacerbate conflict.

- *Avoid personal attacks, name calling, profanity, and emotional overstatement.* Threats and bad language can turn a minor conflict into an all-out war. When people feel attacked, they usually respond defensively. Avoid exaggerating your emotions. If you say you're *irritated* or *annoyed* rather than *furious,* you can still communicate your feelings, but you'll take the sting out of your description.

- *Use self-talk.* Instead of lashing out at someone, the better tactic is to pause, take a slow deep breath, and talk yourself down off your emotional ledge. You may think that talking to yourself is an eccentricity, but thoughts are directly linked to feelings. The messages we tell ourselves play a major role in how we feel and respond to others.[86]

Manage Information Because uncertainty, misinformation, and misunderstanding are often by-products of conflict and disagreement, skills that promote mutual understanding are important components of cooperative conflict management. The following skills help enhance the quality of communication during conflict:

- *Clearly describe the conflict-producing events.* Instead of blurting out complaints in a random order, try to deliver a brief, well-organized, chronological presentation. In the case of our group project example, you could offer your perspective on what created the conflict, sequencing the events and describing them dispassionately so that your fellow group members end up sharing your understanding of the problem.

- *"Own" your statements by using descriptive "I" language.* Use "I" language instead of "you" language to create a supportive climate. "I feel upset when it seems as if little is getting done and we're running the risk of not making our deadline" is an example of an "I" statement you could make to your group members. The statement describes your feelings as your own and keeps the issue manageable.

- *Use effective listening skills.* Managing information is a two-way process. Whether you're describing a conflict situation to someone or that individual is bringing a conflict to your attention, good listening skills are invaluable. Give your full attention to other speakers so that you can fully understand their perspectives, and then respond appropriately.

- *Check your understanding of what others say and do.* Checking perceptions is vital when emotions run high. If you're genuinely unsure about facts, issues, or major ideas addressed during a conflict, ask questions instead of barreling ahead with solutions. Then summarize your understanding of the information, checking key points to make sure that you comprehend the message.

Manage Goals Conflict is goal-driven; people involved in an interpersonal conflict want something, and for some reason—competitiveness, scarce resources, or a lack of understanding—their goals appear to be in conflict. To manage conflict, here are some techniques that will help you seek an accurate understanding of everyone's goals and identify where they overlap:

- *Identify everyone's goals.* Most goals can be phrased in terms of wants or desired outcomes. In the group project example, suppose you express your goal of turning the project in on time to your fellow group members. Next, it's useful to identify the goals of other people involved in the conflict. Use effective describing, listening, and responding skills to determine what each conflict partner wants. Obviously, if goals are kept hidden, it will be difficult to resolve the conflict.

- *Identify where your goals and everyone else's goals overlap.* Authorities on conflict negotiation stress the importance of focusing on shared goals in seeking to manage differences.[87] Suppose that after you explain your goal about the project deadline, another group member states that her or his goal is to make the project the best it can possibly be. These goals may be compatible, so you've identified a commonality that can help unify the group rather than keeping it splintered. But what if the goal of making the project the best it can be means that your group will have to ask the professor for an extension on the deadline? Now you may have competing goals, but at least you've identified a central part of the problem. Framing the problem as "How can we achieve our mutual goal?" rather than arguing over differences of opinion moves the discussion to a more productive level.

Manage the Problem   If you can view conflicts as problems to be solved rather than battles to be won or lost, you'll better manage the issues that confront you in your relationships. Of course, not all conflicts can be easily managed and resolved. But a rational, logical approach to conflict management is more effective than emotionally flinging accusations and opinions at someone. Structuring a disagreement as a problem to solve helps manage emotions that often erupt while also keeping the conversation focused on issues rather than personalities. As you apply a problem-solving approach to managing conflict, consider the following suggestions:

- *Define the problem before trying to solve it.* When a problem needs to be solved, we typically want to head directly for solutions. Resist that temptation, and make sure everyone fully understands the problem at hand before trying to fix it.

- *Think of lots of possible solutions.* The more possible solutions you identify and consider, the greater the likelihood that conflict will be managed successfully. If you're just batting around one or two solutions, you're limiting your options in managing the conflict.

- *Systematically discuss together the pros and the cons of each possible solution, arriving at the best decision.* After you have a list of possible solutions, honestly identify advantages and disadvantages of each solution. Determine which solution or combination of solutions best achieves the goals you and your feuding partners are trying to accomplish.

▼ When communicating to resolve a conflict, try to "own" your communication by using "I" language rather than accusatory "you" language.
Jack Hollingsworth/Photodisc/Getty Images

STUDY GUIDE:

〉 REVIEW, APPLY, AND ASSESS

The Importance of Relationships: Friends, Family, and Colleagues

8.1 Explain how the five Communication Principles for a Lifetime apply to interpersonal communication among friends, family members, and colleagues.

REVIEW: Relationships of all types are important in our lives, but those with friends, family, and colleagues are most critical to our overall enjoyment. The five Communication Principles for a Lifetime can be applied to each form of relationship and can improve how we communicate interpersonally with others.

APPLY: How have your friendships changed since you were younger? How do you expect your long-term friendships to develop as you get older? Has one of your ? relationships, like with a sibling, turned into a friendshi ? as you've both gotten older?

ASSESS: Draw five concentric circles on a blank sheet of paper. (Concentric circles are circles within circles.) Write the word "me" in the center circle, representing the core of the model. Then think about all of your relationships— family members, friends, coworkers, acquaintances, bosses, etc. Place ten of these relationships at various spots on the circles. The people closest to you, in terms of intimacy or trustworthiness, get placed on the inner ring; others are placed farther out, depending on how close you perceive you are to those people. Finally, analyze the placements of different people; if you want someone to move closer in to the center (to *you*), what kind of communication is required to make that change?

Stages of Relationship Development

8.2 Identify and describe the stages of relational escalation and de-escalation.

REVIEW: Research has determined that relationships, particularly intimate or romantic ones, tend to develop in stages of escalation and de-escalation. Interpersonal communication is affected by the stage of a relationship; in turn, movement through the stages is facilitated by interpersonal communication. The five stages of relational escalation are (1) pre-interaction awareness, (2) initiation, (3) exploration, (4) intensification, and (5) intimacy. The five stages of relational de-escalation are

(1) turmoil-stagnation, (2) de-intensification, (3) individualization, (4) separation, and (5) post-interaction.

KEY TERMS:
pre-interaction awareness stage	de-intensification stage
initiation stage	individualization stage
exploration stage	
intensification stage	separation stage
intimacy stage	cyber infidelity
turmoil or stagnation	post-interaction stage

... with the description of relational escalation of the Chapter match for

ASSESS
tionship Stages model that depicts escalation). Assess a relationship using this model; it can be a friendship, intimate relationship, coworker, or so forth. Are both of you on the same level? Is the relationship escalating, stabilizing (meaning no movement upward or downward), or de-escalating? Are some communication changes necessary in the relationship?

Relationship Dissolution (a.k.a. the Breakup)

8.3 Summarize research findings on relationship dissolution, including communication in the on-again/off-again relationship and the postdissolutional relationship.

REVIEW: Not all relationships last, so communication skills are important when a romantic relationship, friendship, or other form of connection ends. Research shows that most people use and prefer a face-to-face channel of communication when being on both the sending and receiving end of relationship dissolution.

KEY TERMS:
relationship dissolution
on-again/off-again relationship
postdissolutional relationship

APPLY: Imagine one of your friends wants to break up with a romantic partner. Using the advice in this chapter, what suggestions would you give your friend for accomplishing the breakup ethically and with as little pain as possible for both parties?

ASSESS: Think of three relationships in your past that have either faded away or ended abruptly. Consider childhood friends, neighbors, classmates, family members, or coworkers. Did these relationship endings involve some form of communication or did life circumstances change the status of these relationships?

Tensions in Relationships: The Dialectical Perspective

8.4 Discuss relational dialectics and three primary tensions in relationships.

REVIEW: One approach to studying interpersonal communication in relationships is the relational dialectics perspective, which examines sets of tensions that emerge in ongoing relationships, especially romantic or intimate ones. Three tensions are particularly critical:

- Integration–separation: autonomy versus connection
- Stability–change: predictab̶i̶l̶i̶t̶y̶

  ̶p̶r̶i̶v̶a̶c̶y̶: openness versus closedness

KEY TERM:
relational dialectics

APPLY: Which of the three tensions described in this chapter have you experienced in your friendships or romantic relationships? How did you resolve the tension, if you have? If you haven't resolved the tension, how are you managing the relationship?

ASSESS: The three relationship tensions described in this chapter are listed as headings below. In the first column, write the name of someone you're currently in a relationship with—it can be a friendship, romantic relationship, family member, etc. Then assess on a 1-to-5 scale (1 = barely applies to us; 5 = always applies to us) how much your relationship reflects each tension. For example, if you write down the name of your best friend, is your handling of the Autonomy vs. Connection tension at a level 1 (we have no tension regarding time spent together versus apart), 2 (occasional tension), or all the way up to a 5 (constant tension)?

Person	Autonomy vs. Connection	Stability vs. Change	Expression vs. Privacy

Managing Interpersonal Conflict

8.5 Summarize the seven types of interpersonal conflict, the key characteristics of conflict management, and the ways in which people can cooperate in conflict situations.

REVIEW: Interpersonal conflict occurs when people cannot agree on a way to meet their needs. Conflict can be constructive or destructive, and it occurs in multiple forms: pseudoconflict, simple conflict, ego conflict, serial arguments, and irresolvable (intractable) conflict. Conflict involves power, which may manifest itself in assertive or aggressive communication. Research has revealed three general styles of managing conflict: nonconfrontational, confrontational, and cooperative. In managing conflict, it's important to manage your emotions, the information surrounding the dispute at hand, competing goals, and the problem itself rather than the people involved.

KEY TERMS:

interpersonal conflict	interpersonal power
constructive conflict	assertive
destructive conflict	communication
pseudoconflict	aggressive
simple conflict	communication
ego conflict	nonconfrontational style
serial arguments	confrontational style
irresolvable (intractable) conflict	cooperative style

APPLY: Have you experienced or witnessed a serial argument or intractable conflict in a relationship? What was the problem? How did the parties respond?

ASSESS:

1. Am I an Aggressive or an Assertive Communicator? Sometimes it's hard to discern the difference between assertive and aggressive communication. To gain some practice, consider the following situations. For each one, first generate aggressive and inappropriate communication. Then rethink the situation and generate an assertive form of communication that would be more effective. We've provided an example to get you started.

Sample Situation: You're expecting a raise at work but find out that a coworker, who has less time on the job than you, received a raise and you didn't.

Aggressive Communication: You interrupt a staff meeting that your boss is holding, storm about the room, and demand an explanation of why you didn't receive the expected raise.

Assertive Communication: You make an appointment with your boss for a meeting. At the meeting, you calmly ask the boss to assess your value to the company, leading up to the question of why you didn't receive the expected raise.

Situation: Two people have been in a monogamous dating relationship for several months when one partner finds out that the other person has cheated.

Situation: A student receives a disappointing grade on a paper. After reading the papers of a few other classmates and finding that poorer-quality papers received higher grades, the student decides to confront the teacher about the grade.

2. What's My Style? In intimate relationships, in which a great deal is on the line, knowing how you usually tend to handle conflict, as well as how your partner handles it, can save you some major heartbreak. Below, we give you a sample situation along with examples of nonconfrontational, confrontational, and cooperative responses. Supply responses reflecting these three conflict management styles for the other two hypothetical conflict situations. (If you're really brave, pose these same situations to your relational partner and compare your responses to hers or his. That exercise could lead to a constructive, proactive discussion about how to handle conflict in your relationship.)

Conflict Situation 1: Your roommate is *wild,* partying every night, coming home late, and disrupting your study time and your sleep. This behavior is starting to affect your ability to get your schoolwork done and concentrate on your studies. You're not a fuddy-duddy, but you're not a nightly partier either. How do you communicate in response to this conflict situation?

> *Nonconfrontational Response:* Ignore it. It's not my problem; it's my roommate's life to live as he (she) pleases. I would rather have more quiet time, but if I bring up my objections, the situation will escalate and get worse, and I'll regret mentioning anything in the first place.
>
> *Confrontational Response:* I have rights; I live in this place and pay my fair share of the rent, so I should be

able to have some peace and quiet so at least one of us doesn't flunk out of college. When my roommate comes home, I'm going to lay down the law on the late-night partying. If the problem persists, I'll threaten to move out.

> *Cooperative Response:* My roommate and I both have rights because we both live in this apartment. When my roommate is sober and alone here at the apartment, not partying with a group of friends, I'll bring up the problem and ask for solutions we can both live with. I want to respect my friend's right to enjoy life, but I want to set limits so my goals can also be reached.

Conflict Situation 2: You work part time at a restaurant near campus. Thus far, the managers have been flexible and understanding about your class schedule and commitments at the university, but now—just when you've got three exams and two papers coming up—they decide to load you up with extra hours. You need this job and want to keep it, so how do you communicate to address the conflict between what you can do and what management wants you to do?

> *Nonconfrontational Response.*
>
> *Confrontational Response:*
>
> *Cooperative Response:*

Conflict Situation 3: You've been dating someone fairly steadily for a few months but have recently developed a romantic interest in a classmate. You'd like to keep dating your current relational partner but renegotiate your relationship so that you can start hanging out with other people, such as the attractive classmate. How do you communicate to manage this situation?

> *Nonconfrontational Response:*
>
> *Confrontational Response:*
>
> *Cooperative Response:*

〉 THE PRINCIPLE POINTS

Principle One:

Be aware of your communication with yourself and others.

- Know your own interests, likes, and dislikes as you expand your circle of friends.
- Awareness and an understanding of self begin in your family.
- Perception checking with colleagues increases your awareness of yourself and your workplace.
- The first stage of relational escalation, the pre-interaction awareness stage, begins with an awareness of the self and the other person you're interested in.

- Be aware that relationships continue to affect o⸺ ⸺ even after they end.
- It's important to know your conflict managemer⸺ ⸺ly if your style differs from that of other conflict partners.
- Self-talk is appropriate in conflict because it can he⸺ ⸺ur emotions and think clearly.
- Check your perceptions of a conflict with trusted ot⸺
- Be aware of your own and others' goals in conflict sit⸺

Principle Two:

Effectively use and interpret verbal messages.

- Language patterns learned as children stay with us into adult⸺
- People in advanced stages of relationships tend to use verbal co⸺ ⸺ss topics that typically aren't discussed in early stages.
- When a relationship terminates or dissolves, most people prefer a ⸺ rather than mediated breakup messages or having the relationship simpl⸺
- Relational partners should use effective verbal communication to wo⸺ ⸺ctics or tensions in a relationship.
- Assertive communication takes a receiver's rights into account; aggres⸺ ⸺on doesn't.
- Managing the verbal expression of your emotions in conflict situations⸺
- Plan your message carefully in a conflict situation.
- Avoid personal attacks, name calling, profanity, and emotional overstatements in conflict situations.
- Use "I" language instead of "you" language in a conflict so as to lessen defensiveness.

Principle Three:

Effectively use and interpret nonverbal messages.

- Nonverbal immediacy behaviors, such as eye contact and a forward body lean, are important in the maintenance of friendships, family relationships, and workplace relationships.
- People in advanced stages of relationships tend to display nonverbal behaviors that typically aren't in evidence in early stages.
- Nonverbal skills are important in your first conversations with people as you attempt to establish and escalate relationships.
- Nonverbal immediacy cues diminish when a relationship de-escalates and then terminates.
- Monitor and adapt your nonverbal behaviors in conflict situations.
- Monitor the nonverbal cues of conflict partners.

Principle Four:

Listen and respond thoughtfully to others.

- Listening is important in friendships, family relationships, and workplace relationships.
- Listening and responding appropriately are key skills that potential employers value.
- Destructive conflict is characterized by a lack of listening.
- Conflict often escalates because the parties don't listen to one another; continue to listen, even if you feel yourself becoming emotional in the conflict.

Principle Five:

Appropriately adapt messages to others.

- It's important to learn to adapt our communication in friendships, family relationships, and workplace relationships.

- Adaptation is critical for couples who face relational tensions.

- Both the on-again/off-again relationship and the push/inpolitional relationship involve a good deal of adaptation in order to be successful.

- In conflict situations, partners often have to adapt to each other and admit they were wrong. Destructive conflict often involves a reluctance to adapt to other people and see the problem from their point of view.

- Be flexible and adapt to other cultures' approaches to conflict. Don't assume that your home culture's approach to conflict management is applicable in conflicts with members of other cultural groups.

- After checking your perceptions of a conflict with trusted others, adapt your communication accordingly.

- One way to adapt in a conflict is to look for overlaps between your goals and the goals of your conflict partners.

CHAPTER

9

UNDERSTANDING GROUP AND TEAM PERFORMANCE

Teamwork is . . . the fuel that allows common people to attain uncommon results.
—ANDREW CARNEGIE

Rawpixel.com/Shutterstock

CHAPTER OUTLINE

LEARNING OBJECTIVES

After studying this chapter, you should be able to

9.1 Describe types of groups and teams, differences between groups and teams, and when participating in groups and teams should be avoided.

9.2 Identify and describe group and team dynamics, including roles, rules, norms, status, power, and cohesiveness.

9.3 Summarize the four stages of group and team development.

Do you like working with others in groups? Although you may be one of those people who relish working on team projects and going to meetings, many people don't like collaborating with others. Here are some typical sentiments people sometimes have about working in groups:

To be effective, a committee should be made up of three people. But to get anything done, one member should be sick and another absent.

A committee is a group of people who individually can do nothing and who collectively decide nothing can be done.

A group task force is a collection of the unfit chosen from the unwilling by the incompetent to do the unnecessary.

Whether you are one of those people who likes group work or one who finds it frustrating and a waste of time, evidence suggests that groups are here to stay. Human beings collaborate.[1] We are raised in groups, educated in groups, and entertained in groups; we worship in groups and work in groups. Today's technology makes it easier for us to collaborate in teams via Facebook and a variety of other technological applications, even when we're not meeting face to face.

There is evidence that you're likely to spend about one-third of your time on the job working in groups or teams and attending meetings or preparing for meetings. Increasingly, those meetings will happen online or via video conferencing.[2] And if you aspire to upper-management leadership positions, you'll spend up to two-thirds of your time in meetings.[3] One study found that more than 80 percent of organizations use teams to accomplish a major portion of the work.[4] Your work will be based on that kindergarten skill called "getting along with others."

To help you with the group and team projects that will inevitably come your way, this chapter offers descriptions of how groups and teams work. In Chapter 10, we'll offer specific strategies for improving group and team performance. As we examine concepts and strategies of group skills and theories, we'll remind you how the core of group communication research can be discussed

▼ We are raised and educated in groups and continue to communicate in groups and teams throughout our lives, so strengthening your group communication skills now will provide lasting benefits. Erik Isakson/Tetra Images/Alamy

in terms of the five principles we've used to frame our presentation of human communication:

1. *Be aware of your communication with yourself and others.* Your awareness of your own behavior and the behavior of other group members is often the first step in understanding why you and other group members behave as you do and adjusting your behavior for improved group performance.

2. *Effectively use and interpret verbal messages.* The verbal messages you and other group members use are pivotal in shaping the roles you assume and how the group accomplishes its work.[5]

3. *Effectively use and interpret nonverbal messages.* The social climate of a group is influenced by the way group members behave nonverbally; eye contact, tone of voice, facial expression, and the use of space and time influence what it feels like to be in a group.

4. *Listen and respond thoughtfully to others.* How group members interact (or don't interact) is directly shaped by group members' skill in listening and responding to what others say and do. One survey found that effective listening was the skill most valued by those who work in groups and teams.[6]

5. *Appropriately adapt messages to others.* The ability to modify messages and adjust to the behavior of others is especially important when communicating with three or more people in a small group.

Groups and Teams Defined

9.1 **Describe types of groups and teams, differences between groups and teams, and when participating in groups and teams should be avoided.**

What makes a group a group? Is a collection of people waiting for an elevator a group? How about students assigned to a class project—do they meet the technical definition of a group? Is there a difference between a group and a team? By exploring these questions, you can better understand what groups and teams do and develop strategies for improving group and team performance.

Communicating in Small Groups

A **small group** consists of three to fifteen people who share a common purpose, feel a sense of belonging to the group, and exert influence on one another.[7] Let's look at this definition more closely.

A Group Consists of a Small Number of People   A small group generally needs at least three people. Two people do not usually exhibit the characteristics of group behavior. A group is not *small* anymore when more than fifteen people meet together. In a larger group, it can become difficult for all members to participate, and a few members often will monopolize the discussion.[8] A large group frequently operates as a collection of subgroups rather than as a single body. Large groups need formal rules, such as parliamentary procedure, to provide structure to manage the group interaction. Without rules, it's unlikely the group will stay focused on the task at hand.

A Group Has a Common Purpose   To be a group, people need to be united by a common goal or purpose. They must all seek the same thing. A collection of people waiting for an elevator may all want to go somewhere, but they probably haven't organized their efforts so that they all are going to the same place. If an instructor assigns you to a class project, you and your classmates do have a common goal: to complete the project and earn a good grade. This class project group would meet our definition of a group.

Groups can be classified according to their purposes into two general categories: primary and secondary. A **primary group** exists to fulfill basic human needs. It's called a primary group because the group meets a primary human need to socialize or just be

small group
Three to fifteen people who share a common purpose, feel a sense of belonging to the group, and exert influence on one another.

primary group
A group, such as a family, that exists to fulfill basic human needs.

social group

A group that exists to provide opportunities for group members to enjoy an activity in the company of others.

secondary group

A group formed to accomplish a specific task or goal.

study group

A group that exists to help its members learn new information and ideas.

therapy group

A group that provides treatment for problems that group members may have.

problem-solving group

A group that meets to seek a solution to a problem and achieve a goal.

focus group

A group that is asked to discuss a particular topic or issue so that others can better understand how the group members respond to the topic or issue presented to them.

virtual group or team

A group or team whose members are not in the same physical location but who are typically connected via some electronic channel.

together. Your family and many **social groups**—groups that provide opportunities for members to enjoy an activity with others—are primary groups.

Secondary groups are more focused on accomplishing a specific task or goal than are primary groups. Secondary groups include:

- **Study groups**, groups that exist to enhance learning;
- **Therapy groups**, groups that provide treatment, or mutual support, including those like Alcoholics Anonymous;
- **Problem-solving groups**, groups that seek to solve a problem by overcoming one or more obstacles to achieve a goal; and
- **Focus groups**, groups of people who are brought together to be interviewed so others can listen and learn from them in order to gather information and opinions.

Group Members Feel a Sense of Belonging   To be a group, the members must realize that they are part of the group. The people waiting for the elevator probably do not feel an obligation to others around them. Group members develop a sense of identity with their group. They know who is in their group and who is not in the group.

Group Members Exert Influence on Others in the Group   When you are in a group, your presence and participation influence other people in the group. Group members are interdependent; what one group member says or does affects other group members. Your comments and even your silence help shape what the group does next. If you meet in person, your nonverbal messages have a powerful effect on personal relationships. Even silence, facial expressions, and eye contact (or lack of it) affect what the group does.

Group Members May Meet Face to Face or Virtually   If you are assigned to work on a class group project, it is likely that you will connect with other group members electronically (such as through instant messaging, email, Facebook, Skype, text, or phone) as much or maybe even more than meeting face to face. You will meet virtually. A **virtual group or team** doesn't meet face to face but is instead connected via some electronic channel. Working as a virtual team has both advantages and disadvantages.[9]

The Advantages of Working in Virtual Teams

- A virtual team can save members travel time and expense.
- Virtual teams can develop the same degree of trust among members as face-to-face groups, especially if the team meets face to face before working virtually.[10]
- In computer-mediated meetings, ideas can be captured easily and recorded quickly and accurately.
- Technology can help structure a group's process and keep the group focused.
- Some team members may feel more comfortable sharing ideas electronically—or even anonymously—than they would in person.

The Disadvantages of Working in Virtual Teams

- Compared to in-person groups, developing trust among virtual group members can take longer.[11]
- When only some members participate virtually, a special effort must be made to integrate long-distance members into the fabric of the team.
- Cultural differences within a virtual group may result in less participation among group members.[12]
- The increased speed of information transfer can allow little time for reflection. Thus, technology may sometimes inadvertently help us make more mistakes, faster.
- When using computer-mediated technology, some group members do not thoroughly evaluate the pros and cons of alternatives.
- The application of technology does not inherently result in better solutions and decisions. Problems are solved and decisions are made by people.[13]

COMMUNICATION & SOCIAL MEDIA

Keep Your Phone Out of Sight

Have you ever been in a meeting and felt tempted to pull out your phone and quickly check your e-mail messages, texts, or Instagram feed? You may want to control that impulse and leave your phone in your pocket. According to a research team's conclusions, using a phone during meetings is perceived as rude.[14] Although you may feel you have a right to sneak a peek at your phone during a meeting, realize that others may take offense. It may give the impression that you are not focused on what the group is doing and prefer to be elsewhere.

A team of researchers found that men and women reacted differently to someone using their phone in a meeting, whether that person was talking on the phone or checking messages. Compared to women, men were almost twice as likely to think it was acceptable to use a phone during a meeting.[15]

If you can't resist pulling out your phone during a meeting, research has found that some behaviors are more offensive than others. Here is a list of the worst phone meeting "sins." At least 50 percent of study respondents found the following behaviors offensive:

- Writing and sending text or email messages
- Making or taking phone calls
- Browsing on the Internet
- Checking to see if you have received a message

About a third of all respondents felt the following behaviors were rude:

- Leaving the meeting to take a call
- Checking for incoming calls
- Glancing at the time[16]

As we noted in Chapter 5, other researchers suggest that simply the presence of a phone during a conversation is distracting. With this in mind, you may want to consider keeping your phone out of sight during face-to-face meetings. Without a phone as a distraction, you may actually be able to pay attention to what's happening in the meeting!

Small group communication is the transactive process of creating meaning among three to fifteen people who share a common purpose, feel a sense of belonging to the group, and exert influence on one another. Regardless of the type of group, communicating in small groups is sometimes a challenge because of the potential for misunderstanding. But don't assume that working in a group will inevitably be a frustrating experience. People accomplish a lot when working together. As anthropologist Margaret Mead said, "Never doubt that a small group of concerned citizens can change the world. Indeed, it's the only thing that ever has." In this chapter and the next, we'll provide concepts and strategies to enhance the quality of your collaborations with others.

small group communication
The transactive process of creating meaning among three to fifteen people who share a common purpose, feel a sense of belonging to the group, and exert influence on each other.

Communicating in Teams

Most of us have participated on a sports team at some time. The goal of a sports team is to win the game or competition. A work team has some of the same characteristics as a sports team.[17] Instead of winning the game, the goal may be to get the contract, build the best mousetrap, or achieve some other objective. A **team** is a coordinated group of people organized to work together to achieve a specific, common goal.[18]

Often the terms *team* and *group* are used interchangeably. Is there a difference? Yes. Given the increased importance teams have in today's workforce, it's important to know precisely how groups and teams are different from each other.[19] Although groups and teams are both made up of a small number of people who work to achieve a goal, teams are often structured deliberately to achieve the goal. Also, teams spend a great deal of time coordinating their efforts to accomplish the goal.[20] Every team is a group, but not every group is highly organized or coordinated enough to meet the definition of a team. Let's consider several specific characteristics of teams.

team
A coordinated group of people organized to work together to achieve a specific common goal.

Teams Develop Clearly Defined Responsibilities for Team Members   On a sports team, most team members have specifically assigned duties, such as shortstop, pitcher, quarterback, or fullback. On a work team, team members' duties and roles are usually explicitly spelled out. Team members may perform more than one function or role, but they nonetheless have well-defined duties.[21]

COMMUNICATION & ETHICS

How Far Would You Go to Achieve a Team Goal?

Without a clear goal, teams falter. But sometimes you may be part of a team whose goal or means of achieving the goal you don't support.

Assume that you're a salesperson and part of a sales team. To get a raise in salary, everyone on the team has to meet the sales goal assigned to the team. To get the sales, one team member doesn't always tell the truth to customers about the company's product. That team member's sales success helps make the whole team look good in terms of sales, but bad in terms of ethics.

What would you do? Would you keep quiet and enjoy the benefits of being part of a "successful" sales team? Or would you bring the unethical behavior of the team member to the attention of your supervisor, even though it would place other team members in jeopardy for knowingly "going along to get along"? The ethical question is: Are team goals more important than individual ethical standards?

Teams Have Clearly Defined Rules for Team Operation   Team members develop explicit rules for how the work should be done. A rule is a followable prescription for acceptable behavior.[22] Just as there are written rules in the game of *Monopoly,* there are usually explicit rules for how a team will function. For example, a team may establish a rule that a member who will be absent from a meeting must tell another team member beforehand. Team members know what the rules are and know how those rules affect the team.

Teams Develop Clear Goals   A third way to characterize a team is to look at the importance and specificity of the team goal.[23] A team goal is usually stated in such a way that the goal can be measured: to win the game, to sell more cornflakes than the competition, or to get to the North Pole before anyone else, for example.

Teams Develop a Way of Coordinating their Efforts   Team members spend time discussing how to accomplish the goals of the team. Their work is coordinated to avoid duplication of effort.[24] A sports team spends considerable time practicing how to work together. Watching a sports team at work is like watching a choreographed dance. Team members have developed a system of working together rather than at cross-purposes. Just as a football team develops a list of the plays to get the ball down the field, a work team develops collaborative strategies to achieve its goal.

Although we have differentiated between groups and teams, don't get the idea that they are completely exclusive entities. Think of groups and teams as existing on a continuum. Some deliberations may more closely follow group behavior, whereas a more coordinated and structured process with clear rules and explicit goals may appear to be more team-like. Because every team is a small group, whenever we refer to a team, we are suggesting that it's a group as well.

When Not to Collaborate in Groups and Teams

Although we've just sung the praises of working in groups and teams, at times

RECAP

Comparing Groups and Teams

	Groups	Teams
Roles and Responsibilities	Individual responsibilities of group members may not always be explicitly defined.	Expectations, roles, and responsibilities of team members are clearly developed and discussed.
Rules	Rules are often not written down or formally developed; rules evolve, depending on the group's needs.	Rules and operating procedures are clearly identified to help the team work efficiently and effectively.
Goals	Group goals may be discussed in general terms.	Clearly spelled-out goals are the focus of what the team does.
Methods	Group members may or may not decide to divide the work among its members.	Team members develop clear methods of collaborating and coordinating their efforts to achieve the team's goals.

one head may be better than two or more. In what situations may it be best *not* to collaborate? The following are four situations in which it is better to work individually rather than collectively:[25]

▼ If conflicts among group members prevent thoughtful discussion, it's probably not a great idea to collaborate. Syda Productions/Fotolia

- *When the group or team has limited time.* Sometimes you may not have time to gather a group together to discuss options; action may be needed immediately. If a very quick decision must be made, for example, in times of extreme crisis or emergency, it may be best to have a leader ready to provide some initial direction.

- *When an expert already has the answer.* If you want to know what tomorrow's weather will be, ask a meteorologist. Don't collaboratively puzzle through questions that can be readily answered by someone else. You don't need a group to hash through the process of finding an answer if an individual can already provide one.

- *When the information is available from other research sources.* Using the power of the Internet, you can find vast amounts of information. Some groups find it useful for individual members to gather information and then meet with the rest of the group to analyze and discuss what they've found. But if you just need information and need it fast, click your mouse or use your smartphone.

- *When the group or team is entrenched in unmanageable conflict.* We don't suggest that you avoid group and team conversations just because they may arouse conflict and disagreement. In fact, it's normal for groups to experience some conflict. But if the conflict is so entrenched that group members can't listen and thoughtfully respond to each other, it may be advisable to take a break from group deliberations. If the conflict is so pervasive that no progress is likely, a more structured conversation, such as mediation or negotiation with a trained facilitator, may be needed to help sort things out.

Group and Team Dynamics

9.2   Identify and describe group and team dynamics, including roles, rules, norms, status, power, and cohesiveness.

Groups and teams are dynamic; their structure changes. The study of group dynamics includes a discussion of the roles, norms, status, power, and cohesiveness of groups. We'll examine each concept and note how it is related to the five Communication Principles for a Lifetime.

Roles

Your **role** is the consistent way you communicate with others in a group. It is based on your expectations of yourself and the expectations others place on you. Do you often become a leader of a group, or are you more comfortable just blending in and taking directions from others? Or are you the one who makes sure the group gets the work done instead of just having a good time? There may also be group members who seem especially gifted at smoothing conflict and disagreement. Research has found that the roles you have assumed in previous groups will likely influence the role you will

role
The consistent way a person communicates with others in a group.

occupy in future groups.[26] But what if there is no pattern to what you typically do in a group? Although you may be influenced by roles you have assumed in the past, your specific role depends on the group dynamics and who else is in the group.

Types of Roles   The following are three classic categories of group roles:

task role

A role that helps a group achieve its goal and accomplish its work.

social role

A role that helps a group manage relationships and affects the group climate.

individual role

A role that focuses attention on the individual rather than on the group.

- **Task roles** are behaviors that help the group achieve its goal and accomplish its work, such as gathering and sharing research conclusions with the group, taking minutes of meetings, and writing ideas on a whiteboard.

- **Social roles** focus on behavior that manages relationships and affects the group climate; these roles help resolve conflict and enhance the flow of communication. Smoothing hurt feelings and helping the group celebrate its accomplishments are examples of social-role behavior.

- **Individual roles** focus attention on the individual rather than on the group. They do not help the group; they emphasize individual accomplishments and issues, not those of the entire group.[27] Dominating group discussions to talk about personal issues or concerns, telling frequent jokes that get the group off track, and constantly complaining or whining about how one's individual needs aren't being met are examples of individual roles.

Leadership Roles   The role of leader, a person who influences others in the group, is a special kind of role, and more than one person can assume it. Some leaders focus on assisting with the team's task and therefore assume more task roles to get the job accomplished. Other leaders assume more social roles to help manage the quality of relationships in the group. Usually, a person who assumes an individual, self-focused role doesn't emerge as a natural leader. Being overly dominant or aggressive or blocking the team's progress may focus attention on an individual, but such self-focused behavior doesn't wear well over time, and people who focus on themselves rather than on the team aren't perceived as effective leaders.

Specific Roles   Helping to develop clear role expectations for you and other team members enhances overall performance.[28] Seventy years ago, group researchers Kenneth Benne and Paul Sheats came up with a list of group roles that remains a classic way of dividing up the roles that group and team members typically assume.[29] As you review the roles and their descriptions, summarized in Table 9.1, note whether you usually assume roles in the task, social, or individual category. Or perhaps you'll see yourself in a variety of roles in all three categories.

TABLE 9.1   A Classification of Group Roles

Task Roles	Description	Example
Initiator/contributor	Offers new ideas or approaches to the group; suggests ways of getting the job done.	"How about developing an agenda to help us organize our work?"
Information seeker	Asks for additional clarification, facts, or other information that helps the group with the issues at hand.	"Can anyone tell me how many times the university has threatened to close the fraternities and sororities on campus because of problems with hazing?"
Opinion seeker	Asks group members to share opinions or express a personal point of view.	"So what do you all think of the new dress code the school board is proposing?"
Information giver	Provides facts, examples, statistics, or other evidence that relates to the task confronting the group.	"Within the past year, the vice president for student affairs has given a special award to three fraternities and one sorority for developing a program to combat underage drinking."
Opinion giver	Offers opinions or beliefs about what the group is discussing.	"I think the new school dress code proposed for first graders is unworkable."
Elaborator	Provides comments or examples to extend or add to the comments of others.	"Tom, that's a good point. I had the same thing happen to me when my children were attending a private school in New York last year."

Task Roles	Description	Example
Coordinator	Clarifies and notes relationships among the ideas and suggestions that have been offered by others.	"Tyrone, your ideas sound a lot like Juanita's suggestion. Juanita, could you elaborate on your idea so that Tyrone can decide whether he agrees or disagrees with you?"
Orienter	Summarizes what has occurred and seeks to keep the group focused on the task at hand.	"I think we're getting a bit off track here. Let's go back to the issue on the agenda."
Evaluator/critic	Assesses the evidence and conclusions that the group is considering.	"How recent are those statistics? I think there are newer figures for us to consider."
Procedural technician	Helps the group accomplish its goal by handling tasks such as distributing reports, writing ideas on a whiteboard, or performing other tasks.	"I'll write your ideas on the board as you suggest them. After the meeting, I'll copy them and summarize them in an e-mail message to each of you."
Recorder	Makes a written record of the group's progress by writing down specific comments, facts, or the minutes of the meeting.	"I'll take the minutes of today's meeting."

Social Roles	Description	Example
Encourager	Offers praise and support and confirms the value of other people and the ideas they contribute.	"You're doing a wonderful job."
Harmonizer	Manages conflict and mediates disputes among group members.	"Tynesha, you and Mandy seem to be agreeing more than you are disagreeing. Both of you have the same goal. Let's brainstorm some strategies that can help you both get what you want."
Compromiser	Resolves conflicts by trying to find an acceptable solution; seeks new alternatives.	"Jane, you want us to meet at 7:00 p.m., and Sue, you'd like us to start at 8:00. What if we started at 7:30? Would that work?"
Gatekeeper	Encourages people who talk too much to contribute less and invites those who are less talkative to participate.	"Tim, we haven't heard what you think. What do you suggest we do?"
Follower	Goes along with the suggestions and ideas of other group members.	"I can support that option. You have summarized the issues about the same way I see them."
Emotion expresser	Verbalizes how the group may be feeling about a specific issue or suggestion.	"We seem to be frustrated that we are not making more progress."
Group observer	Summarizes the group's progress or lack of progress.	"We are making great progress on all the issues except how much salary we should offer."
Tension reliever	Monitors stress within the group and offers suggestions for breaks, using humor or other appropriate strategies.	"Hey, what we need is a good laugh. Here's a joke I saw on the Internet today."

Individual Roles	Description	Example
Aggressor	Deflates or disconfirms the status of other group members or tries to take credit for the work of others.	"Lee, your idea is the pits. We all know that what I suggested two meetings ago is the only way to go."
Blocker	Is negative, stubborn, and disagreeable without an apparent reason.	"I just don't like it. I don't have to tell you why. I just don't like it."
Recognition seeker	Seeks the spotlight by dwelling on his or her personal accomplishments; seeks the praise of others.	"Don't you remember this was my idea? And say, did you see my picture in the paper? I won the grand prize at the science fair."
Self-confessor	Uses the group as a forum to disclose unnecessary personal feelings and personal problems unrelated to the group's task.	"I can't deal with this stuff right now. My parents are being so unfair. They won't let me live off campus next year. They just don't understand me."
Joker	Wants to crack jokes, tell stories, and just have fun instead of focusing on the task or what the group needs.	"Hey, let's forget this project and go to the mall. I'll tell you the gossip I heard about Professor Smith. What a kook!"
Dominator	Tries to take control of the group, talks too much, and uses flattery or aggression to push his or her ideas off on the group.	"Now, here's what we're going to do: Marcie, you will take notes today; Phil, you go get us some pizza; and Russ, I want you to just sit there in case I need you to run an errand."

(continued)

A Classification of Group Roles (*continued*)

Individual Roles	Description	Example
Special-interest pleader	Seeks to get the group to support a pet project or personal agenda.	"My service club would like it if we would support the new downtown renovation project. I'll stand a good chance at club president if I can get you on board."
Help seeker	Seeks to evoke a sympathetic response from others; often expresses insecurity stemming from feelings of low self-worth.	"I don't know if I can participate in this project. I'm not very good with people. I just feel like I don't relate well to others or have many friends."

As you look at the list of roles in Table 9.1, you may think, "Yes, that's what I usually do. That's the role I usually take." You can probably see roles that fit other group members. Most group members don't assume only one or two roles during group meetings. Most of us assume several roles when we interact in a group. A role is worked out jointly between us and the group, and the roles we assume change depending on which group we're in. Your personality and the personality characteristics of other team members also significantly influence role development within teams.[30] Effective group members adapt their behavior to what is happening or needed in the group. In some groups, your expertise may give you the confidence to share information and opinions freely. In other groups, your assumed role may be to maintain social harmony and peace.

Balancing Roles   What are the best or worst roles to assume? We don't recommend that you assume any individual role; by definition, these roles focus attention on an individual rather than on the group. Every group needs a balance of task and social roles, instead of attention drawn to an individual. At the same time, however, don't ignore the contributions of your fellow group members. One study found that one of the most negative things a group member can do is ignore comments another group member makes, isolating a group member.[31]

What is the proper balance between task and social concerns? Some experts recommend a 60–40 balance between task and social roles.[32] In general, more comments need to be about getting the work done than about having fun or managing the social climate, but it is also important to make sure that there are good working relationships among group members. If your group seems unduly focused on the task and members are insensitive to the harmony of the group relationships, the group will not be as effective as it might be. Conversely, an out-of-balance group that focuses just on having a good time is not going to achieve its task goals.

Use two of the Communication Principles for a Lifetime to help you balance roles.

Principle 1: Be aware of your communication:	Monitor what roles are being assumed and not assumed in your group.
Principle 5: Adapt appropriately:	Adapt your behavior to the group's needs by helping meet a need or fill an unfilled role.

Rules

As we noted both in Chapter 1 and earlier in this chapter, *rules* are followable prescriptions that indicate what behavior is expected or preferred.[33] Rules also clearly specify what behavior is inappropriate. By the time students attend college, most of them are quite familiar with rules. Leaders or members of groups and teams often develop rules that specify how people should behave.

In particular, teams often develop ground rules that help them function more smoothly. **Team ground rules** are a way to talk about the behaviors that are expected of group members. Rules are needed to ensure that a team is both efficient and effective. They also help manage uncertainty when working with others. Although most informal groups do not develop explicit, written rules, more formal, highly structured teams may take time to develop such rules as that everyone should attend all meetings, meetings will start on time, and each member should follow through on individual assignments. Making the rules

team ground rules

The behaviors that are expected of team members, often spelled out in explicit rules of acceptable behavior developed by team members working together.

explicit makes it easier to foster appropriate behavior and prevent inappropriate behavior. Research has found that when people are working in virtual teams, in which uncertainty is often high, clear rules help a team operate more efficiently.[34]

Norms

Although not all groups develop explicit rules, most groups and teams develop norms. **Norms** are general standards that determine what is appropriate and inappropriate behavior in a group. As their name implies, norms reflect what's normal behavior in the group; they influence a variety of group member behaviors, such as the type of language that is acceptable, the casualness of members' clothing, or the acceptability of using first names. Is it normal for group members to raise their hands before speaking in your group? Is it acceptable to move around while the group is in session or to get a cup of coffee while someone is talking?

Norms and Rules   How do norms differ from rules? Rules are more explicit. Group and team rules are written down or at least verbalized. Here's an example of a rule: Any member of this team who does not pay his or her dues on time will pay an extra $5 in dues. Norms are more general standards or expectations that are not as clearly spelled out. It may be a norm in your group that no one uses four-letter words; there's probably no written policy that prohibits expletives, and group members may never have said, "No one should ever use a curse word during our discussions," but even without such specific admonitions, members don't use offensive or obscene words.

Sources of Norms   Norms develop on the basis of what you and other team members have experienced in other groups as well as behavior that occurs naturally as group members interact. If after a couple of meetings no one is uttering a swear word, a norm has begun to gel.

The norms that emerge in a group are also strongly influenced by the larger cultural context in which group members live. Norms relating to how attentive the group is to deadlines and punctuality, for example, are anchored in the overall cultural expectations. Some people approach time from a **monochronic time perspective**; they are more likely to develop norms to do only one thing at a time, to pay attention to deadlines and schedules, and to make plans to use time efficiently. Others prefer a **polychronic time perspective**; they do many things at a time, don't worry about deadlines and schedules, believe relationships are more important than work, change plans frequently, and are less concerned about deadlines than are monochronic individuals.[35] Many people from the United States and northern Europe tend to be monochronic; deadlines and timelines are valued.[36] People from Latin America, southern Europe, and the Middle East often tend to be polychronic; deadlines and strict adherence to schedules are less important.[37]

If you find yourself in a group whose members have cultural approaches to time or other norms that are different from yours, what should you do? Consider these suggestions:

- Take time to talk about those differences. Share your concerns and assumptions.
- Don't pounce on other team members and accuse them of being laggards or taskmasters.
- Make the issue a group concern rather than an issue between just one or two people.

Conversation and compromise can accomplish a lot when you find yourself facing cultural differences.

Enforcing Norms   Noticing when someone breaks a norm can help you spot a norm. If a member waltzes into a meeting twenty minutes late and several folks grimace and point toward the clock on the wall, that's a sure sign that a norm has been violated. The severity of the punishment for violating a norm corresponds to the significance of the norm.[38] Mild punishment is usually unspoken—such as silent glances or frowning

norms
Standards that determine what is appropriate and inappropriate behavior in a group.

monochronic time perspective
Preferring to do one thing at a time, to pay attention to deadlines and schedules, and to use time efficiently.

polychronic time perspective
Preferring to do many things at once, to place less emphasis on deadlines and schedules, and to consider relationships to be more important than work and meeting deadlines.

▼ Cultural norms about the use of time are just one source of diversity you may encounter when communicating in groups or teams. How can you start a discussion about group norms? Fotos593/Shutterstock

status

An individual's importance and prestige.

power

The ability to influence other people's behavior.

stares. More serious punishment might include a negative comment about the behavior in front of other group members or even expulsion from the group.

You don't have to worry about whether your group will have norms or not; norms happen. You should, however, monitor the group norms to ensure that your behavior doesn't distract from the work of the group and to notice the possible development of any unproductive group norms (such as spending too much time socializing) that the group should talk about.

Status

As she walks into the room, all eyes are fixed on *her*. Group members watch every move. As the chairperson, she has much influence. Without her support, no new issues will come before the board. She has high status. **Status** refers to an individual's importance and prestige. Your status in a group influences to whom you talk, who talks to you, and even what you talk about. Your perceived importance affects both your verbal and your nonverbal messages. A person with high status typically

- Talks more than low-status members,
- Directs comments to other high-status group members,
- Has more influence on the decisions the group makes,
- Is listened to by group members, and
- Addresses more comments to the entire group than to individuals.[39]

Because high-status people enjoy more privileges, most people want to be in the "in-group"—the group with high status and influence. Being aware of status differences can help you predict who talks to whom. If you can discern status differences, you'll also be better able to predict the type of messages communicated. Although some people underestimate their perceived level of status and influence in a group, research suggests that you are probably quite perceptive at knowing your own status level when communicating with others.[40]

But just because a person has status doesn't mean that his or her ideas are good. Some groups get into trouble because they automatically defer to the person with more status without reviewing the validity of the ideas presented. Don't let status differences influence your perceptions of, and critical thinking about, the merit of the ideas presented. Conversely, don't dismiss ideas simply because the person who suggested them doesn't have high status or prestige. Focus on the quality of the message, not on the messenger.

Power

Status refers to perceived importance, whereas **power** is the ability to influence others' behavior. Although status and power often go hand in hand, a group member can have high status and still not be able to influence how others behave. People have power if they can affect what others do. Their power stems from the resources available to them to influence others. Who does and doesn't have power in a group influences how people relate to one another.

A group in which the power is not balanced may have problems; the "power people" may dominate the discussion. In any group or team, when one or more members dominate the discussion, the group loses the contributions and insights of others. People with less power tend to participate less in group discussion unless they're trying to gain power. A power struggle often creates ripples of conflict and contention through a group. Power struggles also often focus attention on individual group members rather than on the group as a whole. Research supports the conclusion that groups with equal power distribution usually have better-quality outcomes than other groups.[41]

According to a classic discussion of how individuals become powerful, there are five power bases: legitimate, referent, expert, reward, and coercive power. These power bases explain why certain people have power and why others don't.[42]

"I've called this meeting because It's a big ego trip having the authority to call you all together whenever I want to."

Legitimate Power   You have **legitimate power** if someone elected or appointed you to a position of power. Your power source comes from holding a position of responsibility. The president of your university or college has the legitimate power to establish and implement school policy. U.S. senators and your mayor are other examples of people who have legitimate power. A group or team member who has been elected chair or president of the group is given legitimate power to influence how the group operates.

legitimate power
Power that stems from being elected or appointed to a position of authority.

Referent Power   You have **referent power** if people like you. Put simply, people we like have more power over us than people we do not like. If you are working on a committee with your best friend, your friend exerts power over you in the sense that you will tend to give more credence to what your friend recommends than to other recommendations. Just the opposite occurs if you are working with someone you don't like. You will be more likely to ignore advice that comes from someone you don't admire than from someone you do, which means that person has less power to influence you.

referent power
Power that stems from being liked.

Expert Power   Knowledge is power. People who have **expert power** are perceived as informed or knowledgeable. They have more influence in a group or team than do people who are perceived as uninformed. Suppose you are working with a group to develop strategies to clean up the river that runs through your town. Your colleague who is majoring in aquatic biology will probably have more power than other, less knowledgeable group members.

expert power
Power derived from having expertise and information.

Reward Power   People who can grant favors, money, or other rewards have more power than people who can't provide such rewards; those who can bestow rewards have **reward power**. People who have greater power to reward are typically sent more positive, supportive messages than people who don't have the ability to reward others. Someone also has reward power if he or she can take away a punishment or other unpleasant experiences. But reward power is effective only if the person being rewarded finds the reward satisfying or useful. What is rewarding to one person may not be rewarding to someone else.

reward power
Power that comes from the ability to provide rewards or favors.

Coercive Power   You have coercive power if you can punish others. **Coercive power** is the flip side of reward power. This influence comes from the ability to make others uncomfortable. If someone can cut your salary, lower your grade, demote

coercive power
Power that stems from being able to punish others.

Types of Power

Legitimate Power	Power that results from being elected, appointed, or ordained to lead or make decisions for a group or a team
Referent Power	Power that results from being popular and well liked
Expert Power	Power that results from having information or being knowledgeable about issues or ideas
Reward Power	Power that results from having the resources to bestow gifts, money, recognition, or other rewards that group members value
Coercive Power	Power that results from having the ability to punish others

you, put you in jail, or force you to do unpleasant jobs, that person has coercive power. This kind of power results from the perception that the person with the power will actually use the power. If a person has the authority to punish but group members don't perceive that the person will use this power, there really is no coercive power.

Even though we have categorized power into five different types, don't get the idea that group members may exert just one type of power. In reality, group or team members often have more than one type of power. For example, because a group member is the elected leader (legitimate power), he or she may also be able to offer rewards (reward power) or punishments (coercive power).

Cohesiveness

If you have ever read about the Three Musketeers or seen a movie about them, you know that their motto was "All for one, one for all." They were a cohesive group—they liked to be around one another. **Cohesiveness** is the degree of attraction that members of a group feel toward one another and the group.

cohesiveness

The degree of attraction group members feel toward one another and toward their group.

Characteristics of Cohesive Groups   In a highly cohesive group, whether meeting face to face or virtually, members feel a high degree of loyalty to one another; the goal of the group is also the goal of the individual.[43] Cohesive group members listen to one another. Members of a cohesive group are more likely to use words and phrases that have a unique meaning to its members; they are also more likely to tell inside jokes—jokes that mean something only to them.[44] Groups that are cohesive generally are more effective than groups that are not.[45]

Groups become cohesive because of a variety of forces that attract people to the group and to one another. Shared goals, feelings of genuine liking, and similarity of backgrounds and culture are variables that influence group cohesiveness.

How to Enhance Group Cohesiveness   Table 9.2 summarizes some strategies that enhance group cohesiveness and other strategies that make a group less cohesive. The common element in cohesive groups is the manner in which group members communicate with one another. Cohesiveness is more likely to occur if group members have the opportunity to talk with one another freely about a goal all members have in common and if this interaction increases group members' affection and liking for one another. Teams that have greater control over how they conduct their work are also more likely to be cohesive.[46]

TABLE 9.2   Suggestions for Enhancing Group Cohesiveness[47]

Cohesive Groups	Incohesive Groups
Talk about the group in terms of "we" rather than "I"; stress teamwork and collaboration.	Emphasize the individual contributions of group members; stress individual accomplishment.
Reinforce good attendance at group meetings.	Make little effort to encourage group members to attend every meeting.
Establish and maintain group traditions.	Make little effort to develop group traditions.
Set clear short-term and long-term goals.	Avoid setting goals or establishing deadlines.
Encourage everyone in the group to participate in the group task.	Allow only the most talkative or high-status members to participate in the group task.
Celebrate when the group accomplishes either a short-term or a long-term goal.	Discourage group celebration; make sure group meetings are all work and little or no fun.

FIGURE 9.1 All-Channel Small Group Communication Network

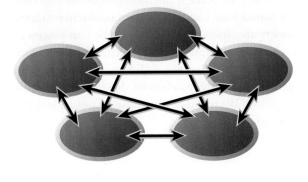

FIGURE 9.3 Wheel Small Group Communication Network

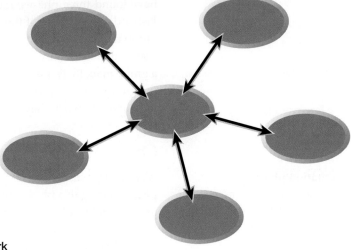

FIGURE 9.2 Chain Small Group Communication Network

Can a group be too cohesive? Yes. Although cohesiveness is usually a good thing, a group can have too much of a good thing. If group members are focused only on having fun and developing a positive, cohesive relationship to the exclusion of getting their work done, productivity can suffer. Strive for group cohesiveness, but balance it with concern for accomplishing the group's task.

A group's **communication interaction pattern** is the consistent pattern of who talks to whom. The all-channel network pattern shown in Figure 9.1, in which everyone talks to everyone else, is most likely to enhance group cohesiveness and productivity.[48] The chain interaction pattern in Figure 9.2 illustrates a form of group communication in which people convey a message to one person at a time rather than communicating with all group members at once. Groups in which a great deal of communication occurs within a **clique**, a smaller group of people within a group who form a common bond among themselves, are also usually less cohesive than groups with communication among all members.

Sometimes, a great deal of communication is directed at the one person in the group who holds a different opinion than the rest of the group. This person is called a **group deviate**. Other group members may spend considerable time trying to change that person's opinion. The wheel interaction pattern, shown in Figure 9.3, occurs when one person is the focal point of communication with all other group members. The focal person in a wheel pattern is not always a group deviate; a quarterback speaking to other football team members is another example of the wheel pattern. However, the wheel pattern, like the chain pattern, is less likely than the all-channel pattern to foster group cohesiveness.

communication interaction pattern
A consistent pattern of who talks to whom.

clique
A smaller, cohesive group within a group.

group deviate
A group member who holds an opinion, attitude, or belief that is different from that of other group members.

Group and Team Development

9.3 Summarize the four stages of group and team development.

Small group communication can be a disorganized, messy process, especially if the all-channel network is the predominant communication pattern. Although the free flow of ideas is a good thing, it may seem as though there is no order or structure to the way group members interact. But what may look like chaotic talk may, in fact, be just a normal aspect of how groups behave.

Researchers have found that some groups go through certain phases or sequences of talk when they meet to solve a problem or make a decision.[49] Some researchers have found three phases; most have found four. Communication researcher Aubrey Fisher developed one of the most descriptive four-phase models.[50] His four phases of group talk are (1) orientation, (2) conflict, (3) emergence, and (4) reinforcement. Once you're able to identify and understand these four phases, you'll have the equivalent of a group map. By listening to what people are saying, you will be able to identify where the group is in the process of development. We will describe these phases so you can identify them when they occur in your group.

Orientation

orientation phase

The first phase of group interaction, in which members become adjusted to one another and to the group's task.

As you might suspect, when people first get together in a group, they enter the **orientation phase**. During this phase, they adjust to at least two things: who's in the group (group process) and what they will be doing (group task).

Research on the orientation phase suggests that your earliest communication is directed at orienting yourself to others as well as to the group's task. What happens during this first phase is often referred to as **primary tension**. This tension results from the uncertainty and discomfort people experience when they meet for the first time.[51] Just as you may have some anxiety when you give a speech, some uncertainty and anxiety occur when group members are trying to figure out who is supposed to do what, who's in charge, and why they are there. Some group members who don't like uncertainty at all and are eager to start sorting things out will suggest an agenda: "Hello, my name is Steve. Let's each introduce ourselves." Other group members are quite content to sit quietly in the background and let others take the lead. As people begin to become acquainted and start talking about the group's purpose, typical groups experience the second phase: conflict.

primary tension

Tension arising from the uncertainty and discomfort that occur when a group first meets.

Conflict

conflict phase

The second phase of group interaction, in which group members experience some degree of disagreement about social and task issues.

As we pointed out, people are different—and nowhere is that more evident than in a group discussion after the group gets down to business. As group members become more comfortable and oriented toward the task and one another, they start asserting opinions about what the group should be doing, how it should be done, and who should be doing it. They have tested the water in the first phase and are now ready to jump in. This second phase, which is characterized by increased disagreement, is known as the **conflict phase**.

task conflict

Conflict that occurs because of differences about how to accomplish what the group is trying to achieve.

Groups may experience **task conflict** in which they disagree about how to accomplish the task at hand, **process conflict** about the procedures and methods of working on the task, or **relational conflict**, in which conflicting opinions about who does what results in personal disagreement.[52] The relational conflict that arises in this phase is sometimes called **secondary tension**. This secondary tension or conflict occurs when there is a struggle for leadership or when the conflict becomes personal and group members disagree with one another.

process conflict

Disagreement about the procedures or methods for accomplishing the task.

relational conflict

Conflict that becomes personal because group members do not like, value, or respect one another.

secondary tension

The conflict that occurs, after the members of a group have become acquainted with one another, over group norms, roles, leadership, and differences among member opinions.

Conflict isn't always bad—it occurs when people are honest about sharing their opinions. If there is no conflict, it usually means that people aren't honest about how they really feel.[53] As journalist Walter Lippman once said, "When we all think alike, then no one is thinking." The conflict phase is necessary for solving problems and maintaining group relationships. When ideas aren't challenged and tested, groups are more likely to make unwise decisions. We are not suggesting that you celebrate when you have conflict, only that you take some comfort in knowing that conflict is an expected part of group deliberations. The amount and intensity of the conflict will vary depending on how important the issues are to the group. The more important the issues are to group members, the greater the intensity of the conflict is likely to be.

Research suggests that when intense conflict arises in your group, especially conflict that results in heightened emotions and tension because of personal or cultural differences, it may be best to "cool it."[54] Taking time to back off rather than continuing to hash out issues verbally may be helpful in managing the tension. Regardless of the issue or trigger for the conflict, when emotions are aroused, rational discussion is hard to achieve. Especially if the group you're in includes people from a variety of cultural backgrounds, it may be best to let the group "breathe" rather than continuing to hammer out meaning with more talk. We're not suggesting that all conflict should be managed by avoiding it. We are suggesting that when emotions become aroused, it's difficult to make headway on the issues. If you don't take a break, you'll likely expand the conflict rather than making progress.

▼ Taking a time-out might help to resolve this team's conflict. What other strategies have you found useful for dealing with conflict in groups? Stockbyte/Getty Images

When conflict in virtual groups and teams stems from differences in cultural values or perceptions, it's important that team members feel connected to the team and empowered to participate rather than feel marginalized or discounted. Research suggests that having virtual team members vote on decisions or the value and importance of contributions is a useful way to keep them engaged with the team.[55]

Emergence

You know you are in the **emergence phase** when the group begins to solidify a common point of view. Decisions emerge, and conflict is reduced. Although conflict may be evident in this third phase, what sets the emergence phase apart from the conflict phase is the way in which group members manage conflict. Norms, roles, and leadership patterns that have been established now help the group get work accomplished. In the emergence phase, the group settles on norms and moves closer to agreement. The group begins to get a clearer glimpse of how issues will be resolved and what the group outcome will be.

Not all of what emerges may be productive. The group could decide that the conflict is so intense that the best decision is to disband the group, or an individual could decide to leave the group.

emergence phase
The third phase of group interaction, in which conflict or disagreement is managed, decisions are made, and group problems begin to be solved or managed.

Reinforcement

Group members become more unified in the **reinforcement phase**. During the orientation, conflict, and emergence phases, group members struggle through getting acquainted, developing cohesiveness, competing for status and prominence, puzzling over what action the group could take, and making decisions. The group eventually emerges from those struggles and develops a new sense of direction. This accomplishment results in a more positive feeling about the group. The group more clearly develops a sense of "we." In fact, one way you can identify the reinforcement phase is when group members use more collective pronouns (*we, us, our*) than personal pronouns (*I, me, my*) when talking about the group.

reinforcement phase
The fourth phase of group interaction, in which group members express positive feelings toward one another and toward the group.

COMMUNICATION & DIVERSITY

The Impact of Individualism and Collectivism on Groups and Teams

As we mentioned in Chapter 6, individualistic cultures tend to focus on individual achievement. Most Americans value individual accomplishment over group or team achievement. In general, people from the dominant cultural groups in the United States, Great Britain, and Australia savor and celebrate individual accomplishment. Collectivistic cultures, which include cultures in Asia, Latin America, and some parts of eastern Europe, emphasize group or team accomplishment rather than individual achievement.[56]

People who hold individualistic cultural values may find it more difficult to work collaboratively than people from collectivistic cultures. The following summary compares individualistic assumptions with collectivistic assumptions about working in groups and teams.[57] These differences can sometimes explain why groups and teams have difficulty collaboratively accomplishing their tasks. If you're from a culture that places a high value on individual achievement, you may find it challenging to work well with others.

Individualistic Assumptions

The best decisions are made by individuals.

Planning should be done by leaders.

Individuals should be rewarded.

Individuals should work primarily for themselves.

Healthy competition among group and team members is more important than teamwork.

Meetings are for sharing information with others.

To get something accomplished, you should work with individual people.

The prime objective of meetings is to advance your own ideas.

Group or team meetings are often a waste of time.

Collectivistic Assumptions

The most effective decisions are made by teams.

Planning is best done by the entire group.

Groups or teams should be rewarded.

Individuals should work primarily for the team.

Teamwork is more important than competition.

Meetings are for making group or team decisions.

To get something accomplished, you should work with the entire group or team.

The prime objective of meetings is to reach consensus or agreement.

Group or team meetings are the best way to achieve a quality goal.

The Process Nature of Group Phases

Even though we have identified four distinct phases that groups can experience, don't get the idea that all groups progress neatly through these phases in exactly the same way. They don't.[58] Some researchers have found that only about one-third of all groups experience these distinct stages.[59] Other studies have had difficulty identifying four phases and found just one or two. Even if you have trouble identifying these phases in your group, you will probably see some elements of the four phases during your group meetings.

Some groups get stuck in one of the phases. For example, have you ever participated in a group that could never quite figure out what it was supposed to do? It was stuck in the orientation phase. Some groups remain in the conflict phase for long periods of time, perhaps bouncing between orientation and conflict. The group either seems torn by personal conflict between group members or just can't reach agreement or make a decision.

As we've noted, the group will eventually reach phase three, when something will emerge, even if it is not a wise decision or high-quality solution. The group may decide, for example, to disband and never meet again because it is so dysfunctional. Although this was not the original objective of the group, something emerged: The group members quit.

Reinforcement is likely to occur because we like to make sense out of what happens to us. Even if the group disbands, we are likely to celebrate its demise or reinforce the decision to disband. Because of our culture's emphasis on efficiency and productivity, many groups quickly gloss over the reinforcement aspects of group celebration. Wise group leaders and participants make sure that accomplishments are celebrated and both group and individual efforts are recognized. The cohesiveness and positive feelings that result from such celebrations will be helpful as the group prepares for its next task.

RECAP

A Map of Group Phases

Phase One: Orientation	• What are we doing here?
	• What is our goal?
	• Who are these people?
	• What is my role?

Phase Two: Conflict	• Who put that person in charge?
	• I see the goal differently.
	• I have different ideas.
	• I have different strategies.

Phase Three: Emergence	• Something happens.
	• Decisions are made.
	• Issues are managed.
	• The group moves forward.

Phase Four: Reinforcement	• The group is aware it is making progress.
	• Members seek to justify their actions.
	• Members reward others.
	• The team celebrates its success or rationalizes its failure.

STUDY GUIDE:

〉 REVIEW, APPLY, AND ASSESS

Groups and Teams Defined

9.1 Describe types of groups and teams, differences between groups and teams, and when participating in groups and teams should be avoided.

REVIEW: Small group communication is the transactive process of creating meaning among a small number (three to fifteen) of people who share a common purpose, feel a sense of belonging to the group, and exert influence on one another. Primary groups, such as family and social groups, exist to fulfill primary human needs to socialize and live together. Secondary groups form to achieve a specific goal. Secondary groups include study, therapy, focus, and problem-solving groups. Groups and teams are similar in that they are collections of a small number of people who meet to achieve a goal. A team can be differentiated from a group in that it is more highly organized and the members' collaborative efforts are more coordinated to achieve the team goal.

KEY TERMS:

small group	problem-solving group
primary group	focus group
social group	virtual group or team
secondary group	small group communication
study group	team
therapy group	

APPLY: What do you find most rewarding about working in groups and teams? What do you find most challenging?

ASSESS: Make a list of all of the groups and teams to which you belong. Analyze your list to determine which groups are most similar to this chapter's definition of a small group. Also identify those groups that function more like a team. Then on a scale of 1 to 10 (with 10 being the most effective and 1 the least effective), assess the effectiveness of each group or team using the criteria discussed in this chapter.

Group and Team Dynamics

9.2 Identify and describe group and team dynamics, including roles, rules, norms, status, power, and cohesiveness.

REVIEW: A variety of factors influence the ever-changing nature of members' interactions in groups and teams. One factor is the role you assume in a group—the consistent way you communicate with others. There are three primary types of roles in small groups and teams: (1) task roles help the group do its work, (2) social roles help the group members relate to one another, and (3) individual roles inappropriately divert the group's focus to individual concerns rather than group concerns. Other factors that affect the dynamic nature of groups and teams include norms (standards of what is normal or expected), rules (explicit statements about appropriate and inappropriate behavior), status (a person's importance or prestige), power (the ability to influence others), and cohesiveness (the degree of loyalty and attraction the group members feel toward one another).

KEY TERMS:

role	power
task role	legitimate power
social role	referent power
individual role	expert power
team ground rules	reward power
norms	coercive power
monochronic time	cohesiveness
perspective	communication interaction
polychronic time	pattern
perspective	clique
status	group deviate

APPLY: Which of the roles described in Table 9.1 do you fill most often in groups? Why do you think you usually take on that role? Which roles would you like to fill more often?

ASSESS: Reflect upon your last group or team meeting. Evaluate the suggestions for enhancing group cohesiveness in Table 9.2 to assess how cohesive your group was. Based on your analysis, evaluate your group on a scale of 1 to 10 as highly cohesive (10) or not at all cohesive (1).

Group and Team Development

9.3 Summarize the four stages of group and team development.

REVIEW: The four stages of group and team development are (1) orientation, (2) conflict, (3) emergence, and (4) reinforcement. During the orientation phase, group members get acquainted with both the task and one another. The second phase, conflict, occurs when group members recognize that they have differing ideas and opinions about both the group's task and its procedures for accomplishing the task. The third phase, emergence, is evident when the group begins to make decisions and starts to complete the task. The reinforcement phase occurs when the group has accomplished its task and takes some time to recognize and confirm the group's actions.

KEY TERMS:

orientation phase
primary tension
conflict phase
task conflict
process conflict

relational conflict
secondary tension
emergence phase
reinforcement phase

APPLY: Do you sometimes feel uncertain and uncomfortable when joining a new group? How do you typically try to resolve discomfort when you meet new group members? How successful is your method?

ASSESS: Communication researchers Katherine Hawkins and Bryant Fillion surveyed personnel managers to find out what they considered the most important skills for successful groups and teams. The skills in the following list are among those that the personnel managers deemed most important. Rate each member of a group you are in on the following skills, using a scale from 1 to 5 (1 = not at all effective, 2 = generally not effective, 3 = uncertain, 4 = effective, and 5 = very effective). Then rate yourself.

Scoring Instructions

Total the score for each group member. A perfect score is 65; the lowest possible score is 13. Your instructor may invite you to share your ratings of other group members anonymously. If you don't share your ratings, simply note how you evaluated your own skills in comparison to other group members.

Skill	Group Member				
	A	B	C	D	E
1. Listens effectively	—	—	—	—	—
2. Understands roles and responsibilities	—	—	—	—	—
3. Actively contributes to the group	—	—	—	—	—

Skill	Group Member				
	A	B	C	D	E
4. Asks clear questions	—	—	—	—	—
5. Establishes and maintains rapport with others	—	—	—	—	—
6. Is sensitive to people with different cultural backgrounds	—	—	—	—	—
7. Uses clear, concise, accurate, and professional language	—	—	—	—	—
8. Communicates well with people who have different professional backgrounds	—	—	—	—	—
9. Gives clear and accurate instructions	—	—	—	—	—
10. Nonverbally presents a positive professional image (through appropriate grooming and attire)	—	—	—	—	—
11. Helps resolve conflicts	—	—	—	—	—
12. Accurately summarizes information for the group	—	—	—	—	—
13. Gives brief, clear, well-organized, and informative presentations to the group when appropriate	—	—	—	—	—
Total	—	—	—	—	—

⟩ THE PRINCIPLE POINTS

Principle One:

Be aware of your communication with yourself and others.

- Be aware of your role and the roles of others in groups and teams.
- Be aware of how you and your group develop and maintain group norms.
- Be mindful of how your power and the power of others influence group interaction.
- Be aware of the forces that affect group and team cohesiveness.
- Be aware of and sensitive to the stages of orientation, conflict, emergence, and reinforcement that influence group interaction.

Principle Two:

Effectively use and interpret verbal messages.

- Be verbally supportive of other team members to foster a collective sense of team spirit.
- Verbally help clarify team goals. Clear, elevating goals are the hallmark of an effective team.
- Express realistic optimism when working with others in groups and teams. Groups and teams with a positive outlook are more effective than those with a pessimistic perspective.
- Help the group or team set clear ground rules and clarify norms that may be ambiguous.
- Talk about your group or team in terms of "we" rather than "I".

Principle Three:

Effectively use and interpret nonverbal messages.

- Nonverbal cues help you understand group and team norms.
- Observe group and team members' use of space, touch, and eye contact to pick up clues about status and power.
- Be supportive of other group members nonverbally as well as verbally. Reinforce statements with positive facial expressions, eye contact, and head nods to indicate agreement when appropriate.

Principle Four:

Listen and respond thoughtfully to others.

- Listening well is a very important way to help a group. Listening skills help you identify your roles and the roles of others.
- Listen to others to help identify group and team norms and rules.
- Listen attentively to other group members to help foster a climate of cohesiveness.

Principle Five:

Appropriately adapt messages to others.

- Adapt to group roles, norms, rules, and status differences.
- Adapt to help the group become oriented to the task, manage conflict, facilitate emergent decisions, and reinforce group behavior.
- Adapt appropriately to cultural differences within the group.

10

ENHANCING GROUP AND TEAM PERFORMANCE

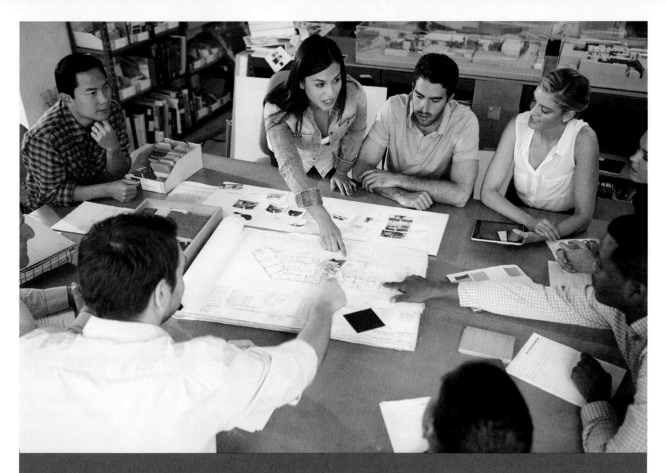

Never doubt that a small group of concerned citizens can change the world; it's the only thing that ever has.

—MARGARET MEAD

Corbisrffancy/Fotolia

→ CHAPTER OUTLINE

- What Effective Group and Team Members Do
- Structuring Group and Team Problem Solving
- Enhancing Group and Team Leadership

- Enhancing Group and Team Meetings
- Study Guide: Review, Apply, and Assess

LEARNING OBJECTIVES

After studying this chapter, you should be able to

10.1 Identify six functions that effective group members perform.

10.2 List and describe the five steps of group problem solving (reflective thinking).

10.3 Compare and contrast the trait, functional, styles, situational, and transformational approaches to understanding leadership.

10.4 Develop and use strategies to structure meetings appropriately, keep meetings on track, and promote appropriate dialogue and interaction.

What's so great about groups? Why does every organization, from the U.S. Congress to the local Parent Teacher Association, use groups, teams, and committees to get things done? The simple fact is: Groups work. Collaborating with other people produces clear benefits that just don't happen when a task is given to an individual. Research clearly supports the following conclusions:

- **Greater Creativity.** Groups and teams come up with more creative solutions to problems than a person does working alone.

- **Enhanced Comprehension.** Working with others in groups improves group members' understanding of the ideas presented.

- **Increased Satisfaction.** Group and team members are more satisfied with the group's conclusions and recommendations if they participated in the discussion than if they did not.

- **More Information.** Groups have access to more information when they tap into the experience of group members.[1]

All these advantages sound wonderful. But these benefits of collaboration don't occur automatically when people work in groups and teams. Sometimes there are significant disadvantages to working collaboratively:

- **Dominance by One Person.** Overly talkative or insensitive, overbearing people may speak too much.

- **Pressure to Conform.** Group members sometimes feel pressure to conform to what other members are doing and saying.

- **Unequal Workload.** It may be easy for some people to loaf and not do their share of the work.

- **More Time.** Working in groups and teams takes more time than working individually.[2]

This chapter is designed to help you maximize the advantages of working in groups and minimize the disadvantages of working collaboratively. We can't claim that if you follow all of the strategies we suggest, your life will be free of unpleasant and unproductive group experiences. (Although one study did find that taking an over-the-counter pain relief pill makes group work less painful.[3]) You don't, however, have to take pain medicine to make group work more tolerable; group members who both understand how groups work (see Chapter 9) and know principles and strategies for enhancing the quality of group work are much more likely to avoid the pitfalls and reap the benefits of working in groups.

Underpinning all the suggestions we offer in this chapter are the same five Communication Principles for a Lifetime that we introduced in Chapter 1 and have been discussing throughout the book. Effective group members are aware of what they are doing. They effectively use verbal and nonverbal messages, listen and respond, and then appropriately adapt their messages to others.

What Effective Group and Team Members Do

10.1 Identify six functions that effective group members perform.

"I hate groups," mutters an exasperated group member who has just finished a two-hour meeting in which nothing was accomplished. "Not me," chirps another group member. "Meetings and team projects are fun. I like the energy and productivity that occur when we work together." What does the second person know that the first one doesn't? As we noted at the start of this chapter, working in groups can have drawbacks, but you can reduce those disadvantages if you and other group members learn some fundamental ways to perform effectively.

Identify a Clear, Elevating Goal

Among the first questions that a vigilant-thinking group asks itself relates to the group's goal: What are we trying to do?[4] According to one research team, the goal should be not only clear, but also *elevating*, or exciting to the group.[5] The group needs to know that it is pursuing a goal that is significant; the goal needs to be something more exciting and important than anything a group member could achieve individually. For example, a professional football team may see itself as a Super Bowl contender at the beginning of preseason. In addition to being exciting, a group's identified goal should also be clear and realistic, as it needs to drive all aspects of what the group does.[6] Without a goal and a results-driven structure to achieve it, group performance sputters. Research has found that it's important not only to set goals, but also to develop contingency plans in case a goal is not reached. Being able to react and adjust the group's plans to achieve a goal is especially important.[7]

Develop a Results-Driven Structure

A group or team may have a clear goal, such as winning the Super Bowl, getting an "A" on a group assignment, or selling more widgets than other groups in the company, but just having a clear, elevating goal doesn't mean that the group will achieve what it wants to achieve. The group also has to carry out actions that contribute to reaching the goal. If you want to win the Super Bowl, you have to invest time in becoming physically fit and working on executing successful football plays. If you want to get an "A" on an assignment, you need to be doing what the instructor wants you to do rather than socializing and just having fun.

A group with a **results-driven structure** is organized around the action steps it needs to take to achieve its goal.[8] To be driven by results means "keeping your eyes on the prize" and then developing a group or team structure to secure that prize. Perhaps you've been part of a group or team that was quite busy but didn't seem to accomplish much; that kind of activity reflects a non-results-driven structure. Results-driven groups focus on verbs—action words—that provide the road map to success.

results-driven structure

A structure that causes a group to focus its efforts on the actions it needs to take to achieve its goals.

Gather and Share Appropriate Information

Another question that vigilant-thinking groups ask is, "Does something need to be changed?" To answer that question, high-performing groups and teams don't just rely on the unsupported opinions of group members. Instead, they gather information and analyze the situation.[9] Keep in mind that sharing information is just as important in virtual groups as it is in face-to-face groups.[10]

To analyze an issue, an effective group should do at least three things:

Gather Accurate Information   Computer programmers are familiar with the acronym GIGO: "Garbage in, garbage out." If you develop a computer program using bad information or a bad program command (garbage), you're likely to get low-quality output (more garbage). Information is the fuel that makes a group function well.[11]

Share Information   Group members have a tendency to share information that everyone in the group already knows. Research has found that better decisions are made when group members make an effort to share information that others may *not* know.[12] So if you are uncertain whether other group members know what you know, don't hesitate to share that information with the entire group.[13]

Draw Accurate Conclusions from Shared Information   Having too little evidence—or no evidence at all—is one reason groups sometimes fail to correctly analyze their current situation.[14] Even if group members do have plenty of evidence, however, it may be bad evidence, or perhaps they have not tested the evidence to see whether it is true, accurate, or relevant.

Group members who use strong evidence to support their well-reasoned arguments are more likely to have their conclusions accepted by the entire group than members who do not.[15] Group members who don't gather and use information effectively are more likely to make bad and less creative decisions than others.[16] Here are some tips for gathering and using information effectively:

- In group deliberations, ask for expert advice sooner rather than later. Seeking expert advice results in better group outcomes.

- If you find that just a few people are doing the talking and sharing information, invite quieter group members to participate. Groups that have more equal participation among members are generally more effective than other groups.

- Don't rush to make a quick decision. To reach a better outcome, take your time and sift through the information you have.

Develop Options

Another hallmark of a vigilantly-thinking group is that the members generate many ideas and potential solutions after gathering information and analyzing a situation. Effective groups don't just settle on one or two ideas and then move on. They list multiple creative approaches.

Sometimes groups get stuck, and ideas just don't flow. If that happens to your group, you may want to take a break from discussing difficult issues or problems rather than continuing to hammer away at them. Taking a break may give you the space you need to properly think through the issues. You may generate a breakthrough solution when you are not actively trying to; perhaps you've had a great idea come to you when you were taking a walk or driving. The principle of self-awareness operates here: As a group member, you have a responsibility to become aware of the group's ability to generate high-quality ideas. Be sensitive to the group's need to take a fresh look at the problem or issue.

Evaluate Ideas

High-performing groups know a good idea when they hear one. They are able to evaluate evidence, opinions, assumptions, and solutions to separate good ideas from bad ones. Low-performing groups are less discriminating. A group that does not critically evaluate ideas because members are too eager to come to a decision just so they can get a job done usually makes low-quality decisions.

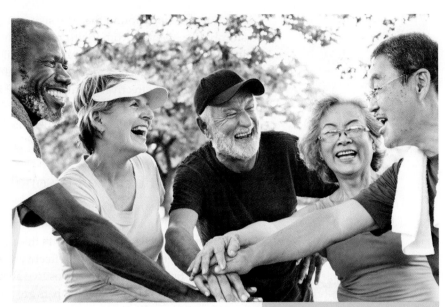

As we've seen, a group of vigilant thinkers examines the advantages and disadvantages of an idea, issue, or opinion.[17] When the group is zeroing in on a particular course of action, the effective group has at least one member who suggests, "Let's consider the positive and negative consequences of this decision." *Research reveals that it's especially important to talk about the negative consequences of a specific proposal.*[18] Some groups use a whiteboard or flipchart and make a written list comparing the pros and the cons. Groups that do so are likely to come up with a better decision than groups that don't systematically evaluate the good and bad aspects of a potential solution or decision.

▲ Members of high-performing groups and teams are likely to enjoy spending time together. A good balance of social and task focus makes it more fun for group members to be together. How else can you make group membership more enjoyable for yourself and other members? Rawpixel.com/Shutterstock

Not only is it a good idea to evaluate the conclusions of the group, but research suggests that it is useful to periodically evaluate the team's process and talk about how well team members coordinate the work. Don't wait until the project is finished to evaluate the team's process; discuss how well the team is achieving its goals as the team is working on a project.[19]

Develop Sensitivity toward Others

Most of the functions we've described so far focus on getting work done effectively and efficiently, but group success is about more than just focusing on the task. Being solely task oriented is not beneficial to the way a group functions. Effective group members need to balance concern for the task with concern for the feelings of others.

Fostering a climate of fairness and supportiveness is essential to developing a well-functioning team.[20] How do you increase your sensitivity toward others?

- Be aware of how your comments might be perceived by others.
- Look for opportunities to confirm the value of others' contributions.
- Nonverbally show that you are genuinely interested in what others are saying.
- Listen to what each group member has to say—even members who hold a minority opinion.

One benefit of working in a group is that you can hear a variety of ideas. If some members' opinions are quickly dismissed because they are not what most other group members think or believe, the group loses the benefit of having many different points of view.

A recent study found that one sign of a competent group is that group members simply like spending time with one another.[21] Another study explicitly noted the importance of trusting one another, clarifying misunderstandings by collaboratively defining important terms, listening effectively, consciously talking about what makes the group effective, sharing personal information, using humor, and laughing together.[22] Competent groups also treat new group members with respect.[23] In summary, competent group members are sensitive to how individual members relate to one another.

Develop a Positive Personal Style

You may have heard the story about a boy who awoke on the morning of his birthday to find only a large pile of manure where he'd hoped to find birthday presents. Undaunted, he smiled and said, "With this much horse manure, there's got to be a pony here somewhere!" Like that boy, effective team members are optimistic: Even in bad times, they find something to be positive about.

One thing effective team members are optimistic about is themselves. Researchers have found that effective teams and team members *believed* that they were effective, that they had the skills and resources to accomplish their task. Teams that were less effective *thought* that they were less effective.[24] Was the team effective due to a self-fulfilling prophecy—did the expectation of being effective cause the team to act effectively? Or did team members think that they were effective because they really were a top-notch team? We're not quite sure what the precise cause-and-effect relationship is between self-perceptions of being effective and actually being effective. We do know, however, that teams that have a positive, can-do attitude perform better than teams whose members have doubts, worries, and uncertainties about whether they will get the job done. The bottom line is that optimism enhances effectiveness.

As we've seen, being driven by results also makes a group member more productive. Furthermore, perhaps not surprisingly, team members also like colleagues who are encouraging, patient, enthusiastic, and friendly. To be perceived as an *ineffective* team member, argue with others frequently, be intolerant and impatient, and cultivate skills that will help you win the "pain-in-the-neck" award. To be an effective team member, you need to find a way to deal with group members who may dominate, block, bully, or have no follow-through. Table 10.1 offers suggestions on how to collaborate with difficult members.

You may wonder whether these attributes of team effectiveness can be enhanced through study and training. There's good news: Evidence suggests that by learning more about teams and participating in training development courses, you can indeed improve your team skills.[25]

RECAP

What Effective Group and Team Members Do

Group Function	Description of Function
Identify a Clear, Elevating Goal	A clear, elevating, or important goal provides an anchor for group discussion.
Develop a Results-Driven Structure	Structure helps the group stay on task and do the things that will help it achieve its goal.
Gather and Share Appropriate Information	Effective teams conduct research, share information with all group members, and take steps to confirm that they have accurate information.
Develop Options	Effective groups expand the number of options before choosing a course of action.
Evaluate Ideas	Effective groups or teams examine the pros and cons of an option before implementing a strategy.
Develop Sensitivity Toward Others	Members of effective groups express sensitivity to the needs and concerns of group members by using appropriate verbal and nonverbal messages, listening, responding, and adapting messages to others.
Develop a Positive Personal Style	Effective group members have optimistic attitudes about the prospects for overall group success and use effective strategies to change ineffective member behavior.

TABLE 10.1   How to Collaborate with Difficult Group Members

Problem	Suggestions
Dominator: A group member talks too much.	1. Consider giving the group member responsibility for a specific task.
	2. Use gatekeeping skills to invite others to talk.
	3. Privately ask the "ververbalizer" to give others an opportunity to talk.
	4. If necessary, the group may collectively decide to confront the domineering member.
Blocker: A group member has a negative attitude and consistently suggests what can't be done.	1. Consider defusing the tension with appropriate humor.
	2. Ask the blocker to play devil's advocate, a role that gives the blocker permission to be negative at certain times rather than all the time.
	3. Ask for evidence to support the blocker's claims.
	4. Gently confront the blocker, noting how his or her negative attitude is affecting the entire group.
No Follow-Through: A group member is irresponsible and doesn't perform assigned tasks.	1. Assign a mentor to help the group member.
	2. Clarify that only those who do the work will be recognized for accomplishing the task.
	3. Privately ask the irresponsible group member to do his or her share of the work.
	4. If need be, confront the irresponsible group member as a group, explaining how the lack of follow-through is hurting the group.
Bully: A group member is unethically aggressive and verbally abusive and tries to take the credit for work others do.	1. Support those who are bullied.
	2. Don't tolerate unethical behavior; describe the offensive behavior to the bully and explain its effect on the group.
	3. As a group, confront the bully, explaining how the bullying behavior is hurting the group's climate.
	4. If need be, seek help from a person of authority outside the group (a supervisor or instructor); sometimes a bully responds only to a person with greater power.

Structuring Group and Team Problem Solving

10.2   **List and describe the five steps of group problem solving (reflective thinking).**

How many of us have uttered the plea, "Just tell me what to do"? When we do, we are usually looking for simple techniques or steps to help us achieve our goal. Several researchers have sought to identify the sequence that works best to help groups solve problems and achieve their goals. In fact, more than seventy methods or sequences of steps and techniques have been prescribed for structuring problem solving in groups and teams.[26] Despite all of these recommendations, however, researchers have concluded that there are no magic techniques that always enable a group of team members to come up with the right solution to a problem. No single prescriptive method or series of steps works best in every situation. There is some good news, though: Research shows that *having some structured sequence of steps or questions works better than having no structure.*[27]

Another important conclusion of group researchers is that whatever structure the group uses must be balanced with interaction.

- **Structure** is the way a group or team discussion is organized to follow a prescribed agenda. Groups and teams need structure to keep them on task and on track.[28] Some group members have a strong preference for organized, structured

structure

The way a group or team discussion is organized, focusing on the group's agenda and the task that needs to be achieved.

FIGURE 10.1 Groups Need a Balance of Structure and Interaction

Structure is achieved through a well organized agenda and a clear discussion plan.

Interaction involves considerable give-and-take discussion to manage relationships and accomplish the task.

conversation.[29] According to research, groups that engage in free-ranging discussion without an agenda change topics about once a minute.[30] Besides having difficulty staying focused, a group without adequate structure or focus is more likely than a well-structured group to take excessive time to do its work, jump at the first solution recommended, find that one or more people dominate discussions, and have problems managing conflict.[31]

- **Interaction** includes give-and-take discussion and the responsiveness of group members to the comments of others. In an interactive group, there are fewer long utterances, more people contribute, and more people take turns talking. People listen and thoughtfully respond to one another. In a highly structured meeting, there is more control over who talks, about what, and for how long; overly structured meetings include less interaction.

interaction
The give-and-take discussion and responsiveness to other group members.

As Figure 10.1 suggests, the key is to find the right balance between structure and interaction. When there is too much interaction, the group experiences the chaos of unbridled talk, which might not be focused; group and team members may need help focusing on one idea at a time rather than bouncing from topic to topic. When there is too much structure, however, the group loses the freedom to listen and respond with sensitivity to what others are saying.

In the pages that follow, we present a set of steps that can help you develop a sequence of things group members should be talking about. These five steps are inspired by educator and philosopher John Dewey, who in 1910 wrote a book called *How We Think*.[32] His book described how individuals go about the problem-solving process. In essence, he described the scientific method that scientists still use to solve problems: defining and analyzing a problem, identifying solutions, picking a solution, and putting the solution into practice. He called this process **reflective thinking**. We present these steps here not as a one-size-fits-all prescription that you should always follow, but as a way of structuring the problem-solving process to manage uncertainty and ensure that the key functions we talked about earlier are accomplished during your discussion. These steps incorporate the ideas we previously presented when describing what effective group members do. In addition to describing each step of the reflective thinking process, we present several techniques to help you structure discussion.

reflective thinking
A problem-solving process based on the scientific method.

Step 1: Identify and Define the Problem

"What's your problem?" As we noted earlier, groups work best when they have identified a clear, elevating goal that unites their effort. Whatever method or technique a group uses, it is essential that the group members know precisely what problem they are trying to solve. To reach a clear statement of the problem, consider asking the following questions:

- What is the specific problem that concerns us?
- What do we want more of or less of?[33]
- What terms, concepts, or ideas do we need to define so as to understand the problem?

It is also helpful to phrase the problem as a question and to clarify the problem.

Develop a Question   Most group experts recommend that an effective way to give your problem-solving task appropriate structure is to phrase your problem in the form of a policy question. A policy question is phrased so that the group will recommend some action (policy) to eliminate, reduce, or manage the problem. Policy questions begin with the words "What should be done about . . ." or "What could be done to improve . . . ."

Here are some examples:

- What should be done to lower the cost of tuition at our university?
- What could be done to decrease property taxes in our state?
- What should be done to make health care more affordable for all U.S. citizens?

Clarify the Problem   One specific technique for clarifying a problem is to use the journalists' six questions method.[34] Most reporters are taught to include the answers to six questions—who, what, when, where, why, and how—when writing a news story. Answering each of these six questions about the problem the group has identified can help further define and limit the problem. For example, a group might ask *who* and *when* questions such as "Who is harmed by the problem?" and "When do the harmful effects of the problem occur?" The group's answers can also help it move to the next step in the process: analyzing the problem.

Step 2: Analyze the Problem

Many groups want to "cut to the chase" quickly and start spinning out solutions without taking the time to analyze the problem thoroughly. Resist this temptation. Analyzing a problem well is an important prerequisite to finding an effective solution. To analyze something is to break it down into smaller pieces. To analyze a problem is to consider the causes, effects, symptoms, history, and other information that will inform the group about how to best solve the problem. Essential questions that can help you analyze problems include the following:

- How long has the problem been in existence?
- How widespread is the problem?
- What are the causes of the problem?
- What are the effects of the problem?
- What are the symptoms of the problem?
- What methods already exist for managing the problem?
- What are the limitations of existing methods?
- What obstacles keep the group from achieving its goal?

Establish Criteria   In addition to considering these questions, group members should develop **criteria**, which are standards for an acceptable solution to a problem. Identifying clear criteria can help you spot a good solution when you see one. Sample criteria for solutions include the following:

criteria
Standards for an acceptable solution.

- The solution should be inexpensive.
- The solution should be implemented by a certain date.
- The solution should be agreed on by all group members.
- The solution should be agreed on by all individuals affected by the recommendations.

Don't rely on your memory when you verbalize criteria. Write down on a highly visible whiteboard, flipchart, or projected image the list of criteria your group has identified. Include the list of criteria in the minutes or notes that summarize the meeting.

Analyze Problem Elements   After you have gathered information and developed criteria, your group may need to develop a systematic way of analyzing the information you've gathered. One technique that can help structure the analysis of your problem

VERBAL

FIGURE 10.2   Force Field Analysis

This analysis was conducted by a group that wanted to increase the number of students who volunteer for community projects. The group's goal is written on the top arrow. Driving forces, shown on the left, are factors that increase the group's chance of achieving its goal. Restraining forces, listed on the right, are factors that reduce the group's ability to get more students to volunteer.

SOURCE: Adapted from Julius E. Etington, *The Winning Trainer* (Houston: Gulf Publishing, 1989).

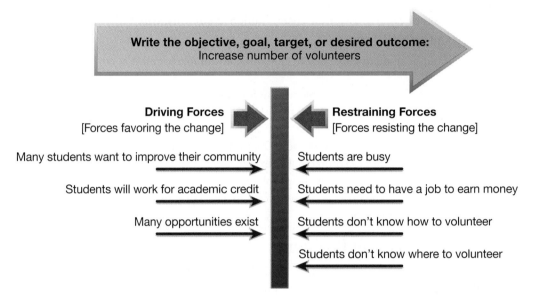

force field analysis technique

A method of analyzing a problem or issue by identifying forces that increase the likelihood that the desired goal will occur (driving forces) and forces that decrease the probability that the goal will occur (restraining forces).

and also help your team identify criteria is the **force field analysis technique** shown in Figure 10.2.[35] This technique works best when your group has identified a clear goal and needs to assess what is happening now that would increase the probability that the goal will be achieved.

After identifying a goal, the group lists all the driving forces currently at work that would help achieve the goal. Then the group does just the opposite: It identifies the restraining forces that are keeping the group from achieving the goal. When complete, the group's task in developing solutions is now clear: Increase the driving forces and decrease the restraining forces.

Step 3: Generate Creative Solutions

Now that you've identified a specific problem, analyzed its causes and history, and established clear criteria for solutions, you're ready to generate creative options to solve the problem. Keep in mind that sometimes it's a group's intuition rather than logical, structured strategies that result in more creative solutions to problems.[36] **Creativity** is the generation, application, combination, and extension of new ideas. Researchers have found that your entire group is more likely to be creative if individual group members are creative, are open to new ideas, have diverse backgrounds, and believe that they can be creative; it's important not to rely on others to be creative but to develop your own creative skill.[37] It's simply not true that only a few gifted and talented people are creative. Creative ideas can come from anyone. Your group is more likely to be creative if you do the following things:[38]

creativity

The generation, application, combination, and extension of new ideas.

- Make sure everyone in the group knows the precise nature of the problem.
- Review and summarize the analysis of the problem.
- Promote a climate of freedom; let people experiment and play with ideas.
- Don't prematurely judge and evaluate the ideas of others.
- Listen to minority points of view; you never know who may have the next great insight.
- Provide enough time for creativity to occur; don't rush the creative process.

Brainstorming is the classic technique for identifying possible solutions to a problem. This technique, in which group members try to generate as many ideas as possible within a set period of time without evaluating them, was developed by an advertising executive about fifty years ago to encourage a group to be creative.[39] You've probably used brainstorming before. Many groups, however, don't use the technique effectively.

Problems with Traditional, Oral Brainstorming The key to making brainstorming work—to come up with as many creative ideas as possible—is to *separate the generation of ideas from the evaluation of ideas.* This means that group members should feel free to offer ideas without fear of criticism, snickering, or being made to feel foolish. Reality, however, may be quite different. When group members start suggesting ideas, there may be verbal or, more likely, nonverbal evaluation of those ideas. People may laugh at the more offbeat suggestions; or when someone announces a suggestion, others may frown, sneer, voice an editorial comment, or talk over the person and ignore the suggestion. Another subtle form of evaluation occurs when some group ideas are praised and some are not. Group members whose ideas are not praised may feel that their ideas are considered stupid. Clearly, when ideas are evaluated as soon as they're offered, brainstorming doesn't work well; members may become reluctant to share ideas. This is especially true of group members who are shy or uncomfortable talking in a group; however, these people may have great ideas that are worth sharing.

Better Brainstorming There are several strategies that can help groups improve on traditional, oral brainstorming. Consider the following suggestions.

Write Down Your Ideas Before Sharing Them With Others Consider having a period of **silent brainstorming**, in which group members work individually before everyone shares their ideas verbally. Another name for silent brainstorming is the **nominal group technique**.[40] For a specified period of time, encourage group members to work individually and write down their ideas. During this time, they are a group in name only (hence the term *nominal*). After group members have brainstormed individually, they share their ideas with the group. For example, each member could be encouraged to present five to ten suggestions for solving the group's problem. Another option is to have group members privately brainstorm and then e-mail their responses to the group leader or other members. However, before any brainstorming begins, make sure group members have a clear understanding of the problem.[41] Electronic brainstorming websites and apps can help virtual groups share ideas without meeting in person.

Piggyback Off the Ideas of Others For groups that do meet in person, group members can brainstorm ideas silently for a few minutes and then move into small groups to share and piggyback ideas before the entire group comes back together. When groups use silent brainstorming, it's usually best to go around the group one at a time to have members share what they have written down. Another creative way to generate ideas is to have group members write each of their ideas or suggestions on a sticky note.[42] Once the ideas are on the sticky notes, group members can stick them to the wall and then arrange them in groups. Seeing other group members' ideas may trigger additional creative ideas.

Evaluate All Ideas After They Are Shared In all variations of brainstorming, the goal is to separate generating or listing ideas from critiquing the ideas. Evaluate the ideas *after* all the group members have finished sharing. When the two parts of brainstorming get mixed together, fewer ideas flow because of group members' fear of being criticized.

Provide Plenty of Time for Brainstorming One research team found that one way to make traditional, oral brainstorming more effective is to give groups more than just a few minutes to generate ideas.[43] Traditional brainstorming groups who generated ideas for more than 10 minutes did just as well as groups using the nominal group

brainstorming
A technique for generating many possible solutions to a problem by withholding evaluation while group members suggest ideas. Ideas are evaluated after suggestions have been offered.

silent brainstorming (nominal group technique)
A method of generating creative ideas; group members brainstorm individually and write down their ideas before meeting together to share them.

technique (in which group members worked individually before sharing ideas collaboratively).[44] Research has confirmed that the nominal group technique has benefits because ideas are generated without others evaluating them. However, with adequate time, traditional brainstorming can also achieve positive results. When given enough time to do their work, traditional brainstorming groups also reported more cohesiveness than teams that used the nominal group technique.[45]

As we've noted, the purpose of brainstorming is to think of as many ideas as possible. To generate a lot of options, encourage members to piggyback off each other's ideas. List all ideas where everybody can see them; referring to the list can fuel more ideas. Try to identify one or more zany or wild ideas—this triggers creativity and may lead to a less zany but workable idea.

Step 4: Select the Best Solution

After the group has generated a long list of ideas, the next step is to evaluate them to determine which ones best meet the criteria the group identified when they analyzed the problem. It's really important that group members have both a clear goal and specific criteria. Without them, the group members will have difficulty recognizing a good solution when they see it.

It is usually easier for groups to expand alternatives (brainstorm) than to narrow alternatives. The methods that groups use to whittle a long list down to a manageable number for more serious debate include these five approaches:

1. *Decision by expert.* Let someone who has high credibility narrow the list.
2. *Rank.* Tell group members to rank their top five choices from 1 to 5.
3. *Rate.* Ask group members to evaluate each solution on a scale from 1 to 5; the solutions that are rated best get the most serious discussion.
4. *Majority vote.* Group members vote for the ideas they like.
5. *Consensus.* Group members seek a solution that all group or team members can accept.

COMMUNICATION & ETHICS

What If Someone Can't Stop Judging?

Sarah likes to be in charge of group meetings. She has lots of good ideas, and other group members benefit from her leadership and wealth of suggestions. But during traditional brainstorming sessions, she can't stop criticizing other people's ideas. One or two group members have asked Sarah not to evaluate others' ideas because they have noticed how some members don't share as frequently because of her criticism, but she just can't seem to stop critiquing ideas during the brainstorming sessions.

Sarah makes important contributions to the group and is a good leader except for this one flaw of continually evaluating what others say. What would you do if you were in this group with Sarah? Would you speak to Sarah, as other group members have done, to ask her to stop critiquing? Or would you say nothing? What are your ethical obligations to help the group perform as effectively as possible?

Some members have suggested asking Sarah to leave the group during brainstorming sessions, because her behavior hurts group creativity. On the basis of what you've read so far in this chapter, what other ideas might help Sarah avoid critiquing ideas as they are generated?

TABLE 10.2 Suggestions for Reaching Group and Team Consensus

Effective Group Members	Ineffective Group Members
Keep the Group Oriented toward Its Goal	
Remind the group what the goal is.	Go off on tangents and do not stay focused on the agenda.
Write facts and key ideas on a flipchart or whiteboard.	Fail to summarize or rely on oral summaries to keep group members focused on the goal.
Talk about the discussion process, and ask questions that keep the group focused on the agenda.	Do little to help clarify group discussion.
Listen to the Ideas of Others	
Clarify misunderstandings.	Do not clarify misunderstandings or check to see whether others understand their message.
Emphasize areas of agreement.	Ignore areas of agreement.
Maintain eye contact when listening to someone and remain focused on the speaker without interrupting.	Do not maintain eye contact with the speaker, do not focus attention on the speaker, or interrupt the speaker.
Promote Honest Dialogue and Discussion	
Seek out differences of opinion.	Do not seek other opinions from group members.
Do not change their minds quickly to avoid conflict.	Quickly agree with other group members to avoid conflict.
Try to involve everyone in the discussion.	Permit one person or just a few people to talk too much and dominate the conversation.

Develop Consensus **Consensus** occurs when there is enough agreement that group members will all support a decision. Consensus doesn't mean that everyone agrees enthusiastically and completely with what the group has decided, but that no one will stand in the way of what the group has decided. The advantage of reaching a consensus decision is that all group members can verbalize support for the decision. But reaching consensus takes time.

The three primary strategies summarized in Table 10.2 can help groups reach consensus:[46]

1. Focus on the goal.[47]
2. Listen.
3. Promote honest discussion.

Avoid Groupthink Be cautious if all group members agree too quickly or too consistently. You may be experiencing groupthink instead of consensus. **Groupthink** occurs when group members seem to agree but primarily just want to avoid conflict. On the surface, it seems as though group members have reached consensus, but it may be an illusion of agreement. Another way of describing groupthink is to call it faulty consensus; too little disagreement often reduces the quality of group decisions. If a group does not seriously examine the pros and cons of an idea, the quality of the decision it makes is likely to suffer because the group has not used its full power to analyze and evaluate ideas.[48]

Failure to test ideas and the resulting groupthink can have serious consequences in the form of wrong, dangerous, or stupid decisions. The following list identifies a few well-known disasters or problems in which groupthink was a key factor:

- In 1986, American TV viewers, including thousands of school children, watched in horror as the *Challenger* space shuttle, carrying the first teacher in space, exploded on their screens. The tragedy resulted from both faulty engineering and groupthink: Some scientists knew that the shuttle might not fly in cold temperatures but, because of pressure to stay on schedule, decided not to stop the launch.[49]

consensus

Agreement among all members of a group or team to support an idea, proposal, or solution.

groupthink

A faulty sense of agreement that occurs when members of a group fail to challenge an idea; a false consensus reached when conflict is minimized and group members do not express concerns or reservations about an idea or proposal.

"All those in favor say 'Aye.'"
"Aye."
"Aye."
"Aye."
"Aye."
"Aye."

- In 1999, several students were killed in a traditional pre–football game bonfire at Texas A&M University. Some people thought the bonfire construction unsafe before the accident occurred, but because of tradition, the bonfire continued to be built and tragedy was the result.[50]

- The commission that investigated the September 11, 2001, terrorist attacks concluded that the nation's lack of preparedness for the attacks was attributable in part to groupthink.[51] The commission found that evidence of a terrorist threat existed before the attacks, yet not enough action was taken to fully address the problem.

News headlines are not the only places to look for examples of groupthink. If you think about it, you'll find plenty of examples in groups and teams you've worked with.

Causes of Groupthink   Groupthink is more likely to occur in your group under the following conditions:

- The group feels apathetic about its task.
- Group members don't expect to be successful.
- One group member has very high credibility—group members tend to believe what he or she says.
- One group member is very persuasive.
- Group members don't usually challenge ideas—it's expected that group members will agree with one another.[52]

Be on the lookout for these symptoms in your groups and teams.

Of course, as the saying goes, "Hindsight is 20/20." After the fact, it can be easy to spot an example of groupthink. The hard part is to be aware of groupthink when it is occurring in your group. Knowing the causes and symptoms of groupthink can help you spot it and then put an end to it.

How to Avoid Groupthink   The first thing to do is to be aware that groupthink is occurring. In addition to awareness, here are several additional strategies to avoid groupthink:[53]

- Don't agree with someone just because that person has high status; examine the evidence and the ideas of others carefully, regardless of their position.
- Consider asking someone from outside the group to evaluate the group's decisions and decision-making process.
- Assign someone to be a devil's advocate—to look for disadvantages to a proposed idea.[54]
- Ask group members to break into smaller teams or pairs to consider both the pros and the cons of a proposed solution.

Step 5: Take Action

Once you have identified your solution or solutions, your group needs to consider the question, "Will it work?" You may want to do a pilot (practice) test or ask a small group of people what they think of your idea before you "go public" with it. Bouncing your proposed solution off an expert and checking to see whether your solution has been successful when others have adopted it can help you test the solution's effectiveness.

If your group has to identify a solution *and* put it into action, your group will need structure to make sure that details don't get overlooked in getting the job done. Perhaps you know the people in the following story:

> This is a story about four people: Everybody, Somebody, Anybody, and Nobody. There was an important job to be done, and Everybody was asked to do it. Everybody was sure Somebody would do it. Anybody could have done it, but Nobody did it. Somebody got angry about that because it was Everybody's job. Everybody thought Anybody could do it, but Nobody realized that Everybody wouldn't do it. It ended up that Everybody blamed Somebody when actually Nobody asked Anybody.

Make a list of who should do what. At the next group meeting, follow up to see whether the assignments have been completed. Effective groups and teams develop an action plan and periodically review it to make sure Anybody asked Somebody.

Enhancing Group and Team Leadership

10.3 Compare and contrast the trait, functional, styles, situational, and transformational approaches to understanding leadership.

Leadership is the ability to influence others through communication to achieve a goal. Some people view a leader as someone who delegates and directs the group. Others see a leader as someone who is primarily responsible for ensuring that whatever task is assigned or designed by the group is completed. Actually, most groups have many leaders, not just one person who influences others. In fact, each group or team member undoubtedly influences what the group does or does not achieve. Regardless of who serves as leader, research suggests that the quality of group and team leadership has a significant effect on how satisfied team members are.[55] Members of an effectively led team feel greater satisfaction, are more productive, and are less likely to be absent than members of less effective groups.[56] The quality of team leadership influences virtually every aspect of what it feels like to be a team member. The prevailing approaches to analyzing the behavior of effective leaders are the trait, functional, styles, situational, and transformational approaches to leadership.

Trait Approach

Are leaders born or made? The **trait approach to leadership** suggests that there are certain attributes or traits that make good leaders. According to this approach, if you are born with these traits or if you cultivate leadership skills, you will be a leader. Research has identified intelligence, confidence, social skills, general administrative skill, physical energy, and enthusiasm as some of the traits effective leaders possess.[57] Researchers have also found that effective leaders develop persuasive arguments and are comfortable expressing their ideas to others.[58] Another research study found support for

RECAP

Reflective-Thinking Steps and Techniques

Steps	Techniques
1. Identify and define the problem.	• Phrase the problem as a policy question. • Use the journalists' six questions method (Who? What? When? Where? Why? How?) to help define the issues.
2. Analyze the problem.	• Use force field analysis to identify driving and restraining forces. • Develop criteria to clarify the issues and help evaluate solutions.
3. Generate creative solutions.	• Use brainstorming. • Use silent brainstorming (nominal group technique) or electronic brainstorming.
4. Select the best solution.	• Narrow alternatives by ranking, rating, majority vote, consensus, or relying on an expert decision. • Reach consensus by being goal oriented, by listening, and by promoting honest dialogue.
5. Take action.	• Develop a clear action plan. • Make a written list of who should do what.

leadership
The ability to influence the behavior of others through communication to achieve a goal.

trait approach to leadership
A view of leadership that identifies specific qualities or characteristics of effective leaders.

▲ According to the trait approach to leadership, personal characteristics such as intelligence, confidence, social skills, physical energy, and enthusiasm make good leaders. Nelson Mandela, who served as President of South Africa and won the Nobel Peace Prize, possessed several traits of an effective leader. However, positive traits alone do not guarantee that someone will be a good leader. REUTERS/Alamy Stock Photo

functional approach to leadership
A view of leadership that identifies the key task and process roles that need to be performed in a group.

task function
A leadership behavior that helps a group accomplish its job.

process function
A leadership behavior that helps maintain a positive group climate.

two of the Communication Principles for a Lifetime presented in this book: Effective leaders are self-aware and adapt to the people they lead and the context in which they lead.[59] Although many leaders do seem to have traits or special skills that can enhance their ability to influence others, just having these traits does not mean that you will be an effective leader. Traits alone will not ensure effective leadership behavior. Leadership is more complicated than that.

Functional Approach

Rather than identifying personality characteristics or other traits, the **functional approach to leadership** categorizes the essential leadership behaviors or functions that need to be performed to enhance the workings of a group. According to the functional approach, there are two broad leadership functions: (1) task functions and (2) process functions. These two functions should look familiar. They are similar to the types of group roles discussed in Chapter 9.

Task Leadership Functions   **Task functions** include behaviors that help the group or team get the work done. Whether the leader is appointed or elected, one of the responsibilities of leaders is to ensure that the group completes the task it is tackling. The functional approach to leadership suggests that several people can share the leadership functions. The following are some of the jobs that often need to be done:

- Helping set the group's agenda
- Recording what the group does
- Determining when meetings begin and end
- Preparing and distributing handouts
- Initiating or proposing new ideas
- Seeking and giving information
- Suggesting options
- Elaborating on the ideas of others
- Evaluating ideas

In most groups, these key functions are assumed by many if not most group members. A group member who rarely helps with any of these tasks often earns the uncoveted title of "slacker."

Process Leadership Functions   **Process functions** are the second major type of function leaders assume in groups. Process leaders seek to maintain a friendly environment that promotes honest, frank discussion. Process leaders have "people skills." They listen sensitively to others and are observant of nonverbal cues. They focus on managing relationships by adapting to the needs of individual members. Another key process leadership task is to seek support from people and resources outside the team. An effective team leader keeps the team informed about how external influences affect the team's work goals.[60] Although a single person can perform all these functions, just as with task leadership, it is more than likely that several people will help maintain the group's process. Specific process roles include the following:

- Energizing the team by encouraging team members to keep at it
- Mediating conflict
- Compromising or helping others to compromise
- Gatekeeping: monitoring discussion to ensure that some members don't talk too much and others too little

In most groups or teams, these process roles are not formally assigned. Although some of the task functions may be explicitly assigned ("Daria, would you make copies of this report?"), process roles are assumed when needed; they emerge according to the needs of the group and the personality, skills, sensitivity, and past experiences of the group members who are present. It is unlikely that you will start a meeting by saying, "Okay, Janice, you're in charge of settling the arguments between Ken and Daryl. And Carl, you try to encourage Muriel and Russell to talk more." Effective leaders look for opportunities to enhance the overall climate of the group. They try to catch people doing something right and then offer sincere praise and recognition.

Styles Approach

The **styles approach to leadership** suggests that leaders operate in one of three primary styles: (1) authoritarian, (2) democratic, or (3) laissez-faire. The methods used to influence group members usually fall into one of these broad categories, outlined in Table 10.3.[61]

styles approach to leadership
A view of leadership that identifies three methods of interacting when leading others: authoritarian, democratic, and laissez-faire.

Authoritarian Leadership   **Authoritarian leaders** influence by giving orders and controlling others. Dictators and military officers assume this leadership style. But you don't have to be in the military or living in a dictatorship to experience an authoritarian leadership style. Perhaps you've felt like mumbling, "Who put *her* in charge?" during a group meeting. Or maybe you have observed that some action needed to be taken and asked someone in the group to do what you thought was needed. As we discussed, groups need a certain amount of structure. The authoritarian leader assumes that he or she knows the type and amount of structure the group needs and proceeds to tell others what to do. Authoritarian leaders may be self-aware

authoritarian leader
One who leads by directing, controlling, telling, and ordering others.

TABLE 10.3 Leadership Styles

Authoritarian	Democratic	Laissez-Faire
The leader makes all policy decisions.	The leader discusses all policy decisions with group members. The group makes decisions by consensus.	The leader gives minimal direction to discussions of policy decisions. Group members must initiate discussions about policy and procedures.
The leader determines what will happen one step at a time; future steps are unclear or uncertain.	The group discusses what steps need to be taken. Group members work together to develop both short-term and long-term action steps.	The leader may supply information about what steps need to be taken, if asked. The leader does not volunteer information.
The leader tells people what to do.	The leader serves as a facilitator to develop a collaborative approach to accomplishing the group's work.	The leader does not participate in creating work assignments.

and may use appropriate verbal and nonverbal messages, but they are not always known for listening and responding to others. They also may not be worried about adapting their messages to those whom they lead. They often speak and expect others to follow. Of the three primary leadership styles, the authoritarian leader is least effective over a long period of time.[62] Yet when a group or team experiences increased stress, a decisive leader is perceived as more charismatic than other types of leaders.[63] Group members don't like an authoritarian leader all the time, but they may tolerate or even appreciate a bold, charismatic leader when there's a need for someone to make an important decision quickly.

Democratic Leadership   The **democratic leader**, as you might guess from the name, consults with the other group members before issuing edicts. The democratic leader listens and adapts messages to others. This type of leader seeks to join in the process of influencing without bulldozing or shoving the group into action its members may resent. Sometimes formal votes are taken in larger groups or assemblies; in smaller groups, the leader or leaders gauge the reaction of the group through dialogue and nonverbal cues. The democratic leader leads by developing a consensus rather than telling people what to do or think.

Laissez-Faire Leadership   The **laissez-faire leader** takes a hands-off, laid-back approach to influencing. This type of leader shies away from actively influencing the group. He or she influences only when pushed to lead. Like the authoritarian leader, this type of leader often does not adapt to the needs of the group. A laissez-faire approach is easiest to spot when an elected or appointed leader simply won't lead. Sometimes, a laissez-faire approach may fit the group's needs. In other instances, laissez-faire leaders fear making a mistake, or they just want to be liked and don't want to ruffle anyone's feathers. But as the slogan goes, "Not to decide is to decide." The laissez-faire leader influences the group by his or her silence or inactivity. The team may have a problem to unravel, but the laissez-faire leader leaves the task entirely to the rest of the group members.

Which leadership style works best? As we discuss next, it depends on the situation. It also depends on the leader and the members. One study found that a democratic, collaborative leadership style works best when the leader is perceived as credible and charismatic.[64] And as we'll see, a more directive, authoritarian style of leadership is generally more effective when group members doubt that they can effectively accomplish the work and value direct assistance and guidance. Remember that leadership in groups and teams is usually shared by several people. Even when someone has been appointed or elected to be "the leader," leadership roles are often assumed by several group members.

Situational Approach

The **situational approach to leadership** views leadership as an interactive process in which such factors as culture, time limitations, group member personalities, and the work the group needs to do determine a particular style of leadership. The situational leadership approach is based on Principle Five: Appropriately adapt messages to others. The effective leader adapts his or her style to fit the needs of the group and the task at hand. Sometimes a group needs a strong, authoritarian leader to make decisions quickly so that the group can achieve its goal. Although most groups prefer a democratic leadership style, during times of crisis a group needs a decisive leader who can help manage uncertainty and provide appropriate structure. An authoritarian style may be acceptable then.[65]

democratic leader
One who leads by developing a consensus among group members; a leader who asks for input and then uses the input when leading and making decisions.

laissez-faire leader
One who fails to lead or who leads or exerts influence only when asked or directed by the group.

situational approach to leadership
A view of leadership as an interactive process in which a leader gauges how to lead based on such factors as the quality of the relationships among group members, the power of the leader, the nature of the task, and the maturity of the group.

Groups with highly structured goals and a high level of stress also may operate best with a more authoritarian leadership style. For example, firefighters who are battling a house fire with a family of five people inside have a clearly structured goal: to save lives. In this situation, the group needs decisive authoritarian leadership. If the group's task is to solve a problem or make a decision collaboratively, the group will likely benefit from a democratic leadership style. If a group's goal is primarily social or creative, a laissez-faire leader may be best. Compared to the firefighters, for example, a book club that is trying to select its next reading selection has less structured goals (there are many possible options) and a less stressful situation (there is no fire!). This less structured and less stressful task calls for a more participative democratic style of leadership or a hands-off, laissez-faire style of leadership. So according to the situational approach, the answer to the question "What's the best leadership style?" is "It depends."[66]

The readiness of the group also plays a major role in which leadership style would work best.[67] *Readiness* refers to a group member's ability to assume responsibility to accomplish a task; his or her overall knowledge, background, and experience; and his or her general level of motivation. Leadership experts Paul Hersey and Ken Blanchard suggest that a directive or more authoritative, "telling" style of leadership seems to work best when groups have a low level of readiness. A high degree of readiness suggests that a more delegating style of leadership would help the group function well. An exceptionally ready or mature group may need minimal direction—more of a laissez-faire leadership style. Wise leaders also consider the cultural backgrounds of those whom they lead. Research supports the important role of culture in influencing the style of leadership that seems to be best suited to a team.[68] Group members from collective cultures seem to appreciate more participative styles of leadership.

surface-level diversity

Human differences that are easily visible to us, such as differences in ethnicity, race, age, sex, gender, and other social and observable features.

deep-level diversity

Human differences that aren't always visible on the surface, such as differences in attitudes, opinions, values, information, culture, and other factors that take time to become evident in groups.

COMMUNICATION & DIVERSITY

Deep and Surface Diversity: Which Differences Make a Difference?

People work in groups because "two heads are better than one." More people bring more—and more varied—approaches to solving a problem or illuminating an issue. But are all differences created equal?

Researchers have found that some differences among group members are more significant than others.[69] **Surface-level diversity** encompasses the human differences that are easily visible to us, such as differences in ethnicity, race, age, sex, gender, and other social and observable features. **Deep-level diversity** involves differences that aren't always visible on the surface, such as differences in attitudes, opinions, values, information, cognitive structure, culture, and other factors that take time to become evident in groups.[70] Group communication researcher Ralph Rodriguez has found that these differences in underlying values or approaches to problems affect a group's performance more than do differences in such surface characteristics as race, gender, and ethnicity. Rodriguez also suggests that groups can enhance the quality of their outcomes if they discuss their differences.[71]

- *Be cautious of making sweeping generalizations about people who are from a culture that appears to be similar to yours*. Researchers have found that we often expect people who look like us at the surface level to agree with us. Yet deep-level differences may be the best predictors of whether someone agrees or disagrees with our perspective.[72]

- *Take time to explore group members' deep-level differences in perspectives and approaches*. These deep-level differences are noticed only after people spend time with one another and are engaged in conversation.

- *Encourage people to share ideas and information via e-mail or text messages*. Because some group members may be quieter than others, the opportunity to respond individually rather than orally in the presence of others may bring out more differences in perspective that can help a group reach a better outcome.

- *Group members need the benefit of different perspectives*. If you're in the surface-level minority or the deep-level minority in a group, make sure that you tactfully yet assertively express your ideas, opinions, facts, and information to the group.

Depending on the situation, a leadership style may emerge naturally from a group. For example, in one-time-only groups, members may allow a more directive leadership approach. However, if a group will be together for some time and the quality of group relations is important to the functioning of the group, a more participative, democratic leadership style is in order.[73]

Transformational Leadership

transformational approach to leadership

A view of leadership that defines a leader as one who leads by shaping the vision of the group and by developing trust through high-quality interpersonal relationships with group members.

One of the newer leadership approaches to emerge is called the **transformational approach to leadership**.[74] The transformational leader influences the group or organization by *transforming* the group—giving it a new vision, energizing or realigning the group culture, or giving the group a new structure. The leader leads by helping members see all the possibilities within the group. The transformational leader also develops a relationship with those whom he or she leads.[75]

Skills of Transformational Leaders   Author Peter Senge suggests three fundamental skills of transformational leadership: (1) Build a shared vision, (2) challenge existing ways of thinking, and (3) be a systems thinker—help a group or team see that everything is connected to everything else.[76] Articulating a shared, or collective, vision is an important part of what a transformational leader does. An authoritarian leader would just tell the group, "Here's your vision; now get to work." The democratic leader would ask, "What vision do you want?" The laissez-faire leader would do nothing about a vision unless asked to do something. The situational leader would say, "Let me see what type of group I'm leading and listen to group members, and then I'll share a vision."

Another skill of transformational leaders is the ability to encourage the development of new ideas. Teams that emphasize the importance of learning and being creative do a better job of both accomplishing tasks and fostering positive, supportive interpersonal relationships.[77] Sometimes viewed as the "guide on the side" rather than the "sage on the stage," transformational leaders prefer to think of themselves as coaches or mentors rather than directive leaders who dictate who does what.

Effects of Transformational Leaders   Research suggests that effectively functioning transformational leaders can enhance team cohesiveness and improve perceptions of team performance.[78] They achieve these benefits by linking with other groups and teams either inside or outside the organization, helping the group span boundaries and stay connected with issues and forces that influence the group.[79] An effective transformational leader can also empower group members to assume responsibility for themselves as well as boost the confidence of group members.

Can transformational leadership skills—or any leadership skills—be taught, the way you can teach someone to drive a car? Some researchers suggest that experience is the best teacher.[80] You can learn how to communicate, listen, relate, and solve problems, but having an opportunity to practice these

RECAP

Leadership Approaches

Approach to Leadership	Guiding Principle
Trait	Leaders possess certain traits or characteristics that contribute to leadership effectiveness.
Functional	Leaders influence others through two primary functions: • Task functions, which help accomplish the work • Process functions, which help establish a positive climate
Styles	Leadership is enacted in three primary styles: • Authoritarian leaders direct and control others. • Democratic leaders solicit input from others and seek to lead by involving others in decisions. • Laissez-faire leaders intentionally influence others only when asked or directed by others to lead.
Situational	Leadership is an interactive process in which a leader adapts his or her approach based on such factors as: • The quality of group member relationships • The nature of the task • Time limitations
Transformational	A leader influences others by: • Developing a shared vision • Using listening and relationship-building skills to create a climate of trust

skills in real-life settings may be the best way to develop your leadership skills. Whether you learn leadership skills and principles from a book or from the "school of life," the role of a good leader is that of a servant, helping others accomplish a goal. This ancient description of a wise leader offers considerable insight into what makes a leader great:

> The wicked leader the people despise.
> The good leader the people revere.
> Of the great leader the people say,
> "We did it ourselves."
> —Lao Tsu

Enhancing Group and Team Meetings

10.4 **Develop and use strategies to structure meetings appropriately, keep meetings on track, and promote appropriate dialogue and interaction.**

Humor columnist Dave Barry said, "If you had to identify, in one word, the reason why the human race has not achieved, and never will achieve, its full potential, that word would be *meetings*."[81] Meetings are an inescapable fact of life for most people and will undoubtedly be inescapable for you as well.

Why does meeting participation inspire such a negative reaction—not just from Dave Barry, but from many people? Often, it's because meeting leaders and participants have not mastered the principles we've stressed as fundamental to communication success in any context. Meetings are more productive if participants are aware of their behaviors and the behaviors of others and if they believe they have the necessary skill to make meetings effective.[82] Using and interpreting verbal and nonverbal messages are also vital skills required for meeting effectiveness, as are listening and responding to messages with sensitivity. Because of the complexity and uncertainty that arise when people collaborate, being able to adapt message content and message structure is essential.[83] We conclude this chapter by providing some tips for managing one of the most likely collaborative contexts you'll encounter: meetings.

What specific problems occur most frequently in meetings? According to a survey of meeting participants, the most common meeting "sin" is getting off the subject.[84] The second-biggest problem is not having clear goals or a meeting agenda. Meeting goers also reported that often meetings were too long, people weren't prepared, nothing really happened, meetings started late, and there were no follow-up action plans.

Meetings need two essential things to be effective: *structure* and *interaction*. Sound familiar? As we noted earlier in this chapter, groups also need a balance of these two things.

Manage Meeting Structure

The essential weapon to combat disorganized, rambling meetings is a clear, well-developed **agenda**, a list of the key issues, ideas, and information that will be discussed, in the order of discussion. How do you develop a well-crafted agenda? Consider these three steps.

agenda

A written plan for achieving the goals of a group meeting, which typically includes items for discussion, action, and information.

Step One: Determine Your Meeting Goals   Every meeting seeks to accomplish something. (If you don't have something to accomplish, don't hold a meeting!) Most meetings have one or more of the following three goals: (1) giving information, (2) discussing information, and (3) taking action.

- *Giving information.* An information-giving meeting is like a briefing or a series of short speeches. If the only task is to share information, you may not really need a meeting at all; a written memo or an e-mail message will suffice. If you want to emphasize the importance of the information by sharing with others face to face, however, then giving information is an appropriate primary meeting goal.

- *Discussing information.* An information-discussion meeting is one in which there is considerable give and take. The key to this type of meeting is not to let it become a series of long-winded speeches. Also, if you're not careful, discussions digress from the topic. The meeting leader or meeting participants should be aware of the goals of the discussion so that comments remain relevant.

- *Taking action.* A meeting may involve making a decision, solving a problem, or implementing a decision or solution. If the purpose of the meeting is to take action, it's helpful if group members know before they arrive for the meeting that they will be asked to take some action.

Step Two: Identify What Needs to be Discussed to Achieve the Goal   After you have determined your goal(s), you need to determine how to structure the meeting to achieve the goal. What topics need to be covered to achieve the goal? What information do you need? What issues do you need to focus on? Brainstorm answers to these questions, but don't worry about the precise order of the items yet; focus on organizing the agenda after you know what you need to discuss.

Step Three: Organize the Agenda   Once you have identified your meeting goals (giving information, discussing information, taking action) and assessed what you need to talk about, take time to arrange the items on your agenda in the most effective way to achieve your goals. Table 10.4 identifies several meeting problems and possible solutions. In addition, here are several specific strategies for organizing effective meetings:[85]

- Organize the agenda around your meeting goals. If you're meeting to solve a problem, you could use the five problem-solving steps as an agenda-setting guide: (1) Identify and define the problem, (2) analyze the problem, (3) generate creative options, (4) select the best option, and (5) take action. A single meeting may focus on only one or two of those steps; don't feel that you have to cram all five problem-solving steps into every meeting.

- Use the subheads "Information Items," "Discussion Items," and "Action Items" as you construct your agenda to signal to group members the goal of the discussion, as shown in the sample meeting agenda.

- Consider putting your most important agenda item first, because what is introduced first usually takes the most time.

TABLE 10.4   Solving Meeting Agenda Problems

Potential Meeting Agenda Problem	Suggested Meeting Agenda Strategy
Meeting participants tend to spend more time on the first or second agenda item than on later items.	Make sure that the early agenda items are something the group needs to spend time on.
Meeting participants want to talk, even if the meeting leader wants them to just listen.	Take advantage of the desire to participate by inviting input and discussion early in the meeting rather than trying to squelch discussion or having to deal with interruptions from group members.
Meeting participants aren't prepared. They haven't done their "homework."	Allow a few minutes for silent reading. Let members get up to speed by reviewing information or quickly looking at key pieces of data.
Meeting participants won't stick to the agenda.	Continue to remind the group of the agenda and the overall goal of the meeting. Make sure to distribute a written agenda ahead of the meeting.
There is an agenda item that may produce conflict and disagreement.	Help the group develop a sense of success by putting one or more noncontroversial items on the agenda ahead of the item that may produce conflict. Build on the group's ability to reach agreement.

- There may be times when you will want to put your most challenging issue for discussion in the middle of the meeting. This gives the group a chance to get oriented at the beginning of the meeting and ease out of the discussion at the end.[86]

- Consider making your first agenda item something that will immediately involve all meeting participants in active discussion. If you start with routine reports (a common practice), you establish a norm of passivity, and boredom is the usual result.

- If you are going to discuss a conflict-producing topic, you may want to put that agenda item after an issue on which you think the group will reach agreement. Groups may be more likely to reach agreement on a contentious issue if they have already reached agreement on another point.

- Start the meeting by asking meeting participants whether they have any other agenda items to consider. That way, you aren't as likely to be surprised by people who want to add something after you've planned the meeting agenda.

- After you've prepared your agenda, estimate how long you think the group will take to discuss each agenda item. Most groups take more time than you would expect to talk about issues and ideas.

Sample Meeting Agenda

Meeting Goals:
1. Discuss new product proposal: evaluate the pros and cons.
2. Decide whether to implement the personnel policy and mentor program.
3. Receive updates from committees.

I. Discussion Items
   A. How should we revise today's agenda?
   B. Identify new problems: What new issues or problems have you identified?
   C. React to new product team proposal (distributed by e-mail): What are the pros and cons of the proposal?

II. Action Items
   A. Should we approve the new personnel policy (distributed by e-mail)?
   B. Issue: Should we implement the new mentor program? If so, what should the program policies be?

III. Information Items
   A. New employee orientation report
   B. Planning committee report
   C. Finance committee report
   D. Announcements

Refer to the sample meeting agenda provided. Notice that the meeting has clear goals. Also notice how many of the agenda items are phrased as questions. Questions give an agenda focus and help to manage discussion.

When your job is to lead the meeting, you have several specific tasks to perform, including the following:

1. Call the group together; find out when is the best time to meet (finding time is often a major problem for busy people).
2. Develop an agenda, using the steps already described.
3. Determine whether there is a **quorum**—the minimum number of people who must be present at a meeting to conduct business.
4. Call the meeting to order.
5. Keep notes (or delegate note-taking). Use a flipchart, dry-erase board, or a computer projection method to make notes visible to members during the meeting. Such written meeting notes become the "group mind" and help keep the group structured.
6. Decide when to take a vote.
7. Prepare a final report or delegate to a group member the preparation of a report or minutes.

quorum
The minimum number of people who must be present at a meeting to conduct business.

Manage Meeting Interaction

Interaction, as you recall, is the back-and-forth dialogue and discussion in which participants engage during meetings. Without interaction, meetings would be like a monologue, a speech, or a seminar rather than a lively discussion. It's important for people in a meeting to be involved in the discussion and share the information with one another.[93] Research has found that meetings that have more equal participation by all participants generally are more effective than meetings dominated by a few

COMMUNICATION & SOCIAL MEDIA

Virtual Meeting Tips

A virtual meeting occurs when you use the Internet or some other electronic means of connecting with others rather than meeting face to face. Using Skype, FaceTime, Google Duo, or another video chatting app has made it increasingly easy to hold a virtual meeting with other team members from around the globe. What are ways to maximize your electronic collaboration? Here are several research-supported tips to help you make the most of mediated meetings:[87]

- *Start live*. If at all possible, make your first meeting a face-to-face meeting. Getting to know your team members in person helps to develop positive relationships at the outset of a longer project in which you will be interacting over a period of time.[88]
- *Develop communication ground rules*. Aside from communicating during a planned virtual meeting, determine how and when you will communicate with other team members.[89] Will you call someone on the phone? Skype? Use only e-mail? Clarify communication expectations about the method of communication and when it's best to reach your fellow team members.
- *Communicate frequently*. One ground rule we suggest is to contact team members when questions or issues arise even if you're not in a scheduled meeting. Don't hesitate to send virtual meeting members short notes and messages. Resist the temptation to hold onto information until you have a longer message. Frequent

communication helps virtual meeting participants get to know one another.

- *Use technology to monitor team progress*. Invite team members to provide periodic reports via e-mail or on the team home page. Also distribute meeting minutes via e-mail very soon after the group has held a virtual meeting.
- *Encourage the development of relationships*. Virtual meetings have a tendency to be task oriented. To foster good team relationships, allow time at the beginning of a virtual meeting for relationship building; during this time, encourage meeting participants to engage in off-task talk, communicating personal information. During the meeting, ensure that every person is heard from and that all are engaged and participating in the meeting.
- *Be positive*. Research suggests that, like members of face-to-face groups, virtual group members who have a positive perception of their own abilities to achieve results are more effective. So fostering a can-do spirit in a group or team is a good thing to do.[90]
- *Share information freely*. Research has found that virtual teams are even less likely to share information than face-to-face groups and teams. If you are meeting in a virtual group, make an extra effort to share information with all group members.[91]
- *Make sure you can use the technology effectively*. Groups that have received training on collaborative technology tools perform better than groups that haven't had training and therefore experience more technology glitches.[92]

people.[94] But too much unfocused interaction can result in a disorganized, chaotic discussion. To keep a meeting on track, meeting leaders and participants need facilitation skills. The most important facilitation skills include being a gatekeeper, using metadiscussion, monitoring discussion time, and structuring discussion techniques to keep discussion focused.

Use Gatekeeping Skills   A gatekeeper encourages less-talkative members to participate and tries to limit long-winded contributions by other group members. Gatekeepers need to be good listeners so that they can help manage the flow of conversation. Gatekeepers make such comments as:

> "Ashley, we haven't heard your ideas yet. Won't you share your thoughts with us?"
>
> or
>
> "Mike, thanks for sharing, but I'd like to hear what others have to say."

Polite, tactful invitations to talk or limit talk usually work. As we noted earlier in this chapter, you may need to speak privately with chronic oververbalizers to let them know that you would appreciate a more balanced discussion.

Use Metadiscussion **Metadiscussion** literally means "discussion about discussion."[95] It's a comment about the discussion process rather than about the topic under consideration. Metadiscussional statements include "I'm not following this conversation. What is our goal?" "Can someone summarize what we've accomplished so far?" and "Peggy, I'm not sure I understand how your observation relates to our meeting goal." These comments contain information and advice about the communication process rather than about the issues being discussed.

Metadiscussional phrases are helpful ways to keep the team or group focused on the task. Obviously, metadiscussional statements should not be phrased to personally attack others. Don't just blurt out "You're off task" or "Oh, let's not talk about that anymore." Instead, use tactful ways of letting other group members know that you'd like to return to the issues at hand. Use "I" messages rather than "you" messages to bring the group back on track. An **"I" message** begins with the word *I*, such as "I am not sure where we are in our discussion" or "I am lost here." A **"you" message** is a way of phrasing a message that makes others feel defensive—for example, "You're not following the agenda" or "Your point doesn't make any sense." Another way to express these same ideas, but with less of a negative edge, is to use "I" messages such as "I'm not sure where we are on the agenda" or "I'm not sure I understand how your point relates to the issue we are discussing." The ability to use the metadiscussion technique is an exceptionally powerful skill because you can offer metadiscussional statements even if you are not the appointed leader.

Monitor Time Being sensitive to the time the group is spending on an issue is yet another skill that is necessary to manage meeting interaction. Think of your agenda as a map, helping you plan where you want to go. Think of the clock as your gas gauge, telling you the amount of fuel you have to get where you want to go. In a meeting, keeping one eye on the clock and one eye on the agenda is analogous to focusing on the map and the gas gauge on a car trip. If you are running low on fuel (time), you will need to either get more gas (budget more time) or recognize that you will not get where you want to go. Begin each meeting by asking how long members can meet. If you have two or three crucial agenda items and one-third of your group has to leave in an hour, you may need to reshuffle your agenda to make sure that you can achieve your goals.

Use Structure to Manage Interaction Another way to manage interaction is to use some of the prescriptive structures talked about earlier. For example, silent brainstorming is a way to gain maximum participation from everyone. Yet another strategy is to ask people to come to the meeting with written responses to questions you posed in the agenda, which group members received in advance of the meeting. This signals that you want people to prepare for the meeting beforehand rather than doing their "homework" at the meeting.

An essential task of the meeting facilitator is to orchestrate meaningful interaction during the meeting so that all group or team members have the opportunity to share. Another structured method of inviting involvement is to have group members first write down their ideas individually and then share them with the group. Having members write before speaking is like providing them with a script, which can be effective in garnering contributions from all group members, not just the people who talk the most or who aren't shy about speaking up.

metadiscussion
Discussion about the discussion process; comments that help the group remain focused on the goals of the group or that point out how the group is doing its work.

"I" message
A message in which you state your perspective or point of view.

"you" message
A message that is likely to create defensiveness in others because it emphasizes how another person has created a problem rather than describing the problem from one's own perspective ("I" message).

RECAP

Strategies for Effective Meetings: Balance Structure and Interaction

How to Give a Meeting Structure

Prepare an effective agenda by

- Determining your meeting goals.
- Identifying what needs to be discussed to achieve the goals.
- Organizing the agenda to achieve the goals.

How to Ensure Managed Interaction

Keep discussion on track by

- Using effective gatekeeping skills.
- Using metadiscussion to help the group focus on the goals.
- Helping the group be sensitive to elapsed time and time remaining for deliberation.
- Using strategies to manage interaction (for example, writing before speaking or silent brainstorming).

Structure _____ **Interaction**

What are the best strategies to make yourself a valuable meeting leader or participant? The five Communication Principles for a Lifetime that we emphasize throughout the book will serve you well. In general, be aware of your own behavior and the behavior of others. Monitor your verbal and nonverbal messages to make sure that you are making comments relevant to the task at hand, but also be sensitive to the needs of the people in your group. You develop that sensitivity by listening to others and responding thoughtfully. Ineffective meeting participants make little effort to link their comments to what others are saying. They also don't adapt to the messages of others. Effective communicators adapt what they say and do to help achieve the goals of the group. There is evidence that putting these principles into practice will enhance group and team performance.[96]

STUDY GUIDE:

〉 REVIEW, APPLY, AND ASSESS

What Effective Group and Team Members Do

10.1 Identify six functions that effective group members perform.

REVIEW: Effective group members identify a clear, elevating goal; develop a results-driven structure; gather, share, and use information effectively; develop options; evaluate ideas; and are sensitive to group social and relationship concerns.

KEY TERM:
results-driven structure

APPLY: After reviewing the list of disadvantages of working in groups, what are specific strategies you could use to minimize any disadvantages from occurring in your group?

ASSESS: Which of the six functions of effective group members do you usually perform? Identify a group function that you usually don't perform and then identify ways you could achieve this function during your next group meeting.

Structuring Group and Team Problem Solving

10.2 List and describe the five steps of group problem solving (reflective thinking).

REVIEW: Although there is no single series of steps that will ensure high performance, five classic steps can help groups organize the problem-solving process: (1) identify and define the problem, (2) analyze the problem, (3) generate creative solutions, (4) select the best solution, and (5) take action.

KEY TERMS:

structure	silent brainstorming
interaction	(nominal group
reflective thinking	technique)
criteria	consensus
force field analysis	groupthink
technique	
creativity	
brainstorming	

APPLY: Reflect on your last group or team meeting. Overall, would the group or team have benefited from having more structure (such as a clear agenda) or more interaction (including participation from every group member)? What could you do to enhance either group structure or group interaction?

ASSESS: Assess which of the five problem solving steps are the easiest for you to perform. Which of the five steps are most challenging for you? Identify strategies for increasing your ability to implement one or more of the five problem solving steps during your next group problem solving discussion.

Enhancing Group and Team Leadership

10.3 Compare and contrast the trait, functional, styles, situational, and transformational approaches to understanding leadership.

REVIEW: High-performing groups have competent group leaders. Researchers have devised several approaches to analyzing leadership. The trait approach to leadership seeks to identify certain characteristics or traits that all leaders possess. The functional approach to leadership suggests that leaders need to be concerned with both task functions and group process functions. A third approach to understanding leadership, the styles approach, identifies leaders as authoritarian, democratic, or laissez-faire. No one style seems to work best all the time. The situational leadership approach suggests that the best leadership style depends on a variety of factors, including the readiness of the group, group members' cultures, the urgency of the problem, and the type of issue the group is discussing. Finally, transformational leadership is an approach that encourages leaders to help shape the group's vision and goals.

KEY TERMS:

leadership	democratic leader
trait approach to leadership	laissez-faire leader
functional approach	situational approach
to leadership	to leadership
task function	surface-level diversity
process function	deep-level diversity
styles approach	transformational approach
to leadership	to leadership
authoritarian leader	

APPLY: What are strategies group members could use to work more effectively if a group leader is using an authoritarian style of leadership and the group would prefer a more participative, democratic leadership style?

ASSESS: Reflect upon the last time you exerted some leadership influence in a group. What was your predominant leadership style? How effective was your leadership?

Enhancing Group and Team Meetings

10.4 **Develop and use strategies to structure meetings appropriately, keep meetings on track, and promote appropriate dialogue and interaction.**

REVIEW: An effective meeting needs a balance of structure and interaction. Groups maintain appropriate structure if meeting planners develop and use an agenda to keep the discussion focused and on track. Meetings also need appropriate amounts of dialogue and discussion. Effective meeting participants monitor the amount of participation from other group or team members and serve as gatekeepers to ensure that ororverbalizers don't monopolize the discussion and quiet members don't feel intimidated.

KEY TERMS:

agenda   "I" message
quorum   "you" message
metadiscussion

APPLY: Using the suggestions and following the examples presented in this chapter, draft a brief agenda for an upcoming meeting of a group you're in.

ASSESS: Reflect on the last meeting you attended. Describe the balance of structure (for example, following an agenda) and interaction (the amount of free-flowing, give-and-take talk during the meeting). Did the meeting need more structure to help group members stay on point or more interaction so that more people participated in the discussion?

Assessing Group and Team Problem-Solving Competencies[97]

Use the evaluation form provided at the end of this chapter to assess the presence or absence of small group communication competencies in a group or team discussion. *Competencies* are specific behaviors that group and team members perform. The assessment form includes nine competencies organized into four general categories. Here's how to use the form:

1. Observe a group or team that is attempting to solve a problem. Write the names of the group members at the top of the form. (If the group includes more than five members, photocopy the form so that each group member can be evaluated.)

2. When using the form, first decide whether each group member has performed each competency. Circle NO if the group member was not observed performing the competency. Circle YES if you did observe the group member performing the competency (for example, defining the problem, analyzing the problem, identifying criteria).

3. For each competency for which you circled YES, determine how effectively the competency was performed. Use a scale from 0 to 3:

   0 = The group member performed this competency but did so inappropriately or inadequately. For example, the person observed tried to define the problem but did so poorly.
   1 = Overall, the person's performance of this competency was adequate.
   2 = The person performed this competency twice.
   3 = The person performed this competency three or more times.

4. Total the score for each group member in each of the following four categories.

   Problem-oriented competencies consist of items 1 and 2. These are behaviors that help the group or team define and analyze the problem. If a group member performed these competencies, his or her point total for this category would range from 0 to 6. The more points the person scores, the better he or she performed this competency.

   Solution-oriented competencies include items 3, 4, and 5; the point total for this category ranges from 0 to 9. These competencies focus on how well the group or team member helped to develop and evaluate a solution to the problem.

   Discussion management competencies include items 6 and 7. These competencies help the group or team remain focused and manage interactions. The point total for this category ranges from 0 to 6.

   Relational competencies are behaviors that focus on dealing with conflict and developing a positive, supportive group climate. Items 8 and 9 reflect this competency; point total for this category ranges from 0 to 6.

5. You can also assess the group's or team's overall ability to perform these competencies. The column marked "Group Assessment" can be used to record your overall impressions of how effectively the group or team behaved. Circle NO if no one in the group performed a particular competency. Circle YES if at least one person in the group or team performed this competency. Then evaluate how well the entire group performed this competency, using the scale already described.

Sometimes it is difficult to make so many judgments about group competencies by just viewing a group discussion once. Many people find that it's easier to make a video recording of the group discussion so that they can observe it more than once.

〉 THE PRINCIPLE POINTS

Principle One:

Be aware of your communication with yourself and others.

- Be sensitive to your group's need for appropriate structure to organize and focus the discussion or interaction and to encourage dialogue.
- Be aware of the appropriate leadership style to meet your group's needs.

Principle Two:

Effectively use and interpret verbal messages.

- Clearly describe the goal of the group.
- Evaluate the merits of ideas by verbalizing both the pros and the cons.
- Use verbal "I" messages to express your need for information and your sensitivity to other group members' feelings.
- Develop and use written agendas to give meetings structure.
- Manage the amount of interaction in a group by encouraging quiet members to participate and overly dominant members to let others express ideas.
- Use metadiscussion to keep a meeting on track.

Principle Three:

Effectively use and interpret nonverbal messages.

- Use appropriate nonverbal messages to establish and maintain a positive group climate.
- When brainstorming, do your best to avoid nonverbally expressing your evaluation of other people's ideas.
- Communicate your sensitivity to other group members through your nonverbal behavior.
- Use appropriate eye contact and other nonverbal cues to regulate the flow of interaction in group and team meetings.

Principle Four:

Listen and respond thoughtfully to others.

- Listen to other group members to determine whether your group is accomplishing the appropriate group functions.
- Listen and respond to others to express your sensitivity to their ideas and opinions.
- To be an effective leader, listen and thoughtfully respond to all members.
- Listen and respond to provide appropriate contributions to group meetings and problem-solving discussions.

Principle Five:

Appropriately adapt messages to others.

- Adapt your leadership and group membership styles to achieve the goals of the group.
- Adapt your messages to help the group identify, define, and analyze the problem; create solutions; select the best solution; and take action.
- Adapt your messages to give group meetings appropriate structure and to foster interaction.

Competent Group Communicator

Problem-Solving Group Communication Competencies	Group Member A		Group Member B	
COMPETENCIES				
Problem-Oriented Competencies				
1. Defined the problem the group attempted to solve.	NO	YES 0 1 2 3	NO	YES 0 1 2 3
2. Analyzed the problem the group attempted to solve. Used relevant information, data, or evidence; discussed the causes, obstacles, history, symptoms, or significance of the problem.	NO	YES 0 1 2 3	NO	YES 0 1 2 3
Solution-Oriented Competencies				
3. Identified criteria for an appropriate solution to the problem.	NO	YES 0 1 2 3	NO	YES 0 1 2 3
4. Generated solutions or alternatives to the problem.	NO	YES 0 1 2 3	NO	YES 0 1 2 3
5. Evaluated solution(s): Identified positive or negative consequences of the proposed solutions.	NO	YES 0 1 2 3	NO	YES 0 1 2 3
Discussion Management Competencies				
6. Maintained task focus: Helped the group stay on, or return to, the task, issue, or topic the group was discussing.	NO	YES 0 1 2 3	NO	YES 0 1 2 3
7. Managed group interaction: Appropriately initiated and terminated discussion, contributed to the discussion, or invited others to contribute to the discussion. Didn't dominate or withdraw.	NO	YES 0 1 2 3	NO	YES 0 1 2 3
Relational Competencies				
8. Managed conflict: Appropriately and constructively helped the group stay focused on issues rather than personalities when conflict occurred.	NO	YES 0 1 2 3	NO	YES 0 1 2 3
9. Maintained climate: Offered positive verbal comments or nonverbal expressions that helped maintain a positive group climate.	NO	YES 0 1 2 3	NO	YES 0 1 2 3

Scoring

NO = Not observed

YES

0 = Overall inappropriate or inadequate performance of competency

1 = Overall adequate performance of competency

2 = Person performed this competency twice

3 = Person performed this competency three or more times

Group Member C		Group Member D		Group Member E		Group Assessment	
NO	YES 0 1 2 3	NO	YES 0 1 2 3	NO	YES 0 1 2 3	NO	YES 0 1 2 3
NO	YES 0 1 2 3	NO	YES 0 1 2 3	NO	YES 0 1 2 3	NO	YES 0 1 2 3
NO	YES 0 1 2 3	NO	YES 0 1 2 3	NO	YES 0 1 2 3	NO	YES 0 1 2 3
NO	YES 0 1 2 3	NO	YES 0 1 2 3	NO	YES 0 1 2 3	NO	YES 0 1 2 3
NO	YES 0 1 2 3	NO	YES 0 1 2 3	NO	YES 0 1 2 3	NO	YES 0 1 2 3
NO	YES 0 1 2 3	NO	YES 0 1 2 3	NO	YES 0 1 2 3	NO	YES 0 1 2 3
NO	YES 0 1 2 3	NO	YES 0 1 2 3	NO	YES 0 1 2 3	NO	YES 0 1 2 3
NO	YES 0 1 2 3	NO	YES 0 1 2 3	NO	YES 0 1 2 3	NO	YES 0 1 2 3
NO	YES 0 1 2 3	NO	YES 0 1 2 3	NO	YES 0 1 2 3	NO	YES 0 1 2 3

Problem-Oriented Competencies (0–6)
Solution-Oriented Competencies (0–9)
Discussion Management Competencies (0–6)
Relational Competencies (0–6)

CHAPTER

11

DEVELOPING YOUR SPEECH

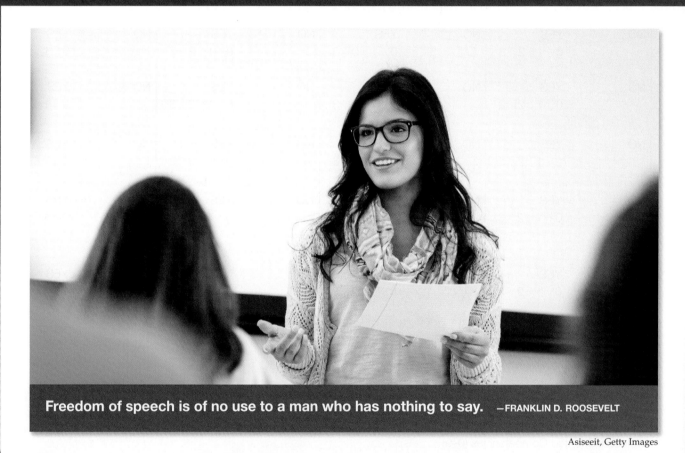

Freedom of speech is of no use to a man who has nothing to say.   —FRANKLIN D. ROOSEVELT

Asiseeit, Getty Images

CHAPTER OUTLINE

- Overviewing the Public Speaking Process
- Building Your Confidence
- Selecting and Narrowing Your Topic
- Identifying Your Purpose

- Developing Your Central Idea
- Generating Main Ideas
- Gathering Supporting Material
- Study Guide: Review, Apply, and Assess

LEARNING OBJECTIVES

After studying this chapter, you should be able to

11.1 List and explain the components of the audience-centered public speaking model.

11.2 Apply specific strategies for becoming a more confident speaker.

11.3 Select and narrow a speech topic that is appropriate to the audience, the occasion, and yourself.

11.4 Write an audience-centered, specific-purpose statement for a speech.

11.5 Develop a central idea for a speech.

11.6 Generate main ideas from a central idea.

11.7 Describe five potential sources and seven types of supporting material for a speech, and use each type effectively.

A good friend of ours who lived in Hong Kong for several years once remarked that she found traveling back to the United States exhausting. Her reason? It was not so much the long plane trip or the thirteen-hour time difference, but, as she explained, "When I begin to hear airport public announcements in English instead of Cantonese, I suddenly feel compelled to pay attention to every word. All that listening wears me out!"

Few of us can take for granted that others will listen to us merely because we are speaking their native language. However, when we study the public speaking process and learn its component skills and principles, we increase the likelihood that others will listen to us out of genuine, compelling interest.

Far from being a rare talent possessed only by an inspired few, the skill of **public speaking** is a teachable, learnable process of developing, supporting, organizing, and orally presenting ideas. The skills you will develop as you learn and practice this process will be of practical use in the future. They will give you an edge in other college courses that require oral presentations. They may help you convince a current or future boss that you deserve a raise. They may even land you a job.

Let's begin our discussion with an overview of the public speaking process. Then we will offer suggestions for building your confidence as a public speaker before focusing specifically on the first five stages of the public speaking process—discovering and narrowing your topic, identifying your purpose, developing a central idea, generating main ideas, and gathering supporting material for your speech—all firmly grounded in the five Communication Principles.

public speaking

A teachable, learnable process of developing, supporting, organizing, and orally presenting ideas.

Overviewing the Public Speaking Process

11.1 List and explain the components of the audience-centered public speaking model.

You don't have to read an entire book on public speaking before you give your first speech. An overview of the public speaking process can help you with your early assignments even if you have to speak before you have a chance to read Chapters 11 through 15. Figure 11.1 illustrates the public speaking process. At the center of the model is "Consider the audience." Double arrows connect this center with every other stage, illustrating that at any point, you may revise your ideas or strategies as you learn more about your audience. Your audience influences every decision you make.

Audience-centered public speakers are inherently sensitive to the diversity of their audiences. While guarding against generalizations that might be offensive, they acknowledge that cultural, ethnic, and other traditions affect the way people process messages. They apply the fundamental principle of appropriately adapting their messages to others. How? They might choose to use pictures to help them communicate. They might select topics and use illustrations with universal themes such as family and friendship. They might adjust

audience-centered public speaker

Someone who considers and adapts to the audience at every stage of the public speaking process.

FIGURE 11.1 An Audience-Centered Model of the Public Speaking Process

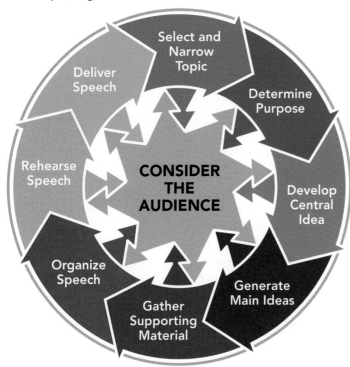

the formality of their delivery and even their clothing to whatever is expected by the majority of the audience members. The fundamental communication principle of adapting to the audience is central to the success of any speech.

Now view the model as a clock, with "Select and narrow topic" at 12 o'clock. From this stage, the process proceeds clockwise in the direction of the arrows, to "Deliver speech." Each stage is one of the tasks of the public speaker:

1. Select and narrow topic.
2. Determine purpose.
3. Develop central idea.
4. Generate main ideas.
5. Gather supporting material.
6. Organize speech.
7. Rehearse speech.
8. Deliver speech.

Building Your Confidence

11.2 **Apply specific strategies for becoming a more confident speaker.**

The previous overview of the stages of the public speaking process should help you understand how to prepare for your first speaking assignment, but if you still feel nervous at the prospect, you are definitely not alone.[1] One study found that more than 80 percent of us feel anxious when we speak to an audience.[2] Other surveys have discovered that the fear of public speaking is more common than the fear of death![3]

public speaking anxiety

Also known as stage fright or speaker anxiety; anxiety about speaking in public that is manifested in physiological symptoms such as rapid heartbeat, butterflies in the stomach, shaking knees and hands, quivering voice, and increased perspiration.

If you are taking a communication class online, you might think you will experience less **public speaking anxiety** than you would if you were speaking to a live audience. But recent research suggests that in fact slightly *more* students report feeling anxious about web-based speech delivery than the number who report anxiety about face-to-face delivery.[4]

What additional factors cause us to feel anxious about speaking in public? Figure 11.2 summarizes the results of studies that have explored the answers to this question.[5]

FIGURE 11.2 Some Reasons We May Feel Anxious about Speaking in Public

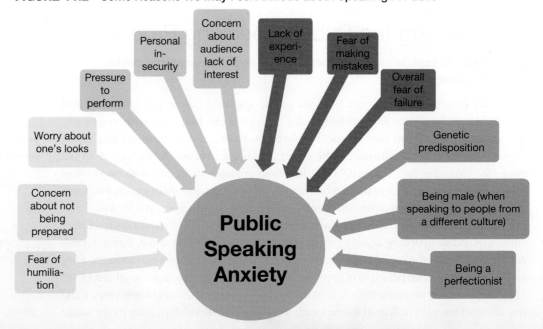

DEVELOPING YOUR SPEECH STEP BY STEP

Considering Your Audience

A well-known Chinese proverb says that a journey of a thousand miles begins with a single step. Developing and delivering a speech may seem like a daunting journey. But if you take it one step at a time and keep your focus on your audience, you'll be rewarded with a well-crafted and well-delivered message.

To help you see how the audience-centered speaking process unfolds, this Developing Your Speech Step by Step feature will provide a window through which you can see how one student prepared and delivered a speech. Dezerae Reyes, an undergraduate student at Texas State University, developed the persuasive speech entitled "The Health Risks of Soft Drinks" that is outlined in Chapter 12.[6] In the pages ahead, we'll walk through the process Dezerae used to develop her speech.

Even before selecting her speech topic, Dezerae thinks about her audience. Because her listeners will include her university classmates and instructor, she knows that she can discuss complex issues, using a fairly advanced vocabulary. Her challenge is to find a topic that will interest her fellow students as well as her instructor.

Fortunately, regardless of the reasons you may feel nervous about speaking in public, you can learn strategies to help you build your confidence. Figure 11.3 outlines these strategies, which are also explained in detail in the following paragraphs.

Understand Public Speaking Anxiety

Regardless of why you may feel anxious, the physical symptoms of public speaking anxiety result from your brain signaling your body to help with a challenging task. Your body responds by increasing your breathing rate and blood flow and by pumping more adrenaline, which in turn results in the all-too-familiar symptoms of a rapid heartbeat, butterflies in the stomach, shaking knees and hands, quivering voice, and increased perspiration.[7]

Although these symptoms may annoy and worry you, the increased oxygen, blood flow, and adrenaline that cause you to feel uncomfortable can actually be helpful. For example, you may find that you speak with heightened enthusiasm. And due to these biological changes, your brain thinks faster and more clearly than you would have believed possible. Overall, your state of increased physical readiness can help you speak better.[8]

▼ Harry Potter creator J. K. Rowling has admitted experiencing public speaking anxiety. We all need to take positive steps to control anxiety before a performance. Seth Wenig/AP Images

FIGURE 11.3 Building Your Confidence

Building Your Confidence

- Understand public speaking anxiety.
- Know how to develop a speech.
- Be prepared.
- Give yourself a mental pep talk.
- Use deep-breathing techniques.
- Focus on your audience.
- Focus on your message.
- Take advantage of opportunities to speak.
- Explore additional resources.

illusion of transparency
The mistaken belief that the physical manifestations of a speaker's nervousness are apparent to an audience.

Keep in mind, too, that most speakers feel more nervous than they look. Although the adage "Never let 'em see you sweat" suggests that our increased perspiration, along with our shaking hands and knocking knees, is likely to be visible to our audience, rarely is that true. Communication researchers call this mistaken belief the **illusion of transparency** and have found that simply informing speakers that their nervousness is not as apparent as they think can improve the quality of their speeches.[9]

Know How to Develop a Speech

Communication researchers have found that instruction in public speaking decreases students' perception of their own public speaking anxiety.[10] By reading the first part of this chapter, you have already taken this first step toward managing your anxiety: learning about the public speaking process. Just knowing what you need to do to develop an effective speech can boost your confidence in being able to do it.

Be Prepared

Being well prepared will decrease your public speaking anxiety. Communication researchers have found that one way for speakers to manage anxiety is to follow the recommended steps for preparing a speech, which include developing a logical and clear outline.[11] Being prepared also involves discovering an appropriate topic and researching that topic thoroughly. Perhaps most importantly, it includes rehearsing your speech. Research suggests that people who spend more time rehearsing experience less public speaking anxiety than those who rehearse less.[12]

When you rehearse your speech, imagine that you are giving it to the audience you will actually address. Stand up. Speak aloud rather than rehearsing silently. If you cannot rehearse in the room where you will deliver the speech, at least imagine that room. If you will be video recording your speech, practice it—and later deliver it—in a professional setting rather than a kitchen or bedroom.[13] Thorough preparation that includes realistic rehearsal will increase your confidence when it is time to deliver your speech.

Give Yourself a Mental Pep Talk

A recent study found that speakers who recast their anxiety as excitement by stating, "I am excited" actually *felt* more excited and were perceived by their listeners as more confident than speakers who tried to tell themselves, "I am calm."[14]

Rather than allowing yourself to dwell on how nervous you are, make a conscious effort to think positively. Remind yourself that you have chosen a topic you know something about. Give yourself a mental pep talk before getting up to speak: "I know I can give this speech. I have prepared and practiced, and I'm going to do a great job." Researchers have suggested that such "prespeaking exercises" may be the most effective antidotes for anxiety both before and during the speech.[15]

Use Deep-Breathing Techniques

Two physical symptoms of nervousness are shallow breathing and rapid heart rate. To counter these symptoms, draw on the breathing techniques employed by practitioners of yoga.[16] Take a few slow, deep breaths before you get up to speak. As you slowly inhale and exhale, try to relax your entire body. These simple strategies will increase your oxygen intake and slow your heart rate, making you feel calmer and more in control.

Focus on Your Audience

Being audience centered is key to reducing public speaking anxiety. As you prepare your speech, consider the needs, goals, and interests of your audience. The more you know about your listeners and how they are likely to respond to your message, the more comfortable you will feel about delivering that message. As you rehearse your speech, visualize your audience members and imagine how they may respond; practice adapting your speech to the responses you imagine. And as you finally deliver your speech, look for positive, reinforcing feedback from audience members.[17] The more you concentrate on your audience, the less you attend to your own nervousness.

Focus on Your Message

Focusing on your message can be another anxiety-reducing strategy. Like focusing on your audience, it keeps you from thinking too much about how nervous you are. In the few minutes before you begin your speech, think about what you are going to say. Mentally review your main ideas. Silently practice your opening lines and your conclusion. Once you start speaking, maintain your focus on your message and your audience rather than on your fears.

Take Advantage of Opportunities to Speak

As you gain public speaking experience, you will feel more in control of your nervousness. Communication researchers have found that most public speakers become progressively more comfortable as they speak, a phenomenon they call **habituation**.[18] Past successes build confidence. Your communication course will provide opportunities for frequent practice, which will increase your skill and confidence.[19]

Explore Additional Resources

For a few people, the above strategies may not be enough help. These people may still experience a level of public speaking anxiety that they consider debilitating. If you believe that you may be such a person, ask your communication instructor for additional resource recommendations. For example, some college or university departments of communication have communication labs that teach students additional strategies to help manage counterproductive anxiety.

RECAP

Building Your Confidence

- Understand public speaking anxiety.
- Know how to develop a speech.
- Be prepared.
- Focus on your audience.
- Focus on your message.
- Give yourself a mental pep talk.
- Use deep-breathing techniques.
- Take advantage of opportunities to speak.
- Explore additional resources.

habituation
The process of becoming more comfortable as you speak.

Selecting and Narrowing Your Topic

11.3 Select and narrow a speech topic that is appropriate to the audience, the occasion, and yourself.

Sometimes a speaker is invited or assigned to speak on a certain topic and doesn't have to think about selecting one. Other times, however, a speaker is given some guidelines—such as time limits and perhaps the general purpose for the speech—but otherwise is free to choose a topic. When that happens to you, as it almost certainly will in your communication class, your task may be made easier by exploring three questions: Who is the audience? What is the occasion? What are my interests and experiences?

Who Is the Audience?

As we have noted several times throughout this book, the principle of appropriately adapting messages to others is central to the communication process. In public speaking, that adaptation begins with topic selection. Who are the members of your audience? What interests and needs do they have in common? Why did they ask you to speak?

One professional speaker calls the answers to such questions "actionable intelligence"—information that you can use as you select your topic.[20] Your college classmates are likely to be interested in such topics as college loans and the job market.

Older adults might be more interested in hearing a speaker address such topics as the cost of prescription drugs and investment tax credits. Thinking about your audience can often yield an appropriate topic.

What Is the Occasion?

You might also consider the occasion for which you are being asked to speak. A Veterans' Day address calls for such topics as patriotism and service to one's country. A university centennial address will focus on the successes in the institution's past and a vision for its future.

What Are My Interests and Experiences?

Self-awareness, another communication principle you already know, can also help you discover a topic. Exploring your own interests, attitudes, and experiences may suggest topics about which you know a great deal and feel passionate about, resulting in a speech you can deliver with energy and genuine enthusiasm. One speaker's thinking about her own interests and experiences quickly produced the following list of possible topics.

> San Antonio, Texas: City of cultural diversity
>
> Ballet Folklorico
>
> Light pollution and dark skies
>
> Working at Schlitterbahn water parks
>
> What a forensic anthropologist does

Even after considering audience, occasion, and personal interests and experiences, you may still find yourself facing a speaking assignment for which you just cannot come up with a satisfactory topic. When that happens, you might try silent brainstorming, scanning web directories and web pages, or listening and reading for topic ideas.

Conducting Silent Brainstorming

Silent brainstorming, which was discussed in Chapter 10 as a technique used by small groups to generate creative ideas, is a useful strategy for generating possible topics for speeches. A silent brainstorming session of about three minutes yielded the twelve potential topics shown in Figure 11.4.

Having generated a list of topics, you can now go back and eliminate the ones that don't have much promise or that you know you would never use. For example, you may not have any real interest in or reason for discussing Joshua Tree National Park. However, perhaps your Irish literature course has given you good background for discussing James Joyce. Keep the topics you like in your class notebook. You can reconsider them for future assignments.

FIGURE 11.4 Brainstorming a Topic

Creating a cluster or concept map such as this one might help you visualize connections between ideas and generate more topic ideas as you brainstorm.

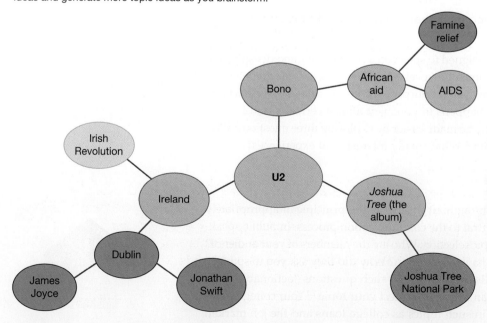

Scanning Web Directories and Web Pages

You know how addicting it can be to surf the web, following various categories and links out of interest and curiosity. What may seem an idle pastime can actually be a good way to discover potential speech topics. For example, a recent random search on Best of the Web (botw.org), starting with the general menu heading *Arts,* yielded the categories and possible topics illustrated in Figure 11.5.

An additional advantage of this strategy is that you now have both possible topics and potential sources for your speech.

Listening and Reading for Topic Ideas

FIGURE 11.5 Possible Topics from a Web Directory Search

It is not unusual to see on television or read in a news source something that triggers an idea for a speech. For example, the following list of topics was suggested by recent headlines:

Conservative European politicians

Likely Supreme Court nominees

World Cup expansion

Amazon Echo versus Google Home

You might also discover a topic in one of your courses. Perhaps you recently had an interesting discussion in your criminology class about minimum mandatory sentencing. It might make a good topic for a speech, and your criminology instructor would probably be happy to suggest additional resources.

Even a subject that comes up in casual conversation with friends may make a good speech topic. Perhaps everyone in your dorm seems to be sniffling and coughing all at once. "It's sick-building syndrome," gasps one. Sick-building syndrome might be an interesting topic for a speech.

The point is to keep your eyes and ears open. You never know when you might see or hear a potential topic. When you do, write it down. Nothing is as frustrating as knowing that you had a good idea for a topic but now can't remember what it was.

Even if you discover potential topics through brainstorming, surfing the web, listening, or reading, you should still consider the communication principles of adapting to your audience and being aware of your own interests and experiences before you make your final topic selection. You will also need to consider the time limits of

DEVELOPING YOUR SPEECH STEP BY STEP

Selecting and Narrowing Your Topic

While surfing the web one afternoon, Dezerae comes across a list of "30 Health Reasons Not to Drink Soda or Diet Soda." As she scans the list, she is startled by the number and severity of health conditions with known links to soft drinks. She vows to cut down on her own consumption. As she ponders this idea, another thought goes through her mind: Maybe the health risks associated with soft drinks would make a good topic for her upcoming persuasive speech. She is personally interested and thinks her audience would be as well.

the speaking assignment. Many good topics need to be narrowed down before they are appropriate for a given assignment. The key to narrowing your topic is sustaining your focus on your audience. One professional speaker advises,

> You have to research the group, look on their website, and talk to people in the group to assess what they need and want to know about a topic . . . .[21]

RECAP

Selecting and Narrowing Your Topic

- Consider the audience, the occasion, and your interests and experiences.
- Practice silent brainstorming.
- Scan web directories and web pages.
- Listen and read for topic ideas.
- Narrow your topic.

With your audience's needs and expectations in mind, you might continue the process of narrowing your topic by constructing the kinds of categories created by web directories. Write your general topic at the top of a list, making each succeeding word or phrase more specific and narrow. Figure 11.6 illustrates how the broad topic *recreation* might be narrowed to a workable topic for a speech.

If you think your audience is unlikely to be interested in *Cruising on a freighter or barge*, you can go back a step and consider other types of cruises—*European river cruises*, for example—that may be more likely to interest your audience.

Identifying Your Purpose

11.4   Write an audience-centered, specific-purpose statement for a speech.

Now that you have a topic in mind, you need to determine your purpose for your speech. A clear purpose can help you select main ideas, an organizational strategy, and supporting material. It can even influence how you deliver your speech. You should determine both your general purpose and your specific purpose for every speech you give.

General Purpose

general purpose
The broad reason for giving a speech: to inform, to persuade, or to entertain an audience.

Your **general purpose** is the broad reason for giving your speech: to inform, to persuade, or to entertain.

- *To inform.* When you inform, you teach. You define, describe, or explain a thing, person, place, concept, or process. Although you may use some humor in your speech or encourage your audience to seek out further information about your topic, your primary purpose for speaking is to give information.

- *To persuade.* If you are using information to try to change or reinforce your audience's ideas or convictions or to urge your audience to do something, your general purpose is persuasive. The insurance representative who tries to get you to buy life insurance, the candidate for state representative who asks for your vote, and the coordinator of Habitat for Humanity who urges your school organization to get involved in building homes all have persuasive general purposes. They may offer information, but they use it to convince you or to get you to do something. Their primary purpose is persuasive.

FIGURE 11.6 Narrowing a Broad Topic

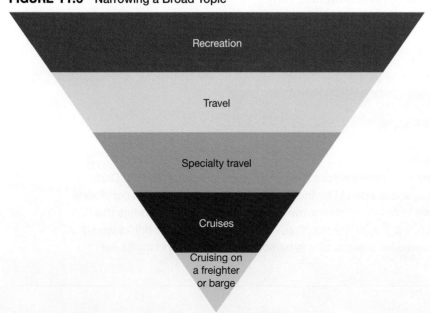

- *To entertain.* The speaker whose purpose is to entertain tries to get the members of his or her audience to smile, laugh, and generally enjoy themselves. For the audience members, learning something or being persuaded about something is secondary to having a good time. Most after-dinner speakers speak to entertain, as do most stand-up comedians and storytellers.

In your speech class, the general purpose for each assignment will probably be set by your instructor. Because the general purpose influences the way you develop and organize your speech, as well as the way you deliver it, it is important to be aware of your general purpose throughout the process of developing and delivering your speech.

Specific Purpose

Knowing whether you want to inform, persuade, or entertain clarifies your general purpose for speaking. You also need to determine your specific purpose. A **specific purpose** is a concise statement of what your listeners should be able to do by the time you finish your speech. In other words, a specific purpose is an audience-centered behavioral goal for your speech. Table 11.1 shows examples of general and specific purposes.

A specific-purpose statement is intended not to become part of your speech, but to guide your own speech preparation. You can begin a specific-purpose statement for any speech with the words:

> At the end of my speech, the audience will . . .

Then you can specify a behavior. For example, if you are giving an informative speech on eating disorders, you might state:

> At the end of my speech, the audience will be able to explain the causes of anorexia.

If your topic is cell phone spyware and your general purpose is to persuade, you might say:

> At the end of my speech, the audience will be able to disable spyware on their cell phones.[22]

Wording your specific purpose as in the examples above will help you keep your audience foremost in your mind during the entire speech preparation process.

Every subsequent decision you make while preparing and delivering your speech should be

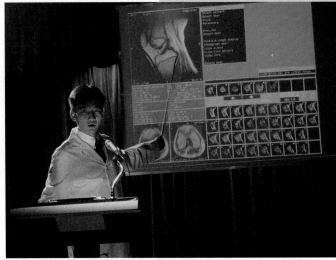

▼ The three main general purposes for public speaking are to inform, to persuade, and to entertain. Which appears to be this speaker's purpose?
CBS Photo Archive/Getty Images

specific purpose
A concise statement of what listeners should be able to do by the time the speaker finishes the speech.

RECAP

Identifying Your Purpose

General Purpose

- To inform — To define, describe, or explain a thing, person, place, concept, or process
- To persuade — To change or reinforce audience members' ideas or convictions, or to urge them to do something
- To entertain — To amuse an audience

Specific Purpose

- Specifies what you want audience members to be able to do by the end of your speech
- Guides you in developing your speech
- Uses the words "At the end of my speech, the audience will . . . "

TABLE 11.1 Examples of General and Specific Purposes

General Purposes	Specific Purposes
To inform	At the end of my speech, the audience will be able to list two benefits for adults learning to play a musical instrument.
To persuade	At the end of my speech, the audience will enroll in a music appreciation course.
To entertain	At the end of my speech, the audience will be laughing at my misadventures as an adult cello student.

COMMUNICATION & ETHICS

Is It Ethical to Buy a Speech?

An online "speech mill" advertises that for $13 per page, "highly qualified writers" will prepare a custom speech for you. The ad goes on to claim that the speeches are "original" and "from scratch," designed to "let you escape the whole preparation process."

Would it be ethical to use this or a similar website to prepare a speech for a class assignment? Why or why not? Are you comfortable with the site's "plagiarism-free guarantee"? Would it be ethical to buy a speech from such a site for a personal occasion, such as a great-aunt's funeral or your cousin's wedding? How do online speechwriters for hire compare, ethically, with professional speechwriters, who are regularly hired by executives and politicians?

guided by your specific purpose. As soon as you have formulated it, add it to the reminders on your smartphone or write it on a note card and keep it with you while you are working on your speech. Think of it as a compass pointing true north—toward your audience. Refer to it often.

Developing Your Central Idea

11.5 Develop a central idea for a speech.

central idea
A definitive point about a topic.

Your specific purpose indicates what you want your *audience* to know or do by the end of your speech, but your **central idea** makes a definitive point about your *topic*. It focuses on the content of the speech. Unlike the specific purpose, which guides your preparation but is *not* stated in your final speech, the central idea *is* stated.

DEVELOPING YOUR SPEECH STEP BY STEP

Identifying Your Purpose

Dezerae's assignment is to prepare and deliver a persuasive speech, so she knows that her general purpose is to persuade—to change or reinforce her audience's ideas, or to urge them to do something. She will talk about the health hazards associated with soft drinks and urge her listeners to cut down on their consumption.

Dezerae knows that her specific purpose should begin with the phrase "At the end of my speech, the audience will . . . ," so she jots down,

At the end of my speech, the audience will know about the health hazards of soft drinks.

As Dezerae considers this draft specific purpose, she sees some problems with it. How can she determine what her audience "knows" at the end of her speech? And what, specifically, should her listeners do with the information she gives them? She edits her purpose statement to read,

At the end of my speech, the audience will list the health hazards associated with soft drinks.

Although more specific, this version is more appropriate for an informative speech than for a persuasive one. Dezerae wants her audience to take action. Maybe a better purpose statement would be,

At the end of my speech, the audience will consume fewer soft drinks.

Dezerae is pleased with this third version. It specifies what she wants her audience members to *do* by the end of her speech.

Sometimes, as in the following example, wording the central idea can be as simple as copying the part of the specific-purpose statement that specifies what the audience should be able to do.

TOPIC: Foreign-language education

SPECIFIC PURPOSE: At the end of my speech, the audience will be able to explain two reasons foreign-language education should begin in the elementary grades.

CENTRAL IDEA: Foreign-language education should begin in the elementary grades.

Figure 11.7 summarizes how the specific purpose and central idea differ. Professional speech coach Judith Humphrey explains the importance of a central idea:

> Ask yourself before writing a speech . . . "What's my point?" Be able to state that message in a single clear sentence. Everything else you say will support that single argument.[23]

To be most useful to both speaker and listeners, the "single clear sentence" to which Humphrey refers should be an audience-centered idea, reflect a single idea, be a complete declarative sentence, and use direct, specific language.

FIGURE 11.7 Specific Purpose Versus Central Idea

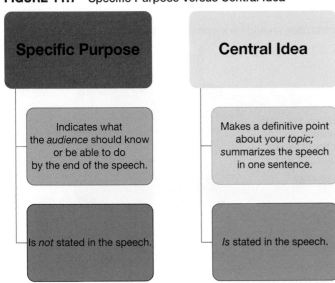

An Audience-Centered Idea

If your specific purpose is focused on your audience, your central idea probably will be, too. It should reflect a topic in which the audience has a reason to be interested and should provide some knowledge that they do not already have or make some claim about the topic that they may not have previously considered. Consider the appropriateness of the central ideas in Figure 11.8 for an audience of students already attending college.

FIGURE 11.8 The central idea should be appropriate for the audience.

X Scholarships from a variety of sources are readily available to first-year college students.

(Inappropriate for audience)

✓ Although you may think of scholarships as a source of money for freshmen, a number of scholarships are only available to students who have completed their first year of college.

(Appropriate for audience)

FIGURE 11.9 The central idea should be a single idea.

X Clubbing and marathon running are two activities that appeal to many college students.

(Two ideas)

✓ **Marathon running appeals to many college students.**

(One idea)

A Single Idea

A central idea should be a single idea. Trying to cover more than one topic, even if the multiple topics are related, only muddles your speech and confuses the audience. The example in Figure 11.9 illustrates this guideline.

A Complete Declarative Sentence

Your central idea should be more than just the word or phrase that is your topic; it should also make a claim about your topic. In addition, avoid wording your central idea as a question. Questions may help you come up with a central idea, but because they don't make any kind of claim, questions themselves are not good central ideas. Figure 11.10 illustrates how a central idea should be a complete **declarative sentence**, not a topic and not a question.

declarative sentence
A complete sentence that makes a statement as opposed to asking a question.

FIGURE 11.10 The central idea should be a complete declarative sentence.

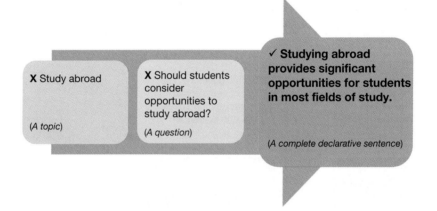

X Study abroad

(A topic)

X Should students consider opportunities to study abroad?

(A question)

✓ **Studying abroad provides significant opportunities for students in most fields of study.**

(A complete declarative sentence)

Direct, Specific Language

As illustrated in Figure 11.11,[24] a good central idea uses direct, specific language rather than qualifiers and vague generalities.

FIGURE 11.11 The central idea should be worded in direct, specific language.

RECAP

The Central Idea Should . . .

Be audience-centered.

Reflect a single topic.

Be a complete declarative sentence.

Use direct, specific language.

X It seems that desert fairy circles may not be what they appear to be.

(Qualified, vague language)

✓ **Although long attributed to fairies, formations dotting the African Namib Desert mark the territory of termites.**

(Direct, specific language)

DEVELOPING YOUR SPEECH STEP BY STEP

Developing Your Central Idea

Dezerae knows from reading Chapter 11 of this book that her central idea should state a single audience-centered idea. She jots down,

Why should people consume fewer soft drinks?

She thinks her first draft is not bad. It is certainly relevant to her purpose. Then she remembers that the central idea should be a *declarative* sentence, not a question. So she revises the question to read,

People should consume fewer soft drinks.

This second draft meets all the criteria for a central idea: It is audience-centered, reflects a single idea, is a complete declarative sentence, and uses direct, specific language.

Generating Main Ideas

11.6 Generate main ideas from a central idea.

If the central idea of a speech is like the thesis statement of a paper, the **main ideas** of a speech correspond to the paragraph topics of a paper. They support or subdivide the central idea and provide more detailed points of focus for developing the speech.

main ideas
Subdivisions of the central idea of a speech that provide detailed points of focus for developing the speech.

Getting from the central idea to related but more specific main ideas can seem challenging, but you can actually use the central idea to generate main ideas. Here's how.

Write the central idea at the top of a sheet of paper or a word-processing document. Then ask yourself three questions:

1. Does the central idea have *logical divisions*?
2. Can I think of several *reasons* the central idea is true?
3. Can I support the central idea with a series of *steps* or a *chronological sequence*?

You should be able to answer yes to one of these questions and to write down the corresponding divisions, reasons, or steps. Let's apply this strategy to several examples.

Does the Central Idea Have *Logical Divisions*?

Suppose that your central idea is "Most accomplished guitarists play three types of guitars." The phrase *three types* is a flag that indicates that this central idea does indeed have logical divisions—in this case, the three types of guitars. You list the three that come to mind:

1. Acoustic
2. Classical
3. Electric

You don't need to use Roman numerals or to worry particularly about the order in which you have listed the types of guitars. Right now, you are simply trying to generate main ideas. They aren't set in concrete, either. You may revise them—and your central idea—several times before you actually deliver the speech. For example, you may decide that you need to include steel guitars in your list, so you revise your central idea to read "four types of guitars" and add "steel" to your list. If your central idea has logical divisions, you may organize those logical divisions topically, spatially, or according to cause–effect or problem–solution, organizational strategies that will be discussed in Chapter 12.

Can You Think of Several *Reasons* the Central Idea Is True?

If your central idea is "Refugee children in developing nations lack educational opportunities," you may not be able to find readily apparent logical divisions.[25] Simply describing the refugee populations of Afghanistan, Somalia, and Myanmar,[26] for example, would not necessarily support the argument that refugee children in developing nations lack educational opportunities. However, the second question—*Can I think of several reasons the central idea is true?*—is more productive. You can develop the central idea with *reasons* why refugee children lack educational opportunities:

1. Developing countries lack educational infrastructure.
2. The focus of international development and support is misguided.

Unlike the list of types of guitars, this list is written in brief complete sentences. You may or may not use full sentences in your own list. The purpose of your first list of main ideas is just to get the ideas in written form, whether using words, phrases, or sentences. You can and will revise them later. If your main ideas are reasons your central idea is true, you will probably organize them according to effect–cause.

Can You Support the Central Idea with a Series of *Steps* or a *Chronological Sequence?*

"Free speech was alternately challenged and defended in the U.S. throughout the twentieth century." This central idea seemed like a pretty good idea when you drafted it, but now what do you do? It does not have any logical divisions. You cannot really come up with reasons it is true. You could, however, support this central idea with a chronological sequence or a history of free speech in the twentieth century. You jot down the following list:

1. 1919: The Supreme Court suggests that speech presenting a "clear and present danger" may be restricted.
2. 1940: Congress declares it illegal to urge the violent overthrow of the federal government.
3. 1964: The Berkeley Free Speech Movement arises from protest over the arrest of student activists.
4. 1989: The Supreme Court defines the burning of the U.S. flag as a speech act.
5. 1997: The Supreme Court defends free speech on the Internet by striking down the Communications Decency Act of 1996.

These five events, arranged in chronological order, could become the main ideas of your speech.

How many main ideas should you have? Your topic and time limit will help you decide. A short speech (three to five minutes) might have only two main ideas. A longer one (eight to ten minutes) might have four or five. If you have more potential main ideas than you can use, decide which main ideas are likely to be most interesting, relevant, and perhaps persuasive to your audience, or combine two or more closely related ideas.

Gathering Supporting Material

11.7 Describe five potential sources and seven types of supporting material for a speech, and use each type effectively.

By the time you have decided on your main ideas, you have a skeleton speech. Your next task is to flesh out that skeleton with **supporting material**, both verbal and visual. Verbal supporting material includes illustrations, explanations, descriptions, definitions, analogies, statistics, and opinions—material that will clarify, amplify, and provide evidence to support your main ideas and your thesis. Visual supporting material includes images, text, video, audio, objects, and people. The speaker who seeks out strong verbal and visual supporting material is adhering to the fundamental communication principles of using verbal and nonverbal messages effectively.

supporting material
Verbal or visual material that clarifies, amplifies, and provides evidence to support the main ideas of a presentation.

▼ A smartphone lets you do Internet research anywhere, but there are also times when you may need to visit a library or interview someone to get information for your speech. scyther5/Shutterstock

Sources of Supporting Material

Like a chef who needs to know where to buy high-quality fresh fruits and vegetables for gourmet recipes, you need to know where to turn for supporting material that will effectively develop your speech and achieve your specific purpose. We will discuss five potential sources of supporting material: personal knowledge and experience, the Internet, online databases, traditional library holdings, and interviews.

Personal Knowledge and Experience   If you were self-aware as you selected your topic, you may have chosen a topic based on your passionate interest in cataloging cat videos or cooking. Or you may have chosen a topic with which you have had some personal experience, such as negotiating a favorable apartment lease. Although most well-researched speeches will include some objective material gathered from the Internet or from library resources, your listeners will respect your authority if they realize that you have firsthand knowledge of your topic.

The Internet   Although easy to use and generally helpful, general search engines such as Google or Bing can yield an overwhelming number of resources. The following relatively simple strategies can help you narrow thousands or even millions of hits to a more workable number:

DEVELOPING YOUR SPEECH STEP BY STEP

Generating Your Main Ideas

With her central idea ("People should consume fewer soft drinks") in hand, Dezerae is ready to generate main ideas for her speech. She applies three questions:

- Does the central idea have logical divisions?
- Can I think of several reasons the central idea is true?
- Can I support my central idea with a series of steps or a chronological sequence?

Dezerae doesn't find logical divisions in her central idea. Nor can she support it with a series of steps or a chronological sequence. But she can certainly list reasons it is true. She begins her list:

1. Soft drinks are high in sugar.
2. High sugar consumption leads to obesity.
3. Obesity puts people at risk for a variety of lifestyle diseases such as heart disease and diabetes.

Dezerae feels confident that she now has three main ideas that both support her central idea and fulfill her specific purpose. Because she also wants her audience to take action (decrease their consumption of soft drinks), she can make that action step her fourth point:

4. You should consume fewer soft drinks.

Now Dezerae feels confident that she has four main ideas that both support her central idea and fulfill her specific purpose.

vertical search engine
A website that indexes information on the World Wide Web in a specialized area.

Boolean search
A web search that ties words together so that a search engine can hunt for the resulting phrase.

- *Vertical search engines.* One way you can narrow your search is to use a **vertical search engine**, a specialized tool that may index, for example, only academic sources (Google Scholar) or job websites (Indeed).

- *Boolean searches.* Another way to narrow a search is to conduct a **Boolean search**, which allows you to enclose phrases in quotation marks or parentheses so that a search yields only those sites on which all words or the phrase appear in that exact order and eliminates sites that contain the words at random. Boolean searches also let you exclude words or phrases from your search or restrict the dates of documents to a specified time frame.

- *Criteria for evaluating web resources.* A third strategy for sorting through information you discover on the Internet has to do with the principles of appropriately interpreting verbal and nonverbal messages. Specifically, you need to evaluate the sites you discover according to a consistent standard. The six criteria in Table 11.2 can serve as such a standard.[27]

Inevitably, one of the first hits in almost any Internet search is *Wikipedia*. Because it is continually updated, *Wikipedia* can provide valuable information about current events and cutting-edge technology. But users should keep in mind that because

TABLE 11.2 Six Criteria for Evaluating Internet Resources

CRITERION	APPLYING THE CRITERION	DRAWING CONCLUSIONS
Accountability: Who is responsible for the site?	• The individual or organization responsible for the site may be clear from the title of the site and/or its URL. • See whether the site is signed. • Follow links or search the author's name to determine his or her expertise and authority. • If the site is unsigned, search for a sponsoring organization. Follow links, search the organization's name, or consider the domain to determine reputability.	• If you cannot identify or verify an author or sponsor, be wary of the site.
Accuracy: Is the information correct?	• Consider whether the author or sponsor is a credible authority. • Assess the care with which the site has been written. • Conduct additional research into the information on the site.	• If the author or sponsor is a credible authority, the information is more likely to be accurate. • A site should be relatively free of writing errors. • You may be able to verify or refute the information by consulting another resource.
Objectivity: Is the site free of bias?	• Consider the interests, philosophical or political biases, and the source of financial support for the author or sponsor of the site. • Does the site include advertisements that might influence its content?	• The more objective the author and sponsor of the site are, the more credible their information may be.

(continued)

Six Criteria for Evaluating Internet Resources *(continued)*

CRITERION	APPLYING THE CRITERION	DRAWING CONCLUSIONS
Timeliness: Is the site current?	• Look at the bottom of the site for a statement indicating when the site was created and when it was last updated. • If you cannot find a date on the site, click on Page Info (for example, from the Tools menu at the top of the browser screen in Firefox) to find a "Last Modified" date. • Enter the title of the site in a search engine. The resulting information should include a date.	• In general, when you are concerned with factual data, the more recent it is, the better.
Usability: Do the layout and design of the site facilitate its use?	• Does the site load fairly quickly? • Is a fee required to gain access to any of the information on the site?	• Balance graphics and any fees against practical efficiency.
Diversity: Is the site inclusive?	• Do language and graphics reflect and respect differences in gender, ethnicity, race, and sexual preference? • Do interactive forums invite divergent perspectives? • Is the site friendly to people with disabilities (e.g., does it offer a large-print or video option)?	• A site should be free of bias, representative of diverse perspectives, and accessible by people with disabilities.

SOURCE: Steven Beebe, et. Al, "Six Criteria for Evaluating Internet Resources", Pearson Ed.,Inc.

anyone, regardless of expertise, can add or edit a *Wikipedia* entry, the site's reliability and appropriateness for academic use are limited.

Online Databases **Online databases** provide access to bibliographic information, abstracts, and full texts for a variety of resources, including periodicals, newspapers, government documents, and even books. Like websites, online databases are accessed via a networked computer. Unlike websites, most databases are restricted to the patrons of libraries that subscribe to them. Your library may subscribe to several or all of the following popular full-text databases:

online database

A subscription-based electronic resource that may offer access to abstracts or the full texts of entries, in addition to bibliographic data.

- *Academic Search Ultimate.* This popular database offers many full-text articles from 1887 to the present, covering a wide variety of subjects.

- *JSTOR.* This multisubject full-text database offers journal articles from the first volume to the present.

- *LexisNexis Academic.* Focusing on business, finance, industry, and law, this database provides many full-text articles from newspapers, magazines, journals, newsletters, and wire services. Dates of coverage vary.

COMMUNICATION & SOCIAL MEDIA

Facebook and the 2016 U.S. Presidential Campaign

Prior to the 1920s, voters in U.S. presidential elections were able to hear and see candidates only face-to-face at political rallies and train whistle stops. In 1924, voters first listened to campaign information on the radio, and in 1952, they viewed ads and speeches on television for the first time.

In 2016, voters for both Donald Trump and Hillary Clinton relied to a significant degree on a new media tool for campaign news: Facebook. A post-election survey conducted by the Pew Research Center revealed that "Nearly one-in-ten of both Trump (7%) and Clinton (8%) voters said Facebook was where they got most of their news about the campaign . . . ."[28]

Sources of Supporting Material

1. *Personal knowledge and experience.* Take advantage of your own expertise.
2. *The Internet.* Use vertical search engines, conduct Boolean searches, and apply evaluation criteria to choose the best information.
3. *Online databases.* For access to abstracts and full texts for a variety of resources, explore the databases to which your library subscribes.
4. *Traditional library holdings.* Get to know your reference librarian for help mining traditional library resources.
5. *Interviews.* When only an expert can provide the information you need, interview that person.

stacks

The collection of books in a library.

reference resources

Material housed in the reference section of a library, such as encyclopedias, dictionaries, atlases, almanacs, and books of quotations.

Traditional Library Holdings Despite the explosion of Internet and database resources in recent years, the more traditional holdings of libraries, both paper and electronic, remain rich sources of supporting material. Spend some time becoming familiar with your library's services and layout so that you know how and where to access books and reference materials.

- *Books.* Libraries' collections of books are called the **stacks**. The stacks are organized by call numbers, which are included in electronic catalog entries. A location guide can tell you the floor or section of the stacks that houses books with the call numbers in which you are interested.

- *Reference resources.* Print **reference resources**—which include encyclopedias, dictionaries, atlases, almanacs, and books of quotations—are indexed with a *ref* prefix on their call numbers to show that they are housed in the reference section of the library. Like periodicals, newspapers, and microfilm, print reference resources are usually available only for in-house research and cannot be checked out. Reference librarians are specialists in the field of information science. They are often able to suggest additional print or electronic resources that you might otherwise overlook. If you plan to use the reference section, visit the library during daytime working hours. A full-time reference librarian is more likely to be on hand and available to help you at that time than in the evenings or on weekends.

Interviews If you need detailed information that only an expert can provide, you may want to interview that person. For example, a member of the city council may be able to explain the reasons for the continuing controversy surrounding granting a liquor license to the new restaurant opening on the edge of campus. Appendix A offers guidelines and strategies for conducting an information-gathering interview.

Types of Supporting Material

If you have explored your own knowledge and insights and those of people you know, discovered material on the Internet, consulted databases, and examined a variety of library resources, you probably have a wealth of potential supporting material. Now you will need to decide what to use in your speech.

Keeping in mind your listeners' knowledge, interests, and expectations will help you determine where an illustration might stir their emotions, where an explanation might help them to understand a point, and where statistics might convince them of the significance of a problem. Let's discuss these and other types of supporting material and consider suggestions for using them effectively.

illustration

A story or anecdote that provides an example of an idea, issue, or problem the speaker is discussing.

Illustrations **Illustrations** offer an example of, or tell a story about, an idea, issue, or problem a speaker is discussing. Illustrations can be as short as a word or phrase or as long as a well-developed paragraph. Sometimes speakers will offer a series of brief illustrations, as President George W. Bush did in his final state of the union address in January 2008:

> In the past seven years, we've also seen images that have sobered us. We've watched throngs of mourners in Lebanon and Pakistan carrying the caskets of beloved leaders taken by the assassin's hand. We've seen wedding guests in blood-soaked finery staggering from a hotel in Jordan, Afghans and Iraqis blown up in

mosques and markets, and trains in London and Madrid ripped apart by bombs. On a clear September day, we saw thousands of our fellow citizens taken from us in an instant.[29]

Other speakers offer longer and more detailed illustrations. Still others will use instead a **hypothetical illustration**—one that has not actually occurred. If you decide to use a hypothetical illustration, it is important to clarify to your audience that the scene you describe never really happened. Notice how Matthew uses the word *imagine,* which lets his audience know that his illustration is hypothetical:

> Imagine an evening outing: You and your two children decide to have a fun night out. You look up to your rearview mirror to see a car slam into the back of your car—WHAM—killing your children. You survive the crash and so does the individual who rear-ended you.[30]

Whether you choose to use brief or extended illustrations, true or hypothetical ones, remember this principle: Everybody likes to hear a story. An illustration almost always ensures audience interest. In addition, communication researchers have found that listeners are less likely to generate counterarguments to a persuasive message supported by examples and personal narratives than one not so supported.[31]

The following suggestions should help you use illustrations effectively in your speeches:

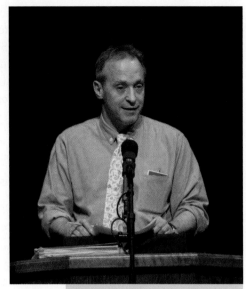

▲ Everybody loves a good story. David Sedaris is famous for illustrations that keep the attention of his audiences. What principles can you use from this chapter to hold your listeners' attention? Adm Golub/Modesto Bee/ZUMAPRESS.com

- Be sure that your illustrations are directly relevant to the idea or point they are supposed to support.
- Choose illustrations that are typical, not exceptions.
- Make your illustrations vivid and specific.
- Use illustrations with which your listeners can identify.
- Remember that the most effective illustrations are often personal ones.

Descriptions　　A **description** provides the details that allow an audience to see, hear, smell, touch, or taste whatever you are talking about. Descriptions can make people and scenes come alive for an audience. In her Nobel Prize acceptance speech, writer Doris Lessing described Africa as she remembered it:

> the banks of the Zambesi, where it rolls between pale grassy banks, it being the dry season, dark-green and glossy, with all the birds of Africa around its banks . . . . elephants, giraffes, lions and the rest . . . the sky at night, still unpolluted, black and wonderful, full of restless stars.[32]

Explanations　　An **explanation** of how something works or why a situation exists can help an audience understand conditions, events, or processes. Discussing the use of solitary confinement in the U.S. juvenile justice system, student speaker Branden explained how this form of punishment came to be used in the first place:

> Solitary confinement in the United States was based on a Quaker belief that prisoners isolated in stone cells with only a Bible would use the time to repent, pray, and find introspection.[33]

Although descriptions and explanations are part of most speeches, they lack the inherent interest factor that illustrations have. The following suggestions may help you keep audiences from yawning:

- Avoid too many descriptions and explanations.
- Keep your descriptions and explanations brief.
- Use specific and concrete language.

hypothetical illustration
An example or story that has not actually occurred.

description
A word picture.

explanation
A statement that makes clear how something is done or why it exists in its present or past form.

definition

A statement of what something means.

classification

A type of definition that first places a term in the general class to which it belongs and then differentiates it from all other members of that class.

operational definition

A definition that shows how a term works or what it does.

analogy

A comparison between two ideas, things, or situations that demonstrates how something unfamiliar is similar to something the audience already understands.

literal analogy

A comparison between two similar things.

figurative analogy

A comparison between two seemingly dissimilar things that share some common feature on which the comparison depends.

statistics

Numerical data that summarize examples.

Definitions A **definition** has two justifiable uses in speeches. First, a speaker should be sure to define any and all specialized, technical, or little-known terms in his or her speech. Such definitions are usually achieved by **classification**, the kind of definition you would find in a dictionary. Alternatively, a speaker may define a term by showing how it works or how it is applied in a specific instance—what is known as an **operational definition**. Before arguing that we need to change our cultural perspective of pain, student speaker Veronica provided an operational definition of *pain*:

> Pain is specifically a physical sensation—you might think of chronic pain or stepping on your five-year-old's Lego . . . .[34]

To use definitions effectively, consider the following suggestions:

- Use definitions only when necessary.
- Be certain that your definitions are understandable.
- Be sure that any definition you provide accurately reflects your use of the word or phrase throughout the speech.

Analogies An **analogy** demonstrates how unfamiliar ideas, things, and situations are similar to something the audience already understands. Speakers can use two types of analogies in their speeches. The first is a **literal analogy**, or comparison of two similar things. Eulogizing former Israeli President Shimon Peres, Barack Obama used a literal analogy to communicate Peres's status among world leaders of the twentieth century:

> In many ways, he reminded me of some other giants of the 20th century that I've had the honor to meet—men like Nelson Mandela; women like Her Majesty, Queen Elizabeth—leaders who have seen so much . . . .[35]

The second type of analogy is a **figurative analogy**, a comparison of two seemingly dissimilar things that in fact share a significant common feature. In her 2016 commencement address at Berkeley, Facebook COO Sheryl Sandberg used a figurative analogy to inspire her listeners to emerge from life's most difficult moments:

> . . . when life sucks you under, you can kick against the bottom, break the surface, and breathe again.[36]

Two suggestions can help you use analogies more effectively in your speeches:

- Be certain that the two things you compare in a literal analogy are very similar.
- Make the similarity between the two things compared in a figurative analogy apparent to the audience.

Statistics **Statistics**, or numerical data, can represent hundreds or thousands of illustrations, helping a speaker express the significance or magnitude of a situation. Statistics can also help a speaker express the relationship of a part to the whole. In her speech on domestic abuse, Ellie used both types of statistics to communicate the inadequacy of funding for shelters:

> . . . 80 percent of shelters had been facing funding cuts, despite the fact that 88 percent have been seeing an increase in their demand. Additionally, more than 20 shelters, aiding thousands of women, have been forced to close entirely . . . .[37]

Skilled speakers learn how to use statistics to their greatest advantage. For example, they try to make numbers more dramatic for their audiences. AFL-CIO president John J. Sweeney dramatized the danger of unsafe bridges in the United States by making a statistic personal:

> Since I was coming to work from Washington to New Rochelle this morning, I asked my staff to check out my route. We found that traveling the I-95 corridor between

Washington, D.C. and New York City, I would cross or come within two-tenths of a mile of 30 bridges that are rated either functionally obsolete or structurally deficient.[38]

Ken Huber, CEO of the innovative medical technology company Grail, dramatized the rapid progress of technology with statistics that his student audience could readily envision:

> Floppy disks were the thumb drives of the 1980s, except it would take over 7,000 floppy disks, or a stack 50 feet high, and cost $35,000, to equal the storage in a one gigabyte thumb drive you buy for 3 bucks today, and [that] easily fits in your pocket.[39]

And student speaker Isaac dramatized a statistic by *compacting* it—expressing it in units more readily understandable to his audience:

> Every hour, the equivalent of 300 football fields of forest is cleared in order to make way for palm oil plantations . . . . That means that in the time it takes me to give this speech, the equivalent of 50 football fields will have already been cleared.[40]

In addition to dramatizing statistics, you can use statistics more effectively if you apply the following suggestions:

- Round off large numbers.
- Use visual aids to present your statistics.
- Cite the sources of your statistics.

Opinions The opinions of others can add authority, drama, and style to a speech. A speaker can use three types of opinions: expert testimony, lay testimony, and literary quotations.

Expert testimony is the type of opinion most frequently employed by speakers. If you lack authority on your topic, cite someone who can offer such expertise. In preparing her speech on the college credit card crisis, Jeni realized that her audience might not believe that the misuse of credit cards by college students is a widespread problem. So Jeni quoted an expert:

> Ruth Suswein, executive director of the Bankcard Holders of America, told the . . . *Pittsburgh Post Gazette,* "I defy you to go on any college campus and find any student who doesn't know some other student who has messed up using credit cards."[41]

expert testimony
The opinion of someone who is an acknowledged expert in the field under discussion.

DEVELOPING YOUR SPEECH STEP BY STEP

Gathering Supporting Material

With a draft of her specific purpose, central idea, and main ideas in hand, Dezerae begins to research the health hazards of soft drinks. The article that launched her topic mentions studies done by Harvard University.

She finds and electronically bookmarks fact sheets and other information from the Harvard studies. She also decides to do a Google search. She finds relevant and convincing data from the Centers for Disease Control and Prevention and the National Institutes of Health. Dezerae creates electronic bookmarks for these additional sources.

She then begins to read each resource more carefully and to take notes. As she does so, she puts quotation marks around any material she copies verbatim and makes sure that she has copied it accurately.

RECAP

Supporting Your Speech

Type of Supporting Material	Guidelines for Use
Illustrations	• Make illustrations directly relevant to the idea or point they support. • Choose illustrations that are typical. • Make illustrations vivid and specific. • Use illustrations with which your listeners can identify. • Remember that the most effective illustrations are often personal ones.
Descriptions and Explanations	• Avoid too many descriptions and explanations. • Keep descriptions and explanations brief. • Use specific and concrete language.
Definitions	• Use definitions only when necessary. • Be certain that definitions are understandable. • Be sure that a definition accurately reflects your use of the word or phrase.
Analogies	• Be certain that the two things you compare in a literal analogy are very similar. • Make apparent to the audience the similarity between the two things compared in a figurative analogy.
Statistics	• Round off large numbers. • Use visual aids. • Cite your sources.
Opinions	• Be certain that any authority you cite is actually an expert on the subject you are discussing. • Identify your sources. • Cite unbiased authorities. • Cite representative opinions, or identify dissenting viewpoints as such. • Quote or paraphrase accurately and in context. • Use literary quotations sparingly.

lay testimony
The opinion of someone who experienced an event or situation firsthand.

literary quotation
A citation from a work of fiction or nonfiction, a poem, or another speech.

After an F5 tornado ravaged Joplin, Missouri, television audiences were moved by the compassionate reporting of Weather Channel journalist Mike Bettes, who was one of the first reporters on the scene. For a speaker, as well as a news organization, such **lay testimony** can provide the most memorable moments of a speech, stirring an audience's emotions.

Finally, speakers may wish to include **literary quotations** in their speeches. Salem State College Professor Robert Brown quoted architect Buckminster Fuller to make a point about how the English language has become increasingly visual and kinesthetic:

As the architectural visionary Buckminster Fuller was fond of saying, "I am a verb." In English, with every innovation that comes to market, we transform things into actions, and nouns into verbs, as when I say: "Let me friend you."[42]

Whether you use expert testimony, lay testimony, or literary quotations, consider the following suggestions for using opinions effectively in your speeches:

• Be certain that any authority you cite is actually an expert on the subject you are discussing.
• Identify your sources.
• Cite unbiased authorities.
• Cite representative opinions, or identify dissenting viewpoints as such.
• Quote or paraphrase your sources accurately and note the context in which the remarks were originally made.
• Use literary quotations sparingly.

As you select your illustrations, descriptions, explanations, definitions, analogies, statistics, and opinions, be guided not only by the suggestions provided in this chapter but also by the five Communication Principles for a Lifetime:

• **Be aware of your communication with yourself and others.** The best supporting material reflects self-awareness, taking advantage of your own knowledge and experience.

• **Effectively use and interpret verbal messages.** Effective verbal supporting material is appropriately worded, concrete, and vivid enough that your audience can visualize what you are talking about.

• **Effectively use and interpret nonverbal messages.** Use visual aids to present statistics.

COMMUNICATION & DIVERSITY

How to Adapt to Your Diverse Audience

Here are some ideas to help you adapt when you speak to an audience of people who have cultural backgrounds different from your own.[43]

- *Adapt your supporting materials.* Telling a good story to illustrate your ideas is an especially effective strategy to appeal to a wide range of audience preferences.
- *Adapt your visual support.* You might want to use more visual aids to illustrate your talk. Pictures and images can communicate universal messages, especially emotional ones.
- *Adapt your speech organization.* People from the predominant culture in North America usually prefer a structured speech that follows an outlined pattern. They also prefer an introduction that previews the

ideas you'll present and a conclusion that crisply summarizes the essential points you've made. A Russian or Eastern European audience would expect a less tightly structured speech, however. When you're in doubt about listener preferences, we recommend being structured and organized.

- *Adapt your delivery style.* One study found that members of some cultures prefer a more formal oratorical style of delivery than the conversational, extemporaneous style that is usually taught in American public speaking classes.[44]

Our overarching suggestion is to be aware of who will be in your audience. Before you develop or deliver your speech, if you're unsure of your listeners' speaking-style preferences, ask for tips and strategies from audience members or people you trust.

- **Listen and respond thoughtfully to others.** If listeners find a speech boring, the speaker has probably not used the fundamental principles of communication as criteria for selecting supporting material.
- **Appropriately adapt messages to others.** Lin-Manuel Miranda, celebrated creator of the hit musical *Hamilton*, told recent graduates at the University of Pennsylvania,

> This act of choosing—the stories we tell versus the stories we leave out—will reverberate across the rest of your life. Don't believe me? Think about how you celebrated this senior week, and contrast that with the version you shared with the parents and grandparents sitting behind you.

Miranda's "act of choosing" will help you select the verbal and visual supporting material that is most appropriately adapted to your audience.

Acknowledgment of Supporting Material

In the United States and most other Western cultures, using the words, sentence structures, or ideas of another person without crediting the source is a serious breach of ethics. Once you have supporting material in hand, you must decide whether and how to acknowledge the source.

Determining What Should Be Acknowledged Some information is so widely known that you may not need to acknowledge a source. For example, you need not cite a source if you say that former FBI official Mark Felt was identified as the long-anonymous Watergate informant "Deep Throat." This fact is general knowledge and is widely available in a variety of sources. If you decide to use any of the following, however, you must acknowledge the source:

- Direct quotations, even if they are only brief phrases
- Others' opinions, assertions, or ideas, even if you paraphrase them rather than quote them verbatim
- Statistics
- Any non-original visual materials, including graphs, tables, and pictures

plagiarism

The presentation of someone else's words or ideas without acknowledging the source.

oral citation

The oral presentation of such information about a source as the author, title, and publication date.

Understanding Plagiarism and its Consequences   Presenting someone else's words or ideas without acknowledging the source constitutes **plagiarism**, a breach of academic honesty that can have dire consequences.

A few years ago, one of your authors heard a student's excellent speech on the importance of detecting cancer early. The only problem was that she heard the same speech again in the following class period! On finding the "speech"—actually a *Reader's Digest* article that was several years old—both students were certain that they had discovered a shortcut to an A. Instead, they failed the assignment, ruined their course grades, and lost their instructor's trust. The consequences of plagiarism in other arenas can be even more severe, including the loss of a job or the end of a promising career.

Acknowledging Sources in Oral Citations   To acknowledge your source, you can integrate an **oral citation** into your speech. In his speech on contaminated water, Nick provided this oral citation:

> *Fortune* of January 25th, 2016, reports that although Congress banned lead water pipes over 30 years ago, more than 3.3 million old pipes remain throughout the country.[45]

STUDY GUIDE:

❯ REVIEW, APPLY, AND ASSESS

Overviewing the Public Speaking Process

11.1 List and explain the components of the audience-centered public speaking model.

REVIEW: The stages of the public speaking process center on consideration of audience members, who influence every decision a speaker makes. A speaker's tasks include selecting and narrowing a topic, identifying a general and specific purpose, developing the central idea, generating main ideas, gathering supporting material, organizing the speech, and rehearsing and delivering the speech.

KEY TERMS:
public speaking
audience-centered public speaker

APPLY: How is the behavior of a speaker who adapts to his or her audience different from that of a speaker who does *not* adapt to the audience?

ASSESS: Pat has been asked to attend Monday night's city council meeting to speak on behalf of neighbors who do not want the council to issue an alcohol use permit to a new restaurant in their neighborhood. What strategies could Pat use to adapt her speech to the members of the city council?

Building Your Confidence

11.2 Apply specific strategies for becoming a more confident speaker.

REVIEW: Understanding public speaking anxiety, knowing how to develop a speech, being prepared, giving yourself mental pep talks, using deep-breathing techniques, and focusing on your audience and message can help you become a more confident speaker, as can taking advantage of opportunities to speak and exploring additional resources.

KEY TERMS:
public speaking anxiety   habituation
illusion of transparency

APPLY: Xavier, one of your best friends from high school, went on to play football for your flagship state university. Now he has been invited back to address the annual football banquet at your old high school. Not having taken an oral communication course yet, Xavier is anxious about his upcoming speech. Based on what you have learned about becoming a more confident speaker, what advice would you give Xavier?

ASSESS: Complete the paper-pencil Personal Report of Public Speaking Anxiety (PRPSA) available at www.jamescmccroskey.com/measures/prpsa.htm to assess your level of communication apprehension. At the end of the communication course in which you are currently enrolled, complete the self-evaluation again to see whether this course has affected your level of communication apprehension.

Selecting and Narrowing Your Topic

11.3 Select and narrow a speech topic that is appropriate to the audience, the occasion, and yourself.

REVIEW: As you begin to prepare your speech, you will first have to select and narrow your topic, keeping in mind the audience, the occasion, and your own interests and experiences. You may find helpful such strategies as silent brainstorming, scanning web directories and websites, and listening and reading for topic ideas.

APPLY: One speaker's self-awareness helped her generate a list of possible topics that began with "San Antonio, Texas: City of cultural diversity." Use your own interests and experiences to help generate a similar list of five to seven topics.

ASSESS: The chair of the Department of Communication Studies visits your required communication class to discuss what you can do with a degree in communication studies. Analyze her choice of topic according to the topic selection guidelines presented in this chapter.

Identifying Your Purpose

11.4 Write an audience-centered, specific-purpose statement for a speech.

REVIEW: Once you have a topic, you need to identify both your general purpose and your specific purpose. General purposes include to inform, to persuade, and to entertain. Specific purposes are determined by the general purpose, the topic, and the audience.

KEY TERMS:

general purpose   specific purpose

APPLY: Given the broad topic "ocean tides," write three specific-purpose statements: one for a speech to inform, one for a speech to persuade, and one for a speech to entertain.

ASSESS: Revise the following draft of a specific-purpose statement so that it better meets the criteria presented in this chapter: To explain why I use public transportation instead of my own car.

Developing Your Central Idea

11.5 Develop a central idea for a speech.

REVIEW: Your central idea will focus on the content of your speech. It should be centered on your audience; reflect a single idea; be a complete declarative sentence; and use direct, specific language.

KEY TERMS:

central idea   declarative sentence

APPLY: Following the guidelines in this chapter, write a central idea for a speech on the topic of buying car insurance.

ASSESS: Revise each of the following central ideas according to the criteria presented in this chapter:

- Bicycling and jewelry making are fun hobbies.
- How do you change your academic major?

Generating Main Ideas

11.6 Generate main ideas from a central idea.

REVIEW: The main ideas of a speech support or subdivide the central idea. They are usually logical divisions of the central idea, reasons the central idea is true, or a series of steps or a chronological sequence that develops the central idea.

KEY TERM:

main ideas

APPLY: Divide the central idea you wrote about buying car insurance into two or more main ideas, using the three questions recommended in this chapter.

ASSESS: Check the main ideas you drafted for the previous "apply" question against the following specific-purpose statement: "At the end of my speech, the audience will explain three criteria for buying car insurance." If your main ideas do not contribute to this specific purpose, make appropriate revisions to either the specific purpose or the main ideas.

Gathering Supporting Material

11.7 Describe five potential sources and seven types of supporting material for a speech, and use each type effectively.

REVIEW: You have at least five potential sources of supporting material: personal knowledge and experience, the Internet, online databases, traditional library holdings, and interviews. Personal knowledge and experience increase the likelihood that the audience will find you a credible speaker. To supplement your own knowledge and experience, you can turn to the vast resources of the Internet. Online databases provide both bibliographic information and full texts to subscribers. You will also most likely use traditional library holdings—books, periodicals, newspapers, and reference resources—as sources of supporting material. And finally, if you need detailed information that only an expert can provide, you may want to interview that person. The types of supporting material available in these sources include illustrations, descriptions, explanations, definitions, analogies, statistics, and opinions. Simple guidelines can help you use each type of supporting material effectively and cite your sources correctly.

KEY TERMS:

supporting material	classification
vertical search engine	operational definition
Boolean search	analogy
online database	literal analogy
stacks	figurative analogy
reference resources	statistics
illustration	expert testimony
hypothetical illustration	lay testimony
description	literary quotation
explanation	plagiarism
definition	oral citation

APPLY: Think back to a recent speech you have heard. Identify an illustration, statistic, or other piece of supporting material from this speech that you found highly memorable.

ASSESS: Use each of the five Communication Principles for a Lifetime to explain *why* the supporting material you identified in the previous "apply" question was memorable.

⟩ THE PRINCIPLE POINTS

Principle One:

Be aware of your communication with yourself and others.

- Understand that public speaking anxiety results from your body working to help you perform better.
- Give yourself a pep talk before getting up to speak.
- Consider your own interests and experiences when selecting a topic.
- Remember that the best supporting material often draws on your own knowledge and experience.

Principle Two:

Effectively use and interpret verbal messages.

- Focus on your message to help you become a more confident speaker.
- Search for topics on the Internet, in the media, and in books.
- Word your specific purpose in terms of your audience to help you keep your focus on them.
- Make sure that your central idea reflects a single topic, is a complete declarative sentence, and uses direct, specific language.
- Consider the accountability, accuracy, objectivity, date, usability, and sensitivity to diversity of verbal material you find on websites.
- Make your illustrations vivid and specific.
- Keep descriptions and explanations brief.
- Describe and explain in specific and concrete language.
- Make your definitions readily understandable, and be certain that they accurately reflect how you use the word or phrase in the speech.
- Round off large numbers to make them more understandable.
- Cite unbiased authorities who represent prevailing opinion.
- Quote or paraphrase accurately and in context.
- Integrate oral citations of your sources into your speech.

Principle Three:

Effectively use and interpret nonverbal messages.

- Remember that nonverbal indicators of public speaking anxiety are rarely visible to an audience.
- Consider the accountability, accuracy, objectivity, date, usability, and sensitivity to diversity of pictures and graphics you find on websites.
- Use visual aids to make statistics more readily understandable to your listeners.

Principle Four:

Listen and respond thoughtfully to others.

- To increase your confidence when speaking in public, seek out information about your listeners and how they are likely to respond to your message.
- Listen for topic ideas in the course of casual conversation with friends.

Principle Five:

Appropriately adapt messages to others.

- As you learn more about your audience, you can revise ideas or strategies for your speech at any point in your preparation process.
- Focus on your audience to increase your confidence.
- Be sensitive to and adapt to the diversity of your audience.
- Consider your audience's interests and expectations as you select the topic for your speech.
- Keep in mind your audience's knowledge, interests, and expectations as you select supporting material for your presentation.

ORGANIZING AND OUTLINING YOUR SPEECH

Don't agonize. Organize. —FLORYNCE R. KENNEDY

Kantver/Fotolia

→ CHAPTER OUTLINE

- Organizing Your Main Ideas
- Organizing Your Supporting Material
- Signposting: Organizing Your Speech for the Ears of Others

- Introducing and Concluding Your Speech
- Outlining Your Speech
- Study Guide: Review, Apply, and Assess

LEARNING OBJECTIVES

After studying this chapter, you should be able to

12.1 List and explain five strategies for organizing the main ideas of a speech.

12.2 Explain how to organize supporting material.

12.3 Use verbal and nonverbal signposts to organize your speech for the ears of others.

12.4 Explain the functions of, and several strategies for, speech introductions and conclusions.

12.5 Develop a preparation outline and speaking notes for a speech.

One study found that college students report spending, on average, nearly half of their total speech preparation time outlining and revising their speeches.[1] This chapter will be key in helping you use that preparation time effectively.

You have already completed the first five stages of audience-centered speech preparation:

1. Select and narrow a topic.
2. Determine your purpose.
3. Develop your central idea.
4. Generate main ideas.
5. Gather supporting material.

Now it is time to put your speech together. You will need to consider first how best to organize your main ideas. Then you will organize your supporting material for maximum effect, and devise signposts to guide your audience through your speech. You will develop an effective introduction and conclusion. Finally, once you have made the necessary decisions about these component parts, you will be ready to outline the entire speech and prepare your speaking notes.

Organizing Your Main Ideas

12.1 **List and explain five strategies for organizing the main ideas of a speech.**

A logically organized speech includes an introduction, a body, and a conclusion. The body presents the most important content of the speech—the main ideas that you generated with the help of your central idea. At least five strategies can help you determine an effective order in which to present those main ideas.

COMMUNICATION & SOCIAL MEDIA

Your Speech as a "Content Sandwich"

Recently developed by LinkedIn as a best practice for blogging, the "content sandwich" can also be a useful model for organizing a speech.[2] Here, adapted for speakers and their listeners, is how to make a content sandwich:

The top bun should draw the audience in. Main ideas and supporting material—lettuce, tomato and cheese—should engage the audience. Signposts are the mustard and mayo that hold the fillings together. And the bottom bun is a call to action.

Organizing Ideas Topically

topical organization

Organization determined by the speaker's discretion or by recency, primacy, or complexity.

If your main ideas are logical divisions of your central idea, you will probably arrange them according to **topical organization**. This strategy is used most frequently. Topical organization may simply be an arbitrary arrangement of main ideas that are fairly equal in importance. For example, if you are giving an informative speech on the various instrument families in the modern symphony orchestra, your main ideas will probably be strings, woodwinds, brass, and percussion. The order in which you discuss these instrument groups may not really matter.

At other times, topical organization is less arbitrary. Three principles may help you arrange your main ideas effectively.

recency

Arrangement of ideas from least important to most important, or from weakest to strongest.

Recency   The principle of **recency** suggests that audiences remember best what they hear *last*. If you want to emphasize the string section of an orchestra, you will purposefully place that instrument family last in your informative speech.

primacy

Arrangement of ideas from most important to least important, or from strongest to weakest.

Primacy   Another principle that can help guide your topical organization is **primacy**, which suggests that you discuss your most convincing or least controversial idea *first*. To adapt to an audience that may be skeptical of some of your ideas, discuss first the points on which you all agree. If you are speaking to an anti-gun-control audience about ways to protect children from violence in schools, don't begin by advocating gun control. Instead, begin by affirming family values and education in the home, perhaps move on to the importance of an antiviolence curriculum and adequate counseling in schools, and only then discuss gun control as a possible preventive measure.

complexity

Arranging ideas from simple to more complex.

chronological organization

Organization by time or sequence.

Complexity   Organization according to **complexity** moves from simple ideas and processes to more complex ones. You have learned many life skills in order of complexity. In first grade, you learned to read easy words first and then moved on to more difficult ones. In third grade, you learned single-digit multiplication tables before moving on to more complex double- and triple-digit multiplication problems. Similarly, if you are giving a speech on how to trace your family's genealogy, you might discuss readily available, user-friendly Internet sources before explaining how to access old courthouse records or parish registries of births, deaths, and baptisms.

▼ Which organization is the best choice for this speaker's presentation about the worldwide operations of his organization? Rawpixel/Shutterstock

Organizing Ideas Chronologically

If you determine that you can best develop your central idea through a series of steps, you will probably organize those steps— your main ideas—chronologically. **Chronological organization** is based on time or sequential order according to when each step or event occurred or should occur. If you are explaining a process, you will want to organize the steps of that process from first to last. If you are providing a historical overview of an event, movement, or policy, you might begin with the end result and trace its history backward in time. Topics that lend themselves to chronological organization include the process for stripping and refinishing a piece of furniture, the five deadliest U.S. tornadoes on record, and the three golden ages of journalism.[3]

Organizing Ideas Spatially

"Go down the hill two blocks and turn left by the florist. Then go three blocks to the next stoplight and turn right. The place you're looking for is about a block farther, on your right." When you offer someone directions, you organize your ideas spatially. **Spatial organization** means arranging items according to their location, position, or direction. It is another strategy by which you might organize main ideas that are logical divisions of your central idea.

Speeches that rely on description are especially good candidates for spatial organization. For example, a discussion of the route taken to the South Pole in 1911 by Norwegian explorer Roald Amundsen or of the molecular structure of DNA would lend itself to spatial organization. You might choose to organize your speech on the three deadliest U.S. tornadoes spatially (according to where each tornado occurred) rather than chronologically (by year).

spatial organization
Organization according to location, position, or direction.

Organizing Ideas to Show Cause and Effect

Cause and effect organization actually refers to two related patterns: identifying a situation and then discussing the resulting effects (cause–effect), and presenting a situation and then exploring its causes (effect–cause).

If your main ideas are *logical divisions* of your central idea, you might organize them according to cause–effect. A speaker discussing the consequences of overworked medical residents might use a cause–effect pattern, first establishing that medical residents are overworked and then that resident exhaustion is a major contributor to medical malpractice.[4]

If your main ideas are *reasons* your central idea is true, you will probably organize them according to effect–cause. A speaker exploring the reasons for the slave trade in southeast Asian fisheries would probably use an effect–cause pattern, first documenting the existence of this slave trade and then exploring its various causes.[5]

As the recency principle would suggest, a cause–effect pattern emphasizes effects; an effect–cause pattern emphasizes causes.

cause and effect organization
Organization by discussing a situation and its effects, or a situation and its causes.

Organizing Ideas by Problem and Solution

If, instead of exploring causes or consequences of a problem or issue, you want either to explore how best to solve the problem or to advocate a particular solution, you will probably choose **problem and solution organization**. This strategy is appropriate for organizing logical divisions of a central idea. For example, if you are speaking on how listeners can protect themselves from mountain lion attacks in the western United States, you might first establish that a significant problem exists, and then talk about solutions to that problem. Or if you are talking about ending discrimination against overweight people, you could first establish that such discrimination exists and then talk about solutions that would end the discrimination.

problem and solution organization
Organization by discussing first a problem and then various solutions.

You can use problem and solution organization for either informative or persuasive speeches. When your general purpose is to persuade, you will go on to urge your audience to support or adopt one or more of the solutions you discuss.

How do you decide which organizational pattern to use? For example, both the mountain lion and the weight discrimination topics lend themselves to organization

COMMUNICATION & DIVERSITY

Acknowledging Cultural Differences in Organizing Messages

What's the shortest distance between two points? Going in a straight line, of course. In organizing a message, it may seem that the most logical strategy is to develop a structure that moves from one idea to the next in a logical, "straight" way. But not every culture organizes ideas using that logic. In fact, each culture teaches its members particular patterns of thought and organization that are considered appropriate for various occasions and audiences.

In general, speakers in the United States tend to be more linear and direct than Semitic, Asian, Romance language, or Russian speakers.[6] Semitic language speakers support their main points by pursuing tangents that might seem "off topic" to many U.S. listeners. Asians may allude to a main point only through a circuitous route of illustrations and parables. And speakers from Romance language and Russian cultures tend to begin with a basic principle and then move to facts and illustrations that only gradually are related to the main point. The models in Figure 12.1 illustrate these culturally diverse patterns of organization.[7]

Of course, these generalizations are very broad. As an effective speaker who seeks to adapt to your audience, you should investigate and perhaps acknowledge, or even consider adopting, the customary organizational strategy of your particular audience. In addition, when you are listening to a speech, recognizing the existence of cultural differences can help you appreciate and understand the organization of a speaker from a culture other than your own.

FIGURE 12.1 Organizational Patterns by Culture

SOURCE: Lieberman, Devorah, *Public Speaking in the Multicultural Environment*, 2nd ed., © 1997. Reprinted and electronically reproduced by permission of Pearson Education, Inc., Hoboken, New Jersey.

U.S.   Semitic   Asian   Romance   Russian

RECAP

Organizing Your Main Ideas

Strategy	Description	Applicable to Main Ideas That Are . . .
Topical	Arbitrary arrangement of topics or organization according to recency, primacy, or complexity	Logical divisions
Chronological	Organization by time or sequence	Steps or a chronological sequence
Spatial	Organization according to location or position	Logical divisions
Cause and effect	Organization by discussing a situation and its causes (effect and cause) or a situation and its effects (cause and effect)	Reasons (effect and cause) Logical divisions (cause and effect)
Problem and solution	Organization by discussing a problem and then various solutions	Logical divisions

by cause and effect, as well as problem and solution. You could discuss mountain lion attacks as an effect and explore the causes of the increased frequency of such attacks in recent years, or you could talk about discrimination against overweight people as a cause and discuss the harmful effects of such discrimination. Your specific purpose can help you make the decision. If you want your audience to be able to explain how to end discrimination against overweight people, select the problem–solution organizational strategy. If you want your audience to be able to explain the harmful effects of discrimination against those who are overweight, use the cause and effect strategy. Let both your general and your specific purpose continue to guide your speech as you organize your main ideas.

COMMUNICATION & ETHICS

The Ethics of Primacy and Recency

Nico knows that according to the principle of recency, he should discuss last what he wants his audience to remember best. In his speech on the risk of counterfeit prescription drugs, however, Nico thinks that it may be more ethical to reveal immediately to his audience how costly the problem is in terms of both dollars and human lives. Is it ethical for Nico to save that important statistic for last?

Organizing Your Supporting Material

12.2 Explain how to organize supporting material.

After you have organized your main ideas, you are ready to organize the supporting material for each idea. Suppose you have two brief illustrations, a statistic, and an opinion in support of your first main idea. How can you organize these materials to communicate your verbal message most effectively?

The now-familiar strategies of chronology, primacy, recency, and complexity can also help you organize your supporting material. For example, you might arrange a group of brief illustrations *chronologically*. At other times, you might apply the principle of *recency* and save your most convincing statistic for last. If you decide to present first the opinion with which you are certain your audience will agree, you apply the principle of *primacy*. Or you might arrange two explanations according to the principle of *complexity*, presenting the simplest one first and working up to the more complex one.

At other times, you may need to turn to an organizational strategy more specifically adapted to supporting material: specificity or soft-to-hard evidence.

- **Specificity.** Your supporting material may include specific illustrations and statistics, as well as more general explanations and opinions. The principle of **specificity** suggests that you offer first a specific illustration or statistic, followed by a general explanation or opinion or—as Cara did in her speech on recruiting black faculty at U.S. colleges and universities—first a general explanation or opinion, followed by a specific illustration or statistic:

    > According to education professor Kimberly Griffin, "Getting to a certain percentage of black faculty by a certain time is a tough road." Most U.S. colleges currently average between 2 percent and 4 percent black faculty.[8]

- **Soft-to-Hard Evidence.** Another principle that can help you organize your supporting material is moving from "soft" to "hard" evidence. Illustrations, descriptions, explanations, definitions, analogies, and opinions are usually considered **soft evidence**, whereas statistics are **hard evidence**. In explaining to his student audience what motivated him to market an early blood-based screening test for cancer, Grail CEO Jeff Huber moved from a personal illustration (soft) to a statistic (hard):

    > [My wife] Laura's cancer is just one story out of millions. There are eight million cancer deaths, every year.[9]

specificity
Organization from specific information to a more general statement, or from a general statement to specific information.

soft evidence
Illustrations, descriptions, explanations, definitions, analogies, and opinions.

hard evidence
Statistics.

RECAP

Organizing Your Supporting Material

Strategy	Description
Chronology	Organization by time or sequence
Recency	Most important material last
Primacy	Most convincing or least controversial material first
Complexity	From simple to more complex material
Specificity	From specific information to general overview or from general overview to specific information
Soft-to-Hard Evidence	From hypothetical illustrations and opinions to facts and statistics

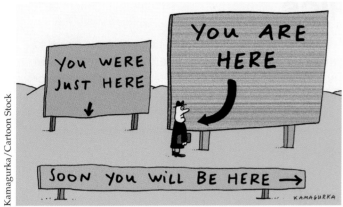

Kamagurka/Cartoon Stock

Signposting: Organizing Your Speech for the Ears of Others

12.3 Use verbal and nonverbal signposts to organize your speech for the ears of others.

You now have a fairly complete, logically organized plan for your speech, but if you tried to deliver it at this point, your audience would probably become confused. What are your main ideas? How is one main idea related to the next? What supporting material develops which main idea? To adapt your logically organized message to your audience, you need to provide **signposts**, organizational cues for the audience's ears. You do this by adding previews, transitions, and summaries that provide coherence as you move from one idea to the next throughout the speech.

Previews

A **preview** "tells them what you're going to tell them"; it is a statement of what is to come. Previews help your audience members anticipate and remember the main ideas of your speech. They also help you move smoothly from the introduction to the body of your speech and from one main idea to the next.

Initial Preview The **initial preview** is usually presented in conjunction with the central idea. Consider student speaker Anastasia's speech on abuse of homeschooled students. After stating her central idea that the system allows severe abuse to go unnoticed, she previewed her three main ideas:

> Today, we'll look at the problem of severe abuse in homeschooling environments, the deregulation that led to it, and how we can ensure that [homeschooled] children . . . are protected in the future.[10]

Internal Preview In addition to providing an initial preview, a speaker may also offer, at various points throughout a speech, an **internal preview**. Internal previews introduce and outline ideas that will be developed as the speech progresses. Student speaker Carson provided an internal preview just before the second main idea of her speech on the U.S. Chamber of Commerce, the top-spending lobbyist in Washington:

> With coercion as its top priority, we are left to question how the [U.S. Chamber of Commerce] is allowed to continue manipulating the public. There are two causes: the legal status of the organization and public misconception.[11]

When Carson delivered this preview, her listeners knew that she was going to explain two possible causes of the problem she had described and documented. Her internal preview generated anticipation, which increased the likelihood that her audience would hear and later remember these causes.

Verbal and Nonverbal Transitions

A **transition** is a verbal or nonverbal signpost that a speaker is moving from one idea to the next.

Verbal Transition To use verbal messages effectively, include **verbal transitions**, words or phrases that show relationships between ideas in your speech. They include simple enumeration (*first, second, third*); synonyms or pronouns that refer to earlier key words or

signpost
A verbal or nonverbal organizational signal.

preview
A statement of what is to come.

initial preview
First statement of the main ideas of a speech, usually presented with or near the central idea.

internal preview
A preview within the speech that introduces ideas still to come.

transition
A word, phrase, or nonverbal cue that indicates movement from one idea to the next or the relationship between ideas.

verbal transition
A word or phrase that indicates the relationship between two ideas.

ideas (the word *they* at the beginning of this sentence refers to the phrase "verbal transitions" in the previous sentence); and words and phrases that show relationships between ideas (*in addition, not only . . . but also, in other words, in summary, therefore, however*). As you begin to rehearse your speech, you might need to experiment with various verbal transitions to achieve a flow that seems natural and logical to you. If none of the verbal alternatives seems quite right, consider a nonverbal transition.

Nonverbal Transition   Sometimes used alone and sometimes used in combination with verbal transitions, an effective **nonverbal transition** might take the form of a facial expression, a pause, a change in vocal pitch or speaking rate, or movement. Most good speakers will use a combination of verbal and nonverbal transitions to signpost their progression from one idea to the next throughout their speeches.

Summaries

Like a preview, a **summary**—a recap of what has been said—provides an opportunity for the audience to grasp a speaker's most important ideas. Most speakers use two types of summaries: internal summaries and a final summary.

Internal Summary   After you have discussed two or three main ideas, you might want to provide an **internal summary** to ensure that the audience keeps these ideas firmly in mind before you move on to another main idea. You can combine an internal summary with an internal preview. In her speech comparing the Brothers Grimm and Disney versions of *Cinderella*, Grace combined an internal summary and preview in this way:

> So now that we've talked a little bit about the differences in the characters between the two versions and the differences in the royal ball scene, I'd like to discuss the way that Disney omitted some violence from their version of *Cinderella* compared to the Brothers Grimm version.[12]

Final Summary   In your conclusion, you may want to provide your audience with a final opportunity to hear and remember your main ideas. Whereas your initial preview gave your audience members their first exposure to your main ideas, your **final summary** will give them their last exposure to those ideas. Near the end of student speaker Kellen's speech on prescription drug pricing, he provided this final summary of his three main ideas:

> Today, by looking at the problems, causes, and solutions of prescription pricing, we can see how the lack of regulation creates outrageously unnecessary expenses for individuals, families, and our nation.[13]

Signposting with previews, transitions, and summaries applies the fundamental principles of using both verbal and nonverbal messages effectively and of adapting your message to others. It increases the likelihood that your audience will grasp your main ideas and the logic of your organizational strategy.

Introducing and Concluding Your Speech

12.4   Explain the functions of, and several strategies for, speech introductions and conclusions.

At this point, you have developed and organized the ideas and content of the body of your speech, but you might not have thought about how you are going to begin and end the speech. That's okay. Even though you will deliver your introduction first, you usually plan it last. This is because you need to know what you're introducing—especially your

▲ Simply telling listeners you are making your first (or second or third) point can help them understand the organization of your speech. R. Gino Santa Maria/Shutterstock

nonverbal transition

A facial expression, vocal cue, or physical movement that indicates that a speaker is moving from one idea to the next.

summary

A recap of what has been said.

internal summary

A recap within the speech of what has been said so far.

final summary

A recap of all the main points of a speech, usually occurring just before or during the conclusion.

▲ In the introduction to his retirement speech, NFL quarterback Peyton Manning used an anecdote about his first professional football game to capture his audience's attention. David Zalubowski/ASSOCIATED PRESS

central idea and main ideas. Once you do, it is time to plan how you will introduce and conclude your speech. Although your introduction and conclusion make up a relatively small percentage of the total speech, they provide your audience with first and final impressions of you and your speech. They are important considerations in adapting your message to others.

Introductions

Your **introduction** should convince your audience to listen to you. More specifically, it must perform six functions: getting the audience's attention, introducing the topic, giving the audience a reason to listen, establishing your credibility, stating your central idea, and previewing your main ideas. Let's briefly consider each of these functions.

Get the Audience's Attention   If an introduction does not capture the attention of audience members, the rest of the speech may be wasted on them. You have to use verbal messages effectively to wake up your listeners and make them want to hear more.

There are several good ways to gain an audience's attention. One commonly used and quite effective way is to open with an illustration or personal anecdote. When NFL quarterback Peyton Manning announced his retirement from the Denver Broncos, he opened his speech with this anecdote:

> In my very first NFL game, I completed my first pass to Hall of Fame running back Marshall Faulk. I threw a touchdown in that same game to Marvin Harrison, who would be inducted into the Hall of Fame. . . . [14]

Other strategies for gaining an audience's attention are to ask a rhetorical question, relate a startling fact or statistic, or quote an expert or a literary text. Writer Zadie Smith opened her 2016 commencement address at Grinnell College by asking the graduates two rhetorical questions:

> You did it. You made it. How do you feel? More importantly, what do you want?[15]

Still other speakers might capture their audience's attention by referring to the occasion, historical or recent events, or something said by a preceding speaker. Speaking to the press at the 2016 International Auto Show in New York, Renault-Nissan Alliance Chair and CEO Carlos Ghosn began by acknowledging the occasion:

> We're here today to mark our industry's rite of spring: The kick-off of the New York International Auto Show.[16]

Although not all of these strategies will work for all speeches, at least one of them should be an option for any speech you make. With a little practice, you may be able to choose from several good possibilities for a single speech.

introduction

Opening lines of a speech, which must catch the audience's attention, introduce the topic, give the audience a reason to listen, establish the speaker's credibility, state the central idea, and preview the main ideas.

Introduce the Topic   Within the first few seconds of listening to you, your audience should have a pretty good idea of what your topic is.

Give the Audience a Reason to Listen   Not only do you have to get your audience's attention and introduce your topic, but you also have to motivate your listeners to continue to listen. Show your listeners how your topic affects them and those they care about. Student speaker Rebecca combined a hypothetical illustration, rhetorical question, and startling statistic to engage her audience in her speech on mental illness in adolescents:

> Imagine you're sitting in your favorite class, and you're looking around at the people around you. What do you notice? Probably what they're wearing. Who they're talking to. What they're doing. What you can't see is that, for every five of those students, one of them has some sort of a mental illness.[17]

By the end of your introduction, your audience should be thinking, "This concerns *me*!"

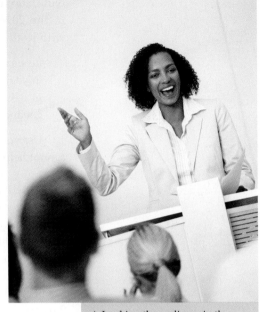

Establish Your Credibility   A credible speaker is one whom the audience judges to be believable, competent, and trustworthy. Be aware of the skills, talents, and experiences you have had that are related to your topic. You can increase your credibility by telling your audience about your expertise. For example, in your introduction to a persuasive speech on studying abroad, you might say:

> I know firsthand how studying abroad can broaden your worldview, increase your understanding of another culture, and enrich your academic studies. Last fall, I studied at the Sorbonne in Paris.

▲ Looking the audience in the eye with a friendly smile as you deliver your well-prepared introduction can help establish your credibility. GlobalStock/ Getty Images

State Your Central Idea   You should usually state your central idea at or near the end of your introduction, as in the following example from Aaron's speech on post-traumatic stress disorder:

> Hundreds of combat veterans . . . are being dismissed from the Armed Services without the medical benefits needed to treat combat stress.[18]

Preview Your Main Ideas   Previewing your main ideas allows your listeners to anticipate and begin to listen for those main ideas. You can provide your initial preview immediately after stating your central idea. Here is the initial preview of main ideas that followed Aaron's central idea, as quoted above:

> So in today's speech we will uncover the problems associated with the denial of benefits to discharged veterans suffering from post-traumatic stress disorder. Next we will investigate the causes of these problems before finally understanding what can be done to solve this flaw in the policies of the VA.[19]

Conclusions

Your introduction creates a critically important first impression, and your **conclusion** leaves an equally important final impression. Long after you finish speaking, your audience will hear the echo of your effective final words. An effective conclusion serves four functions: to summarize the speech, to reemphasize the central idea in a memorable way, to motivate the audience to respond, and to provide closure. Let's consider each of these functions.

conclusion
Closing lines of a speech, which leave a final impression.

Summarize the Speech   The conclusion offers a speaker a last chance to repeat his or her main ideas. Most speakers summarize their main ideas between the body of the speech and its conclusion or in the first part of the conclusion.

Reemphasize the Central Idea in a Memorable Way   The conclusions of a number of famous speeches contain many of the lines we remember best:

> . . . and that government of the people, by the people, for the people, shall not perish from the earth. (*Abraham Lincoln*)[20]
> Old soldiers never die; they just fade away. (*General Douglas MacArthur*)[21]

Note, too, the brevity of these memorable lines. As Aaron Beverly, a competitor in the 2016 Toastmasters World Championship of Public Speaking, remarked with irony,

> Leave a lasting memory using as few words as possible and strive with every fiber in your being to avoid being the type of person who rambles on and on with no end in sight, more likely than not causing listeners to sit and think to themselves, Oh my goodness can somebody please make this stop.[22]

Use your final verbal message effectively. Word your thoughts so that your audience cannot help but remember them.

Motivate the Audience to Respond Think back to your specific purpose. What do you want your audience to be able to do by the end of your speech? If your purpose is to inform, you may want your audience to think about your topic or seek more information about it. If your purpose is to persuade, you may want your audience to take some sort of action, such as write a letter, make a phone call, or volunteer for a cause. Your conclusion is where you can motivate your audience to respond. Student speaker Kevin concluded his speech on the importance of bystander intervention in addressing the epidemic of sexual assault, with both a call and opportunity for action:

> Five minutes ago, I told you I was going to ask you to pledge to be an effective bystander before we walked out of this room. So here we go. If you're willing to take the pledge, raise your hand. Awesome. Keep your hands up, and I'll say the pledge for us. "I pledge to recognize that non-consensual sex is sexual assault, to identify situations in which sexual assault may occur, to intervene in situations where consent has not been or cannot be given, to create an environment in which sexual assault is unacceptable and survivors are supported." That's the pledge. Now follow through.[23]

closure
The sense that a speech is finished.

▼ Effective speakers often save their most important idea—the one they want the audience to walk away with—for last. iofoto/Shutterstock

Provide Closure Have you ever listened to a speech and felt surprised or uncertain when it ended? If so, you were listening to a speaker who did not achieve the last purpose of an effective conclusion: providing **closure**, or a sense that the speech is finished.

You can provide closure by referring to your introduction and finishing a story, answering a rhetorical question, or reminding your audience of where you started. Seeking support for Girl Scouting from the Metropolitan Club of New York, Sylvia Acevedo, Interim CEO of Girl Scouts of the U.S.A., opened her speech by noting,

> It's an exciting time for someone like me who, because of Girl Scouts, had the opportunity to reach for the stars to become a rocket scientist and have an amazing career that spans technology, philanthropy, and education.[24]

After exploring ways for her audience to become involved in supporting the Girl Scouts, Acevedo ended her speech with this line:

> After all, it's not really rocket science.

You can also achieve closure by using verbal and nonverbal signposts. For example, you might use such verbal transitions as *finally* or *in conclusion* as you move into your conclusion. You might also pause before you begin the conclusion, slow your speaking rate as you deliver your final sentence, or signal by falling vocal inflection that you are making your final statement. Experiment with these strategies until you are certain that your speech "sounds finished."

RECAP	
The Purposes of Introductions and Conclusions	
Your introduction should . . .	Get your audience's attention.
	Introduce your topic.
	Give your audience a reason to listen.
	Establish your credibility.
	State your central idea.
	Preview your main ideas.
Your conclusion should . . .	Summarize your speech.
	Reemphasize your central idea in a memorable way.
	Motivate your audience to respond.
	Provide closure.

Outlining Your Speech

12.5 Develop a preparation outline and speaking notes for a speech.

With your introduction and conclusion planned, you are almost ready to begin rehearsing your speech. By this point, you should have your preparation outline nearly complete. A **preparation outline** is a fairly detailed outline of your central idea, main ideas, and supporting material. It may also include your specific purpose, introduction, and conclusion. A second outline, which you will prepare shortly, makes up the speaking notes from which you will eventually deliver your speech.

preparation outline
A detailed outline of a speech that includes the central idea, main ideas, and supporting material, and may also include the specific purpose, introduction, and conclusion.

Preparation Outline

A detailed preparation outline can help you ensure that your main ideas are clearly related to your central idea and are logically and adequately supported. When you create a preparation outline, you are applying the first fundamental principle of communication: becoming increasingly aware of your communication. In addition to helping you judge the unity and coherence of your speech, the preparation outline also serves as an early rehearsal outline and is usually handed in as part of a class requirement.

Instructors who require you to turn in a preparation outline will probably have their own specific requirements. For example, some instructors ask for the introduction and conclusion as part of the outline, whereas others want only an outline of the body of the speech. Some instructors ask that you incorporate signposts into the outline or write your specific purpose at the top of the outline. Be certain that you carefully listen to and follow your instructor's specific requirements regarding which elements to include.

Almost certainly, your instructor will require that you use **standard outline format**. Standard outline format lets you become more aware of the exact relationships among various main ideas, subpoints, and supporting material in your speech. Even if you haven't had much experience with formal outlines, the following guidelines can help you produce a correct outline.

standard outline format
Conventional use of numbered and lettered headings and subheadings to indicate the relationships among parts of a speech.

Use Standard Numbering   Outlines are numbered with Roman and Arabic numerals and uppercase and lowercase letters followed by periods, as follows:

I. First main idea
   A. First subdivision of I
   B. Second subdivision of I

      1. First subdivision of B
      2. Second subdivision of B
         (a) First subdivision of 2
         (b) Second subdivision of 2
  II. Second main idea

You will probably not need to subdivide beyond the level of lowercase letters in most speech outlines.

Use at Least Two Subdivisions, If Any, for Each Point   You cannot divide anything into fewer than two parts. On an outline, every I should be followed by a II, every A should be followed by a B, and so on. If you have only one subdivision, fold it into the level above it.

Line Up Your Outline Correctly   Main ideas, indicated by Roman numerals, are written closest to the left margin. The *periods* following these Roman numerals need to line up so that the first letters of the first words also line up:

    I. First main idea
   II. Second main idea
  III. Third main idea

Letters or numbers of subdivisions begin directly underneath the first letter of the first *word* of the point above:

    I. First main idea
       A. First subdivision of I
       B. Second subdivision of I

If a main idea or subdivision takes up more than one line, the second line begins under the first letter of the first word of the preceding line:

    I. First main idea
       A. A rather lengthy subdivision that runs more than one line
       B. Second subdivision

Within Each Level, Make the Headings Grammatically Parallel   Regardless of whether you write your preparation outline in complete sentences or in phrases, be consistent within each level. In other words, if I is a complete sentence, II should also be a complete sentence. If A is an infinitive phrase (one that begins with *to* plus a verb, such as "to guarantee greater security"), B should also be an infinitive phrase.

In this chapter, we have included a sample preparation outline for the speech Dezerae Reyes has prepared in the Developing Your Speech Step by Step feature.[25] As you review this outline, please keep in mind that your instructor may have additional or alternative requirements for what your preparation outline should include or how it should be formatted.

Speaking Notes

As you rehearse your speech, you will need to look at your preparation outline less and less. You should now have both the structure and the content of your speech quite well in mind. At this point, you are ready to develop a shorter outline to serve as your speaking notes.

Speaking notes should provide all the information you will need to make your speech as you have planned, but should not be so detailed that you will be tempted to read rather than speak to your audience. Here are a few suggestions for developing speaking notes.

Use Note Cards, a Smartphone, or a Tablet   Your speaking notes should be small enough to hold in one hand, quiet to handle, and readily legible.

Sample Preparation Outline

Purpose

At the end of my speech, the audience will consume fewer soft drinks.

Writing her purpose statement at the top of the outline will help Dezerae keep it in mind, but always follow your instructor's specific requirements for how to format your preparation outline.

Introduction

Imagine that your doctor calls you, and she says, "Hey, I know you're stressed, but I have a solution for you. I'm going to prescribe a daily pill that will give you all the energy you need to go through your day, and it's also really affordable for students, and it tastes pretty good, too. But it has side effects: It's mildly addictive, it will burn your mouth, and you'll start to feel sick and sluggish after a while—but it will get the job done." Most of us would not consider that situation. But we have, because that "pill" I just described is soda. And I used to feel those experiences myself. I used to be a daily—even hourly—soda drinker. But I've made the decision to stop drinking soda, and the change has been significant.

Dezerae catches her listeners' attention by combining a hypothetical illustration and personal anecdote. Other strategies for effectively getting your audience's attention were discussed earlier in the chapter.

Central Idea

So today I'm going to tell you just how bad drinking soda is, in the hopes that you can also transition from soda to healthier drinks.

Dezerae writes out and labels her central idea and the initial preview that follows. Again, follow your instructor's requirements.

Preview

First, I'm going to tell you about the biggest problem associated with soda; second, how that problem can cause weight gain and obesity; and finally, how it can cause disease.

Body

I. Let's discuss the biggest problem with drinking soda: It is high in sugar.

   A. I know we know that soda contains sugar, but I don't think we know the significance of just how much. With one 20-ounce soda, we are consuming more than our daily sugar intake recommendation.
   B. In 2014, the World Health Organization suggested that sugars should make up only about 5 percent of daily calorie intake (6 teaspoons or 25 grams).
   C. So if we convert that: 3 teaspoons = 1 tablespoons 6 teaspoons = 2 tablespoons.
   D. On the other hand, I have a 20-ounce Coca Cola, which has 65 grams of sugar. The amount of sugar in this soda: 4 grams = 1 teaspoon, 65 grams divided by 4 = 16.25 teaspoons, 16.25 teaspoons = almost 5 1/2 tablespoons.

As Dezerae calculates the measurements orally, she uses presentation aids to help her audience visualize the amounts.

The first main idea of the speech is indicated by the Roman numeral I. This main idea has four subpoints, indicated by A, B, C, and D.

The World Health Organization says that the average American consumes 19.25 teaspoons of sugar every day, which is far higher than the 6 we're supposed to consume.

Signpost: Now that you know about the problem of high sugar consumption, how does that lead to obesity?

II. Consuming such a vast amount of excess calories from foods and drinks high in free sugars contributes to unhealthy weight gain, which can lead to obesity.

   A. According to the Obesity Society, added sugar consumption has increased by 30 percent over the last three decades.
   B. According to the U.S. Department of Health and Human Services, 68.8 percent of adults age 20 or older are overweight or obese. And drinks like soda are partially to blame because they add so much sugar to our already sugary diets.

Dezerae provides written citations of her orally cited sources in the references section at the end of her outline. Make sure you follow your instructor's requirements for including and formatting source citations in your outline.

(continued)

Sample Preparation Outline *(continued)*

Signpost: So high soda consumption can cause obesity, which in turn can lead to disease.

Dezerae continues to use signposts to organize her speech for the ears of her listeners—in this case, transitioning from her second main idea (II) to her third (III).

III. Being overweight and/or obese can put you at risk for a variety of lifestyle diseases, such as heart disease and diabetes.

   A. According to the American Heart Association, drinking sugar-sweetened beverages every day is associated with an increase in a particular type of body fat that may affect a person's risk for developing heart disease and even diabetes.

   B. It's important that we know this fact because heart disease, which is a lifestyle disease, is the number one killer in the U.S. for both men and women, according to the Centers for Disease Control and Prevention. And this is a big reason I stopped drinking soda. Several years ago, I witnessed one of my own family members have a heart attack and eventually pass away from heart disease. I decided to reduce my risk while I still could.

Signpost: Now you know how excess sugar consumption from drinking soda can damage your health.

Conclusion

In order to decrease these health risks, drink less soda and drink healthier alternatives instead. So if you're craving soda, whether that be today, next week, or next month, try drinking a sparkling flavored water. There's no sugar, but it's still carbonated and it's flavored. Even better, drink a glass of water, tea, or even coffee for a week, and you'll start to feel a difference in your body. If you want to take the first step today, I'll be passing out sparkling flavored water at the end of class. I hope this sparkling water is the first step of many steps to a healthier, happier life.

In her conclusion, Dezerae brings closure to her speech with an action step that reflects the specific purpose of her speech. By telling her audience that she will have healthier drinks available at the end of class, she both reemphasizes her central idea in a memorable way and motivates her audience to respond.

References

Following her instructor's requirements, Dezerae includes a list of her references in her preparation outline, formatted in APA style.

30 health reasons not to drink soda or diet soda. (n.d.). Retrieved from http://hccua .org/health/healthandwellness.cfm?id=311

Beverages. (2014). Retrieved from www.sugarstacks.com/beverages.htm

Gunnars, K. (n.d.). *Daily intake of sugar - how much sugar should you eat per day?* Retrieved from https://authoritynutrition.com/how-much-sugar-per-day/

Healthy diet. (September 2015). Retrieved from World Health Organization site: www.who.int/mediacentre/factsheets/fs394/en/

How sweet is it? (2012). Retrieved from Harvard University site: https://cdn1.sph .harvard.edu/wp-content/uploads/sites/30/2012/10/how-sweet-is-it-color.pdf

Leading causes of death. (2016). Retrieved from Centers for Disease Control and Prevention site: www.cdc.gov/nchs/fastats/leading-causes-of-death.htm

Overweight and obesity statistics. (2012). Retrieved from National Institute of Diabetes and Digestive and Kidney Diseases site: www.niddk.nih.gov/health-information/health-statistics/Pages/ overweight-obesity-statistics.aspx

Soft drinks and disease. (2016). Retrieved from Harvard University T. H. Chan School of Public Health site: www.hsph.harvard.edu/nutritionsource/ healthy-drinks/soft-drinks-and-disease

Sugary drinks and the obesity epidemic. (2012). Retrieved from Harvard University T. H. Chan School of Public Health site: https://cdn1.sph.harvard.edu/ wp-content/uploads/sites/30/2012/10/sugary-drinks-and-obesity-fact-sheet -june-2012-the-nutrition-source.pdf

Sample Preparation Outline *(continued)*

U.S. adult consumption of added sugars increased by more than 30% over three decades.
(2014). Retrieved from Obesity Society site: www.obesity.org/news/
press-releases/us-adult

Note cards are generally preferable to sheets of paper because they do not rustle when you handle them, and they are small enough to hold in one hand. Prepare your note cards according to logical blocks of material, using one note card for your introduction, one or two for the body of your speech, and one for your conclusion. Number your note cards in case they get out of order while you are speaking. If you choose instead to put your speaking notes on an electronic device, you should be able to scroll through your outline as you progress through the speech. Regardless of whether you use note cards or an electronic device, be sure your font is large enough to read easily.

Use Standard Outline Format   Standard outline format will help you find your exact place when you glance down at your speaking notes. You will know, for example, that your second main idea is indicated by "II."

Include Your Introduction and Conclusion in Abbreviated Form   Even if your instructor does not require you to include your introduction and conclusion on your preparation outline, include shortened versions of them in your speaking notes. You might even feel more comfortable delivering the speech if you have your first and last sentences written out in front of you.

Include Your Central Idea, But Not Your Purpose Statement   Be sure to include your central idea in your speaking notes. Do not include your purpose statement because you will not actually say it during your speech.

Include Supporting Material and Signposts   Write out in full any statistics and direct quotations and their sources. Write down your key signposts—your initial preview, for example—to ensure that you will not grope awkwardly as you move from one idea to another.

Include Delivery Cues   Writing such cues as "Louder," "Pause," or "Walk two steps left" will remind you to communicate the nonverbal messages you have planned. Use a different color font or ink so that you don't confuse your delivery cues with your verbal content.

Figure 12.2 illustrates speaking notes for Dezerae's speech on the health risks of soft drinks.

RECAP

Two Types of Speech Outlines

Type	Purpose
Preparation Outline	Allows speaker to examine speech for completeness, unity, coherence, and overall effectiveness. May serve as first rehearsal outline.
Speaking Notes	Include supporting material, signposts, and delivery cues.

FIGURE 12.2   Sample Speaking Notes

Preview

1. Today I'm going to discuss [hold up one finger] first the biggest problem with drinking soda;
2. [hold up two fingers] second, how that problem can cause obesity and disease;
3. [hold up three fingers] finally, how you can consume fewer sodas.

Body

I. High in sugar.
   A. 20 ounce soda = > daily sugar recommendation
   B. World Health Organization:
      - Healthy diet = < 10% energy intake from sugars
      - (12 teaspoons = 4 tablespoons, based on 2,000 daily calorie diet)

CHAPTER 12

〉 REVIEW, APPLY, AND ASSESS

Organizing Your Main Ideas

12.1 List and explain five strategies for organizing the main ideas of a speech.

REVIEW: Once you have found supporting material, you are ready to organize your ideas and information. Depending on your topic, purpose, and audience, you can organize the main ideas of your speech chronologically, topically, spatially, by cause and effect, or by problem and solution.

KEY TERMS:

topical organization
recency
primacy
complexity
chronological organization

spatial organization
cause and effect
    organization
problem and solution
    organization

APPLY: For each of the five patterns of organization discussed, suggest a topic that might be organized according to that pattern.

ASSESS: Take notes as you listen to a speech, either live or online. Then organize your notes into an outline that you think reflects both the speaker's organization and the intended relationship among ideas and supporting material.

Organizing Your Supporting Material

12.2 Explain how to organize supporting material.

REVIEW: You can often organize supporting material according to one of the same patterns used to organize main ideas: chronology, recency, primacy, or complexity. You can also organize supporting material by specificity or from soft to hard evidence.

KEY TERMS:

specificity
soft evidence

hard evidence

APPLY: Select one of the speeches in Appendix B. Identify the supporting material for one main idea in this speech.

What principle did the speaker use to organize his or her supporting material?

ASSESS: Reread the Communication & Ethics feature box in this chapter. Based on how you responded to the question posed there, discuss whether either primacy or recency may be a more ethical choice than the other.

Organizing Your Speech for the Ears of Others

12.3 Use verbal and nonverbal signposts to organize your speech for the ears of others.

REVIEW: With your speech organized, you will want to add signposts—previews, transitions, and summaries—to make your organization clearly apparent to your audience.

KEY TERMS:

signpost
preview
initial preview
internal preview
transition

verbal transition
nonverbal transition
summary
internal summary
final summary

APPLY: In a recent speech, class lecture, or TED talk you have viewed online, identify one or more signposts.

ASSESS: For one of the speeches in Appendix B, find at least one example of each of the following:

- A transition word or phrase
- An internal preview
- An internal summary

Introducing and Concluding Your Speech

12.4 Explain the functions of, and several strategies for, speech introductions and conclusions.

REVIEW: A carefully planned introduction will capture your audience's attention, introduce your topic, give the audience a reason to listen, establish your credibility, state your central idea, and preview your main ideas. An equally carefully planned conclusion will summarize your speech, reemphasize the central idea in a memorable way, motivate your audience to respond, and provide closure.

KEY TERMS:

introduction   closure
conclusion

APPLY: Draft an introduction for a speech on one of the following topics:

- Strategies for surviving a tornado
- Private-school vouchers
- Mars up close
- Celebrities and the press

In addition to introducing the topic and previewing your main ideas, be sure to plan strategies for getting the attention of audience members and giving them a reason to listen. Also devise a way to establish your own credibility as a speaker on that topic.

ASSESS: Give an example of a memorable speech introduction you've heard. Explain how that introduction effectively caught your attention and gave you a reason to listen.

Outlining Your Speech

12.5 Develop a preparation outline and speaking notes for a speech.

REVIEW: A final step before beginning to rehearse your speech is to prepare a detailed preparation outline and speaking notes. Your preparation outline should follow the guidelines provided by your instructor.

KEY TERMS:

preparation outline   standard outline format

APPLY: What alternative method of formatting might work for speakers who do not wish to use a standard outline for their speaking notes?

ASSESS: Why do you think it is important not to read your speaking notes?

⟩ THE PRINCIPLE POINTS

Principle One:

Be aware of your communication with yourself and others.

- Be aware of the skills, talents, and experiences you have that can enhance your credibility with your listeners.
- Use a preparation outline to demonstrate to yourself that your main ideas are clearly related to your central idea and are logically and adequately supported.

Principle Two:

Effectively use and interpret verbal messages.

- To communicate your verbal message effectively, organize your speech logically.
- Use verbal transitions to show relationships between ideas in your speech.
- Introduce your topic and preview your main ideas in your introduction.
- Use anecdotes, rhetorical questions, startling facts or statistics, or other techniques to capture your listeners' attention when you begin your talk.
- In your conclusion, summarize your speech and reemphasize your main idea in a memorable way.

Principle Three:

Effectively use and interpret nonverbal messages.

- Use nonverbal transitions—pauses, facial expressions, altered vocal pitch or speaking rate, and movement—to indicate when you are moving from one idea to the next.
- Use nonverbal cues—such as pausing, slowing your rate of speech, and letting your vocal inflection fall—to signal closure in the final sentence or two of your conclusion.
- Add delivery cues and reminders to your final speaking notes.

Principle Four:

Listen and respond thoughtfully to others.

- As you listen to speeches, be aware that their organization may reflect patterns considered appropriate in cultures other than your own.

Principle Five:

Appropriately adapt messages to others.

- Investigate and consider using the customary organizational strategy of your audience's culture.
- In most cases, discuss last the idea that you most want your audience to remember.
- If you know that your audience members will be skeptical of some of your ideas, present first the ideas on which you and the audience can agree.
- Provide signposts as organizational cues for your audience.
- Use your introduction and conclusion to help adapt your speech to your audience.

DELIVERING YOUR SPEECH

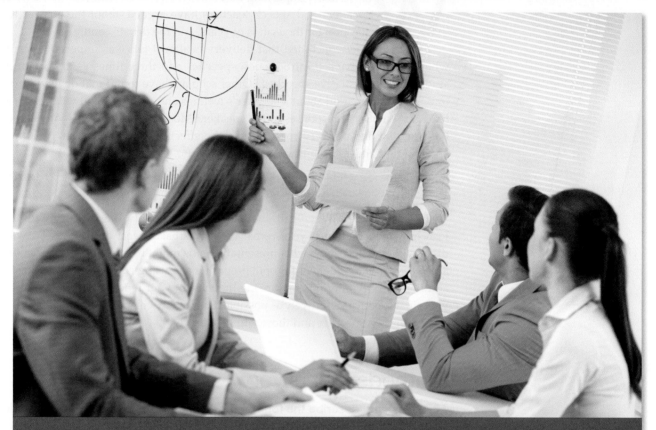

O the orator's joys! To inflate the chest, to roll the thunder of the voice out from the ribs and throat, to make the people rage, weep, hate, desire. —WALT WHITMAN

Pressmaster/Shutterstock

→ CHAPTER OUTLINE

- Methods of Delivery
- Effective Verbal Delivery
- Effective Nonverbal Delivery
- Effective Presentation Aids

- Some Final Tips for Rehearsing and Delivering Your Speech
- Criteria for Evaluating Speeches
- Study Guide: Review, Apply, and Assess

LEARNING OBJECTIVES

After studying this chapter, you should be able to

13.1 List and describe the four methods of delivery, and provide suggestions for effectively using each one.

13.2 List and explain three criteria for effective verbal delivery.

13.3 Identify and illustrate characteristics of effective nonverbal delivery.

13.4 Discuss how to prepare and use presentation aids effectively.

13.5 Make the most of your rehearsal time, and deliver your speech effectively.

13.6 Understand and apply criteria for evaluating speeches.

Which is more important, the content of a speech or the way it is delivered? Speakers and speech teachers have argued about the answer to this question for thousands of years, and the debate continues.

One researcher concluded that delivery is almost twice as important as content when students give self-introduction speeches and three times as important when students give persuasive speeches.[1] Other scholars have found that delivery provides important information about a speaker's feelings and emotions and will in turn affect listeners' emotional responses to the speaker.[2] Most speech teachers today agree that both content and delivery contribute to the effectiveness of a speech. As a modern speechwriter and communication coach suggests,

> In the real world—the world where you and I do business—content and delivery are always related. And woe be to the communicator who forgets this.[3]

In this chapter, we will discuss how you can apply the five Communication Principles for a Lifetime to your verbal and nonverbal delivery of speeches. We will also discuss how to determine what presentation aids might be effective for your audience, and we will offer guidelines for both preparing and using various presentation aids. In addition, we will offer tips for making the most of your rehearsal time and delivering your final speech as effectively as possible. Finally, we will talk briefly about evaluating both your own speeches and those you hear.

Methods of Delivery

13.1 **List and describe the four methods of delivery, and provide suggestions for effectively using each one.**

Different audiences expect and prefer different delivery styles. For example, if you are using a microphone to speak to an audience of 1,000 people, your listeners may expect a relatively formal delivery style. On the other hand, your communication class would probably find it odd if you delivered a formal oration to your twenty-five classmates.

People from different cultures also have different expectations of what is considered effective speech delivery. Listeners from Japan and China, for example, prefer subdued gestures to a more flamboyant delivery. British listeners expect a speaker to stay behind a lectern and use relatively few gestures.

Speakers should consider and adapt to their audience's expectations, their topic, and the speaking situation as they select from four basic methods of delivery: manuscript speaking, memorized speaking, impromptu speaking, and extemporaneous speaking.

Manuscript Speaking

Perhaps you remember the first speech you ever had to give, maybe as long ago as elementary school. Chances are that you wrote out your message and read it to your audience. Unfortunately, **manuscript speaking** is rarely done well enough to be interesting. Most speakers who rely on a manuscript read it either in a monotone or with a pattern of vocal inflection that makes the speech "sound read." They are so afraid of losing their place that they keep their eyes glued to the manuscript and seldom look at the audience. These challenges are significant enough that most speakers should avoid reading from a manuscript most of the time.

Occasions when effective verbal messages depend on careful and exact phrasing are the few exceptions to the general rule of avoiding manuscript speaking. For example, because an awkward statement made by the U.S. Secretary of State could cause an international crisis, his or her remarks on critical issues are usually carefully scripted. If you ever have to speak on a sensitive, critical, or controversial issue, you too might need to deliver a manuscript speech. If so, consider the suggestions in Figure 13.1.

Memorized Speaking

After that first speech you read in elementary school, you probably became a savvier speaker. Perhaps the next time you had to give a speech, you wrote it out and memorized it. You thought that no one would be able to tell. What you didn't know then, but probably do now, is that most **memorized speaking** sounds stiff and recited. In addition, you run the risk of forgetting parts of your speech and having to search awkwardly for words in front of your audience. By memorizing your speech, you also forfeit the ability to adapt to your audience while you are speaking.

On occasion, speaking from memory is justifiable. If you must deliver a short speech within a narrow time limit, memorizing and rehearsing it will allow you to time it more accurately. The three guidelines in Figure 13.2 can help you use nonverbal messages effectively when you deliver a speech from memory.

FIGURE 13.1 Tips for Effective Manuscript Speaking

Practice with your manuscript before you deliver your speech.

Type your manuscript in short, easy-to-scan phrases on the upper two-thirds of the paper so you won't have to look too far down the page.

Unobtrusively use your index finger to keep your place in the text.

EFFECTIVE MANUSCRIPT SPEAKING

manuscript speaking
Reading a presentation from a written text.

memorized speaking
Delivering a speech word for word from memory without using notes.

FIGURE 13.2 Tips for Effective Memorized Speaking

Listen to a recording of your speech to ensure that your vocal inflection sounds like a conversation rather than a recitation.

Avoid speaking too rapidly.

Use gestures and movement.

EFFECTIVE MEMORIZED SPEAKING

FIGURE 13.3 Tips for Effective Impromptu Speaking

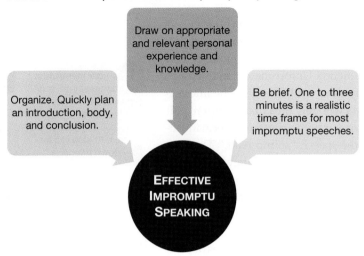

Impromptu Speaking

During President Bill Clinton's 1993 healthcare speech before a joint session of Congress, the teleprompter scrolled the wrong text for nine minutes. Drawing on his years of experience, the president kept speaking. As political advisor and commentator Paul Begala marveled, "Nine minutes the guy went without a note, and no one could tell."[4]

Although you may plan your speeches, there are times—as illustrated by Clinton's experience—when the best plans go awry. A more likely possibility is that you will be asked to answer a question or respond to an argument without advance warning or time to prepare. At such times, you will have to call on your skills in **impromptu speaking**, or speaking "off the cuff."

Having a solid grasp of the topic on which you are asked to speak can help you in such instances. The six additional guidelines in Figure 13.3 can also help you avoid fumbling for words or rambling.

impromptu speaking
Delivering a presentation without advance preparation.

Extemporaneous Speaking

We have saved for last the method of speaking most appropriate for most circumstances, preferred by most audiences, and most often taught in public speaking classes: **extemporaneous speaking**. The extemporaneous speech is a well-developed and well-organized message delivered in an interesting and vivid manner. It reflects your understanding of how to use both verbal and nonverbal messages effectively and your ability to adapt these messages to your audience. Although we offer numerous guidelines for extemporaneous speaking in this text, consider the three tips in Figure 13.4 before you rehearse and deliver your speech.

extemporaneous speaking
Delivering a well-developed, well-organized, carefully rehearsed speech without having memorized the exact wording.

RECAP

Methods of Delivery

Manuscript	Reading a speech from a written text
Memorized	Giving a speech word for word from memory without using notes
Impromptu	Delivering a speech without advance preparation
Extemporaneous	Speaking from a written or memorized outline without having memorized the exact wording of the speech

FIGURE 13.4 Tips for Effective Extemporaneous Speaking

Effective Verbal Delivery

13.2 List and explain three criteria for effective verbal delivery.

In an examination of some 125 years' worth of student speeches prepared for intercollegiate competition, researchers Leah White and Lucas Messer found remarkable consistency in students' use of stylized language. White and Messer explain, "Style and delivery are often tightly connected. Speeches rich in language strategies lend themselves to engaging deliveries."[5] Although you will not write out most speeches word for word, you will want to plan and rehearse words, phrases, and sentences that clearly, accurately, and memorably communicate your ideas. Let's examine some guidelines for effectively using and understanding words and word structures in a speech.

Using Words Clearly

Clarity is essential to making meaning. Clear words are specific and concrete, simple, and vivid. Building on our discussion in Chapter 3 of the power of verbal messages, we will examine each of these characteristics in turn.

Specific, Concrete Words A **specific word** refers to an individual member of a general class—for example, *ammonite* as opposed to the more general term *fossil*, or *sodium* as opposed to *chemical*. Specific words are often **concrete words**, appealing to one of the five senses and communicating an image clearly, as Figure 13.5 demonstrates.

In each case, the second word is more specific and concrete than the first and better communicates the image the speaker intends. For maximum clarity in your speeches, use more specific, concrete words than general, abstract ones.

Simple Words **Simple words** are generally an asset to a speaker. An audience will immediately understand them. In his classic essay "Politics and the English Language," George Orwell includes this prescription for simplicity:

> Never use a long word where a short one will do. . . . Never use a foreign phrase, a scientific word, or a jargon word if you can think of an everyday English equivalent.[6]

Selected thoughtfully, simple words can communicate with both accuracy and power.

Vivid Words **Vivid words** add color and interest to your language. Like concrete words, they help you communicate mental images more accurately and interestingly. Most speakers who try to make their language more vivid think first of adding adjectives to nouns—for example, *distressed oak table* instead of *table*, or *scruffy tabby cat* instead of *cat*.

specific word
A word that refers to an individual member of a general class.

concrete word
A word that refers to an object or describes an action or characteristic in the most specific way possible.

simple word
A word known to most people who speak the same language.

vivid word
A colorful word.

FIGURE 13.5 Which word in each of the following pairs creates a more specific mental picture?

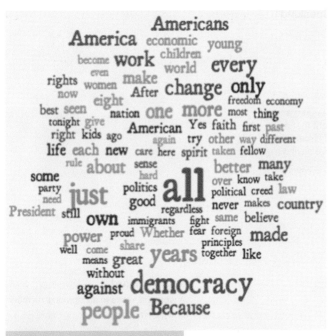

▲ This word cloud visualizes the frequency with which Barack Obama used various words in his presidential farewell address in January 2017. Note that many of the words in larger font, which are those Obama used most, are simple words that tend to evoke vivid emotions. How can you use simple, specific words to drive home your messages?
Source: Based on Barack Obama's speech delivered on January 10, 2017, in Chicago, IL. Susan J. Beebe/Pearson Education

thesaurus

A list of synonyms.

correct word

A word that means what the speaker intends and is grammatically correct in the phrase or sentence in which it appears.

unbiased word

A word that does not stereotype, discriminate against, or insult any gender, ethnic, cultural, or religious group.

In these examples, the first phrase is certainly more vivid. However, what is less frequently considered and potentially more powerful is substituting vivid verbs for "blah" verbs—for example, *sprout* instead of *grow*, and *devour* instead of *eat*.

When searching for a vivid word, you might want to consult a **thesaurus**, or collection of synonyms. But do not assume that the most obscure or unusual synonym you find will necessarily be the most vivid. Sometimes a simple word can evoke a vivid image for your audience.

Using Words Accurately

In addition to using words clearly, using words accurately is essential to ensuring understanding. The most accurate words are correct and unbiased.

Correct Words   Perhaps most obviously, you should use **correct words** when you speak. Grammatical and usage errors communicate a lack of preparation and can lower your credibility with your audience. Be aware of errors that you make habitually. If you are uncertain about how to use a word, look it up in a dictionary or ask someone who knows. If you are stumped by whether to say, "Neither the people nor the president *knows* how to solve the problem" or "Neither the people nor the president *know* how to solve the problem," seek assistance from a good English handbook. (By the way, the first sentence is the correct one.)

Unbiased Words   **Unbiased words** do not disparage, either intentionally or unintentionally, any gender or racial, cultural, or religious group, nor do they offend any audience member who may belong to one of these groups.

Although speakers can fairly easily avoid overtly offensive language, they must be more mindful to avoid language that subtly stereotypes or discriminates. As National Transportation Safety Board Chair Deborah Hersman told attendees at the International Women in Aviation Conference,

> I don't want to hear anybody say "I saw a woman mechanic!"
> Or "I saw an all-woman flight crew!"
> Or "I saw a woman engineer!"
> Or "I saw a woman CEO!"
> Or "I saw a woman in space exploration!"
> Not because there are none of us there, but because there are so many of us there![7]

When possible, adapt to your audience by choosing unbiased gender-neutral language.

Crafting Memorable Word Structures

We have discussed the importance of using words that are clear and accurate. Now we will turn our attention to crafting memorable word structures that create the figurative language, drama, and cadences needed to provide what one marketing communication specialist calls "ear appeal."[8]

Figurative Language   One way to make your message memorable is to use **figurative language**, including **metaphors** (implied comparisons), **similes** (overt comparisons using *like* or *as*), and **personification** (the attribution of human qualities to nonhuman things or ideas). Such language is

VERBAL

RECAP

Using Words Well

Use specific, concrete words to communicate clearly and specifically.

Use simple words to be understood readily.

Use vivid words to add color and interest to your language.

Use correct words to enhance your credibility.

Use unbiased words to avoid offending people of any gender or from any ethnic, cultural, or religious group.

memorable because it is used in a way that is a little different from its ordinary, expected usage. Figure 13.6 provides examples of each type of figurative language.

Drama   Another way to make the word structures in your speech more memorable is to use language to create **drama** by phrasing something in an unexpected way. Three specific devices that can help you achieve verbal drama are omission, inversion, and suspension:

- *Omission.* When you strip a phrase or sentence of nonessential words that the audience expects or with which they are so familiar that they will mentally fill them in, you are using **omission**. Journalist Bill Moyers described modifications of a major American newspaper with the succinct phrase "More money, less news."[10]

- *Inversion.* **Inversion**—reversing the normal order of words in a phrase or sentence—can also create drama in a speech. In his 2017 presidential inaugural address, Donald Trump inverted the usual subject–verb sentence pattern to verb-subject to make this declaration emphatic and memorable: "Now arrives the hour of action."[11]

- *Suspension.* A third way to create drama through sentence structures is to employ verbal **suspension**, saving an important word or phrase for the end of a sentence rather than placing it at the beginning. In an address delivered shortly after his election, Donald Trump used suspension to focus on restoring America: "Now begins a great national campaign . . . to restore the full promise of America for all of our people."[12]

Cadence   A final way to create memorable word structures is to use **cadence**, or language rhythm, in your speech. A speaker does so not by speaking in a singsong pattern, but by using such stylistic devices as parallelism, antithesis, repetition, and alliteration:

- *Parallelism.* **Parallelism** occurs when two or more clauses or sentences have the same grammatical pattern. In his presidential farewell address, Barack Obama used parallelism in his final charge to the American people:

  > I am asking you to hold fast to that faith written into our founding documents; that idea whispered by slaves and abolitionists; that spirit sung by immigrants and homesteaders. . . .[13]

figurative language
Language that deviates from the ordinary, expected meaning of words to make a description or comparison unique, vivid, and memorable.

metaphor
An implied comparison between two things.

simile
An overt comparison between two things that uses the word *like* or *as*.

personification
The attribution of human qualities to inanimate things or ideas.

drama
A characteristic of a speech created when something is phrased in a way that differs from the way the audience expects.

omission
Leaving out a word or phrase the audience expects to hear.

inversion
Reversing the normal word order of a phrase or sentence.

suspension
Withholding a key word or phrase until the end of a sentence.

cadence
The rhythm of language.

parallelism
Using the same grammatical structure for two or more clauses or sentences.

FIGURE 13.6   Figurative Language[9]

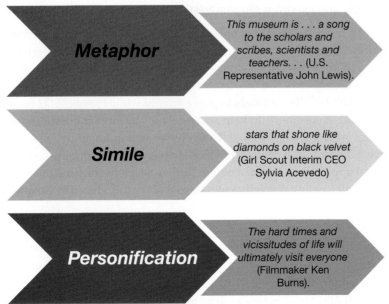

Metaphor — This museum is . . . a song to the scholars and scribes, scientists and teachers. . . (U.S. Representative John Lewis).

Simile — stars that shone like diamonds on black velvet (Girl Scout Interim CEO Sylvia Acevedo)

Personification — The hard times and vicissitudes of life will ultimately visit everyone (Filmmaker Ken Burns).

RECAP

Crafting Memorable Word Structures

To make your message memorable, use . . .

Figurative Language

Metaphor	Making an implied comparison
Simile	Making a comparison using *like* or *as*
Personification	Attributing human qualities to nonhuman things or ideas

Drama

Omission	Leaving nonessential words out of a phrase or sentence
Inversion	Reversing the normal order of words in a phrase or sentence
Suspension	Withholding the key ideas in a phrase or sentence until the end

Cadence

Parallelism	Using two or more clauses or sentences with the same grammatical structure
Antithesis	Using a two-part parallel structure in which the second part contrasts in meaning with the first
Repetition	Using a key word or phrase more than once
Alliteration	Repeating a consonant sound

antithesis
Contrasting the meanings of the two parts of a parallel structure.

repetition
Emphasizing a key word or phrase by using it more than once.

alliteration
The repetition of a consonant sound (usually the first consonant) several times in a phrase, clause, or sentence.

eye contact
Looking at an audience during a presentation.

The parallel noun phrases, *that faith*, *that idea*, and *that spirit*, helped Obama's final words soar.

- *Antithesis.* Similar to parallelism, except that the two structures contrast in meaning, **antithesis** is often marked by the conjunctions "not only. . . but (also)." In a speech marking the fiftieth anniversary of John F. Kennedy's "Moon Shot" speech, Vice President Joe Biden noted that Kennedy's character "was a reflection not only of his generation, but of America's character."[14]

- *Repetition.* **Repetition** of an important word or phrase can add emphasis to a key idea and memorability to your message. At the close of his commencement address at the University of Illinois in 2016, Grail CEO Jeff Huber repeated his denial of the cliché *Things happen for a reason*:

> Things don't "happen for a reason." But you can find purpose and meaning in things that do happen.
> Things don't happen for a reason. But how you respond can reveal your true character.
> Things don't happen for a reason. But they do often happen because nobody has yet found a better way.[15]

- *Alliteration.* A final strategy for creating cadence is to use **alliteration**, the repetition of an initial consonant sound several times in a phrase, clause, or sentence. Coca-Cola Chair and CEO Muhtar Kent used alliteration to preview his three main ideas:

> At Coca-Cola, we're focused on the "Three Ws" of Women, Water and Wellbeing.[16]

Repeating the *w* sound added cadence—and memorability—to Kent's three main ideas.

Effective Nonverbal Delivery

13.3 Identify and illustrate characteristics of effective nonverbal delivery.

At this point, you understand how important it is to deliver your speech effectively and what delivery style most audiences today prefer. You are familiar with the four methods of delivery and know how to maximize the use of each one. You also have some ideas about how to use effective and memorable language. Still, you may wonder, "What do I do with my hands?" "Is it all right to move around while I speak?" "How can I make my voice sound interesting?" To help answer these and similar questions, and to help you use nonverbal messages more effectively, we will examine five major categories of nonverbal delivery: eye contact, physical delivery, facial expression, vocal delivery, and personal appearance. This discussion further develops the fundamental principle of using and interpreting nonverbal messages that we introduced in Chapter 4.

Eye Contact

Of all the nonverbal delivery variables discussed in this chapter, the most important one in a public speaking situation for North Americans is **eye contact**. Eye contact with your audience members lets them know that you are interested in and ready to talk to them. It also permits you to determine whether they are responding to you.

COMMUNICATION & DIVERSITY

The Academic Quarter

When speaking at a Polish university a few years ago, one of your authors expected to begin promptly at 11:00 a.m., as announced in the program and on posters. By 11:10, it was clear that the speech would not begin on time, and your author began to despair of having any audience at all.

In Poland, it turns out, both students and professors expect to adhere to the "academic quarter." In other words, most lectures begin at least fifteen minutes (a quarter of an hour) after the announced starting time.

If your author had asked a Polish professor about the audience's expectations, he would have known about this custom in advance. One way to avoid such misunderstandings is to talk with people you know who are familiar with the cultural expectations. Another way is to observe other speakers presenting to similar audiences. Ask specific questions, including the following:

1. Where does the audience expect me to stand while speaking?
2. Do listeners expect direct eye contact?
3. When will the audience expect me to start and stop my talk?
4. Will listeners find movement and gestures distracting or welcome?
5. Do listeners expect presentation aids?

Keep cultural differences in mind as you rehearse and deliver speeches to diverse audiences.

In addition, most listeners will think that you are more capable and trustworthy if you look them in the eye than if you avoid eye contact. Some studies document a relationship between eye contact and speaker credibility, as well as between eye contact and listener learning.[17]

How much eye contact do you need? One study found that speakers with less than 50 percent eye contact are considered unfriendly, uninformed, inexperienced, and even dishonest by their listeners.[18] On the other hand, is there such a thing as too much eye contact? For North American audiences, the answer is probably not. Be aware, though, that not all people from all cultures prefer as much eye contact as North Americans do. Asians, for example, generally prefer less.

If you are recording your speeches for an online class, you will need to establish eye contact with the device you're using to record your speech, which can be challenging. Although doing so may seem easier than looking at a live audience, more than two-thirds of respondents in a recent study felt that it was actually more difficult.[19] The following suggestions can help you use eye contact more effectively when you speak in public:

- Establish eye contact with your audience before you say anything. Eye contact sends listeners a message to tune in as you start your talk.
- Maintain eye contact with your audience as you deliver your opening sentence without looking at your notes.
- Try to establish eye contact with people throughout your audience, not just with the front row or only one or two people. Briefly look into the eyes of an individual, and then transfer your eye contact to someone else.
- Do not look over your listeners' heads. They will notice if you do so and may even turn around to try to find out what you are looking at.

Physical Delivery

Gestures, movement, and posture are the three key elements of **physical delivery**. A good speaker knows how to use effective gestures, make meaningful movements, and maintain appropriate posture while speaking to an audience.

Gestures The hand and arm movements you use while speaking are called **gestures**. Nearly all people from all cultures use some gestures when they speak. In fact, research

physical delivery
A person's gestures, movement, and posture, which influence how a message is interpreted.

gestures
Movements of the hands and arms to communicate ideas.

▲ This speaker's gesture acknowledging his fellow graduates is simple, natural, and definite. Focusing on your audience and your message during rehearsals can help you to gesture effectively when you deliver your speech to an audience. Comstock/Getty Image

suggests that gesturing is instinctive and that it is intrinsic to speaking and thinking.[20] Yet even if you gesture easily and appropriately in the course of everyday conversation, you may feel awkward about what to do with your hands when you are in front of an audience. To minimize this challenge, consider the following guidelines:

- Focus on the message you want to communicate. As in ordinary conversation, when you speak in public, your hands should help emphasize or reinforce your verbal message. Your gestures should coincide with what you are saying.

- Again, as in conversation, let your gestures flow with your message. They should appear natural, not tense or rigid.

- Be definite. If you want to gesture, go ahead and gesture. Avoid making minor hand movements that will be masked by the lectern or that may appear to your audience as accidental brief jerks.

- Vary your gestures. Try not to use the same hand or one all-purpose gesture all the time. Think of the different gestures you can use, depending on whether you want to enumerate, point, describe, or emphasize ideas.

- Don't overdo your gestures. You want your audience to focus not on your gestures, but on your message.

- Make your gestures appropriate to your audience and the situation. When speaking to a large audience in a relatively formal setting, use bolder, more sweeping, and more dramatic gestures than you would use when speaking to a small audience in an informal setting. Also consider the culture-based expectations of your audience. Americans in general tend to use more gestures than speakers from other cultures. If you are speaking to a culturally diverse audience, you may want to tone down your gestures.

movement

A change of location during a presentation.

Movement Another element of physical delivery is **movement**. You may wonder, "Should I walk around during my speech, or should I stay in one place?" "Should I stay behind the lectern, or could I stand beside or in front of it?" "Can I move around among the audience?" The following criteria may help you answer these questions:

- Like gestures, any movement should be purposeful. It should be consistent with the verbal content of your message; otherwise, it will appear to be aimless wandering. You might signal the beginning of a new idea or major point in your speech with movement, or you might move to signal a transition from a serious idea to a more humorous one. The bottom line is that your use of movement should make sense to your listeners. No movement at all is better than random, distracting movement.

- If a physical barrier such as a lectern, a row of chairs, or an overhead projector makes you feel cut off from your listeners, move closer to the audience. Studies suggest that physical proximity enhances learning.[21]

- Adapt to the cultural expectations of your audience. British listeners, for example, have commented to us that American lecturers tend to stand too close to an audience when speaking. If you think that movement will make your audience uncomfortable, stay in one carefully chosen spot to deliver your speech.

Posture **Posture** is the third element of physical delivery to consider when delivering a speech. One study suggests that your posture may reflect on your credibility as a speaker.[22] Certainly, slouching lazily across a lectern does not communicate enthusiasm for or interest in your audience or your topic. On the other hand, you should adapt your posture to your topic, your audience, and the level of formality of the speaking occasion. For example, during a very informal speech, it may be perfectly appropriate, as well as comfortable and natural, to lean against the edge of a desk.

Few speech teachers or texts advocate specific speaking postures. Instead, you should observe some commonsense guidelines about posture:

- Avoid slouching, shifting from one foot to the other, or drooping your head.
- Unless you have a disability, do not sit while delivering a speech. An exception might be perching on or leaning against the edge of a desk or stool (which would still elevate you slightly above your audience) during a very informal speech.

posture
A speaker's stance.

Like your gestures and movement, your posture should not call attention to itself. Rather, it should reflect your interest in and attention to your audience and your message.

Facial Expression

Your **facial expression** plays a key role in expressing your thoughts, emotions, and attitudes.[23] Your audience sees your face before they hear what you are going to say, giving you the opportunity to set the tone for your message even before you begin to speak. Social psychologist Paul Ekman has found that facial expressions of primary emotions are virtually universal, so even a culturally diverse audience will be able to read your facial expressions clearly.[24]

facial expression
An arrangement of the facial muscles to communicate thoughts, emotions, and attitudes.

Throughout your speech, your facial expression, like your body language and eye contact, should be appropriate to your message. Relate somber news wearing a serious expression. Tell a humorous story with a smile. To communicate interest in your listeners, keep your expression alert and friendly. To ensure that you are maximizing the use of this important nonverbal delivery cue, rehearse your speech in front of a mirror; better yet, record and analyze video of yourself rehearsing your speech. Consider as objectively as possible whether your face is reflecting the emotional tone of your ideas.

Vocal Delivery

We have already discussed the importance of selecting words and phrases that will most effectively communicate your ideas, information, and images. We referred to this element of delivery as verbal delivery. **Vocal delivery**, on the other hand, involves nonverbal vocal cues—not the words you say, but the way you say them. Effective vocal delivery requires you to speak so that your audience can understand you and will remain interested in what you are saying. Nonverbal vocal elements include volume, pitch, rate, and articulation.

vocal delivery
Nonverbal voice cues, including volume, pitch, rate, and articulation.

Volume **Volume** is the softness or loudness of your voice. It is the most fundamental determinant of audience understanding. If you do not speak loudly enough, even the most brilliant presentation will be ineffective, because the audience simply will not hear you. In addition, volume can signal important ideas in your speech; for example, you can deliver a key idea either more loudly or more softly than you have been speaking. Consider these guidelines to help you appropriately adapt the volume of your voice to your audience's needs:

volume
The softness or loudness of a speaker's voice.

- Speak loudly enough so that the audience members farthest from you can hear you without straining. Doing so will ensure that everyone else in the room can hear you, too.

- Vary the volume of your voice in a purposeful way. Indicate important ideas by turning your volume up or down.
- Be aware of whether you need a microphone to amplify your volume. If you do and one is available, use it.

There are three kinds of microphones, only one of which demands much technique:

1. *Lavaliere or Wireless Hand-Held.* Both lavaliere and wireless hand-held microphones allow a speaker to move freely while speaking. Often worn on the front of a shirt or a jacket lapel by news reporters and interviewees, a lavaliere microphone requires no particular care other than not thumping it or accidentally knocking it off.

2. *Boom.* A boom microphone is used by filmmakers. It hangs over the heads of the speakers and is controlled remotely, so the speakers need not be particularly concerned with it.

3. *Stationary.* A stationary microphone may be attached to a lectern, sit on a desk, or stand on the floor. Generally, today's stationary microphones are multidirectional. Even so, you will have to keep your mouth at about the same distance from the microphone at all times to avoid distracting fluctuations in the volume of sound. You can turn your head from side to side and use gestures, but you will have to limit other movements.

Under ideal circumstances, you will be able to practice with your microphone. If you have the chance, figure out where to stand for the best sound quality and to determine how sensitive the mike is to extraneous noise. Practice will accustom you to any voice distortion or echo that might occur so that these sound qualities do not surprise you during your presentation.

pitch
How high or low a speaker's voice is.

Pitch Whereas volume is the loudness or softness of your voice, **pitch** refers to how high or low your voice is. To some extent, pitch is determined by physiology. The faster the folds in your vocal cords vibrate, the higher the habitual pitch of your voice. In general, female vocal folds vibrate much faster than do those of males. You can, however, raise or lower your habitual pitch within a certain range.

inflection
Variation in vocal pitch.

Variation in pitch, called **inflection**, is a key factor in communicating the meaning of your words. You know that a startled "Oh!" in response to something someone has told you communicates something quite different from a lower-pitched, questioning "Oh?" Your vocal inflection indicates your emotional response to what you have heard.

Vocal inflection also helps to keep an audience interested in your message. If you speak in a monotone, without changing your pitch, the audience will probably become bored quickly. To help you monitor and practice your pitch and inflection as you prepare to speak, record and play back your speech at least once as you rehearse. Listen carefully to your pitch and inflection. If you think that you are speaking in too much of a monotone, practice again with exaggerated variations in pitch. Eventually, you will find a happy medium.

rate
How fast or slowly a speaker speaks.

Rate Another vocal variable is **rate**, or speed. How fast do you talk? Most speakers average between 120 and 180 words per minute. Good speakers vary their rate to add interest to their delivery and to emphasize key ideas. To determine whether your speaking rate is appropriate and purposeful, become conscious of it. Record your presentation during rehearsal and listen critically to your speech speed. If it seems too fast, make a conscious effort to slow down. Use more **pauses** after questions and before important ideas. If you are speaking too slowly, make a conscious effort to speed up.

pause
A few seconds of silence during a speech, used both to slow a fast pace and to signal a key idea.

Articulation **Articulation** is the enunciation of sounds. As a speaker, you want to articulate distinctly to ensure that your audience can determine what words you are using. Sometimes we fall into the habit of mumbling or slurring—saying *wanna* instead of *want to*, or *chesterdrawers* instead of *chest of drawers*. Some nonstandard articulation

articulation
The production of clear and distinct speech sounds.

DEVELOPING YOUR SPEECH STEP BY STEP

Rehearsing Your Speech

Dezerae begins to rehearse her speech. From the beginning, she stands and speaks aloud, practicing gestures and movement that seem appropriate to her message.

At first, Dezerae rehearses from her preparation outline (see Chapter 12). These early rehearsals go quite well, but the speech runs a little short. Dezerae knows that she tends to speak fairly rapidly, so she decides to plan more pauses throughout the speech—some to allow her listeners to think about an important point she has just made, and others to provide nonverbal transitions. When she prepares her speaking notes, Dezerae writes the delivery cue "Pause" in several strategic places.

---

may be part of a speaker's **dialect**, a speech style common to an ethnic group or a geographic region. One dialect with which most of us are familiar is the dialect of the southern United States, characterized by a distinctive drawl.

Although most native speakers of English can understand different English dialects, studies have shown that North American listeners assign more favorable ratings to, and can recall more information presented by, speakers with dialects similar to their own.[25] If your dialect is significantly different from that of your listeners, or you suspect that it could be potentially distracting, you may want to work to improve your articulation or standardize your dialect. To do so, be aware of words or phrases that you have a tendency to drawl, slur, or chop. Once you have identified them, practice saying them distinctly and correctly.

dialect
A consistent style of pronunciation and articulation that is common to an ethnic group or geographic region.

Appearance

What would you wear to deliver a speech to your class? To address your city council? The fact that you would probably wear something different for each of these occasions suggests that you are already aware of the importance of a speaker's **appearance**. There is considerable evidence that your personal appearance affects how your audience will respond to you and your message. If you violate your audience's expectations, you will be less successful in achieving your purpose. The following guidelines may make selecting a wardrobe a bit easier when you are next called on to speak:

appearance
A speaker's dress and grooming.

- Never wear anything potentially distracting, such as a T-shirt with writing on it. You want your audience to listen to you, not read your shirt.

- Consider appropriate clothing to be a presentation aid. For example, if you are a nurse or an emergency technician, wear your uniform when you speak about your profession. (We will discuss presentation aids in more detail shortly.)

- Take cues from your audience. If you know that they will be dressed in business attire, dress similarly. If anything, you want to be a bit more dressed up than members of your audience.

- When in doubt about what to wear, select something conservative.

RECAP

Characteristics of Effective Nonverbal Delivery

- Eye contact should be established before you say anything and should be sustained as much as possible throughout your speech.

- Gestures should be relaxed, definite, varied, and appropriate to your audience and the speaking situation.

- Movement should be purposeful and adapted to the audience's cultural expectations.

- Posture should feel natural and should be appropriate to your topic, your audience, and the occasion.

- Facial expression should be alert, friendly, and appropriate to your message.

- Volume should be loud enough that you can be easily heard and should be purposefully varied.

- Pitch should be varied so that the inflection in your voice helps sustain your audience's interest.

- Rate should be neither too fast nor too slow and can be varied to add interest and emphasize key ideas.

- Articulation should be clear and distinct.

- Appearance should conform to what the audience expects.

Effective Presentation Aids

13.4   Discuss how to prepare and use presentation aids effectively.

We have already discussed two elements of delivery: verbal delivery and nonverbal delivery. A third element used with increasing frequency in this era of sophisticated computer presentation software is the **presentation aid**. The term *presentation aid* refers to anything your audience can listen to or look at to help them understand your ideas. Images, text, video, audio, objects, models, and people are some of the types of presentation aids frequently used by speakers.

As long as they *aid* the speaker, rather than *replace* the speaker or the speech, presentation aids can be invaluable. They help you gain and maintain your audience's attention.[26] They communicate your organization of ideas. They illustrate sequences of events or procedures. They help your audience understand and remember your message. In addition, chances are that for at least one of the assignments in your communication class, you will be required to use a presentation aid. Because presentation aids are valuable supplements to your speeches and because students of communication are so often required to use them, let's discuss first the types of available presentation aids. Then we will discuss guidelines for using computer-generated presentation aids and, finally, provide some general suggestions for using presentation aids effectively.

presentation aid

Any tangible item used to help communicate ideas to an audience.

Types of Presentation Aids

If you are required to use a presentation aid for an assignment or you think that a presentation aid might enhance your message, you have a number of options from which to select. You could use drawings, photographs, maps, graphs, charts, text, video, audio, objects, models, or people.

Images   The most commonly used presentation aids are two-dimensional images: drawings, photographs, maps, graphs, and charts.

- **Drawings.** You can use simple drawings to help illustrate or explain ideas that you are talking about. For example, you could sketch the tunnels of a fire ant mound to show your audience why it is so difficult to eradicate an entire ant colony. You could sketch the plants and animals that are crucial to the life cycle of the Florida Everglades. You could ask a friend to help you prepare a drawing, or you could use computer software to generate a simple image. Your drawings do not have to be original artwork. Just be sure to credit your source if you use someone else's sketch. A good way to display your drawing to your audience is to scan it and then put it into a computer-generated slide. Keep your drawings large and simple. Line drawings are often more effective than more detailed ones.

- **Photographs.** If you are giving a speech on urban forestry, you might want to show your audience high-quality photographs of trees that are appropriate for urban sites in your area. In this case, photographs would show color and detail that would be nearly impossible to achieve with drawings.

  The biggest challenge to using photographs as presentation aids is size; most printed photos are simply too small to be seen clearly from a distance. If you want to use photographs, store them on a flash drive. Then, when you want to display the photos, you can bring them up on a computer screen and use a video projection system to enlarge them for your audience.

- **Maps.** Like photographs, most maps are too small to be useful as presentation aids; to be effective, they must be enlarged in some way. You can accomplish this by scanning and transferring your map to a computer-generated slide. Be sure to highlight the areas or routes you are going to talk about in your speech.

- **Charts.** Charts can summarize and organize a great deal of information in a small space. Consider using a chart any time you need to present information that could be organized under several headings or in several columns. The chart in Figure 13.7 displays the growing percentage of online American adults using Facebook.[27] You can prepare charts quite easily by using the table feature in your word-processing program. Again, be sure your chart is large enough to be seen easily. Make it visually simple and do not put too much information in one chart.

- **Graphs.** Graphs are effective ways to present statistical relationships to your audience and help make data more concrete. You are probably already familiar with the three basic types of graphs:

  1. *Bar graph.* A **bar graph** consists of bars of various lengths that represent percentages or numbers. It is useful for making comparisons.
  2. *Pie graph.* A round **pie graph** shows how data are divided proportionately.
  3. *Line graph.* A **line graph** can show both trends over a period of time and relationships among variables.

We recommend that you use raw data and a computer program like Microsoft Word or Excel to generate graphs. Your graphs should be simple and uncluttered. Figure 13.8 illustrates the three basic types of graphs. These examples were created using the charts function in Microsoft Word.

FIGURE 13.7 Chart

Percentage of Online American Adults Using Facebook	
2014	71%
2016	79%

bar graph

A graph consisting of bars of various lengths that represent numbers or percentages.

pie graph

A circular graph that shows how a set of data is divided proportionately.

line graph

A graph that shows trends over a period of time and relationships among variables.

FIGURE 13.8 Three Types of Graphs: (A) Bar Graph, (B) Pie Graph, and (C) Line Graph

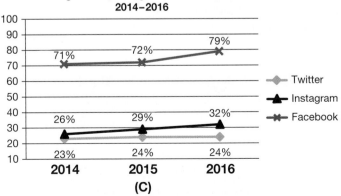

COMMUNICATION & SOCIAL MEDIA

Communicating Social Media Statistics with Computer-Generated Presentation Aids

In your preparation outline for your speech on social media use, you have included the following statistics:

79% of adult Americans online in 2016 reported using Facebook, indicating a steady annual rise in usage. Fewer than half that number use either Instagram or Twitter, with those user numbers remaining fairly flat over the past few years.[28]

But will your audience be able to comprehend these statistics by just hearing them? For maximum impact, you could supplement the statistics with computer-generated presentation aids. Figure 13.8 illustrates three computer-generated graphs of these statistics. The bar graph compares numbers of users of the three sites; the pie graph displays the number of Facebook users; and the line graph traces the numbers of users of all three sites over a three-year period.

Text In addition to—or instead of—using images, many speakers use a word, phrase, or bulleted outline as a presentation aid. Although some speakers still occasionally display text on chalkboards, dry-erase boards, flipcharts, or posters, most speakers today use slides created with PowerPoint or similar presentation software. Although presentation software helps you adapt your message to audiences who increasingly expect sophisticated technical support, do not use it simply to project your speaking notes. Rather than letting your slides *become* your presentation, use them to *supplement* it. Figure 13.9 offers suggestions for effectively using text as a presentation aid.

Video and Audio If you want to use audio presentation aids—say, music or excerpts from speeches or interviews—you might want to play a CD or an MP3 file. Both are readily available, and their sound can be amplified. Similarly, modern video technologies allow you to show scenes from a movie, an excerpt from a training film, or a brief original video. Make sure any recordings stored on DVDs, smartphones, or tablets, or streamed from the Internet, offer good picture and sound quality and permit freeze-frame viewing. Most audio and video devices allow you to replay a scene several times if you want your audience to listen or watch for different specific elements.

FIGURE 13.9 Effectively Using Text as a Presentation Aid

Using Text Effectively

Make certain the text conveys significant information.

Don't use too much text. Some experts suggest no more than seven lines of text on any single slide.

Make informed and mindful decisions about fonts, color, and layout. A light background with darker-colored words in a simple 28-point or larger font usually works well.

FIGURE 13.10 Effectively Using Video and Audio Presentation Aids

Using Video and Audio Effectively

Use only brief clips and excerpts. Audio and video should always supplement, rather than supplant, your speech.

Have the equipment set up and ready to go in the room in which you are speaking.

Be certain the volume is amplified enough that your audience can hear it without straining.

Be certain your audience can see your video. If you have an audience of 25 to 30 people, you can use a 25-inch screen for video. For larger audiences, you will need to use several television monitors or projection technology.

If you plan to use an audio or video presentation aid, consider the suggestions provided in Figure 13.10.

Objects and Models The first type of presentation aid you ever used—perhaps as long ago as preschool "show and tell"—was probably an object. You took to school your favorite teddy bear or the new remote-control car you got for your birthday. Remember how the kids crowded around to see what you had brought?

Because listeners of all ages like tangible, real things, using objects as presentation aids can still help you engage your audience. In his speech on the lead danger from water pipes, student speaker Nick held up two water bottles as he said,

> I have two water bottles here. The brown water is from Flint, Michigan, and the clear water is from my apartment in the nearby city of Detroit. Which bottle contains a dangerous level of lead? The answer? Both do.[29]

He had his audience's full attention. Figure 13.11 includes guidelines for effectively using objects and models as presentation aids.

If it is not possible to bring an object to class, you may be able to substitute a model. For example, you cannot bring a 1956 Ford Thunderbird into a classroom, but you may be able to construct and bring a model. You probably could not acquire a dog's heart to bring to class, but you might be able to find a model to use for your explanation of how heartworms damage that vital organ. If you use a model as a presentation aid, be sure it is large enough to be seen by all members of your audience.

People You might not think of people as potential presentation aids, but they can be. George W. Bush used ordinary people as visual aids for some of his most important presidential speeches, "asking them to stand and then telling stories of their sacrifices or heroism . . . a way of coming down from the stage,

FIGURE 13.11 Effectively Using Objects and Models as Presentation Aids

Using Objects and Models Effectively

Make certain the object or model is neither too large nor too small. If it is too large, it may be unwieldy; if it is too small, your audience won't be able to see it.

Don't use dangerous or illegal objects as presentation aids. They may make your audience members uneasy or actually put them at risk.

COMMUNICATION & ETHICS

Profanity in an Audio Presentation Aid

Matt wants to talk to his college classmates about the use of profanity in rap music. He plans to play audio clips of several profane song lyrics to illustrate his point. Should Matt play these songs, even though doing so might offend several members of his audience? Why or why not?

RECAP

Types of Presentation Aids

- Keep *drawings* simple and large.
- Be sure that *photographs* are large enough to be seen easily.
- Highlight on a *map* the geographic areas you will discuss.
- Limit the amount of information you put on any single *chart*.
- Keep *graphs* simple and uncluttered.
- Use only brief *video* and *audio* clips, make sure they can be easily seen or heard, and have equipment ready to go before you speak.
- Use *objects* and *models* that you can handle easily and that are safe and legal.
- Rehearse with *people* who will serve as presentation aids, and don't let them steal the show.

as it were, and mingling with the crowd."[30] In other instances, people can model costumes, play an instrument, or demonstrate a dance. If you are going to ask someone to assist you by acting as a presentation aid for a speech, consider the guidelines provided in Figure 13.12.

Additional Guidelines for Preparing and Using Presentation Aids

In addition to the specific guidelines provided for various types of presentation aids, the following general guidelines can help you prepare and use all types of presentation aids more effectively.

Select the Right Presentation Aids   As is evident from the above discussion, you have a number of options for presentation aids. If you are trying to decide which to use, consider these suggestions:

1. Be constantly aware of your specific purpose. Be certain that your presentation aid contributes to it.
2. Adapt to your listeners. Let their interests, experiences, and knowledge guide your selection of presentation aids. For example, an audience of accountants would readily understand arbitrage charts that might be incomprehensible to a more general

FIGURE 13.12   Effectively Using People as Presentation Aids

Using People Effectively

↓

Rehearse with the person who will be helping you.

↓

Don't have the person stand beside you, doing nothing. Wait and introduce the person to your audience when needed.

↓

Don't let your presentation aid steal the show. Make his or her role specific and fairly brief. As the speaker, you should remain the "person of the hour."

audience. If you will be speaking to a large audience, be certain that everyone will be able to see or hear your presentation aid.

3. Consider your own skill and experience. Use equipment with which you have had experience, or allow yourself ample time to practice.

4. Take into account the room in which you will speak. If it has large windows and no shades, for example, do not plan to use a visual presentation aid that will require a darkened room. If you plan to use PowerPoint slides, be sure that both hardware and software are available and in good working order.

Use Presentation Aids Thoughtfully One speechwriter and presentation coach warns against this bleak but all-too-common scenario:

> The presenter says, "And now, I'd like to talk about quality." And lo and behold . . . the word *quality* flashes on a screen. Now, folks, does this slide offer any new information? Does it clarify a complex point? Does it strengthen the bond between presenter and audience? You know the answer: a resounding "no."[31]

Be sure that the aids you use help you communicate your message.

Rehearse with Your Presentation Aids The day of your speech should not be the first time you deliver your presentation while holding up your model, advancing your PowerPoint slides, or cueing your video clip. Practice setting up and using your presentation aids until you feel at ease with them. Consider during rehearsal what you would do at various stages of the speech if you had to carry on without a particular presentation aid. For example, what if the wifi stops working, your equipment fails to show up, or the electricity goes off? Have contingency plans.

Maintain Eye Contact with Your Audience, Not with Your Presentation Aids You can glance at your presentation aids during your talk, but do not talk to them. Keep looking at your audience.

Explain Your Presentation Aids Always talk about and explain your presentation aids. Do not assume that the audience will understand their relevance and how to interpret them.

Time the Display of Your Presentation Aids to Coincide with Your Discussion of Them Don't put a presentation aid in front of your audience until you are ready to use it. Likewise, remove or cover your presentation aid after you finish with it. Keeping presentation aids in front of an audience before or after you use them will only serve to distract from your message.

Do Not Pass Objects, Pictures, or Other Small Items among Audience Members Passing things around distracts audience members. Either people are focused on whatever they are looking at, or they are counting the number of people who will handle the object before it reaches them. If the item is too small for everyone to see it when you hold it up, it is not a good presentation aid.

▼ Although this speaker has developed a compelling PowerPoint presentation aid, she is losing eye contact with her audience as she presents it. How can you learn to handle your presentation aids with confidence, while maintaining effective eye contact with your audience? Creativa Images/ Shutterstock

Use Handouts Effectively   Handing out papers during your speech can distract your audience. If possible, wait to distribute handouts until after you have spoken. If your audience needs to refer to the material while you are speaking about it, go ahead and pass out the handouts; then, at various points in your speech, tell audience members where in the handout they should focus.

Use Small Children and Animals with Caution   Small children and even the best-trained animals are unpredictable. In a strange environment, in front of an audience, they may not behave in their usual way. The risk of having a child or animal detract from your message may be too great to justify using either as a presentation aid.

Some Final Tips for Rehearsing and Delivering Your Speech

13.5   Make the most of your rehearsal time, and deliver your speech effectively.

Throughout this chapter, we have described and offered suggestions for effective verbal and nonverbal delivery and use of presentation aids. In addition to those tips, the following suggestions will help you make the most of your rehearsal time and ultimately deliver your speech successfully:

- *Finish your preparation outline several days before you must deliver the speech.* Begin to rehearse from the preparation outline. Revise the speech as necessary, and then outline your speaking notes. Continue to rehearse and modify your speaking notes as necessary.

- *Practice, practice, practice.* Rehearse aloud as often as possible. Only by rehearsing will you gain confidence in both the content of the speech and your delivery of it. As the author of the bestselling book *Quiet: The Power of Introverts in a World That Can't Stop Talking* points out,

  > If you went to a job interview without fixing your tie or applying your lipstick in front of the mirror, you would hope that there's no scarlet lip gloss smeared across your teeth, but how could you know for sure? Better to take the guesswork out of it.[32]

- *Use good delivery skills while rehearsing.* Rehearse your speech standing up. Pay attention to your gestures, posture, eye contact, facial expression, and vocal delivery, as well as the verbal message. Rehearse with your presentation aids.

- *If possible, practice your speech for someone.* Researchers in one study found that students who practice their speeches before an audience score higher on evaluations than those who practice without an audience.[33]

- *Use audio or video technology to record your speech, but try not to be overly critical when you listen to or watch yourself, as many of us tend to be.* Notice whether you use too many filler sounds or words, such as "uh," "er," "okay," "you know," and "like." Realize, however, that you're developing a delivery style unique to you, so don't try to change too much.

- *Prepare the room and equipment.* You may want to rearrange the furniture or any equipment. If you are using technology, check to see that it is working properly, and set up your presentation aids carefully.

He took every chance to practice his talk.

- *Re-create the speaking situation in your final rehearsals.* Try to rehearse in a room similar to the one in which you will deliver the speech. Use the speaking notes you will use the day you deliver the speech. Give the presentation without stopping. The more realistic the rehearsal, the more confidence you will gain.

- *Get plenty of rest the night before you speak.* Being well rested is more valuable than squeezing in a frantic, last-minute rehearsal.

- *Arrive early.* If you do not know for certain the location of the room in which you will make your presentation, give yourself plenty of time to find it. Set up and check your presentation aids.

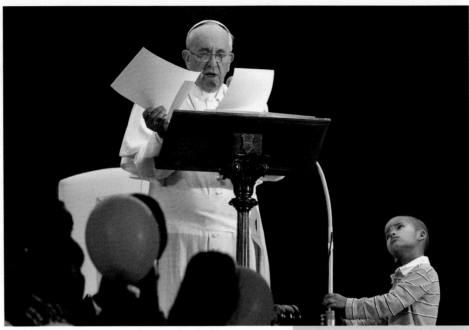

▲ When a small boy insisted on participating in one of Pope Francis's early speeches, the Pope seemed delighted rather than distracted. How can you prepare to deliver your speech with similar composure? TIZIANA FABI/ Stringer/Getty Images

- *Review and apply the suggestions offered in Chapter 11 for becoming a more confident speaker.* As the moment for delivering your speech nears, remind yourself of the effort you have spent preparing it. Visualize yourself delivering the speech effectively. Silently practice your opening lines. Think about your audience. Breathe deeply. Relax.

- *If something unforeseen (a ringing cell phone, for example) briefly interrupts your speech, remain composed as you pause briefly and then pick up where you left off.* If the incident is amusing, you can laugh along with your audience. When the presidential seal fell off Barack Obama's lectern and crashed to the stage during a speech, he quipped, "That's all right, all of you know who I am."[34]

- *After you have delivered your speech, seek feedback from members of your audience.* Use the information you gain to improve your next presentation.

DEVELOPING YOUR SPEECH STEP BY STEP

Delivering Your Speech

The long-awaited day of Dezerae's speech has arrived at last. She got a full night's sleep last night and ate a light breakfast before setting out for class.

As she waits to speak, Dezerae visualizes herself delivering her speech calmly and confidently. When her name is called, she rises, walks to the front of the room, and establishes eye contact with her audience before she begins to speak. Dezerae focuses on adapting her message to her listeners. She looks at individual members of her audience, uses purposeful and well-timed gestures, and speaks loudly and clearly.

Even before she hears her classmates' applause, Dezerae knows that her speech has gone well.

Criteria for Evaluating Speeches

13.6 Understand and apply criteria for evaluating speeches.

What makes a speech successful? Our purpose here is not to take you through the centuries of dialogue and debate about this issue, but rather to offer practical ways to evaluate your own speeches as well as those of others.

Your instructor will probably use a rubric or evaluation form that lists precise criteria. Underlying any list of what a successful speaker should do, however, are two fundamental goals: A successful speech should be *effective*, and it should be *ethical*.

- *Effective.* To be effective, a speech should be understandable to listeners and should achieve the speaker's intended purpose.[35]

- *Ethical.* A good speaker is an ethical speaker—one who tells the truth, cites sources for nonoriginal words and ideas, and is sensitive and responsive to listeners. Even if a message can be understood clearly and achieves the speaker's purpose, if the speaker has used unethical means to achieve that purpose, the speech is not successful.

〉 REVIEW, APPLY, AND ASSESS

Methods of Delivery

13.1 List and describe the four methods of delivery, and provide suggestions for effectively using each one.

REVIEW: As you consider how you will deliver your presentation speech, you will select from four methods of delivery: manuscript speaking, memorized speaking, impromptu speaking, and extemporaneous speaking. Extemporaneous speaking is the style taught today in most presentational public speaking classes and preferred by most audiences.

KEY TERMS:

manuscript speaking
memorized speaking
impromptu speaking
extemporaneous speaking

APPLY: Answering an instructor's question or presenting a summary of a small group discussion to the larger class may call for impromptu speaking skills. Based on your observations and experiences in such situations, what tips can you add to those provided in Figure 13.3?

Effective Verbal Delivery

13.2 List and explain three criteria for effective verbal delivery.

REVIEW: Once you know what method of delivery you will use, you should think about and rehearse words, phrases, and sentences that will best communicate your intended message and give it a distinct and memorable style. The most effective language is clear, accurate, and memorable.

KEY TERMS:

specific word
concrete word
simple word
vivid word
thesaurus
correct word
unbiased word
figurative language
metaphor
simile
personification
drama
omission
inversion
suspension
cadence
parallelism
antithesis
repetition
alliteration

APPLY: A friend asks you for advice on making the word choice in her speech as effective as possible. Offer her at least three suggestions based on the criteria in this chapter for using words effectively.

Effective Nonverbal Delivery

13.3 Identify and illustrate characteristics of effective nonverbal delivery.

REVIEW: Nonverbal variables are critical to effective delivery. Physical delivery includes a speaker's gestures, movement, and posture. Eye contact is perhaps the most important delivery variable, determining to a large extent your credibility with your audience. Facial expression plays a key role in expressing your thoughts, emotions, and attitudes. Vocal delivery includes such elements as volume, pitch, rate, and articulation. Finally, your personal appearance can affect how your audience responds to you and your message.

KEY TERMS:

eye contact
physical delivery
gestures
movement
posture
facial expression
vocal delivery
volume
pitch
inflection
rate
pause
articulation
dialect
appearance

APPLY: Which of the characteristics of nonverbal delivery described so far—eye contact, gesturing, movement, posture, or facial expression—are you confident you can use effectively? Which are most challenging for you? Which of the tips in this chapter do you plan to use to help you overcome your challenges?

ASSESS: For a speech you have viewed either live or online, consider the speaker's nonverbal delivery. Did he or she make appropriate eye contact with the audience? Did the speaker use appropriate volume and vocal variation? Did he or she use gestures effectively? Explain your responses.

Effective Presentation Aids

13.4   Discuss how to prepare and use presentation aids effectively.

REVIEW: Presentation aids include images, text, video, audio, objects, models, and people. All presentation aids should be easy to see and simple. Also be sure to select the right presentation aids, use presentations aids thoughtfully, rehearse with your presentation aid, explain your presentation aid, time the use of your presentation aid, refrain from passing things around or using handouts indiscriminately, and remember that small children and animals are unpredictable presentation aids.

KEY TERMS:

presentation aid	pie graph
bar graph	line graph

APPLY: What is the least effective use of presentation aids you've witnessed? Based on this chapter, what advice would you give to that speaker to help improve his or her use of presentation aids?

Some Final Tips for Rehearsing and Delivering Your Speech

13.5   Make the most of your rehearsal time, and deliver your speech effectively.

REVIEW: Final suggestions for rehearsing your speech include allowing ample time, rehearsing it aloud while standing up, practicing your speech for someone, recording and listening to or watching your speech, and re-creating the actual speaking situation in your final rehearsals. Make sure you get plenty of rest the night before you speak, arrive early, and apply the suggestions offered in Chapter 11 for becoming a more confident speaker.

APPLY: How can you determine when you have rehearsed long enough that you can extemporaneously deliver your key ideas to your listeners, but not so long that you are giving a memorized speech?

ASSESS: Record your speech while you rehearse. When reviewing the recording, objectively and critically observe your gestures, posture, eye contact, facial expression, and vocal delivery, as well as your verbal message. Make necessary adjustments.

Criteria for Evaluating Speeches

13.6   Understand and apply criteria for evaluating speeches.

REVIEW: Underlying any list of what a successful speaker should do are two fundamental goals: A successful presentation should be effective, and it should be ethical.

APPLY: What kinds of comments from classmates evaluating your speeches would you find most helpful? What types of remarks would be *least* useful? Explain your answers.

ASSESS: Is it ethical to make only positive comments and no suggestions for improvement when evaluating a classmate's speech? Explain your answer.

〉 THE PRINCIPLE POINTS

Principle One:
Be aware of your communication with yourself and others.

- As you become increasingly comfortable rehearsing an extemporaneous speech, you can decrease your reliance on your notes.
- Usage and articulation errors communicate a lack of preparation. If you are uncertain how to use or pronounce a word or phrase, look it up or ask someone.
- Use a microphone if you need one and one is available. Be sure to rehearse with it.
- Be aware of your speaking rate, and adjust it if necessary.
- Be certain that your presentation aids contribute to your specific purpose.

Principle Two:
Effectively use and interpret verbal messages.

- When exact wording is critical, you may want to deliver a manuscript or memorized speech.
- Do not try to memorize an extemporaneous speech word for word; vary the ways in which you express ideas and information.
- Phrase your ideas so that they will be clear, accurate, and memorable.

Principle Three:

Effectively use and interpret nonverbal messages.

- When you deliver a manuscript speech, try to look at an entire sentence at a time so that you can maintain eye contact with your audience as you deliver the sentence.
- Do not read a manuscript speech too rapidly; vary the rhythm, inflection, and pace of delivery so that the speech does not sound as though it is being read.
- Deliver a memorized speech at a moderate pace, and avoid patterns of vocal inflection that make the speech sound recited.
- Use gestures and movement to add interest and emphasis to both manuscript and memorized speeches.
- To heighten your credibility and increase listener learning, use eye contact to let your audience know that you are interested in and ready to talk to them.
- Use gestures to reinforce your verbal message.
- Move during your speech to signal the beginning of a new idea or major point or to signal a transition between a serious idea and a humorous one.
- Speak loudly enough to be heard easily by all members of your audience.
- Vary the volume of your voice to emphasize ideas and sustain the audience's interest.
- Vary your speaking rate to add interest to your delivery and emphasize key ideas.
- Articulate your words clearly.

Principle Four:

Listen and respond thoughtfully to others.

- Use eye contact to help you determine how your audience members are responding to you.
- If possible, rehearse your speech in front of someone and seek feedback about both your content and your delivery.

Principle Five:

Appropriately adapt messages to others.

- Although audiences today generally expect speakers to use everyday language and a conversational delivery style, you will need to adapt your delivery to audiences of different sizes and from different cultures.
- Let your audience's interests, experiences, and knowledge guide your preparation and selection of presentation aids.

14

SPEAKING TO INFORM

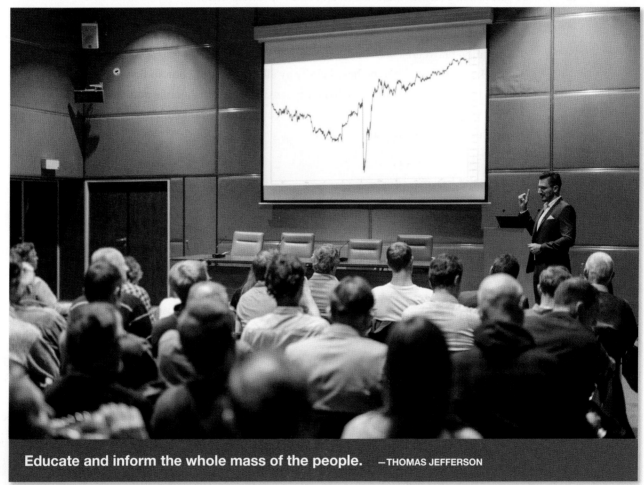

Educate and inform the whole mass of the people. —THOMAS JEFFERSON

Matej Kastelic/Shutterstock

→ CHAPTER OUTLINE

- Types of Informative Speeches
- Strategies for Organizing Your Informative Speech
- Strategies for Making Your Informative Speech Clear
- Strategies for Making Your Informative Speech Interesting

- Strategies for Making Your Informative Speech Memorable
- Study Guide: Review, Apply, and Assess

LEARNING OBJECTIVES

After studying this chapter, you should be able to

14.1 Describe five types of informative speeches.

14.2 Identify and use appropriate strategies for organizing informative speeches.

14.3 Identify and use strategies for making informative speeches clear.

14.4 Identify and use strategies for making informative speeches interesting.

14.5 Identify and use strategies for making informative speeches memorable.

One survey of both speech teachers and students who had taken a communication course found that the single most important skill taught in a public speaking class is how to give an informative speech.[1] Given the importance in our lives of sending and receiving information, this finding is not surprising.

Important as it may be, informing or teaching others can also be a challenge because of one simple fact: *Presenting information does not mean that communication has occurred.* One of the cofounders of Common Craft, a company known for explaining complex ideas and processes in short, easy-to-understand videos, says that

> Creating a great explanation involves stepping out of your own shoes and into the audience's. It is a process built on empathy, on being able to understand and share the feelings of another.[2]

In other words, a speaker must be audience-centered to communicate information successfully.

In this chapter, we will examine different types of informative tasks and identify specific strategies to help you organize your messages and make them clear, interesting, and memorable. Throughout our discussion, we will continue to apply the five Communication Principles for a Lifetime.

Types of Informative Speeches

14.1 Describe five types of informative speeches.

The purpose of a message to **inform** is to share information with others to enhance their knowledge or understanding of the objects, procedures, people, events, or ideas you discuss. Identifying which of the five types of informative speeches you are giving can help you select and narrow your topic, organize your message, and choose appropriate supporting material.

inform
To share information with others to enhance their knowledge or understanding of the information, concepts, and ideas you present.

Speeches about Objects

A speech about an object might be about anything tangible—anything you can see or touch. You may or may not show the actual object to your audience while you are talking about it. Objects that could form the basis of an interesting speech include the following:

Items from your own collection (antiques, vintage vinyl, baseball cards)

Brunelleschi's Dome

Celtic harps

Isle of Skye

The Franklin Delano Roosevelt Memorial in Washington, D.C.

Speeches about Procedures

A speech about a procedure discusses how something works (for example, how blood travels through the human circulatory system) or describes a process that produces a particular outcome (such as how grapes become wine). At the close of such a presentation, your audience should be able to describe, understand, or perform the procedure you have described. Here are some examples of procedures that could be topics of effective informative speeches:

> How to access and use a Virtual Private Network (VPN)
>
> How state laws are made
>
> How to refinish furniture
>
> How to select a cell phone provider
>
> How to garden organically
>
> How to select and purchase stocks

Notice that all these examples start with the word *how.* A speech about a procedure usually focuses on how a process is completed or how something can be accomplished. Speeches about procedures are often presented in workshops or other training situations in which people learn skills.

One good way to teach people a skill is to follow the acronym T-E-A-C-H, as shown in Figure 14.1.[3]

Many speeches about procedures include visual aids. Whether you are teaching people how to install a WiFi router or how to give a speech, showing them how to do something—the *Example* step of the T-E-A-C-H acronym—is almost always more effective than just telling them how to do it.

Speeches about People

Most of us enjoy hearing about the lives of real people, whether famous or unknown, living or dead, who have some special quality. The key to making an

FIGURE 14.1   Remember TEACH to teach.

The letters in the acronym TEACH stand for Tell-Example-Apply-Coach-Help and summarize an effective process you can use to teach people new skills.

T
- TELL: Describe what you want your listeners to know.

E
- EXAMPLE: Show listeners an example of how to perform the skill.

A
- APPLY: Give listeners an opportunity to apply the knowledge by performing the skill.

C
- COACH: Provide positive coaching to encourage listeners.

H
- HELP: Help listeners learn by correcting mistakes.

COMMUNICATION & ETHICS

Confidential or Potentially Dangerous Information

Mike, a computer engineering major, understands how a computer hacker recently accessed confidential personal information files on faculty members at his university. The procedure is actually simple enough that even people without sophisticated technical ability could understand and replicate it. Mike thinks that the procedure might be a good topic for an interesting informative speech. Meanwhile, Mike's classmate Paul, a chemistry major, considers whether to give an informative speech on how to create homemade explosives. If you are privy to confidential or potentially dangerous information, is it ethical to share it with others in an informative speech?

effective biographical speech is to be selective. Don't try to cover every detail of your subject's life. Relate the key elements in the person's career, personality, or other significant life features so that you build to a particular point, rather than just recite facts about the individual. One speaker gave a memorable speech about his friend:

> To enter Charlie's home was to enter a world of order and efficiency. His den reflected his many years as an Air Force officer; it was orderly and neat. He always knew exactly where everything was. When he finished reading the morning paper, he folded it so neatly by his favorite chair that you would hardly know that it had been read. Yet for all of his efficiency, you knew the minute you walked into his home that he cared for others, that he cared for you. His jokes, his stories, his skill in listening to others drew people to him. He never met a stranger. He looked for opportunities to help others.

Notice how the details capture Charlie's personality and charm. Speeches about people should give your listeners the feeling that the person is a unique, authentic individual.

One specific type of speech about a person is an introduction of another speaker and his or her topic. There are two cardinal rules for introducing another speaker: Be brief and be accurate. Remember that the audience has come to hear the main speaker, not you. In addition, be certain that you know how to pronounce the speaker's name.

Speeches about Events

Have you experienced a natural disaster such as an earthquake, hurricane, or tornado? Have you witnessed the inauguration of a president, governor, or senator? A major event,

▼ You may have seen a recording of the CBS news bulletin on the assassination of John F. Kennedy. Legendary newscaster Walter Cronkite's ability to describe the event while reflecting the incredible emotion of the moment has made that broadcast a classic. Just as Cronkite was able to do, your purpose as an informative speaker describing an event is to make that event come alive for your listeners.
CBS Photo Archive/Getty Images

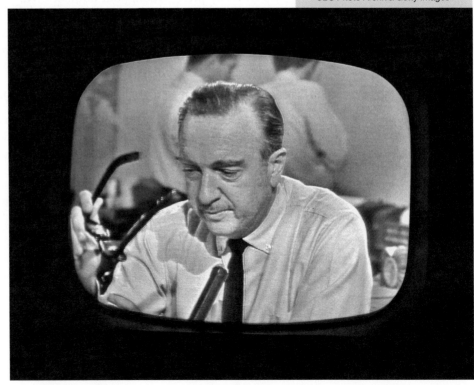

whether it is one you have experienced firsthand or one you have researched, can form the basis of a fascinating informative speech. Your goal as a speaker is to describe the event in concrete, tangible terms, bringing the experience to life for your audience.

Speeches about Ideas

By nature, speeches about ideas are more abstract than other types of speeches. The following principles, concepts, and theories might make good topics for idea speeches:

Principles of time management

Freedom of speech

Evolution

Theories of communication

Buddhism

Animal rights

As you look at this list, you may think that these topics seem boring, but as British writer G. K. Chesterton once said, "There is no such thing on earth as an uninteresting subject; the only thing that can exist is an uninterested person."[4] The selection and use of illustrations, examples, and anecdotes to make an otherwise abstract idea seem both interesting and relevant to your listeners are keys to gaining and maintaining interest in your speech about an idea.

Strategies for Organizing Your Informative Speech

14.2   Identify and use appropriate strategies for organizing informative speeches.

As with any presentation, your audience will better understand your informative speech if you organize your ideas logically.[5] Regardless of the length or complexity of your message, you must follow a logical pattern to be understood. The topic of your informative speech may lend itself to a particular organizational pattern.

Organizing Speeches about Objects

Speeches about objects may be organized topically; a topical pattern is structured around the logical divisions of the object you're describing. Here is a sample topical outline for a speech about an object—a nuclear power plant:

I. The reactor core
   A. The nuclear fuel in the core
   B. The placement of the fuel in the core

II. The reactor vessel
   A. The walls of a reactor vessel
   B. The function of the coolant in the reactor vessel

III. The reactor control rods
   A. The description of the control rods
   B. The function of the control rods

Speeches about objects may also be organized chronologically. A speaker might, for example, focus on the history and development of nuclear power plants, and such a speech would probably be organized chronologically. Or, depending on the speaker's specific purpose, the speech could be organized spatially, describing the physical layout of a nuclear power plant.

Organizing Speeches about Procedures

Speeches about procedures are usually organized chronologically, according to the steps involved in the process. Anita chose a chronological organization for her explanation of how to develop a new training curriculum in teamwork skills:

   I. Conduct a needs assessment of your department.
      A. Identify the method of assessing department needs.
      B. Implement the needs assessment.

  II. Identify the topics that should be presented in the training.
      A. Specify topics that all members of the department need.
      B. Specify topics that only some members of the department need.

 III. Write training objectives.
      A. Write objectives that are measurable.
      B. Write objectives that are specific.
      C. Write objectives that are attainable.

  IV. Develop lesson plans for the training.
      A. Identify the training methods you will use.
      B. Identify the materials you will need.

Notice that Anita grouped the tasks into four steps. Her audience members will remember these four general steps of the curriculum development process much more easily than if each individual task had been listed as a separate step.

Organizing Speeches about People

One way to talk about a person's life is in chronological order: birth, school, career, family, professional achievements, death. However, if you are interested in presenting a specific theme, such as "Winston Churchill, master of English prose," you may decide instead to organize Churchill's life experiences topically:

   I. Journalist
  II. Author
 III. Orator

▼ Chefs who teach classes in person or on television, such as Bobby Flay, often arrange their speeches chronologically, to show the procedure of following a recipe from start to finish. What procedures could you describe to an audience?
Vespasian/Alamy

Organizing Speeches about Events

Most speeches about an event follow a chronological arrangement, but a speech about an event might also describe the complex issues or causes behind it and be organized topically. For example, if you were to talk about the Civil War, you might choose to focus on three causes of the war:

I. Political
II. Economic
III. Social

Although these main points are topical, specific subpoints may be organized chronologically. However you choose to organize your speech about an event, remember that your goal should be to ensure that your audience is enthralled by your vivid description.

Organizing Speeches about Ideas

Most speeches about ideas are organized topically (by logical subdivisions of the central idea) or according to complexity (from simple ideas to more complex ones). The following example illustrates how Thompson used a topical organization for his informative speech about the three major branches of philosophical study:

I. Metaphysics
   A. The study of ontology
   B. The study of cosmology

II. Epistemology
   A. Knowledge derived from thinking
   B. Knowledge derived from experiencing

III. Logic
   A. Types of reasoning
   B. Types of proof

Table 14.1 summarizes typical organizational patterns used for major categories of informational speech topics.

TABLE 14.1 Organizing Informative Speeches

Speech Type	Description	Typical Organizational Patterns	Sample Topics
OBJECTS	Present information about tangible things	Topical Spatial Chronological	The Rosetta Stone Electronic tablets International Space Station

PROCEDURES	Review how something works, or describe a process	Chronological
		Topical
		Complexity
			How to . . .
			  clone a dog
			  trap lobsters

PEOPLE	Describe either a famous person or a personal acquaintance	Chronological Topical	Rosa Parks Indira Gandhi Young grandmother
EVENTS	Describe something that has happened, is happening, or will happen	Chronological Topical Complexity Spatial	Chinese New Year Cinco de Mayo
IDEAS	Present abstract information or information about principles, concepts, theories, or issues	Topical Complexity	Communism Microeconomic theory Tao Te Ching

Strategies for Making Your Informative Speech Clear

14.3 Identify and use strategies for making informative speeches clear.

Think of the best teacher you ever had. He or she probably possessed a special talent for making information clear, interesting, and memorable. Some speakers, like some teachers, are better than others at presenting information clearly.

A message is clear when the listener understands it in the way the speaker intended. As described in the Communication & Diversity feature, translating your speech into the audience's language is a basic step toward helping listeners understand.

How else do you make your messages clear to others?[6] You can help your audience make sense of your message by expressing your ideas simply, presenting information at a reasonable pace, and relating new information to what the audience already knows.

Simplify Ideas

Your job as a public speaker is to communicate with your audience, not to see how many complex words and ideas you can cram into your speech. The simpler your ideas and phrases, the greater the chance that your audience will understand and remember them.

COMMUNICATION & DIVERSITY

Using an Interpreter

It is quite possible that you may at some time be asked to speak to an audience of people who do not understand English or who cannot hear. In such a situation, you will need an interpreter to translate your message so that your audience can understand you. When using an interpreter, consider the following tips:

1. *Edit your message to fit within the time limit.* A speech that may take you thirty minutes to deliver without an interpreter will take at least an hour to present with an interpreter.

2. *Slow your speaking rate a bit.* Pause after every two or three sentences to give the interpreter time to translate your message.

3. *Don't say anything that you don't want your audience to hear.* Don't assume that your audience doesn't understand you just because you're using an interpreter.

4. *Give your interpreter a written copy of any facts, figures, or other detailed data.*

5. *Use humor with caution.* Humor often doesn't translate well. Even a very skilled interpreter may have difficulty communicating the intended meaning of your humor.

6. *Avoid slang, jargon, or terms that will be unfamiliar to your listeners or the interpreter.*

7. *When possible, talk with your interpreter before you deliver your speech.* Tell him or her the general points you will present. Give the interpreter an outline or, if you are using a manuscript, a transcript of your speech.

Vladimir Mucibabic/Shutterstock

Let's say that you decide to talk about state-of-the-art wireless earbuds. Given the lack of headphone jacks on some current smartphone models, that's a fine topic, but don't try to make your audience as sophisticated as you are about wireless earbuds in a five-minute speech. Discuss only major features and name one or two leaders in the field. Don't load your speech with complex details. Edit ruthlessly.

Pace Your Information Flow

If you present too much new information too quickly, you may overwhelm your listeners, and their ability to understand may falter. Arrange your supporting material so that you present an even flow of information rather than bunching up many significant details around one point. Remember that signposts offer your listeners both a break from listening to new information and help in processing that information. Preview your main ideas in your introduction, and use frequent internal summaries.[7]

Relate New Information to Old

Most of us learn by building on what we already know. As a speaker, you can apply this learning principle to help make your informative speech clear. Professional speaker and trainer John Zimmer explains,

> It is always helpful to anchor your (new) ideas to something with which the audience is familiar. That is why metaphors and analogies are so powerful.[8]

RECAP

Strategies for Making an Informative Speech Clear

Simplify ideas.

Pace the information flow.

Relate new information to old.

For example, tell bewildered new students how their first year of college will be similar to high school and how it will be different. Or describe to young 4-H members how raising cattle is similar to taking care of any animal; they all need food, water, and shelter. By building on the familiar, you can help your listeners understand how your new concept or information relates to their experience.

Strategies for Making Your Informative Speech Interesting

14.4 **Identify and use strategies for making informative speeches interesting.**

> He had them. No one moved. They hung on every word.

How can you create such interest when *you* speak? Here are several strategies to keep your audiences yearning for more.

Relate to Your Listeners' Interests

Your listeners may be interested in your topic for a variety of reasons. It may affect them directly, it may add to their knowledge, it may satisfy their curiosity, or it may entertain them. These reasons are not mutually exclusive. For example, if you were speaking at your local public library on how integration affected black businesses in your town, your audience of community members would be interested because your talk would affect them directly, add to their knowledge and satisfy their curiosity.[9]

Another way to make your message interesting is to think about why you yourself are interested in the topic. Once you are aware of your own interests and background, you can often find ways to establish common bonds with your audience.

Use Attention-Getting Supporting Material

Consider the following tips for selecting supporting material to best capture and sustain your listeners' attention:

- Research suggests that you can increase audience interest if you first provide a simple overview with an analogy, model, picture, or vivid description.[10]
- As you discuss the object, process, person, event, or idea, keep in mind the *who, what, when, where, and why* questions outlined in Figure 14.2.

Theresa McCracken/CartoonStock

Establish a Motive for Your Audience to Listen to You

There will be a test covering my lecture tomorrow. It will count as 50 percent of your semester grade.

Such statements may not make a teacher popular, but they will certainly motivate the class to listen. Lacking a teacher's power to assign grades, you will need to find more

FIGURE 14.2 Attention-Getting Supporting Material: Who, What, When, Where, and Why?

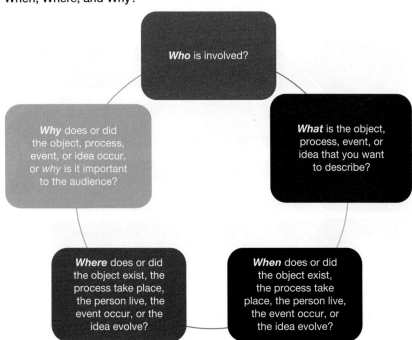

Who is involved?

What is the object, process, event, or idea that you want to describe?

When does or did the object exist, the process take place, the person live, the event occur, or the idea evolve?

Where does or did the object exist, the process take place, the person live, the event occur, or the idea evolve?

Why does or did the object, process, event, or idea occur, or *why* is it important to the audience?

creative ways to get your audience to listen to you. We suggest you use the following strategies of questioning, engaging, and relating:

- *Question:* One way to arouse the interest of your listeners is to ask them a question, such as one of the following:

  "How many of you are interested in saving tuition dollars this year?"

  "Who would like to save money on their income taxes?"

  "How many of you would like to learn an effective way of preparing your next speech?"

  These questions could stimulate your listeners' interest and motivate them to give you their attention.

- *Engage:* A second way to capture your listeners' interest is to begin your speech with an anecdote, a startling statistic, or some other attention-getting strategy.
- *Relate:* Finally, you can tell your listeners explicitly how the information in your speech will be of value to them.

Use Word Pictures

word picture
A vivid description that invites listeners to draw on their senses.

A **word picture** is a vivid description that helps your listeners form a mental image by appealing to one or more of their senses of sight, sound, smell, touch, and taste. Such powerful images can gain and hold an audience's attention. Use as many of your senses as possible to construct effective word pictures, as illustrated in Figure 14.3.

In addition to providing sensory images, you can enhance a word picture by describing the emotion a listener might feel if he or she were to experience the situation you relate. Use specific adjectives rather than general terms such as *happy* or *sad*. One speaker, talking about receiving her first speech assignment, described her reaction with these words:

My heart stopped. Panic began to rise up inside. Me? . . . For the next five days I lived in dreaded anticipation of the forthcoming event.[11]

FIGURE 14.3 Appealing to Your Audience's Senses with Word Pictures

Sight — Use lively language to describe the flaws, foibles, bumps, and beauties of the people, places, and things you want your audience to see.

Sound — Use colorful, onomatopoetic words, such as *buzz*, *snort*, *hum*, *crackle*, or *hiss*, to imitate the sound you want your listeners to hear with their "mental ear."

Smell — The first day of school may evoke the scents of new shoe leather, unused crayons, and freshly painted classrooms. The associated smells greatly enhance the overall word picture.

Touch — Rather than saying that something is rough or smooth, use a simile, such as "the rock was rough as sandpaper" or "the pebble was as smooth as a baby's skin."

Taste — Thinking about your grandmother may evoke memories of her buttery homemade noodles or her sweet, fudgy nut brownies. Such description can help you paint for your listeners an accurate, vivid image of your grandmother.

COMMUNICATION & SOCIAL MEDIA

"Killer" Presentations on Social Media

When making an informative presentation via social media, incorporating interesting supporting material is just as important as when you are addressing an audience face-to-face. Social media writer and speaker Rebekah Radice considers an engaging anecdote a key "best practice" for social media presentations: The most memorable presentations are those that tell a story rather than include a lot of text and statistics.[12]

Notice how such words and phrases as "my heart stopped," "panic," and "dreaded anticipation" effectively invoke the speaker's terror at the prospect of giving a speech, much more so than had she simply said, "I was scared."

Create Interesting Presentation Aids

Each day, audiences are exposed to a barrage of messages conveyed through such highly visual electronic media as streaming video. They have grown to depend on more than words alone to help them remember ideas and information. Research suggests that presentation aids can help you get and maintain audience members' attention, as well as increase their retention of the information in your speech.[13] When you need to present summaries of data, a well-crafted line graph can quickly and memorably reinforce the words and numbers you cite.

Use Humor

"Humor is the spice of speeches," says comedian Michael Klepper. "Too little and your message may be bland or lifeless, too much and it can burn the mouth."[14] The challenge is to use just the right kind of humor in the right amounts. The following suggestions can help you use humor wisely:[15]

- *Be certain your humor is appropriate to your listeners.* Because your audience "gives attempts at humor their success or failure," you should avoid topics or language that might offend your listeners and create so much emotional noise for them that they cannot focus on your message.[16]

- *Use humor to make a point.* Don't tell a joke just for the sake of getting a laugh. Make sure that your story or punch line relates to your message. Here's an example of how one presenter used a brief joke to make a point about the value of teamwork:

  > I read recently about a veterinarian and a taxidermist who decided to share a shop in a small town in Ohio. The sign in the front window read: "Either way, you get your dog back."
  >
  > There is an important lesson there. We need to work together to solve our problems. People from marketing need to work with operations people. Designers need to work with engineers. Then, when we find a problem that one part of the organization can't solve, someone else may suggest a solution. It doesn't matter who comes up with the solution. The important thing is to "get your dog back."[17]

- *Poke fun at yourself.* Audiences love it when you tell a funny or embarrassing story about yourself. In addition, if the joke's on you, you don't have to worry about whether you will offend someone else.[18]

▲ Judicious use of humor will help keep your audience's attention and can help them remember and understand your points. Before using humor, be sure to evaluate carefully whether the joke or story you want to use is appropriate for the occasion and the audience, and whether you have the ability to tell it well.

Digital Vision/Getty Images

- *Use humorous quotations.* You don't have to be a comedy writer to be funny. Quote humorous proverbs, poetry, or sayings from others. Remember, however, that what may be funny to you may not be funny to your audience. Try out your quotes and jokes on others before you present them from behind the lectern. And don't try to pass off a quotation from someone else as one of your own; always give credit for the quotations you use.

- *Use cartoons.* A cartoon may be an effective way to make a point. Make sure that your cartoon is large enough to be seen by everyone in the audience. As with any humor, though, don't overdo your use of cartoons.

RECAP

Strategies for Making an Informative Speech Interesting

Relate to your listeners' interests.

Use attention-catching supporting material.

Establish a motive for your audience to listen to you.

Use word pictures.

Create interesting presentation aids.

Use humor.

Strategies for Making Your Informative Speech Memorable

14.5 Identify and use strategies for making informative speeches memorable.

If you have made your message clear and interesting, you're well on your way to ensuring that your audience members will remember what you say. Presenting a well-organized message will also help your listeners remember what you say. In this section, we'll discuss several additional strategies for making your speech memorable.

Build in Redundancy

Seldom do writers need to repeat themselves. If readers don't quite understand a passage, they can go back and read it again. However, most speech teachers advise their students to structure their speeches as follows:

1. *Tell them what you're going to tell them.* In the introduction of your speech, provide a broad overview of the purpose of your message. Identify the major points you will present.
2. *Tell them.* In the body of your speech, develop each of the main points mentioned during your introduction.
3. *Tell them what you've told them.* Finally, in your conclusion, summarize the key ideas discussed in the body of your speech.

Use Adult Learning Principles

People remember what is important to them, so it is not surprising that one key to making your message memorable is to adapt it to your listeners. If your audience comprises adult listeners, you should make sure that you deliver your message in the way that adults learn best. **Adult learning principles** suggest that adults prefer the following:[19]

- Relevant information that they can use immediately
- Active involvement in the learning process
- Connections between the new information and their life experiences

adult learning principles
Preferences of adult learners for what and how they learn.

Most people with office jobs have in-boxes (or "in-piles") on their desks, where they place work that needs to be done. Similarly, adult learners tend to have "mental in-boxes"; as audience members, they have mental agendas of what they want or need to gain from listening to a speech. Remember these characteristics of adult learners, as well as the importance of adapting your message to others. If you tailor your information to address *their* agenda, you will make your message memorable and also have more success in informing your audience.

Reinforce Key Ideas Verbally

Suppose you have four suggestions for helping your listeners chair a meeting, and your last suggestion is the most important one. How can you make sure that your audience knows that? Just tell them. You can reinforce an idea by using a phrase such as "This is the most important point" or "Be sure to remember this next point; it's the most crucial one." Be careful, however, not to overuse this technique. If you claim that every other point is a key point, soon your audience will not believe you.

Reinforce Key Ideas Nonverbally

You can also signal the importance of a point with nonverbal emphasis. Gestures can accent or emphasize key phrases, just as italics do in written communication. A well-placed pause can emphasize and reinforce a point. Pausing just before or after you make an important point will focus attention on your thought. Raising or lowering your voice can also reinforce a key idea.

Movement can also help to emphasize major ideas. Moving from behind the lectern to tell a personal anecdote can signal that something special and more intimate is about to be shared. Remember that your movement and gestures should be meaningful and natural, rather than seeming arbitrary or forced. Your need to emphasize an idea can provide the motivation to make a meaningful movement.

The sample informative speech about a person (Elvis Presley) that appears at the end of this chapter is organized chronologically. In this speech, student speaker Angelitta Armijo applies a number of strategies for making an informative speech clear, interesting, and memorable:

- *Clear.* Angelitta makes her speech clear by providing signposts at strategic points to give her audience opportunities to process new information.
- *Interesting.* Angelitta took an important step in making her speech interesting when she initially selected her topic. By speaking on a subject in which she is personally interested and to which her listeners can relate, Angelitta captures and sustains their attention.
- *Memorable.* Finally, Angelitta makes her speech memorable by relating key information to her listeners and using main ideas to focus that information, by dramatizing statistics, and by closing with a line that her listeners will relate to Elvis.

RECAP

Strategies for Making an Informative Speech Memorable

Build in redundancy.

Use adult learning principles.

Reinforce key ideas verbally.

Reinforce key ideas nonverbally.

Sample Informative Speech

Elvis

Angelitta Armijo[20]
Texas State University

Can you imagine being a singer with 150 different albums and singles that have been certified gold, platinum, or multiplatinum? Neither can I. But according to Elvis.com, that's the reality for Elvis Presley.

Although Elvis is no longer with us, his influence on the rock industry remains prevalent today. After all, he paved the way for groups such as the Beatles and Led Zeppelin. I personally have been an Elvis fan for as long as I can remember. I grew up on him, and I own many of his albums on CD, cassette, and vinyl. I also own every movie that he's ever starred in, including some of his TV specials, which I'll talk about later.

Elvis Presley was an American kid who grew up on the wrong side of the tracks and later became the King of Rock 'N' Roll. To better understand Elvis, you need to know about his early days of life before he was famous, his early career, and his shift in career focus, which was prevalent until the end of his life.

Let's begin with Elvis's humble beginnings. Elvis was born into a poor family, but he kept his eyes on his dreams and his love of music. Elvis Aaron Presley was born January 8, 1935, in Tupelo, Mississippi, to Gladys and Vernon Presley. Actually, Elvis was born as a twin but his brother, Jesse Garon, died at birth, leaving Elvis to be raised as an only child, according to the A&E Network. Also according to A&E Network, Elvis was very dedicated to his family and especially to his mother, whom he loved very much. His family encouraged him to be active in church, and it was in church that he discovered his love of singing and music. When he was ten years old, he received his first guitar, and throughout his childhood and young adult life, he was involved in many talent shows.

According to Elvis.com, the family moved to Memphis in 1948 to seek financial and job security. Soon after graduating high school in 1953 in Memphis, Elvis became a truck driver. It was during his truck driving years that Elvis recorded a few songs at Sun Records for his mother for her birthday. It was at Sun Records where his career began, because Sam Phillips asked him to record more songs, in hopes of finding a star.

So now that you know about Elvis's beginnings, we can discuss his rise to fame and early successes. Elvis's career began at Sun Records and grew as his fans wanted to see him on stage, on TV, and on the silver screen. According to *Rolling Stone*, one of the recordings requested by Sam Phillips, "That's Alright Momma," became Elvis's first single in 1954. This single, and many of Elvis's other singles, showed the influence of blues music, which he discovered in Memphis. By 1955, Elvis was signed to RCA, a premier record label. In 1956, his first album was released, titled *Elvis Presley*. According to Elvis.com, this record was #1 on the Billboard Pop Charts for 10 weeks and was also Elvis's first gold album, selling over a million copies.

Throughout the rest of the '50s, Elvis appeared on many variety shows such as the *Ed Sullivan Show* and starred in his first movie, *Love Me Tender*. In 1960, after two years in the army, Elvis taped a special *Welcome Home Elvis* edition of Frank Sinatra's TV show. He received $125,000 for appearing on the show—which, according to Elvis.com, was a record sum of money for an appearance at that time. According to IMDb, Elvis released 27 films throughout the '60s. This was obviously his career focus at that time. He also put out many soundtracks for these movies; some of them include *GI Blues*, *Blue Hawaii*, and *Viva Las Vegas*.

Angelitta introduces her speech with a rhetorical question.

Angelitta establishes a motive for her audience to listen to her by sharing her personal interest in Elvis.

Angelitta previews the three main ideas of her presentation, organized chronologically.

Angelitta provides her audience with details about Elvis's early life, having selected those that influenced his music career.

Angelitta provides a signpost to summarize her first main idea and preview her second one.

Angelitta knows that the key to making an effective biographical speech is to be selective. To support her second main idea, she has selected the key events of Elvis's meteoric rise to fame.

(continued)

Sample Informative Speech *(continued)*

After covering Elvis's early life and career, we can now discuss his career change. The obvious shift from movies to music came with Elvis's 1968 *Comeback Tour Special*, initially entitled *Elvis*. Elvis used the 1968 *Comeback Special* to be taken more seriously, and he ended the special on a personal note, by closing with the song *If I Can Dream*. This song was in response to the tragedies that had occurred in the 1960s, such as the assassination of JFK, Martin Luther King Jr., and Bobby Kennedy, all men whom Elvis respected. This was a sign he was ready to be taken more seriously. His movies changed as well; he finished up his acting career with a few movies that were less cheesy and had more serious plots.

In 1973, Elvis made history. His *Aloha from Hawaii Special* was broadcast via satellite to 40 countries and viewed by 1 to 1.5 billion people, according to Elvis.com. Also according to Elvis.com, 51% of Americans viewed the *Aloha from Hawaii Special*. That means it was seen in more American households than the walk on the moon was! Elvis continued to sell out shows and venues such as Madison Square Garden and Las Vegas until his career ended in 1977 with his death.

You can see that Elvis's life is something for the history books. He came from humble beginnings and catapulted himself into a thriving career to become the King of Rock 'N' Roll. Now you know about his life before fame, his early fame and rise to stardom, and a career shift that he focused on. Now—as Elvis would say—"Thank you, thank you very much."

Angelitta provides another signpost to summarize her second main idea and preview her third one.

Again, Angelitta is selective in relating details about Elvis's later career, focusing on those that emphasize the increasingly serious nature of his work.

Having provided data about the viewership of Elvis's 1973 *Aloha from Hawaii Special*, Angelitta makes these numbers more dramatic for her listeners by comparing them with the numbers of American households who watched the first moon walk.

After summarizing her main ideas, Angelitta provides closure to her speech with Elvis's signature sign-off.

STUDY GUIDE:

❯ REVIEW, APPLY, AND ASSESS ────────

Types of Informative Speeches

14.1 Describe five types of informative speeches.

REVIEW: There are five basic types of informative speeches. A speech about an object might be about anything tangible, whereas a speech about a procedure discusses how something works or describes a process that produces a particular outcome. Speeches about people can be about either the famous or the little known. Speeches about events describe major occurrences or personal experiences and speeches about ideas are often abstract and generally discuss principles, concepts, or theories.

KEY TERM:
inform

APPLY: Which type of informative speech have you heard most often? Which type do you think you are most likely to give?

Strategies for Organizing Your Informative Speech

14.2 Identify and use appropriate strategies for organizing informative speeches.

REVIEW: Strategies for organizing your informative speech will vary according to the type of informative speech and your specific purpose. A speech about an object may be organized topically, chronologically, or spatially. A speech about a procedure will usually be organized chronologically. Speeches about either people or events are also usually organized chronologically but can be organized topically. A speech about an idea will probably be organized topically.

APPLY: How could you organize a speech about a brain-imaging project in which you have been involved?

ASSESS: Use the following checklist to assess the *organization* of an informative speech you have developed for your communication class:

_____ Introduction that states the central idea

_____ Body organized in a logical way

_____ Conclusion that restates the central idea and provides closure

Strategies for Making Your Informative Speech Clear

14.3 Identify and use strategies for making informative speeches clear.

REVIEW: To make your message clear, use simple rather than complex ideas, pace the flow of your information, and relate new information to old ideas.

ASSESS: Use the following checklist to assess the *clarity* of an informative speech you have developed for your communication class:

_____ Clear, one-sentence declarative central idea

_____ Main ideas relate to the central idea as natural divisions, reasons, or chronological steps

_____ Preview of main ideas in the speech's introduction

_____ Main ideas developed in the body of the speech

_____ Summary of the main ideas in the speech's conclusion

Strategies for Making Your Informative Speech Interesting

14.4 Identify and use strategies for making informative speeches interesting.

REVIEW: To increase interest in your speech, relate information to your listeners' interests, find and use attention-getting supporting material, establish a motive for your audience to listen to you, use vivid word pictures, create intriguing and clear presentation aids, and use humor appropriately.

KEY TERM:
word picture

APPLY: Think about something you have seen or experienced recently. Draft a word picture that describes the image or experience.

ASSESS: Before giving a speech to your class in which you share a humorous or interesting story that includes information about a friend, should you ask that friend's permission? Explain your answer.

335

Strategies for Making Your Informative Speech Memorable

14.5   Identify and use strategies for making informative speeches memorable.

REVIEW: To make messages memorable, build in some redundancy (tell your audience what you're going to tell them, tell them, and then tell them what you've told them), apply principles of adult learning, and reinforce key ideas both verbally and nonverbally.

KEY TERM:
adult learning principles

APPLY: What strategies does your public speaking teacher use in class to make information memorable?

ASSESS: Use the following checklist to help ensure that an informative speech you have developed for your communication class is *memorable*:

_____ Adapted to the needs, interests, and background of audience

_____ Evident connection between new information and listeners' life experiences

_____ Redundancy and reinforcement of key ideas

_____ Nonverbal reinforcement of key ideas

〉 THE PRINCIPLE POINTS

Principle One:

Be aware of your communication with yourself and others.

- To determine how best to organize your message, be conscious of the type of informative speech you are developing (speech about an object, a procedure, a person, an event, or an idea).
- Be mindful of strategies that will make your informative messages clear, interesting, and memorable.

Principle Two:

Effectively use and interpret verbal messages.

- Use supporting material such as stories, examples, and illustrations to gain and maintain attention.
- Create word pictures to make images and stories interesting and memorable.
- Pace the flow of the information you present to enhance message clarity.
- Relate new information to old information to increase clarity and retention.
- To help make your message memorable, reinforce ideas verbally.
- Use simple rather than complex ideas to make your message clear.
- Build in message redundancy to enhance message retention.

Principle Three:

Effectively use and interpret nonverbal messages.

- Use presentation aids to make messages clear, interesting, and memorable.
- Observe the nonverbal behavior of your audience to help you determine whether your message has been communicated clearly.
- Nonverbally reinforce ideas to make your message memorable.

Principle Four:

Listen and respond thoughtfully to others.

- Before you deliver your speech to an audience, talk and listen to audience members to help you customize your message for them.

Principle Five:

Appropriately adapt messages to others.

- To enhance message clarity, adapt the structure and flow of your speech to your listeners.

SPEAKING TO PERSUADE

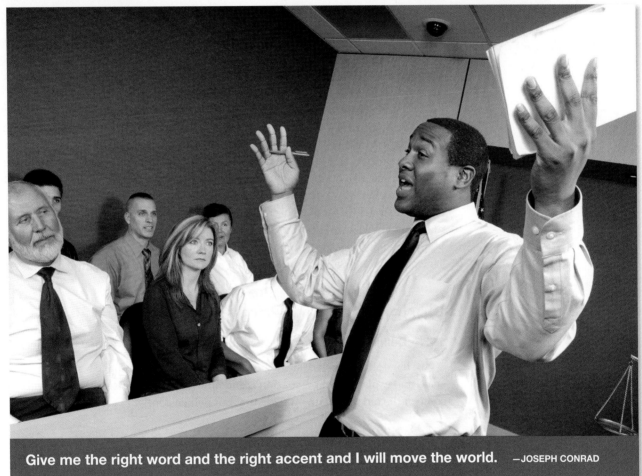

Give me the right word and the right accent and I will move the world. —JOSEPH CONRAD

Junial Enterprises/Shutterstock

→ CHAPTER OUTLINE

- Understanding Persuasion
- Developing Your Audience-Centered Persuasive Speech
- Supporting Your Persuasive Message with Credibility, Logic, and Emotion

- Organizing Your Persuasive Message
- Adapting Ideas to People and People to Ideas
- Study Guide: Review, Apply, and Assess

LEARNING OBJECTIVES

After studying this chapter, you should be able to

15.1 Define persuasion and describe five ways listeners may be motivated.

15.2 Explain how to select and narrow a persuasive topic, identify a persuasive purpose, and develop and support a persuasive proposition.

15.3 Use credibility, logical reasoning, and emotional appeals to make your persuasive speech more effective.

15.4 Organize your persuasive message.

15.5 Provide specific suggestions for adapting to receptive audiences, neutral audiences, and unreceptive audiences.

You don't have to be an attorney, an advertiser, or a politician to use the highly valued skill of persuasion. Whether you're asking your roommate to help you clean the kitchen, seeking an extension on your term paper from your professor, or trying to convince your city council to support a library expansion, you too need the power to persuade.

In 333 BCE, Aristotle was among the first to write a comprehensive guide to persuasion. His work, *Rhetoric*, was used by other Greek and Roman writers who sought to summarize principles and strategies of persuasion. The chapter you are reading draws on some of that classic advice and updates it with contemporary research. We first define persuasion, noting how it is both similar to and different from informing others. We then explore how persuasion works by explaining how to motivate an audience. We also offer strategies for developing a persuasive speech; present ideas to help you organize your persuasive message; provide methods to help you move an audience with your credibility, logic, reasoning, and emotional appeals; and help you adapt your message not only to receptive audiences but also to those who are neutral or unreceptive.

Understanding Persuasion

15.1 Define persuasion and describe five ways listeners may be motivated.

As we have already noted, since the time of Aristotle, people have been trying to understand and explain what persuasion is and how it works. In this section, we will examine some of the most fundamental ideas about persuasion.

Persuasion Defined

Persuasion is the process of attempting to change or reinforce attitudes, beliefs, values, or behavior. When we persuade, we are urging someone to modify or maintain the way he or she thinks, feels, or behaves.

Using force to achieve your goal is **coercion**, not persuasion. Weapons, threats, and other unethical strategies may momentarily achieve what you want, but such means are certainly not appropriate or ethical. Efforts to persuade should be grounded in giving people options, rather than forcing them to respond in a certain way.

The Psychology of Persuasion

How does persuasion work? What makes you dial the phone to have a piping hot pepperoni pizza delivered to your door after you watch a television commercial for pizza? What motivates people to do things that they wouldn't do unless they were persuaded to do so? Let's look at five explanations of why people respond to efforts to persuade.

persuasion
The process of attempting to change or reinforce a listener's attitudes, beliefs, values, or behavior.

coercion
The use of force to get another person to think or behave as you wish; coercion is unethical because it takes away free choice.

COMMUNICATION & ETHICS

Hidden Agendas

David told a group of local businesspeople at a Chamber of Commerce meeting that he wanted to inform them about some of the new and exciting ideas his startup software company was developing. His real purpose, however, was to get people to invest in his company. Was it ethical of David not to tell his listeners that he really wanted them to become investors? Why or why not?

Cognitive Dissonance   When you are presented with information that is inconsistent with your current attitudes, beliefs, values, or behavior, you experience a kind of mental discomfort called **cognitive dissonance**. For example, if you frequently drive when you are drowsy and then learn that driving when drowsy is a major contributor to traffic accidents, this theory predicts that you will experience cognitive dissonance. The incompatibility between your customary behavior and your new knowledge will make you feel uncomfortable. Your discomfort may prompt you to change your thoughts, likes or dislikes, feelings, or behavior so that you can restore your comfort level or sense of balance. In this case, you may decide to stop driving when drowsy.

cognitive dissonance
The sense of mental disorganization or imbalance that may prompt a person to change when new information conflicts with previously organized thought patterns.

Skilled persuasive speakers know that creating dissonance and then offering their listeners a way to restore balance is an effective persuasive strategy. For example, student speaker Sean wants to persuade his listeners to take greater safety precautions in preparing food. He begins by focusing on the health threat posed by bacteria in even the cleanest kitchens:

> Right now, as you sit and listen to me speak about kitchen bacteria, millions of them are probably reproducing in your kitchen, simply waiting for the perfect opportunity to join you for lunch.[1]

Sean is deliberately creating dissonance. He knows that his audience members value their health and that they have always assumed their kitchens to be relatively clean. His next task is to restore his listeners' sense of balance. He assures them that solutions exist and that "they are simple and you can start them as early as today." If the audience members implement such simple actions as washing their hands frequently, using paper towels, and washing sponges and dishcloths along with the dishes, they can resolve their dissonance and once again feel secure about their kitchen safety. The need to resolve dissonance provides one explanation of why people may respond to a speaker's attempts to persuade.

Needs   Need is one of the best motivators. A shopper who just broke the heel off a shoe is much more likely to buy new shoes than someone who is just browsing. When you are a speaker, the better you understand what your listeners need, the better you can adapt to them. And the more you can adapt, the greater the chance that you can persuade them to change an attitude, belief, or value or get them to take some action.

The classic theory that outlines our basic needs was developed by Abraham Maslow.[2] If you've taken a psychology course, you have undoubtedly encountered this theory, which has important applications for persuasion. Maslow suggested that a **hierarchy of needs**, illustrated in Figure 15.1, motivates the behavior of all people:

hierarchy of needs
Abraham Maslow's classic theory that humans have five levels of needs and that lower-level needs must be met before people can be concerned about higher-level needs.

- *Physiological needs.* At the bottom of the hierarchy are basic physiological needs (such as needs for food, water, and air), which have to be satisfied before we can attend to any other concern.
- *Safety needs.* Once our physiological needs have been met, we think next about safety needs. We need to feel safe and be able to protect those we love.
- *Social needs.* If we are comfortable and secure, we attend next to social needs, including the need to be loved and the need to belong to a group.

FIGURE 15.1 Maslow's Hierarchy of Needs

SOURCE : Maslow, Abraham (1954). *Motivation and Personality.* New York: HarperCollins.

- *Self-esteem needs.* The next level of need is for self-esteem, or our judgment of self-worth.
- *Self-actualization needs.* Finally, if the first four levels of need have been satisfied, we may attend to the need for self-actualization, or achieving our highest potential.

Understanding and applying the hierarchy of needs helps you adapt to your audience. One practical application is to do everything in your power to ensure that your audience's physiological needs are met. For example, if your listeners are sweating and fanning themselves, they are unlikely to be very interested in whether Bigfoot exists or whether the city should reopen River Park. If you can turn on the air conditioning or fans, you will

stand a greater chance of persuading your audience than if you continue your speech in that stifling atmosphere.

Another way you can apply the hierarchy of needs is by appealing to an audience's basic need for safety. For example, Mike knows that most of his audience members have young friends or family members who routinely ride school buses. As he begins to talk about the problem of safety hazards on school buses, he appeals to the audience's need to protect those they love.

Fear Appeals   One of the oldest ways to convince people to change their minds or their behavior is by scaring them into compliance. Fear works. The appeal to fear often takes the form of a verbal message—an "if–then" statement. *If* you do (or don't do) X, *then* something awful will happen to you:

- If you don't get a flu shot, then you will probably catch the flu.
- If you text and drive, then you are more likely to die in an automobile accident.
- If you smoke cigarettes, then you are at greater risk for lung cancer.

These statements are all examples of fear appeals. A variety of research studies support the principles outlined in Figure 15.2 for using fear as a motivator.[3]

The effectiveness of fear appeals is based on both cognitive dissonance and Maslow's hierarchy of needs. The fear aroused creates dissonance. Taking action reduces the fear and can meet a need, such as living a long life, being safe from harm, having good friends, or achieving a fulfilling career.

Of course, you have an ethical responsibility not to overstate your case or fabricate evidence when using a fear appeal. The persuader always has an ethical responsibility to be truthful when trying to arouse fear in the listener.

Positive Motivation   A political candidate's Facebook page declares: "Vote for me! You'll have lower taxes and higher wages, and your children will be better educated." Does this politician's promise sound familiar? It sounds like what most politicians offer: better days ahead if you'll vote for that candidate. Politicians, salespeople, and most other successful persuaders know that one way to change or reinforce your attitudes, beliefs, values, or behavior is to use positive motivation.

Positive motivational appeals are verbal messages promising that good things will happen if the speaker's advice is followed. The key to using positive motivation is to know what your listeners value. Most Americans value a comfortable, prosperous life; stimulating, exciting activity; a sense of accomplishment; world, community, and

FIGURE 15.2 Using Fear to Motivate Listeners

Make the threat applicable to listeners' loved ones.	*"If your parents don't have a smoke alarm in their house, they are ten times more likely to die in a house fire."*
Make the threat credible.	*"Doctors agree that lack of sleep poses a threat to students' health and academic performance."*
Make the threat imminent.	*"An overly fatty diet coupled with lack of exercise is the primary cause of heart disease in the United States. Eat less fat and get more exercise, or you may die prematurely."*
Make the threat strong.	*"After the category 5 hurricane comes ashore, most of the coastal area will remain uninhabitable for weeks if not months."*

elaboration likelihood model (ELM)

A contemporary theory that people can be persuaded both directly and indirectly.

▼ According to the elaboration likelihood model, we are often persuaded by indirect factors that are not central to the product or message. What indirect factors do the advertisers of this product hope will persuade shoppers to buy it? Vladimir Wrangel/Fotolia

personal peace; and overall happiness and contentment. In a persuasive speech, you can motivate your listeners to respond to your message by describing what advantages they will experience if they follow your advice.

The Elaboration Likelihood Model (ELM) One of the newest frameworks for understanding persuasion is called the **elaboration likelihood model (ELM)**.[4] ELM theory, which focuses on how audience members interpret persuasive messages, includes a category of factors that researchers call *indirect* or *peripheral*. If you respond to the catchy music, creative logo, or attractive spokesperson in an advertisement, you have been indirectly persuaded. When hearing a speech by one of your classmates, you may be influenced by the speaker's stylish outfit or impressive PowerPoint template. If you can't identify exactly why you were persuaded, you were probably persuaded by peripheral factors.

Advertisers have long been aware of the effectiveness of indirect persuasion. One researcher points out,

> In current advertising practice, it is rare to find magazine ads that lead off with a direct verbal claim such as "[Brand X] gets clothes clean." Instead of straightforward claims that a brand possesses some attribute or delivers some benefit, one encounters pictures of . . . measuring cups full of blue sky.[5]

Like consumers, voters can also be persuaded indirectly—by a political party preference, or by a candidate's favorability or image.[6]

Because ELM theory is a more audience-centered model than other persuasive theories, it can be especially valuable in helping you understand how you have been indirectly persuaded. And as a speaker, you should be aware of any peripheral factors that could be adapted to influence your listeners, such as your delivery, appearance, and general impression of preparedness.

Developing Your Audience-Centered Persuasive Speech

15.2 Explain how to select and narrow a persuasive topic, identify a persuasive purpose, and develop and support a persuasive proposition.

Now that you have an understanding of what persuasion is and is not, you're probably wondering how best to develop a persuasive message. The audience-centered model of public speaking, which we introduced in Chapter 11, can help you design and deliver a persuasive speech, just as it can an informative one. As Figure 15.3 illustrates, you should prepare for a persuasive speech in the same way that you would for any speech: by considering the needs, interests, and background of your audience. Ethically adapting to listeners is important in any communication situation, but it is especially important in persuading others.

Narrowing Your Topic

As with any speech, after you've thought about your audience, the next step is to select and narrow your topic. The best persuasive topic is one about which you feel strongly. If your listeners sense that you are committed to, and excited about, your topic, chances are that they will be interested and involved as well.

The principle of appropriately adapting messages to others can help guide your choice of a persuasive topic. Know the local, state, national, and international issues that interest and affect your listeners:

* Should the city build a new power plant?
* Should convicted child molesters be permitted to live in any neighborhood they like?
* Should the United States drop economic sanctions against Iran?

These and other significant controversial issues make excellent persuasive speech topics. Avoid frivolous topics, such as "why you should make your own potholders," when so many important issues challenge the world and your listeners.

Remain informed about important issues of the day. Blogs, Facebook posts, and tweets can provide ideas for persuasive speeches. Other potential sources include talk radio, daily newspapers, and online news sites. After you have chosen a topic for your persuasive message, staying up to date on current events can help you narrow your topic and find interesting and appropriate supporting material for your speech.

FIGURE 15.3 Audience-Centered Model of the Public Speaking Process

Identifying Your Purpose

Attitudes, beliefs, and values, identified in Chapter 2 as components of a person's self-concept, are also integral to understanding how to persuade others.

FIGURE 15.4   Targeting Attitudes, Beliefs, and Values in Specific Purpose Statements

Attitudes—our likes and dislikes—are much more likely to change than are our beliefs or values. Our sense of what is right and wrong—our values—are least likely to change.

| Attitude

A learned predisposition to respond favorably or unfavorably to something | • At the end of my speech, the audience will favor making downtown streets one-way to regulate traffic flow.
• At the end of my speech, the audience will agree that the community needs a new elementary school. |
| Belief

Ways in which you structure reality | • At the end of my speech, the audience will testify that ghosts exist.
• At the end of my speech, the audience will acknowledge that the increase in highway traffic deaths is related to the increase in the speed limit for large trucks. |
| Value

Enduring concepts of right and wrong | • At the end of my speech, the audience will campaign for the Green Party ticket in the upcoming election.
• At the end of my speech, the audience will support the right of art museums to display whatever kinds of art the museum directors deem appropriate. |

When your general purpose is to persuade, your specific purpose should target your listeners' attitudes, beliefs, or values, or their behavior.

Figure 15.4 defines attitudes, beliefs, and values; provides examples of specific purpose statements that target each one; and illustrates that attitudes lie fairly close to the surface of our convictions, with values the most deeply ingrained in the center of the model.

Be aware of whether your specific purpose targets an attitude, a belief, a value, or a behavior, and be realistic in assessing what you will need to do in your speech to effect change. Recall, too, from our definition of *persuasion* that you can try to *reinforce* attitudes, beliefs, values, and behavior that audience members already hold, or you can try to *change* their attitudes, beliefs, values, or behavior. Reinforcing what listeners already know or think is relatively easy; it's more of a challenge to change their minds.

Developing Your Central Idea as a Persuasive Proposition

After clarifying their specific purpose, most persuasive speakers find it useful to cast their central idea as a **proposition**, a statement with which they want their audience to agree. A well-worded proposition is a verbal message that can help you fine-tune your persuasive objective and develop strategies for convincing your audience that your proposition is true. There are three categories of propositions: propositions of fact, propositions of value, and propositions of policy. Let's examine each type in more detail.

Propositions of Fact   A **proposition of fact** is a claim that something is or is not the case or that something did or did not happen. A speaker who uses a proposition of fact as the central idea of a persuasive speech focuses on changing or reinforcing the listeners' beliefs—what they think is true.

Propositions of Value   As the word *value* suggests, a **proposition of value** calls for the listener to judge the worth or importance of something. A simple example is "Tattoos are beautiful." Other value propositions compare two ideas, things, or actions and suggest that one is better than the other.

proposition
A claim with which you want your audience to agree.

proposition of fact
A claim that something is or is not the case or that something did or did not happen.

proposition of value
A claim that calls for the listener to judge the worth or importance of something.

FIGURE 15.5 Persuasive Propositions

Proposition of **Fact**

Asbestos exists in our elementary school.

Proposition of **Value**

Closing the school to remove asbestos is safer than having the work done with the school open.

Proposition of **Policy**

We should close the elementary school for six months while asbestos is removed from the building.

Propositions of Policy The third type of proposition, the proposition of policy, advocates a specific action, such as changing a regulation, procedure, or behavior. **Propositions of policy** include the word *should*.

Figure 15.5 provides an example of each of the three types of persuasive propositions.

With your specific purpose and central idea in hand, you are ready to move to the next stages in the public speaking process. In most cases, you can draw your main ideas from several reasons *why* the persuasive proposition is true. Then you will be ready to begin selecting supporting material.

proposition of policy
A claim advocating a specific action to change a regulation, procedure, or behavior.

rhetoric
The process of discovering the available means of persuasion.

ethos
The credibility or ethical character of a speaker.

logos
Logical arguments.

pathos
Emotional appeals.

Supporting Your Persuasive Message with Credibility, Logic, and Emotion

15.3 Use credibility, logical reasoning, and emotional appeals to make your persuasive speech more effective.

Aristotle defined **rhetoric** as the process of "discovering the available means of persuasion."[7] What exactly are those "available means"? They are the various strategies you can use to support your persuasive proposition. Aristotle suggested three: (1) **ethos**, emphasizing the credibility or ethical character of a speaker; (2) **logos**, using logical arguments; and (3) **pathos**, using emotional appeals to move an audience.

Ethos: Establishing Your Credibility

If you were going to buy a new computer, to whom would you turn for advice? Perhaps you would consult your brother, who is a computer geek, or your roommate, who is a computer science major? Alternatively, you could seek advice from *Consumer Reports*, a monthly publication providing reviews and ratings of various consumer products. In other words, you would turn to a source that you consider credible.

For centuries, teachers and researchers have sought to understand the factors that audiences consider in deciding whether a speaker is credible. Aristotle thought that a public speaker should be ethical, possess good character, display common sense, and be concerned for the well-being of his audience. Quintilian, a Roman teacher of public speaking, advised that a speaker should be "a good man speaking well." These ancient speculations about the elements that enhance a speaker's credibility are reflected in our modern understanding of **credibility**. When you give a speech, your credibility depends upon the audience's perception of your competence, trustworthiness, and dynamism. Your listeners, not you, determine whether you have credibility.

credibility
An audience's perception of a speaker's competence, trustworthiness, and dynamism.

competence
An aspect of a speaker's credibility that reflects whether the speaker is perceived as informed, skilled, and knowledgeable.

Competence One clear factor in credibility is **competence**. A speaker should be informed, skilled, or knowledgeable about the subject he or she is discussing. You will be more persuasive if you can convince your listeners that you know something about your topic. How can you do that?

You can use verbal messages effectively by talking about your relevant personal experience with the topic. If you have taken and enjoyed a cruise, for instance, you can tell your audience about the highlights of your trip. You can also cite evidence to support your ideas. Even if you have not taken a cruise yourself, you can be prepared with information about what a good value a cruise is—how much it costs and what is included—in comparison to how much the same trip would cost if one were to travel by air and stay and eat in hotels.

Trustworthiness A second factor in credibility is **trustworthiness**. While delivering a speech, you need to convey honesty and sincerity to your audience. You cannot simply say, "Trust me." You have to earn the audience's trust by demonstrating that you are interested in and experienced with your topic. Again, speaking from personal experience makes you appear to be a more trustworthy speaker. Conversely, having something to gain by persuading your listeners may make you suspect in their eyes, which is why salespeople and politicians often lack credibility; if you do what they say, they will clearly benefit by earning sales commissions or being elected to public office.

Dynamism A third factor in credibility is a speaker's **dynamism**, or energy. Dynamism is often projected through delivery. If we apply the communication principle of using and understanding nonverbal messages effectively, a speaker who maintains eye contact, has enthusiastic vocal inflection, and moves and gestures purposefully is likely to be seen as dynamic. **Charisma** is a form of dynamism. A charismatic speaker possesses charm, talent, magnetism, and other qualities that make the person attractive and energetic. Many people considered President Franklin Roosevelt and Pope John Paul II charismatic speakers.

▲ Audiences often perceive a dynamic, charismatic speaker, such as this one, as credible. What steps can you take to be more dynamic in your delivery, or to assure your audience of your competence or trustworthiness? Stockbyte/Getty Images

Stages of Credibility You have opportunities before, during, and after your speech to enhance your credibility. **Initial credibility** is the impression your listeners have of you before you even begin to speak. They grant you initial credibility on the basis of such factors as your appearance and your credentials. **Derived credibility** is the perception your listeners form as you deliver your speech. And **terminal credibility** is the perception of your credibility that your listeners have when you finish your speech. Figure 15.6 provides specific suggestions for enhancing your credibility at each of these three stages.

trustworthiness

An aspect of a speaker's credibility that reflects whether the speaker is perceived as believable and honest.

dynamism

An aspect of a speaker's credibility that reflects whether the speaker is perceived as energetic.

charisma

Talent, charm, and attractiveness.

initial credibility

The impression of a speaker's credibility that listeners have before the speaker begins to speak.

derived credibility

The impression of a speaker's credibility based on what the speaker says and does during the speech.

terminal credibility

The final impression listeners have of a speaker's credibility, after the speech has been concluded.

FIGURE 15.6 Enhancing Your Credibility

To enhance **initial credibility** (before you speak) → To enhance **derived credibility** (as you speak) → To enhance **terminal credibility** (after you speak)

- Dress appropriately
- Prepare a summary of your qualifications for the person who introduces you.

- Establish common ground with listeners.
- Support your arguments with evidence.
- Organize your message well.

- Prepare a strong conclusion.
- Deliver your conclusion well.
- Maintain eye contact after your closing sentence.

Logos: Using Evidence and Reasoning

In addition to being considered a credible speaker, you will gain influence with your audience if you can effectively use logically structured arguments supported with evidence. As we noted earlier, Aristotle called logical arguments *logos*, which, translated from Greek, means "the word." Using words effectively to communicate your arguments to your listeners is vital to persuading thoughtful and informed listeners.[8]

The goal is to provide logical proof for your arguments. **Proof** consists of both evidence and reasoning. **Evidence** is another word for the illustrations, definitions, statistics, and opinions that are your supporting material. **Reasoning** is the process of drawing conclusions from your evidence. There are three major ways to draw logical conclusions: inductively, deductively, and causally.

proof
Evidence plus reasoning.

evidence
The material used to support a point or premise.

reasoning
The process of drawing a conclusion from evidence.

inductive reasoning
Using specific instances or examples to reach a probable general conclusion.

reasoning by analogy
A special kind of inductive reasoning that draws a comparison between two ideas, things, or situations that share some essential common feature.

Inductive Reasoning   Reasoning that arrives at a general conclusion from specific instances or examples is known as **inductive reasoning**. You reason inductively when you claim that a conclusion is probably true because of specific evidence.

Reasoning by analogy is a special type of inductive reasoning. An analogy demonstrates how an unfamiliar idea, thing, or situation is similar to something the audience already understands. If you develop an original analogy, rather than quote one you find in a printed source, you are reasoning inductively. Here's an example of reasoning by analogy: Mandatory rear seatbelt laws that were enacted in Missouri saved lives; therefore, Kansas should also develop mandatory rear seatbelt laws. The key to arguing by analogy is to claim that the two things you are comparing (such as driving habits in Missouri and Kansas) are similar, so your argument is sound. Here's another example: England has a relaxed policy toward violence being shown on television and has experienced no major rise in violent crimes; therefore, the United States should relax its policy on showing violence on TV.

deductive reasoning
Moving from a general statement or principle to reach a certain specific conclusion.

syllogism
A three-part argument, including a major premise, a minor premise, and a conclusion.

Deductive Reasoning   Reasoning from a general statement or principle to reach a specific conclusion is called **deductive reasoning**. Deductive reasoning can be structured as a **syllogism**, a three-part argument that consists of a major premise, a minor premise, and a conclusion. For example, if you were attempting to convince your audience to vote for an upcoming school bond issue, your syllogism might look like the following:

MAJOR PREMISE: Keeping schools in good repair extends the number of years that school buildings can be used.

MINOR PREMISE: The proposed school bond issue provides money for school repairs.

CONCLUSION: The proposed school bond issue will extend the number of years that we can use our current school buildings.

Contemporary logicians note that when you reason deductively, the certainty of your conclusion rests primarily on the validity of the major premise and secondarily on the truth of the minor premise. If you can prove that keeping schools in good repair extends the useful life of school buildings, and if it is true that the proposed bond issue provides money for school repairs, your conclusion will be certain.

causal reasoning
Relating two or more events in such a way as to conclude that one or more of the events caused the others.

Causal Reasoning   You use **causal reasoning** when you relate two or more events in such a way as to conclude that one or more of the events probably caused the others. For example, you might argue that public inoculation programs during the twentieth century eradicated smallpox.

As we noted in Chapter 12 when we discussed cause and effect as an organizational strategy, there are two ways to structure a causal argument. One is by reasoning from

COMMUNICATION & DIVERSITY

"Elementary Reasoning, My Dear Watson"

Although we frequently use the word *diversity* to refer to readily discernible differences in sex, race, culture, and age, diversity can also involve differences in perspective or point of view. As the following narrative shows, people may draw different conclusions from the same evidence.

Sherlock Holmes and Dr. Watson went on a camping trip. After a good meal and a bottle of wine, they lay down for the night and went to sleep. Some hours later, Holmes awoke and nudged his faithful friend.

"Watson, look up at the sky and tell me what you see."

Watson replied, "I see millions and millions of stars."

"What does that tell you?" inquired Holmes.

Watson pondered for a minute. "Astronomically, it tells me that there are millions of galaxies and potentially billions of planets. Astrologically, I observe that Saturn is in Leo. Horologically, I deduce that the time is approximately a quarter past three. Theologically, I can see that God is all powerful and that we are small and insignificant. Meteorologically, I suspect that we will have a beautiful day tomorrow. What does it tell you?"

Holmes was silent for a moment and then spoke. "Watson, you idiot! Someone has stolen our tent!"

---

cause to effect—that is, predicting a result from a known fact. For example, you know that it has rained more than an inch over the last few days, so you predict that the aquifer level will rise. The inch of rain is the cause, and the rising aquifer is the effect. The other way to structure a causal argument is by reasoning from a known effect to the cause. National Transportation Safety Board accident investigators reason from effect to cause when they reconstruct airplane wreckage to determine the cause of an air disaster.

The key to developing any causal argument is to be certain that a causal relationship actually exists between the two factors you are investigating. A few summers ago, a young science student took part in a bird population project involving counting chimney swifts in a given area just before sunset. He counted the most chimney swifts on the Fourth of July. It would not have been valid, however, to argue that fireworks (or parades or hot dogs or anything else connected with the Fourth of July) caused an increase in the number of chimney swifts seen in the area. The Fourth of July holiday and the bird count were not related by cause and effect.

Logical Fallacies   Unfortunately, not all people who try to persuade you will use sound evidence and reasoning. Some will try to develop arguments in ways that are irrelevant or inappropriate. Such reasoning is called a **logical fallacy**. To be a better-informed consumer, as well as a more ethical persuasive speaker, you should be aware of some of the following common logical fallacies.

logical fallacy

Attempting to persuade without adequate evidence or with arguments that are irrelevant or inappropriate.

RECAP

Inductive, Deductive, and Causal Reasoning

Type of Reasoning	Reasoning begins with . . .	Reasoning ends with . . .	Conclusion is . . .	Example
Inductive	specific examples	a general conclusion	probable or not probable	Dell, HP, and Acer computers are all reliable. Therefore, PCs are reliable.
Deductive	a general statement	a specific conclusion	certain or not certain	All professors at this college have advanced degrees. Tom Bryson is a professor at this college. Therefore, Tom Bryson has an advanced degree.
Causal	something known	a speculation about causes or effects of what is known	likely or not likely	The number of people with undergraduate degrees has risen steadily since 1960. This increasing number has caused a glut in the job market of people with degrees.

causal fallacy

Making a faulty cause and effect connection between two things or events.

bandwagon fallacy

Suggesting that because everyone believes something or does something, it must be valid, accurate, or effective.

either–or fallacy

Oversimplifying an issue as offering only two choices.

hasty generalization

Reaching a conclusion without adequate supporting evidence.

personal attack

Attacking irrelevant personal characteristics of someone connected with an idea, rather than addressing the idea itself.

red herring

Using irrelevant facts or information to distract someone from the issue under discussion.

appeal to misplaced authority

Using someone without the appropriate credentials or expertise to endorse an idea or product.

non sequitur

Presenting an idea or conclusion that does not logically follow the previous idea or conclusion; Latin for "it does not follow."

- *Causal fallacy.* Trying to link the Fourth of July with the chimney swift count would be an example of a **causal fallacy**, or, to use its Latin term, *post hoc, ergo propter hoc* ("after this; therefore, because of this"). Simply because one event follows another does not mean that the two are related.

- *Bandwagon fallacy.* "Jumping on the bandwagon" is a colloquial expression for thinking or doing something just because everybody else is. Someone who argues that "everybody thinks that, so you should too" is using the **bandwagon fallacy**. Speakers using the bandwagon fallacy often use the word *everybody*:

  Everybody knows that taxes are too high.

  Everybody agrees that the government should support a strong military.

- *Either–or fallacy.* "Either we support the bond issue, or we end up busing our students to another school district!" shouts Lupe in a moment of heated debate among the members of the school board. This **either–or fallacy** ignores the possibility of other solutions to the district's problem of dilapidated buildings (for example, purchasing portable classroom buildings or establishing new attendance zones within the district).

- *Hasty generalization.* A person who draws a conclusion from too little evidence or nonexistent evidence is making a **hasty generalization**. For example, one person's failing a math test does not necessarily mean that the test was too difficult or unfair.

- *Personal attack.* Using a **personal attack** as a substitute for a refutation of issues is also a logical fallacy. This approach is also known as an *ad hominem* argument, a Latin phrase that means "to the man." For example, "The new federal health care plan is a bad idea because it was proposed by that crazy senator" is a personal attack. Do not dismiss an idea solely because you have something against the person who presents it.

- *Red herring.* Someone who argues against an issue by bringing up irrelevant facts or arguments is using a **red herring**. This fallacy takes its name from the old trick of distracting dogs who are following a scent by dragging a smoked herring across a trail. Speakers use a red herring when they want to distract an audience from certain issues. A congressional representative, indicted for misuse of federal funds, would be using a red herring if he or she called a press conference and spent most of the time talking about a colleague's sexual indiscretions.

- *Appeal to misplaced authority.* When advertisers trot out baseball players to endorse breakfast cereal or movie stars to pitch credit cards, they are guilty of an **appeal to misplaced authority**. Although baseball players may know a great deal about the game of baseball, they are no more knowledgeable than most of us about breakfast cereal. Movie stars may be experts at acting, but they probably are not experts in the field of personal finance.

- *Non sequitur.* If you argue that students should give blood because it is nearly time for final exams, you are guilty of using a **non sequitur** (Latin for "it does not follow") because your reason has nothing to do with your argument.

Persuasive speakers who provide logical proof (evidence and reasoning) for their arguments and who avoid logical fallacies heighten their chances for success with their audience. But good speakers also know that evidence and reasoning are not their only tools. Emotion is another powerful strategy for moving an audience to support a persuasive proposition.

Pathos: Using Emotion

People often make decisions based not on logic but on emotion. Advertisers know all about it; just think of soft-drink commercials. There is little rational reason for people to spend any part of their food budget on soft drinks that are "empty calories." So soft-drink advertisers turn instead to emotional appeals, striving to connect feelings of pleasure with their product. Smiling people, upbeat music, and good times are usually part of the formula for selling soft drinks.

One way to make an emotional appeal is with emotion-arousing verbal messages. Words such as *mother, flag, freedom*, and *slavery* trigger emotional responses in listeners. Patriotic slogans, such as "Remember the Alamo" and "Give me liberty, or give me death," are examples of phrases that have successfully aroused emotions in listeners.

Another way to appeal to emotions is to use concrete illustrations and descriptions. Although illustrations and descriptions are themselves types of evidence or supporting material, their effect is often emotional, as in the following example:

> Michelle Hutchinson carefully placed her three-year-old daughter into her child safety seat. She was certain that Dana was secure. Within minutes Michelle was involved in a minor accident, and the seat belt that was never designed to hold a child safety seat allowed the seat to lunge forward, crushing the three-year-old's skull on the dash. Dana died three days later.[9]

Effective use of nonverbal messages can also appeal to audience members' emotions. Visual aids—pictures, slides, or video—can provide emotion-arousing images. A photograph of a dirty, ragged child alone in a big city can evoke sadness and pain. A video clip of an airplane crash can arouse fear and horror. A picture of a smiling baby makes most of us smile, too. As a speaker, you can use visual aids to evoke both positive and negative emotions.

When you use emotional appeals, you have an obligation to be ethical and forthright. Making false claims, misusing evidence or images, or relying exclusively on emotion without any evidence or reasoning violates standards of ethical public speaking.

Give me Liberty or Give me Death!!

©Glenn and Gary McCoy/Distributed by Universal Uclick via CartoonStock.com

Glenn and Gary McCoy/CartoonStock

RECAP

Tips for Using Emotion to Persuade

- Use emotion-arousing words.
- Use concrete illustrations and descriptions to create emotional images.
- Use visual aids to evoke both positive and negative emotions.
- Be ethical and forthright. Avoid making false claims, misusing evidence or images, or relying exclusively on emotion.

Organizing Your Persuasive Message

15.4 Organize your persuasive message.

An audience-centered persuasive speaker adapts the organization of the speech to the audience's needs, attitudes, beliefs, behaviors, and background. Most persuasive speeches are organized according to one of four strategies: problem–solution, cause-and-effect, refutation, or the motivated sequence. The first two strategies were also discussed in Chapter 12; the last is a special variation of the problem–solution format.

Problem–Solution

When you use a problem–solution organization for your persuasive message, apply the principle of appropriately adapting messages to others. If you are speaking to an apathetic audience or one that is not aware that a problem exists, emphasize the problem portion of the message. If your audience is already aware of the problem, emphasize the solution or solutions. In either case, your challenge will be to provide ample evidence that your perception of the problem is accurate and reasonable. You'll also need to convince your listeners that the solution or solutions you advocate are the most appropriate ones to solve the problem.

Notice how student speaker Nicholas organizes his speech "The Death of Reading" in a problem–solution pattern:[10]

I. PROBLEM: Reading is a dying activity.
  A. Each year more than 500 courts hear arguments to ban books.
  B. Since 1990, more than 2,000 libraries across America have closed.
  C. Leisure reading has decreased more than 50 percent since 1975.

II. SOLUTIONS:
  A. Teach children that reading as an activity has worth and beauty.
  B. Teach children that books in and of themselves only express ideas and should not be banned.
  C. Support programs such as "One City, One Book" that encourage community involvement and literary discussion.
  D. Give books as gifts.
  E. Allow others to see you read.

The sample persuasive speech at the end of this chapter is an example of a message organized by first stating the problem and then presenting some specific solutions.

Cause and Effect

If two or more situations are causally related, a cause-and-effect strategy can work well for a persuasive speech. Here is an example of a persuasive outline organized from cause to effect:[11]

I. CAUSE: The foster care system is in crisis.
  A. Since 1987, there has been a 90 percent increase in the number of children placed in foster care nationally.
  B. During that same time, there has been a 3 percent decrease in the number of licensed foster homes.

II. EFFECT: Children in foster care are at risk.
  A. Children in the foster care system are five times more likely to die as a result of abuse than children in the general population.
  B. Eighty percent of federal prisoners spent time in our nation's foster care system as children.

▼ This speaker uses a graph to persuade his audience that a new marketing plan has affected profits. How would relating cause and effect help you to persuade your audience? Thinkstock Images/ Getty Images

An effect may have more than one cause. For example, standardized test scores may be low in your state both because of low per-pupil expenditures and because of a lack of parental involvement in the schools. To argue that only one of the two factors causes the low test scores would probably be inaccurate.

It is also possible for two situations to coexist but not be causally related. Suppose that standardized test scores are indeed low in your state and that your state has a lottery. Both situations exist, but one does not cause the other.

Refutation

Refutation is an organizational strategy in which you identify likely objections to your proposition and then refute those objections with arguments and evidence. This third way to organize your persuasive speech is especially useful when you are facing an unreceptive audience—one that does not agree with your point of view or your specific proposition.

refutation

Organization according to objections your listeners may have to your ideas and arguments.

You will be most likely to organize your persuasive message by refutation if you know your listeners' chief objections to your proposition. In fact, if you do not acknowledge such objections, the audience will probably think about them during your speech anyway. Credible facts and statistics will generally be more effective in supporting your points of refutation than will emotional arguments.

One speaker organized a persuasive speech on organ donation by providing the following refutations for four common misconceptions about the process:[12]

I. Anyone who decides to become a donor can reconsider that decision at any time.
II. Doctors will do everything to save the life of an organ donor that they would do for a non-donor.
III. No one who views the body of an organ donor will be able to tell that organs have been removed.
IV. Families of organ donors do not pay for any procedure related to the organ donation.

The Motivated Sequence

The **motivated sequence**, devised by Alan Monroe, is a five-step organizational plan that integrates the problem–solution method with principles that have been confirmed by research and practical experience.[13] The five steps are attention, need, satisfaction, visualization, and action.

motivated sequence

Alan H. Monroe's five-step plan for organizing a persuasive message: attention, need, satisfaction, visualization, and action.

Attention Your first task in applying the motivated sequence is to get your listeners' attention. (This is also the first stage in appropriately adapting your message to others.) You already know attention-getting strategies for introductions: rhetorical questions, illustrations, startling facts or statistics, quotations, humorous stories, and references to historical or recent events. The attention step is, in essence, your application of one of these strategies.

Samin begins his persuasive speech about landmines with this attention-catching illustration:

> In Angola, little Tusnia became yet another one of the town's orphans. She was out in the field playing with her friends when she stumbled onto the ground and screamed. Her mother went running to see what happened, stepped in the wrong place, and was mutilated instantly. Parts from her body were found as far as 30 meters from the explosion site.[14]

Need After getting your audience's attention, establish why your topic, problem, or issue should concern your listeners. Tell your audience about the problem. Adapt your message to them by convincing them that the problem affects them directly. Argue that there is a need for change. During the need step (which corresponds to the problem step in a problem–solution strategy), you should develop logical arguments backed by evidence. At this point, you can create dissonance or use a credible fear appeal to motivate listeners to respond to your solution. Samin outlines his need step as follows:

> Citizens of countries with landmines face two major problems: risk of death or serious injury, and disruption of daily routines.

Satisfaction After you explain and document a need or problem, identify your plan (or solution) and explain how it will satisfy the need. You need not go into painstaking detail. Present enough information for your listeners to gain a general understanding of how the problem may be solved. Samin recommends two solutions in his satisfaction step:

> One possible solution is to spread awareness. Luckily, this process has already been started by the United Nations Children Fund or UNICEF. . . . And a second solution is to teach successful de-mining technology to indigenous populations.

visualization
A word picture of the future.

positive visualization
A word picture of how much better things will be if a solution is implemented.

negative visualization
A word picture of how much worse things will be if a solution is not implemented; a fear appeal.

Visualization   Now you need to give your audience a sense of what it would be like if your solution were adopted or, conversely, not adopted. **Visualization**—a word picture of the future—applies the fundamental principle of using and understanding verbal messages effectively. An appropriate presentation aid can also help your audience visualize the implications of your persuasive message. With a **positive visualization** approach, you paint a rosy picture of how wonderful the future will be if your satisfaction step is implemented. With a **negative visualization** approach, you paint a bleak picture of how terrible the future will be if nothing changes; you use a fear appeal to motivate your listeners to do what you suggest to avoid further problems. You might also combine the two approaches: The problem will be solved if your solution is adopted, but things will get increasingly worse if it is not. An ethical speaker makes sure that the positive or negative visualization message is accurate and not overstated. Samin offers positive visualization to communicate what can happen if his second solution is implemented:

> Perhaps in the future Tusnia can use this technology to start de-mining Angola so that the horrific atrocity that she faced will not happen to anyone else.

Action   The final step of the motivated sequence requires you to adapt your solution to your audience. Offer your listeners some specific action they can take to solve the problem you have discussed. Identify exactly what you want them to do. Give them simple, clear, and easy-to-follow steps. At the end of your speech, provide a web site to go to for more information, an address to which they can write a letter of support, or a petition to sign. Samin suggests a specific action step his listeners can take to solve the problem of landmines:

> First, sign the People's Treaty to Support the Convention on Cluster Munitions, which is a de-mining effort. Second, Help the International Campaign to Ban Landmines by donating money to their cause.

Figure 15.7 illustrates the steps in the motivated sequence. You can adapt this strategy to both your topic and the needs of your audience. For example, if you are speaking to a knowledgeable, receptive audience, you do not need to spend a great deal of time on the need step. Your listeners already know that the need is serious. However, they may feel helpless to do anything about it. In this case, you would want to emphasize the satisfaction and action steps.

On the other hand, if you are speaking to neutral or apathetic audience members, you will need to spend time getting their attention and proving that a problem exists, is significant, and affects them personally. In this case, you will emphasize the attention, need, and visualization steps.

The organizational strategies for persuasive speeches are summarized in Table 15.1. Is there one best way to organize a persuasive message? The answer is no. The organizational strategy you select must depend on your audience, message, and desired objective. Just remember that your decision can have a major effect on your listeners' response to your message.

FIGURE 15.7   The Motivated Sequence

TABLE 15.1 Organizational Patterns for Persuasive Speeches

Organizational Pattern	Definition	Example
Problem–Solution	Organization by discussing a problem and then its various solutions	I. Tooth decay threatens children's dental health. II. Inexpensive, easy-to-apply sealants make teeth resistant to decay.
Cause and Effect	Organization by discussing a situation and its causes, or a situation and its effects	I. Most HMOs refuse to pay for treatment they deem "experimental." II. Patients die who might have been saved by "experimental" treatment.
Refutation	Organization according to objections your listeners may have to your ideas and arguments	I. Although you may think that college football players get too much financial aid, they work hard for it, spending twenty to thirty hours a week in training and on the field. II. Although you may think that college football players don't spend much time on academics, they have two hours of enforced study every weeknight.
Motivated Sequence	Alan H. Monroe's five-step plan for organizing a persuasive message: attention, need, satisfaction, visualization, and action	I. Attention: "An apple a day keeps the doctor busy." What has happened to the old adage about keeping the doctor away? Why has it changed? II. Need: Pesticides are poisoning our fresh fruits and vegetables. III. Satisfaction: Growers must seek environmentally friendly alternatives to pesticides. IV. Visualization: Remember the apple poisoned by Snow White's wicked stepmother? You may be feeding such apples to your own children. V. Action: Buy organically grown fruits and vegetables.

COMMUNICATION & SOCIAL MEDIA

The Motivated Sequence in Advertising

Strategies for organizing persuasive messages are used not just by public speakers but also by advertisers. Many ads use the motivated sequence, at least in part, to persuade.

After you've studied the description of the motivated sequence, search YouTube for a product advertisement that is organized according to the motivated sequence.

Analyze the ad, identify its target audience, and prepare a brief written explanation of how the video uses the motivated sequence. If you have an online class discussion board, post your written analysis and a link to the video.

Be sure to bookmark the video URL, as your instructor may also ask you to be prepared to show the commercial you found to your class, to discuss the target audience, and to present your outline of the motivated sequence.[15]

Adapting Ideas to People and People to Ideas

15.5 Provide specific suggestions for adapting to receptive audiences, neutral audiences, and unreceptive audiences.

Scholar Donald C. Bryant's definition of rhetoric emphasizes the principle of appropriately adapting a message to an audience, which he calls the process of adjusting ideas to people and people to ideas.[16] With this thought, we've now come full circle in the process of developing a persuasive message. As we have emphasized throughout our discussion of public speaking, analyzing your audience members and adapting to them is at the heart of the speech-making process; it's one of the fundamental Communication Principles for a Lifetime. In a persuasive speech, adapting begins with identifying your specific purpose and understanding whether you are trying to change or reinforce attitudes, beliefs, values, or behavior. It continues when you select an organizational strategy.

For example, if your audience members are unreceptive toward your ideas, you might organize your speech by refutation and address their objections directly. In addition, research studies and experienced speakers can offer other useful suggestions to help you adapt to your audience. Let's look at some specific strategies for persuading receptive, neutral, and unreceptive audiences.

The Receptive Audience

It is usually a pleasure to address an audience that already supports you and your message. In these situations, you can explore your ideas in depth and can be fairly certain of a successful appeal to action. The following suggestions can help you engage receptive audience members:

- *Identify with your audience.* Emphasize your similarities and common interests. A good place to do so is often in the introduction of your speech.
- *State your speaking objective overtly.* Tell your audience members exactly what you want them to do, and ask them for an immediate show of support. If your listeners are already receptive, you do not have to worry that being overt will antagonize them. Rather, it will give you more time to rouse them to passionate commitment and action.
- *Use emotional appeals.* If your listeners already support your position, you can spend less time providing detailed evidence and instead focus on using strong emotional appeals to move them to action.

The Neutral Audience

Many audiences will fall somewhere between being wildly enthusiastic and being hostile and will simply be neutral. The listeners' neutrality may take the form of indifference: They know about the topic or issue, but they do not see how it affects them, or they cannot make up their minds about it. Alternatively, their neutrality may take the form of ignorance: They just do not know much about the topic. Regardless of whether they are indifferent or ignorant, your challenge is to get them interested in your message. Otherwise, they may escape by sleeping through your speech or engaging in such self-distracting activities as texting or surfing the web. The following suggestions can help you engage your neutral audience members:

- *Hook your neutral audience with an especially engaging introduction or attention step.* Brian provided such an introduction to his persuasive speech about the number of Americans who live with chronic pain:

    "I can't shower because the water feels like molten lava. Every time someone turns on a ceiling fan, it feels like razor blades are cutting through my legs. I'm dying." Meet David Bogan, financial advisor from Deptford, New Jersey; Porsche, boat, and homeowner; and a victim of a debilitating car accident that has not only rendered him two years of chronic leg pain, but a fall from the pinnacle of success. Bogan has nothing now. Life to him, life with searing pain, is a worthless tease of agony and distress.[17]

- *Appeal to common ground.* Another strategy for persuading neutral audiences is to refer to universal beliefs or common concerns. For example, protecting the environment and having access to good health care might be common concerns.
- *Appeal to your listeners' interests.* Show how the topic affects not only them but also people they care about. For example, parents will be interested in issues and policies that affect their children.
- *Limit your persuasive purpose.* Be realistic about what you can accomplish. People who are neutral at the beginning of your speech are unlikely to change their opinion in just a few minutes. Persuasion is unlikely to occur all at once or after only one presentation of arguments and issues.

The Unreceptive Audience

As a speaker, you will find that one of your biggest challenges is to persuade audience members who are unreceptive toward you or your message. If they are unreceptive toward you personally, you need to find ways to enhance your credibility and persuade them to listen to you. If they are unreceptive toward your point of view, the following strategies may help:

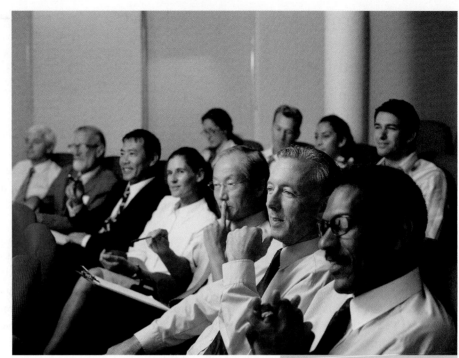

▲ Most audiences will start out fairly neutral toward your persuasive goal. To persuade such an audience, you can establish common ground between their needs and your goals and appeal to their interests. Digital Vision/Photodisc/Getty Images

- *Focus on universal beliefs and concerns.* Do not immediately announce your persuasive purpose. Explicitly telling your unreceptive listeners that you plan to change their minds can make them defensive. Instead, refer to areas of agreement, as you would with a neutral audience. Rather than saying, "I'm here this morning to convince you that we should raise city taxes," you might say, "I think we can agree that we have an important common goal: achieving the best quality of life possible here in our small community."

- *Following the principle of primacy, advance your strongest arguments first.* If you save your best argument for last (the recency principle), your audience may already have stopped listening.

- *Acknowledge the opposing points of view that audience members may hold.* Summarize the reasons they may oppose your point of view; then cite evidence and use arguments to refute the opposition and support your conclusion. In speaking to students seeking to hold down tuition costs, a dean might say, "I am aware that many of you struggle to pay for your education. You work nights, take out loans, and live frugally." Then the dean could go on to identify how the university could provide additional financial assistance to students.

- *Be especially aware of, and effectively use, nonverbal messages.* One study suggests that unreceptive audiences may more negatively evaluate speakers who do not gesture than they do those who use gestures.[18]

In the following persuasive speech on private ambulance companies, Blake Bergeron argues a proposition of policy. He supports his speech by being a knowledgeable, well-prepared speaker; using evidence and reasoning; and making emotional appeals. He organizes his persuasive speech according to cause and effect, and problem–solution patterns.

RECAP

Adapting Ideas to People and People to Ideas

Persuading the Receptive Audience	Persuading the Neutral Audience	Persuading the Unreceptive Audience
• Identify with your audience.	• Gain and maintain your audience's attention.	• Do not tell listeners that you are going to try to convince them to support your position.
• Emphasize common interests.	• Refer to beliefs and concerns that are important to listeners.	• Present your strongest arguments first.
• Provide a clear objective; tell your listeners what you want them to do.	• Show how the topic affects people your listeners care about.	• Acknowledge opposing points of view.
• Appropriately use emotional appeals.	• Be realistic about what you can accomplish.	• Use appropriate gestures.

Sample Persuasive Speech

Private Ambulances

Blake Bergeron[19]
The University of Texas

When 81-year-old Tennessee resident Donna Maher woke up with chest pain and shortness of breath, she knew what to do: dial 911. After she was told paramedics would leave as quickly as they could, *Jacobin Magazine* on January 5, 2017, describes surveillance footage showing Rural/Metro employee Cortney Bryson receiving the dispatch and lighting a cigarette. In those moments, Donna slips into a coma and ten days later, passes away.

This second-rate response from a first responder is horrifying, but to be expected. Rural/Metro is a private company with no loyalty to the county or its residents. The June 25, 2016, *New York Times* laments that one in four of the ambulances we pay taxes for is owned and operated by private corporations with little oversight. Danielle Ivory, one of the authors of that *New York Times* article, reveals in a February 13, 2017, interview that the financial crisis left municipalities cash-strapped and unable to provide basic ambulance services. But where cities saw disaster, corporate giants like Rural/Metro, Transcare, and American Medical Response saw opportunity and stepped in, bringing with them a complete disregard for our safety. *The Week* on July 6, 2016, warns that, from the ambulance workers who slept through an emergency call, to the company who sent a $761 collections notice to an infant, private ambulances are in a state of emergency. With more than 50 million calls going to private ambulances this year, it's clear: We need greater protections from the dangers of private ambulances. So, let's first look at why residents are left helpless, next understand this corporate takeover's effects, and finally learn how we can fight back—because when you dial 911, big business shouldn't answer.

In 2010, Lifestar Response employee Jim Ralston approached CEO Danny Platt about rampant medical fraud occurring in the company. His response: It's fine; "we['re] profitable." Lifestar's attacks persist for two reasons: unsystematic oversight and consumer deception.

First, corporations exploit a lack of standardization within emergency services. The August 3, 2016, *Democracy Now* elaborates that since privatization really started after the financial crisis, regulations haven't caught up—a problem exacerbated by the fact that there is no national standard for what emergency services have to report, or what even constitutes a late arrival time. Companies take advantage of this lack of oversight and coerce municipalities to keep regulations as lax as possible. *Alternet* on August 5, 2016, warns that the municipality loses all forms of agency. Like Edgewater, Colorado—this municipality is supposed to charge Rural/Metro for response times over seven minutes, but with no reporting requirements, enforcement is impossible. Without standard metrics, we don't know if companies actually do their jobs.

Blake captures his listeners' attention with an illustration.

Blake moves from his opening illustration to facts and statistics that make it clear to his audience that "This issue concerns you."

Blake states his central idea in a single concise declarative statement. He then previews his main ideas in an organizational pattern that moves from cause to effect and then to solution.

Sample Persuasive Speech (*continued*)

Second, we're unprotected because private ambulances keep us in the dark. The February 2017 *Journal of Emergency Medical Services* reveals that 72 percent of U.S. ambulance use is not medically needed, something companies do not want us to know. Private ambulances capitalize on our simplistic view of emergency response, urging us to call them as soon as things get rough. But to make things worse, we think this necessity is paid for by taxes. It's not. The *Bradenton Herald* on January 8, 2017, reveals that the average ambulance costs us approximately $1,000. But when residents think costs are covered, why would companies tell us about subscription services, or when ambulances are not needed? By keeping us blind, they've created the perfect storm, feeding on an illusion they know they can exploit.

Blake poses a rhetorical question to his listeners to help sustain their attention.

For fourteen years, New York's Chez Valenta was forced by his company to participate in the practice of "ER Shopping," where one paramedic is a lookout while the other steals whatever he or she can from the emergency room. Chez's former employer embodies two effects of this corporate takeover: poor quality of service and increased risk of bankruptcy.

First, private ambulances bring about deadly consequences. *EMS1* on January 15, 2017, asserts a company is at "level zero" when no fully staffed or stocked ambulances are available. Because private ambulances are motivated to keep profits high and costs low, they experience as much as 400 percent more level zeros. *EMS1* on July 29, 2016, narrates that in 2015, Pamela and her husband Larry were riding their motorcycle together when they ran into a tree. Pamela, who was mildly injured, frantically dialed 911, who dispatched the ambulance provider, Opportunity EMS. They were at level zero, sent a crew without proper equipment, and caused Pamela to watch her husband die right in front of her. It's normally hard to point fingers for a patient's death, but for Pamela it couldn't be clearer. They left her a widow.

At this point in the speech, another specific illustration increases the likelihood that audience members will think, "This could happen to me."

Second, privatization dramatically increases the risk of bankruptcy. The July 2, 2016, *Des Moines Register* cautions that privatization is risky because businesses go bankrupt far more often than municipalities do. And when emergency services go bankrupt, as five have in the past year, we're left stranded. The February 14, 2017, *Wall Street Journal* calls out Transcare. In February 2016, some 1,700 people woke up jobless, approximately 5,000 emergency calls went unanswered, and dozens of city officials scrambled to figure out what to do when 911 dispatchers across ten cities heard one message: "out of service." Their last line of defense fell out from under them. It's familiar. Lax regulations and prioritization of profits left us wrecked in 2008; nearly a decade later and those same symptoms turn us into prey in our most vulnerable moments.

Jay Robbins was one of Transcare's 200 employees. As a first responder who was at Ground Zero on 9/11, he cries, "Transcare betrayed us." Look, we can't abolish private ambulances because some municipalities have no other option, but we can change how these corporations operate, in two ways: by establishing enforcement standards and by increasing preparedness.

Blake offers an internal preview of the solution section of his speech.

(continued)

Sample Persuasive Speech *(continued)*

First, corporations exploit a lack of standardization. So I've worked with Lisa Horton from Aurora, Colorado, to create a standard based on Aurora's contract with Falck Ambulance. Under these guidelines, ambulances would be required to reveal all response times and pay strict penalties for times over seven minutes and the number of instances of level zero. We can take these standards to our local governments and demand revamped regulations. Write down your name, email, and address, and I'll mail the guidelines to your city or county's government. Private ambulances are in all 50 states, meaning that your city may not be private, but some city in your state is; it's up to us to keep residents safe. Municipalities are pretty slow, y'all. So, we've got to get the ball rolling now. Starting this movement on the local level is the only way to ensure our interests get met.

Second, since private ambulances stay silent, let's shed some light on how to properly handle emergencies. First, since ambulances have $45 a year subscriptions, call yours and find out. Next, I've got simple questions to determine whether you actually need an ambulance. If you just need transportation to the ER, call a taxi, rideshare, friend, whatever. If you broke your arm, but there's no blood, a rideshare would definitely be cheaper and probably be faster. Fort Worth, Texas, launched a campaign with that message and in just one year, cut down on over 10,000 rides. To help spread the word, I've created a toolkit. It's got a pamphlet, magnet, flyer— literally everything you need to remind yourself and others. We've been told since we were young that if there's an emergency, dial 911, but now it's time we ensure companies enter this industry not to provide a quick buck, but to provide a pivotal public service.

When *New York Times* reporter Danielle Ivory visited Transcare's bankruptcy auction, she found herself in awe. She describes seeing "expired medical supplies," broken heart monitors, and former employees brought to tears wondering what to do now. Today, we've examined the causes, effects, and solutions so we can all better protect ourselves from private ambulances. While a Tennessee county may have lost one of their very own, hopefully we can ensure that this story doesn't have to tell itself again.

Blake suggests a specific action step for his first solution.

Blake provides tools to help his listeners enact a second solution.

Blake provides closure by referring in his final sentence to his opening illustration.

STUDY GUIDE:

⟩ REVIEW, APPLY, AND ASSESS

Understanding Persuasion

15.1 Define persuasion and describe five ways listeners may be motivated.

REVIEW: Persuasion is the process of attempting to change or reinforce attitudes, beliefs, values, or behaviors. Cognitive dissonance, a sense of mental disorganization or imbalance that arises when new information conflicts with previously organized thought patterns, may prompt a person to change his or her attitudes, beliefs, values, or behavior. Maslow's classic hierarchy of needs attempts to explain why people may be motivated to respond to persuasive appeals. Both fear appeals and positive motivational appeals can prompt listeners to respond to a persuasive message. The elaboration likelihood model (ELM) explains how listeners may be motivated by such peripheral factors as the speaker's appearance.

KEY TERMS:

persuasion	hierarchy of needs
coercion	elaboration likelihood
cognitive dissonance	model (ELM)

APPLY: Describe a time when you experienced cognitive dissonance, whether as a result of persuasive communication or not, and explain how you resolved the feeling.

ASSESS: Using the definition of *persuasion* provided in this chapter, explain what makes the end-of-chapter speech "Private Ambulances" a persuasive speech.

Developing Your Audience-Centered Persuasive Speech

15.2 Explain how to select and narrow a persuasive topic, identify a persuasive purpose, and develop and support a persuasive proposition.

REVIEW: Your specific persuasive purpose targets your audience's attitudes, beliefs, values, or behavior. Attitudes are learned predispositions to respond favorably or unfavorably toward something. A belief is one's sense of what is true or false. Values are enduring conceptions of right or wrong or good or bad. Of the three, attitudes are most susceptible to change, and values are least likely to change. After clarifying your specific purpose, you can word your central idea as a proposition of fact, value, or policy.

KEY TERMS:

proposition	proposition of value
proposition of fact	proposition of policy

APPLY:

1. Brainstorm three topics that would make a good persuasive speech for an audience of your communication classmates. Explain whether these topics target your audience members' attitudes, beliefs, values, or behavior.

2. State an attitude, a belief, and a value that you hold related to the topic of transportation. Use your attitude, belief, and value to develop a proposition of fact, a proposition of value, and a proposition of policy that could each be a central idea for a persuasive speech.

ASSESS: Use the following checklist to assess your choice of topic and purpose for a persuasive speech you develop for your communication class:

_____ Topic focused on an important issue

_____ Topic narrowed to fit time limits

_____ Persuasive general purpose—to change or reinforce listeners' attitudes, beliefs, values, or behavior

_____ Audience-centered specific purpose

_____ General and specific purposes achieved

_____ Central idea is a clear, declarative one-sentence summary of the speech

_____ Central idea is a proposition of fact, value, or policy

Supporting Your Persuasive Message with Credibility, Logic, and Emotion

15.3 Use credibility, logical reasoning, and emotional appeals to make your persuasive speech more effective.

REVIEW: Support for your persuasive proposition can include credibility, logic, and emotion. Credibility is your audience's perception of your competence, trustworthiness, and dynamism. Enhancing your initial credibility before you speak, your derived credibility during your speech, and your terminal credibility after your speech will help you improve your overall credibility as a speaker. Reasoning, the process of drawing a conclusion from evidence, is integral to your persuasive process. The three primary types of reasoning are inductive, deductive, and causal. You can also reason by analogy. You can be a more effective and ethical persuader by avoiding such reasoning fallacies as the causal fallacy, bandwagon fallacy, either–or fallacy, hasty generalization, personal attack, red herring, appeal to misplaced authority, and non sequitur. In addition to persuading others because of who you are (ethos) or how well you reason (logos), you can move an audience to respond by using emotional appeals (pathos).

KEY TERMS:

rhetoric	inductive reasoning
ethos	reasoning by analogy
logos	deductive reasoning
pathos	syllogism
credibility	causal reasoning
competence	logical fallacy
trustworthiness	causal fallacy
dynamism	bandwagon fallacy
charisma	either–or fallacy
initial credibility	hasty generalization
derived credibility	personal attack
terminal credibility	red herring
proof	appeal to misplaced
evidence	authority
reasoning	non sequitur

APPLY: Imagine you are giving a speech to your classmates near the end of the term. What specific strategies can you use to enhance your credibility with this audience?

ASSESS: Use the following checklist to assess the credibility, logical reasoning, and emotional appeals in a persuasive speech you develop for your communication class:

_____ Ethos evident in speaker's appearance, credentials, preparation, and delivery

_____ Logos evident in logically reasoned arguments supported by evidence

_____ Pathos evident in emotion-arousing words and phrases, concrete illustrations and descriptions, and evocative presentation aids

Organizing Your Persuasive Message

15.4 Organize your persuasive message.

REVIEW: Ways to organize your persuasive message include problem–solution, cause and effect, refutation, and the motivated sequence. The motivated sequence

includes five steps: attention, need, satisfaction, visualization, and action.

KEY TERMS:

refutation	positive visualization
motivated sequence	negative visualization
visualization	

APPLY: You want your listeners to support a local ordinance that will restrict noise after 10:00 p.m. in your community. Using the motivated sequence, identify a way to catch their attention, establish a need, identify a solution, visualize the benefits of this proposal, and present a specific action step they could take to help the ordinance pass.

ASSESS: Use the following checklist to assess the organization of a persuasive speech you develop for your communication class:

_____ Introduction caught attention, established motive for audience to listen, stated central idea, and previewed main ideas

_____ Body organized in a logical way—for example, according to problem–solution, cause and effect, refutation, or the motivated sequence

_____ Conclusion restated central idea, summarized main ideas, and provided closure

_____ Positive and negative emotions and visualization evoked by presentation aids, if any

Adapting Ideas to People and People to Ideas

15.5 Provide specific suggestions for adapting to receptive audiences, neutral audiences, and unreceptive audiences.

REVIEW: Be prepared to adapt your persuasive messages to receptive, neutral, and unreceptive audiences. If your listeners are receptive, identify with them, be overt in stating your speaking objective, and use emotional appeals. If they are neutral, hook them with your introduction, refer to universal beliefs and common concerns, show them how the topic affects them and those they care about, and be realistic about what you can accomplish. If your listeners are unreceptive, focus on areas of agreement, present your strongest arguments first, acknowledge opposing points of view, and use appropriate gestures.

APPLY: You want to persuade members of your communication class to buy snacks from the campus World Environment Club, whose members donate profits to save South American rainforests. Most of your classmates do not even know or care much about rainforests half a world away and some have stereotyped the Environment Club as a bunch of out-of-touch hippies. What persuasive speaking strategies would be helpful in achieving your goal?

ASSESS: For a speech you are preparing for your communication class, consider whether your classmates are a receptive, neutral, or unreceptive audience. What specific strategies offered in this chapter will help you adapt to your audience?

〉 THE PRINCIPLE POINTS

Principle One:

Be aware of your communication with yourself and others.

- Know whether the specific purpose of your persuasive speech is to change or reinforce an attitude, a belief, a value, or a behavior, and be realistic in assessing what you need to do to affect change.
- Relate personal experiences to show that you are a competent and trustworthy speaker.
- To help enhance your initial credibility, have a brief summary of your qualifications and accomplishments ready for the person who will introduce you.
- To be a better informed consumer of persuasive messages, as well as a more ethical persuasive speaker, be aware of, and avoid using, common logical fallacies.

Principle Two:

Effectively use and interpret verbal messages.

- To create negative visualization, describe in detail how bleak or terrible the future will be if your solution is not implemented.
- To create positive visualization, describe in detail how wonderful the future will be if your solution is implemented.
- To select and narrow a topic for your persuasive speech, stay current on important issues of the day by paying attention to print and electronic media.
- Word your central idea as a proposition to help fine-tune your speaking objective and develop strategies for persuading your listeners.
- To bolster your audience's opinion of your competence, cite evidence to support your ideas.
- To enhance your terminal credibility, prepare a thoughtful conclusion.
- Provide logical proof (evidence and reasoning) for your arguments and avoid logical fallacies to heighten your chances for success with your audience.
- Use emotion-arousing words and concrete illustrations and descriptions to appeal to an audience's emotions.

Principle Three:

Effectively use and interpret nonverbal messages.

- Maintain eye contact, use enthusiastic vocal inflection, and move and gesture purposefully to increase the likelihood that your audience will view you as dynamic.
- Dress appropriately to enhance your credibility.
- To enhance your terminal credibility, maintain eye contact through and even after your closing sentence.
- Use presentation aids to help evoke both positive and negative emotions as well as positive and negative visualization.
- Use gestures when speaking to an unreceptive audience.

Principle Four:

Listen and respond thoughtfully to others.

- As a speaker, the better you understand what your listeners need, the better you can adapt to them and the greater the chance that you can persuade them to change an attitude, belief, or value or get them to take some action.

- If your audience is receptive to your ideas, you can identify with them, state your speaking objective overtly, and use emotional appeals.

- If your audience is neutral, hook them with an engaging introduction, appeal to common ground and their interests, and limit your persuasive purpose.

- If your audience is unreceptive to your ideas, you might organize your speech by refutation and address their objections directly.

Principle Five:

Appropriately adapt messages to others.

- As you develop your persuasive purpose, consider the background and cultural expectations of your listeners.

- To motivate your listeners, appeal to their basic needs.

- Do everything possible to ensure that your audience's physiological and safety needs are met.

- If your audience is aware of the problem you are discussing, emphasize the solution or solutions in your problem–solution speech.

- In the need step of your motivated-sequence speech, establish why your topic, problem, or issue should concern your listeners. Convince audience members that the problem affects them directly.

- In the action step of the motivated-sequence speech, suggest a specific action your listeners can take to solve the problem you have discussed.

- If you are speaking to a knowledgeable, receptive audience, do not spend a great deal of time on the need step of the motivated sequence; instead, emphasize the satisfaction and action steps.

- Make the most of your opportunity to speak to a receptive audience by identifying with them.

- If your audience is receptive, state your speaking objective overtly, tell your listeners exactly what you want them to do, and ask them for an immediate show of support.

- Use emotional appeals with a receptive audience.

- If you are speaking to a neutral audience, emphasize the attention, need, and visualization steps of the motivated sequence.

- To persuade a neutral audience, appeal to universal beliefs and concerns.

- Show a neutral audience how your topic affects them and the people they love.

- If you are speaking to an apathetic audience or one that is not even aware that a problem exists, emphasize the problem portion of your problem–solution speech.

- Be realistic about what you can accomplish with neutral and unreceptive audiences.

- If your audience is unreceptive, focus on areas of agreement.

- If your audience is unreceptive, advance your strongest arguments first.

- Acknowledge and then refute the opposing points of view held by an unreceptive audience.

APPENDIX

INTERVIEWING

APPENDIX OBJECTIVES

After studying this appendix, you should be able to

A.1 Define what an interview is, and identify five
different kinds of interviews.

A.2 Describe the three phases of a well-structured
interview.

A.3 Identify and describe how to be interviewed for a job,
including how to develop a well-worded résumé.

A.4 Identify and describe how to be interviewed
in an information-gathering interview.

A.5 Explain how to conduct an interview.

We imagine that you won't be as unwise as the job applicant who put on his résumé that his availability for work was limited because Friday, Saturday, and Sunday were "drinking time" or the one who tried to explain away an arrest found during a background check by admitting, "We stole a pig, but it was a really small pig." Nonetheless, you can still benefit from reading tips, strategies, and suggestions for polishing your interviewing skills.[1]

An **interview** is a form of oral interaction structured to achieve a goal; it often involves just two people who take turns speaking and listening, but it can include more than two people. An effective interview is not a random conversation; rather, the person conducting the interview has carefully framed the objectives of the interview and developed a structured plan for achieving those objectives. The person being interviewed should also prepare by considering the kinds of questions he or she may be asked and being ready to give appropriate responses.

In this introduction to interviewing, we'll discuss communication strategies that can enhance your job interview skills, whether interviewing in person or via Skype, FaceTime, or another video messaging application. We'll also offer tips about how to participate in an information-gathering interview. We'll conclude the appendix by identifying strategies that can help you polish your talents if you are the person interviewing others.

Whether you are a recent high school graduate or have been in the workforce for several years and have come back to school to finish your degree and pursue a new career, the Communication Principles for a Lifetime that we've emphasized in this book can help you enhance your interviewing skills.

interview

A form of oral interaction structured to achieve a goal; it involves two or more people who take turns speaking and listening.

Types of Interviews

A.1 **Define what an interview is, and identify five different kinds of interviews.**

The planned or structured nature of the interview sets it apart from other communication situations, yet interviews sometimes include elements of interpersonal, group, and presentational communication. Interviews embody interpersonal communication in that there are two or more people participating in the interview who must establish a relationship. If the goal of the interview is to find a solution to a vexing problem, the interview may resemble elements of a group discussion in which a problem is defined and analyzed and solutions are generated, evaluated, and then implemented. Preparing for a job interview is like a public speaking situation; you focus on your audience (the interviewer), keep your purpose in mind as you research the company you're interviewing with, organize your ideas, and even rehearse your responses to questions you think you may be asked.

When people think of the term *interview*, what most commonly comes to mind is a job interview. Yet interviews can also be a means of gathering information, sharing job performance feedback, solving problems, and persuading others. Even though we are focusing primarily on employment and information-gathering interviews, the strategies we present can help you with *any* interview situation.

Information-Gathering Interview

information-gathering interview

An interview, such as an opinion poll, whose purpose is to seek information from another person.

Just as the name suggests, **information-gathering interviews** are designed to seek information from the person being interviewed. *Public-opinion polls* are one type of information-gathering interview. When you leave an organization, you may be asked to participate in an *exit interview*, an interview designed to assess why you are leaving the company. A reporter for an online publication, newspaper, radio, or TV station interviews people to gather information for a story.

The people who are most skilled at conducting information-gathering interviews do their homework before the interview. They come prepared with specific questions and have already conducted background research. In addition to preparing questions, a skilled information-gathering interviewer listens and develops questions that stem from the information that is shared during the interview.

Appraisal Interview

An **appraisal interview**, sometimes called a performance review, occurs when a supervisor or employer shares information with you about your job performance. Such an interview enables you to see how others perceive your effectiveness and helps you determine whether you are likely to get a promotion or a layoff. During an appraisal interview, you can typically express your observations about the organization and your goals for the future. Usually, a supervisor prepares a written report summarizing your strengths and weaknesses and then meets with you to review it.

When you are receiving feedback from a supervisor, the best approach is to listen and gather as much information about the supervisor's perceptions as possible. In an evaluation situation, especially if the feedback is negative, it is easy to become defensive. Instead, you should try to manage your emotions and use the information to your benefit. If you disagree with your supervisor's evaluation, consider using the conflict management skills we discussed in Chapter 8. In addition, provide specific examples to support your position. Just saying that you don't like the review is likely to do more harm than good.

appraisal interview
An interview during which a supervisor or employer shares information with an employee about his or her job performance.

Problem-Solving Interview

A **problem-solving interview** is designed to resolve a problem that affects one or both parties involved in the interview. A disciplinary interview to consider corrective action toward an employee or students is one type of problem-solving interview. Grievance interviews are also problem-solving interviews; one person brings a grievance or complaint against another person, and solutions are sought to resolve the problem or conflict.

The strategies presented in Chapter 10 for structuring a problem-solving group discussion can also help you organize a problem-solving interview. Before seeking to solve or manage a problem, first define the issues; then analyze the causes, history, and symptoms of the problem. Rather than focusing on only one solution, brainstorm several possible solutions, and then evaluate the pros and the cons of the potential solutions before settling on a single solution.

problem-solving interview
An interview, such as a grievance or disciplinary interview, that is designed to solve a problem.

Persuasion Interview

During a **persuasion interview**, one person seeks to change or reinforce the attitudes, beliefs, values, or behavior of one or more other people. The sales interview is a classic example of an interview in which the goal is to persuade. A political campaign interview is another example of a persuasion interview.

Our discussion in Chapter 15 of the principles and strategies of persuading others can help you prepare for a persuasion interview. The advantage of trying to persuade someone during an interview rather than in a speech is the size of the audience; during a persuasive interview, you may have an audience of one. It is especially important to analyze and adapt to your listener when seeking to persuade.

persuasion interview
An interview that attempts to change or reinforce attitudes, beliefs, values, or behavior, such as a sales interview.

Job Interview

A **job interview** is a focused, structured conversation whose goal is to assess a person's credentials and skills for employment. The job interview may involve elements of each of the types of interviews we've already discussed. Information is both gathered and shared, and a job interview will certainly solve a problem if you're the one looking for a job and you are hired. Elements of persuasion are also involved in a job interview. If

job interview
A focused, structured conversation whose goal is to assess a person's credentials and skills for employment.

you are seeking a job, you're trying to persuade the interviewer to hire you; if you are the interviewer and you're interviewing an exceptionally talented person, your job is to persuade the interviewee to join your organization.

Regardless of the purpose or format of the interview, the five Communication Principles for a Lifetime that we've used to organize our discussion of interpersonal, group and team, and presentational communication situations will serve you well when you participate in an interview. Whether you are the interviewer or the interviewee, it is important to be aware of how you are coming across to others. Using and interpreting verbal and nonverbal messages are critical to having a successful interview. In our definition of an interview, we noted that all individuals involved both talk and listen. Adapting to others is also essential. Effective interview participants listen, respond, and speak extemporaneously rather than delivering overly scripted, planned messages.

Phases of an Interview

A.2   Describe the three phases of a well-structured interview.

Just as a speech or term paper has a beginning, a middle, and an end, so does a well-structured interview. No matter what type, most interviews have three phases:

1. *The opening.* The interviewer puts the interviewee at ease and presents an overview of the interview agenda.
2. *The body.* During the longest part of an interview, the interviewer asks questions, and the interviewee listens and responds. The interviewee may also ask questions.
3. *The conclusion.* The interviewer summarizes what will happen next and usually gives the interviewee an opportunity to ask any final questions.

It is the responsibility of the interviewer, the person leading the interview, to develop a structure for the interview. But it's also helpful for the interviewee to understand the overall structure in advance to know what to expect both before and during the interview. So whether you're the interviewer or the interviewee, understanding the interview structure we discuss in this appendix should be of value to you.

The Opening

The opening of any interview is crucial because it creates a climate for positive and open communication. When interviewing someone, you should strive to establish rapport and to clarify the goals of the interview.

To establish rapport, start the conversation with something that will put the interviewee at ease. The discussion could be about something as simple as the weather, recent events both of you attended, or other light topics. Make direct eye contact, smile appropriately, and offer a firm handshake to establish a warm atmosphere.

Besides making the interviewee comfortable, the interviewer should clarify the goals of the interview by explicitly stating the general purpose for the meeting. After the opening conversation, it may be helpful for the interviewer to provide a general overview of the nature and purpose of the interview and an estimate of how long it will last. Clarifying a meeting's purpose helps both parties get their bearings and check their understanding. A good interviewer makes sure that everyone is on the same wavelength before the actual questioning begins.

Both the interviewer and the interviewee should arrive a few minutes early for the interview. The interviewee should be prepared, however, to wait patiently if necessary. If you are the interviewer and have decided to use a recording device, set it up. You may keep it out of sight once the interviewee has seen it, but *never* try to hide the fact that you are recording the interview—such a ploy is unethical and in some states, illegal. If you are going to take written notes, get out your paper and pen. Now you are ready to begin asking your prepared questions.

The Body: Asking Questions

Once the interviewee has been put at ease during the opening of the interview, the bulk of the interview will consist of the interviewer asking the interviewee questions. Even though both parties listen and speak, the interviewer has the primary responsibility for questioning. If the interviewer has done a good job of identifying and clarifying his or her objectives and gathering information, the key questions to be asked are usually fairly obvious.

Question Types   Interview questions fall into one of four categories: open, closed, probing, or hypothetical.[2] A typical interview usually includes some of each type.

Open Questions   **Open questions** are broad and unstructured questions that allow interviewees considerable freedom to determine the amount and kind of information they will provide. Because they encourage the interviewee to share information almost without restriction, open questions are useful in determining opinions, values, and perspective. Such questions as "What are your long- and short-term career goals?" "Why do you seek employment here?" and "How do you feel about gun control?" prompt personal and wide-ranging responses.

Closed Questions   **Closed questions** limit the range of possible responses. They may ask for a simple yes or no—"Do you enjoy working in teams?"—or they may allow interviewees to select responses from a number of specific alternatives: "How often do you go to the movies? (1) Less than once a month, (2) Once a month, (3) Twice a month, (4) Once a week." Closed questions enable the interviewer to gather specific information by restricting interviewees' freedom to express personal views or elaborate on responses. Closed questions are most often used when an interviewer is trying to obtain a maximum amount of information in a short period of time.

Probing Questions   **Probing questions** encourage interviewees to clarify or elaborate on partial or superficial responses. Through the use of these questions, interviewers attempt to clarify or direct responses. Such questions as "Could you elaborate on your coursework in the area of communication?" "Do you mean to say that you already own three vacuum cleaners?" and "Will you tell me more about your relationship with your supervisor?" call for further information in a particular area. Often spontaneous, probing questions follow up on the key questions that interviewers have prepared in advance.

Hypothetical Questions   Interviewers use **hypothetical questions** when they describe a set of conditions and ask interviewees what they would do if they were in that situation. Such questions are generally used either to gauge reactions to emotion-arousing or value-laden circumstances or to reveal an interviewee's likely responses to real situations. A police officer might ask an eyewitness to a murder, "What if I told you that the man you identified as the murderer in the line-up was the mayor?" During an exit interview, a personnel manager might ask, "If we promoted you to chief sanitary engineer and paid you $4 an hour more, would you consider staying with Bob's Landfill and Landscaping?"

open question

A question that is broad and unstructured and that allows the respondent considerable freedom to determine the amount and kind of information provided.

closed question

A question that limits the range of possible responses and requires a simple, direct, and brief answer.

probing question

A question that encourages the interviewee to clarify or elaborate on partial or superficial responses and that usually takes the discussion in a desired direction.

hypothetical question

A question used to gauge an interviewee's reaction to an emotion-arousing or value-laden situation or to reveal an interviewee's likely reactions to a real situation.

RECAP

Types of Interview Questions

	Uses	Example
Open Question	Prompts wide-ranging responses. Answers reveal interviewee's opinions, values, and perspectives.	Tell me about your previous job duties. How would you describe your son's problems in school?
Closed Question	Requests simple yes or no response or forces interviewee to select a response from limited options.	Have you been skiing in the past month? Which one of the following drinks would you buy? a. Coke b. Pepsi c. 7-Up
Probing Question	Encourages clarification of, or elaboration on, previous responses. Leads response in a specific direction.	Can you tell me more about the pain in your side? We've talked about your mother. Can you describe how you felt about your father's long absences from home when you were a child?
Hypothetical Question	Gauges reactions to emotional or value-laden situations. Elicits response to a real or imaginary situation.	How would you support your opponent if she were elected chair of the board? What would you do if your secretary lost an important file?

FIGURE A.1 The Funnel Sequence

Getting at specific pieces of information through use of direct questioning

funnel sequence
A questioning sequence that begins with broad, open questions and proceeds toward more closed questions.

inverted funnel sequence
A questioning sequence that begins with closed questions and proceeds to more open questions, intended to encourage an interviewee to respond easily early in the interview.

tunnel sequence
A way of structuring interview questions so that parallel open or closed questions (or a combination of open and closed questions) are asked to gather a large amount of information in a short amount of time; no probing questions are asked.

Questioning Sequences Open, closed, probing, and hypothetical questions may be used in any combination, as long as their sequence is thoughtfully planned. Depending on the purpose, these questions may be arranged into three basic sequences: funnel, inverted funnel, and tunnel.

The Funnel Sequence As Figure A.1 shows, the **funnel sequence** begins with broad, open questions and proceeds to more closed questions. The advantage of this format is that it allows an interviewee to express views and feelings without restriction, at least early in an interview. For example, it may be more useful to begin a grievance interview with the question "How would you describe your relationship with your supervisor?" than with "What makes you think that your supervisor treats you like an idiot?" The first question allows the free expression of feelings, whereas the second clearly reflects an interviewer's bias, immediately forcing the discussion in a negative direction. The following series of questions provides an example of a funnel sequence that might be used for an information-gathering interview.

1. Why do you find communication interesting?
2. What area of communication are you primarily interested in?
3. How long have you studied interpersonal communication?
4. Why do you think interpersonal attraction theory is useful?
5. What would you do to test interpersonal attraction theory?

Notice that the questions start by asking for general information and then focus on more specific ideas.

The Inverted Funnel Sequence The opposite of the funnel sequence is the **inverted funnel sequence**, as shown in Figure A.2, which begins with closed questions and proceeds to more open questions. An interview designed to gather information about a worker's grievance might be based on the inverted funnel and might include the following series of questions:

1. Do you believe that your supervisor wants to fire you?
2. What makes you think that you'll be fired soon?
3. What do you think has caused this problem between you and your supervisor?
4. How has this problem affected your work?
5. How would you describe the general working climate in your department?

The relatively closed questions that begin the inverted funnel sequence are intended to encourage an interviewee to respond easily, because they require only brief answers (yes or no, short lists, and the like). As the sequence progresses, the questions become more open and thus require more elaborate answers and greater disclosure.

The inverted funnel sequence is appropriate when an interviewer wants to direct the interview along specific lines and encourage an interviewee to respond with short, easily composed answers. An interviewer can follow up with more general questions to solicit increasingly broad information—the "big picture."

FIGURE A.2 The Inverted Funnel Sequence

Building the "big picture" with repeated questioning, integrating previous responses

The Tunnel Sequence Finally, the **tunnel sequence** consists of a series of related open or closed questions or a combination of the two; the sequence is intended to gather a wide range of information. This sequence does not include probing questions; it goes into less depth than the other two sequences. An interviewer may use the tunnel sequence to gather information about attitudes and opinions without regard for the reasons behind an interviewee's answers or the intensity of the interviewee's feelings. The following is a typical tunnel sequence:

1. What are the three major issues in the presidential campaign this year?
2. Which candidate would you vote for if the election were held today?
3. Who will you vote for in the race for U.S. senator?

4. Are you a registered voter in this state?

5. What do you think of the proposition to set up a nuclear waste dump in this state?

The tunnel sequence is most appropriate when an interviewer wants some general information on a variety of topics in a relatively short period of time.

Although these sequences have been discussed as if they were independent and easily distinguishable, a good questioning strategy will probably combine one or more of these question sequences. The key to effective interviewing is to prepare a set of questions that will get the amount and kinds of information you need. An interviewer should remain flexible enough to add, subtract, and revise questions as a discussion proceeds. Such an approach ensures that the objectives of the interview will be accomplished.

As you conduct the interview, use the questions you have prepared as a general guide but not a rigid schedule. If the person you are interviewing mentions an interesting angle you did not think of, don't be afraid to pursue the point. Listen carefully to the person's answers, and ask for clarification of any ideas you don't understand.

The Conclusion

Opinion polls, marketing surveys, and sales pitches often end rather abruptly with a "Thank you for taking the time to help me." Many other kinds of interviews require follow-up meetings or some form of future contact. For this reason, and for reasons of common courtesy, the conclusion of an interview is very important. Conclusions can summarize the interview and establish a basis for a continued relationship as well as bringing the meeting to a close.

Summarizing   A primary function of the conclusion is to summarize the proceedings. All parties should be aware of and agree on what happened during the meeting. To ensure understanding and agreement, an interviewer summarizes the highlights of the discussion, asking for and offering clarification if necessary.

Continuing the Relationship   Another function of the conclusion is to encourage a continued, friendly relationship. The positive communication climate developed during the interview should be carried into its conclusion. The interviewer may need to establish interpersonal harmony if he or she asked questions that resulted in conflict or made the interviewee uncomfortable. Comments such as "I'm glad we had a chance to talk about this problem" or "Thank you for sharing and listening" enable both parties to feel like they have had a positive and productive encounter.

Clarifying Expectations   An interviewer can tell the interviewee when to expect further contact or action, if appropriate. A job applicant wants to know when to expect a phone call about a follow-up interview or a job offer. An expert, interviewed by a journalist, wants to know how his or her comments will be used and when the story is likely to be published.

Ending the Meeting   At the end of virtually any interview, good manners require both the interviewer and the interviewee to say, "Thank you."

RECAP

Organizing an Interview

Phase	Goals
Opening	Put the interviewee at ease.
	Review the purpose.
	Establish rapport.
	Provide an orientation.
Body	Use questions appropriate to the interview type and objective:
	• Use open questions to elicit wide-ranging responses.
	• Use closed questions to get specific responses.
	• Use probing questions to seek clarification or elaboration.
	• Use hypothetical questions to gauge a reaction to an imaginary situation.
	Design questioning sequences appropriate to the interview purpose:
	• Use the funnel sequence to elicit general comments first and specific information later.
	• Use the inverted funnel sequence to elicit specific information first and more general comments later.
	• Use the tunnel sequence to gather lots of information without probing too deeply.
Conclusion	Summarize the proceedings.
	Encourage friendly relations.
	Arrange further contact(s).
	Exchange thank-yous.

Because an interview requires mutual effort, both parties deserve recognition. One final suggestion: Do not prolong the interview beyond the time limits of your appointment.

How to Be Interviewed for a Job

A.3 **Identify and describe how to be interviewed for a job, including how to develop a well-worded résumé.**

Woody Allen once said, "80 percent of success is showing up." We suggest that you do more than just show up for a job interview, however. Like giving an effective speech, having a successful job interview involves thoughtful preparation and careful planning. According to *CareerBuilder*, a popular website for job hunters, it takes an average of seventeen interviews to get one job offer.[3] To increase your odds of getting hired after an interview, we present research-based suggestions and strategies that can help you make your first impression your best impression when looking for employment.

Be Aware of Your Skills and Abilities

The first communication principle we introduced in this book is to be aware of your communication. Before you interview for a job, it is important to be aware not only of your communication as you interact with others, but also of your unique skills, talents, and abilities. Many people select a career because they think that they might like to *be* a lawyer, doctor, or teacher. But rather than thinking about what you want to be, we suggest considering what you like to *do*. Ask yourself these questions:

What do I like to do in my free time?

What are my best skills and talents?

What education and training do I have?

What experiences or previous jobs have I had?

In addition to answering these questions, write down responses to complete this statement: "I can . . . . " For example, you might respond, "I can cook, write, and relate well to others." List as many answers as possible. Here's another statement to complete: "I have . . . . " You might answer, "I have traveled, worked on a farm, and sold magazine subscriptions." Responding to the "I can" and "I have" statements will help you develop an awareness of your skills and experiences that will help you respond readily when you are asked about them during an interview. Reflecting on your interests can help you decide which career will best suit your talents; you will also be able to develop a résumé that reflects your best abilities.

Prepare Your Résumé

résumé

A written, concise, well-organized description of a person's qualifications for a job.

A **résumé** is a written, concise, well-organized description of your qualifications for a job. A résumé is essentially your professional story. And like a story, it has a main character (you), a story background (your credentials), and a plot (your professional work history). How long should a résumé be? Many employers don't expect a résumé to be longer than two printed pages; some will look only at a one-page résumé. (Résumés of experienced career professionals may be longer than two pages, however.) Today most résumés are posted and distributed online via such sites as LinkedIn, Glassdoor, Indeed, or Monster.com.

Throughout our discussion of presentational speaking we emphasized the importance of analyzing and adapting to your audience. The same principle of being audience-centered holds true when preparing your résumé. The specific decisions you make about what to include on a résumé should be based on your understanding of the people who will review it. The best résumés are ethically adapted to showcase how your skills and experiences can meet the needs of prospective employers.

One of the best ways to understand what qualifications potential employers seek is to network with those who may have a job for you.[4] **Networking** is the process of communicating with others, sharing information, developing new career contacts, and learning about the needs of prospective employers. You can network using your own contacts or you can reach out to family, friends, and colleagues for their contacts.

Although your résumé is important in helping you land a job, its key function is to help you get an interview. How you perform in the interview will determine whether you get the job. Employers rarely hire someone only on the basis of a résumé. Most employers spend less than a minute—and some only a few seconds—looking at each résumé. In fact, many résumés are never even read by a human being—they are first reviewed by a computer software program to confirm your compatibility for the position. Therefore, your résumé should be clear and easy to read and should focus on the essential information an employer seeks.

Elements of a Résumé   Most employers will be looking for standard information on your résumé. (Study the sample résumé that appears in this appendix.[5]) Most résumés include the following information:

- *Personal information.* Employers will look for your name, address, phone numbers, e-mail address, and website address (if you have one). Provide phone numbers where you can be reached during both the day and the evening.
- *Career objective.* Many employers will want to see your career objective. Make it brief, clear, and focused. Customize your career objective for each different position you seek. Communicate truthfully about how your goals mesh with the goals and needs of the employer.
- *Education.* Include your major, your degree, your graduation date, and the institution you attended.
- *Experience.* Describe your relevant work experience, listing your most recent job first. Include the names of employers, dates when you worked, and a very brief description of your duties.
- *Honors and special accomplishments.* List any awards, honors, offices held, or other leadership responsibilities.
- *Optional information.* If you have volunteer experience, have traveled, or have computer skills or other pertinent experience, be sure to include it if it is relevant to your objective and the job.
- *References.* List the names, phone numbers, and e-mail addresses of people who can speak positively about your skills and abilities. Or you may indicate that your references are available on request.

Formatting Your Résumé   Most résumés are sent electronically today, so it's important to use techniques to make sure your résumé is accurately transmitted and, once it gets to an employer, stands out in the e-crowd. Career-search expert Katherine Hansen has several useful tips for submitting your résumé online:[6]

- *Use their words.* Many résumés are first "read" by a computer software program that scans your résumé for keywords that are mentioned in the job posting or are used frequently in your career field. To avoid having your résumé screened out or never even reaching a human being, make liberal use of appropriate keywords as well as specific action verbs. As you write your résumé, remember the importance of staying truthful.
- *Keep it simple.* Text formatting, such as boldfaced text, larger fonts in headings, or lines to divide sections, helps people find key information in your résumé more quickly. However, that same formatting can create problems when you submit your résumé electronically. Many larger employers have online applications that require you to paste your résumé into a blank form, for example. You may also decide to paste all or part of your résumé into an e-mail when responding to a job board posting. For these purposes, you need a plain-text résumé, with no formatting.[7]

networking
The process of communicating with others to share information, develop career contacts, and learn the needs of prospective employers.

- *Be (a little) creative with plain text.* You can use bullets, asterisks (*), lower-case letter o's (o), and carets (>) to format lists of accomplishments in a plain-text résumé. It's also possible to create lines or boxes using text characters such as equal signs (======), plus signs (++++++), and tildes (~~~~~~~~), but don't overdo it.

- *Prepare to be published.* Smaller employers may not use electronic scanning, and larger employers who do use it may still print the résumés of those who make the "short list" of applicants. So in addition to your plain-text résumé, you may want to prepare a version of your résumé with formatting that looks good to the human eye as well as the electronic eye. You can submit your formatted résumé as an e-mail attachment or upload it to an online application. Numerous print and online résumé guides can provide formatting tips. No matter what format you choose, one task is essential: Before submitting your résumé to employers, carefully review a printed copy to spot and correct any errors that could cause you to be rejected.

- *Publish yourself.* In some career fields, employers expect you to establish your own website or social media profile where you provide your résumé in HTML format, along with a portfolio of work samples. Although the HTML format permits you to use more graphics, remember that unless you are a graphic designer, the purpose of any graphics should be to help tell your story simply and effectively, not to dazzle the reader with your design talent.

- *Adapt.* Rather than preparing only one résumé and sending it to every job posting, follow our Communication Principle Five and customize your story for each audience. Appropriately adapt not only the content of your résumé but also the format to ensure that it meets each prospective employer's requirements.

When developing your résumé, be sure to use specific action verbs to describe your experience. Also use these action words during interviews. Rather than using a general verb such as "I *worked* on a project," use more descriptive action words that clarify the role you assumed. Consider using some of the following words when listing or describing your activities or accomplishments:

accelerated	evaluated	promoted
accepted	expanded	proposed
accomplished	expedited	provided
achieved	facilitated	recommended
adapted	found	reduced
administered	generated	researched
analyzed	guided	resulted in
approved	improved	reviewed
built	increased	revised
completed	initiated	selected
conceived	instructed	solved
conducted	interpreted	stimulated
controlled	maintained	structured
coordinated	managed	supervised
created	mastered	tested
delegated	motivated	trained
demonstrated	negotiated	translated
designed	operated	traveled
developed	organized	updated
directed	originated	utilized
effected	participated	won
eliminated	planned	

Sample Résumé

MARIA SANCHEZ
3124 West Sixth Street
San Marcos, TX 78666
(512) 555-0102
(512) 555-0010
mariasanchez@emailprovider.com

PROFESSIONAL OBJECTIVE:	Seeking a position in human resources as a training specialist.
EDUCATION:	Bachelor of Arts Degree Major: Communication Studies Minor: English Texas State University Graduation Date: May 20XX
PROFESSIONAL EXPERIENCE:	20XX–Present, Intern, GSD&M, Austin, Texas • Assisted in creating a leadership training program • Designed flyers and display ads using desktop publishing software • Made cold calls to prospective clients 20XX–August 20XX, Intern, Target Market, Houston, Texas • Developed a sales training seminar • Coordinated initial plan for writing advertising copy for Crest Inc.'s advertising campaign 20XX–20XX, Supervisor, S&B Associates, San Marcos, Texas • Supervised three employees editing training materials 20XX–20XX, Advertising Sales and Reporter, *University Star*, San Marcos, Texas • Sold ads for university paper and worked as social events reporter
OTHER EXPERIENCE:	20XX–20XX, Summer job at Target, San Marcos, Texas 20XX–20XX, Summer job at YMCA, Austin, Texas
SKILLS:	Team Leadership, Photography, Computer Proficiency, Research and Analysis, Public Speaking, Customer Service
ACCOMPLISHMENTS & HONORS:	Paid for majority of my college education while maintaining a 3.5 grade point average, Presidential Scholarship, Vice President of Texas State University Communication Club, Editor/Historian of MortarBoard, John Marshall High School Vice President of Junior Class, Yearbook Coordinator
PROFESSIONAL ORGANIZATIONS:	Lambda Pi Eta, American Society for Training and Development, Communication Club, National Communication Association
INTERESTS:	Photography, tennis, softball, theater
REFERENCES:	Available at your request

Identify the Needs of Your Potential Employer

After you have analyzed your skills and abilities and have prepared a well-crafted résumé, try to anticipate the needs and goals of your potential employer. A good interviewee adapts his or her message to the interviewer.

How do you find information about an organization that will help you adapt your message to fit its needs? In a word: research. Gather as much information as you can about not only the person who will interview you but also the needs and goals of the organization or company where you want to work. As a starting point, search for information about the organization online. Virtually every organization these days has a web presence. But do more than just look at the organization's home page; click on the various links to learn more about what the organization does.

Look and Communicate Your Best

The opportunity to assess your appearance and the way in which you express yourself nonverbally is one of the most important reasons an interviewer wants to meet with you face to face.

Dress for Success   As we discussed in Chapter 4, don't forget about the power of nonverbal messages in making a good impression. Dressing for success is crucial. Regardless of the type or level of the job for which you are applying, most experts suggest that you dress conservatively and give special attention to your grooming. For most professional positions, men will be expected to wear a coat and tie or a suit and well-polished shoes. Women will be expected to wear a dress, suit, or other coordinated attire. There are many jobs, of course, for which wearing a business suit to the interview would be overkill (such as manual labor), but if you're not certain what to wear, it's better to err on the side of dressing up rather than dressing down.

Communicate Your Best   What determines whether you are hired for the job? In short, it's the way you communicate. By the time you get to an interview, your interviewer has already determined that you have at least the minimum qualifications for the job. Your ability to apply the Communication Principles for a Lifetime that we've reiterated throughout the book is key to making a good impression on your interviewer. In Chapter 1, when we discussed why it's important to learn about communication, we noted that the top three key factors that employers look for in a job applicant focus on your communication skill.[8] Your ability to listen, respond, and relate to your interviewer is one of the best predictors of whether you will be hired for a job. Among the areas an interviewer is trying to assess by observing your behavior are the following:

- *Self-expression.* Are you clear or are you vague when you respond to questions? Do you make effective eye contact? Do you talk too much or too little?
- *Maturity.* Are you likely to make good judgments and effective decisions?
- *Personality.* What's your overall style of relating to people? Are you outgoing, shy, quiet, overbearing, enthusiastic, warm, friendly?
- *Experience.* Can you do the job? Do you have a track record that suggests you can effectively do what needs to be done?
- *Enthusiasm.* Do you seem interested in this job and the organization? Do you seem to be genuine and authentic, or is your enthusiasm phony?
- *Goals.* Where are you heading in life? Are your short-term and long-term goals compatible with the needs of the organization?

If you are being interviewed via Skype, FaceTime, or some other video conferencing technology, keep in mind that gestures and facial expressions may seem amplified when viewed by others on a screen. Consider minimizing your gestures and expressions (as most newscasters do) when communicating via video. Practice your video interview ahead of time by recording yourself with your smartphone or another digital device. By watching the recording, you can gain the perspective that others will have when they participate in your video interview.

Marketing experts know the importance of developing a brand name (such as Coke, Kleenex, or Starbucks) to make a product memorable and distinctive. A **personal brand** works the same way. Your personal brand is the impression you leave when the interview has concluded. As career counselor Delores Dean notes, "The goal in branding is to leave behind an impression of you that will be remembered. You must stand out above the rest and be the best."[9] How do you develop yourself as a memorable brand? One way is to use both nonverbal and verbal messages effectively. Nonverbally, you can make sure that you are remembered through your appearance. Pay special attention to what you wear and how you interact nonverbally with the interviewer. Verbally, if you project a positive attitude when you speak, you can leave a lasting, positive impression. A memorable, appropriate, and well-told brief story in response to a question can also help you be remembered. The goal of the interview is not only to *make* a positive impression, but also to *leave* a positive impression that will be remembered when the interviewer sifts through his or her notes and memories of multiple interviews.

personal brand
The clear impression an interviewee leaves when the interview has concluded.

Polish Your Online Appearance

Journalist Andy Simmons noted, "Every American has, at some point, appeared naked, drunk, unconscious, rude, crude or felonious online. Okay, maybe not everyone, but surf the Net and that's the impression you'll get."[10] Simmons's point is that it's important to make sure your online impression is as presentable as your live-and-in-person appearance. If you have a Facebook or other social media profile, make sure that it contains no embarrassing photos or quotes that might damage your reputation. Keep in mind that employers are searching online to see whether applicants are as credible as their résumés or personal impressions suggest.[11] According to *Career-Builder*, when employers used the Internet to check the facts on people's résumés, here's what they found:

- 31 percent had lied about their qualifications.
- 24 percent had some link to criminal behavior.
- 19 percent had made negative comments about a past employer.
- 19 percent had bragged about drinking or using illegal drugs.
- 15 percent had shared confidential information about their former employers.
- 11 percent had posted unflattering or sexually explicit photos.
- 8 percent had used an obscene or unprofessional online screen name.

Monster.com reported that among the most common lies on a résumé include education, employment dates, job titles, and technical skills.[12] Although you may think no one will check or know if you fudge information on your résumé, it's easy for employers to double-check its accuracy. Career counselor Liz Ryan cautioned, "People think that they can make up and embellish details about companies that have been sold or gone out of business. But LinkedIn, Facebook and our wide-ranging networks will put a quick stop to most efforts to change history in our favor."[13]

So always be truthful, and monitor your online presence. Don't assume that no one will find out about something you have fabricated on your résumé or a "friend" of yours has posted about you online. Increasingly, employers are using social networks such as Facebook and Twitter to see whether your cyberpersonality is consistent with the well-scrubbed, polished appearance you presented in your interview and on your résumé. We provide specific tips and suggestions for putting your best online image forward in the Communication and Social Media box.

COMMUNICATION & SOCIAL MEDIA

Putting Your Best Facebook Image Forward

Perhaps you should think twice before posting that photo from last night's wild party to your Facebook page or retweeting that slightly offensive joke. According to one source, almost half of all employers will routinely review social media sites such as Facebook and Twitter to gain a broader picture of you and your skills.[14] Another source suggests that more than 90 percent of employers will search social media sites for clues about you.[15] So if you're looking for a job, make sure your social media accounts put your best image forward. Among the top reasons an employer did not hire someone after conducting research online include finding inappropriate content posted, evidence of excessive drinking or using drugs, negative comments about previous employers, or lies about qualifications.[16] Here are several tips for making sure your social media profiles don't become an obstacle to your employment.[17]

> *Privacy.* Review your Facebook and other social media privacy settings to make sure that you are in control of the information that you want others to see.

> *Photos.* Review the photos posted on your social media sites to remove unflattering ones or images that might highlight your party skills but not your work skills. Consider updating your profile photo to project the professional image you wish to promote.

> *Monitor What You and Others Post About You.* Review what you and others have posted, including comments on blogs and other social media outlets, to ensure that your posts don't detract from your credibility as a potential employee. Consider what

you have posted from the perspective of someone who may hire you.

Review Your Friends List and Those Whom You Have Tagged. Even if you have carefully scrubbed your profile information on your Facebook account or on another site, unless you have carefully adjusted your privacy settings, a prospective employer may glean information you'd rather not make available through your friends' pages or through those you have tagged.

Google Yourself. One of the first things many prospective employers do is search for your name using Google. We recommend that you preemptively Google yourself to find out what a prospective employer may see and read about you. By signing up for a Google Alert, you'll find out when your name pops up on the Internet. Consider how you might need to modify your online presence to relay a more positive image. Of course, there may be some information you cannot change. But some Internet content you can alter, such as the information you submit on your own social media accounts.

Monitor Your Online Name. Avoid what you and your friends may think are cute or funny screen names, such as Imlazyandbored or hottotrot. It's unlikely a prospective employer will be amused and therefore, it's less likely you'll be hired. One final tip: Check to make sure your voice mail greeting on your smartphone is professional and appropriate. Using a fake accent, giving yourself a "cute" name, attempting humor that may offend, or referencing inappropriate ethnic, cultural, or sexual orientation stereotypes will not enhance your credibility or employability.

Listen, Respond, and Ask Appropriate Questions

Because an interview is a structured, planned discussion, it is important to demonstrate effective listening and responding skills. Stay focused on what your interviewer is asking you. Remember to stop, look, and listen for both the details and the major points of the questions.

When you respond to questions, you should project genuine enthusiasm and competence. Don't put on an act: Be yourself while being professional. Be friendly and pleasant without being overly effusive or giddy. Communication researcher Mary Minto found that how you respond to an interviewer's questions could be even more important than what you say.[18] Your tone of voice, use of pauses and gestures, and posture are vital in expressing your personality and overall mood. Talking rapidly and nonstop without periodically pausing, for example, communicates that you are not sensitive to others.

One of the best ways to prepare for an interview is to anticipate an interviewer's questions. Table A.1 lists typical questions that may be asked during an interview.[19] We don't recommend that you memorize "canned" or overly rehearsed answers, but it

TABLE A.1 Typical Questions Asked during Job Interviews

I. Education

1. Why did you select your major area of study?
2. Why did you select your college/university?
3. If you were starting college again, what would you do differently? Why?
4. What subjects were most and least interesting? Useful? Why?
5. Other than the courses you studied, what is the most important thing you learned from your college experience?
6. How did you finance your college education?

II. Experience

7. What do you see as your strengths as an employee?
8. You say that a strength you have is ___. Give me some indication, perhaps an example, that illustrates this strength.
9. What special skills would you bring to this position?
10. Describe your last few work experiences. Why did you leave each one?
11. What were the best and worst aspects of your last job?
12. What were some of your achievements and disappointments in your last job?
13. Do you see yourself as a leader/manager of people? Why?
14. What kinds of work situations would you like to avoid? Why?
15. What frustrations have you encountered in your work experience? How have you handled these frustrations?
16. What do you look for in a boss?
17. Most employees and bosses have some disagreements. What are some things that you and your boss have disagreed about?

III. Position and Company

18. Why did you select this company?
19. Why did you decide to apply for this particular position?
20. How do you see yourself being qualified for this position?
21. Are you willing to relocate?

IV. Self-Evaluation

22. Tell me a little bit about yourself. Describe yourself.
23. What do you see as your personal strengths? Talents? How do you know that you possess these? Give examples of each.
24. What do you see as your weak points? Areas for improvement? Things you have difficulty doing? What have you done to deal with these weak areas?
25. Describe a specific work problem you had. Explain what you did to solve this problem.
26. What do you consider to be your greatest work achievement? Why?

V. Goals

27. Where do you see yourself being in your profession in five years? In ten years? How did you establish these goals? What will you need to do to achieve these goals?
28. What are your salary expectations for this position? Starting salary? Salary in five years?

may be helpful to think about possible responses to these questions. Also be prepared to answer questions about your unique experiences, such as military service, vocational training, or membership on sports teams.

Make sure you get a good night's sleep before the interview and eat sensibly (don't skip breakfast; don't stuff yourself at lunch) so that you can stay alert. Long interviews can be physically demanding.

Consider the interview an opportunity to ask questions as well as to answer them; toward the end of an interview, most interviewers will give you an opportunity to ask whatever questions you'd like. Asking questions about an organization is a way to display enthusiasm for the job as well as a means of assessing whether you really want to join the organization. You will want to know the following:

- Will there be any job training for this position?
- What are the opportunities for advancement?
- What is the atmosphere like in the workplace? (You will also be able to observe the workplace during the interview.)

- What hours do people work?
- Is there flexibility in scheduling the work day?
- When do you anticipate making a decision about this position?

The very first question you ask should *not* be "How much does this job pay?" Usually, the interviewer will discuss salary and benefits with you during the interview. If it is a preliminary interview and there is a chance that you will be called back for another interview, you may want to defer questions about salary and benefits until you know that the organization is seriously considering you for the position.

During the interview, maintain eye contact and speak assertively. The goal in an interview is to project a positive attitude to the interviewer. As motivational speaker Zig Ziglar once noted, "Your attitude, not your aptitude, will determine your altitude."

Follow Up after the Interview

After the interview, it is wise to write a brief letter or e-mail to thank the interviewer and to provide any additional information that may have been requested. You may also want to send a thank-you note to others in the organization, such as a secretary or administrative assistant, for helping you arrange the interview. If the interviewer asked for references, make sure to let your reference providers know as soon as possible that they may be contacted. If you are asking them to send letters of recommendation to the organization, expedite the process by providing addressed, stamped envelopes or the appropriate e-mail addresses and a copy of your résumé so that they can personalize their letters with specific information.

Is it appropriate to call the person who interviewed you to ask when a decision will be made about hiring someone? Some employers abide by the philosophy "Don't call us, we'll call you," but many others would interpret your call as a sign of your interest in the position and a testament to your ability to follow through. You may want to take the direct approach and simply ask the interviewer toward the end of the interview, "Would it be all right if I called you in a few days to find out if you have made a decision or if you need additional information?" If the interviewer tells you that a decision will be made by a certain date and then that date passes by, it is probably okay to call and find out whether the job has been offered to someone else and to express your continued interest in the position if it hasn't been filled.

How to Be Interviewed in an Information-Gathering Interview

A.4   Identify and describe how to be interviewed in an information-gathering interview.

The bulk of the responsibility for an effective information-gathering interview falls on the person who is doing the interviewing. If you are the interviewer in an information-gathering interview, review the suggestions we offer in this appendix for structuring the interview. Most information-gathering interviews follow this general structure.

If you are the person being interviewed, however, your primary responsibilities are to be prepared, to listen carefully, and to respond appropriately to questions. In addition, a good interviewee knows what to expect in an information-gathering interview. You should prepare responses to anticipated questions, pay close attention to requests for specific information, and answer questions directly and accurately.

Prepare for the Interview

In most cases, interviewees have some advance knowledge of the purpose and objective of interviews, especially if someone is seeking specific information or advice. You can therefore anticipate probable topics of discussion. If you are uncertain what the interview is about, it is appropriate to ask the person who will interview you how best to prepare for the questions he or she plans to ask. Yes, sometimes news programs have an interviewer pop up in an office, thrust a microphone in an interviewee's face, and ask a pointed question. In most cases, however, NBC news anchor Brian Williams (or his equivalent) is not going to ambush you.

Depending on the nature of the interview, you might want to brush up on the facts you may be asked about. Jot down a few notes to remind you of names, dates, and places. In some cases, you may want to do some background reading on the topic of the interview.

Finally, think about not only what you will say in the interview but also how you will respond nonverbally. Be on time. Maintain an attitude of interest with eye contact, attentive body positions, alert facial expressions, and an appropriately firm handshake.

Listen Effectively

Interviewing situations require you to listen to determine the amount and depth of information desired. If your responses are to be appropriate and useful, you must know what is being requested. If questions are unclear, ask for clarification or elaboration. By doing so, you can respond more fully and relevantly.

Successful interviewees practice empathy. Interviewers are people, and interviewing situations are interpersonal encounters. Effective interviewees consider situations from interviewers' points of view, listen "between the lines" of what someone says to focus on underlying emotions, and watch for nonverbal cues. When interviewees listen to all facets of the communication, they can better adapt to the situation.

Respond Appropriately

Just as questioning is the primary responsibility of an interviewer, responding is the primary responsibility of an interviewee. Keep answers direct, honest, and appropriate in depth and relevance. For example, in response to the question "How would you describe the quality of your relationship with your family?" don't give a fifteen-minute speech about your problems with your ex-spouse, keeping the children in clothes, and finding dependable home care for your aging parents. To make sure that you give the best possible answer, listen carefully when a question is posed and, if necessary, take a few moments to think before you answer. A response that is well thought out, straightforward, and relevant will be much more appreciated than one that is hasty, evasive, and unrelated to the question.

Using language and vocabulary that are appropriate to the situation is also important. The use of too much slang or technical terminology in an attempt to impress an interviewer can easily backfire by distracting the interviewer or distorting communication. Direct and simple language promotes understanding.

Finally, be flexible and adapt to the needs of the interviewing situation. Some interviewers will ask questions to throw you off guard. If that happens to you, take a moment to think before you respond. Try to discover the reason for the question and respond to the best of your ability. Listen carefully for the content *and* intent of questions so that you provide the information requested, especially when the interviewer changes topics. Flexibility and adaptability depend on good listening, empathy, accurate reading and interpretation of nonverbal communication, and practice. Just remember: "Engage brain before opening mouth."

The Responsibilities of the Interviewer

A.5 Explain how to conduct an interview.

So far, we've emphasized how to behave when you are the person being interviewed. As you assume leadership positions in your profession and community, you will undoubtedly be called on to interview others. In addition to knowing how to structure the opening, body, and conclusion of an interview, which we discussed earlier, there are several other characteristics of effective interviewers, whether you are seeking to hire an employee or simply gathering information.

Be Aware of Biases and Prejudices

First and foremost, an interviewer must be aware of his or her own biases and prejudices. Each person has a set of experiences, beliefs, attitudes, and values that influence how that person receives, interprets, and evaluates incoming stimuli. If accurate and useful information is to be shared in an interview, an interviewer must be aware of his or her own perceptual processes so as to make accurate and objective interpretations. An otherwise qualified candidate for a job shouldn't be eliminated from consideration just because the interviewer has a bias against red-haired people, for example.

Adapt to an Interviewee's Behavior

Skilled interviewers observe, evaluate, and adapt to the communication behavior of their interviewees. Because no two interviews—and no two interviewees—are exactly alike, interviewers adapt their communication behavior accordingly. A flexible communication style is a necessity. Interviewers should have predetermined plans, but they should not be thrown off balance if an interviewee suddenly turns the tables and asks, "How much money do *you* make for *your* job?"

Adaptability also includes the use of appropriate language and vocabulary. You should consciously choose language and vocabulary that interviewees will understand. Little is gained by using technical, ambiguous, or vague terms. Words should be straightforward, simple, and specific but not so simple that interviewees feel "talked down" to. Empathy is important in determining the most appropriate language and vocabulary to use.

Deal Wisely with Sensitive Content

When planning questions for an interview, consider possible sensitive topics that should be avoided. A question in a grievance interview such as "Why were you fired from your last job?" will provoke a defensive reaction.

Good judgment and careful word choice play crucial roles. One ill-chosen question can destroy the positive and open communication developed in an opening. Effective interviewers avoid potentially troublesome topics and attempt to put interviewees at ease. They discuss sensitive issues *if and only if* they are related to the purpose of the interviews. When a sensitive subject must be discussed, experienced interviewers choose their words carefully; for example, the question "Why were you fired?" might be rephrased as "How would you describe your relationship with your previous supervisor?"

Listen Effectively

The admonition to listen effectively has appeared frequently in this appendix. Effective listening is at the heart of any interview. No matter how well interviewers have prepared, the time will have been wasted if they are poor listeners. They need strong listening skills to make sure that they are receiving the amount and kind of information they need. They must be able to identify partial or irrelevant responses.

Highly developed listening skills also increase the ability to accurately perceive and interpret unintentional messages and beliefs, attitudes, and values. Interviewers learn a great deal from nonverbal as well as verbal communication.

Record Information

The information accumulated from an interview is useless if it is not recorded completely and accurately. A partial or inaccurate report can lead to poor decisions and mistaken actions. Take appropriate, legible, written notes. If you plan to record audio or video, ask the interviewee in advance for permission to do so.

Ask Appropriate Questions

The success of most interviews will be determined by the quality of the questions asked during the conversation. Think of questions as "mental can openers" designed to reveal how the other person thinks and behaves. Earlier, we discussed question types (open, closed, probing, and hypothetical) and question sequences (funnel, inverted funnel, and tunnel). Some of your questions should be planned. Other questions may evolve from the discussion. The best questions during an interview emerge from simply listening to what the other person is saying and then probing or following up on information and ideas verbalized.

If you are interviewing a job applicant, be aware that there are certain questions that you should *not* ask. These questions are inappropriate because they ask for information that either laws or court interpretations of laws suggest could lead to illegal discrimination. Here's a list of topics you should not bring up during an employment interview when you're asking the questions:[20]

arrest records	insurance claims
less-than-honorable discharges	judgments
gender and marital status	citizenship or national origin
maiden name	mother's maiden name
number of children	place of birth
ages of children	disabilities
number of preschool children	handicap
spouse's name	illnesses or accidents
spouse's education	hospitalizations
spouse's income	current or prior medication/treatment
form of birth control	workers' compensation claims
family plans	weight
child care arrangements	religion
car accidents	church affiliation
lawsuits	social organizations
legal complaints	loans
ownership of home	wage assignments or garnishments
rental status	bankruptcy
length of residence	credit cards
date of high school graduation	form of transportation
age	ownership of car
sexual orientation	

STUDY GUIDE:

› REVIEW, APPLY, AND ASSESS

Types of Interviews

A.1 Define what an interview is, and identify five different kinds of interviews.

REVIEW: An interview is a form of oral interaction that is structured to achieve a goal and that involves two or more people who take turns speaking and listening. We have identified five types of interview situations: the information-gathering interview, the appraisal interview, the problem-solving interview, the persuasion interview, and the job interview.

KEY TERMS:

interview
information-gathering
  interview
appraisal interview

problem-solving interview
persuasion interview
job interview

APPLY: It may seem as though the supervisor does most of the preparation for an appraisal interview, but what should an employee do to prepare before an appraisal interview?

ASSESS: Reflect on the last time you were interviewed. What kind of interview was it? How would you evaluate your overall interview skills? What interview skills (if any) do you think you need to improve?

Phases of an Interview

A.2 Describe the three phases of a well-structured interview.

REVIEW: All interviews have an opening, in which the interviewee is put at ease; a body, during which questions are asked and answered; and a conclusion, which brings the interview to a comfortable close.

KEY TERMS:

open question
closed question
probing question
hypothetical question

funnel sequence
inverted funnel sequence
tunnel sequence

APPLY: Imagine that you're an employer who is interviewing candidates for a social media blogger position at your organization. Write a series of interview questions

that follow either the funnel sequence or the inverted funnel sequence.

ASSESS: Review the list of key terms for this section and identify the question types in which you are most skilled in asking and answering. Also, identify the types of questions in which you may need to enhance your skill in either asking or answering.

How to Be Interviewed for a Job

A.3 Identify and describe how to be interviewed for a job, including how to develop a well-worded résumé.

REVIEW: When you are seeking employment, start by becoming aware of your skills and abilities; then use your personal inventory to develop a well-written résumé. Focus on the needs of your prospective employer: Research the organization where you seek a job. During the interview, listen carefully to the questions asked by the interviewer and respond appropriately. After the interview, it may be appropriate to send a thank-you note to the interviewer.

KEY TERMS:

résumé
networking

personal brand

APPLY: Before submitting your résumé to a prospective employer, use the following checklist to ensure that it meets the criteria of an effective résumé.

_____ Name, address, and all contact numbers are accurate.
_____ My career objective matches the advertised need of the employer.
_____ My employment dates are accurate.
_____ I've described the projects I've completed and skills I possess using action verbs and appropriate keywords.
_____ My résumé is clearly formatted.
_____ There are no spelling errors.
_____ There are no grammar or punctuation errors.

ASSESS: Conduct a social media audit of all the information available about you online. What needs to be changed, edited, or modified to improve your online image?

How to Be Interviewed in an Information-Gathering Interview

A.4 Identify and describe how to be interviewed in an information-gathering interview.

REVIEW: When you are preparing to be interviewed for an information-gathering interview, there are three primary tasks. First, prepare for the interview by reviewing information you think that the interviewer will ask you about. Second, listen closely to the questions you are being asked. Finally, respond appropriately by keeping answers direct and honest. Don't ramble. Observe the interviewer's nonverbal responses to determine whether you are answering the questions appropriately.

APPLY: A visit to your doctor or dentist for a regular checkup is, in part, an interview in which the practitioner gathers information from you. How can you prepare for the typical questions you'll be asked at your next checkup?

ASSESS: Watch an information-gathering interview on *60 Minutes, Charlie Rose, Today,* or another news or news magazine program. Identify the types of questions that the interviewer asks (open, closed, probing, or hypothetical). On the basis of the information presented in this appendix, evaluate the effectiveness of both the interviewer and the interviewee.

Responsibilities of the Interviewer

A.5 Explain how to conduct an interview.

REVIEW: When you interview others, don't let your own biases and prejudices interfere with your job of listening and responding to the interviewee. Although it's useful to have a list of questions, be prepared to adapt to the interviewee's behavior. The best interviews have a spontaneous flow rather than a rigid structure. Don't ask illegal questions during a job interview, and handle sensitive questions with tact and diplomacy. Listening well is the hallmark of an effective interviewer. Develop a strategy to record the information you gather from the interview. Finally, the key to any interview is the quality of the questions asked. As the interviewer, you are responsible for asking clear, appropriate, and answerable questions.

APPLY: As an interviewer, what are some ways you could adapt a planned list of questions to specific interviewees?

ASSESS: Imagine that you are an employer interviewing a job applicant. The applicant's answers to your first few questions have not impressed you, and you are growing fairly certain that this is not the right person for the job. How should you proceed in the interview?

〉 THE PRINCIPLE POINTS

Principle One:

Be aware of your communication with yourself and others.

- Take inventory of your skills and abilities to help you determine the job opportunities and careers that are best for you.
- Use your analysis of your talents to help you develop your résumé.
- During an interview, monitor your messages to ensure that you are communicating clearly and effectively.

Principle Two:

Effectively use and interpret verbal messages.

- Speak clearly, and respond to each question you are asked during an interview.
- Use action-oriented words on your résumé and during an interview to describe your accomplishments.
- Organize your résumé to include key elements of your education, experience, and special qualifications.
- When conducting an employment interview, don't ask illegal or unethical questions.

Principle Three:

Effectively use and interpret nonverbal messages.

- Pay special attention to your appearance when you interview for a job; dress conservatively and appear neat and well groomed.
- Speak with confidence, use appropriate eye contact, and communicate interest and enthusiasm during the interview.
- When you interview someone, monitor your interviewee's nonverbal messages for clues about the individual's personality and ability to work with people.
- As an interviewer, observe, evaluate, and then appropriately adapt to the communication behavior of the interviewee.

Principle Four:

Listen and respond thoughtfully to others.

- When you are interviewed for a job, be sure to stop, look, and listen to the interviewer's questions and comments.
- Listen for both the details of the message and the major points or key ideas.
- When interviewing others, consider listening among your most important tasks.

Principle Five:

Appropriately adapt messages to others.

- Learn as much as you can about any prospective employer so that you can describe how your abilities best fit with the needs of the organization to which you are applying.
- Appropriately adapt your communication behavior during an interview, whether you are the interviewer or the interviewee, on the basis of what you learn and observe during the interview.

SAMPLE SPEECHES FOR DISCUSSION AND EVALUATION

Informative Speech

Audism

by Cimmi Alvarez[1]

Dr. Elisabeth Zinser was excited to take over the president's office at Gallaudet University, the only Deaf university in the world, in March of 1988. She wanted to advance the university's rich legacy, but struggled to relate to her soon-to-be students—because, unlike her students, she was not Deaf. The October 23, 1988, *New York Times* reports that Dr. Zinser was chosen over two qualified Deaf candidates, and in response, the student body, most of whom are Deaf, rose up and protested in opposition. Shortly after, the university announced its first Deaf president since its founding in April of 1864: Dr. I. King Jordan. This was a major win for the Deaf community, and a crucial step toward recognizing and rectifying the historic oppression of the Deaf. Today, however, hearing culture continues to dominate society, and audism prevails. In 1975, Tom Humphries coined the term "audism" or "the notion that one is superior based on one's ability to hear." Thomas Holcomb explains in his 2013 book *Introduction to American Deaf Culture*, "In short, audism is the hearing way of dominating, restructuring and exercising authority over the Deaf community." You may have been amazed when you saw a viral video: "deaf baby hears for the first time." But as the June 13, 2016, *Daily Dot* elucidates, such videos casually reinforce audism. New technologies, like cochlear implants, validate the hearing world's view that the Deaf should change how they communicate, to conform to hearing society. Although our community frequently speaks out against discrimination like racism, sexism, and homophobia, we ignore a different form of oppression: audism. So let's learn what audism is by first, examining its historical roots; next, exploring its current form; and finally, discussing implications, because our ability to hear does not excuse our failure to listen.

In a December 2, 2016, personal interview with David Simmons, an instructor on my college campus, I asked what he thought the hearing community needed to learn, and he answered, "Respect." Let's start with American Sign Language, or ASL. To understand the history of audism, we must begin with the actions of HEARING PEOPLE and then understand the culture of DEAF PEOPLE. [While giving her speech, Cimmi signs all words and phrases printed in all caps.]

First, Alexander Graham Bell—yes, the guy who invented the telephone—was a major opponent of signed language in the classroom. Bell believed that since his Deaf wife and mother could speak, all Deaf children should learn to speak. The January 29, 2014, *Rooted in Rights* explains that Bell used his influence to advocate for conformity.

In 1880, educators of the Deaf, though none were Deaf themselves, gathered at the Congress of Milan. There, Bell spoke for three days and promoted oralism, the practice of forcing the Deaf to speak and read lips, as the best way to educate the Deaf. Meanwhile, advocates of ASL, also all hearing, were given only three hours to make counter arguments. The Congress of Milan voted to ban signed languages in the classroom and began a 100-year policy of audism—schools did not hire Deaf teachers, students spoke only in the classroom, and the use of any sign was punished, sometimes with physical violence.

Next, audism grew from an ignorance about Deaf culture. Thomas Holcomb explains in his previously cited book that the Deaf view themselves as a linguistic minority group with a distinct culture, a culture that requires the use of sign language and views deafness as a positive trait rather than a disability. The August 11, 2016, Americans with Disabilities Act defines disability as "a physical or mental impairment that substantially limits one or more major life activities"—activities like holding a job, getting married, or having families, which Deaf people do all the time. Deaf people view their deafness as a language barrier rather than a disability. Audism is rooted in the able-bodied community, leading many hearing scientists and doctors to view deafness as a disability that needs to be cured, rather than what it is: a linguistic subculture. The 1990 AMERICANS with DISABILITIES ACT was supposed to ensure that people with disabilities would receive equal education and occupational opportunities. And yet audism persists and is felt heavily in EDUCATION and the OFFICE.

First, the Deaf still lack the resources to access quality education. Partly due to ADA's emphasis on accommodation, states are cutting Deaf education funding. The July 4, 2016, *Casper Star Tribune* posits that in Wyoming forty percent of a 1.6-million-dollar education budget cut is coming from Deaf programs. Thus, the June 24, 2015, Rochester Institute of Technology points out that Deaf education has been shifted out of residential schools, with eighty-five percent of Deaf students now attending their local public schools. But public schools are fighting for funding as it is. Thomas Holcomb explains in his previously cited book that many Deaf high school graduates have limited English skills and poor ASL fluency because their education is based solely on English, with limited measurable success in meeting communicative, linguistic, and educational needs.

Next, Deaf individuals face deeply rooted oppression in the workplace. Historically, Deaf people were labeled "Deaf and Dumb," and assumed incapable of the cognitive ability to perform everyday work. During the two World Wars, the Deaf were not allowed to serve in the military, a ban that still exists today. The March 10, 2017, *Silent Grapevine* points out that for decades, the Deaf were pigeonholed into blue collar jobs: carpenters, laborers, mechanics, and farmers. The October 26, 2016, *Huffington Post* furthers that today more than half of Deaf employees have faced discrimination at some point in their career due to their deafness. As a result, the December 16, 2015, *Communication Service for the Deaf* posits that despite advances in technology and the protection of the ADA, almost seventy-five percent of Deaf individuals are unemployed.

There is an ASL sign for audism: It is a combination of the signs for DEAF and OPPRESSION. It is a subtlety lost among most in the hearing community, but can better be understood with two implications.

First, audism reveals how we are primed to confuse speech with language. Dirksen L. Bauman, a professor at Gallaudet University, writes in his 2004 paper *Audism* that language is what binds us together as humans, but we have been operating under a definition that confuses language with speech. We don't view signing as a language equal to that of spoken languages. Audism is harder to overcome than other forms of oppression because of how deafness affects language. In fact, the September 16, 2015, *Huffington Post* reports that on September 5th and 6th of that year, more than 1,500 people showed up in Washington, D. C., for a two-day protest of audism in the workplace. But mainstream media never showed up. A major civil rights protest happened in the nation's capital, but the Deaf were not loud enough, did not speak the language of "we the people," and were considered irrelevant. MLK called riots the "language of the unheard," a language the Deaf might have to learn if they hope to overcome their oppressors.

Next, the ADA itself is entrenched in audism. The August 8, 2016, U.S. Department of Agriculture explains that the ADA was designed to ensure that people with disabilities have greater access to American society, currently encouraging "reasonable" accommodations to hearing systems, such as requiring schools to hire ASL interpreters, but not developing superior alternatives to these systems. And while ADA has opened access, the progress is short-lived. The November 18, 2016, *Vice* points out that President Trump's stance on governmental agencies means that cuts are likely for the Department of Justice's civil rights division, which enforces the ADA. A weakened ADA and lack of oversight could mean cuts to Deaf education and inclusion programs. *Vice* continues that, most extremely, many Deaf individuals fear mandatory cochlear implantation designed to cut costs of specialized education and enforcement of the ADA. In Trump's era, the rights of the disabled are at greater risk than ever before, allowing legal audism to spread, essentially starting a new era of hearing-based Jim Crow.

For decades, the competitive forensics community has fought against oppression in many different forms. But, today we learned about the plight of a silent minority—the Deaf—by looking at historical and current oppression and discussing the implications of audism. WE WORK to GIVE a VOICE to the VOICELESS, BUT SOMETIMES we SHOULD LISTEN or WATCH instead.

Persuasive Speech
Doctors and Sex Abuse
by Cole Hanzlicek[2]

A 32-year-old woman in California visits plastic surgeon Mark Knight for a routine post-surgery checkup. Her husband and two sons wait in the car; it won't take long, she says. *The Atlanta Journal Constitution* on September 22, 2016, elaborates, "Dr. Knight calls himself an artist, one whose 'gifted hands' sculpt bodies to perfection." [In this appointment, though,] "his hands strayed." As a part of its yearlong investigation, *The Atlanta Journal Constitution*, or the *AJC*, discovered that Mark Knight is a predatory physician, and not the only one lurking in our medical system. *CBS News* on August 24, 2016, reveals that Knight joins the more than 2,400 doctors nationwide who have sexually abused their patients since 1999. But perhaps more shockingly, Knight, along with half of those abusive doctors, still practices today. Half. And *The Chicago Tribune* of July 6, 2016, clarifies that these numbers represent only reported cases, leaving countless victims unknown. All the while, sexually abusive doctors hide behind their white coats. What's worse, the *AJC* on November 16, 2016, reports that 49 states have failed to take comprehensive legal action against this system of abuse. When these atrocities are committed by the very professionals we turn to when we are at our weakest and most vulnerable, and ignored by our state governments, the burden falls on us to hold these predators accountable; because for God knows how long, no one else has. So let's first understand why this abuse goes unnoticed and unpunished, next recognize the devastating impact predatory physicians have, before finally developing solutions. In 2002, *The Boston Globe* uncovered a decades-long legacy of sexual abuse in the Catholic Church, exposing an institution built on faith and trust. Today, alongside the work of the *AJC*, we'll do the same.

At the onset of their investigation, the *AJC* requested records of abuse from all 50 states. However, in a personal interview on January 27, 2017, lead *AJC* journalist Danny Robbins explains that in response, state medical boards claimed no such records existed. But after months of searching, the *AJC* uncovered thousands. States hid these records for two reasons: cultural trust in physicians and dangerous holes in state legislation.

First, we can't fathom that a doctor would ever cross the line from professional to predator. CNN on July 12, 2016, explains, "in our culture, we [praise and respect] doctors, we're not trained to question them," and predatory physicians take advantage of that trust. *ABC News* on February 24, 2017, notes the example of U.S. Olympic gymnastic team physician Larry Nassar, who for the last twenty years assaulted over sixty gymnasts. For his victims, Nassar was a friendly face, a break from the pressures of Olympic training. But when these patients began to feel uncomfortable at his advances, he didn't step away. No, he told them his actions were part of a special treatment to relieve back pain, exploiting their trust.

Next, gaps in the law leave patients vulnerable. *NBC News* on August 24, 2016, explains that because our society needs doctors, and it's really hard to become a doctor, state legislators turn a blind eye when they abuse. In fact, the *AJC* on November 17, 2016, graded all fifty states in five areas where the law should protect patients from abuse. But, for public access to records of abuse, 38 states received failing grades. Thirty-four states have failed to remove predatory physicians from practice. And, in 47 states, there is little to no requirement for law enforcement to investigate abuse as a criminal act. Not every state fails every category, but with the exception of Delaware, every state fails at least one—and predatory physicians capitalize on it.

Even when abusive doctors do lose their state license to practice, the *AJC* on July 5, 2016, reveals that they can just go to the next state—like Oscar Almeida, who inappropriately touched four patients in Alabama and lost his license to practice there, so he went to Mississippi, where the medical board claimed he "would be an asset to the state." This state-sanctioned system of abuse results in two effects: damaging patient health and institutional blindness.

First, the normalization of abuse endangers patient health. The *AJC* on December 9, 2016, explains, "[victims of abuse often] keep silent for fear they won't be believed" by their peers. In response, many stop going to the doctor completely; but for some, even escape does not guarantee their safety. The *AJC* continues, in 2012, 23-year-old Elgin Stafford accused University of California doctor Robert Kevess of sexual abuse. But "as [Elgin] faced the possibility of seeing Kevess in court, the 23-year-old disappeared and [days later] was found floating in a waterway." For Elgin, the betrayal of his doctor and the fear of his peers' silence was too much to bear.

Second, institutions become blind to the cycle of abuse. *NPR* on August 24, 2016, reports that medical regulators' refusal to punish these abusive doctors essentially grants them the consent of the state. Local Delaware newspaper *The Norwalk Reflector*, on December 29, 2016, tells the story of pediatrician Earl Bradley, who in 1994 molested a two-year-old girl. To investigators, Bradley claimed the victim's mother was trying to extort him for money, and medical regulators agreed; after all, they said, "[Bradley] specialized in welfare patients, so a shakedown was a distinct possibility." The case was closed, and over the next fifteen years, Bradley would go on to abuse, molest, and rape 1,200 children.

Thankfully, in 2009, Delaware police arrested Earl Bradley, and he is now serving life in prison. Since his arrest, Delaware has worked to become the safest state in the country for patients. And on March 1, 2017, the *AJC* reported that California has followed their lead. As states across the country begin to do their part, let's do ours.

First, let's end our blind trust in doctors. On this handout, I've compiled a list of the worst doctors highlighted by the *AJC* for the most egregious offenses in all 50 states. Also, visit the website of the Federation of State Medical Boards, *docinfo.org*. Search your doctors; it'll tell you if they have faced any disciplinary actions. If an abusive doctor is practicing near you, please give me your email, and I will send you a warning flyer you can quickly personalize and distribute. After learning that an abusive doctor continues to practice just blocks away from my university, I placed flyers all over my campus exposing his past. These doctors shouldn't be allowed to practice, but because they are, let's make sure they never see another patient again.

Finally, take action in your state legislature. Earlier, I discussed the five legal problem areas identified by the *AJC*. Here is a map of the United States; if your state is green, great—your state is effectively covering all five areas. If your state is yellow, orange, or red—we've got some work to do. Using the grading system of the *AJC*, I've compiled a list of every state's worst problem area, so write down your information, and I will send you a Personalized Advocacy Pack. It's got contact information for your state representative, a phone script, and sample legislation modeled after Delaware's. If we advocate in every state represented in this room, we can turn the tide of abuse across the country.

When doctors take the Hippocratic Oath, they vow to "abstain from harm." Right now, more than 1,200 doctors across the country are violating that oath, and right now, the *AJC* is working to expose all of them. Today, we examined the causes, effects, and solutions to this state-protected system of abuse. We put our lives in our doctor's hands. But ensuring that they uphold their oath is in our hands now.

Notes

Chapter 1

1 R. Emanuel, J. Adams, K. Baker, E. K. Daufin, C. Ellington, E. Fitts, J. Himsel, L. Holladay, and D. Okeowo, "How College Students Spend Their Time Communicating," *International Journal of Listening* 22 (2008): 12–28; E. T. Klemmer and F. W. Snyder, "Measurement of Time Spent Communicating," *Journal of Communication* 20 (1972): 142.

2 We thank our friend Tom Burkholder, University of Nevada, Las Vegas, for this idea.

3 J. C. Humes, *The Sir Winston Method: The Five Secrets of Speaking the Language of Leadership* (New York: William Morrow, 1991).

4 V. Marchant, "Listen Up!" *Time* (June 28, 1999): 72.

5 A. Vangelisti and J. Daly, "Correlates of Speaking Skills in the United States: A National Assessment," *Communication Education* 38 (1989): 132–43.

6 M. Cronin, ed., "The Need for Required Oral Communication Education in the Undergraduate General Education Curriculum," unpublished paper, 1993, available from the National Communication Association, Washington, DC.

7 J. Ayres and T. S. Hopf, "The Long-Term Effect of Visualization in the Classroom: A Brief Research Report," *Communication Education* 39 (1990): 75–78.

8 See J. C. McCroskey and M. Beatty, "The Communibiological Perspective: Implications for Communication in Instruction," *Communication Education* 49 (2000): 1; also see J. C. McCroskey, J. A. Daly, M. M. Martin, and M. J. Beatty, eds., *Communication and Personality: Trait Perspectives* (Cresskill, NJ: Hampton Press, 1998).

9 J. H. McConnell, *Are You Communicating? You Can't Manage without It* (New York: McGraw-Hill, 1995).

10 Value Investors Portal, "Warren Buffet on Communication Skills," *YouTube*, December 6, 2010, accessed May 14, 2013, www.youtube.com/watch?v=tpgcEYpLzP0.

11 Hart Research Associates, "Falling Short? College Learning and Career Success," *Association of American Colleges and Universities*, January 20, 2015, accessed February 12, 2017, www.aacu.org; Hart Research Associates, "Employer Priorities for Most Important College Learning Outcomes," *Association of American Colleges and Universities*, January 20, 2015, accessed February 12, 2017, www.aacu.org; "Staffing in Special Markets," *Society for Human Resources Management*, September 3, 2016, accessed February 12, 2017, www.shrm.org. Also see: J. L. Winsor, D. Curtis, and R. D. Stephens, "National Preferences in Business and Communication Education: A Survey Update," *Journal of the Association of Communication Administration* 3 (1997): 170–179. For a summary of the values and virtues of studying communication, see S. P. Morreale and J. C. Pearson, "Why Communication Education Is Important: The Centrality of the Discipline in the 21st Century," *Communication Education* 57.2 (2008): 224–240; also see S. P. Morreale, D. W. Worley, and B. Hugenberg, "The Basic Communication Course at Two- and Four-Year U.S. Colleges and Universities: Study VIII—The 40th Anniversary," *Communication Education* 59.4 (2010): 405–430; Hart Research Associates "Raising the Bar: Employers' Views on College Learning in the Wake of the Economic Downturn," Washington, DC, Association of American Colleges and Universities (January 10, 2010); D. Sellnow, "Integrated Composition and Communication: Addressing the Needs of the 21st Century," paper presented at the Rhetoric Society of America annual conference, Minneapolis, Minnesota (May 2010).

12 Career Services, "What Skills and Attributes Employers Seek When Hiring Students," *University of Wisconsin–River Falls*, accessed June 7, 2007, www.uwrf.edu/ccslskills/htm; C. Luckenbaugh and K. Gray, "Employers Describe Perfect Job Candidate," *Association of Colleges and Employers Survey*, accessed June 4, 2007, www.naceweb.org/press/display.asp?year=2003&prid=169; R. S. Hansen and K. Handson, "What Do Employers Really Want? Top Skills and Values Employers Seek from Job Seekers," *Quintessential Careers*, accessed June 4, 2007, www.quintcareers.com/job_skills_values.html. For evidence that communication skills can be developed, see R. F. Brown, C. L. Bylurd, J. A. Gueguen, C. Diamond, J. Eddington, and D. Kissane, "Developing Patient-Centered Communication Skills Training for Oncologists: Describing the Content and Efficacy of Training," *Communication Education* 59.3 (2010): 235–48; G. Sulcas and J. English, "A Case for Focus on Professional Communication Skills at Senior Undergraduate Level in Engineering and the Built Environment," *Southern African Linguistics & Applied Language Studies* 28.3 (2010): 219–26.

13 For a discussion of the prominence of LinkedIn in the job market see: S. Rivera, "You Heard it Here First: LinkedIn is the New (and Improved) Facebook," *Study Breaks*, (November 2016): 34.

14 P. Gillooly, "Why You Need Social Media," *The New York Times*, Business (December 4, 2016): 8.

15 M. M. Robles, "Executive Perceptions of the Top 10 Soft Skills Needed in Today's Workplace," *Business Communication Quarterly* 75, no. 4 (2012): 453–65.

16 K. E. Davis and M. Todd, "Assessing Friendship: Prototypes, Paradigm Cases, and Relationship Description," in *Understanding Personal Relationships,* edited by S. W. Duck and D. Perlman (London: Sage, 1985); B. Wellman, "From Social Support to Social Network," in *Social Support: Theory, Research and Applications,* edited by I. G. Sarason and B. R. Sarason (Dordrecht, Netherlands: Nijhoff, 1985); R. Hopper, M. L. Knapp, and L. Scott, "Couples' Personal Idioms: Exploring Intimate Talk," *Journal of Communication* 31 (1981): 23–33.

17 M. Argyle and M. Hendershot, *The Anatomy of Relationships* (London: Penguin Books, 1985): 14.

18 D. Goleman, "Emotional Intelligence: Issues in Paradigm Building," in *The Emotionally Intelligent Workplace,* edited by C. Chemiss and D. Goleman (San Francisco: Jossey-Bass, 2001): 13.

19 V. Satir, *People Making* (Palo Alto, CA: Science and Behavior Books, 1972): 1.

20 M. Argyle, *The Psychology of Happiness* (London: Routledge, 2001).

21 J. Lynch, *The Broken Heart: The Medical Consequences of Loneliness* (New York: Basic Books, 1977).

22 D. P. Phillips, "Deathday and Birthday: An Unexpected Connection," in *Statistics: A Guide to the Unknown,* edited by J. M. Tanur (San Francisco: Holden-Day, 1972); also see F. Korbin and G. Hendershot, "Do Family Ties Reduce Mortality? Evidence from the United States 1968," *Journal of Marriage and the Family* 39 (1977): 737–46; K. Heller and K. S. Rook, "Distinguishing the Theoretical Functions of Social Ties: Implications of Support Interventions," in *Handbook of Personal Relationships* 2e, edited by S. W. Duck, K. Dindia, W. Ickes, R. Milardo, R. S. L. Mills, and B. R. Sarason (Chichester, UK: Wiley, 1997); B. R. Samson, L. G. Sarason, and R. A. R. Gurung, "Close Personal Relationships and Health Outcomes: A Key to the Role of Social Support," in *Handbook of Personal Relationships* 2e, edited by S. W. Duck, K. Dindia, W. Ickes, R. Milardo, R. S. L. Mills, and B. R. Sarason (Chichester, UK: Wiley, 1997); S. Duck, *Relating to Others* (Buckingham, UK: Open University Press, 1999): 1.

23 Pamela Paul, "Does Facebook Make Someone Social Offline?" *New York Times* (January 30, 2011): Style 8; also see

S. Craig Watkins and H. Erin Lee, "Got Facebook? Investigating What's Social About Social Media," *University of Texas at Austin*, accessed January 31, 2011, www.theyoungandthedigital.com/wp-content/uploads/2010/11/watkins_lee_facebookstudy-nov-18.pdf.

24 F. E. X. Dance and C. Larson, *Speech Communication: Concepts and Behavior* (New York: Holt, Rinehart and Winston, 1972).

25 Dance and Larson, *Speech Communication.*

26 J. T. Masterson, S. A. Beebe, and N. H. Watson, *Invitation to Effective Speech Communication* (Glenview, IL: Scott, Foresman, 1989).

27 M. Gladwell, *Blink: The Power of Thinking without Thinking* (New York: Little, Brown, 2005).

28 L. Barker, R. Edwards, C. Gaines, K. Gladney, and F. Holley, "An Investigation of Proportional Time Spent in Various Communication Activities of College Students," *Journal of Applied Communication Research* 8 (1981): 101–9.

29 D. Barnlund, *Interpersonal Communication: Survey and Studies* (Boston: Houghton Mifflin, 1968).

30 See, for instance, C. R. Berger and J. J. Bradac, *Language and Social Knowledge: Uncertainty in Interpersonal Relations* (London: Arnold, 1982).

31 O. Wiio, *Wiio's Laws—and Some Others* (Espoo, Finland: Welin-Goos, 1978).

32 T. Watzlawick, J. B. Bavelas, and D. Jackson, *The Pragmatics of Human Communication* (New York: W. W. Norton, 1967).

33 D. Thompson, R. Filik "Sarcasm in Written Communication: Emoticons are Efficient Markers of Intention" in *Journal of Computer-Mediated Communication*, 21 (2016): 105–20.

34 S. B. Shimanoff, *Communication Rules: Theory and Research* (Beverly Hills, CA: Sage, 1980).

35 H. Lasswell, "The Structure and Function of Communication in Society," in *The Communication of Ideas*, edited by L. Bryson (New York: Institute for Religious and Social Studies, 1948): 37.

36 See V. E. Cronen, W. B. Pearce, and L. M. Harris, "The Coordinated Management of Meaning: A Theory of Communication," in *Human Communication Theory: Comparative Essays,* edited by F. E. X. Dance (New York: Harper & Row, 1982): 61–89.

37 This section is based on Masterson, Beebe, and Watson, *Invitation to Effective Speech Communication.* We are especially indebted to J. T. Masterson for this discussion.

38 See R. P. Wolff, *About Philosophy* (Upper Saddle River, NJ: Prentice Hall, 2000): 308–35.

39 C. S. Lewis, *The Abolition of Man* (New York: Macmillan, 1947); also see A. M. Nicholi Jr., *The Question of God: C. S. Lewis and Sigmund Freud Debate God, Love, Sex, and the Meaning of Life* (New York: Free Press, 2002).

40 C. Christians and M. Traber, *Communication Ethics and Universal Values* (Beverly Hills, CA: Sage, 1997); also see S. Bok, *Common Values* (Columbia: University of Missouri Press, 2002).

41 Christians and Traber, *Communication Ethics and Universal Values.*

42 For additional discussion of the ethical values taught in the world's religions, see H. Smith, *The World's Religions* (San Francisco: HarperSanFrancisco, 1991).

43 Adapted from W. Ham, *Man's Living Religions* (Independence, MO: Herald Publishing House, 1966): 39–40.

44 "NCA Credo for Communication Ethics," *National Communication Association*, 1999, accessed June 27, 2001, www.natcom.org/conferences/Ethicslethicsconfcred099.htm.

45 M. Holden, "Dating with Tinder," http: askmen.com, accessed January 28, 2017.

46 A. Sullivan, "Put Down Your Phone," *New York*, (September 19, 2016): 35.

47 E. Darics, "The Blurring Boundaries Between Synchronicity and Asynchronicity: New Communicative Situations in Work-Related Instant Messaging" in *International Journal of Business Communication*, 51:4 (2014): 337–58.

48 A. Sullivan, "Put Down Your Phone."

49 M. Anderson, "6 facts about Americans and their smartphones," Pew Research Center (April 5, 2015), www.pewresearch.org/fact-tank/2015/04/01/6-facts-about-americans-and-their-smartphones, accessed April 20, 2017.

50 A. Sullivan, "Put Down Your Phone."

51 A. Sullivan, "Put Down Your Phone."

52 M. Seo, J. Kim, and P. David, "Always Connected or Always Distracted? ADHD Symptoms and Social Assurance Explain Problematic Use of Mobile Phone and Multicommunicating," *Journal of Computer-Mediated Communication*, 20 (2015): 667–81.

53 N. S. Baron, *Always On: Language in an Online and Mobile World* (New York: Oxford University Press, 2008); also see D. Crystal, *txtng: The gr8 db8* (Oxford, UK: Oxford University Press, 2008); S. Turkle, *Alone Together: Why We Expect More from Technology and Less from Each Other* (New York: Basic Books, 2011); M. A. Dourin, "College Students' Text Messaging, Use of Textese, and Literacy Skills," *Journal of Assisted Learning* 27.1 (2011): 67.

54 Watkins and Lee, "Got Facebook?"

55 A. Smith, "6 New Facts about Facebook," *Pew Research Center*, accessed February 3, 2014, www.pewresearch.org/fact-tank.

56 T. Philbin, "Instagram Quotes Are the Death of Complex Thought," *Study Breaks* (November 2016), p. 34.

57 Zephora Digital Marketing. The Top 20 Valuable Facebook Statistics—Updated January 2017. https://zephoria.com/top-15-valuable-facebook-statistics, accessed January 29, 2017.

58 A. Sullivan, "Put Down Your Phone."

59 C. Smith, "Facebook by the Numbers," *Digital Market Ramblings*, accessed March 28, 2014, expandedramblings.com/index.php/by-the-numbers-17-amazing-facebook-stats/#.UzWMY1xNw8M.

60 Zephora Digital Marketing. The Top 20 Valuable Facebook Statistics—Updated January 2017. https://zephoria.com/top-15-valuable-facebook-statistics, accessed January 29, 2017.

61 Smith, "Facebook by the Numbers."

62 Smith, "Facebook by the Numbers."

63 Watkins and Lee, "Got Facebook?"; Zephora Digital Marketing. The Top 20 Valuable Facebook Statistics—Updated January 2017. https://zephoria.com/top-15-valuable-facebook-statistics, accessed January 29, 2017.

64 Zephora Digital Marketing. The Top 20 Valuable Facebook Statistics—Updated January 2017. https://zephoria.com/top-15-valuable-facebook-statistics, accessed January 29, 2017.

65 Watkins and Lee, "Got Facebook?"; T. Philbin, "Instagram Quotes Are the Death of Complex Thought."

66 D. J. Saul, "3 Million Teens Leave Facebook in 3 Years: The 2014 Facebook Demographic Report," January 15, 2014, accessed March 28, 2014, istrategylabs.com/2014/01/3-million-teens-leave-facebook-in-3-years-the-2014-facebook-demographic-report/.

67 Zephora Digital Marketing. The Top 20 Valuable Facebook Statistics—Updated January 2017. https://zephoria.com/top-15-valuable-facebook-statistics, accessed January 29, 2017.

68 Watkins and Lee, "Got Facebook?"

69 A. Smith, "6 New Facts about Facebook."

70 R. Kraut, M. Patterson, V. Lundmark, S. Kiesler, M. Tridas, and W. Scherlis, "Internet Paradox: A Social Technology That Reduces Social Involvement and Psychological Well-Being?" *American Psychologist* 53 (1998): 1017–31.

71 R. Kraut, S. Kiesler, B. Boneva, J. Cummings, V. Helgeson, and A. Crawford, "Internet Paradox Revisited," *Journal of Social Issues* 58 (2002): 49–74; P. E. N. Howard, L. Raine, and S. Jones, "Days and Nights on the Internet: The Impact of a Diffusing Technology," *American Behavioral Scientist* 45 (2001): 383–404; M. A. Mazur and R. J. Bums, "Perceptions of Relational Interdependence in Online Relationships: The Effects of Communication Apprehension and Introversion," *Communication Research Reports* 17.4 (2000): 397–406.

72 Y. Amichai-Hamburger, *The Social Net: Human Behavior in Cyberspace* (Oxford, UK: Oxford University Press, 2005); K. Y. A. McKenna and J. A. Bargh, "Plan 9 from Cyberspace: The Implications of the Internet for Personality and Social Psychology," *Personality and Social Psychology Review* 4 (2000): 57–75.

73 S. Turkle, *Alone Together*: 1.

74 A. Sedghi, "Facebook: 10 Years of Social Networking, in Numbers," *The Guardian*, February 4, 2014, accessed March 28, 2014, www.theguardian.com/news/datablog/2014/feb/04/facebook-in-numbers-statistics.

75 Watkins and Lee, "Got Facebook?"

76 B. Jin and J. F. Pena, "Mobile Communication in Romantic Relationships: Mobile Phone Use, Relational Uncertainty, Love, Commitment, and Attachment Styles," *Communication Reports* 23.1 (2010): 39–51.

77 Zephora Digital Marketing. The Top 20 Valuable Facebook Statistics—Updated January 2017. https://zephoria.com/top-15-valuable-facebook-statistics, accessed January 29, 2017.

78 We appreciate and acknowledge our friend and colleague M. Redmond for his contributions to our understanding of interpersonal communication. For more information, see S. A. Beebe, S. J. Beebe, and M. V. Redmond, *Interpersonal Communication: Relating to Others* 8e (Boston: Pearson, 2017).

79 For an excellent discussion of the power of dialogue to enrich the quality of communication, see D. Yankelovich, *The Magic of Dialogue: Transforming Conflict into Cooperation* (New York: Simon & Schuster, 1999).

80 S. A. Beebe and J. T. Masterson, *Communicating in Small Groups: Principles and Practices* 11e (Boston: Pearson, 2015).

81 M. S. Poole and I. Ahmed, "Group Decision Support Systems," in *21st Century Communication: A Reference Handbook*, edited by W. Eadie (Thousand Oaks, CA: Sage, 2010); also see M. C. Poole, "Collaboration, Integration, and Transformation: Directions for Research on Communication and Information Technologies," *Journal of Computer-Mediated Communication* 14 (2009): 753–763.

82 See: D. Ofri, The Conversation Placebo, *The New York Times* Sunday Review (January 22, 2017): 2.

83 For an excellent review of intrapersonal communication theory and research, see D. Voate, *Intrapersonal Communication: Different Voices, Different Minds* (Hillsdale, NJ: Lawrence Erlbaum, 1994).

84 D. Quinn, *My Ishmael* (New York: Bantam Books, 1996).

85 B. Plester and C. Wood, "Exploring Relationships between Traditional and New Media Literacies: British Preteen Texters at School," *Journal of Computer-Mediated Communication* 14 (2009): 1108–29.

86 Robert Fulghum, *All I Really Need to Know I Learned in Kindergarten* (New York: Ballantine Books, 1988).

87 Barker et al., "An Investigation of Proportional Time Spent in Various Communication Activities of College Students."

Chapter 2

1 J. Knight-McCord, D. Cleary, N. Grant, A. Herron, S. Jumbo, T. Lacey, T. Livingston, S. Robinson, R. Smith, and R. Emanuel, "What Social Media Sites Do College Students Use Most?" *Journal of Undergraduate Ethnic Minority Psychology* 2 (2016): 21–26.

2 S. R. Covey, *The Seven Habits of Highly Effective People*, Anniversary Edition (New York: Simon & Schuster, 2013): 74.

3 D. W. Johnson, *Reaching Out: Interpersonal Effectiveness and Self-Actualization* 11e (Boston: Pearson, 2012): 51.

4 E. Young, "Who Do You Think You Are?" *New Scientist* 229 (2016): 30.

5 S. E. Wood, E. Green Wood, and D. Boyd, *Mastering the World of Psychology* 6e (Boston: Pearson, 2017): 115.

6 N. R. Branscombe and R. A. Baron, *Social Psychology* 14e (Boston: Pearson, 2016).

7 C. Scaffidi Abbate, S. Boca, and G. H. E. Gendolla, "Self-Awareness, Perspective-Taking, and Egocentrism," *Self & Identity* 15 (2016): 371–380; S. M. McNaughton, "Developing Pre-Requisites for Empathy: Increasing Awareness of Self, the Body, and the Perspectives of Others," *Teaching in Higher Education* 21 (2016): 501–515; Young, "Who Do You Think You Are?"; A. Sutton, "Measuring the Effects of Self-Awareness: Construction of the Self-Awareness Outcomes Questionnaire," *Europe's Journal of Psychology* 12 (2016): 645–658.

8 K. Horney, *Neurosis and Human Growth* (New York: W. W. Norton, 1991): 17.

9 A. Elliott, *Concepts of the Self* 3e (Cambridge, UK: Polity Press, 2013); K. J. Gergen, *The Saturated Self: Dilemmas of Identity in Contemporary Life* (New York: Basic Books, 2000); B. Goss, *Processing Communication: Information Processing in Intrapersonal Communication* (Belmont, CA: Wadsworth, 1982): 72.

10 S. Harter and W. M. Bukowski, *The Construction of the Self* 2e (New York: Guilford, 2015); D. O. Oyserman, K. E. Elmore, and G. S. Smith, "Self, Self-Concept, and Identity," in *Handbook of Self and Identity* 2e, edited by M. R. Leary and J. Price Tangney (New York: Guilford, 2013): 69–104.

11 G. Bukobza, "The Epistemological Basis of Selfhood," *New Ideas in Psychology* 25 (2007): 39.

12 Bukobza, "The Epistemological Basis of Selfhood," 37–65.

13 For more information on self-concept and culture, see A. A. Pekerti and D. C. Thomas, "The Role of Self-Concept in Cross-Cultural Communication," *International Journal of Cross Cultural Management* 15 (2015): 167–193; C. M. Brown, A. A. Shilling, and S. W. Park, "A Comparison of Self-Complexity in the United States and South Korea," *Self & Identity* 16 (2017): 16–36; S. E. Cross and J. S. Gore, "Cultural Models of the Self," in *Handbook of Self and Identity*, 587–614; C. Kanagawa, S. E. Cross, and H. R. Markus, "'Who Am I?' The Cultural Psychology of the Conceptual Self," *Personality and Social Psychology Bulletin* 27 (2001): 90–103.

14 W. James, *Principles of Psychology* (New York: Henry Holt, 1890).

15 M. Ura and K. S. J. Preston, "The Influence of Thin-Ideal Internalization on Women's Body Image, Self-Esteem, and Appearance Avoidance: Covariance Structure Analysis," *American Communication Journal* 17 (2015): 15–26; J. Veldhuis, E. A. Konjin, and J. C. Seidell, "Counteracting Media's Thin-Body Ideal for Adolescent Girls: Informing Is More Effective Than Warning," *Media Psychology* 17 (2014): 154–184; M. Tiggemann, "The Status of Media Effects on Body Image Research: Commentary on Articles in the Thematic Issue on Body Image and Media," *Media Psychology* 17 (2014): 127–133.

16 L. Shu-Yueh, "The Effects of Cosmetic Surgery Reality Shows on Women's Beliefs of Beauty Privileges, Perceptions of Cosmetic Surgery, and Desires for Cosmetic Enhancements," *American Communication Journal* 16 (2014): 1–14; V. Quick, R. McWilliams, and C. Byrd-Bredbenner, "Fatty, Fatty, Two-By-Four: Weight-Teasing History and Disturbed Eating in Young Adult Women," *American Journal of Public Health* 103 (2013): 508–515.

17 M. Cordes, S. Vocks, R. Dtising, A. Bauer, and M. Waldorf, "Male Body Image and Visual Attention Towards Oneself and Other Men," *Psychology of Men & Masculinity* 17 (2016): 243–254; L. DeFeciani, "Eating Disorders and Body Image Concerns among Male Athletes," *Clinical Social Work Journal* 44 (2016): 114–123; M-E. Brierley, K. R. Brooks, J. Mond, R. J. Stevenson, and I. D. Stephen, "The Body and the Beautiful: Health, Attractiveness, and Body Composition in Men's and Women's Bodies," *PLoS One* 11 (2016): 1–16; Z. Sylvia, T. K. King, and B. J. Morse, "Virtual Ideals: The Effect of Video Game Play on Male Body Image," *Computers in Human Behavior* 37 (2014): 183–188; L. A. Ricciardelli and M. P. McCabe, "Body Image Development in Adolescent Boys," in *Body Image: A Handbook of Science, Practice, and Prevention* 2e, edited by T. F. Cash and L. Smolak (New York: Guilford, 2013): 85–92.

18 K. P. McIntyre, B. A. Mattingly, and G. W. Lewandowski, "When 'We' Changes 'Me,'" *Journal of Social & Personal Relationships* 32 (2015): 857.

19 C. H. Cooley, *Human Nature and the Social Order* (New York: Scribner's, 1912).

20 G. H. Mead, *Mind, Self, and Society* (Chicago: University of Chicago Press, 1934); A. Aron and N. Nardone, "Self and Close Relationships," in *Handbook of Self and Identity*, 520–541.

20 R. M. Dailey, "Testing Components of Confirmation: How Acceptance and Challenge from Mothers, Fathers, and Siblings Are Related to Adolescent Self-Concept," *Communication Monographs* 77 (2010): 592–617.

22 J. N. Martin and T. K. Nakayama, *Experiencing Intercultural Communication* 6e (New York: McGraw-Hill, 2017).

23 M. A. Hogg, "Social Identity and the Psychology of Groups," in *Handbook of Self and Identity*, 502–519.

24 D. K. Ivy, *GenderSpeak: Communicating in a Gendered World* 6e (Dubuque, IA: Kendall Hunt, 2017); M. Forman-Brunnell and J. D. Whitney (Eds.), *Dolls Studies: The Many Meanings of Girls' Toys and Play* (London: Peter Lang, 2015); D. Ehrensaft, *Gender Born, Gender Made: Raising Healthy Gender-Nonconforming Children* (New York: The Experiment, 2011); J. E. O. Blakemore and R. E. Centers, "Characteristics of Boys' and Girls' Toys," *Sex Roles* 53 (2005): 619–634.

25 J. E. Stake, "Gender Differences and Similarities in Self-Concept within Everyday Life Contexts," *Psychology of Women Quarterly* 16 (1992): 349–363.

26 S. Lamb, L. M. Brown, and M. Tappan, *Packaging Boyhood: Saving Our Sons from Superheroes, Slackers, and Other Media Stereotypes* (New York: St. Martin's, 2009); S. Lamb and L. M. Brown, *Packaging Girlhood: Rescuing Our Daughters from Marketers' Schemes* (New York: St. Martin's, 2006).

27 Elliott, *Concepts of the Self*; A. Elliott and P. du Gay, *Identity in Question* (Thousand Oaks, CA: Sage, 2009); J. Jorgenson, "Reflexivity in Feminist Research Practice: Hearing the Unsaid," *Women & Language* 34 (2011): 115–118; C. E. Medved and L. H. Turner, "Qualitative Research: Practicing Reflexivity," *Women & Language* 34 (2011): 109–112.

28 M. McKay and P. Fanning, *Self-Esteem: A Proven Program of Cognitive Techniques for Assessing, Improving, and Maintaining Your Self-Esteem* 4e (Oakland, CA: New Harbinger Publications, 2016).

29 G. Steinem, *Revolution from Within: A Book of Self-Esteem* (Boston: Little, Brown, 1993): 26.

30 J. D. Campbell, P. D. Trapnell, S. J. Heine, I. M. Katz, L. F. Lavallee, and D. R. Lehman, "Self-Concept Clarity: Measurement, Personality Correlates, and Cultural Boundaries," *Journal of Personality and Social Psychology* 70 (1996): 141–156.

31 For more information on self-concept clarity, see A. E. Wong, R. R. Vallacher, and A. Nowak, "Intrinsic Dynamics of State Self-Esteem: The Role of Self-Concept Clarity," *Personality & Individual Differences* 100 (2016): 167–172; C. Fullwood, B. M. James, and C-H. Chen-Wilson, "Self-Concept Clarity and Online Self-Presentation in Adolescents," *CyberPsychology, Behavior & Social Networking* 19 (2016): 716–720; R. E. Fite, M. I. H. Lindeman, A. P. Rogers, E. Voyles, and A. M. Durik, "Knowing Oneself and Long-Term Goal Pursuit: Relations among Self-Concept Clarity, Conscientiousness, and Grit," *Personality & Individual Differences* 108 (2017): 191–194; A. Pilarska, "How Do Self-Concept Differentiation and Self-Concept Clarity Interrelate in Predicting Sense of Personal Identity?" *Personality & Individual Differences* 102 (2016): 85–89; K. P. McIntyre, B. A. Mattingly, G. W. Lewandowski, and A. Simpson, "Workplace Self-Expansion: Implications for Job Satisfaction, Commitment, Self-Concept Clarity, and Self-Esteem among the Employed and Unemployed," *Basic & Applied Social Psychology* 36 (2014): 59–69; J. D. Campbell, "Self-Esteem and Clarity of the Self-Concept," *Journal of Personality and Social Psychology* 59 (1990): 538–549.

32 L. Rill, E. Baiocchi, M. Hopper, K. Denker, and L. N. Olson, "Exploration of the Relationship Between Self-Esteem, Commitment, and Verbal Aggressiveness in Romantic Dating Relationships," *Communication Reports* 22 (2009): 102–113; T. DeHart and B. W. Pelham, "Fluctuations in State Implicit Self-Esteem in Response to Daily Negative Events," *Journal of Experimental Social Psychology* 43 (2007): 157–165.

33 A. J. Holmstrom, J. C. Russell, and D. D. Clare, "Assessing the Role of Job-Search Self-Efficacy in the Relationship between Esteem Support and Job-Search Behavior among Two Populations of Job Seekers," *Communication Studies* 66 (2015): 277–300; A. J. Holmstrom, J. C. Russell, and D. D. Clare, "Esteem Support Messages Received during the Job Search: A Test of the CETESM," *Communication Monographs* 80 (2013): 220–242.

34 Ivy, *GenderSpeak*.

35 W. Bleidom, J. J. A. Denissen, J. E. Gebauer, R. C. Arslan, P. J. Rentfrow, J. Potter, and S. D. Gosling, "Age and Gender Differences in Self-Esteem—A Cross-Cultural Window," *Journal of Personality & Social Psychology* 111 (2016): 396–410; C. Mason, K. Mason, and A. Mathews, "Aspiring to Lead: An Investigation into the Interactions between Self-Esteem, Patriarchal Attitudes, Gender, and Christian Leadership," *Journal of Psychology & Theology* 44 (2016): 244–256; B. M. Hill, S. M. Ogletree, and K. M. McCrary, "Body Modifications in College Students: Considering Gender, Self-Esteem, Body Appreciation, and Reasons for Tattoos," *College Student Journal* 50 (2016): 246–52; S. Sprecher, J. E. Brooks, and W. Avogo, "Self-Esteem among Young Adults: Differences and Similarities Based on Gender, Age, and Cohort (1990–2012)," *Sex Roles* 69 (2013): 264–275; G. D. Webster, L. A. Kirkpatrick, J. B. Neziek, C. V. Smith, and E. L. Paddock, "Different Slopes for Different Folks: Self-Esteem Instability and Gender as Moderators of the Relationship between Self-Esteem and Attitudinal Aggression," *Self and Identity* 6 (2007): 74–94.

36 K. Kay and C. Shipman, *The Confidence Code: The Science and Art of Self-Assurance—What Women Should Know* (New York: Harper Business, 2014); S. Sandberg, *Lean In: Women, Work, and the Will to Lead* (New York: Alfred A. Knopf, 2013); M. Brzezinski, *Knowing Your Value: Women, Money, and Getting What You're Worth* (New York: Weinstein Books, 2011).

37 E. Pila, A. Stamiris, A. Castonguay, and C. M. Sabiston, "Body-Related Envy: A Social Comparison Perspective in Sport and Exercise," *Journal of Sport & Exercise* 36 (2014): 93–106; V. Hoorens and C. Van Damme, "What Do People Infer from Social Comparisons? Bridges between Social Comparison and Person Perception," *Social & Personality Psychology Compass* 6 (2012): 607–618; B. Butzer and N. A. Kuiper, "Relationships between the Frequency of Social Comparisons and Self-Concept Clarity, Intolerance of Uncertainty, Anxiety, and Depression," *Personality and Individual Differences* 41 (2006): 167–176; L. Festinger, "A Theory of Social Comparison Processes," *Human Relations* 2 (1954): 117–140.

38 Knight-McCord et al., "What Social Media Sites Do College Students Use Most?"; S. Greenwood, A. Perrin, and M. Duggan, "Social Media Update 2016," *Pew Research Internet Project*, November 11, 2016, www.pewinternet.org/2016/11/11/social-media-update-2016.

39 B. K. Johnson and S. Knobloch-Westerwick, "When Misery Avoids Company: Selective Social Comparisons to Photographic Online Profiles," *Human Communication Research* 43 (2017): 54–75; J. Liu, C. Li, N. Carcioppolo, and M. North, "Do Our Facebook Friends Make Us Feel Worse? A Study of Social Comparison and Emotion," *Human Communication Research* 42 (2016): 619–640; J. Fox and M. A. Vendemia, "Selective Self-Presentation and Social Comparison through Photographs on Social Networking Sites," *CyberPsychology, Behavior & Social Networking* 19 (2016): 593–600; C-C. Yang, "Instagram Use, Loneliness, and Social Comparison Orientation: Interact and Browse on Social Media, But Don't Compare," *CyberPsychology, Behavior & Social Networking* 19 (2016): 703–708; H. Appel, J. Crusius, and A. L. Gerlach, "Social Comparison, Envy, and Depression on Facebook: A Study Looking at the Effects of High Comparison Standards on Depressed Individuals," *Journal of Social & Clinical Psychology* 34 (2015): 277–289; K. Wilcox and A. T. Stephen, "Are Close Friends the Enemy? Online Social Networks, Self-Esteem, and Self-Control," *Journal of Consumer Research* Supplement (2014): S63–S76; N. Haferkamp and N. C. Kramer, "Social Comparison 2.0: Examining the Effects of Online Profiles on Social-Networking Sites," *CyberPsychology, Behavior, & Social Networking* 14 (2011): 309–314.

40 P. M. Valkenburg, J. Peter, and A. P. Schouten, "Friend Networking Sites and Their Relationship to Adolescents' Well-Being and Social Self-Esteem," *CyberPsychology & Behavior* 9 (2006): 484–490; A. L. Gonzales and J. T. Hancock, "Mirror, Mirror on My Facebook Wall: Effects of Exposure to Facebook on Self-Esteem," *CyberPsychology, Behavior, & Social Networking* 14 (2011): 79–83;

N. B. Ellison, C. Steinfield, and C. Lampe, "The Benefits of Facebook 'Friends': Social Capital and College Students' Use of Online Social Networking Sites," *Journal of Computer-Mediated Communication* 12 (2007): 1143–1168.

41 M. Iqani and J. E. Schroeder, "#Selfie: Digital Self-Portraits as Commodity Form and Consumption Practice," *Consumption, Markets & Culture* 19 (2016): 405–415.

42 K. Pounders, C. M. Kowalczyk, and K. Stowers, "Insight into the Motivation of Selfie Postings: Impression Management and Self-Esteem," *European Journal of Marketing* 50 (2016): 1879–1892.

43 K. E. Lommerud, D. R. Straume, and S. Vagstad, "Mommy Tracks and Public Policy: On Self-Fulfilling Prophecies and Gender Gaps in Hiring and Promotion," *Journal of Economic Behavior & Organization* 116 (2016): 540–554; S. Wurm, L. M. Warner, J. P. Ziegelmann, J. K. Wolff, and B. Schuz, "How Do Negative Self-Perceptions of Aging Become a Self-Fulfilling Prophecy?" *Psychology & Aging* 28 (2013): 1088–1097; S. Madon, J. Willard, M. Guyll, and K. C. Scherr, "Self-Fulfilling Prophecies: Mechanisms, Power, and Links to Social Problems," *Social & Personality Psychology Compass* 5 (2011): 578–590; L. Jussim and K. D. Harber, "Teacher Expectations and Self-Fulfilling Prophecies: Knowns and Unknowns, Resolved and Unresolved Controversies," *Personality and Social Psychology Review* 9 (2005): 131–155; L. Jussim, K. D. Harber, J. T. Crawford, T. R. Cain, and F. Cohen, "Social Reality Makes the Social Mind: Self-Fulfilling Prophecy, Stereotypes, Bias, and Accuracy," *Interaction Studies* 6 (2005): 85–102; S. Madon, M. Guyll, R. Spoth, and J. Willard, "Self-Fulfilling Prophecies," *Psychological Science* 15 (2004): 837–845.

44 A. Eryilmaz and H. Atak, "Investigation of Starting Romantic Intimacy in Emerging Adulthood in Terms of Self-Esteem, Gender, and Gender Roles," *Educational Sciences: Theory & Practice* 11 (2011): 595–600; S. Zhang and L. Stafford, "Perceived Face Threat of Honest but Hurtful Evaluative Messages in Romantic Relationships," *Western Journal of Communication* 72 (2008): 19–39; M. H. Kernis, C. E. Lakey, and W. L. Heppner, "Secure Versus Fragile High Self-Esteem as a Predictor of Verbal Defensiveness: Converging Findings across Three Different Markers," *Journal of Personality* 76 (2008): 477–512.

45 Goss, *Processing Communication*, 72.

46 J. Roessler, "Thinking, Inner Speech, and Self-Awareness," *Review of Philosophy and Psychology* 7 (2016): 541–557; E. J. Oliver, D. Marklan, and J. Hardy, "Interpretation of Self-Talk and Post-Lecture Affective States of Higher Education Students: A Self-Determination Theory Perspective," *British Journal of Educational Psychology* 80 (2010): 307–323; J. Hardy, R. Roberts, and L. Hardy, "Awareness and Motivation to Change Negative Self-Talk," *Sport Psychologist* 23 (2009): 435–450; L. C. Lederman, "The Impact of Gender on the Self and Self-Talk," in *Women and Men Communicating: Challenges and Changes* 2e, edited by L. P. Arliss and D. J. Borisoff (Prospect Heights, IL: Waveland, 2001), 78–89; J. R. Johnson, "The Role of Inner Speech in Human Communication," *Communication Education* 33 (1984): 211–222; J. Ayres, "The Power of Positive Thinking," *Communication Education* 37 (1988): 289–296.

47 A. T. Latinjak, M. Torregrosa, and J. Renom, "Combining Self Talk and Performance Feedback: Their Effectiveness with Adult Tennis Players," *Sport Psychologist* 25 (2011): 18–31; N. Zourbanos et al., "The Social Side of Self-Talk: Relationships between Perceptions of Support Received from the Coach and Athletes' Self-Talk," *Psychology of Sport & Exercise* 12 (2011): 407–414; A. V. Tovares, "Managing the Voices: Athlete Self-Talk as a Dialogic Process," *Journal of Language & Social Psychology* 29 (2010): 261–277.

48 D. Wang, "A Study of the Relationship between Narcissism, Extraversion, Drive for Entertainment, and Narcissistic Behavior on Social Networking Sites," *Computers in Human Behavior* 66 (2017): 138–148; H. Cai, V. S. Y. Kwan, and C. Sedikides, "A Sociocultural Approach to Narcissism: The Case of Modern China," *European Journal of Personality* 26 (2012): 529–535; M. S. Wilson and C. G. Sibley, "'Narcissism Creep?' Evidence for Age-Related Differences in Narcissism in the New Zealand General Populations," *New Zealand Journal of Psychology* 40 (2011): 89–95.

49 J. M. Twenge, *Generation Me: Why Today's Young Americans Are More Confident, Assertive, Entitled—and More Miserable Than Ever Before* (Rev/Upd. ed; New York: Atria, 2014), 2; J. M. Twenge, "The Narcissism Epidemic: Narcissism Is on the Rise among Individuals and in American Culture," *Psychology Today*, August 12, 2013, retrieved June 15, 2014, www.psychologytoday.com; F. Rhodewalt, "Contemporary Perspectives on Narcissism and the Narcissistic Personality Type," in *Handbook of Self and Identity*, 571–586.

50 J. M. Twenge, S. Konrath, J. D. Foster, W. K. Campbell, and B. J. Bushman, "Egos Inflating over Time: A Cross-Temporal Meta-Analysis of the Narcissistic Personality Inventory," *Journal of Personality* 76 (2008): 875–901; S. Konrath, J. M. Twenge, W. K. Campbell, J. D. Foster, and B. J. Bushman, "This Generation Is More Special Than the Others: A Cross-Temporal Meta-Analysis of the Narcissistic Personality Inventory," paper presented at the conference on Educating the Next Generation of College Students, University of San Diego, February 27, 2007.

51 S. Mehdizadeh, "Self-Presentation 2.0: Narcissism and Self-Esteem on Facebook," *CyberPsychology, Behavior, & Social Networking* 13 (2010): 357–364.

52 W. Hart, J. Adams, K. A. Burton, and G. K. Tortoriello, "Narcissism and Self-Presentation: Profiling Grandiose and Vulnerable Narcissists' Self-Presentation Tactic Use," *Personality & Individual Differences* 104 (2017): 48–57; S. M. Bergman, M. E. Fearrington, S. W. Davenport, and J. Bergman, "Millennials, Narcissism, and Social Networking: What Narcissists Do on Social Networking Sites and Why," *Personality & Individual Differences* 50 (2011): 706–711; E. Y. Ong, R. P. Ang, J. Ho, J. C. Lim, D. H. Goh, C. S. Lee, and A. Y. Chua, "Narcissism, Extraversion, and Adolescents' Self-Presentation on Facebook," *Journal of Personality and Social Psychology* 43 (2011): 838–852.

53 For other research on narcissism and self-esteem, see M. J. C. Guedes, "Mirror, Mirror on the Wall, Am I the Greatest Performer of All? Narcissism and Self-Reported and Objective Performance," *Personality & Individual Differences* 108 (2017): 182–185; J. M. Twenge and W. K. Campbell, *The Narcissism Epidemic: Living in the Age of Entitlement* (New York: Free Press, 2011); J. K. Bosson, C. E. Lakey, W. K. Campbell, V. Zeigler-Hill, C. H. Jordan, and M. H. Kernis, "Untangling the Links between Narcissism and Self-Esteem: A Theoretical and Empirical Review," *Social and Personality Psychology Compass* 2 (2008): 1415–1439; V. Zeigler-Hill, "Discrepancies between Implicit and Explicit Self-Esteem: Implications for Narcissism and Self-Esteem Instability," *Journal of Personality* 74 (2006): 119–144; E. Hoover, "Here's You Looking at You, Kid: Study Says Many Students Are Narcissists," *The Chronicle of Higher Education* (March 9, 2007).

54 McKay and Fanning, *Self-Esteem*.

55 B. R. Schlenkere, S. A. Wowra, R. M. Johnson, and M. L. Miller, "The Impact of Imagined Audiences on Self-Appraisals," *Personal Relationships* 15 (2008): 247–260; see J. Ayres and T. S. Hopf, "The Long-Term Effect of Visualization in the Classroom: A Brief Research Report," *Communication Education* 39 (1990): 75–78; J. Ayres and T. S. Hopf, "Visualization: Is It More Than Extra-Attention?" *Communication Education* 38 (1989): 1–5.

56 J. Ayres, T. S. Hopf, and D. M. Ayres, "An Examination of Whether Imaging Ability Enhances the Effectiveness of an Intervention Designed to Reduce Speech Anxiety," *Communication Education* 43 (1994): 252–258.

57 McKay and Fanning, *Self-Esteem*.

58 A concept related to bravado and confidence is *communication bravado*, introduced by K. Quintanilla and J. Mallard, "Understanding the Role of Communication Bravado: An Important Issue for Trainers/Educators," *Texas Speech Communication Journal* 33 (2008): 44–49.

59 B. N. Frisby, R. J. Sidelinger, and M. Booth-Butterfield, "No Harm, No Foul: A Social Exchange Perspective on Individual and Relational Outcomes Associated with Relational Baggage," *Western Journal of Communication* 79 (2015): 555–572; R. J. Sidelinger and M. Booth-Butterfield, "Starting Off on the Wrong Foot: An Analysis of Mate Value, Commitment, and Partner 'Baggage' in Romantic Relationships," *Human Communication* 12 (2009): 403–419.

60 P. R. Hinton, *The Psychology of Interpersonal Perception* (New York: Routledge, 1993).

61 E. B. Goldstein and J. R. Brockmole, *Sensation and Perception* 10e (Belmont, CA: Cengage Learning/Wadsworth, 2016); A. S. Rancer, F. F. Jordan-Jackson, and D. A. Infante, "Observers' Perceptions of an Interpersonal Dispute as a Function of Mode of Presentation," *Communication Reports* 16 (2003): 35–48; D. A. Kenny, *Interpersonal Perception: A Social Relations Analysis* (New York: Guilford Press, 1994).

62 M. Merleau-Ponty, *Phenomenology of Perception* (New York: Routledge, 2013); Z. Wang, M. Huifang, J. Yexin, and L. Fan, "Smile Big or Not? Effects of Smile Intensity on Perceptions of Warmth and Competence," *Journal of Consumer Research* 43 (2017): 7887–7805; L. Vingilis-Jaremko, D. Maurer, G. Rhodes, and L. Jeffery, "The Influence of Averageness on Adults' Perceptions of Attractiveness: The Effect of Early Visual Deprivation," *Perception* 45 (2016): 1399–1411.

63 U. Lyngs, E. Cohen, W. T. Hattori, M. Newson, and D. T. Levin, "Hearing in Color: How Expectations Distort Perception of Skin Tone," *Journal of Experimental Psychology: Human Perception and Performance* 42 (2016): 2068–2076; B. Fink, P. J. Matts, S. Roder, R. Johnson, and M. Burquest, "Differences in Visual Perception of Age and Attractiveness of Female Facial and Body Skin," *International Journal of Cosmetic Science* 33 (2011): 126–131; S. F. O'Neil and M. A. Webster, "Adaptation and the Perception of Facial Age," *Visual Cognition* 19 (2011): 534–550.

64 C. M. Steele, *Whistling Vivaldi: How Stereotypes Affect Us and What We Can Do* (New York: W. W. Norton, 2011); L. C. Aguilar, *Ouch! That Stereotype Hurts . . . Communicating Respectfully in a Diverse World* (Bedford, TX: Walk the Talk Company, 2006); D. J. Schneider, A. H. Hastorf, and P. C. Ellsworth, *Person Perception* 2e (Reading, MA: Addison-Wesley, 1979).

65 R. Asgary, B. Sckell, A. Alcabes, R. Naderi, P. Adongo, and G. Ogedegbe, "Perceptions, Attitudes, and Experience Regarding mHealth among Homeless Persons in New York City Shelters," *Journal of Health Communication* 20 (2015): 1473–1480; M. L. Shier, M. E. Jones, and J. R. Graham, "Perspectives of Employed People Experiencing Homelessness of Self and Being Homeless: Challenging Socially Constructed Perceptions and Stereotypes," *Journal of Sociology & Social Welfare* 37 (2010): 13–37; A. J. Kosor and L. Kendal-Wilson, "Older Homeless Women: Reframing the Stereotype of the Bag Lady," *Affilia* 17 (2002): 354–370.

66 D. T. Kenrick, S. L. Neuberg, and R. B. Cialdini, *Social Psychology: Goals in Interaction* 6e (Boston: Pearson, 2014), 360.

67 C. Duerringer, "Be a Man—Buy a Car! Articulating Masculinity with Consumerism in *Man's Last Stand*," *Southern Communication Journal* 80 (2015): 137–152; M. Kimmel, *Angry White Men: American Masculinity at the End of an Era* (New York: Nation Books, 2015); C. Spears Brown, *Parenting Beyond Pink and Blue: How to Raise Your Kids Free of Gender Stereotypes* (New York: Ten Speed Press, 2014); A. P. Smiler, *Challenging Casanova: Beyond the Stereotype of the Promiscuous Young Male* (San Francisco: Jossey-Bass, 2012); M. Salesses, *Different Racisms: On Stereotypes, the Individual, and Asian American Masculinity* (New York: Thought Catalog, 2013).

68 C. N. Macrae, G. V. Bodenhausen, A. B. Milne, and J. Jetten, "Out of Mind But Back in Sight: Stereotypes on the Rebound," *Journal of Personality and Social Psychology* 67 (1994): 808–817.

69 This chapter benefited from the fine scholarship and work of M. V. Redmond, coauthor of *Interpersonal Communication: Relating to Others* 8e (Boston: Pearson, 2017).

Chapter 3

1 A. Grace, N. Kemp, F. H. Martin, and R. Parrila, "Undergraduates' Attitudes to Text Messaging Language Use and Intrusions of Textisms into Formal Writing," *New Media & Society* 17 (2015): 792–809; D. Wray, "An Exploration of the Views of Teachers Concerning the Effects of Texting on Children's Literacy Development," *Journal of Information Technology Education* 14 (2015): 271–282; D. K. Ivy and S. T. Wahl, *Nonverbal Communication for a Lifetime* 2e (Dubuque, IA: Kendall Hunt, 2014); D. Powell and M. Dixon, "Does SMS Text Messaging Help or Harm Adults' Knowledge of Standard Spelling," *Journal of Computer Assisted Learning* 28 (2011): 58–66; L. D. Rosen, J. Chang, L. Erwin, L. M. Carrier, and N. A. Cheever, "The Relationship between 'Textisms' and Formal and Informal Writing among Young Adults," *Communication Research* 37 (2010): 420–440.

2 R. E. Tamargo Guzzardo, J. R. Kroff Valdés, and P. E. Dussias, "Examining the Relationship between Comprehension and Production Processes in Code-Switched Language," *Journal of Memory & Language* 89 (2016): 138–161; A. N. Amicucci, "How They Really Talk," *Journal of Adolescent & Adult Literacy* 57 (2014): 483–491; K. H. Turner, "Flipping the Switch: Code-Switching from Text Speak to Standard English," *English Journal* 98 (2009): 60–65.

3 Hart Research Associates, "Falling Short? College Learning and Career Success," *Association of American Colleges and Universities*, January 20, 2015, accessed February 12, 2017, www.aacu.org; Hart Research Associates, "Employer Priorities for Most Important College Learning Outcomes," *Association of American Colleges and Universities*, January 20, 2015, accessed February 12, 2017, www.aacu.org; "Staffing in Special Markets," *Society for Human Resources Management*, September 3, 2016, accessed February 12, 2017, www.shrm.org.

4 B. Spitzberg and J. P. Dillard, "Social Skills and Communication," in *Interpersonal Communication Research: Advances through Meta-Analysis*, edited by M. Allen, R. W. Preiss, B. M. Gayle, and N. Burrell (Mahwah, NJ: Lawrence Erlbaum, 2002), 89–107.

5 B. L. Whorf, "Science and Linguistics," in *Language, Thought, and Reality*, edited by J. B. Carroll (Cambridge: Massachusetts Institute of Technology Press, 1956).

6 R. F. Verderber and K. S. Verderber, "Elements of Language," in *Making Connections: Readings in Relational Communication* 5e, edited by K. M. Galvin (New York: Oxford University Press, 2011), 51–60.

7 *Oxford Desk Dictionary and Thesaurus, American Edition* (New York: Oxford University Press, 2007).

8 Y. Neuman, Y. Cohen, and D. Assaf, "How Do We Understand the Meaning of Connotations? A Cognitive Computational Model," *Semiotica* 2015 (2015): 1–16; "What's in a Name? Denotation, Connotation, and 'A Boy Named Sue'," *Communication Teacher* 25 (2011): 136–138.

9 P. Ferre, M. Guasch, T. Garcia-Chico, and R. Sanchez-Casas, "Are There Qualitative Differences in the Representation of Abstract and Concrete Words? Within-Language and Cross-Language Evidence from the Semantic Priming Paradigm," *Quarterly Journal of Experimental Psychology* 68 (2015): 2402–2418; S.-T. Kousta, G. Vigliocco, D. P. Vinson, M. Andrews, and E. Del Campo, "The Representation of Abstract Words: Why Emotion Matters," *Journal of Experimental Psychology* 140 (2011): 14–34.

10 E. R. Fyle, N. M. McNeil, and B. Rittle-Johnson, "Easy as ABCABC: Abstract Language Facilitates Performance on a Concrete Patterning Task," *Child Development* 86 (2015): 927–935; L. M. Bauer, E. L. Olheiser, and J. Altarriba, "Word Type Effects in False Recall: Concrete, Abstract, and Emotion Word Critical Lures," *American Journal of Psychology* 122 (2009): 469–481; A. Parker and N. Dagnall, "Concreteness Effects Revisited: The Influence of Dynamic Visual Noise on Memory for Concrete and Abstract Words," *Memory* 17 (2008): 397–410.

11 A. G. Smith, ed., *Communication and Culture* (New York: Holt, Rinehart and Winston, 1966).

12 D. K. Ivy, *GenderSpeak: Communicating in a Gendered World* 6e (Dubuque, IA: Kendall Hunt, 2017).

13 Number of Monthly Active Twitter Users Worldwide from 1st Quarter 2010 to 4th Quarter 2016 (in Millions), accessed February 24, 2017, www.statista.com.

14 B. L. Ott, "The Age of Twitter: Donald J. Trump and the Politics of Debasement," *Critical Studies in Media Communication* 34 (2017): 59–68.

15 M. Zappavigna, *Discourse of Twitter and Social Media: How We Use Language to Create Affiliation on the Web* Reprint Edition (New York: Bloomsbury Academic: 2012).

16 D. Murthy, S. Bowman, A. J. Gross, and M. McGarry, "Do We Tweet Differently from Our Mobile Devices? A Study of Language Differences on Mobile and Web-Based Twitter Platforms," *Journal of Communication,* 65 (2015): 816–837; Y. Hu, K. Talamadupula, and S. Kambhampati, "Dude, Srsly?: The Suprisingly Formal Nature of Twitter's Language," *ICWSM,* Proceedings of the 7th International Conference on Weblogs and Social Media (2013): 244–253.

17 J. Close Conoley, "Sticks and Stones Can Break My Bones and Words Can Really Hurt Me," *School Psychology Review* 37 (2008): 217–220.

18 Y. Osward, *Every Word Has Power: Switch on Your Language and Turn on Your Life* (New York: Atria Books/Simon & Schuster, 2008); P. Denton, *The Power of Our Words: Teacher Language That Helps Children Learn* (Turners Falls, MA: Northwest Foundation for Children, 2007).

19 E. Sher, *The Emotionary: A Dictionary of Words That Don't Exist for Feelings That Do* (New York: Razorbill/Penguin Random House, 2016), 57.

20 C. M. Frisby, "Sticks 'n' Stones May Break My Bones, but Words They Hurt Like Hell: Derogatory Words in Popular Songs," *Media Report to Women* 38 (2010): 12–18; H. A. Schroth, J. Bain-Chekal, and D. F. Caldwell, "Sticks and Stones May Break Bones and Words Can Hurt Me: Words and Phrases That Trigger Emotions in Negotiations and Their Effects," *International Journal of Conflict Management* 16 (2005): 102–127; A. Palayiwa, P. Sheeran, and A. Thompson, "'Words Will Never Hurt Me!': Implementation Intentions Regulate Attention to Stigmatizing Comments About Appearance," *Journal of Social and Clinical Psychology* 29 (2010): 575–598; A. Ellis, *A New Guide to Rational Living* (North Hollywood, CA: Wilshire Books, 1977).

21 J. L. Dibble, N. M. Punyanunt-Carter, A. Morris, and R. Hair, "A New Look for the 'Little Black Book': Prospective Sex Partners, Back Burner Relationships, and Modern Communication Technology," in *Contemporary Studies of Sexuality & Communication: Theoretical & Applied Perspectives,* edited by J. Manning and C. M. Noland (Dubuque, IA: Kendall Hunt, 2016), 189–202.

22 A. M. Croom, "Slurs, Stereotypes, and In-Equality: A Critical Review of 'How Epithets and Stereotypes Are Racially Unequal'," *Language Sciences* 52 (2015): 139–154; D. Archer, "Slurs, Insults, (Backhanded) Compliments, and Other Strategic Facework Moves," *Language Sciences* 52 (2015): 82–97; C. J. O'Dea, S. S. Miller, E. B. Andres, M. H. Ray, D. F. Till, and D. A. Saucier, "Out of Bounds: Factors Affecting the Perceived Offensiveness of Racial Slurs," *Language Sciences* 52 (2015): 155–164; J. Rahman, "Missing the Target: Group Practices That Launch and Deflect Slurs," *Language Sciences* 52 (2015): 70–81;. M. Harris, "Flying Solo: Negotiating the Matrix of Racism and Sexism in Higher Education," *Women & Language* 35 (2012): 103–107; J. Hartigan, *What Can You Say? America's National Conversation on Race* (Stanford, CA: Stanford University Press, 2010).

23 S. Koeser, E. A. Kuhn, and S. Sczesny, "Just Reading? How Gender-Fair Language Triggers Readers' Use of Gender-Fair Forms," *Journal of Language & Social Psychology* 34 (2015): 343–357; K. M. Douglas and R. M. Sutton, "'A Giant Leap for Mankind,' But What about Women? The Role of System-Justifying Ideologies in Predicting Attitudes toward Sexist Language," *Journal of Language & Social Psychology* 33 (2014): 667–680; A. Taylor, M. J. Hardman, and C. Wright, *Making the Invisible Visible: Gender in Language* (Bloomington, IN: IUniverse LLC, 2013); R. K. Mallett and D. E. Wagner, "The Unexpectedly Positive Consequences of Confronting Sexism," *Journal of Experimental Social Psychology* 47 (2011): 215–220; G. He, "An Analysis of Sexism in English," *Journal of Language Teaching and Research* 1 (2010): 332–335.

24 M. Budziszewska, K. Hansen, and M. Bilewicz, "Backlash over Gender-Fair Language: The Impact of Feminine Job Titles on Men's and Women's Perception of Women," *Journal of Language & Social Psychology* 33 (2014): 681–691; C. Kramarae, "Muted Group Theory and Communication: Asking Dangerous Questions," *Women & Language* 28 (2005): 55–61; S. Ardener, "Muted Groups: The Genesis of an Idea and Its Praxis," *Women & Language* 28 (2005): 50–54; J. K. Swim, R. Mallett, and C. Stangor, "Understanding Subtle Sexism: Detection and Use of Sexist Language," *Sex Roles* 51 (2004): 117–128; J. Briere and C. Lanktree, "Sex-Role Related Effects of Sex Bias in Language," *Sex Roles* 9 (1983): 625–632; L. Brooks, "Sexist Language in Occupational Information: Does It Make a Difference?" *Journal of Vocational Behavior* 23 (1983): 227–232.

25 S. Killerman, *The Social Justice Advocate's Handbook: A Guide to Gender* (Austin, TX: Impetus Books, 2013); B. D. Earp, "The Extinction of Masculine Generics," *Journal for Communication & Culture* 2 (2012): 4–19; J. Flanigan, "The Use and Evolution of Gender Neutral Language in an Intentional Community," *Women & Language* 36 (2013): 27–41.

26 R. Kaveney, "Why Trans Is In, But Tranny Is Out," accessed February 24, 2017, www.theguardian.com; Earp, "The Extinction of Masculine Generics"; Killerman, *The Social Justice Advocate's Handbook*; P. Gygax, U. Gabriel, O. Sarrasin, J. Oakhill, and A. Garnham, "Some Grammatical Rules Are More Difficult Than Others: The Case of the Generic Interpretation of the Masculine," *European Journal of Psychology of Education* 24 (2009): 235–246; M. A. Clason, "Feminism, Generic 'He,' and the *TNIV* Bible Translation Debate," *Critical Discourse Studies* 3 (2006): 23–35; J. L. Stinger and R. Hopper, "Generic *He* in Conversation?" *Quarterly Journal of Speech* 84 (1998): 209–221; J. Gastil, "Generic Pronouns and Sexist Language: The Oxymoronic Character of Masculine Generics," *Sex Roles* 23 (1990): 629–641; D. K. Ivy, L. Bullis-Moore, K. Norvell, P. Backlund, and M. Javidi, "The Lawyer, the Babysitter, and the Student: Inclusive Language Usage and Instruction," *Women & Language* 18 (1994): 13–21; W. Martyna, "What Does 'He' Mean? Use of the Generic Masculine," *Journal of Communication* 28 (1978): 131–138.

27 "Supplemental Material: Writing Clearly and Concisely, General Guidelines for Reducing Bias," *Publication Manual of the American Psychological Association* 6e, 2009, accessed February 24, 2017, www.apastyle.org.

28 L. Madson and R. M. Hessling, "Does Alternating between Masculine and Feminine Pronouns Eliminate Perceived Gender Bias in a Text?" *Sex Roles* 41 (1999): 559–576; D. Kennedy, "Review Essay: She or He in Textbooks," *Women & Language* 15 (1992): 46–49.

29 L. Madson and J. Shoda, "Alternating between Masculine and Feminine Pronouns: Does Essay Topic Affect Readers' Perceptions?" *Sex Roles* 54 (2006): 275–285; T. Strahan, "'They' in Australian English: Non-Gender-Specific or Specifically Non-Gendered?" *Australian Journal of Linguistics* 28 (2008): 17–29.

30 A. Hess, "Multiple Choice," *The New York Times Magazine* (April 3, 2016): 13–15; Killerman, *The Social Justice Advocate's Handbook*.

31 Ivy, *GenderSpeak*.

32 Ivy, *GenderSpeak*.

33 Ivy, *GenderSpeak*.

34 R. Goldman, "Here's a List of 58 Gender Options for Facebook Users," *ABC News*, February 13, 2014, accessed February 17, 2014, abcnews.go.com; K. Steinmetz, "A Comprehensive Guide to Facebook's New Options for Gender Identity," February 14, 2014, *Time*, accessed February 18, 2014, techland.time.com; P. Weber, "Confused by All the New Facebook Genders? Here's What They Mean," *Slate*, February 21, 2014, accessed March 14, 2014, www.slate.com/blogs/lexicon_valley/2014/02/21/gender_facebook_now_has_56_categories_to_choose_from_including_cisgender.html.

35 "Trans 101: Cisgender," *Basic Rights Oregon*, October 9, 2011, accessed February 18, 2014, www.basicrights.org.

36 Our understanding of asexual identity was informed by a student panel organized by Dr. Maureen Keeley, Texas State University, as part of the annual Communication Week programming, March 2014; J. S. Decker, "How to Tell If You Are Asexual," September 20, 2014, accessed June 18, 2014, time.com.

37 *The Asexual Visibility and Education Network*, accessed June 19, 2014, www.asexuality.org.

38 M. Fischer, "It's Judith Butler's World," *New York* (July 13–26, 2016): 38–44; D. S. Strasser and K. Hobson, "'You Had Sex, Right?': Theorizing Desire, Identity, Reciprocity, and Sex in Queer Friendships," in *Contemporary Studies of Sexuality & Communication*, 169–187; J. Sanders, "The Questioning Continuum: Seeking Sexuality as a Lifelong Process," *Bitch* (Spring 2016): 71–73.

39 S. Criniti and E. R. Green, "Understanding Transgender Identities and Experiences," in *Contemporary Studies of Sexuality & Communication*, 125–142; L. G. Spencer, IV, "Introduction: Centering Transgender Studies and Gender Identity in Communication Scholarship," in *Transgender Communication Studies: Histories, Trends, and Trajectories*, edited by L. G. Spencer, IV, and J. C. Capuzza (Lanham, MD: Lexington, 2015); A. Silman, "Laverne Cox Talks Battling Transphobia on 'Orange Is the New Black'," accessed June 26, 2015, www.salon.com.

40 Ivy, *GenderSpeak*.

41 J. Hall and B. LaFrance, "'That's Gay': Sexual Prejudice, Gender Identity, Norms, and Homophobic Communication," *Communication Quarterly* 60 (2012): 35–58; M. R. Woodford, M. L. Howell, A. Kulick, and P. Silverschanz, "'That's So Gay': Heterosexual Male Undergraduates and the Perpetuation of Sexual Orientation Microaggressions," *Campus Journal of Interpersonal Violence* 28 (2013): 416–435; M. R. Woodford, M. L. Howell, P. Silverschanz, and L. Yu, "'That's So Gay': Examining the Covariates of Hearing This Expression among Gay, Lesbian, and Bisexual College Students," *Journal of American College Health* 60 (2012): 429–434; N. Updike, "That's So Gay!" *Salon*, September 14, 2000, salon.com; Associated Press, "'That's So Gay' Prompts a Lawsuit: Student Sent to Principal's Office Insists It Was Not a Homophobic Putdown," *MSNBC*, February 28, 2007, msnbc.com.

42 P. C. McCabe, E. A. Dragowski, and F. Rubinson, "What Is Homophobic Bias Anyway? Defining and Recognizing Microaggressions and Harassment of LGBTQ Youth," *Journal of School Violence* 12 (2013): 7–26; M. Kantor, *Homophobia: The State of Sexual Bigotry Today* 2e (Santa Barbara, CA: Praeger, 2009); G. Griffin, "Understanding Heterosexism: The Subtle Continuum of Homophobia," *Women & Language* 21 (1998): 33–39.

43 J. F. Nussbaum (Ed.), *Communication across the Lifespan* (International Communication Association Conference Theme Book Series, vol. 3; New York: Peter Lang, 2016); A. Applewhite, *This Chair Rocks: A Manifesto Against Ageism* (Networked Books, 2016); T. D. Nelson (Ed.), *Ageism: Stereotyping and Prejudice Against Older Persons* (Cambridge: Massachusetts Institute of Technology Press, 2004).

44 N. Isenberg, *White Trash: The 400-Year Untold History of Class in America* (New York: Viking, 2016); B. Jensen, *Reading Classes: On Culture and Classism in America* (Ithaca, NY: ILR Press, 2012); R. K. S. Macaulay, *Talk That Counts: Age, Gender, and Social Class Differences in Discourse* (New York: Oxford University Press, 2005); M. Argyle, *The Psychology of Social Class* (New York: Routledge, 1993).

45 J. S. Seiter, J. Larsen, and J. Skinner, "'Handicapped' or 'Handicapable'? The Effects of Language about Persons with Disabilities on Perceptions of Source Credibility and Persuasiveness," *Communication Reports* 11 (1998): 21–31.

46 J. St. Pierre, "Cripping Communication: Speech, Disability, and Exclusion in Liberal Humanist and Posthumanist Discourse," *Communication Theory* 25 (2015): 330–348; A. Kafer, *Feminist, Queer, Crip* (Bloomington: Indiana University Press, 2013), 14.

47 J. R. Gibb, "Defensive Communication," *Journal of Communication* 11 (1961): 141–148. For other research on communication climate, see G. L. Bradley and A. C. Campbell, "Managing Difficult Workplace Conversations: Goals, Strategies, and Outcomes," *International Journal of Business Communication* 53 (2016): 443–464; G. L. Forward, K. Czech, and C. M. Lee, "Assessing Gibb's Supportive and Defensive Communication Climate: An Examination of Measurement and Construct Validity," *Communication Research Reports* 28 (2011): 1–15; J. M. Reagle, "'Be Nice': Wikipedia Norms for Supportive Communication," *New Review of Hypermedia & Multimedia* 16 (2010): 161–180.

48 Forward, Czech, and Lee, "Assessing Gibb's Supportive and Defensive Communication Climate," 2.

49 J. H. Kim and J. Kim, "The Dynamics of Polarization and Compromise in Conflict Situations: The Interaction between Cultural Traits and Majority-Minority Influence," *Communication Monographs* 84 (2017): 128–141.

50 L. H. Turner, "Message from the President," *Spectra* (November, 2011), accessed February 25, 2017, www.natcom.org.

51 B. Clark, "50 Trigger Words and Phrases for Powerful Multimedia Content," *copyblogger*, April 20, 2009, www.copyblogger .com/trigger-words; E. T. Booth, "Assign This: Trigger Words," *Spectra* (Washington, DC: National Communication Association, June/July 2007).

52 S. M. McNaughton, "Developing Pre-Requisites for Empathy: Increasing Awareness of Self, the Body, and the Perspectives of Others," *Teaching in Higher Education* 21 (2016): 501–515; P. Bloom, *Against Empathy: The Case for Rational Compassion* (New York: ECCO/HarperCollins, 2016); R. Krznaric, *Empathy: Why It Matters and How to Get It* (New York: Perigee Books, 2014); L. V. Oceja, M. W. Heerdink, E. L. Stocks, T. Ambrona, B. Lopez-Perez, and S. Salgado, "Empathy, Awareness of Others, and Action: How Feeling Empathy for One-Among-Others Motivates Helping the Others," *Basic & Applied Social Psychology* 36 (2014): 111–124; P. L. Lockwood, A. Seara-Cardoso, and E. Viding, "Emotion Regulation Moderates the Association between Empathy and Prosocial Behavior," *PloS ONE* 9.5 (2014): e96555; K. McLaren, *The Art of Empathy: A Complete Guide to Life's Most Essential Skill* (Louisville, CO: Sounds True Publishers, 2013); A. J. Clark, "Empathy and Sympathy: Therapeutic Distinctions in Counseling," *Journal of Mental Health Counseling* 32 (2010): 95–101; J. Hakansson and H. Montgomery, "Empathy as an Interpersonal Phenomenon," *Journal of Social and Personal Relationships* 20 (2003): 267–284; M. V. Redmond, "The Functions of Empathy (Decentering) in Human Relations," *Human Relations* 42 (1993): 593–606.

53 D. B. Whiteside and L. J. Barclay, "The Face of Fairness: Self-Awareness as a Means to Promote Fairness among Managers with Low Empathy," *Journal of Business Ethics* 137 (2016): 721–730; L. M. Carrier, A. Spradlin, J. P. Bunce, and L. D. Rosen, "Virtual Empathy: Positive and Negative Impacts of Going Online upon Empathy in Young Adults," *Computers in Human Behavior* 52 (2015): 39–48; C. Levesque, M-F. Lafontaine, A. Caron, J. L. Flescha, and S. Bjornson, "Dyadic Empathy, Dyadic Coping, and Relationship Satisfaction: A Dyadic Model," *Europe's Journal of Psychology* 10 (2014): 118–134; D. Johnson, "Helpful Listening and Responding," in *Making Connections*, 70–76; D. F. Barone, P. S. Hutchings, H. J. Kimmel, H. L. Traub, J. T. Cooper, and C. M. Marshall, "Increasing Empathic Accuracy through Practice and Feedback in a Clinical Interviewing Course," *Journal of Social and Clinical Psychology* 24 (2005): 156–171.

54 T. Challies, "The Art and Science of the Humblebrag," *Challies .com*, October 22, 2013, accessed June 19, 2014, www .challies.com; *The Rachel Maddow Show*, MSNBC, June 23, 2012, Television.

Chapter 4

1 M. Kaneko and J. Mesch, "Eye Gaze in Creative Sign Language," *Sign Language Studies* 13 (2013): 372–400; M. Fox, *Talking Hands: What Sign Language Reveals About the Mind* (New York: Simon & Schuster, 2008); R. B. Grossman and J. Kegl, "Moving Faces: Categorization of Dynamic Facial Expressions in American Sign Language by Deaf and Hearing Participants," *Journal of Nonverbal Behavior* 31 (2007): 23–38.

2 S. L. Aloia and D. H. Solomon, "Emotions Associated with Verbal Aggression Expression and Suppression," *Western Journal of Communication* 80 (2016): 3–20; C. Civile and S. Obhi, "Power Eliminates the Influence of Body Posture on Facial Emotion Recognition," *Journal of Nonverbal Behavior* 40 (2016): 283–299; U. Hess, C. Blaison, and K. Kafetsios, "Judging Facial Emotion Expressions in Context: The Influence of Culture and Self-Construal Orientation," *Journal of Nonverbal Behavior* 40 (2016): 55–64; G. Garcia, M. P. Greenfield, M. Michikyan, J. Morris, W. G. Small, & E. Zgourou, "Five Days at Outdoor Education Camp without Screens Improves Preteen Skills with Nonverbal Emotion," *Computers in Human Behavior* 39 (2014): 387–392; T. Banziger, S. Patel, & K. Scherer, "The Role of Perceived Voice and Speech Characteristics in Vocal Emotion Communication," *Journal of Nonverbal Behavior* 38 (2014): 31–52.

3 A. Mehrabian, *Nonverbal Communication* (Chicago: Aldine-Atherton, 1972).

4 R. L. Birdwhistell, *Kinesics and Context* (Philadelphia: University of Pennsylvania Press, 1970).

5 D. Re and N. Rule, "Making a (False) Impression: The Role of Business Experience in First Impressions of CEO Leadership Ability," *Journal of Nonverbal Behavior* 40 (2016): 235–245.

6 R. Petrician, A. Todorov, and C. Grady, "Personality at Face Value: Facial Appearance Predicts Self and Other Personality Judgments among Strangers and Spouses," *Journal of Nonverbal Behavior* 38 (2014): 259–277.

7 N. O. Rule and N. Ambady, "She's Got the Look: Inferences from Female Chief Executive Officers' Faces Predict Their Success," *Sex Roles* 61 (2009): 644–652; L. P. Naumann, S. Vazire, P. J. Rentfrow, and S. D. Gosling, "Personality Judgments Based on Physical Appearance," *Personality and Social Psychology Bulletin* 35 (2009): 1661–1671.

8 R. Ryan, *60 Seconds and You're Hired* Rev. Ed. (New York: Penguin, 2016); G. L. Stewart, S. L. Dustin, M. R. Barrick, and T. C. Darnold, "Exploring the Handshake in Employment Interviews," *Journal of Applied Psychology* 93 (2008): 1139–1146.

9 D. K. Ivy and S. T. Wahl, *Nonverbal Communication for a Lifetime* 2e (Dubuque, IA: Kendall Hunt, 2014); E. Krumhuber, K. Likowski, and P. Weyers, "Facial Mimicry of Spontaneous and Deliberate Duchenne and Non-Duchenne Smiles," *Journal of Nonverbal Behavior* 38 (2014): 1–11; S. Farley, "Nonverbal Reactions to an Attractive Stranger: The Role of Mimicry in Communicating Preferred Social Distance," *Journal of Nonverbal Behavior* 38 (2014): 195–208.; R. C. Schmidt, S. Morr, P. Fitzpatrick, and M. J. Richardson, "Measuring the Dynamics of Interactional Synchrony," *Journal of Nonverbal Behavior* 36 (2012): 263–279; D. Lakens and M. Stel, "If They Move in Sync, They Must Feel in Sync: Movement Synchrony Leads to Attributions of Rapport and Entitativity," *Social Cognition* 29 (2011): 1–14; K. Wilt, K. Funkhouser, and W. Revelle, "The Dynamic Relationships of Affective Synchrony to Perceptions of Situations," *Journal of Research in Personality* 45 (2011): 309–321; J. L. Lakin, V. W. Jefferis, C. M. Cheng, and T. L. Chartrand, "The Chameleon Effect as Social Glue: Evidence for the Evolutionary Significance of Nonconscious Mimicry," *Journal of Nonverbal Behavior* 27 (2003): 145–161; N. Guéguen, "The Mimicker Is a Mirror of Myself: Impact of Mimicking on Self-Consciousness and Social Anxiety," *Social Behavior and Personality* 39 (2011): 725–728; N. Guéguen, "The Effects of Incidental Similarity with a Stranger on Mimicry Behavior," *The Open Behavioral Science Journal* 6 (2012): 15–22; N. Guéguen, A. Martin, and S. Meineri, "Mimicry and Helping Behavior: An Evaluation of Mimicry on Explicit Helping Request," *The Journal of Social Psychology* 15 (2011): 1–4; J. Holler and J. Wilkin, "Co-Speech Gesture Mimicry in the Process of Collaborative Referring During Face-to-Face Interaction," *Journal of Nonverbal Behavior* 35 (2011): 133–153.

10 C. Rush, *The Mere Mortal's Guide to Fine Dining* (New York: Broadway Books, 2006); C. Jacob and N. Guegen, "The Effect of Physical Distance between Patrons and Servers on Tipping," *Journal of Hospitality & Tourism Research* 36 (2012): 25–31.

11 M. Argyle, *Bodily Communication* (New York: Methuen, 1988).

12 J. N. Martin and T. K. Nakayama, *Experiencing Intercultural Communication* 6e (New York: McGraw-Hill, 2017); D. Matsumoto and H. S. Hwang, "Cultural Influences on Nonverbal Behavior," in *Nonverbal Communication: Science and Applications*, edited by D. Matsumoto, M. G. Frank, and H. S. Hwang (Thousand Oaks, CA: Sage, 2013a), 97–120; P. A. Andersen, "Tactile Traditions: Cultural Differences and Similarities in Haptic Communication," in *The Handbook of Touch: Neuroscience, Behavioral, and Health Perspectives*, edited by M. J. Hertenstein and S. J. Weiss (New York: Springer, 2011), 351–371; M. Jung and H. N. Fouts, "Multiple Caregivers' Touch Interactions with Young Children among the Bofi Foragers in Central Africa," *International Journal of Psychology* 46 (2011): 24–32; P. Yang, "Nonverbal Gender Differences: Examining Gestures of University-Educated Mandarin Chinese Speakers," *Text & Talk* 30 (2010): 333–357; P. Szarota, "The Mystery of the European Smile: A Comparison Based on Individual Photographs Provided by Internet Users," *Journal of Nonverbal Behavior* 34 (2010): 249–256; D. Matsumoto, A. Olide, J. Schug, B. Willingham, and M. Callan, "Cross-Cultural Judgments of Spontaneous Facial Expressions of Emotion," *Journal of Nonverbal Behavior* 33 (2009): 213–238; H. A. Elfenbein, "Learning in Emotion Judgments: Training and the Cross-Cultural Understanding of Facial Expressions," *Journal of Nonverbal Behavior* 30 (2006): 21–36; R. E. Axtell, *Gestures: Do's and Taboos of Body Language around the World* (New York: Wiley, 1998).

13 D. Matsumoto and H. Hwang, "Cultural Similarities and Differences in Emblematic Gestures," *Journal of Nonverbal Behavior* 37 (2013b): 1–27; E. Vennekens-Kelly, *Subtle Differences, Big Faux Pas: Test Your Cultural Competence* (Scottsdale, AZ: Summertime, 2012); L. A. Samovar, R. E. Porter, E. R. McDaniel, and C. S. Roy, "Approaches to Intercultural Communication," in *Intercultural Communication: A Reader* 14e, edited by L. A. Samovar, R. E. Porter, E. R. McDaniel, and C. S. Roy (Belmont, CA: Wadsworth, 2014), 1–4.

14 See J. K. Burgoon and S. B. Jones, "Toward a Theory of Personal Space Expectations and Their Violations," *Human Communication Research* 2 (1976): 131–146. For discussions and applications of expectancy violations theory, see C. N. Wright and M. E. Roloff, "You Should Just Know Why I'm Upset: Expectancy Violation Theory and the Influence of Mind Reading Expectations (MRE) on Responses to Relational Problems," *Communication Research Reports* 32 (2015): 10–19; A. Miller-Ott and L. Kelly, "The Presence of Cell Phones in Romantic Partner Face-to-Face Interactions: An Expectancy Violation Theory Approach," *Southern Communication Journal* 80 (2015): 253–270; W. Walther-Martin, "Media-Generated Expectancy Violations: A Study of Political Humor, Race, and Source Perceptions," *Western Journal of Communication* 79 (2015): 492–507; L. K. Odom, E. S. Parcell, B. M. A. Baker, and V. Cronin-Fisher, "Communication and Female Date Initiation: Differences in Perceptions Based on Assertiveness of Instructor," *Iowa Journal of Communication* 47 (2015): 177–196; B. W. Chiles and M. E. Roloff, "Apologies, Expectations, and Violations: An Analysis of Confirmed and Disconfirmed Expectations for Responses to Apologies," *Communication Reports* 27 (2014): 65–77; R. J. Sidelinger, "Using Relevant Humor to Moderate Inappropriate Conversations: Maintaining Student Communication Satisfaction in the Classroom," *Communication Research Reports* 31 (2014): 292–301; E. L. Cohen, "Expectancy Violations in Relationships with Friends and Media Figures," *Communication Research Reports* 27 (2010): 97–111.

15 I. Marini, X. Wang, C. Etzbach, and A. Del Castillo, "Ethnic, Gender, and Contact Differences in Intimacy Attitudes toward Wheelchair Users," *Rehabilitation Counseling Bulletin* 56 (2013): 135–145; D. W. Worley, "Communication and Students with Disabilities on College Campuses," in *Handbook of Communication and People with Disabilities*, edited by D. O. Braithwaite and T. L. Thompson (Mahwah, NJ: Erlbaum, 2000), 125–140.

16 J. Fast, *Body Language* (New York: M. Evans, 1970).

17 A. Flomenbaum, "Accenture Report: 87% of Consumers Use Second Screen Devices While Watching TV," April 20, 2015, accessed March 4, 20127, www.adweek.com; 2015 Accenture Digital Consumer Survey, accessed March 4, 2017, www.accenture.com; "The Second Screen: A Growing Phenomenon in the Multimedia Industry," white paper, *Beenius*, accessed June 21, 2014, www.beenius.tv; J. Bercovici, "The Second-Screen Trend Is Bigger Than Twitter Vs. Facebook," *Forbes*, October 10, 2013, accessed June 21, 2014, www.forbes.com; HUB Research, "What's TV Worth?" April 11, 2013, accessed June 21, 2014, hubresearchllc.com/download-report/2013-whats-tv-worth.

18 P. Ekman and W. V. Friesen, "The Repertoire of Nonverbal Behavior: Categories, Origins, Usage, and Coding," *Semiotica* 1 (1969): 49–98.

19 American Society for Aesthetic Plastic Surgery, "American Society for Aesthetic Plastic Surgery Reports More Than $13.5 Billion Spent for First Time Ever," March 8, 2016, accessed March 5, 2017, www.surgery.org/media/news-releases/american-society-for-aesthetic-plastic-surgery; U. Lyngs, E. Cohen, W. T. Hattori, M. Newson, and D. T. Levin, "Hearing in Color: How Expectations Distort Perception of Skin Tone," *Journal of Experimental Psychology: Human Perception and Performance* 42 (2016): 2068–2076.

20 M. Cordes, S. Vocks, R. Dtising, A. Bauer, and M. Waldorf, "Male Body Image and Visual Attention Towards Oneself and Other Men," *Psychology of Men & Masculinity* 17 (2016): 243–254; L. DeFeciani, "Eating Disorders and Body Image Concerns among Male Athletes," *Clinical Social Work Journal* 44 (2016): 114–123; M-E. Brierley, K. R. Brooks, J. Mond, R. J. Stevenson, and I. D. Stephen, "The Body and the Beautiful: Health, Attractiveness, and Body Composition in Men's and Women's Bodies," *PLoS ONE* 11 (2016): 1–16; M. Ura and K. S. J. Preston, "The Influence of Thin-Ideal Internalization on Women's Body Image, Self-Esteem, and Appearance Avoidance: Covariance Structure Analysis," *American Communication Journal* 17 (2015): 15–26; V. Quick, R. McWilliams, and C. Byrd-Bredbenner, "Fatty, Fatty, Two-By-Four: Weight-Teasing History and Disturbed Eating in Young Adult Women," *American Journal of Public Health* 103 (2013): 508–515; Z. Sylvia, T. K. King, and B. J. Morse, "Virtual Ideals: The Effect of Video Game Play on Male Body Image," *Computers in Human Behavior* 37 (2014): 183–188; L. A. Ricciardelli and M. P. McCabe, "Body Image Development in Adolescent Boys," in *Body Image: A Book of Science, Practice, and Prevention* 2e, edited by T. F. Cash and L. Smolak (New York: Guilford, 2013), 85–92; A. A. Poorani, "Who Determines the Ideal Body? A Summary of Research Findings on Body Image," *New Media & Mass Communication* 2 (2012): 1–12; M. Krcmar, S. Giles, and D. Helme, "Understanding the Process: How Mediated and Peer Norms Affect Young Women's Body Esteem," *Communication Quarterly* 56 (2008): 111–130; J. S. Wrench and J. L Knapp, "The Effects of Body Image Perceptions and Sociocommunicative Orientations on Self-Esteem, Depression, and Identification and Involvement in the Gay Community," *Journal of Homosexuality* 55 (2008): 471–503.

21 J. Gibson and J. Gore, "Is He a Hero or a Weirdo? How Norm Violations Influence the Halo Effect," *Gender Issues* 33 (2016): 299–310; W. J. Lammers, S. Davis, O. Davidson, and K. Hogue, "Impact of Positive, Negative, and No Personality Descriptors on the Attractiveness Halo Effect," *Psi Chi Journal of Psychological Research* 21 (2016): 29–34.

22 B. Verhulst, M. Lodge, and H. Lavine, "The Attractiveness Halo: Why Some Candidates Are Perceived More Favorably Than Others," *Journal of Nonverbal Behavior* 34 (2010): 111–117; L. P. Naumann, S. Vazire, P. J. Rentfrow, and S. D. Gosling, "Personality Judgments Based on Physical Appearance," *Personality & Social Psychology Bulletin* 35 (2009): 1661–1671; T. H. Feeley, "Evidence of Halo Effects in Student Evaluations of Communication Instruction," *Communication Education* 51 (2002): 225–236.

23 M. Parry, "Researchers Find Ratemyprofessors.com Useful, If Not Chili-Pepper Hot," *The Chronicle of Higher Education* (December 2, 2011): A4; R. Wilson, "Being Hot Leaves Some Professors Cold," *The Chronicle of Higher Education* (August 13, 2010): A1, A9; K. Soper, "RateMyProfessor'sAppearance.com," *The Chronicle of Higher Education* (September 17, 2010): B24; T. A. Moriarty, "They Love Me, They Love Me Not," *The Chronicle of Higher Education* (April 24, 2009): A27; R. Toor, "Can't We Be Smart and Look Good, Too?" *The Chronicle Review* (April 3, 2009): B4–B5; C. Edwards, A. Edwards, Q. Qing, and S. T. Wahl, "The Influence of Computer-Mediated Word-of-Mouth Communication on Student Perceptions of Instructors and Attitudes toward Learning Course Content," *Communication Education* 56 (2007): 255–277.

24 M. L. Knapp, J. A. Hall, and T. G. Horgan, *Nonverbal Communication in Human Interaction* 8e (Belmont, CA: Wadsworth/Cengage Learning, 2013); M. Aliakbari and K. Abdollahi, "Does It Matter What We Wear? A Sociolinguistic Study of Clothing and Human Values," *International Journal of Linguistics* 5 (2013): 34–45.

25 C. A. Zestcott, M. G. Bean, and J. Stone, "Evidence of Negative Implicit Attitudes toward Individuals with a Tattoo Near the Face," *Group Processes & Intergroup Relations* 20 (2017): 186–201; L. Dunden and A. Francis, "Inking and Thinking: Honor Students and Tattoos," *College Student Journal* 50 (2016): 219–223; B. M. Hill, S. M. Ogletree, and K. M. McCrary, "Body Modifications in College Students: Considering Gender, Self-Esteem, Body Appreciation, and Reasons for Tattoos," *College Student Journal* 50 (2016): 246–252; A. R. Timming, "Visible Tattoos in the Service Sector: A New Challenge to Recruitment and Selection," *Work, Employment and Society* 29 (2014): 60–78; J. Rowsell, G. Kress, and B. Street, "Visual Optics: Interpreting Body Art, Three Ways," *Visual Communication* 12 (2013): 97–122; W. Lim, D. Ting, E. Leo, and C. Jayanthy, "Contemporary Perceptions of Body Modifications and Its Acceptability in the Asian Society: A Case of Tattoos and Body Piercings," *Asian Social Science* 9 (2013): 37–42; K. Doss and A. S. Ebesu Hubbard, "The Communicative Value of Tattoos: The Role of Public Self-Consciousness on Tattoo Visibility," *Communication Research Reports* 26 (2009): 62–74.

26 N. Armstrong and M. Wagner, *Field Guide to Gestures: How to Identify and Interpret Virtually Every Gesture Known to Man* (Philadelphia: Quirk Books, 2003).

27 A. Arroyo and S. R. Brunner, "Negative Body Talk as an Outcome of Friends' Fitness Posts on Social Networking Sites: Body Surveillance and Social Comparison as Potential Moderators," *Journal of Applied Communication Research* 44 (2016): 216–235.

28 E. M. Lamberg and L. M. Muratori, "Cell Phones Change the Way We Walk," *Gait & Posture* 35 (2012): 688–690.

29 K. M. Quintanilla and S. T. Wahl, *Business and Professional Communication: Keys for Workplace Excellence* 3e (Thousand Oaks, CA: Sage, 2016); R. Lawson, "I Just Love the Attention: Implicit Preference for Direct Eye Contact," *Visual Cognition* 23 (2015): 450–488; D. Tang and B. Schmeichel, "Look Me in the Eye: Manipulated Eye Gaze Affects Dominance Mindsets," *Journal of Nonverbal Behavior* 39 (2015): 181–194; S. Mann, A. Vrij, S. Leal, P. A. Granhag, L. Warmelink, and D. Forrester, "Windows to the Soul? Deliberate Eye Contact as a Cue to Deceit." *Journal of Nonverbal Behavior* 36 (2012): 205–215; T. Field, J. E. Malphurs, R. Yando, D. Bendell, K. Carraway, and R. Cohen, "Legal Interviewers Use Children's Affect and Eye Contact Cues to Assess Credibility of Their Testimony," *Early Child Development & Care* 180 (2010): 397–404; A. Vrij, S. Mann, S. Leal, and R. Fisher, "'Look into My Eyes': Can an Instruction to Maintain Eye Contact Facilitate Lie Detection?" *Psychology, Crime, & Law* 16 (2010): 327–348; S. A. Beebe, "Eye Contact: A Nonverbal Determinant of Speaker Credibility," *Speech Teacher* 23 (1974): 21–25.

30 Knapp, Hall, and Horgan, *Nonverbal Communication in Human Interaction*.

31 S. C. Koch, C. G. Baehne, L. Kruse, F. Zimmermann, and J. Zumbach, "Visual Dominance and Visual Egalitarianism: Individual and Group-Level Influences of Sex and Status in Group Interactions," *Journal of Nonverbal Behavior* 34 (2010): 137–153; J. A. Hall, "Women's and Men's Nonverbal Communication: Similarities, Differences, Stereotypes, and Origins," in *The SAGE Handbook of Nonverbal Communication,* edited by V. Manusov and M. L. Patterson (Thousand Oaks, CA: Sage, 2006).

32 P. Ekman and W. Friesen, *Unmasking the Face* (Englewood Cliffs, NJ: Prentice Hall, 1975); R. L. Birdwhistell, "The Language of the Body: The Natural Environment of Words," in *Human Communication: Theoretical Explorations,* edited by A. Silverstein (New York: Wiley, 1974), 203–220.

33 C. Darwin, *Expression of Emotions in Man and Animals* (London, UK: Appleton; reprinted University of Chicago Press, 1965).

34 Z. Wang, M. Huifang, J. Yexin, and L. Fan, "Smile Big or Not? Effects of Smile Intensity on Perceptions of Warmth and Competence," *Journal of Consumer Research* 43 (2017): 787–805; U. Hess, K. Kafetsios, H. Mauersberger, C. Blaison, and C.-L. Kessler, "Signal and Noise in the Perception of Facial Emotion Expressions: From Labs to Life," *Personality and Social Psychology Bulletin* 42 (2016): 1092–1110; Civile and Obhi, "Power Eliminates the Influence of Body Posture on Facial Emotion Recognition"; Hess, Blaison, and Kafetsios, "Judging Facial Emotion Expressions in Context"; S. Gunnery and J. Hall, "The Duchenne Smile and Persuasion," *Journal of Nonverbal Behavior* 38 (2014): 181–194; A. G. Halberstadt, P. A. Dennis, and U. Hess, "The Influence of Family Expressiveness, Individuals' Own Emotionality, and Self-Expressiveness on Perceptions of Others' Facial Expressions," *Journal of Nonverbal Behavior* 35 (2011): 35–50; K. U. Likowski, P. Weyers, B. Seibt, C. Stohr, P. Pauli, and A. Muhlberger, "Sad and Lonely? Sad Mood Suppresses Facial Mimicry," *Journal of Nonverbal Behavior* 35 (2011): 101–117; M. Gagnon, P. Gosselin, I. Hudon-ven der Buhs, K. Larocque, and K. Milliard, "Children's Recognition and Discrimination of Fear and Disgust Facial Expressions," *Journal of Nonverbal Behavior* 34 (2010): 27–42; J. P. Forgas and R. East, "How Real Is That Smile? Mood Effects on Accepting or Rejecting the Veracity of Emotional Facial Expressions," *Journal of Nonverbal Behavior* 32 (2009): 157–170; D. Matsumoto and B. Willingham, "Attitudes and Social Cognition: Spontaneous Facial Expressions of Emotion of Congenitally and Noncongenitally Blind Individuals," *Journal of Personality and Social Psychology* 96 (2009): 1–10; J. Beavin Bavelas and N. Chovil, "Nonverbal and Verbal Communication: Hand Gestures and Facial Displays as Part of Language Use in Face-to-Face Dialogue," in *The SAGE Handbook of Nonverbal Communication,* edited by V. Manusov and M. L. Patterson (Thousand Oaks, CA: Sage, 2006), 97–115.

35 Z. H. Gong and E. P. Bucy, "When Style Obscures Substance: Visual Attention to Display Appropriateness in the 2012 Presidential Debates," *Communication Monographs* 83 (2016): 349–372; C. M. Hurley and M. G. Frank, "Executing Facial Control During Deception Situations," *Journal of Nonverbal Behavior* 35 (2011): 119–131; M. Mendolia, "Explicit Use of Categorical and Dimensional Strategies to Decode Facial Expressions of Emotion," *Journal of Nonverbal Behavior* 31 (2007): 57–75; A. P. Atkinson, J. Tipples, D. M. Burt, and A. W. Young, "Asymmetric Interference Between Sex and Emotion in Face Perception," *Perception and Psychophysics* 67 (2005): 1199–1213.

36 P. Collett, "The Seven Faces of Donald Trump—a Psychologist's View," *The Guardian* (January 15, 2017), accessed March 11, 2017, www.theguardian.com.

37 Ekman and Friesen, *Unmasking the Face*.

38 D. Shichuran, T. Yong, and A. M. Martinez, "Compound Facial Expressions of Emotion," *Proceedings of the National Academy of Sciences* 111 (2014): 1454–1462.

39 P. M. Cole, "Children's Spontaneous Control of Facial Expression," *Child Development* 57 (1986): 1309–1321.

40 K. Floyd, *The Loneliness Cure: Six Strategies for Finding Real Connections in Your Life* (Fort Collins, CO: Adams Media, 2016); J. Hart, "Healing Touch, Therapeutic Touch, and Reiki: Energy Medicine Advances in the Medical Community," *Alternative & Complementary Therapies* 18 (2012): 309–313; K. Bundgaard and K. B. Nielsen, "The Art of Holding Hands: A Fieldwork Study Outlining the Significance of Physical Touch in Facilities for Short-Term Stay," *International Journal for Human Caring* 15 (2011): 34–41; R. Feldman, "Maternal Touch and the Developing Infant," in *The Handbook of Touch: Neuroscience, Behavioral, and Health Perspectives,* edited by M. J. Hertenstein and S. J. Weiss (New York: Springer, 2011), 373–408; K. Floyd, P. M. Pauley, and C. Hesse, "State and Trait Affectionate Communication Buffer Adults' Stress Reactions," *Communication Monographs* 77 (2010): 618–636; T. Field, "Touch Deprivation and Aggression against Self Among Adolescents," in *Developmental Psychobiology of Aggression,* edited by D. M. Stoff and E. J. Susman (New York: Cambridge University Press, 2005), 117–140.

41 C. Hesse and A. C. Mikkelson, "Affection Deprivation in Romantic Relationships," *Communication Quarterly* 65 (2017): 20–38; K. Floyd, "Affection Deprivation Is Associated with Physical Pain and Poor Sleep Quality," *Communication Studies* 67 (2016): 379–398.

42 Ivy and Wahl, *Nonverbal Communication for a Lifetime*.

43 D. H. Mansson, F. Marko, K. Bachrata, Z. Daniskova, J. Gajdosikova Zeleiova, V. Janis, and A. S. Sharov, "Young Adults' Trait Affection Given and Received as Functions of Hofstede's Dimensions of Cultures and National Origin," *Journal of Intercultural Communication Research* 45 (2016): 404–418; Andersen, "Tactile Traditions."

44 Matsumoto and Hwang, "Cultural Influences on Nonverbal Behavior"; R. DiBiase and J. Gunnoe, "Gender and Culture Differences in Touching Behavior," *Journal of Social Psychology* 144 (2004): 49–62; E. T. Hall, *The Hidden Dimension* (Garden City, NY: Anchor, 1990); E. T. Hall, *Beyond Culture* (New York: Doubleday, 1981); M. S. Remland, T. S. Jones, and H. Brinkman, "Interpersonal Distance, Body Orientation and Touch: Effect of Culture, Gender, and Age," *Journal of Social Psychology* 135 (1995): 281–295.

45 M. Morningstar, M. A. Dirks, and S. Huang, "Vocal Cues Underlying Youth and Adult Portrayals of Socio-Emotional Expressions," *Journal of Nonverbal Behavior* 41 (2017): 1–29; J. Davidson, "Where the Top Notes Go," *New York* (October 3–16, 2016): 114–118; V. Andre, C. Petr, N. Andre, M. Hausberger, and A. Lemasson, "Voice Features of Telephone Operators Predict Auditory Preferences of Consumers," *Interaction Studies* 17 (2016): 77–97; V. Hughes, S. Wood, and P. Foulkes, "Strength of Forensic Voice Comparison Evidence from the Acoustics of Filled Pauses," *International Journal of Speech, Language & the Law* 23 (2016): 99–132; C. Rezlescu, T. Penton, V. Walsh, H. Tsujimura, S. K. Scott, and M. J. Banissy, "Dominant Versus Attractive Faces: The Contribution of Visual and Auditory Information to Integrated Person Impressions," *Journal of Nonverbal Behavior* 39 (2015): 355–370; A. N. Edgar, "Looking White, Sounding Black: Adele and Musical Authenticity," *Communication Currents, a Publication of the National Communication Association* 9 (2014); M. G. Frank, A. Maroulis, and D. J. Griffin, "The Voice," in *Nonverbal Communication: Science and Application,* edited by D. Matsumoto, M. G. Frank, and H. S. Hwang (Thousand Oaks, CA: Sage, 2013), 53–74; M. Imhof, "Listening to Voices and Judging People," *International Journal of Listening* 24 (2010): 19–33; A. Karpf, *The Human Voice: How This Extraordinary Instrument Reveals Essential Clues About Who We Are* (New York: Bloomsbury, 2006).

46 A. M. Goberman, S. Hughes, and T. Haydock, "Acoustic Characteristics of Public Speaking: Anxiety and Practice Effects," *Speech Communication* 53 (2011): 867–876; F. Roberts, A. L. Francis, and M. Morgan, "The Interaction of Inter-Turn Silence with Prosodic Cues in Listener Perceptions of 'Trouble' in Conversation," *Speech Communication* 48 (2006): 1079–1093; T. DeGroot and S. J. Motowidlo, "Why Visual and Vocal Interview Cues Can Affect Interviewers' Judgments and Predict Job Performance,"

Journal of Applied Psychology 84 (1999): 986–993; N. Christenfeld, "Does It Hurt to Say Um?" *Journal of Nonverbal Behavior* 19 (1995): 171–186.

47 M. Zuckerman and V. Sinicropi, "When Physical and Vocal Attractiveness Differ: Effects on Favorability of Interpersonal Impressions," *Journal of Nonverbal Behavior* 35 (2011): 75–86.

48 A. Hancock and G. Haskin, "Speech-Language Pathologists' Knowledge and Attitudes Regarding Lesbian, Gay, Bisexual, Transgender, and Queer (LGBTQ) Populations," *American Journal of Speech-Language Pathology* 24 (2015): 206–221; J. Sawyer, J. L. Perry, and A. Dobbins-Scaramelli, "A Survey of the Awareness of Speech Services Among Transgender and Transsexual Individuals and Speech-Language Pathologists," *International Journal of Transgenderism* 15 (2014): 146–163; L. Garabedian and A. Hancock, "Transgender Voice and Communication Treatment: A Retrospective Chart Review of 25 Cases," *International Journal of Language and Communication Disorders* 48 (2013): 54–65.

49 K. Erlandson, "Stay Out of My Space," *Journal of College & University Student Housing* 387 (2012): 46–61; M. Costa, "Territorial Behavior in Public Settings," *Environment & Behavior* 44 (2012): 713–721; T. Bringslimark, T. Hartig, and G. Grindal Patil, "Adaptation to Windowlessness: Do Office Workers Compensate for a Lack of Visual Access to the Outdoors?" *Environment & Behavior* 43 (2011): 469–487; F. U. J. Paul, M. K. Mandal, K. Ramachandran, and M. R. Panwar, "Interpersonal Behavior in an Isolated and Confined Environment," *Environment & Behavior* 42 (2010): 707–717; A. Vogler and J. Jorgensen, "Windows to the World, Doors to Space: The Psychology of Space Architecture," *Leonardo* 38 (2005): 390–399; P. Harris and D. Sachau, "Is Cleanliness Next to Godliness? The Role of Housekeeping in Impression Formation," *Environment & Behavior* 37 (2005): 81–99.

50 J. Kim and R. DeDear, "Workspace Satisfaction: The Privacy-Communication Trade-Off in Open-Plan Offices," *Journal of Environmental Psychology* (2013): 18–26; I. Vilnai-Yavetz, A. Rafaeli, and C. Schneider-Yaacov, "Instrumentality, Aesthetics, and Symbolism of Office Design," *Environment & Behavior* 37 (2005): 533–551; J. Sandberg, "Want to Know Someone's Job Status? Look at Desk Location," *Corpus Christi Caller Times* (March 2, 2003): D4.

51 C. C. Andrade, M. L. Lima, A. S. Devlin, and B. Hernandez, "Is It the Place or the People? Disentangling the Effects of Hospitals' Physical and Social Environments on Well-Being," *Environment & Behavior* 48 (2016): 299–323; L. Biemiller, "To College Employees, the Work Environment Is All-Important," *The Chronicle of Higher Education* (July 18, 2008): B12, B14, B17; S. D. Gosling, S. J. Ko, T. Mannarelli, and M. E. Morris, "A Room with a Cue: Personality Judgments Based on Offices and Bedrooms," *Journal of Personality and Social Psychology* 82 (2002): 379–398; A. Lohmann, X. B. Arriaga, and W. Goodfriend, "Close Relationships and Placemaking: Do Objects in a Couple's Home Reflect Couplehood?" *Personal Relationships* 10 (2003): 437–449.

52 L. Scannel, M. Hodgson, J. G. M. Villarreal, and R. Gifford, "The Role of Acoustics in the Perceived Suitability of, and Well-Being in, Informal Learning Spaces," *Environment & Behavior* 48 (2026): 769–795; A. Joseph, Y.-S. Choi, and X. Quan, "Impact of Physical Environment of Residential Health, Care, and Support Facilities (RHCSF) on Staff and Residents: A Systematic Review of Literature," *Environment & Behavior* 48 (2016): 1203–1241; A. Fenko and C. Loock, "The Influence of Ambient Scent and Music on Patients' Anxiety in a Waiting Room of a Plastic Surgeon," *Health Environments Research & Design Journal* 7 (2014): 33–59.

53 P. Dev and L. Haynes, "Teacher Perspectives on Suitable Learning Environments for Students with Disabilities: What Have We Learned from Inclusive, Resource, and Self-Contained Classrooms?" *International Journal of Interdisciplinary Social Sciences: Annual Review* 9 (2015): 53–64; A. S. Sief, A. Pruski, and A. Bennia, "A New Approach for Handling Element Accessbility Problems Faced by Persons with a Wheelchair," *Journal of Automation, Mobile Robotics & Intelligent Systems* 10 (2016): 27–39;

P. Monaghan, "Design for Disability Will Become the Norm," *The Chronicle Review* (February 12, 2010): B6–B7; T. R. Vandenbark, "Tending a Wild Garden: Library Web Design for Persons with Disabilities," *Information Technology & Libraries* 29 (2010): 23–29; D. K. White et al., "Are Features of the Neighborhood Environment Associated with Disability in Older Adults?" *Disabilities & Retention* 32 (2010): 639–645.

54 For more information on design for people with disabilities, see G. Pullin, *Design Meets Disability* (Cambridge, MA: MIT Press, 2011).

55 Matsumoto and Hwang, "Cultural Influences on Nonverbal Behavior"; M. Pearce and R. Woodford-Smith, "The (Dis)location of Time and Space: Trans-Cultural Collaborations in Tokyo," *Journal of Media Practice* 13 (2012): 197–213.

56 Hall, *The Hidden Dimension*; H. Overhill, "Apple Pie Proxemics: Edward T. Hall in the Kitchen Work Triangle," *Design Issues* 30 (2014): 67–82

57 Farley, "Nonverbal Reactions to an Attractive Stranger"; S. Li and Y. Li, "How Far Is Far Enough? A Measure of Information Privacy in Terms of Interpersonal Distance," *Environment & Behavior* 39 (2007): 317–331; D. Matsumoto, "Culture and Nonverbal Behavior," in *The SAGE Handbook of Nonverbal Communication*, edited by V. Manusov and M. L. Patterson (Thousand Oaks, CA: Sage, 2006), 219–235; C. M. J. Beaulieu, "Intercultural Study of Personal Space: A Case Study," *Journal of Applied Social Psychology* 34 (2004): 794–805.

58 A. Schneeweis, "Power, Gender, and Ethnic Spaces," *Journal of Communication Inquiry* 40 (2016): 88–105; S. Canagarajah, "Agency and Power in Intercultural Communication: Negotiating English in Translocal Spaces," *Language & Intercultural Communication* 13 (2013): 202–224; T. T. Prabhu, "Proxemics: Some Challenges and Strategies in Nonverbal Communication," *IUP Journal of Soft Skills* 4 (2010): 7–14; L. Van Doorn, "Perception of Time and Space of (Formerly) Homeless People," *Journal of Human Behavior in the Social Environment* 20 (2010): 218–238; D. R. Carney, J. A. Hall, and L. Smith LeBeau, "Beliefs about the Nonverbal Expression of Social Power," *Journal of Nonverbal Behavior* 29 (2005): 105–123.

59 D. K. Ivy, *GenderSpeak: Communicating in a Gendered World* 6e (Dubuque, IA: Kendall Hunt); V. Santilli and A. N. Miller, "The Effects of Gender and Power Distance on Nonverbal Immediacy in Symmetrical and Asymmetrical Power Conditions: A Cross-Cultural Study of Classrooms and Friendships," *Journal of International and Intercultural Communication* 4 (2011): 3–22; M. Costa, "Interpersonal Distances in Group Walking," *Journal of Nonverbal Behavior* 34 (2010): 15–26; J. A. Hall, "Women's and Men's Nonverbal Communication: Similarities, Differences, Stereotypes, and Origins," in *The SAGE Handbook of Nonverbal Communication*, edited by V. Manusov and M. L. Patterson (Thousand Oaks, CA: Sage, 2006), 201–218.

60 G. Brown and S. L. Robinson, "Reactions to Territorial Infringement," *Organization Science* 22 (2011): 210–224; J. Koen and K. Durrheim, "A Naturalistic Observational Study of Informal Segregation: Seating Patterns in Lectures," *Environment & Behavior* 42 (2010): 448–468; N. Kaya and B. Burgess, "Territoriality: Seat Preferences in Different Types of Classrooms," *Environment & Behavior* 39 (2007): 859–876; S. M. Lyman and M. B. Scott, "Territoriality: A Neglected Sociological Dimension," in *The Nonverbal Communication Reader: Classic and Contemporary Reading* 2e, edited by L. K. Guerro, J. DeVito, and M. L. Hecht (Prospect Heights, IL: Waveland, 1999), 175–183.

61 C. Baraniuk, "Ghosts in the Machine," *New Scientist* 227 (2015): 38–41; N. M. Doering and S. Poeschl, "Nonverbal Cues in Mobile Phone Text Messages: The Effects of Chronemics and Proxemics," in *The Reconstruction of Space and Time: Mobile Communication Practices*, edited by R. Ling and S. Campbell (New Brunswick, NJ: Transaction Publishers, 2009); V. Cho and H. Hung, "The Effectiveness of Short Message Service for Communication with Concerns of Privacy Protection and Conflict Avoidance," *Journal of Computer-Mediated Communication* 16 (2011): 250–270; Ivy and

Wahl, *Nonverbal Communication for a Lifetime*; Knapp, Hall, and Horgan, *Nonverbal Communication in Human Interaction*.

62 Mehrabian, *Nonverbal Communication*.

63 For applications of Mehrabian's immediacy principle, see M. D. Dixson, M. R. Greenwell, C. Rogers-Stacy, R. Weister, and S. Lauer, "Nonverbal Immediacy Behaviors and Online Student Engagement: Bringing Past Instructional Research into the Present Virtual Classroom," *Communication Education* 66 (2017): 37–53; S. Kelly, C. Rice, B. Wyatt, J. Ducking, and Z. Denton, "Teacher Immediacy and Decreased Student Quantitative Reasoning Anxiety: The Mediating Effect of Perception," *Communication Education* 64 (2015): 171–186; R. J. Sidelinger and D. M. Bolen, "Compulsive Communication in the Classroom: Is the Talkaholic Teacher a Misbehaving Instructor?" *Western Journal of Communication* 79 (2015): 174–196; G. D. Bodie, S. M. Jones, A. J. Vickery, L. Hatcher, and K. Cannava, "Examining the Construct Validity of Enacted Support: A Multitrait-Multimethod Analysis of Three Perspectives for Judging Immediacy and Listening Behaviors," *Communication Monographs* 81 (2014): 495–523; L. Martin and T. P. Mottet, "The Effect of Instructor Nonverbal Immediacy Behaviors and Feedback Sensitivity on Hispanic Students' Affective Learning Outcomes in Ninth-Grade Writing Conferences," *Communication Education* 60 (2011): 1–19; P. L. Witt and J. Kerssen-Griep, "Instructional Feedback I: The Interaction of Facework and Immediacy on Students' Perceptions of Instructor Credibility," *Communication Education* 60 (2011): 75–94; F-Y. F. Wei and Y. K. Wang, "Students' Silent Messages: Can Teacher Verbal and Nonverbal Immediacy Moderate Student Use of Text Messaging in Class?" *Communication Education* 59 (2010): 475–496.

64 Argyle, *Bodily Communication*.

65 P. A. Andersen, *Nonverbal Communication: Forms and Functions* 2e (Long Grove, IL: Waveland, 2008): 168.

66 Lakens and Stel, "If They Move in Sync, They Must Feel in Sync"; Wilt, Funkhouser, and Revelle, "The Dynamic Relationships of Affective Synchrony to Perceptions of Situations"; K. McGinty, D. Knox, and M. E. Zusman, "Nonverbal and Verbal Communication in 'Involved' and 'Casual' Relationships among College Students," *College Student Journal* 37 (2003): 68–71; B. Le Poire, A. Duggan, C. Shepard, and J. Burgoon, "Relational Messages Associated with Nonverbal Involvement, Pleasantness, and Expressiveness in Romantic Couples," *Communication Research Reports* 19 (2002): 195–206.

67 J. K. Burgoon and N. E. Dunbar, "Nonverbal Expressions of Dominance and Power in Human Relationships," in *The SAGE Handbook of Nonverbal Communication*, edited by V. Manusov and M. L. Patterson (Thousand Oaks, CA: 2006), 279–297; D. R. Carney and L. Smith LeBeau, "Beliefs about the Nonverbal Expression of Social Power," *Journal of Nonverbal Behavior* 29 (2005): 105–123; M. Schmid Mast and J. A. Hall, "Who Is the Boss and Who Is Not? Accuracy of Judging Status," *Journal of Nonverbal Behavior* 28 (2004): 145–165; M. Helweg-Larsen, S. J. Cunningham, A. Carrico, and A. M. Pergram, "To Nod or Not to Nod: An Observational Study of Nonverbal Communication and Status in Female and Male College Students," *Psychology of Women Quarterly* 28 (2004): 358–361; L. Z. Tiedens and A. R. Fragale, "Power Moves: Complementarity in Dominant and Submissive Nonverbal Behavior," *Journal of Personality and Social Psychology* 84 (2003): 558–568; Mehrabian, *Nonverbal Communication*.

68 M. L. Knapp, M. S. McGlone, D. L. Griffin, and W. Earnest, *Lying and Deception in Human Interaction* 2e (Dubuque, IA: Kendall Hunt, 2015); J. K. Burgoon, J. G. Proudfoot, R. Schuetzler, and D. W. Wilson, "Patterns of Nonverbal Behavior Associated with Truth and Deception: Illustrations from Three Experiments," *Journal of Nonverbal Behavior* 38 (2014): 325–354; M. G. Frank and E. Svetieva, "Deception," in *Nonverbal Communication: Science and Application*, edited by D. Matsumoto, M. G. Frank, and H. S. Hwang (Thousand Oaks, CA: Sage, 2013), 121–144; M. L. Knapp, J. A. Hall, and T. G. Horgan, *Nonverbal Communication in Human Interaction* 8e (Belmont, CA: Wadsworth, 2013);

A. Vrij, "Nonverbal Communication and Deception," in *The SAGE Handbook of Nonverbal Communication*, edited by V. Manusov and M. L. Patterson (Thousand Oaks, CA: Sage, 2006).

69 Ivy and Wahl, *Nonverbal Communication for a Lifetime*; S. Mann, A. Vrij, S. Leal, P. A. Granhag, L. Warmelink, and D. Forrester, "Windows to the Soul? Deliberate Eye Contact as a Cue to Deceit," *Journal of Nonverbal Behavior* 36 (2013): 205–215; F. M. Marchak, "Detecting False Intent Using Eye Blink Measures," *Frontiers in Psychology* 4 (2013): 736.

70 M. Boltz, R. Dyer, and A. Miller, "Are You Lying to Me? Temporal Cues for Deception," *Journal of Language and Social Psychology* 29 (2010): 458–466; L. Anolli and R. Ciceri, "The Voice of Deception: Vocal Strategies of Naive and Able Liars," *Journal of Nonverbal Behavior* 21 (1997): 259–284.

71 H. R. Bosker, A. F. Pinget, H. Quene, T. Sanders, and N. H. deJong, "What Makes Speech Sound Fluent? The Contributions of Pauses, Speed, and Repairs," *Language Testing* 30 (2012): 159–175; L. K. Guerrero and K. Floyd, *Nonverbal Communication in Close Relationships* (Mahwah, NJ: Erlbaum, 2006).

72 J. K. Burgoon, R. Schuetzler, and D. W. Wilson, "Kinesic Patterning in Deceptive and Truthful Interactions," *Journal of Nonverbal Behavior* 39 (2015): 1–25.

73 J. Tierney, "At Airports, a Misplaced Faith in Body Language," *The New York Times*, March 23, 2014, accessed April 1, 2014, www.nytimes.com/2014; C. F. Bond, Jr., and B. M. DePaulo, "Accuracy of Deception Judgments," *Review of Personality and Social Psychology* 10 (2006): 214–234.

Chapter 5

1 A. K. Przybylski and N. Weinstein, "Can You Connect with Me Now? How the Presence of Mobile Communication Technology Influences Face-to-Face Conversation Quality," *Journal of Social and Personal Relationships* 30.3 (2012): 237–246. R. J. Allred and J. P. Crowley, "The 'Mere Presence' Hypothesis: Investigating the Nonverbal Effects of Cell-Phone Presence on Conversation Satisfaction," *Communication Studies* 68:1 (January-March, 2017): 1–21.

2 R. Emanuel, J. Adams, K. Baker, E. K. Daufin, C. Ellington, F. Fits, J. Himsel, L. Holladay, and D. Okeowo, "How College Students Spend Their Time Communicating," *International Journal of Listening* 22 (2008): 13–28; also see L. Barker et al., "An Investigation of Proportional Time Spent in Various Communication Activities for College Students," *Journal of Applied Communication Research* 8 (1981): 101–1 09; also see K. Dindia and B. L. Kennedy, "Communication in Everyday Life: A Descriptive Study Using Mobile Electronic Data Collection," paper presented at the annual conference of the National Communication Association, Chicago (November 2004); L. Cooper and T. Buchanan, "Listening Competency on Campus: A Psychometric Analysis of Student Learning," *The International Journal of Listening* 24 (2010): 141–163.

3 For an excellent review of listening research, see M. L. Beall, J. Gill-Rosier, J. Tate, and A. Matten, "State of the Context: Listening in Education," *International Journal of Listening* 22 (2008): 123–132; also see A. D. Wolvin, "Listening Engagement: Intersecting Theoretical Perspectives," in *Listening and Human Communication in the 21st Century*, edited by A. D. Wolvin (Oxford, UK: Wiley-Blackwell, 2010): 7–30.

4 One study found that only 5 percent of colleges and universities offered a course in listening. See K. G. Wacker and K. Hawkins, "Curricula Comparison for Classes in Listening," *International Journal of Listening* 9 (1995), pp. 14–28.

5 G. Bodie, M. E. Pence, M. Rold, M. D. Chapman, J. Lejune, and L. Anzalone, "Listening Competence in Initial Interactions II: Applying Trait Centrality to Discover the Relative Placement of Listening Competence Among Implicit Competency Theories" in *Communication Studies*, 66:5 (2015): 528–548.

6 For additional support for the importance of listening in interpersonal relationships, see L. Sparks, S. S. Travis, and S. R. Thompson, "Listening for the Communication Signals of Humor, Narratives, and Self-Disclosure in the Family

Caregiver Interview," *Health & Social Work* 30.4 (2005): 340–343; S. Wright, "The Beauty of Silence: Deep Listening Is a Key Nursing Skill That Can Be Learned with Practice," *Nursing Standard* 20.50 (2006): 18–20; M. R. Jalongo, "Listening in Early Childhood: An Interdisciplinary Review of the Literature," *International Journal of Listening* 24.1 (2010): 1–18.

7   J. Hackenbracht and K. Gasper, "I'm All Ears: The Need to Belong Motivates Listening to Emotional Disclosure," *Journal of Experimental Social Psychology* 49 (2013): 915–921; G. S. Bodie, C. C. Gearhart, J. P. Denham, and A. J. Vickery, "The Temporal Stability and Situational Contingency of Active-Empathic Listening," *Western Journal of Communication* 77.2 (2013): 113–138.

8   For a provocative discussion of the role of empathy and compassion in our interactions with others, see P. Bloom, *Against Empathy: The Case for Rational Compassion* (New York: ECCO/HarperCollins, 2016).

9   C. Jacobs and D. Coghlan, "Sound of Silence: On Listening in Organizational Learning," *Human Relations* 58.1 (2005):115–138.

10 P. Skaldeman, "Converging or Diverging Views of Self and Other: Judgment of Relationship Quality in Married and Divorced Couples," *Journal of Divorce & Remarriage* 44 (2006): 145–160.

11 For a review of the role of listening in business contexts, see J. Flynn, T. R. Valikoski, and J. Grau, "Listening in the Business Context: Reviewing the State of Research," *International Journal of Listening* 22 (2008): 141–151.

12 For a review of literature documenting the importance of listening in the health professions, see D. L. Roter and J. A. Hall, *Doctors Talking with Patients/Patients Talking with Doctors: Improving Communication in Medical Visits* (Westport, CT: Praeger, 2006); J. Davis, C. R. Thompson, A. Foley, C. D. Bond, and J. DeWitt, "An Examination of Listening Concepts in the Healthcare Context: Differences Among Nurses, Physicians, and Administrators," *International Journal of Listening* 22 (2008): 152–167.

13 K. W. Hawkins and B. P. Fullion, "Perceived Communication Skill Needs for Work Groups," *Communication Research Reports* 16 (1999): 167–174.

14 J. Brownell, "Perceptions of Effective Listeners: A Management Study," *Journal of Business Communication* (Fall 1990): 401–415; D. A. Romig, *Side by Side Leadership* (Austin, TX: Bard, 2001).

15 J. Burnside-Lawry, "Listening and Participatory Communication: A Model to Assess Organizational Listening Competency," *The International Journal of Listening* 26 (2012): 102–121; C. Jacobs and D. Coghlan, "Sound of Silence."

16 R. Bommelje, J. M. Houston, and R. Smither, "Personality Characteristics of Effective Listeners: A Five Factor Perspective," *International Journal of Listening* 17 (2003): 32–46.

17 M. S. Conaway, "Listening: Learning Tool and Retention Agent," in *Improving Reading and Study Skills*, edited by A. S. Algier and K. W. Algier (San Francisco: Jossey-Bass, 1996): 51–63.

18 For a review of how listening is discussed in public speaking textbooks, see W. C. Adams and E. S. Cox, "The Teaching of Listening as an Integral Part of an Oral Activity: An Examination of Public-Speaking Texts," *International Journal of Listening* 24.2 (2010): 89–105.

19 Adapted from the International Listening Association's definition of *listening*, which may be found on its website, www.listen.org; for a theoretical explanation of the attending listening process, see L. A. Januskik, "Building Listening Theory: The Validation of the Conversational Listening Span," *Communication Studies* 5.2 (June 2007): 139; see also G. D. Bodie, K. St. Cyr, M. Pence, M. Rold, and J. Honeycutt, "Listening Competence in Initial Interactions I: Distinguishing Between What Listening Is and What Listeners Do," *The International Journal of Listening* 26 (2012): 1–28.

20 S. C. Bentley, "Listening in the 21st Century," *International Journal of Listening* 14 (2000): 129–142; also see A. D. Wolvin and C. G. Coakley, "Listening Education in the 21st Century," *International Journal of Listening* 14 (2001): 143–152. For an excellent literature review of definitions and perspectives on defining

listening, see S. Bentley, "Benchmarking Listening Behaviors: Is Effective Listening What the Speaker Says It Is?" *International Journal of Listening* 11.1 (2008): 51–68.

21 D. Mount and A. Mattila, "Last Chance to Listen: Listening Behaviors and Their Effect on Call Center Satisfaction," *Journal of Hospitality & Tourism Research* 26.2 (2002): 124–137.

22 A. Mulanx and W. G. Powers, "Listening Fidelity Development and Relationship to Receiver Apprehension and Locus of Control," *International Journal of Listening* 17 (2003): 69–78.

23 W. L. Randall, S. M. Prior, and M. Skarborn, "How Listeners Shape What Tellers Tell: Patterns of Interaction in Lifestory Interviews and Their Impact on Reminiscence by Elderly Interviewees," *Journal of Aging Studies* 20.4 (2006): 381–396.

24 A. Zohoori, "A Cross-Cultural Comparison of the HURIER Listening Profile Among Iranian and U. S. Students," *International Journal of Listening* 27 (2013): 50–60.

25 K. W. Watson, L. L. Barker, and J. B. Weaver, *The Listener Style Inventory* (New Orleans: Spectra, 1995); D. Worthington, G. D. Bodie, and C. Gearhart, "The Listening Styles Profile Revised (LSP-R): A Scale Revision and Validation," paper presented at the Eastern Communication Association, Arlington, VA (2011); G. D. Bodie and D. L. Worthington, "Revisiting the Listening Styles Profile (LSP-16): A Confirmatory Factor Analytic Approach to Scale Validation and Reliability Estimation," *International Journal of Listening* 24.2 (2010): 69–88; G. D. Bodie, C. C. Gearhart, and D. L. Worthington, "The Listening Styles Profile-Revised (LSP-R): A Scale Revision and Evidence for Validity," *Communication Quarterly* 61.1 (2014): 72–90; G. D. Bodie, J. P. Denham, and C. C. Gearhart, "Listening as a Goal-Directed Activity," *Western Journal of Communication* 78.5 (2014): 668–684.

26 Bodie, Denham and Gearhart, "Listening as a Goal-Directed Activity"; G. D. Bodie, C. C. Gearhart, J. P. Denham and A. J. Vickery "The Temporal Stability and Situational Contingency of Active-Empathetic Listening" in *Western Journal of Communication*, 77:2 (2013): 113–138.

27 D. L. Worthington, "Exploring the Relationship between Listening Style Preference and Personality," *International Journal of Listening* 17 (2003): 68–87; D. L. Worthington, "Exploring Juror's Listening Processes: The Effect of Listening Style Preference on Juror Decision Making," *International Journal of Listening* 17 (2003): 20–37.

28 Worthington, "Exploring Juror's Listening Processes."

29 Worthington, "Exploring Juror's Listening Processes."

30 Worthington, "Exploring Juror's Listening Processes."

31 J. B. Weaver III and M. Kirtley, "Listening Styles and Empathy," *Southern Communication Journal* 2 (1995): 131–141.

32 Bodie, Denham, and Gearhart, "Listening as a Goal-Directed Activity."

33 S. L. Sargent and J. B. Weaver, "Correlates Between Communication Apprehension and Listening Style Preferences," *Communication Research Reports* 14 (1997): 74–78.

34 M. K. Johnston, J. B. Weaver, K. W. Watson, and L. L. Barker, "Listening Styles: Biological or Psychological Differences?" *International Journal of Listening* 14 (2000): 14–31.

35 See C. Kiewitz, J. B. Weaver III, B. Brosius, and G. Weimann, "Cultural Differences in Listening Style Preferences: A Comparison of Young Adults in Germany, Israel, and the United States," *International Journal of Public Opinion Research* 9 (1997): 233–248; N. Dragon and J. C. Sherblom, "The Influence of Cultural Individualism and Collectivism on U.S. and Post Soviet Listening Styles," *Human Communication* 11 (2008): 177–192.

36 L. L. Barker and K. W. Watson, *Listen Up* (New York: St. Martin's Press, 2000); also see M. Imhof, "Who Are We as We Listen? Individual Listening Profiles in Varying Contexts," *International Journal of Listening* 18 (2004): 36–45.

37 Imhof, "Who Are We as We Listen?"

38 Bodie, Denham, and Gearhart, "Listening as a Goal-Directed Activity."

39 W. Winter, A. J. Ferreira, and N. Bowers, "Decision-Making in Married and Unrelated Couples," *Family Process* 12 (1973): 83–94.

40 R. Montgomery, *Listening Made Easy* (New York: Amacom, 1981); also see O. Hargie, C. Sanders, and D. Dickson, *Social Skills in Interpersonal Communication* (London, UK: Routledge, 1994); O. Hargie, ed., *The Handbook of Communication Skills* (London, UK: Routledge, 1997).

41 R. G. Owens, "Handling Strong Emotions," in *The Handbook of Communication Skills*, edited by O. Hargie (London: Croom Helm/New York University Press, 1986).

42 D. Goleman, *Emotional Intelligence: Why It Can Matter More Than IQ* (New York: Bantam Books, 1995); also see D. Goleman, "Emotional Intelligence: Issues in Paradigm Building," in *The Emotionally Intelligent Workplace*, edited by C. Cherniss and D. Goleman (San Francisco: Jossey-Bass, 2001): 13.

43 For an excellent review of emotional intelligence research, see D. Grewal and P. Salovey, "Feeling Smart: The Science of Emotional Intelligence," *American Scientist* 93 (2005): 330–339. Also see J. Keaton and L. Kelly, "Emotional Intelligence as a Mediator of Family Communication Patterns and Reticence," *Communication Reports* 21.2 (2008): 104–116; R. Pishghadam, "Emotional and Verbal Intelligences in Language Learning," *Iranian Journal of Language Studies* 3.1 (2009): 43–64.

44 Goleman, *Emotional Intelligence*; Grewal and Salovey, "Feeling Smart."

45 J. L. Gonzalez-Balado, ed., *Mother Teresa: In My Own Words* (New York: Gramercy Books, 1997).

46 R. G. Nichols, "Factors in Listening Comprehension," *Speech Monographs* 15 (1948): 154–163; G. M. Goldhaber and C. H. Weaver, "Listener Comprehension of Compressed Speech When the Difficulty, Rate of Presentation, and Sex of the Listener Are Varied," *Speech Monographs* 35 (1968): 20–25.

47 M. Fitch-Hauser, D. A. Barker, and A. Hughes, "Receiver Apprehension and Listening Comprehension: A Linear or Curvilinear Relationship?" *Southern Communication Journal* 56 (1988): 62–71; P. E. King and R. R. Behnke, "Patterns of State Anxiety in Listening Performance," *Southern Communication Journal* 70.1 (2004): 72–81.

48 Fitch-Hauser et al., "Receiver Apprehension and Listening Comprehension."

49 C. R. Sawyer, K. Gayle, A. Topa, and W. Powers, "Listening Fidelity Among Native and Nonnative English-Speaking Undergraduates as a Function of Listening Apprehension and Gender" in *Communication Research Reports* 31 (2014): 62–71.

50 Fitch-Hauser et al., "Receiver Apprehension and Listening Comprehension."

51 K. J. Anderson and C. Leaper, "Meta-Analyses of Gender Effects on Conversational Interruption: Who, What, When, Where, and How," *Sex Roles* 39 (1998): 225–252.

52 For a review of the literature on gender, listening, and communication, see D. K. Ivy, *GenderSpeak* 5e (Boston: Pearson, 2012).

53 B. R. Burleson, L. K. Hanasono, G. D. Bodie, A. J. Holmstrom, J. D. McCullough, J. J. Rack, and J. Gill Rosier, "Are Gender Differences in Responses to Supportive Communication a Matter of Ability, Motivation, or Both? Reading Patterns of Situation Effects Through the Lens of a Dual-Process Theory," *Communication Quarterly* 59 (2011): 37–60.

54 Sargent and Weaver, "Correlates Between Communication Apprehension and Listening Style Preferences,"

55 J. Silverman, "Attentional Styles and the Study of Sex Differences," in *Attention: Contemporary Theory and Analysis,* edited by D. I. Mostofsky (New York: Appleton-Century-Crofts, 1970): 61–79.

56 K. Watson, L. Barker, and J. Weaver, "The Listening Styles Profile (LPP16): Development and Validation of an Instrument to Assess Four Listening Styles," *Journal of International Listening Association* (1995), research cited on *20/20*, ABC television network, September 1998.

57 J. O. Yum, "The Impact of Confucianism on Interpersonal Relationships and Communication Patterns in East Asia," in *Intercultural Communication: A Reader*, edited by L. A. Samovar and R. E. Porter (Belmont, CA: Wadsworth, 2000): 86.

58 T. S. Lebra, *Japanese Patterns of Behavior* (Honolulu: University Press of Hawaii, 1976).

59 Imhof, "Who Are We as We Listen?"

60 Bodie et al., "Listening Competence in Initial Interactions I."

61 Bodie et al., "Listening Competence in Initial Interactions I."

62 A. Carruthers, "Listening, Hearing and Changing," *Business Communication* 5 (2004): 3.

63 There is evidence that we sometimes use cognitive strategies about which we are not always aware to help us when listening. For more information, see L. Janusik and S. A. Keaton, "Toward Developing a Cross-Cultural Metacognition Instrument for Listening in First Language (L^1) Contexts: The (Janusik – Keaton) Metacognitive Listening Instrument" in *Journal of Intercultural Communication Research*, 44:4 (2015): 288–306.

64 K. K. Halone and L. L. Pecchioni, "Relational Listening: A Grounded Theoretical Model," *Communication Reports* 14 (2001): 59–71.

65 I. W. Johnson, C. G. Pearce, T. L. Tuten, and L. Sinclair, "Self-Imposed Silence and Perceived Listening Effectiveness," *Business Communication Quarterly* 66 (2003): 23–45.

66 M. V. Redmond, "The Functions of Empathy (Decentering) in Human Relations," *Human Relations* 42 (1993): 593–606.

67 A. Mehrabian, *Nonverbal Communication* (Chicago: Aldine Atherton, 1970); A. Mehrabian, *Silent Messages* (Belmont, CA: Wadsworth, 1981); also see D. Lapakko, "Three Cheers for Language: A Closer Examination of a Widely Cited Study of Nonverbal Communication," *Communication Education* 46 (1997): 63–67.

68 I. M. Imhof, "Listening to Voices and Judging People," *International Journal of Listening* 24.1 (2010): 19–33.

69 H. J. Ferguson and R. Breheny, "Listeners' Eyes Reveal Spontaneous Sensitivity to Others' Perspectives," *Journal of Experimental Social Psychology* 48 (2012): 257–263.

70 M. Argyle and M. Cook, *Gaze and Mutual Gaze* (Cambridge, UK: Cambridge University Press, 1976).

71 Hargie et al., *Social Skills in Interpersonal Communication;* Hargie, *The Handbook of Communication Skills.*

72 For an excellent review of listening skills and research supporting listening skill development, see J. Brownell, "The Skills of Listening-Centered Communication," in *Listening and Human Communication in the 21st Century*, edited by A. D. Wolvin (Oxford, UK: Wiley-Blackwell, 2010): 141–157.

73 Gearhart, Denham and Bodie, "Listening as a Goal-Directed Activity."

74 A. D. Wolvin and S. D. Cohen, "An Inventory of Listening Competency Dimensions," *The International Journal of Listening* 26 (2012): 64–66.

75 For a review of literature about measuring empathy, see G. D. Bodie, "The Active Empathic Listening Scale (AELS): Conceptualization and Validity Evidence," *Communication Quarterly* 59 (2011): 277–295.

76 See R. G. Nichols and L. A. Stevens, "Listening to People," *Harvard Business Review* 35 (September–October 1957): 85–92.

77 W. T. Mickelson and S. A. Welch, "A Listening Competence Comparison of Working Professionals," *International Journal of Listening* 27.2 (2013): 85–99.

78 K. McComb and F. M. Jablin, "Verbal Correlates of Interviewer Empathic Listening and Employment Interview Outcomes," *Communication Monographs* 51 (1984): 353–371.

79 A. Clark, "Communication Confidence and Listening Competence: An Investigation of the Relationships of Willingness to Communicate, Communication Apprehension, and Receiver Apprehension to Comprehension of Content and Emotional Meaning in Spoken Messages," *Communication Education* 38 (1989): 237–248.

80 Halone and Pecchioni, "Relational Listening." J. Vickery, S. A. Keaton, and G. D. Bodie, "Intrapersonal Communication and Listening Goals: An Examination of Attributes and Functions of Imagined Interactions and Active-Empathic Listening Behaviors," *Western Communication Journal* 80, 1 (2015): 20–38.

81 Pearce et al., "Assessment of the Listening Styles Inventory."

82 Pearce et al., "Assessment of the Listening Styles Inventory."

83 G. D. Bodie, "The Nature of Supportive Listening II: The Role of Verbal Person Centeredness and Nonverbal Immediacy," *Western Journal of Communication* 76 (2012): 250–269.

84 E. A. Doohan, "Listening Behaviors of Married Couples: An Exploration of Nonverbal Presentation to a Relational Insider," *International Journal of Listening* 21 (2007): 24–41.

85 W. R. Miller, K. E. Hedrick, and D. R. Orlofsky, "The Helpful Responses Questionnaire: A Procedure for Measuring Therapeutic Empathy," *Journal of Clinical Psychology* 47 (1991): 444–448; A. Paukert, B. Stagner, and K. Hope, "The Assessment of Active Listening Skills in Helpline Volunteers," *Stress, Trauma, and Crisis* 7 (2004): 61–76; D. H. Levitt, "Active Listening and Counselor Self-Efficacy: Emphasis on One Micro-Skill in Beginning Counselor Training," *Clinical Supervisor* 20 (2001): 101–115; V. B. Van Hasselt, M. T. Baker, S. J. Romano, K. M. Schlessinger, M. Zuker, R. Dragone, and A. L. Perera, "Crisis (Hostage) Negotiation Training: A Preliminary Evaluation of Program Efficacy," *Criminal Justice and Behavior* 33 (2006): 56–69; H. Weger Jr., G. R. Castle, and M. C. Emmett, "Active Listening in Peer Interviews: The Influence on Perceptions of Listening Skill," *International Journal of Listening* 24 (2010): 34–49.

86 Weger et al., "Active Listening in Peer Interviews; also see M. R. Wood, "What Makes for Successful Speaker-Listener Technique? Two Case Studies," *Family Journal* 18.1 (2010): 50-54.

87 Vickery, Keaton, and Bodie, "Intrapersonal Communication and Listening Goals."

88 K. Crawford, "Following You: Disciplines of Listening in Social Media," *Journal of Media & Cultural Studies* 23 (2009): 525–535.

89 For a classic discussion of empathy and interpretive listening, see J. Stewart, "Interpretive Listening: An Alternative to Empathy," *Communication Education* 32 (1983): 379–391; Bommelje et al., "Personality Characteristics of Effective Listeners"; J. Håkansson and H. Montgomery, "Empathy as an Interpersonal Phenomenon," *Journal of Social & Personal Relationships* 20 (2003): 267–284.

90 Goleman, *Emotional Intelligence.*

91 A. de Saint-Exupéry, as quoted in Goleman, *Emotional Intelligence.*

92 P. Toller, "Learning to Listen, Learning to Hear: A Training Approach," *Time to Listen to Children: Personal and Professional Communication,* edited by C. Birgit (Florence, KY: Taylor, Frances/Routledge, 1999): 48–61; T. Drollinger, L. B. Comer, and P. T. Warrington, "Development and Validation of the Active Empathetic Listening Scale," *Psychology & Marketing* 23.2 (2006): 161–180; S. L. Do and D. L. Schallert, "Emotions and Classroom Talk: Toward a Model of the Role of Affect in Students' Experiences of Classroom Discussions," *Journal of Educational Psychology* 96.4 (2004): 619–634.

93 H. J. M. Nouwen, "Listening as Spiritual Hospitality," in *Bread for the Journey* (New York: HarperCollins, 1997).

94 C. R. Rogers, "Empathic: An Unappreciated Way of Being," in *A Way of Being* (Boston: Houghton Mifflin, 1980): 137–163.

95 J. C. McCroskey and M. J. Beatty, "The Communibiological Perspective: Implications for Communication in Instruction," *Communication Education* 49 (2000): 1–6; M. J. Beatty and J. C. McCroskey, "Theory, Scientific Evidence and the Communibiological Paradigm: Reflections on Misguided Criticism," *Communication Education* 49 (2001): 36–44.

96 M. E. Pence and A. J. Vickery, "The Roles of Personality and Trait Emotion Intelligence in the Active-Empathic Listening Process: Evidence from Correlational and Regression Analyses," *The International Journal of Listening* 26 (2012): 159–174.

97 D. F. Barone, P. S. Hutchings, H. J. Kimmel, H. L. Traub, J. T. Cooper, and C. M. Marshall, "Increasing Empathic Accuracy through Practice and Feedback in a Clinical Interviewing Course," *Journal of Social and Clinical Psychology* 24 (2005): 156–171.

98 Weaver and Kirtley, "Listening Styles and Empathy."

99 Goleman, *Emotional Intelligence.*

100 G. Bodie, A. J. Vickery, K. Cannava, and S. M. Jones "The Role of 'Active Listening' in Informal Helping Conversations: Impact on Perceptions of Listener Helpfulness, Sensitivity, and Discloser Emotional Improvement" in *Western Journal of Communication,* 79:2 (2015): 151–173.

101 Hargie et al., *Social Skills in Interpersonal Communication;* R. Boulton, *People Skills* (New York: 1981). We also acknowledge others who have presented excellent applications of listening and responding skills in interpersonal and group contexts: D. A. Romig and L. J. Romig, *Structured Teamwork* (D Guide) (Austin, TX: Performance Resources, 1990); S. Deep and L. Sussman, *Smart Moves* (Reading, MA: Addison-Wesley, 1990); P. R. Scholtes, *The Team Handbook* (Madison, WI: Joiner Associates, 1988); Hargie, *The Handbook of Communication Skills.*

102 S. M. Jones, "Supportive Listening," *The International Journal of Listening* 25 (2011): 85–103.

103 Our discussion of appropriate and inappropriate social support responses is taken from B. D. Burleson, "Emotional Support Skill," in *Handbook of Communication and Social Interaction Skills,* edited by O. Greene and B. R. Burleson (Mahwah, NJ: Lawrence Erlbaum, 2003): 566–568. See also G. D. Bodie, A. J. Vickery, and C. C Gearhart, "The Nature of Supportive Listening, I: Exploring the Relation between Supportive Listeners and Supportive People," *International Journal of Listening* 27 (1): 39–49.

104 A. M. Nicotera, J. Steele, A. Catalani, and N. Simpson, "Conceptualization and Test of an Aggression Competence Model," *Communication Research Reports* 29 (2012): 12–25.

105 L. B. Comer and T. Drollinger, "Active Empathic Listening and Selling Success: A Conceptual Framework," *Journal of Personal Selling & Sales Management* 19 (1999): 15–29; S. B. Castleberry, C. D. Shepherd, and R. Ridnour, "Effective Interpersonal Listening in the Personal Selling Environment: Conceptualization, Measurement, and Nomological Validity," *Journal of Marketing Theory and Practice* (Winter 1999): 30–38.

106 F.C.B. Hansen, H. Resnick, and J. Galea, "Better Listening: Paraphrasing and Perception Checking—A Study of the Effectiveness of a Multimedia Skills Training Program," *Journal of Technology in Human Services* 20 (2002): 317–331; D. Ifert Johnson and K. Long, "Evaluating the Effectiveness of Listening Instruction in Introductory Communication Courses," paper presented at the International Communication Association (2008).

107 R. Lemieux and M. R. Tighe, "Attachment Styles and the Evaluation of Comforting Responses: A Receiver Perspective," *Communication Research Reports* 21 (2004): 144–153; also see W. Samter, "How Gender and Cognitive Complexity Influence the Provision of Emotional Support: A Study of Indirect Effects," *Communication Reports* 15 (2002): 5-16.

Chapter 6

1 Research documents several culture-based differences in communication, including approaches to leadership, deception, and conflict management styles. See N. Ensari and S. E. Murphy, "Cross-Cultural Variations in Leadership Perceptions and Attribution of Charisma to the Leader," *Organizational Behavior and Human Decision Processes* 92 (2003): 52–66; M. K. Lapinski and T. R. Levine, "Culture and Information Manipulation Theory: The Effects of Self-Construal and Locus of Benefit on Information Manipulation," *Communication Studies* 5 (2000): 55–73; D. Cai and E. L. Fink, "Conflict Style Differences between Individualists and Collectivists," *Communication Monographs* 69 (2002): 67–87; M. S. Kim and A. S. Ebesu Hubbard, "Intercultural

Communication in the Global Village: How to Understand 'The Other'," *Journal of Intercultural Communication Research* 36.3 (2007): 223–235.

2 For a discussion of the role of self-awareness as a strategy for enhancing intercultural competence, see R. C. Weigl, "Intercultural Competence through Cultural Self-Study: A Strategy for Adult Learners," *International Journal of Intercultural Relations* 33 (2009): 346–360.

3 T. Friedman, *Thank You for Being Late: An Optimist's Guide to Thriving in the Age of Accelerations* (New York: Farrar, Straus, and Girous, 2016).

4 For a review of research identifying the importance of adapting to cultural differences, see Y. Hu and W. Fan, "An Exploratory Study on Intercultural Communication Research Contents and Methods: A Survey Based on the International and Domestic Journal Papers Published from 2001 to 2005," *International Journal of Intercultural Relations* 35 (2011): 554–566.

5 D. K. Ivy, *GenderSpeak: Personal Effectiveness in Gender Communication* 6e (Dubuque, Iowa: Kendall Hunt Publishers, 2016).

6 J. Gray, *Men Are from Mars, Women Are from Venus* (New York: HarperCollins, 1992).

7 D. K. Ivy, *GenderSpeak*. D. J. Canary and T. R. Emmers Sommer, *Sex and Gender Differences in Personal Relationships* (New York: Guilford, 1997).

8 D. Tannen, *You Just Don't Understand* (New York: William Morrow, 1990).

9 S. D. Farley, A. M. Ashcraft, M. F. Stasson, and R. L. Nusbaum, "Nonverbal Reactions to Conversational Interruption: A Test of Complementarity Theory and the Status/Gender Parallel," *Journal of Nonverbal Behavior* 34.4 (2010): 193–206.

10 A. C. Selbe, *Are You from Another Planet or What?* Workshop presented at the Joint Service Family Readiness Matters Conference, Phoenix, AZ (July 1999).

11 R. B. Rubin, E. M. Perse, and C. A. Barbato, "Conceptualization and Measurement of Interpersonal Communication Motives," *Human Communication Research* 14 (1988): 602–628; D. Tannen, *That's Not What I Meant!* (London: Dent, 1986).

12 P. Weber, "Confused by All the New Facebook Genders? Here's What They Mean," *Slate*, February 21, 2014, accessed March 22, 2014, www.slate.com/blogs/lexicon_valley/2014/02/21/gender_facebook_now_has_56_categories_to_choose_from_including_cisgender.html.

13 "A Survey of LGBT Americans: Attitudes, Experiences and Values in Changing Times," *Pew Research Social & Demographic Trends*, June 13, 2013, accessed March 18, 2014, www.pewsocial-trends.org/2013/06/13/a-survey-of-lgbt-americans; T. Mottet, "The Role of Sexual Orientation in Predicting Outcome: Value and Anticipated Communication Behaviors," *Communication Quarterly* 43 (Summer 2000): 223–239; for an excellent review of literature summarizing attitudes toward gay men and lesbians, see J. Soliz, E. Ribarsky, M. M. Harrigan, and S. Tye-Williams, "Perceptions of Communication with Gay and Lesbian Family Members: Predictors of Relational Satisfaction and Implications for Outgroup Attitudes," *Communication Quarterly* 58.1 (2010): 77–95.

14 "A Survey of LGBT Americans."

15 G. M. Herek, "Heterosexuals' Attitudes Toward Lesbian and Gay Men: Correlates and Gender Differences," *Journal of Sex Research* 25 (1988): 451–477.

16 Herek, "Heterosexuals' Attitudes Toward Lesbian and Gay Men"; M. S. Weinberg and C. J. Williams, *Male Homosexuals: Their Problems and Adaptations* (New York: Free Press, 1974); Mottet, "The Role of Sexual Orientation in Predicting Outcome."

17 "A Survey of LGBT Americans."

18 J. Soliz, E. Ribarsky, M. M. Harrigan, and S. Tye-Williams, "Perceptions of Communication with Gay and Lesbian Family Members: Predictors of Relational Satisfaction and Implications for Outgroup Attitudes," *Communication Quarterly* 58.1 (2010): 77–95.

19 "Removing Bias in Language; Sexuality," *American Psychological Association*, accessed March 2006, www.apastyle.org/sexuality.html; J. W. Peters, "The Decline and Fall of the 'H' Word," *The New York Times*, Sunday Styles (March 23, 2014): 10.

20 A. Williams and P. Garrett, "Communication Evaluations across the Life Span: From Adolescent Storm and Stress to Elder Aches and 'Pains'," *Journal of Language and Social Psychology* 21 (June 2002): 101–126; also see D. Cai, H. Giles, and K. Noels, "Elderly Perceptions of Communication with Older and Younger Adults in China: Implications for Mental Health," *Journal of Applied Communication Research* 26 (1998): 32–51.

21 J. Montepare, E. Koff, D. Zaitchik, and M. Albert, "The Use of Body Movements and Gestures as Cues to Emotions in Younger and Older Adults," *Journal of Nonverbal Behavior* 23 (1999): 133–152.

22 J. Harwood, E. B. Ryan, H. Giles, and S. Tysoski, "Evaluations of Patronizing Speech and Three Response Styles in a Non-Service-Providing Context," *Journal of Applied Communication Research* 25 (1997): 170–195.

23 T. C. Segrin, "Age Moderates the Relationship between Social Support and Psychosocial Problems," paper presented at the International Communication Association, San Diego, CA (May 2003).

24 N. Howe and W. Strauss, *Millennials Rising: The Next Great Generation* (New York: Vintage Books, 2000).

25 Howe and Strauss, *Millennials Rising*.

26 K. Meyers and K. Sadaghiani, "Millennials in the Workplace: A Communication Perspective on Millennials' Organizational Relationships and Performance," *Journal of Business & Psychology* 25.2 (2010): 225–238.

27 "Millennials in Adulthood: Detached from Institutions, Networked with Friends," *Pew Research Social & Demographic Trends*, March 7, 2014, accessed March 20, 2014, www.pewsocialtrends.org/2014/03/07/millennials-in-adulthood.

28 Information summarized from Howe and Strauss, *Millennials Rising*.

29 Our discussion of generational differences and communication is also based on J. Smith, "The Millennials Are Coming," workshop presented at Texas State University, San Marcos, TX (2006).

30 Howe and Strauss, *Millennials Rising*; H. Karp, C. Fuller, and D. Sirias, *Bridging the Boomer-Xer Gap: Creating Authentic Teams for High Performance at Work* (Palo Alto, CA: Davies-Black, 2002).

31 Although the term race used to refer to a person's genetic background, today it includes socially-constructed perceptions based on a variety of factors including geography and culture. See: *Random House Webster's Unabridged Dictionary* (New York: Random House, 1998), 1590. For a description of the evolving definition of race see: *English Oxford Living Dictionaries* https://en.oxforddictionaries.com/definition/race accessed February 11, 2017.

32 R. Lewontin, "The Apportionment of Human Diversity," *Evolutionary Biology* 6 (1973): 381–397.

33 S. Saulny, "Black? White? Asian? More Young Americans Choose All of the Above," *The New York Times* (January 30, 2011): 1, 20–21.

34 D. Matsumoto and L. Juang, *Culture and Psychology* (Belmont, CA: Wadsworth/Thomson, 2004), 16; also see H. A. Yee, H. H. Fairchild, F. Weizmann, and E. G. Wyatt, "Addressing Psychology's Problems with Race," *American Psychologist* 48 (1994): 1132–1140.

35 B. J. Allen, *Differences Matter: Communicating Social Identity* (Long Grove, IL: Waveland Press, 2004).

36 S. Roberts, *Who We Are Now: The Changing Face of America in the Twenty-First Century* (New York: Henry Holt, 2004).

37 T. Friedman, *The World Is Flat: A Brief History of the Twenty-First Century* (New York: Farrar, Straus and Giroux, 2005).

38 Adapted from *Information Please Almanac* (Boston: Houghton Mifflin, 1990) and *World Almanac and Book of Facts* (New York: World Almanac, 1991), as cited by Lustig and Koester, *Intercultural Competence*, 11.

39 For a discussion of globalization and change see: T. Friedman, *Thank You for Being Late: An Optimist's Guide to Thriving in the Age of Accelerations*, (New York: Farrar, Straus, and Girous, 2016).

40 A. G. Smith, ed., *Communication and Culture* (New York: Holt, Rinehart and Winston, 1966).

41 M. E. Ryan, "Another Way to Teach Migrant Students," *Los Angeles Times* (March 31, 1991): B20, as cited by M. W. Lustig and J. Koester, *Intercultural Competence: Interpersonal Communication across Cultures* (Boston: Allyn & Bacon, 2009), 11.

42 Roberts, *Who We Are Now,* 126.

43 "One in Three US Residents Member of a Minority Group," Marketing Charts, May 21, 2007, accessed September 25, 2014, www.marketingcharts.com/traditional/one-in-three-us-residents-a-member-of-a-minority-group-418.

44 Roberts, *Who We Are Now,* 122; A. Caldwell, "Census: More Than Half of Texans Are Minorities," *Austin American-Statesman* (August 11, 2005): lB.

45 L. A. Jacobsen, M. Kent, M. Lee, and M. Mather, "Population Bulletin: America's Aging Population," Population Reference Bureau, February 2011, 66(1), 4, www.prb.org/pdf11/aging-in-America.pdf.

46 S. Saulny, "Black? White? Asian?"

47 G. Chen and W. J. Starosta, "A Review of the Concept of Intercultural Sensitivity," *Human Communication* 1 (1997): 7.

48 "One Nation, One Language?" *U.S. News & World Report* (September 25, 1995): 40, as cited by Lustig and Koester, *Intercultural Competence,* 10.

49 "One in Three US Residents Member of a Minority Group." "Increasing Diversity of U.S. Population," *Boston Globe/Boston/Production/BostonGlobe.com/WebPages/Homepage/homepage.ad-layer.story-asset.dwp*

50 S. Jaschik, "Women Lead in Doctorates," *Inside Higher Ed*, September 14, 2010, accessed September 25, 2014, www.insidehighered.com/news/2010/09/14/doctorates.

51 "Gay and Lesbian Population: Los Angeles County and the City of Los Angeles. *Los Angeles Almanac*, accessed May 26, 2008, www.laalmanac.com/population/po55.htm.

52 By 2050 No One Race/Ethnic Category Will Be a Majority, www.nacme.org/publications/data_book/DECK1Increasing Diversity.pdf, accessed January 26, 2017.

53 By 2050 No One Race/Ethnic Category Will Be a Majority, www.nacme.org/publications/data_book/DECK1Increasing Diversity.pdf, accessed January 26, 2017.

54 E. T. Hall, *Beyond Culture* (Garden City, NY: Doubleday, 1976).

55 For example, see A. V. Matveeve and P. E. Nelson, "Cross Cultural Competence and Multicultural Team Performance: Perceptions of American and Russian Managers," *International Journal of Cross Cultural Management* 4 (2004): 253–270.

56 G. Hofstede, *Culture's Consequences: International Differences in Work Related Values* (Beverly Hills, CA: Sage, 1980); G. Hofstede and G. J. Hofstede, *Cultures and Organizations: Software of the Mind* 3e (New York: McGraw-Hill, 2010).

57 H. J. Ladegaard, "Global Culture—Myth or Reality? Perceptions of 'National Cultures' in Global Corporation," *Journal of Intercultural Communication Research* 36.2 (2007): 139–163; also see T. R. Levine, H. S. Park, and R. K Kim, "Some Conceptual and Theoretical Challenges for Cross-Cultural Communication Research in the 21st Century," *Journal of Intercultural Communication Research* 36.3 (2007): 205–221.

58 E. R. Pedersen, C. Neighbors, M. E. Larimer, and C. M. Lee, "Measuring Sojourner Adjustment Among American Students Studying Abroad," *International Journal of Intercultural Relations* 35 (2011): 881–889; G/Gap. The Effects of Intercultural Training upon the Organizational Performance of Multinational Corporations in China," *International Journal of Business Anthropology* 1: 97–116.

59 For an excellent overview of issues in teaching intercultural communication, see Levine et al., "Some Conceptual and Theoretical Challenges for Cross-Cultural Communication Research in the 21st Century."

60 C. Ward, S. Bochner, and A. Furnham, *The Psychology of Culture Shock* (Hove, UK: Routledge, 2001).

61 T. L. Sandel, "'Oh, I'm Here!': Social Media's Impact on the Cross-cultural Adaptation of Students Studying Abroad," *Journal of Intercultural Communication Research*, 45(1) (2014): 1–29.

62 C. H. Dodd, *Dynamics of Intercultural Communication* (New York: McGraw-Hill, 1998).

63 P. Coy, "The Future of Work," *Business Week* (August 20 and 27, 2007): 43.

64 See J. B. Walther, "Interpersonal Effects in Computer-Mediated Interaction: A Relational Perspective," *Communication Research* 19 (1992): 52–90; J. B. Walther, "Relational Aspects of Computer-Mediated Communication: Experimental and Longitudinal Observations," *Organizational Science* 6 (1995): 186–203; J. B. Walther, J. F. Anderson, and D. Park, "Interpersonal Effects in Computer-Mediated Interaction: A Meta-Analysis of Social and Anti-Social Communication," *Communication Research* 21 (1994): 460–487.

65 M. E. Heilman, S. Caleo, and M. L. Halim, "Just the Thought of It!: Effects of Anticipating Computer-mediated Communication on Gender Stereotyping," *Journal of Experimental Social Psychology* 46.4 (2010): 672–675; M. Hansen, S. Fabriz, S. Stehle "Cultural Cues in Students' Computer-Mediated Communication: Influences on E-mail Style, Perception of the Sender, and Willingness to Help in *Journal of Computer-Mediated Communication,* 20 (2015): 278–294.

66 J. Park, Y. M. Baek, and M. Cha "Cross-Cultural Comparison of Nonverbal Cues in Emoticons on Twitter: Evidence from Big Data Analysis" in *Journal of Communication,* 64 (2014): 333–354.

67 Y. Mao and C. L. Hade "Relating Intercultural Communication Sensitivity to Conflict Management Styles, Technology Use, and Organizational Communication Satisfaction in Multinational Organizations in China" in *Journal of Intercultural Communication Research* 44:2, (2015): 132–150.

68 Hall, *Beyond Culture.*

69 L. A. Samovar, R. E. Porter, and L. A. Stefani, *Communication between Cultures* (Belmont, CA: Wadsworth, 1998).

70 Hofstede, *Culture's Consequences*; Hofstede and Hofstede, *Cultures and Organizations* 3e.

71 G. Hofstede, "Dimensionalizing Cultures: The Hofstede Model in Context," *Online Readings in Psychology and Culture* 2 (2011): 1–25; also see: D. H. Mansson, F. Marko, K. Bachrata, Z. Daniskova, J. Gajdosikova Zeleiova, V. Janis, and A. S. Sharov, "Young Adults' Trait Affection Given and Received as Functions of Hofstede's Dimensions of Cultures and National Origin," *Journal of Intercultural Communication Research* 45, 5 (2016): 404–418.

72 S. Ting-Toomey, "Applying Dimensional Values in Understanding Intercultural Communication," *Communication Monographs* 77.2 (2010): 169–180.

73 For research about the effect of individualistic and collectivistic cultural values on communication and conflict management, see R. Kaushal and C. T. Kwantes, "The Role of Culture and Personality in Choice of Conflict Management Strategy," *International Journal of Intercultural Relations* 30 (2006): 579–603.

74 A.S. Waterman's *The Psychology of Individualism*, Praeger, 1984, 4-5.

75 W. B. Gudykunst, *Bridging Differences: Effective Intergroup Communication* (Newbury Park, CA: Sage, 1998).

76 H. C. Triandis, "The Many Dimensions of Culture," *Academy of Management Executive* 18 (2004): 88–93.

77 M. Voronov and J. A. Singer, "The Myth of Individualism-Collectivism: A Critical Review," *Journal of Social Psychology* 142 (2002): 461–480.

78 For an excellent review of Hofstede's work, see J. W. Bing, "Hofstede's Consequences: The Impact of His Work on Consulting and Business Practices," *Academy of Management Executive* 18 (2004): 80–87.

79 Hofstede, *Culture's Consequence*; Hofstede and Hofstede, *Cultures and Organizations* 3e.

80 G. Hofstede, "Cultural Dimensions in Management and Planning," *Asia Pacific Journal of Management* (January 1984): 81–98; Hofstede and Hofstede, *Cultures and Organizations* 3e.

81 For a discussion of a nation's long- and short-term time orientation, see Hofstede and Hofstede, *Cultures and Organizations* 3e, 210–238.

82 Hofstede and Hofstede, *Cultures and Organizations* 3e.

83 *The Declaration of Independence.* http://www.ushistory.org/declaration/document/ accessed January 23, 2017.

84 Hofstede, "Dimensionalizing Cultures."

85 Hofstede, "Dimensionalizing Cultures."

86 Hofstede, "Dimensionalizing Cultures."

87 J. W. Neuliep, "Assessing the Reliability and Validity of the Generalized Ethnocentrism Scale," *Journal of Intercultural Communication Research* 31 (2002): 201–215. For additional research on the role of ethnocentrism in communication, see Y. Lin, A. Rancer, and A. Sunhee Lim, "Ethnocentrism and Intercultural Willingness to Communicate: A Cross-Cultural Comparison Between Korean and American College Students," *Journal of Intercultural Communication Research* 32 (2003): 117–128.

88 See Ensari and Murphy, "Cross-Cultural Variations in Leadership Perceptions and Attribution of Charisma to the Leader"; Lapinski and Levine, "Culture and Information Manipulation Theory"; Cai and Fink, "Conflict Style Differences between Individualists and Collectivists."

89 C. Kluckhohn and S. Murray, 1953, as quoted by J. S. Caputo, H. C. Hazel, and C. McMahon, *Interpersonal Communication* (Boston: Allyn & Bacon, 1994), 304.

90 Y. Kashima, E. S. Kashima, U. Kim, and M. Gelfand, "Describing the Social World: How Is a Person, a Group, and a Relationship Described in the East and in the West?" *Journal of Experimental Social Psychology* 42 (2006): 388–396.

91 D. E. Brown, "Human Universals and Their Implications," in *Being Humans: Anthropological Universality and Particularity in Transdisciplinary Perspectives,* edited by N. Roughley (New York: Walter de Gruyter, 2000, 156–174). For an applied discussion of these universals, see S. Pinker, *The Blank Slate: The Modern Denial of Human Nature* (London: Penguin Books, 2002).

92 D. W. Kale, "Ethics in Intercultural Communication," in *Intercultural Communication: A Reader* 6e, edited by L. A. Samovar and R. E. Porter (Belmont, CA: Wadsworth, 1991).

93 L. A. Samovar and R. E. Porter, *Communication between Cultures* (Stamford, CT: Wadsworth and Thomson Learning, 2001), 29.

94 C. S. Lewis, *The Abolition of Man* (New York: Macmillan, 1944).

95 M. Hansen, S. Fabriz, and S. Stehle, "Cultural Cues in Students' Computer-Mediated Communication: Influences on E-mail Style, Perception of the Sender, and Willingness to Help," *Journal of Computer-Mediated Communication,* 20 (2015): 278–294.

96 M. Gladwell, *Blink: The Power of Thinking without Thinking* (New York: Little, Brown, 2005).

97 S. Kamekar, M. B. Kolsawalla, and T. Mazareth, "Occupational Prestige as a Function of Occupant's Gender," *Journal of Applied Social Psychology* 19 (1988): 681–688.

98 E. Roosevelt, as cited by Lustig and Koester, *Intercultural Competence.*

99 S. Ting-Toomey, "Intercultural Conflict Training: Theory-Practice Approaches and Research Challenges," *Journal of Intercultural Communication Research* 36.3 (2007): 255–271.

100 J. G. DeJaeghere and Y. Cao, "Developing U. S. Teachers' Intercultural Competence: Does Professional Development Matter?" *International Journal of Intercultural Relations* 33 (2009): 437–447.

101 P. Holmes and G. O'Neill, "Developing and Evaluating Intercultural Competence: Ethnographies of Intercultural Encounters," *International Journal of Intercultural Relations* 36 (2012): 707–718.

102 For a discussion of how intercultural competence has been applied to educational context, see P. Bayless, *Assessing the Intercultural Sensitivity of Elementary Teachers in Bilingual Schools in a Texas School District,* doctoral dissertation, University of Minnesota, Minneapolis (2009).

103 M. R. Hammer, M. J. Bennett, and R. Wiseman, "Measuring Intercultural Sensitivity: The Intercultural Development Inventory," *International Journal of Intercultural Relations* 27 (2003): 422.

104 Hammer, et al., "Measuring Intercultural Sensitivity," 421–443.

105 For additional research about the validity of measuring intercultural adaptation, see J. F. Greenholtz, "Does Intercultural Sensitivity Cross Cultures? Validity Issues in Porting Instruments across Languages and Cultures," *International Journal of Intercultural Relations* 29 (2005): 73–89.

106 R. Vollhardt, "Enhanced External and Culturally Sensitive Attributions after Extended Intercultural Contact," *British Journal of Social Psychology* 49.2 (2010): 363–383.

107 A. N. Miller and J. A. Samp, "Planning Intercultural Interaction: Extending Anxiety Uncertainty Management Theory," *Communication Research Reports* 24.2 (2007): 87–95.

108 Taking initiative when interacting with others from another culture can enhance intercultural competence. See E. S. Yakunina, I. K. Weigold, A. Weigold, S. Hercegovac, and N. Elsayed, "The Multicultural Personality: Does It Predict International Students' Openness to Diversity and Adjustment?" *International Journal of Intercultural Relations* 36 (2010): 533–540.

109 W. B. Gudykunst and Y. Kim, *Communicating with Strangers* (New York: Random House, 1984); Gudykunst, *Bridging Differences.*

110 Miller and Samp, "Planning Intercultural Interaction."

111 B. J. Lough, "International Volunteers' Perceptions of Intercultural Competence," *International Journal of Intercultural Relations* 35 (2011): 452–464.

112 For a classic discussion of egocentrism and ethnocentrism, see T. W. Adorno, E. Frenkel-Brunswik, D. J. Levinson, and R. N. Sanford, *The Authoritarian Personality* (New York: Harper & Brothers, 1950).

113 Neuliep, "Assessing the Reliability and Validity of the Generalized Ethnocentrism Scale"; Lin et al., "Ethnocentrism and Intercultural Willingness to Communicate."

114 M. V. Redmond, "The Functions of Empathy (Decentering) in Human Relations," *Human Relations* 42 (1993): 593–606; also see M. V. Redmond, "A Multidimensional Theory and Measure of Social Decentering," *Journal of Research in Personality* 1 (1995): 35–88; for an excellent discussion of the role of emotions in establishing empathy, see D. Goleman, *Emotional Intelligence* (New York: Bantam, 1995).

115 See B. J. Broome, "Building Shared Meaning: Implications of a Relational Approach to Empathy for Teaching Intercultural Communication," *Communication Education* 40 (1991): 235–249. Much of this discussion is based on the treatment of social decentering and empathy in S. A. Beebe, S. J. Beebe, and M. V. Redmond, *Interpersonal Communication: Relating to Others* 6e (Boston: Pearson, 2011).

116 F. Walter, M. S. Cole, and R. H. Humphrey, "Emotional Intelligence: *Sine Qua Non* of Leadership or Folderol?" *Academy of Management Perspectives* (2011): 45–59; Y. C. Lin, A. S. Y. Chen, and Y. C. Song, "Does Your Intelligence Help to Survive in a Foreign Jungle? The Effects of Cultural Intelligence and Emotional Intelligence on Cross-Cultural Adjustment," *International Journal of Intercultural Relations* 36 (2012): 541–552.

117 For an excellent discussion of empathy as it relates to intercultural communication, see D. W. Augsburger, *Pastoral Counseling across Cultures* (Philadelphia: Westminster Press, 1986), 28–30.

118 H. J. M. Nouwen, *Bread for the Journey* (New York: HarperCollins, 1997).

119 C. Gallois, T. Ogay, and H. Giles, "Communication Accommodation Theory: A Look Back and a Look Ahead," In W. B. Gudykunst, ed. *Theorizing about Intercultural Communication,* (Thousand Oaks, CA: Sage, 2005): 121–148; also see: M. Hansen, S. Fabriz, and S. Stehle, "Cultural Cues."

120 J. R. C. Kuntz, J. R. Kuntz, D. Elenkov, and A. Nabirukhina, "Characterizing Ethical Cases: A Cross-Cultural Investigation of Individual Differences, Organizational Climate, and Leadership on Ethical Decision-Making," *Journal of Business Ethics* (2013): 317–331.

121 R. H. Farrell, ed., *Off the Record: The Private Papers of Harry S. Truman* (New York: Harper & Row, 1980), 310.

122 S. M. Fowler, "Training across Cultures: What Intercultural Trainers Bring to Diversity Training," *International Journal of Intercultural Relations* 30 (2006): 401–411.

123 See, for example, A. Molinsky, "Cross-Cultural Code-Switching: The Psychological Challenges of Adapting Behavior in Foreign Cultural Interactions," *Academy of Management Review* (2007): 622–640.

124 L. J. Carrell, "Diversity in the Communication Curriculum: Impact on Student Empathy," *Communication Education* 46 (1997): 234–244.

125 Ting-Toomey, "Intercultural Conflict Training"; D. F. Barone, P. S. Hutchings, H. J. Kimmel, H. L. Traub, J. T. Cooper, and C. M. Marshall, "Increasing Empathic Accuracy through Practice and Feedback in a Clinical Interviewing Course," *Journal of Social and Clinical Psychology* 24 (2005): 156–171; J. Hamilton and R. Woodward-Kron, "Developing Cultural Awareness and Intercultural Communication through Multimedia: A Case Study from Medicine and Health Sciences," *System* 38.4 (2010): 560–568.

Chapter 7

1 J. S. Wrench and N. M. Punyanunt-Carter, "From the Front Porch to Swiping Right: The Impact of Technology on Modern Dating," in *The Impact of Social Media in Modern Romantic Relationships*, edited by N. M. Punyanunt-Carter and J. S. Wrench (Lanham, MD: Lexington, 2017): 1–12; C. Rudder, *Dataclysm: Love, Sex, Race, and Identity—What Our Online Lives Tell Us about Our Offline Selves* (New York: Broadway Books, 2015); A. Ramirez, E. M. Bryant Sumner, C. Fleuriet, and M. Cole, "When Online Dating Partners Meet Offline: The Effect of Modality Switching on Relational Communication between Online Daters," *Journal of Computer-Mediated Communication* 20 (2015): 99–114; J. K. Stuller, "Leveling Up: Geek Women Are Connecting More Than Ever," *Bitch* (Winter, 2015): 39–43; B. D. Grill, "From Telex to Twitter: Relational Communication Skills for a Wireless World," in *Making Connections: Readings in Relational Communication* 5e, edited by K. M. Galvin (New York: Oxford University Press, 2011), 89–96; J. B. Walther and A. Ramirez Jr., "New Technologies and New Directions in Online Relating," in *New Directions in Interpersonal Communication Research*, edited by S. W. Smith and S. R. Wilson (Los Angeles: Sage, 2010), 264–284.

2 K. M. Galvin and C. A. Wilkinson, "The Communication Process: Impersonal and Interpersonal," in *Making Connections* 5e, 5–12.

3 E. Berscheid, "Interpersonal Attraction," in *The Handbook of Social Psychology*, edited by G. Lindzey and E. Aronson (New York: Random House, 1985), 413–484, as reported in J. A. Simpson and B. A. Harris, "Interpersonal Attraction," in *Perspectives on Close Relationships*, edited by A. L. Weber and J. H. Harvey (Boston: Allyn & Bacon, 1994), 45–66; W. G. Graziano and J. W. Bruce, "Attraction and the Initiation of Relationships: A Review of the Empirical Literature," in *Handbook of Relationship Initiation*, edited by S. Sprecher, A. Wenzel, and J. Harvey (New York: Psychology Press, 2008), 269–295; S. Sprecher and D. Felmlee, "Insider Perspectives on Attraction," in *Handbook of Relationship Initiation*, 297–313.

4 D. K. Ivy and S. T. Wahl, *Nonverbal Communication for a Lifetime* 2e (Dubuque, IA: Kendall Hunt, 2014); L. K. Guerrero and K. Floyd, *Nonverbal Communication in Close Relationships* (Mahwah, NJ: Erlbaum, 2006); J. H. Harvey and A. L. Weber, *Odyssey of the Heart: Close Relationships in the 21st Century* 2e (Mahwah, NJ: Erlbaum, 2002).

5 D. K. Ivy, *Genderspeak: Personal Effectiveness in Gender Communication* 5e (Boston: Pearson, 2012); F. Gaiba, "Straight Women and Gay Men Friends: A Qualitative Study," *Dissertation Abstracts International: Section A. Humanities and Social Sciences* 69 (2008): 262; L. M. Tillmann-Healy, *Between Gay and Straight: Understanding Friendship across Sexual Orientation* (Walnut Creek, CA: AltaMira Press, 2001); R. Hopcke and L. Rafaty, *Straight Women, Gay Men: Absolutely Fabulous Friendships* 2e (Berkeley, CA: Wildcat Canyon Press, 2001); R. Hopcke and L. Rafaty, *A Couple of Friends: The Remarkable Friendship between Straight Women and Gay Men* (Berkeley, CA: Wildcat Canyon Press, 1999).

6 N. H. Bartlett, H. M. Patterson, D. P. VanderLaan, and P. L. Vasey, "The Relation between Women's Body Esteem and Friendships with Gay Men," *Body Image* 6 (2009): 235–241.

7 M. Boler, "Hypes, Hopes, and Actualities: New Digital Cartesianism and Bodies in Cyberspace," in *The New Media and Cybercultures Anthology*, edited by P. K. Nayar (Malden, MA: Wiley-Blackwell, 2010), 185–208; D. Currier, "Assembling Bodies in Cyberspace: Technologies, Bodies, and Sexual Difference," in *The New Media and Cybercultures Anthology*, 254–267; J. A. McCown, D. Fisher, R. Page, and M. Homant, "Internet Relationships: People Who Meet People," *Cyberpsychology & Behavior* 4 (2001): 593–596; A. Cooper and L. Sportolari, "Romance in Cyberspace: Understanding Online Attraction," *Journal of Sex Education and Therapy* 22 (1997): 7–14; K. Y. A. McKenna, A. S. Green, and M. E. J. Gleason, "Relationship Formation on the Internet: What's the Big Attraction?" *Journal of Social Issues* 58 (2002): 9–31.

8 A. Cooper, I. P. McLoughlin, and K. M. Campbell, "Sexuality in Cyberspace: Update for the 21st Century," *Cyberpsychology & Behavior* 32 (2000): 521–536.

9 C. D. Wotipka and A. C. High, "An Idealized Self or the Real Me? Predicting Attraction to Online Dating Profiles Using Selective Self-Presentation and Warranting," *Communication Monographs* 83 (2016): 281–302; C. L. Toma and J. T. Hancock, "Looks and Lies: The Role of Physical Attractiveness in Online Dating Self-Presentation and Deception," *Communication Research* 37 (2010): 335–351; C. L. Toma and J. D. D'Angelo, "Connecting Profile-to-Profile: How People Self-Present and Form Impressions of Others through Online Dating Profiles," in *The Impact of Social Media in Modern Romantic Relationships*, 147–161; J. E. Brooks and H. A. Neville, "Interracial Attraction among College Men," *Journal of Social & Personal Relationships* 34 (2017): 166–183; K. A. Gibson, A. E. Thompson, and L. F. O'Sullivan, "Love Thy Neighbour: Personality Traits, Relationship Quality, and Attraction to Others as Predictors of Infidelity among Young Adults," *Canadian Journal of Human Sexuality*, 25 (2016): 186–198.

10 Wrench and Punyanunt-Carter, "From the Front Porch to Swiping Right"; V. Santiago Arias, N. M. Punyanunt-Carter, and J. S. Wrench, "Future Directions for Swiping Right: The Impact of Technology on Modern Dating," in *The Impact of Social Media in Modern Romantic Relationships*, 261–272.

11 L. K. Guerrero, P. A. Andersen, and W. A. Afifi, *Close Encounters: Communicating in Relationships* 5e (Los Angeles: Sage, 2017), 54.

12 S. W. Duck, *Personal Relationships and Personal Constructs: A Study of Friendship Formation* (New York: Wiley, 1973).

13 S. A. Takeuchi, "On the Matching Phenomenon in Courtship: A Probability Matching Theory of Mate Selection," *Marriage and Family Review* 40 (2006): 25–51; G. B. Forbes, L. E. Adams-Curtis, B. Rade, and P. Jaberg, "Body Dissatisfaction in Women and Men: The Role of Gender-Typing and Self-Esteem," *Sex Roles* 44 (2001): 461–484; D. Bar-Tal and L. Saxe, "Perceptions of Similarity and Dissimilarity of Attractive Couples and Individuals," *Journal of Personality and Social Psychology* 33 (1976): 772–781.

14 D. M. Amodio and C. J. Showers, "'Similarity Breeds Liking' Revisited: The Moderating Role of Commitment," *Journal of Social and Personal Relationships* 22 (2005): 817–836.

15 Y. Cheng and D. Gruhn, "Perceived Similarity in Emotional Reaction Profiles between the Self and a Close Other as a Predictor of Emotional Well-Being," *Journal of Social & Personal Relationships* 33 (2016): 711–732; R. Singh, D. T. Wegener, K. Sankaran, S. Singh, P. K. F. Lin, M. X. Seow, J. S. Q. Teng, and S. Shuli, "On the Importance of Trust in Interpersonal Attraction from Attitude Similarity," *Journal of Social & Personal Relationships* 32 (2015): 829–850; L. Frischlich, D. Rieger, T. Dratsch, and G. Bente, "Meet Joe Black? The Effects of Mortality Salience on the Desire to Date In-Group Versus Out-Group Members Online,"

Journal of Social & Personal Relationships 32 (2015): 509–528; Y. Ng, C. Kulik, and P. Bordia, "The Moderating Role of Intergroup Contact in Race Composition, Perceived Similarity, and Applicant Attraction Relationships," *Journal of Business & Psychology* 31 (2016): 415–431; S. Sprecher, "Effects of Actual (Manipulated) and Perceived Similarity on Liking in Get-Acquainted Interactions: The Role of Communication," *Communication Monographs* 81 (2014): 4–27.

16 P. M. Sias, H. Pedersen, E. B. Gallagher, and I. Kopaneva, "Workplace Friendship in the Electronically Connected Organization," *Human Communication Research* 38 (2012): 253–279; A. C. High and D. H. Solomon, "Locating Computer-Mediated Social Support within Online Communication Environments," in *Computer-Mediated Communication in Personal Relationships*, edited by K. B. Wright and L. M. Webb (New York: Peter Lang, 2010), 119–136; A. Kappas and N. C. Kramer (Eds.), *Face-to-Face Communication over the Internet: Emotions in a Web of Culture, Language, and Technology* (Cambridge, UK: Cambridge University Press, 2011); McKenna et al., "Relationship Formation on the Internet."

17 M. T. Whitty and J. K. Gavin, "Age/Sex/Location: Uncovering the Social Cues in the Development of On-Line Relationships," *Cyberpsychology and Behavior* 4 (2001): 623–630.

18 Fehr, "Friendship Formation;" Ivy and Wahl, *Nonverbal Communication for a Lifetime* 2e.

19 A. J. Johnson, E. Bostwick, and M. Bassick, "Long-Distance Versus Geographically Close Romantic Relationships: The Effects of Social Media on the Development and Maintenance of These Relationships," in *The Impact of Social Media in Modern Romantic Relationships*, 113–129; C. J. Billedo, P. Kerkhof, and C. Finkenauer, "The Use of Social Networking Sites for Relationship Maintenance in Long-Distance and Geographically Close Romantic Relationships," *Cyberpsychology, Behavior and Social Networking* 18 (2015): 152–157; J. L. Borelli, H. F. Rasmussen, M. L. Burkhart, and D. A. Sbarra, "Relational Savoring in Long-Distance Romantic Relationships," *Journal of Social & Personal Relationships* 32 (2015): 1083–1108.

20 C. L. Jiang and J. T. Hancock, "Absence Makes the Communication Grow Fonder: Geographic Separation, Interpersonal Media, and Intimacy in Dating Relationships," *Journal of Communication* 63 (2013): 556–577; K. C. Maguire, D. Heinemann-LaFave, and E. Sahlstein, "'To Be Connected, Yet Not at All': Relational Presence, Absence, and Maintenance in the Context of a Wartime Deployment," *Western Journal of Communication* 77 (2013): 249–271; K. C. Maguire and T. A. Kinney, "When Distance Is Problematic: Communication, Coping, and Relational Satisfaction in Female College Students' Long-Distance Dating Relationships," *Journal of Applied Communication Research* 38 (2010): 27–46; L. Stafford, "Geographic Distance and Communication During Courtship," *Communication Research* 37 (2010): 275–297.

21 M. Prensky, "Digital Natives, Digital Immigrants," *On the Horizon* 9 (2001); *Digital Native*, accessed July 6, 2011, www.digitalnative.org/wiki.

22 L. Sharabi and J. P. Caughlin, "Usage Patterns of Social Media across Stages of Romantic Relationships," in *The Impact of Social Media in Modern Romantic Relationships*, 15–29; N. S. Rodriguez and J. Huemmer, "Male Same-Sex Dating in the Digital Age," in *The Impact of Social Media in Modern Romantic Relationships*, 81–89; P. B. Brandtzaeg, "Social Networking Sites: Their Users and Social Implications—A Longitudinal Study," *Journal of Computer-Mediated Communication* 17 (2012): 467–488; D. Ballard-Reisch, B. Rozzell, L. Heldman, and D. Kamerer, "Microchannels and CMC: Short Paths to Developing, Maintaining, and Dissolving Relationships," in *Computer Mediated Communication in Personal Relationships*, 56–78; K. Shonbeck, "Communicating in a Connected World," in *Making Connections* 5e, 393–400.

23 P. M. Markey and C. N. Markey, "Romantic Ideals, Romantic Obtainment, and Relationship Experiences: The Complementarity of Interpersonal Traits among Romantic Partners," *Journal of Social and Personal Relationships* 24 (2007): 517–533; Guerrero et al., *Close Encounters*.

24 R. Watson, M. Daffern, and S. Thomas, "The Impact of Interpersonal Style and Interpersonal Complementarity on the Therapeutic Alliance between Therapists and Offenders in Sex Offender Treatment," *Sexual Abuse: Journal of Research and Treatment* 29 (2017): 107–127.

25 D. Re and N. Rule, "Making a (False) Impression: The Role of Business Experience in First Impressions of CEO Leadership Ability," *Journal of Nonverbal Behavior* 40 (2016): 235–245; R. Petrican, A. Todorov, and C. Grady, "Personality at Face Value: Facial Appearance Predicts Self and Other Personality Judgments among Strangers and Spouses," *Journal of Nonverbal Behavior* 38 (2014): 259–277; H. Fisher, "The First Three Minutes," *O: The Oprah Winfrey Magazine* (November 2009): 140.

26 A. Mehrabian, *Nonverbal Communication* (Chicago: Aldine-Atherton, 1972).

27 M. Jia, C. Jiuqing, and C. L. Hale, "Workplace Emotion and Communication: Supervisor Nonverbal Immediacy, Employees' Emotion Experience, and Their Communication Motives," *Management Communication Quarterly* 31 (2017): 69–87; G. Bodie, K. E. Cannava, A. J. Vickery, and S. M. Jones, "Patterns of Nonverbal Adaptation in Supportive Interactions," *Communication Studies* 67 (2016): 3–19; A. M. Ledbetter and A. T. Keating, "Maintaining Facebook Friendships: Everyday Talk as a Mediator of Threats to Closeness," *Western Journal of Communication* 79 (2015): 197–217; R. Ranganath, D. Jurafsky, and D. A. McFarland, "Detecting Friendly, Flirtatious, Awkward, and Assertive Speech in Speed-Dates," *Computer Speech & Language* 27 (2013): 89–115; J. Deyo, P. Walt, and L. Davis, "Rapidly Recognizing Relationships: Observing Speed Dating in the South," *Qualitative Research Reports in Communication* 12 (2011): 71–78; M. L. Houser, S. M. Horan, and L. A. Furler, "Dating in the Fast Lane: How Communication Predicts Speed-Dating Success," *Journal of Social and Personal Relationships* 25 (2008): 749–768; P. W. Eastwick and E. J. Finkel, "Speed-Dating: A Powerful and Flexible Paradigm for Studying Romantic Relationship Initiation," in *Handbook of Relationship Initiation*, 297–313.

28 P. Collett, *The Book of Tells* (London: Bantam, 2004); J. A. Daly, E. Hogg, D. Sacks, M. Smith, and L. Zimring, "Sex and Relationship Affect Social Self-Grooming," in *The Nonverbal Communication Reader: Classic and Contemporary Readings* 2e, edited by L. K. Guerrero, J. DeVito, and M. L. Hecht (Prospect Heights, IL: Waveland, 1999), 56–61.

29 J. A. Hall, "Interpreting Social-Sexual Communication: Relational Framing Theory and Social-Sexual Communication, Attraction, and Intent," *Human Communication Research* 42 (2016): 138–164; J. A. Hall and C. Xing, "The Verbal and Nonverbal Correlates of the Five Flirting Styles," *Journal of Nonverbal Behavior* 39 (2015): 41–68; J. Hall, C. Xing, and S. Brooks, "Accurately Detecting Flirting," *Communication Research* 542 (2015): 939–958; Guerrero et al., *Close Encounters.*

30 K. Kaspar and J. Krull, "Incidental Haptic Stimulation in the Context of Flirt Behavior," *Journal of Nonverbal Behavior* 37 (2013): 165–173; J. A. Hall, S. Carter, M. J. Cody, and J. M. Albright, "Individual Differences in the Communication of Romantic Interest: Development of the Flirting Styles Inventory," *Communication Quarterly* 58 (2010): 365–393.

31 A. Smith, "15% of American Adults Have Used Online Dating Sites or Mobile Dating Apps," Pew Research Center (2016), accessed March 11, 2017, from http://pewinternet.org; A. Smith and M. Duggan, "Online Dating and Relationships," Pew Research Center (2013), accessed March 11, 2017, from http://pewinternet.org; E. L. Cohen, N. D. Bowman, and K. Borchert, "Private Flirts, Public Friends: Understanding Romantic Jealous Responses to an Ambiguous Social Networking Site Message as a Function of Message Access Exclusivity," *Computers in Human Behavior* 35 (2014): 533–541; C. Fleuriet, M. Cole, and L. K. Guerrero, "Exploring Facebook: Attachment Style and Nonverbal Message Characteristics as Predictors of Anticipated Emotional Reactions to Facebook Postings," *Journal of Nonverbal Behavior* 38 (2014): 429–450.

32 M. T. Whitty, "Cyber-Flirting: An Examination of Men's and Women's Flirting Behaviour Both Offline and on the Internet," *Behaviour Change* 21 (2004): 115–126. For more information on flirting and conveying attraction, see D. D. Henningsen, M. L. M. Henningsen, E. McWorthy, C. McWorthy, and L. McWorthy, "Exploring the Effects of Sex and Mode of Presentation in Perceptions of Dating Goals in Video-Dating," *Journal of Communication* 61 (2011): 641–658; D. D. Henningsen, F. Kartch, N. Orr, and A. Brown, "The Perceptions of Verbal and Nonverbal Flirting Cues in Cross-Sex Interactions," *Human Communication* 12 (2009): 371–381; J. M. Albright, "How Do I Love Thee and Thee and Thee: Self-Presentation, Deception, and Multiple Relationships Online," in *Online M@tchmaking*, edited by M. T. Whitty, A. Baker, and J. A. Inman (New York: Palgrave Macmillan, 2007), 81–93; D. D. Henningsen, M. Braz, and E. Davies, "Why Do We Flirt?" *Journal of Business Communication* 45 (2008): 483–502; M. T. Whitty and A. N. Carr, "Cyberspace as Potential Space: Considering the Web as a Playground to Cyber-Flirt," *Human Relations* 56 (2003): 869–891.

33 "Netflix and chill," Wikipedia, accessed March 11, 2017, from https://en.wikipedia.org.

34 A. Gregory, "Flirtmoji," *Bitch* (Fall 2016): 14; J. King-Slutzky, "An Emoji Guide for the Text Message Clueless," accessed March 11, 2017, from www.nerve.com; https://flirtmoji.com.

35 L. Stafford and J. D. Hillyer, "Information and Communication Technologies in Personal Relationships," *Review of Communication* 12 (2012): 290–213; M. Lipinski-Harten and R. W. Tafarodi, "A Comparison of Conversational Quality in Online and Face-to-Face First Encounters," *Journal of Language and Social Psychology* 31 (2012): 331–341; J. P. Caughlin and L. L. Sharabi, "A Communicative Interdependence Perspective of Close Relationships: The Connections between Mediated and Unmediated Interactions Matter," *Journal of Communication* 63 (2013): 873–893.

36 S. Sprecher and S. Metts, "Logging on, Hooking up: The Changing Nature of Romantic Relationship Initiation and Romantic Relating," in *Human Bonding: The Science of Affectional Ties*, edited by C. Hazan and M. I. Campa (New York: Guilford, 2013), 197–225; A. L. Vangelisti, "Interpersonal Processes in Romantic Relationships," in *The SAGE Handbook of Interpersonal Communication* 4e, edited by M. L. Knapp and J. A. Daly (Thousand Oaks, CA: Sage, 2011), 597–632; J. B. Walther, "Theories of Computer-Mediated Communication and Interpersonal Relations," in *The SAGE Handbook of Interpersonal Communication*, 443–480.

37 D. A. Stinson, J. J. Cameron, and K. J. Robinson, "The Good, the Bad, and the Risky," *Journal of Social & Personal Relationships* 32 (2015): 1109–1136; L. K. Odom, E. Sahlstein Parcell, B. M. A. Baker, and V. Cronin-Fisher, "Communication and Female Date Initiation: Differences in Perceptions Based on Assertiveness of Initiator," *Iowa Journal of Communication* 47 (2015): 177–196; D. Menaker, *A Good Talk: The Story and Skill of Conversation* (New York: Twelve Publishers, 2011); D. Menaker, "How to Break the Ice," *O: The Oprah Winfrey Magazine* (January 2010): 121; D. Pillet-Shore, "Doing Introductions: The Work Involved in Meeting Someone New," *Communication Monographs* 78 (2011): 73–95.

38 S. Turkle, *Reclaiming Conversation: The Power of Talk in a Digital Age* (New York: Penguin, 2016).

39 M. Sunnafrank and A. Ramirez, "At First Sight: Persistent Relational Effects of Get-Acquainted Conversations," *Journal of Social and Personal Relationships* 21 (2004): 361–379.

40 C. R. Berger and R. J. Calabrese, "Some Explorations in Initial Interaction and Beyond: Toward a Developmental Theory of Interpersonal Communication," *Human Communication Research* 1 (1975): 99–112; C. R. Berger and J. J. Bradac, *Language and Social Knowledge: Uncertainty in Interpersonal Relations* (Baltimore: Edward Arnold, 1982); H. Yifeng, "Hands-On Experience with Uncertainty Reduction Theory: An Effective and Engaging Classroom Activity," *Florida Communication Journal* 43 (2015): 119–123; M. L. Antheunis, A. P. Schouten, P. M. Valkenburg, and J. Peter, "Interactive Uncertainty Reduction Strategies and

Verbal Affection in Computer-Mediated Communication," *Communication Research* 39 (2012): 757–780; C. Palmieri, K. Prestano, R. Gandley, E. Overton, and Q. Zhang, "The Facebook Phenomenon: Online Self-Disclosure and Uncertainty Reduction," *China Media Research* 8 (2012): 48–53.

41 For more research on relational uncertainty, a topic related to uncertainty reduction theory, we refer you to the work of Leanne Knobloch and others; see L. K. Knobloch, A. T. Ebata, P. C. McGlaughlin, and J. A. Theiss, "Generalized Anxiety and Relational Uncertainty as Predictors of Topic Avoidance During Reintegration Following Military Deployment," *Communication Monographs* 80 (2013): 452–477; L. K. Knobloch and J. A. Theiss, "Relational Uncertainty and Relationship Talk within Courtship: A Longitudinal Actor-Partner Interdependence Model," *Communication Monographs* 78 (2011): 3–26; L. K. Knobloch, "Relational Uncertainty and Interpersonal Communication," in *New Directions in Interpersonal Communication Research*, 69–93; L. K. Knobloch, "Uncertainty Reduction Theory: Communicating under Conditions of Ambiguity," in *Engaging Theories in Interpersonal Communication: Multiple Perspectives*, edited by L. A. Baxter and D. O. Braithwaite (Los Angeles: Sage, 2008), 133–144; P. Schrodt and K. E. Phillips, "Self-Disclosure and Relational Uncertainty as Mediators of Family Communication Patterns and Relational Outcomes in Sibling Relationships," *Communication Monographs* 83 (2016): 486–504; R. M. Dailey, L. LeFebvre, B. Crook, and N. Brody, "Relational Uncertainty and Communication in On-Again/Off-Again Romantic Relationships: Assessing Changes and Patterns across Recalled Turning Points," *Western Journal of Communication* 80 (2016): 239–263; E. M. Boucher, "Doubt Begets Doubt: Causal Uncertainty as a Predictor of Relational Uncertainty in Romantic Relationships," *Communication Reports* 28 (2015): 12–23; M. A. Pytlak, L. M. Zerega, and M. L. Houser, "Jealousy Evocation: Understanding Commitment, Satisfaction, and Uncertainty as Predictors of Jealousy-Evoking Behaviors," *Communication Quarterly* 63 (2014): 310–328; M. C. Stewart, M. Dainton, and A. K. Goodboy, "Maintaining Relationships on Facebook: Associations with Uncertainty, Jealousy, and Satisfaction," *Communication Reports* 27 (2014): 13–26.

42 N. B. Ellison, J. T. Hancock, and C. L. Toma, "Profile as Promise: A Framework for Conceptualizing Veracity in Online Dating Self-Presentations," *New Media & Society* 14 (2012): 45–62; R. E. Guadagno, B. M. Okdie, and S. A. Kruse, "Dating Deception: Gender, Online Dating, and Exaggerated Self-Presentation," *Computers in Human Behavior* 28 (2012): 642–647; J. A. Hall, N. Park, S. Hayeon, and J. C. Michael, "Strategic Misrepresentation in Online Dating: The Effects of Gender, Self-Monitoring, and Personality Traits," *Journal of Social & Personal Relationships* 27 (2010): 117–135; J. T. Hancock and C. L. Toma, "Putting Your Best Face Forward: The Accuracy of Online Dating Photographs," *Journal of Communication* 59 (2009): 367–386; C. L. Toma and J. T. Hancock, "A New Twist on Love's Labor: Self-Presentation in Online Dating Profiles," in *Computer-Mediated Communication in Personal Relationships*, 41–55.

43 C. L. Kleinke, F. B. Meeker, and R. A. Staneski, "Preference for Opening Lines: Comparing Ratings by Men and Women," *Sex Roles* 15 (1986): 585–600; E. Weber, *How to Pick Up Girls!* (New York: Bantam Books, 1970).

44 C. Senko and V. Fyffe, "An Evolutionary Perspective on Effective vs. Ineffective Pick-up Lines," *Journal of Social Psychology* 150 (2010): 648–667.

45 D. Dickson and O. Hargie, "Questioning," in *The Handbook of Communication Skills* 3e, edited by O. Hargie (London: Routledge, 2006), 121–145.

46 Sharabi and Caughlin, "Usage Patterns of Social Media across Stages of Romantic Relationships."

47 W. Hart, J. Adams, K. A. Burton, and G. K. Tortoriello, "Narcissism and Self-Presentation: Profiling Grandiose and Vulnerable Narcissists' Self-Presentation Tactic Use," *Personality & Individual Differences* 104 (2017): 48–57; D. Wang, "A Study of the Relationship between Narcissism, Extraversion, Drive for

Entertainment, and Narcissistic Behavior on Social Networking Sites," *Computers in Human Behavior* 66 (2017): 138–148.

48 A. L. Vangelisti, M. L. Knapp, and J. A. Daly, "Conversational Narcissism," *Communication Monographs* 57 (1990): 251–274; J. M. Twenge, S. Konrath, J. D. Foster, W. K. Campbell, and B. J. Bushman, "Egos Inflating over Time: A Cross-Temporal Meta-Analysis of the Narcissistic Personality Inventory," *Journal of Personality* 76 (2008): 875–901; J. M. Twenge, *Generation Me: Why Today's Young Americans Are More Confident, Assertive, Entitled—and More Miserable Than Ever Before* Revised/Updated (New York: Free Press, 2013); J. M. Twenge and W. K. Campbell, *The Narcissism Epidemic: Living in the Age of Entitlement* (New York: Free Press, 2011); J. M. Twenge, "The Narcissism Epidemic: Narcissism Is on the Rise among Individuals and in American Culture," August 12, 2013, accessed June 15, 2014, www.psychtoday.com; F. Rhodewalt, "Contemporary Perspectives on Narcissism and the Narcissistic Personality Type," in *Handbook of Self and Identity*, edited by M. R. Leary and J. Price Tangney (New York: Guilford, 2013), 571–586.

49 J. Lamkin, J. A. Lavner, and A. Shaffer, "Narcissism and Observed Communication in Couples," *Personality & Individual Differences* 105 (2017): 224–228; W. T. Behary and D. J. Siegel, *Disarming the Narcissist: Surviving and Thriving with the Self-Absorbed* (Oakland, CA: New Harbinger Publications, 2013); C. Malkin, *Rethinking Narcissism: The Secret to Recognizing and Coping with Narcissists* (New York: Harper, 2016); C. Derber, *The Pursuit of Attention: Power and Ego in Everyday Life* (New York: Oxford University Press, 2000).

50 J. Holmes, "Complimenting—A Positive Politeness Strategy," in *Language and Gender: A Reader*, edited by J. Coates (Malden, MA: Blackwell, 1998), 100–120.

51 J. C. Mirivel, *The Art of Positive Communication: Theory and Practice* (New York: Peter Lang, 2014); M. Strobel, *The Compliment Quotient: Boost Your Spirits, Spark Your Relationships, and Uplift the World* (New York: Wise Roads Press, 2011); C. Matheson, *The Art of the Compliment: Using Kind Words with Grace and Style* (New York: Skyhorse Publishing, 2009); D. C. Marigold, J. G. Holmes, and M. Ross, "More Than Words: Compliments from Romantic Partners Foster Security in Low Self-Esteem Individuals," *Journal of Personality and Social Psychology* 92 (2007): 232–248; E. M. Doohan and V. Manusov, "The Communication of Compliments in Romantic Relationships: An Investigation of Relational Satisfaction and Sex Differences and Similarities in Compliment Behavior," *Western Journal of Communication* 68 (2004): 170–194; C. Parisi and P. Wogan, "Compliment Topics and Gender," *Women & Language* 29 (2006): 21–28.

52 M. Beck, "Why It's Harder to Receive Than to Give," *O: The Oprah Winfrey Magazine* (September 2006): 81–83.

53 "The Health Benefits of Strong Relationships," *Harvard Women's Health Watch* 18 (December 2010): 1.

54 A. Ledbetter, "Relational Maintenance Behavior and Shared TV Viewing as Mediators of the Association between Romanticism and Romantic Relationship Quality," *Communication Studies* 68 (2017): 95–114; C. Fowler and J. Gasiorek, "Depressive Symptoms, Excessive Reassurance Seeking, and Relationship Maintenance," *Journal of Social & Personal Relationships* 34 (2017): 91–113; J. E. Foster and A. R. Thorson, "'I'm Too Stressed to 'Like' Your Post!': Exploring the Connections among Facebook Relational Maintenance, Stress, and Closeness," *Iowa Journal of Communication* 48 (2016): 76–95; M. Burke and R. E. Kraut, "The Relationship between Facebook Use and Well-Being Depends on Communication Type and Tie Strength," *Journal of Computer-Mediated Communication* 21 (2016): 265–281; D. J. Weigel, C. B. Lalasz, and D. A. Weiser, "Maintaining Relationships: The Role of Implicit Relationship Theories and Partner Fit," *Communication Reports* 29 (2016): 23–34; M. Dainton and A. Stokes, "College Students' Romantic Relationships on Facebook: Linking the Gratification for Maintenance to Facebook Maintenance Activity and the Experience of Jealousy," *Communication Quarterly* 63 (2015): 365–383; S. LaBelle and S. A. Myers, "The Use

55 Harvey and Weber, *Odyssey of the Heart*, 105–106.

56 S. Jourard, *The Transparent Self* (Princeton, NJ: Van Nostrand, 1971).

57 D. W. Johnson, *Reaching Out: Interpersonal Effectiveness and Self-Actualization* 11e (Boston: Pearson, 2012), 48–49.

58 E. K. Ruppel, C. Gross, A. Stoll, B. S. Peck, M. Allen, and S.-Y. Kim, "Reflecting on Connecting: Meta-Analysis of Differences between Computer-Mediated and Face-to-Face Self-Disclosure," *Journal of Computer-Mediated Communication* 22 (2017): 18–34; S. A. Rains, S. R. Brunner, and K. Oman, "Self-Disclosure and New Communication Technologies," *Journal of Social and Personal Relationships* 33 (2016): 42–61; J. Kim and K. Dindia, "Online Self-Disclosure: A Review of Research," in *Computer-Mediated Communication in Personal Relationships*, 156–180; C. M. H. Bane, M. Cornish, N. Erspamer, and L. Kampman, "Self-Disclosure through Weblogs and Perceptions of Online and 'Real-Life' Friendships among Female Bloggers," *Cyberpsychology, Behavior, & Social Networking* 13 (2010): 131–139; R. West and L. H. Turner, "Technology and Interpersonal Communication," in *Making Connections* 5e, 379–386.

59 K. Shonbeck, "Thoughts on CMC by an E-mailer, IMer, Blog Reader, and Facebooker," in *Making Connections: Readings in Relational Communication* 4e, edited by K. M. Galvin and P. Cooper (Los Angeles: Roxbury, 2006), 372–378.

60 V. J. Derlega, B. Winstead, A. Mathews, and A. L. Braitman, "Why Does Someone Reveal Highly Personal Information? Attributions for and against Self-Disclosure in Close Relationships," *Communication Research Reports* 25 (2008): 115–130.

61 W. Xie and C. Kang, "See You, See Me: Teenagers' Self-Disclosure and Regret of Posting on Social Network Sites," *Computers in Human Behavior* 52 (2015): 398–407; J. E. Wendorf and F. Yang, "Benefits of a Negative Post: Effects of Computer-Mediated Venting on Relationship Maintenance," *Computers in Human Behavior* 52 (2015): 271–277.

62 Sandra Petronio's body of work on communication privacy management (CPM theory) is our most significant source of information on this topic; see S. Petronio, *Boundaries of Privacy: Dialectics of Disclosure* (Albany: SUNY Press, 2002); S. Petronio, "Brief Status Report on Communication Privacy Management Theory," *Journal of Family Communication* 13 (2013): 6–14; J. T. Child and S. Petronio, "Unpacking the Paradoxes of Privacy in CMC Relationships: The Challenges of Blogging and Relational Communication on the Internet," in *Computer-Mediated Communication in Personal Relationships*, 21–40; A. M. Hosek and J. Thompson, "Communication Privacy Management and College Instruction: Exploring the Rules and Boundaries That Frame Instructor Private Disclosures," *Communication Education* 58 (2009), 327–349; S. Petronio and W. T. Durham, "Communication Privacy Management Theory," in *Exploring Theories in Interpersonal Communication*, edited by L. A. Baxter and D. O. Braithwaite (Los Angeles: Sage, 2008), 309–322; S. Petronio, "Translational Research Endeavors and the Practices of Communication Privacy Management," *Journal of Applied Communication Research* 35 (2007): 218–222; S. Petronio, "The Boundaries of Privacy: Praxis of Everyday Life," in *Balancing Secrets of Private Disclosure*, edited by S. Petronio (Mahwah, NJ: Lawrence Erlbaum, 2000), 37–49; L. B. Rosenfeld, "Overview of the Ways Privacy, Secrecy, and Disclosure Are Balanced in Today's Society," in *Balancing Secrets of Private Disclosure*, 3–17. For other research on CPM, see the entire volume 13, year 2013, of the *Journal of Family Communication*, including the introductory piece: M. C. Morr Serewicz, "Introducing the Special Issue on Communication Privacy Management Theory and Family Privacy Regulation," *Journal of Family Communication* 13 (2013): 1–5. For related research on privacy and disclosure, see K. C. C. Yang, A. Pulido, and Y. Kang, "Exploring the Relationship between Privacy Concerns and Social Media Use among College Students: A Communication Privacy Management Perspective," *Intercultural Communication Studies* 25

(2016): 46–62; S.-A. A. Jin, "Peeling Back the Multiple Layers of Twitter's Private Disclosure Onion: The Roles of Virtual Identity Discrepancy and Personality Traits in Communication Privacy Management on Twitter," *New Media & Society* 15 (2013): 813–833; V. Cho and H. Hung, "The Effectiveness of Short Message Service for Communication with Concerns of Privacy Protection and Conflict Avoidance," *Journal of Computer-Mediated Communication* 16 (2011): 250–270; E. Butler, E. McCann, and J. Thomas, "Privacy Setting Awareness on Facebook and Its Effect on User-Posted Content," *Human Communication* 14 (2011): 39–55; T. Afifi and K. Steuber, "The Revelation Risk Model (RRM): Factors That Predict the Revelation of Secrets and the Strategies Used to Reveal Them," *Communication Monographs* 76 (2009): 144–176.

63 L. G. Spencer, IV, "Coming Out, Bringing Out: God's Love, Transgender Identity, and Difference," in *Transgender Communication Studies,* edited by L. G. Spencer, IV, and J. C. Capuzza (New York: Lexington, 2016), 187–198; K. M. Norwood and P. J. Lannutti, "Families' Experiences with Transgender Identity and Transition: A Family Stress Perspective," in *Transgender Communication Studies,* 51–68; K. B. Carnelley, E. G. Hepper, C. Hicks, and W. Turner, "Perceived Parental Reactions to Coming Out, Attachment, and Romantic Relationship Views," *Attachment and Human Development* 13 (2011): 217–236; M. Vaughan and C. Waehler, "Coming Out Growth: Conceptualizing and Measuring Stress-Related Growth Associated with Coming Out to Others as a Sexual Minority," *Journal of Adult Development* 17 (2010): 94–109; L. Heatherington and J. A. Lavner, "Coming to Terms with Coming Out: Review and Recommendations for Family Systems-Focused Research," *Journal of Family Psychology* 22 (2008): 329–343; M. L. Rasmussen, "The Problem of Coming Out," *Theory into Practice* 43 (2004): 144–151.

64 B. L. Lane and C. W. Piercy, "Making Sense of Becoming Facebook Official: Implications for Identity and Time," in *The Impact of Social Media in Modern Romantic Relationships,* 31–45.

65 I. Altman and D. Taylor, *Social Penetration: The Development of Relationships* (New York: Holt, Rinehart and Winston, 1973).

66 J. Luft, *Group Process: An Introduction to Group Dynamics* (Palo Alto, CA: Mayfield, 1970).

67 P. D. Bolls, "Understanding Emotion from a Superordinate Dimensional Perspective: A Productive Way Forward for Communication Processes and Effects Studies," *Communication Monographs* 77 (2010): 146–152.

68 D. Keltner, J. Tracy, D. A. Sauter, D. C. Cordaro, and G. McNeil, "Expression of Emotions," in *Handbook of Emotions,* edited by L. Feldman Barrett, M. Lewis, and J. M. Haviland-Jones (New York: Guilford, 2016); S. Metts and S. Planalp, "Emotional Experience and Expression: Current Trends and Future Directions in Interpersonal Relationship Research," in *The SAGE Handbook of Interpersonal Communication,* 283–316; E. L. MacGeorge, B. Feng, and B. R. Burleson, "Supportive Communication," in *The SAGE Handbook of Interpersonal Communication,* 317–354.

69 U. Hess, C. Blaison, and K. Kafetsios, "Judging Facial Emotion Expressions in Context: The Influence of Culture and Self-Construal Orientation," *Journal of Nonverbal Behavior* 40 (2016): 55–64; Y. Xiaoqian, T. J. Andrews, and A. W. Young, "Cultural Similarities and Differences in Perceiving and Recognizing Facial Expressions of Basic Emotions," *Journal of Experimental Psychology: Human Perception & Performance* 42 (2016): 423–440; Y. Kimura, "Expressing Emotions in Teaching: Inducement, Suppression, and Disclosure as Caring Profession," *Educational Studies in Japan: International Yearbook* 5 (2010): 63–78.

70 P. A. Andersen, "In Different Dimensions: Nonverbal Communication and Culture," in *Intercultural Communication: A Reader* 14e, edited by L. A. Samovar, R. E. Porter, E. R. McDaniel, and C. Sexton Roy (Belmont, CA: Wadsworth/Cengage Learning, 2014), 229–241.

71 D. Hample, A. S. Richards, and C. Skubisz, "Blurting," *Communication Monographs* 80 (2013): 503–532.

72 Hample et al., "Blurting," 507.

73 U. Hess, R. B. Adams Jr., K. Grammer, and R. E. Kleck, "Face Gender and Emotion Expression: Are Angry Women More Like Men?" *Journal of Vision* 9 (2009): 1–8; A. Campbell and S. Muncer, "Intent to Harm or Injure? Gender and the Expression of Anger," *Aggressive Behavior* 34 (2008): 282–293; T. B. Kashdan, A. Mishra, W. E. Breen, and J. J. Froh, "Gender Differences in Gratitude: Examining Appraisals, Narratives, the Willingness to Express Emotions, and Changes in Psychological Needs," *Journal of Personality* 77 (2009): 1–40; R. W. Simon and L. E. Nath, "Gender and Emotion in the United States: Do Men and Women Differ in Self-Reports of Feelings and Expressive Behavior?" *American Journal of Sociology* 109 (2004): 1137–1176.

74 M. S. Kimmel, *Angry White Men: American Masculinity at the End of an Era* (New York: Nation Books, 2015); M. S. Kimmel, *Guyland: The Perilous World Where Boys Become Men* (New York: Harper Paperbacks, 2009).

75 Jourard, *The Transparent Self.*

76 B. B. Burleson, "Introduction to the Special Issue: Psychological Mediators of Sex Differences in Emotional Support," *Communication Reports* 15 (2002), 1–4; W. Pollack, *Real Boys: Rescuing Our Sons from the Myths of Boyhood* (New York: Owl Books, 1999); O. Silverstein and B. Rashbaum, *The Courage to Raise Good Men* (New York: Penguin, 1995).

77 C. Hesse and E. A. Rauscher, "Privacy Tendencies and Revealing/Concealing: The Moderating Role of Emotional Competence," *Communication Quarterly* 61 (2013): 91–112.

78 E. L. MacGeorge, L. M. Guntzviller, K. S. Brisini, L. C. Bailey, S. K. Salmon, K. Severen, S. E. Branch, H. M. Lillie, C. K. Lindley, R. G. Pastor, and R. D. Cummings, "The Influence of Emotional Support Quality on Advice Evaluation and Outcomes," *Communication Quarterly* 65 (2017): 80–96; A. Joseph, T. D. Afifi, and A. Denes, "(Unmet) Standards for Emotional Support and Their Short- and Medium-Term Consequences," *Communication Monographs* 83 (2016): 163–193; J. S. Priem and D. Haunani Solomon, "Emotional Support and Physiological Stress Recovery: The Role of Support Matching, Adequacy, and Invisibility," *Communication Monographs* 82 (2015): 88–112; G. D. Bodie, B. R. Burleson, and S. M. Jones, "Explaining the Relationships among Supportive Message Quality, Evaluations, and Outcomes: A Dual-Process Approach," *Communication Monographs* 79 (2012): 1–22.

79 J. G. Myrick, A. E. Holton, I. Himelboim, and B. Love, "#Stupidcancer: Exploring a Typology of Social Support and the Role of Emotional Expression in a Social Media Community," *Health Communication* 31 (2016): 596–605.

Chapter 8

1 N. L. Galambos and L. A. Kotylak, "Transformations in Parent-Child Relationships from Adolescence to Adulthood," in *Relationship Pathways: From Adolescence to Young Adulthood,* edited by B. P. Laursen and W. A. Collins (Thousand Oaks, CA: Sage, 2011), 23–42; W. K. Rawlins, *The Compass of Friendship: Narratives, Identities, and Dialogues* (Los Angeles: Sage, 2009); M. Monsour, *Women and Men as Friends: Relationships across the Life Span in the 21st Century* (Mahwah, NJ: Lawrence Erlbaum, 2002); M. Paul, *The Friendship Crisis: Finding, Making, and Keeping Friends When You're Not a Kid Anymore* (New York: Rodale Books, 2005).

2 N. Way, *Deep Secrets: Boys' Friendships and the Crisis of Connection* (Cambridge, MA: Harvard University Press, 2013); R. Blieszner, "Close Relationships over Time," as reported in J. A. Simpson and B. A. Harris, "Interpersonal Attraction," in *Perspectives on Close Relationships,* edited by A. L. Weber and J. H. Harvey (Boston: Allyn & Bacon, 1994), 1–18.

3 C. A. Hafen, B. Laursen, and D. DeLay, "Transformations in Friend Relationships across the Transition into Adolescence," in B. P. Laursen and W. A. Collins, Eds., *Relationship Pathways: From Adolescence to Young Adulthood,* 69–90.

4 J. Yager, *Friendshifts: The Power of Friendship and How It Shapes Our Lives* (Stamford, CT: Hannacroix Creek Books, 2013);

C. M. Chow, H. Roelse, D. Buhrmeister, and M. K. Underwood, "Transformations in Friend Relationships across the Transition into Adulthood," in B. P. Laursen and W. A. Collins, Eds., *Relationship Pathways: From Adolescence to Young Adulthood*, 91–112; W. Rawlins, "Being There for Friends," in *Making Connections: Readings in Relational Communication* 4e, edited by K. M. Galvin and P. Cooper (Los Angeles: Roxbury, 2006), 329–332.

5   H. Reeder, "'He's Like a Brother': The Social Construction of Satisfying Cross-Sex Friendship Roles," *Sexuality & Culture* 21 (2017): 142–162; S. Nelson, *Frientimacy: How to Deepen Friendships for Lifelong Health and Happiness* (Berkeley, CA: Seal Press, 2016); B. McEwan and L. K. Guerrero, "Freshmen Engagement through Communication: Predicting Friendship Formation Strategies and Perceived Availability of Network Resources from Communication Skills," *Communication Studies* 61 (2010): 445–463; B. Fehr, "Friendship Formation," in *Handbook of Relationship Initiation*, edited by S. Sprecher, A. Wenzel, and J. Harvey (New York: Psychology Press, 2008), 29–54; G. Foster, "Making Friends: A Nonexperimental Analysis of Social Pair Formation," *Human Relations* 58 (2005): 1443–1465; A. J. Johnson, E. Wittenberg, M. M. Villagran, M. Mazur, and P. Villagran, "Relational Progression as a Dialectic: Examining Turning Points in Communication among Friends," *Communication Monographs* 70 (2003): 230–249.

6   J. Harwood, *Understanding Communication and Aging* (Los Angeles: Sage, 2007); L. Gee, *Friends: Why Men and Women Are from the Same Planet* (New York: Bloomsbury, 2004); Monsour, *Women and Men as Friends*.

7   L. H. Turner and R. West, "The Challenge of Defining 'Family,'" in *The SAGE Handbook of Family Communication*, edited by L. H. Turner and R. West (Thousand Oaks, CA: Sage, 2014), 10–25; E. A. Suter, L. A. Baxter, L. M. Seurer, and L. J. Thomas, "Discursive Constructions of the Meaning of 'Family' in Online Narratives of Foster Adoptive Parents," *Communication Monographs* 81 (2014): 59–78; "A Woman's Nation Changes Everything," in *The Shriver Report* (Washington, DC: Center for American Progress, 2009), accessed October 29, 2009, awomansnation.com; "Women in America: Indicators of Social and Economic Well-Being," *White House*, March 1, 2011, accessed March 13, 2011, www.whitehouse.gov; K. Galvin and C. Bylund, "First Marriage Families: Gender and Communication," in *Women and Men Communicating: Challenges and Changes* 2e, edited by L. P. Arliss and D. J. Borisoff (Prospect Heights, IL: Waveland, 2001), 132–148; V. Satir, "The Rules You Live By," in *Making Connections* 4e, 168–174; R. S. Miller, *Intimate Relationships* 6e (New York: McGraw-Hill, 2011).

8   *Miami Herald* (July 9, 1982): 12A.

9   "Stepfamily Statistics," *The Stepfamily Foundation*, accessed March 14, 2017, www.stepfamily.org; P. Schrodt, "Coparental Communication with Nonresidential Parents as a Predictor of Children's Feelings of Being Caught in Stepfamilies," *Communication Reports* 29 (2016): 63–74; M. L. Thorsen and V. King, "My Mother's Husband," *Journal of Social & Personal Relationships* 33 (2016): 835–851; K. Floyd and M. T. Morman, *Widening the Family Circle* 2e (Thousand Oaks, CA: Sage, 2013).

10 E. A. Suter, "Communication in Lesbian and Gay Families," in L. H. Turner and R. West, Eds., *The SAGE Handbook of Family Communication* 4e, 235–247; J. Dixon and D. S. Dougherty, "A Language Convergence/Meaning Divergence Analysis Exploring How LGBTQ and Single Employees Manage Traditional Family Expectations in the Workplace," *Journal of Applied Communication Research* 42 (2014): 1–19; J. Koenig Kellas and E. A. Suter, "Accounting for Lesbian-Headed Families: Lesbian Mothers' Responses to Discursive Challenges," *Communication Monographs* 79 (2012): 475–498.

11 V. Satir, *The New Peoplemaking* (Mountain View, CA: Science & Behavior Books, 1988), 4.

12 D. M. Keating, J. C. Russell, J. Cornacchione, and S. W. Smith, "Family Communication Patterns and Difficult Family Conversations," *Journal of Applied Communication Research* 41 (2013): 160–180; J. P. Caughlin, A. F. Koerner, P. Schrodt, and M. A. Fitzpatrick, "Interpersonal Communication in Family Relationships," in *The SAGE Handbook of Interpersonal Communication* 4e, edited by M. L. Knapp and J. A. Daly (Thousand Oaks, CA: Sage, 2011), 679–714.

13 P. Schrodt, P. L. Witt, and A. S. Messersmith, "A Meta-Analytical Review of Family Communication Patterns and Their Associations with Information Processing, Behavioral, and Psychosocial Outcomes," *Communication Monographs* 75 (2008): 248–269.

14 L. K. Knobloch, A. T. Ebata, P. C. McGlaughlin, and J. A. Theiss, "Generalized Anxiety and Relational Uncertainty as Predictors of Topic Avoidance During Reintegration Following Military Deployment," *Communication Monographs* 80 (2013): 452–477; L. K. Knobloch and S. R. Wilson, "Communication in Military Families across the Deployment Cycle," in L. H. Turner and R. West, Eds., *The SAGE Handbook of Family Communication* 4e, 370–385.

15 C. Wilson, "A New Way to Work," *Sound & Communications* 62 (2016): 38–39.

16 S. Jana, A. Pande, A. Chan, and P. Mohapatra, "Mobile Video Chat: Issues and Challenges," *IEEE Communications Magazine* 51 (2013): 144–151.

17 S. Yarosh and G. D. Abowd, "Mediated Parent-Child Contact in Work-Separated Families," *Proceedings of the SIGCHI Conference on Human Factors in Computing Systems* (2011): 1185–1194.

18 L. K. Knobloch, E. D. Basinger, E. C. Wehrman, A. T. Ebata, and P. C. McGlaughlin, "Communication of Military Couples during Deployment and Reunion: Changes, Challenges, Benefits, and Advice," *Journal of Family Communication* 16 (2016): 160–179; S. P. Carter and K. D. Renshaw, "Spousal Communication during Military Deployments," *Journal of Family Issues* 37 (2016): 2309–2332; K. C. Maguire and E. Sahlstein Parcell, "Communication and the Coping Paradox: The Case of Army Spouses and Wartime Deployment," *Southern Communication Journal* 80 (2015): 365–376; J. Rea, A. Behnke, N. Huff, and K. Allen, "The Role of Online Communication in the Lives of Military Spouses," *Contemporary Family Therapy: An International Journal* 27 (2015): 329–339; J. A. Laser and P. M. Stephens, "Working with Military Families through Deployment and Beyond," *Clinical Social Work Journal* 39 (2011): 28–38.

19 J. M. Gottman, J. S. Gottman, and C. L. Atkins, "The Comprehensive Soldier Fitness Program: Family Skills Components," *American Psychologist* 66 (2011): 52–57.

20 A. L. Joseph and T. D. Afifi, "Military Wives' Stressful Disclosures to Their Deployed Husbands: The Role of Protective Buffering," *Journal of Applied Communication Research* 38 (2010): 412–434.

21 Hart Research Associates, "Falling Short? College Learning and Career Success," *Association of American Colleges and Universities*, January 20, 2015, accessed February 12, 2017, www.aacu.org; Hart Research Associates, "Employer Priorities for Most Important College Learning Outcomes," *Association of American Colleges and Universities*, January 20, 2015, accessed February 12, 2017, www.aacu.org; "Staffing in Special Markets," *Society for Human Resources Management*, September 3, 2016, accessed February 12, 2017, www.shrm.org.

22 P. M. Sias, H. Pedersen, E. B. Gallagher, and I. Kopaneva, "Workplace Friendship in the Electronically Connected Organization," *Human Communication Research* 38 (2012): 253–279.

23 K. K. Myers, D. R. Seibold, and H. S. Park, "Interpersonal Communication in the Workplace," in *The SAGE Handbook of Interpersonal Communication* 4e, 527–562; R. B. Adler, J. M. Elmhorst, and K. Lucas, *Communication at Work* 11e (New York: McGraw-Hill, 2012); D. O'Hair, G. W. Friedrich, and L. A. Dixon, *Strategic Communication in Business and the Professions* 8e (Boston: Pearson, 2015).

24 M. L. Knapp and A. Vangelisti, "Relationship Stages: A Communication Perspective," in K. M. Galvin and P. Cooper, Eds.,

Making Connections 4e, 132–139; M. L. Knapp, A. L. Vangelisti, and J. P. Caughlin, *Interpersonal Communication and Human Relationships* 7e (Boston: Pearson, 2014); K. N. Dunleavy and M. Booth-Butterfield, "Idiomatic Communication in the Stages of Coming Together and Falling Apart," *Communication Quarterly* 57 (2009): 416–432; P. A. Mongeau and M. L. Miller Henningsen, "Stage Theories of Relationship Development: Charting the Course of Interpersonal Communication," in *Engaging Theories in Interpersonal Communication: Multiple Perspectives*, edited by L. A. Baxter and D. O. Braithwaite (Los Angeles: Sage, 2008), 363–375; L. K. Guerrero, P. A. Andersen, and W. A. Afifi, *Close Encounters: Communication in Relationships* 5e (Thousand Oaks, CA: Sage, 2017).

25 L. Sharabi and J. P. Caughlin, "Usage Patterns of Social Media across Stages of Romantic Relationships," in *The Impact of Social Media in Modern Romantic Relationships*, edited by N. M. Punyanunt-Carter and J. S. Wrench (Lanham, MD: Lexington, 2017): 15–29; C.-C. Yang, B. B. Brown, and M. T. Braun, "From Facebook to Cell Calls: Layers of Electronic Intimacy in College Students' Interpersonal Relationships," *New Media & Society* 16 (2014): 5–23; J. Fox and C. Anderegg, "Romantic Relationship Stages and Social Networking Sites: Uncertainty Reduction Strategies and Perceived Relational Norms on Facebook," *Cyberpsychology, Behavior and Social Networking* 17 (2014): 685–691; J. Fox, K. M. Warber, and D. C. Makstaller, "The Role of Facebook in Romantic Relationship Development: An Exploration of Knapp's Relational Stage Model," *Journal of Social & Personal Relationships* 30 (2013): 771–794.

26 D. Hauani Solomon, K. M. Weber, and K. R. Steuber, "Turbulence in Relational Transitions," in *New Directions in Interpersonal Communication Research*, edited by S. W. Smith and S. R. Wilson (Los Angeles: Sage, 2010), 115–134; R. M. Dailey, A. D. Hampel, and J. B. Roberts, "Relational Maintenance in On-Again/Off-Again Relationships: An Assessment of How Relational Maintenance, Uncertainty, and Commitment Vary by Relationship Type and Status," *Communication Monographs* 77 (2010): 75–101; R. M. Dailey, K. Rossetto, R. A. Pfiester, and C. A. Surra, "A Qualitative Analysis of On-Again/Off-Again Romantic Relationships: 'It's Up and Down, All Around'," *Journal of Social & Personal Relationships* 26 (2009): 443–466; R. M. Dailey, R. A. Pfiester, B. Jin, G. Beck, and G. Clark, "On-Again/Off-Again Dating Relationships: How Are They Different from Other Dating Relationships?" *Personal Relationships* 16 (2009): 23–47.

27 Knapp and Vangelisti, "Relationship Stages"; Knapp et al., *Interpersonal Communication and Human Relationships*.

28 B. L. Lane and C. W. Piercy, "Making Sense of Becoming Facebook Official: Implications for Identity and Time," in *The Impact of Social Media in Modern Romantic Relationships*, edited by N. M. Punyanunt-Carter and J. S. Wrench (Lanham, MD: Lexington, 2017): 31–45.

29 S. W. Duck, "A Topography of Relationship Disengagement and Dissolution," in *Personal Relationships 4: Dissolving Relationships*, edited by S. W. Duck (New York: Academic Press, 1982); Guerrero et al., *Close Encounters*.

30 B. Laursen and C. A. Hafen, "Future Directions in the Study of Close Relationships: Conflict Is Bad (Except When It's Not)," *Social Development* 19 (2010): 858–872.

31 C. Harasymchuk and B. Fehr, "A Prototype Analysis of Relational Boredom," *Journal of Social & Personal Relationships* 30 (2012): 627–646.

32 B. Kring, "Cyber Infidelity: The New Seduction," *Journal of Sex & Marital Therapy* 42 (2016): 751–753; A. Ferron, Y. Lussier, and S. Sabourin, "Spousal Problems Arising from Internet Usage: Cyber Infidelity and Sexting," *Integrating Science & Practice* 3 (2013): 27–31; V. S. Millner, "Internet Infidelity: A Case of Intimacy with Detachment," *Family Journal* 16 (2008): 78–82; B. H. Henline, L. K. Lamke, and M. D. Howard, "Exploring Perceptions of Online Infidelity," *Personal Relationships* 14 (2007): 113–128; K. M. Hertlein and F. P. Piercy, "Internet Infidelity:

A Critical Review of the Literature," *Family Journal* 14 (2006): 366–371.

33 M. Rabbitt, "Is Infidelity Obsolete?" *Women's Health* (July/August 2010): 144.

34 S. J. Watkins and S. D. Boon, "Expectations Regarding Partner Fidelity in Dating Relationships," *Journal of Social & Personal Relationships* 33 (2016): 237–256; E. A. Utley, "Rethinking the Other Woman: Exploring Power in Intimate Heterosexual Triangular Relationships," *Women's Studies in Communication* 39 (2016): 177–192; C. C. Malachowski and B. N. Frisby, "The Aftermath of Hurtful Events: Cognitive, Communicative, and Relational Outcomes," *Communication Quarterly* 63 (2015): 187–203.

35 I. Tsapelas, H. E. Fisher, and A. Aron, "Infidelity: When, Where, Why," in *The Dark Side of Close Relationships II*, edited by W. R. Cupach and B. H. Spitzberg (New York: Routledge, 2011), 175–196; E. Nersesian-Solé, "What He's Hiding from You," *Women's Health* (November 2010): 98–100; J. A. Samp and J. L. Monahan, "Alcohol-Influenced Nonverbal Behaviors During Discussions about a Relationship Problem," *Journal of Nonverbal Behavior* 33 (2009): 193–211; F. S. Christopher and S. Sprecher, "Sexuality in Marriage, Dating, and Other Relationships: A Decade Review," in *Speaking of Sexuality: Interdisciplinary Readings*, edited by J. K. Davidson Sr. and N. B. Moore (Los Angeles: Roxbury, 2005): 54–71.

36 M. L. Hans, B. D. Selvidge, K. A. Tinker, and L. M. Webb, "Online Performances of Gender: Blogs, Gender-Bending, and Cybersex as Relational Examples," in *Computer-Mediated Communication in Personal Relationships*, edited by K. B. Wright and L. M. Webb (New York: Peter Lang, 2010), 302–323.

37 K. Y. A. McKenna, A. S. Green, and P. K. Smith, "Demarginalizing the Sexual Self," *Journal of Sex Research* 38 (2001): 302–316; A. Cooper, I. P. McLoughlin, and K. M. Campbell, "Sexuality in Cyberspace: Update for the 21st Century," *Cyberpsychology & Behavior* 3 (2000): 521–536.

38 Duck, "A Topography of Relationship Disengagement and Dissolution."

39 V. Lukacs and A. Quan-Haase, "Romantic Breakups on Facebook: New Scales for Studying Post-Breakup Behaviors, Digital Distress, and Surveillance," *Information, Communication & Society* 18 (2015): 492–508.

40 D. M. Frost, J. D. Rubin, and N. Darcangelo, "Making Meaning of Significant Events in Past Relationships," *Journal of Social & Personal Relationships* 33 (2016): 938–960.

41 L. E. LeFebvre, K. G. Blackburn, and N. Brody, "Navigating Romantic Relationships on Facebook: Extending the Relationship Dissolution Model to Social Networking Environments," *Journal of Social & Personal Relationships* 32 (2015): 78–98; K. G. Blackburn, N. Brody, and L. E. LeFebvre, "The I's, We's, and She/He's of Breakups: Public and Private Pronoun Usage in Relationship Dissolution Accounts," *Journal of Language & Social Psychology* 33 (2014): 202–213; L. A. Lee and D. A. Sbarra, "The Predictors and Consequences of Relationship Dissolution: Breaking Down Silos," in *Human Bonding: The Science of Affectional Ties*, edited by C. Hazan and M. I. Campa (New York: Guilford, 2013), 308–342.

42 L. E. LeFebvre, "Phantom Lovers: Ghosting as a Relationship Dissolution Strategy in the Technological Age," in *The Impact of Social Media in Modern Romantic Relationships*, 219–235; K. Ramirez, "'Baby, WTF? Where Are You?!?' The Act of 'Ghosting' Explained," *Island Waves* (April 18, 2013), 5; A. Syrtash, "Are You Guilty of Ghosting?," *Yahoo*, September 9, 2012, accessed April 20, 2013, shine.yahoo.com.

43 T. Levine and S. L. Fitzpatrick, "You Know Why; The Question Is How? Relationships between Reasons and Methods in Romantic Breakups," paper presented at the meeting of the International Communication Association (May 2005), New York City, New York.

44 Knapp et al., *Interpersonal Communication and Human Relationships*; M. L. Knapp and A. L. Vangelisti, "Relational Decline,"

in *Making Connections* 4e, 269–273; W. R. Cupach, "Dialectical Process in the Disengagement of Interpersonal Relationships," in *Making Connections* 4e, 274–280; M. Pelaez, T. Field, M. Diego, O. Deeds, and J. Delgado, "Insecurity, Control, and Disinterest Behaviors Are Related to Breakup Distress in University Students," *College Student Journal* 45 (2010): 333–340; D. Davis, P. R. Shaver, and M. L. Vernon, "Physical, Emotional, and Behavioral Reactions to Breaking Up: The Roles of Gender, Age, Emotional Involvement, and Attachment Style," *Personality and Social Psychology Bulletin* 29 (2003): 871–884.

45 L. Locker Jr., W. D. McIntosh, A. A. Hackney, J. H. Wilson, and K. E. Wiegand, "The Breakup of Romantic Relationships: Situational Predictors of Perception of Recovery," *North American Journal of Psychology* 12 (2010): 565–578; D. Cullingson, *Breaking Up Blues: A Guide to Survival* (New York: Routledge, 2008); S. P. Banks, D. M. Altendorf, J. O. Greene, and M. Cody, "An Examination of Relationship Disengagement: Perceptions, Breakup Strategies, and Outcomes," *Western Journal of Speech Communication* 51 (1987): 19–41.

46 K. Matthews, "The Dear John Talk and Other Dreaded Conversations: Eight Ways to Make Them Easier, Kinder, Gentler," *O: The Oprah Winfrey Magazine* (August 2007): 144, 146.

47 D. K. Ivy, *GenderSpeak: Communicating in a Gendered World* 6e (Dubuque, IA: Kendall Hunt, 2017).

48 K. Tan, C. R. Agnew, L. E. VanderDrift, and S. M. Harvey, "Committed to Us: Predicting Relationship Closeness Following Nonmarital Romantic Relationship Breakup," *Journal of Social & Personal Relationships* 32 (2015): 456–471; M. O'Connor, "Winning the Breakup: A Generation Defines Itself by Post-Relationship Peacocking," *New York* (December 1–14, 2014), 28–32.

49 R. M. Dailey, K. R. Rossetto, A. A. McCracken, B. Jin, and E. W. Green, "Negotiating Breakups and Renewals in On-Again/Off-Again Dating Relationships: Traversing the Transitions," *Communication Quarterly* 60 (2012): 165–189; R. M. Dailey, B. Jin, A. Pfiester, and G. Beck, "On-Again/Off-Again Dating Relationships: What Keeps Partners Coming Back?" *Journal of Social Psychology* 151 (2011): 417–440; R. M. Dailey, A. V. Middleton, and E. W. Green, "Perceived Relational Stability in On-Again/Off-Again Relationships," *Journal of Social & Personal Relationships* 28 (2011): 1–25; Dailey et al., "Relational Maintenance in On-Again/Off-Again Relationships"; Dailey et al., "On-Again/Off-Again Dating Relationships"; Dailey et al., "A Qualitative Analysis of On-Again/Off-Again Romantic Relationships."

50 R. M. Dailey, L. E. LeFebvre, B. Crook, and N. Brody, "Relational Uncertainty and Communication in On-Again/Off-Again Romantic Relationships: Assessing Changes and Patterns across Recalled Turning Points," *Western Journal of Communication* 80 (2016): 239–263; R. M. Dailey, A. A. McCracken, B. Jin, K. R. Rossetto, and E. W. Green, "Negotiating Breakups and Renewals: Types of On-Again/Off-Again Dating Relationships," *Western Journal of Communication* 77 (2013): 382–410; S. A. Robbins and A. F. Merrill, "Understanding Posttransgressional Relationship Closeness: The Roles of Perceived Severity, Rumination, and Communication Competence," *Communication Research Reports* 31 (2014): 23–32.

51 N. Brody, L. E. LeFebvre, and K. G. Blackburn, "Post-Dissolution Surveillance on Social Networking Sites," in *The Impact of Social Media in Modern Romantic Relationships*, 237–257; P. J. Lannutti and K. A. Cameron, "Beyond the Breakup: Heterosexual and Homosexual Post-Dissolutional Relationships," *Communication Quarterly* 50 (2002): 153–170.

52 K. Koenig Kellas and S. Sato, "'The Worst Part Is, We Don't Even Talk Anymore': Post-Dissolutional Communication in Break Up Stories," in *Making Connections: Readings in Relational Communication* 5e, edited by K. M. Galvin (New York: Oxford University Press, 2011), 297–309; A. N. Lambert and P. C. Hughes, "The Influence of Goodwill, Secure Attachment, and Positively Toned Disengagement Strategy on Reports of Communication Satisfaction in Nonmarital Post-Dissolution Relationships," *Communication Research Reports* 27 (2010): 171–183; J. Koenig Kellas, D. Bean, C. Cunningham, and K. Y. Cheng, "The Ex-Files: Trajectories, Turning Points, and Adjustment in the Development of Post-Dissolutional Relationships," *Journal of Social & Personal Relationships* 25 (2008): 23–50.

53 L. A. Baxter, *Voicing Relationships: A Dialogic Perspective* (Thousand Oaks, CA: Sage, 2011); L. A. Baxter and D. O. Braithwaite, "Relational Dialectics Theory, Applied," in S. W. Smith and S. R. Wilson, Eds., *New Directions in Interpersonal Communication Research*, 48–66; L. A. Baxter and D. O. Braithwaite, "Relational Dialectics Theory: Crafting Meaning from Competing Discourses," in L. A. Baxter and D. O. Braithwaite, Eds., *Engaging Theories in Interpersonal Communication*, 349–361; L. A. Baxter and B. M. Montgomery, *Relating: Dialogues and Dialectics* (New York: Guilford, 1996); L. A. Baxter and B. M. Montgomery, "Rethinking Communication in Personal Relationships from a Dialectical Perspective," in *Communication and Personal Relationships*, edited by K. Dindia and S. Duck (New York: Wiley, 2000), 31–53.

54 For extensions and applications of relational dialectics theory, see S. L. Faulkner and P. D. Ruby, "Feminist Identity in Romantic Relationships: A Relational Dialectics Analysis of E-Mail Discourse as Collaborative Found Poetry," *Women's Studies in Communication* 38 (2015): 206–226; J. Fox, J. L. Osborn, and K. W. Warber, "Relational Dialectics and Social Networking Sites: The Role of Facebook in Romantic Relationship Escalation, Maintenance, Conflict, and Dissolution," *Computers in Human Behavior* 35 (2014): 527–534; C. K. Rudick and K. B. Golsan, "Revisiting the Relational Communication Perspective: Drawing upon Relational Dialectics Theory to Map an Expanded Research Agenda for Communication and Instruction Scholarship," *Western Journal of Communication* 78 (2014): 255–273; J. R. Pederson, "Competing Discourses of Forgiveness: A Dialogic Perspective," *Communication Studies* 65 (2014): 353–369; R. Amati and A. G. Hannawa, "Relational Dialectics Theory: Disentangling Physician-Perceived Tensions of End-of-Life Communication," *Health Communication* 29 (2014): 962–973; N. O'Boyle, "Front Row Friendships: Relational Dialectics and Identity Negotiations by Mature Students at University," *Communication Education* 63 (2014): 169–191; J. Simmons, R. Lowery-Hart, S. T. Wahl, and M. C. McBride, "Understanding the African-American Student Experience in Higher Education through a Relational Dialectics Perspective," *Communication Education* 62 (2013): 376–394; E. Sahlstein, K. C. Maguire, and L. Timmerman, "Contradictions and Praxis Contextualized by Wartime Deployment: Wives' Perspectives Revealed through Relational Dialectics," *Communication Monographs* 76 (2009): 421–442.

55 J. L. Semlak and J. C. Pearson, "Big Macs/Peanut Butter and Jelly: An Exploration of Dialectical Contradictions Experienced by the Sandwich Generation," *Communication Research Reports* 28 (2011): 296–307; E. Sahlstein and T. Dun, "'I Wanted Time to Myself and He Wanted to Be Together All the Time': Constructing Breakups as Managing Autonomy-Connection," *Qualitative Research Reports in Communication* 9 (2008): 37–45.

56 B. McEwan and D. Horn, "ILY & Can U Pick up Some Milk: Effects of Relational Maintenance via Text Messaging on Relational Satisfaction and Closeness in Dating Partners," *Southern Communication Journal* 81 (2016): 168–181; A. Miller-Ott and L. Kelly, "The Presence of Cell Phones in Romantic Partner Face-to-Face Interactions: An Expectancy Violation Theory Approach," *Southern Communication Journal* 80 (2015): 253–270; R. L. Duran, L. Kelly, and T. Rotaru, "Mobile Phones in Romantic Relationships and the Dialectic of Autonomy Versus Connection," *Communication Quarterly* 59 (2011): 19–36; J. A. Hall and N. K. Baym, "Calling and Texting (Too Much): Mobile Maintenance Expectations, (Over) Dependence, Entrapment, and Friendship Satisfaction," *New Media & Society* 14 (2011): 316–331.

57 C. Prentice, "Relational Dialectics among In-Laws," *Journal of Family Communication* 9 (2009): 67–89.

58 T. A. Coffelt, "Is Sexual Communication Challenging between Mothers and Daughters?" *Journal of Family Communication* 10 (2010): 116–130; P. W. Toller and D. O. Braithwaite, "Grieving Together and Apart: Bereaved Parents' Contradictions of Marital Interaction," *Journal of Applied Communication Research* 37 (2009): 257–277; Sahlstein and Maguire, "Contradictions and Praxis Conceptualized by Wartime Deployment"; A. F. Herrmann, "How Did We Get This Far Apart? Disengagement, Relational Dialectics, and Narrative Control," *Qualitative Inquiry* 13 (2007): 989–1007.

59 S. M. Horan, "Further Understanding Sexual Communication," *Journal of Social & Personal Relationships* 33 (2016): 449–468.

60 W. A. Donohue and D. A. Cai, "Interpersonal Conflict: An Overview," in *Managing Interpersonal Conflict: Advances through Meta-Analysis*, edited by N. A. Burrell, M. Allen, B. M. Gayle, and R. W. Preiss (New York: Routledge, 2014), 22–41; S. Ting-Toomey and J. G. Oetzel, "Introduction to Interpersonal/International Conflict," in *The SAGE Handbook of Conflict Communication: Integrating Theory, Research, and Practice* 2e, edited by J. G. Oetzel and S. Ting-Toomey (Thousand Oaks, CA: Sage, 2013), 99–104.

61 M. Deutsch, "Cooperation and Competition," in *The Handbook of Conflict Resolution: Theory and Practice*, edited by M. Deutsch, P. T. Coleman, and E. C. Marcus (New York: Jossey-Bass, 2006), 23–42.

62 Deutsch, "Cooperation and Competition."

63 W. W. Wilmot and J. L. Hocker, *Interpersonal Conflict* 9e (New York: McGraw-Hill, 2013).

64 G. R. Miller and M. Steinberg, *Between People: A New Analysis of Interpersonal Communication* (Chicago: Science Research Associates, 1975).

65 S. Morrison and P. Schrodt, "The Perceived Threat and Resolvability of Serial Arguments as Correlates of Relational Uncertainty in Romantic Relationships," *Communication Studies* 68 (2017): 56–71; A. J. Johnson and I. A. Cionea, "Serial Arguments in Interpersonal Relationships: Relational Dynamics and Interdependence," in *Communicating Interpersonal Conflict in Close Relationships*, edited by J. A. Samp (New York: Routledge, 2016), 111–127; J. L. Bevan, M. Cummings, M. L. Engert, and L. Sparks, "Romantic Serial Argument Perceived Resolvability, Goals, Rumination, and Conflict Strategy Usage: A Preliminary Longitudinal Study," *Communicating Interpersonal Conflict in Close Relationships*, 128–143; M. E. Roloff, R. M. Reznik, C. Waite Miller, and K. L. Johnson, "'I Thought We Settled This?!' Antecedents and Consequences of Resolution of an Initial Episode in a Serial Argument," *Argumentation & Advocacy* 52 (2015): 8–31; M. R. Roloff and K. L. Johnson, "Serial Arguing over the Relational Life Course: Antecedents and Consequences," in *Stability and Change in Relationships* (Cambridge, UK: Cambridge University Press, 2002), 107–128, as cited in M. R. Roloff and R. M. Reznik, "Communication During Serial Arguments," in *Studies in Applied Interpersonal Communication*, edited by M. T. Motley (Thousand Oaks, CA: Sage, 2008), 97; M. R. Roloff, "Conflict and Communication: A Roadmap through the Literature," *Managing Interpersonal Conflict*, 42–58.

66 P. T. Coleman, "Intractable Conflict," *The Handbook of Conflict Resolution*, 533–559; C. Waite Miller, "Irresolvable Interpersonal Conflicts: Students' Perceptions of Common Topics, Possible Reasons for Persistence, and Communication Patterns," *Making Connections*, 240–247.

67 J. Fox and J. Frampton, "Social Media Stressors in Romantic Relationships," *The Impact of Social Media on Modern Romantic Relationships*, 181–195; S. M. Horan, T. D. Guinn, and S. Banghart, "Understanding Relationships among the Dark Triad Personality Profile and Romantic Partners' Conflict Communication," *Communication Quarterly* 63 (2015): 156–170; D. Aldeis and T. D. Afifi, "Putative Secrets and Conflict in Romantic Relationships Over Time," *Communication Monographs* 82 (2015): 224–251; N. A. Burrell and J. D. Shields, "An Overview of Interpersonal Conflict Management Issues in Personal, Intimate, and Social Contexts," *Managing Interpersonal Conflict*, 251–254; C. Segrin, A. Hanzal, and T. J. Domschke, "Accuracy and Bias in Newlywed Couples' Perceptions of Conflict Styles and the Association with Marital Satisfaction," *Communication Monographs* 76 (2009): 207–233; R. Domingue and D. Mollen, "Attachment and Conflict Communication in Adult Romantic Relationships," *Journal of Social & Personal Relationships* 26 (2009): 678–696.

68 N. E. Dunbar, B. L. Lane, and G. Abra, "Power in Close Relationships: A Dyadic Power Theory Perspective," *Communicating Interpersonal Conflict in Close Relationships*, 75–92; P. T. Coleman, "Power and Conflict," *The Handbook of Conflict Resolution*, 120–143.

69 C. R. Berger, "Social Power and Interpersonal Communication," in *Explorations in Interpersonal Communication*, edited by G. R. Miller (Newbury Park, CA: Sage, 1976).

70 Y. Mao and C. L. Hale, "Relating Intercultural Communication Sensitivity to Conflict Management Styles, Technology Use, and Organizational Communication Satisfaction in Multinational Organizations in China," *Journal of Intercultural Communication Research* 44 (2015): 132–150; S. Ting-Toomey, "Managing Intercultural Conflicts Effectively," in *Intercultural Communication: A Reader* 14e, edited by L. A. Samovar, R. E. Porter, E. R. McDaniel, and C. Sexton Roy (Belmont, CA: Wadsworth/Cengage Learning, 2014), 355–367; S. Ting-Toomey and L. C. Chung, *Understanding Intercultural Communication* 2e (New York: Oxford University Press, 2011); S. Ting-Toomey and J. G. Oetzel, "Culture-Based Situational Conflict Model: An Update and Expansion," *The SAGE Handbook of Conflict Communication*, 763–790; M. D. Hazen and R. Shi, "Harmony, Conflict, and the Process of Argument in Chinese Societies," in *Intercultural Communication: A Reader* 13e, edited by L. A. Samovar and R. E. Porter (Belmont, CA: Wadsworth/Cengage Learning, 2011), 445–456; S. E. Quasha and F. Tsukada, "International Marriages in Japan: Cultural Conflict and Harmony," *Intercultural Communication* 13e, 126–143; P. R. Kimmel, "Culture and Conflict," *The Handbook of Conflict Resolution*, 625–648; P. Pederson, "Multicultural Conflict Resolution," *The Handbook of Conflict Resolution*, 649–670; D. Tjosvold, K. Leung, and D. W. Johnson, "Cooperative and Competitive Conflict in China," *The Handbook of Conflict Resolution*, 671–692.

71 R. Miller, *Intimate Relationships* 7e (New York: McGraw-Hill, 2014).

72 M. Schuessler Harper, *Keeping Quiet: Self-Silencing and Its Association with Relational and Individual Functioning among Adolescent Romantic Couples*, unpublished doctoral dissertation, University of Tennessee, Knoxville, 2004; "Unhealthy for Women Not to Speak Up During Marital Spats," *Harvard Women's Health Watch* (January 2008): 6–7; T. Parker-Pope, "Marital Spats, Taken to Heart," *New York Times*, October 7, 2007, nytimes.com.

73 L. S. Aloia and D. Haunani Solomon, "Cognitive and Physiological Systems Linked to Childhood Exposure to Family Verbal Aggression and Reactions to Conflict in Adulthood," *Communicating Interpersonal Conflict in Close Relationships*, 11–27; O. Hargie, *Skilled Interpersonal Communication: Research, Theory, and Practice* 6e (London: Routledge, 2017).

74 A. S. Rancer and T. A. Avtgis, *Argumentative and Aggressive Communication: Theory, Research, and Application* 2e (Thousand Oaks, CA: Sage, 2014). For more research on verbal aggression, see R. R. Roper, A. J. Johnson, and E. N. Bostwick, "A Target's Perspective: Verbal Aggressiveness, Coping Strategies, and Relational Harm," *Communication Research Reports* 34 (2017): 21–28; L. S. Aloia and D. Haunani Solomon, "Sex Differences in the Perceived Appropriateness of Receiving Verbal Aggression," *Communication Research Reports* 34 (2017): 1–10; N. S. Hoskins, A. Woszidlo, and A. Kunkel, "Words Can Hurt the Ones You Love: Interpersonal Trust as It Relates to Listening Anxiety and Verbal Aggression," *Iowa Journal of Communication* 48 (2016): 96–112; L. S. Aloia and D. Haunani Solomon, "Emotions Associated with Verbal Aggression Expression and Suppression," *Western Journal of Communication* 80 (2016): 3–20.

75 G. D. Paul and L. L. Putnam, "Moral Foundations of Forgiving in the Workplace," *Western Journal of Communication* 81 (2017): 43–63; P. Hopeck and T. R. Harrison, "Reframing, Refocusing, Referring, Reconciling, and Reflecting: Exploring Conflict Resolution Strategies in End-of-Life Situations," *Health Communication* 32 (2017): 240–246; A. L. Mello and L. A. Delise, "Cognitive Diversity to Team Outcomes: The Roles of Cohesion and Conflict Management," *Small Group Research* 46 (2015): 204–226.

76 P. Schrodt, P. L. Witt, and J. R. Shimkowski, "A Meta-Analytical Review of the Demand/Withdraw Pattern of Interaction and Its Associations with Individual, Relational, and Communicative Outcomes," *Communication Monographs* 81 (2014): 28–58; Satir, *The New Peoplemaking*; Wilmot and Hocker, *Interpersonal Conflict*.

77 L. L. Putnam and C. E. Wilson, "Communicative Strategies in Organizational Conflicts: Reliability and Validity of a Measurement Scale," in *Communication Yearbook* 6, edited by M. Burgoon (Beverly Hills, CA: Sage, 1982).

78 C. Gunsoy, S. E. Cross, A. K. Uskul, G. Adams, and B. Gercek-Swing, "Avoid or Fight Back? Cultural Differences in Responses to Conflict and the Role of Collectivism, Honor, and Enemy Perception," *Journal of Cross-Cultural Psychology* 46 (2015): 1081-1102; C-C. Cheng and C. Tardy, "A Cross-Cultural Study of Silence in Marital Conflict," *Media Report Overseas* 6 (2010): 95–105; J. Oduor-Frimpong, "Semiotic Silence: Its Uses as a Conflict Management Strategy in Intimate Relationships," *Semiotica* 167 (2007): 283–308; D. J. Canary and S. Lakey, *Strategic Conflict* (New York: Routledge, 2012); B. A. Budjac Corvette, *Conflict Management: A Practical Guide to Developing Negotiation Strategies* (New York: Prentice Hall, 2006).

79 M. A. Gross, L. K. Guerrero, and J. K. Alberts, "Perceptions of Conflict Strategies and Communication Competence in Task-Oriented Dyads," *Journal of Applied Communication Research* 32 (2004): 249–270.

80 R. Fisher, W. Ury, and B. Patton, *Getting to Yes: Negotiating Agreement without Giving In* Revised Edition (New York: Penguin Books, 2011).

81 This information is based on several excellent discussions of conflict management skills. We acknowledge R. C. Arnett, L. McManus, and A. McKendree, *Conflict between Persons: The Origins of Leadership* (Dubuque, IA: Kendall Hunt, 2014); W. R. Cupach, D. J. Canary, and B. H. Spitzberg, *Competence in Interpersonal Conflict* 2e (Long Grove, IL: Waveland, 2009); Wilmot and Hocker, *Interpersonal Conflict*; O. Hargie, *Skilled Interpersonal Communication*; O. Hargie, *The Handbook of Communication Skills* 3e (London: Routledge, 2006); O. Hargie, C. Saunders, and D. Dickson, *Social Skills in Interpersonal Communication* 3e (London: Routledge, 1994); Fisher et al., *Getting to Yes*.

82 E. Liu and M. E. Roloff, "To Avoid or Not to Avoid: When Emotions Overflow," *Communication Research Reports* 32 (2015): 332–339.

83 B. M. Gayle and R. W. Preiss, "Language Intensity Plus: A Methodological Approach to Validate Emotions in Conflicts," *Communication Reports* 12 (1999): 43–50; Wilmot and Hocker, *Interpersonal Conflict*.

84 A. S. Ebesu Hubbard, B. Hendrickson, K. S. Fehrenbach, and J. Sur, "Effects of Timing and Sincerity of Apology on Satisfaction and Changes in Negative Feelings During Conflicts," *Western Journal of Communication* 77 (2013): 305–322; Z. Qin and M. Andreychik, "Relational Closeness in Conflict: Effects on Interpersonal Goals, Emotion, and Conflict Styles," *Journal of International Communication* 19 (2013): 107–116; L. K. Guerrero, "Emotion and Communication in Conflict Interaction," *The SAGE Handbook of Conflict Communication*, 105–131; E. G. Lindner, "Emotion and Conflict: Why It Is Impossible to Understand How Emotions Affect Conflict and How Conflict Affects Emotions," *The Handbook of Conflict Resolution*, 268–293; C. R. Knee, C. Lonsbary, A. Canevello, and H. Patrick, "Self-Determination and Conflict in Romantic Relationships," *Journal of Personality and Social Psychology* 89 (2005): 997–1009.

85 A. Ellis, *A New Guide to Rational Living* (North Hollywood, CA: Wilshire Books, 1977).

86 J. Roessler, "Thinking, Inner Speech, and Self-Awareness," *Review of Philosophy and Psychology* 7 (2016): 541–557; L. C. Lederman, "The Impact of Gender on the Self and Self-Talk," in L. P. Arliss and D. J. Borisoff, Eds., *Women and Men Communicating: Challenges and Changes* 2e, 78–89; Ellis, *A New Guide to Rational Living*.

87 Fisher et al., *Getting to Yes*.

Chapter 9

1 For a comprehensive review of group process research, see G. Randsley de Moura, T. Leader, J. Pelletier, and D. Abrams, "Prospects for Group Processes and Intergroup Relations Research: A Review of 70 Years' Progress," *Group Processes & Intergroup Relations* 11 (2008): 575–596; Also see: S. Sloman and P. Fernback, *The Knowledge Illusion: Why We Never Think Alone* (New York: Riverhead Books, 2017).

2 R. K. Mosvick and R. B. Nelson, *We've Got to Start Meeting Like This[!]* (Glenview, IL: Scott, Foresman, 1987). Also see: B. Lam, "The Wasted Workday," *The Atlantic*, December 4, 2014, accessed April 15, 2017, www.theatlantic.com/business/archive/2014/12/the-wasted-workday/383380/.

3 Mosvick and Nelson, *We've Got to Start Meeting Like This[!]* Also see: S. Duckweiler, "How Much Time Do We Spend in Meetings?: The Ugly Truth About Meetings," *The Muse*, accessed April 15, 2017, www.themuse.com/advice/how-much-time-do-we-spend-in-meetings-hint-its-scary.

4 D. C. Strubler and K. M. York, "An Exploratory Study of the Team Characteristics Model Using Organizational Teams," *Small Group Research* 38 (2007): 670–695.

5 K. Halvorsen, "Team Decision Making in the Workplace: A Systematic Review of Discourse Analytic Studies," *Journal of Applied Linguistics and Professional Practice* 3 (2013): 273–296.

6 K. W. Hawkins and B. P. Fillion, "Perceived Communication Skill Needs for Work Groups," *Communication Research Reports* 16 (1999): 167–174; also see S. Burkhalter, J. Gastil, and T. Kelshaw, "A Conceptual Definition and Theoretical Model of Public Deliberation in Small Face-to-Face Groups," *Communication Theory* 12 (2002): 398–422.

7 S. A. Beebe and J. T. Masterson, *Communicating in Small Groups: Principles and Practices* 11e (Boston: Pearson, 2015).

8 J. S. Mueller, "Why Individuals in Larger Teams Perform Worse," *Organizational Behavior and Human Decision Processes* 117 (2012): 111–124.

9 B. Bell and S. W. J. Kozlowski, "A Typology of Virtual Teams: Implications for Effective Leadership," *Group & Organizational Management* 27 (2002): 14–49; A. Thatcher, "Small Group Decision-Making in Face-to-Face and Computer-Mediated Environments: The Role of Personality," *Behavior & Information Technology* 22 (2003): 203–218; D. R. Lemus, D. R. Seibold, A. J. Flanagin, and M. J. Metzger, "Argument and Decision Making in Computer Mediated Groups," *Journal of Communication* 54 (2004): 302–320; E. V. Hobman, P. Bordia, B. Irmer, and A. Chang, "The Expression of Conflict in Computer-Mediated and Face-to-Face Groups," *Small Group Research* 33 (2002): 439–464; R. Benbunan-Fich, S. R. Hiltz, and M. Turoff, "A Comparative Content Analysis of Face-to-Face vs. Asynchronous Group Decision Making," *Decision Support Systems* 34 (2002): 457–469; D. S. Staples and J. Webster, "Exploring Traditional and Virtual Team Members' 'Best Practices': A Social Cognitive Theory Perspective," *Small Group Research* 38 (2007): 60–97; S. Z. Schiller and M. Mandviwalla, "Virtual Team Research: An Analysis of Theory Use and a Framework for Theory Appropriation," *Small Group Research* 38 (2007): 12–59; J. T. Polzer, C. B. Crisp, S. L. Jarvenpaa, and J. W. Kim, "Extending the Faultline Model to Geographically Dispersed Teams: How Colocated Subgroups Can Impair Group Functioning," *Academy of Management Journal* 4 (2006): 679–692; also see

C. Garon and K. Wegryn, *Managing Without Walls: Maximize Success with Virtual, Global and Cross-Cultural Teams* (Lewisville, TX: MC Press, 2006); T. Brake, *Where in the World Is My Team? Making Success of Your Virtual Global Workplace* (San Francisco: Jossey-Bass, 2008); D. Derosa and R. Lepsinger, *Virtual Team Success: A Practical Guide for Working and Leading from a Distance* (San Francisco: Jossey-Bass, 2010).

10 J. M. Wilson, S. G. Straus, and B. McEvily, "All in Due Time: The Development of Trust in Computer-Mediated and Face-to-Face Teams," *Organizational Behavior and Human Decision Processes* 99 (2006): 16–33; also see C. A. Nystrom and V. Asproth, "Virtual Teams—Support for Technical Communication?," *Journal of Organisational Transformation & Social Change* 10 (2013): 64–80; M. del C. Triana, B. L. Kirkman, and M. F. Wagstaff, "Does the Order of Fact-to-Face and Computer-Mediated Communication Matter in Diverse Project Teams? An Investigation of Communication Order Effects on Minority Inclusion and Participation," *Journal of Business Psychology* 27 (2013): 57–70.

11 Wilson et al., "All in Due Time."

12 N. N. Bazarova and Y. C. Yuan, "Expertise Recognition and Influence in Intercultural Groups: Differences between Fact-to-Face and Computer-Mediated Communication," *Journal of Computer-Mediated Communication* 18 (2013): 437–453.

13 C. E. Timmerman and C. R. Scott, "Virtually Working: Communicative and Structural Predictors of Media Use and Key Outcomes in Virtual Work Teams," *Communication Monographs* 73 (2006): 108–136.

14 M. Washington, E. Okoro, and P. Cardon, "Perceptions of Civility for Mobile Phone Use in Formal and Informal Meetings" in *Business and Professional Communication*, 77 (2013), pp. 52–64.

15 Washington, Okoro, and Cardon, "Perceptions of Civility for Mobile Phone Use."

16 Washington, Okoro, and Cardon, "Perceptions of Civility for Mobile Phone Use."

17 N. Katz and G. Koenig, "Sports Teams as a Model for Workplace Teams: Lessons and Liabilities," *Academy of Management Executive* 15 (2001): 56–67; L. G. Snyder, "Teaching Teams about Teamwork: Preparation, Practice, and Performance Review," *Business Communication Quarterly* (2009): 74–79.

18 Our discussion of teams and teamwork is from Beebe and Masterson, *Communicating in Small Groups;* for an excellent review of teamwork theoretical models, see V. Rousseau, C. Aube, and A. Savoie, "Teamwork Behaviors: A Review and an Integration of Frameworks," *Small Group Research* 27 (2006): 540–570.

19 T. D. Fletcher and D. A. Major, "The Effects of Communication Modality on Performance and Self-Ratings of Teamwork Components," *Journal of Computer Mediated Communication* 11 (2006): 557–576.

20 A. G. Sheard and A. P. Kakabadse, "From Loose Groups to Effective Teams: The Nine Key Factors of the Team Landscape," *Journal of Management Development* 21 (2002): 133–151; also see R. A. Meyers and D. R. Seibold, "Making Foundational Assumptions Transparent: Framing the Discussion About Group Communication and Influence," *Human Communication Research* 35 (2009): 286–295.

21 See F. C. Broadbeck and T. Breitermeyer, "Effects of Individual versus Mixed Individual and Group Experience in Rule Induction on Group Member Learning and Group Performance," *Journal of Experimental Social Psychology* 36 (2002): 621–648.

22 S. B. Shimanoff, *Communication Rules: Theory and Research* (Beverly Hills, CA: Sage, 1980).

23 M. Hoegl, "Goal Setting and Team Performance in Innovative Projects: On the Moderating Role of Teamwork Quality," *Small Group Research* 34 (2003): 3–19; A. W. Woolley, M. E. Gerbasi, C. F. Chabris, S. M. Kosslyn, and J. R. Hackman, "Bringing in the Experts: How Team Composition and Collaborative Planning Jointly Shape Analytic Effectiveness," *Small Group Research* 39 (2008): 352–371; H. Van Mierlo and A. Kleingeld, "Goals, Strategies, and Group Performance: Some Limits of Goal Setting in Groups," *Small Group Research* 41 (2010): 524–555; H. V.

Mierlo and E. A. J. Van Hooft, "A Group-Level Conceptualization of the 2 X 2 Achievement Goal Framework: Antecedents and Motivational Outcomes," *Group & Organization Management* 40 (2015): 776–808; M. P. Healey, T. Vuori, and G. Hodgkinson, "When Teams Agree While Disagreeing: Reflection and Refection in Shared Cognition," *Academy of Management Review* 40 (2015): 399–422; L. Alexander and D. V. Knippernberg, "Teams in Pursuit of Radical Innovation: A Goal Orientation Perspective," *Academy of Management Review*, 39 (2014) 423–438.

24 R. Rico, M. Sanchez-Manzanares, F. Gil, and C. Gibson, "Team Impact Coordination Processes: A Team Knowledge-Based Approach," *Academy of Management Review* 33 (2008): 163–184; M. Schaeffner, H. Huettermann, D. Gebert, S. Boerner, E. Kearney, and L. Song, "Swim or Sink Together: Collective Team Member Alignment for Separating Task and Relationship Conflicts," *Group and Organization Management*, 40 (2015): 467–499.

25 Beebe and Masterson, *Communicating in Small Groups.*

26 J. E. Mathieu, S. I. Tannenbaum, M. R. Kukenberger, J. S. Donsbach, and G. M. Alliger, "Team Role Experience and Orientation: A Measure and Tests of Construct Validity," *Group & Organization Management* 40 (2015): 6–34.

27 M. Priesemuth, A. Arnuad, and M. Schminke, "Bad Behavior in Groups: The Impact of Overall Justice Climate and Functional Dependence on Counterproductive Work Behavior in Work Units," *Group & Organization Management* 38 (2013): 230–257.

28 C. Savelsbergh, J. M. P. Gevers, B. I. J. M. van der Heijden, and R. F. Poell, "Team Role Stress: Relationships with Team Learning and Performance in Project Teams," *Group & Organization Management* 37 (2012): 67–100.

29 K. D. Benne and P. Sheats, "Functional Roles of Group Members," *Journal of Social Issues* 4 (1948): 41–49; for a good review of role development in groups, see A. P. Hare, "Types of Roles in Small Groups: A Bit of History and a Current Perspective," *Small Group Research* 28 (1994): 433–438; A. J. Salazar, "An Analysis of the Development and Evolution of Roles in the Small Group," *Small Group Research* 27 (1996): 475–503.

30 T. Halfhill, E. Sundstrom, J. Lahner, W. Calderone, and T. M. Nielsen, "Group Personality Composition and Group Effectiveness: An Integrative Review of Empirical Research," *Small Group Research* 36 (2005): 83–105.

31 G. M. Wittenbaum, H. C. Shulman, and M. E. Braz, "Social Ostracism in Task Groups: The Effects of Group Composition," *Small Group Research* 41 (2010): 330–353.

32 R. F. Bales, *Interaction Process Analysis* (Chicago: University of Chicago Press, 1976).

33 Shimanoff, *Communication Rules.*

34 M. E. Scott, "'Communicate through the Roof': A Case Study Analysis of the Communicative Rules and Resources of an Effective Global Virtual Team," *Communication Quarterly* 61 (2013): 301–318.

35 For a discussion of monochronic and polychronic time, see E. T. Hall, *The Silent Language* (New York: Doubleday, 1959).

36 M. J. Waller, M. E. Zellmer-Bruhn, and R. C. Giambatista, "Watching the Clock: Group Pacing Behavior under Dynamic Deadlines," *Academy of Management Journal* 45 (2002): 1046–1055.

37 Hall, *The Silent Language.*

38 M. Shaw, *Group Dynamics: The Psychology of Small Group Behavior* (New York: McGraw-Hill, 1981), 281.

39 J. I. Hurwitz, A. F. Zander, and B. Hymovitch, "Some Effects of Power on the Relations among Group Members," in *Group Dynamics: Research and Theory*, edited by D. Cartwright and A. Zander (New York: Harper & Row, 1953), 483–492; D. C. Barnlund and C. Harland, "Propinquity and Prestige as Determinants of Communication Networks," *Sociometry* 26 (1963): 467–479; G. C. Homans, *The Human Group* (New York: Harcourt Brace and World, 1992); H. H. Kelly, "Communication in Experimentally Created Hierarchies," *Human Relations* 4 (1951): 36–56.

40 C. Anderson, J. S. Beer, J. Chatman, S. Srivastava, and S. E. Spataro, "Knowing Your Place: Self-Perceptions of Status in Face-to-Face Groups," *Journal of Personality and Social Psychology* 91 (2006): 1094–1110.

41 M. R. Singer, *Intercultural Communication: A Perceptual Approach* (Englewood Cliffs, NJ: Prentice Hall, 1987), 118.

42 J. R. P. French and B. H. Raven, "The Bases of Social Power," in *Group Dynamics: Research and Theory*, edited by D. Cartwright and A. Zander (New York: Harper & Row, 1953), 607–623.

43 A. V. Carron and L. R. Brawley, "Cohesion: Conceptual and Measurement Issues," *Small Group Research* 43 (2012): 726–743; O. Saafein and G. Shaykhian, "Factors Affecting Virtual Team Performance in Telecommunication Support Environment," *Telematics and Informatics* 31 (2014): 459–462.

44 D. Neumann, "Small Group Cohesion and Frequency of Idiom Use," paper presented at the annual meeting of the National Communication Association, Chicago, November 2004; G. Yilmaz, "The Tale of We, You and I: Interpersonal Effects on Pronoun Use in Virtual Teams," *The Florida Communication Journal*, 42 (2014).

45 C. R. Evans and K. L. Dion, "Group Cohesion and Performance: A Meta-Analysis," *Small Group Research* 43 (2012): 690–701; S. M. Gully, D. J. Devine, and D. J. Whitney, "A Meta-Analysis of Cohesion and Performance: Effects of Level of Analysis and Task Interdependence," *Small Group Research* 43 (2012): 702–725.

46 M. R. Barrick, B. H. Bradley, A. L. Kristof-Brown, and A. E. Colbert, "The Moderating Role of Top Management Team Interdependence: Implications for Real Teams and Working Groups," *Academy of Management Journal* 50 (2007): 544–557.

47 Adapted from E. G. Bormann and N. C. Bormann, *Effective Small Group Communication* (Minneapolis: Burgess, 1980), 70–72.

48 N. C. Sauer and S. Kauffeld, "Meetings as Networks: Applying Social Network Analysis to Team Interaction," *Communication Methods and Measures*, 7 (2013): 26-47; M. Priesemuth, A. Arnuad, and M. Schminke, "Bad Behavior in Groups: The Impact of Overall Justice Climate and Functional Dependence on Counterproductive Work Behavior in Work Units," *Group & Organization Management* 38 (2013): 230–257.

49 C. Savelsbergh, J. M. P. Gevers, B. I. J. M. van der Heijden, and R. F. Poell, "Team Role Stress: Relationships with Team Learning and Performance in Project Teams," *Group & Organization Management* 37 (2012): 67–100.

50 B. A. Fisher, "Decision Emergence: Phases in Group Decision Making," *Speech Monographs* 37 (1970): 60.

51 For a discussion of primary tension and group phases, see E. Bormann, *Discussion and Group Methods* (New York: Harper & Row, 1975).

52 P. J. Boyle, D. Hanlon, and J. E. Russo, "The Value of Task Conflict to Group Decisions," *Journal of Behavioral Decision Making* 25 (2012): 217–227; F. R. C. de Wit, K. A. Jehn, and D. Scheepers, "Task Conflict, Information Processing, and Decision-Making: The Damaging Effect of Relationship Conflict," *Organizational Behavior and Human Decision Processes* 122 (2013): 177–189.

53 For an examination of the practical role of conflict in jury deliberations, see M. S. Poole and M. Dobosh, "Exploring Conflict Management Processes in Jury Deliberations through Interaction Analysis," *Small Group Research* 41 (2010): 408–426.

54 M. A. Von Glinow, D. Shapiro, and J. Brett, "Can We Talk, and Should We? Managing Emotional Conflict in Multicultural Teams," *Academy of Management Review* 29 (2004): 578–592.

55 M. Janssens and J. M. Brett, "Cultural Intelligence in Global Teams: A Fusion Model of Collaboration," *Group & Organization Management* 31 (2006): 124–153.

56 G. Hofstede, *Culture's Consequences: International Differences in Work Related Values* (Beverly Hills, CA: Sage, 1980); G. Hofstede, *Cultures and Organizations: Software of the Mind* (London: McGraw-Hill, 1991).

57 Adapted from J. Mole, *Mind Your Manners: Managing Business Cultures in Europe* (New York: Nicholas Brealey, 1995).

58 S. A. Wheelan and T. Williams, "Mapping Dynamic Interaction Patterns in Work Groups," *Small Group Research* 34 (2003): 433–467; S. A. Wheelan, B. Davidson and F. Tilin, "Group Development Across Time: Reality or Illusion?" *Small Group Research*, 34 (2003): 223–245.

59 M. S. Poole, "Decision Development in Small Groups: A Multiple Sequence Model of Group Decision Development," *Communication Monographs* 50 (1983): 321–341; also see C. Pavitt and K. Kline Johnson, "Scheidel and Crowell Revisited: A Descriptive Study of Group Proposal Sequencing," *Communication Monographs* 69 (2002): 19–32.

Chapter 10

1 See N. R. F. Maier, "Assets and Liabilities in Group Problem Solving: The Need for an Integrative Function," *Psychological Review* 74 (1967): 239–249; M. Argyle, *Cooperation: The Basis of Sociability* (London: Routledge, 1991); H. A. M. Wilke and R. W. Meertens, *Group Performance* (London: Routledge, 1994); S. Sloman and P. Fernbach, *The Knowledge Illusion: Why We Never Think Alone* (New York: Riverhead Books, 2017).

2 Maier, "Assets and Liabilities in Group Problem Solving"; Argyle, *Cooperation*; Wilke and Meertens, *Group Performance*.

3 C. N. DeWall, D. S. Chester, and D. S. White, "Can Acetaminophen Reduce the Pain of Decision-Making?" *Journal of Experimental Social Psychology* 56 (2015): 117–120.

4 D. F. Crown, "The Use of Group and Groupcentric Individual Goals for Culturally Heterogeneous and Homogeneous Task Groups: An Assessment of European Work Teams," *Small Group Research* 38 (2007): 489–508.

5 C. E. Larson and F. M. J. LaFasto, *Teamwork: What Must Go Right/ What Can Go Wrong* (Beverly Hills, CA: Sage, 1989); also see D. D. Chrislip and C. E. Larson, *Collaborative Leadership* (San Francisco: Jossey-Bass, 1994); D. A. Romig, *Breakthrough Teamwork: Outstanding Results Using Structured Teamwork* (Chicago: Irwin, 1996); M. A. Marks, J. E. Mathieu, and S. J. Zaccaro, "A Temporally Based Framework and Taxonomy of Team Processes," *Academy of Management Review* 26 (2001): 356–376; N. Katz, "Sports Teams as a Model for Workplace Teams: Lessons and Liabilities," *Academy of Management Executive* 15 (2001): 56–67.

6 Larson and LaFasto, *Teamwork*; Chrislip and Larson, *Collaborative Leadership*; Romig, *Breakthrough Teamwork*; Y. Gong, T.-Y. Kim, D.-R. Lee, and J. Zhu, "A Multilevel Model of Team Goal Orientation, Information Exchange, and Creativity," *Academy of Management Journal* 56 (2013): 827–851; A. N. Pieterse, D. van Knippenberg, and D. van Knippenberg, "Cultural Diversity and Team Performance: The Role of Team Member Goal Orientation," *Academy of Management Journal* 56 (2013): 782–804.

7 L. A. DeChurch and C. D. Haas, "Examining Team Planning through an Episodic Lens: Effects of Deliberate, Contingency, and Reactive Planning on Team Effectiveness," *Small Group Research* 39 (2008): 542–568.

8 Larson and LaFasto, *Teamwork*.

9 C. M. J. H. Savelsbergh, B. I. J. M. van der Heijden, and R. F. Poell, "The Development and Empirical Validation of a Multidimensional Measurement Instrument for Team Learning Behaviors," *Small Group Research* 40 (2009): 578–607.

10 J. R. Mesmer-Magnus, L. A. DeChurch, M. Jimenez-Rodriguez, and J. Wildman, "A Meta-Analytic Investigation of Virtuality and Information Sharing in Teams," *Organizational Behavior and Human Decision Processes* 115 (2011): 214–225.

11 T. Reimer, A. Reimer, and V. B. Hinsz, "Naive Groups Can Solve the Hidden-Profile Problem," *Human Communication Research* 36 (2010): 443–467.

12 For a review of research about the importance of sharing information to reach a high-quality decision or solution, see J. A. Bonito, M. H. DeCamp, and E. K. Ruppel, "The Process of Information Sharing in Small Groups: Application of a Local Model," *Communication Monographs* 75 (2008): 136–157; W. P. van Ginkel and D. van Knippenberg, "Group Information Elaboration and Group Decision Making: The Role of Shared Task Representations," *Organizational Behavior and Human Decision Processes* 105 (2008): 82–97; T. Reimer, S. Kuendig, U. Hoffrage, E. Park, and V. Hinsz, "Effects of Information Environment on Group Discussions and Decisions in the Hidden-Profile Paradigm,"

Communication Monographs 74 (2007): 1–28; W. P. van Ginkel and D. van Knippenberg, "Knowledge about the Distribution of Information and Group Decision Making: When and Why Does It Work?" *Organizational Behavior and Human Decision Processes* 108 (2009): 218–229.

13 M. Alsharo, "Knowledge Sharing in Virtual Teams: The Impact on Trust, Collaboration, and Team Effectiveness," Unpublished doctoral dissertation, Department of Computer Science and Information Systems, University of Colorado (2013); E. Jones and J. Kelly, "The Psychological Costs of Knowledge Specialization in Groups: Unique Expertise Leaves You Out of the Loop," *Organizational Behavior and Human Decision Processes* 121 (2013): 174–182; H. C. Xie, "The Role of Computer Mediated Communication Competence on Unique Information Pooling and Decision Quality in Virtual Teams," Unpublished M.A. thesis, Michigan State University, (2015).

14 O. S. Chernyshenko, A. G. Miner, M. R. Baumann, and J. A. Sniezek, "The Impact of Information Distribution, Ownership, and Discussion on Group Member Judgment: The Differential Cue Weighting Model," *Organizational Behavior and Human Decision Processes* 91 (2003): 12–25.

15 D. R. Seibold and R. A. Meyers, "Group Argument: A Structuration Perspective and Research Program," *Small Group Research* 38 (2007): 312–336.

16 S. Y. Sung and J. N. Choi, "Effects of Team Knowledge Management on the Creativity and Financial Performance of Organizational Teams," *Organizational Behavior and Human Decision Processes* 118 (2012): 4–13.

17 M. Orlirtzky and R. Y. Hirokawa, "To Err Is Human, to Correct for It Divine: A Meta-Analysis of Research Testing the Functional Theory of Group Decision-Making Effectiveness," *Small Group Research* 32.3 (2001): 313–341.

18 Orlitzky and Hirokawa, "To Err Is Human, to Correct for It Divine"; B. L. Smith, "Interpersonal Behaviors That Damage the Productivity of Creative Problem Solving Groups," *Journal of Creative Behavior* 27 (1993): 171–187.

19 H. Ding and X. Ding, "Project Management, Critical Praxis, and Process-Oriented Approach to Teamwork," *Business Communication Quarterly* 71 (2008): 456–471; P. Lofstrand and I. Zakrisson, "Competitive Versus Non-Competitive Goals in Group Decision-Making," *Small Group Research* 45:4 (2014): 451–464.

20 A. B. Henley and K. H. Price, "Want a Better Team? Foster a Climate of Fairness," *Academy of Management Executive* 16 (2002): 153–155.

21 J. L. Thompson, "Building Collective Communication Competence in Interdisciplinary Research Teams," *Journal of Applied Communication Research* 37 (2009): 278–297.

22 P. K. Kim, C. D. Cooper, K. T. Dirks, and D. L. Ferrin, "Repairing Trust with Individuals versus Groups," *Organizational Behavior and Human Decision Processes* 120 (2013): 1–14.

23 A. Kane and F. Rink, "When and How Groups Utilize Dissenting Newcomer Knowledge: Newcomers' Future Prospects Condition the Effect of Language-Based Identity Strategies," *Group Processes and Intergroup Relations* (2016): 1–17.

24 A. T. Pescosolido, "Group Efficacy over Time on Group Performance and Development," *Small Group Research* 34 (2003): 20–43.

25 J. S. Prichard and M. J. Ashleigh, "The Effects of Team-Skills Training on Transactive Memory and Performance," *Small Group Research* 38 (2007): 696–726; T. L. Rapp and J. E. Mathieu, "Evaluating an Individually Self-Administered Generic Teamwork Skills Training Program across Time and Levels," *Small Group Communication* 38 (2007): 532–555.

26 S. A. Beebe and J. T. Masterson, *Communicating in Small Groups: Principles and Practices* 11e (Boston: Pearson, 2015); A. B. VanGundy, *Techniques of Structured Problem Solving* 2e (New York: Van Nostrand Reinhold, 1988).

27 J. K. Brilhart and L. M. Jochem, "Effects of Different Patterns on Outcomes of Problem-Solving Discussion," *Journal of Applied Psychology* 48 (1964): 174–179; W. E. Jurma, "Effects of Leader Structuring Style and Task Orientation Characteristics of Group Members," *Communication Monographs* 49 (1979): 282–295; S. Jarboe, "A Comparison of Input-Output, Process-Output, and Input-Process-Output Models of Small Group Problem-Solving Effectiveness," *Communication Monographs* 55 (1988): 121–142; VanGundy, *Techniques of Structured Problem Solving.*

28 S. A. Beebe, "Structure-Interaction Theory: Conceptual, Contextual and Strategic Influences on Human Communication," *Russian Journal of Linguistics Vestnik Rudn: Special Issue: Intercultural Communication Theory and Practice* 19, 4 (2015): 7–21; E. Crawford and J. Lepine, "A Configural Theory of Team Processes: Accounting for the Structure of Taskwork and Teamwork," *Academy of Management Review* 38 (2013): 32–48.

29 Y. Liu and P. McLeod, "Individual Preference for Procedural Order and Process Accountability in Group Problem-Solving," *Small Group Research* 45 (2014): 154–175.

30 D. M. Berg, "A Descriptive Analysis of the Distribution and Duration of Themes Discussed by Task-Oriented Small Groups," *Speech Monographs* 34 (1967): 172–175; E. G. Bormann and N. C. Bormann, *Effective Small Group Communication* 2e (Minneapolis: Burgess, 1976), 132; M. S. Poole, "Decision Development in Small Groups III: A Multiple Sequence Model of Group Decision Development," *Communication Monographs* 50 (1983): 321–341; Y. Liu and P. McLeod, "Individual Preference for Procedural Order and Process Accountability in Group Problem-Solving."

31 For an excellent summary of the literature documenting these problems, see Sunwolf and D. R. Seibold, "The Impact of Formal Procedures on Group Processes, Members, and Task Outcomes," in *The Handbook of Group Communication Theory and Research*, edited by L. Frey (Thousand Oaks, CA: Sage, 1999), 395–431.

32 J. Dewey, *How We Think* (Boston: D.C. Heath, 1910).

33 For an excellent discussion of how to define and clarify problems including viewing problems as something we want more of or less of see: D. A. Romig, *Breakthrough Teamwork: Outstanding Results Using Breakthrough Teamwork* (Austin, TX: Irwin, 1996).

34 This explanation of the journalists' six questions method is based on a discussion by J. E. Eitington, *The Winning Trainer* (Houston: Gulf Publishing, 1989), 157.

35 Based on the research of K. Lewin, "Frontiers in Group Dynamics," *Human Relations* 1 (1947): 5–42.

36 K. Dijkstra, J. Van Der Pligt, and G. Van Kleef, "Deliberation Versus Intuition: Decomposing the Role of Expertise in Judgement and Decision Making," *Journal of Behavioral Decision Making* 26 (2013): 285–294.

37 M. C. Schilpzand, D. M. Herold, and C. E. Shalley, "Members' Openness to Experience and Teams' Creative Performance," *Small Group Research* 42 (2011): 55–76; S. J. Shin, T.-Y. Kim, J.-Y. Lee, and L. Bian, "Cognitive Team Diversity and Individual Team Member Creativity: A Cross-Level Interaction," *Academy of Management Journal* 55 (2012): 197–212; P. Alahuhta, E. Nordback, A. Sivunen, and T. Suraka, "Fostering Team Creativity in Virtual Worlds," *Journal of Virtual Worlds Research* 7:3 (2014).

38 See S. Taggar, "Individual Creativity and Group Ability to Utilize Individual Creative Resources: A Multilevel Model," *Academy of Management Journal* 45 (2002): 315–330; C. E. Johnson and M. A. Hackman, *Creative Communication: Principles and Applications* (Prospect Heights, IL: Waveland, 1995).

39 A. F. Osborn, *Applied Imagination* (New York: Scribner's, 1962).

40 A. L. Delberg, A. H. Van de Ven, and D. H. Gustason, *Group Techniques for Program Planning: A Guide to Nominal Group and Delphi Processes* (Glenview, IL: Scott, Foresman, 1975), 7–16.

41 O. Goldenberg, J. Larson Jr., and J. Wiley, "Goal Instructions, Response Format, and Idea Generation," *Small Group Research* 44 (2013): 227–256.

42 D. Straker, *Rapid Problem Solving with Post-it Notes* (Tucson: Fisher Books, 1997).

43 D. H. Henningsen and M. Henningsen, "Generating Ideas About the Uses of Brainstorming: Reconsidering the Losses and Gains of Brainstorming Groups Relative to Nominal Groups," *Southern Communication Journal* 78:1 (2013): 42–55.

44 D. H. Henningsen and M. Henningsen, "Generating Ideas About the Uses of Brainstorming."

45 D. H. Henningsen and M. Henningsen, "Generating Ideas About the Uses of Brainstorming."

46 Adapted from Beebe and Masterson, *Communicating in Small Groups.*

47 M. A. Roberto, "Strategic Decision-Making Processes: Beyond the Efficiency-Consensus Trade-Off," *Group & Organizational Management* 29 (2004): 625–658.

48 J. S. Rijnbout and B. M. McKimmie, "Deviance in Organizational Group Decision-Making: The Role of Information Processing, Confidence, and Elaboration," *Group Processes & Intergroup Relations* 15 (2012): 813–828.

49 R. Y. Hirokawa, D. S. Gouran, and A. Martz, "Understanding the Sources of Faulty Group Decision Making: A Lesson from the *Challenger* Disaster," *Small Group Behavior* 19 (1988): 411–433.

50 R. K. M. Haurwitz, "Faculty Doubted Bonfire's Stability," *Austin American-Statesman* (December 10, 1999): A1, A2.

51 D. Jehl, "Panel Unanimous: 'Groupthink' Backed Prewar Assumptions, Report Concludes," *The New York Times* (July 10, 2004), 1; also see *The 9/11 Commission Report: Final Report of the National Commission on Terrorist Attacks upon the United States* (Washington, DC: National Commission on Terrorist Attacks, 2004).

52 J. F. Veiga, "The Frequency of Self-Limiting Behavior in Groups: A Measure and an Explanation," *Human Relationships* 44 (1991): 877–895.

53 I. L. Janis, *Victims of Groupthink* (Boston: Houghton Mifflin, 1973).

54 R. Y. Hirokawa and D. R. Scheerhorn, "Communication and Faulty Group Decision-Making," in *Communication and Group Decision-Making*, edited by R. Y. Hirokawa, S. Poole, and M. S. Poole (Beverly Hills, CA: Sage, 1996), 63–80.

55 C. M. Mason and M. R. Griffin, "Group Task Satisfaction: The Group's Attitude to Its Task and Work Environment," *Group & Organizational Management* 30 (2005): 625–652; also see: K. Parry, M. Cohen, and S. Bhattacharya, "Rise of the Machines: A Critical Consideration of Automated Leadership Decision Making in Organizations," *Group & Organization Management* 41 (2016): 1–24.

56 M. S. Limon and B. H. La France, "Communication Traits and Leadership Emergence: Examining the Impact of Argumentativeness, Communication Apprehension, and Verbal Aggressiveness in Work Groups," *Southern Communication Journal* 70 (2005): 123–133; also see A. M. L. Raes, U. Glunk, M. G. Heijltjes, and R. A. Roe, "Top Management Team and Middle Managers: Making Sense of Leadership," *Small Group Research* 38 (2007): 360–386.

57 See B. M. Bass, *Stodgill's Handbook of Leadership* (New York: Free Press, 1981).

58 A. Srivastava, K. M. Bartol, and E. A. Locke, "Empowering Leadership in Management Teams: Effects of Knowledge Sharing, Efficacy, and Performance," *Academy of Management Journal* 49 (2006): 1239–1251.

59 G. J. Calanes, "In Their Own Words: An Exploratory Study of Bona Fide Group Leaders," *Small Group Research* 34 (2003): 741–770.

60 P. Balkundi and D. Harrison, "Ties, Leaders, and Time in Teams: Strong Inference about Network Structure's Effects on Team Viability and Performance," *Academy of Management Journal* 49 (2006): 49–68.

61 R. White and R. Lippitt, "Leader Behavior and Member Reaction in Three Social Climates," in *Group Dynamics* 3e, edited by D. Cartwright and A. Zander (New York: Harper & Row, 1968): 319.

62 M. Van Vugt, S. F. Jepson, C. M. Hart, and D. De Cremer, "Autocratic Leadership in Social Dilemmas: A Threat to Group Stability," *Journal of Experimental and Social Psychology* 40 (2004): 1–13.

63 S. Halverson, S. E. Murphy, and R. E. Riggio, "Charismatic Leadership in Crisis Situations: A Laboratory Investigation of Stress and Crisis," *Small Group Research* 35 (2004): 495–514.

64 D. S. DeRue, C. M. Barnes, and F. P. Morgeson, "Understanding the Motivational Contingencies of Team Leadership," *Small Group Research* 41 (2010): 621–651.

65 S. S. K. Lam, X. P. Chen, and J. Schaubroeck, "Participative Decision Making and Employee Performance in Different Cultures: The Moderating Effects of Allocentrism/Idiocentrism and Efficacy," *Academy of Management Journal* 45 (2002): 905–914.

66 D. C. Korten, "Situational Determinants of Leadership Structure," *Journal of Conflict Resolution* 6 (1962): 222–235.

67 P. Hersey, K. Blanchard, and D. Johnson, *Management of Organizational Behavior: Utilizing Human Resources* 9e (Englewood Cliffs, NJ: Prentice–Hall, 2007).

68 For an excellent discussion of transformational leadership applied to teams, see S. D. Dionne, F. J. Yammarino, L. E. Atwater, and W. D. Spangler, "Transformational Leadership and Team Performance," *Journal of Organizational Change Management* 17 (2004): 177–193.

69 See K. W. Phillips, G. B. Northcraft, and M. A. Neale, "Surface-Level Diversity Collide: The Effects on Dissenting Group Members," *Organizational Behavior and Human Decision Processes* 9 (2006): 143–160; J. R. Larson, "Deep Diversity and Strong Synergy: Modeling the Impact of Variability in Members' Problem-Solving Strategies on Group Problem-Solving Performance," *Small Group Research* 3 (2007): 413–436.

70 A. Mello and L. Delise, "Cognitive Diversity to Team Outcomes: The Roles of Cohesion and Conflict Management," *Small Group Research* 46:2 (2015): 204–226.

71 R. Rodriguez, "Challenging Demographic Reductionism: A Pilot Study Investigating Diversity in Group Composition," *Small Group Research* 26 (1998): 744–759.

72 Phillips et al., "Surface-Level Diversity Collide."

73 R. F. Fiedler, *A Theory of Leadership Effectiveness* (New York: McGraw-Hill, 1967): 144.

74 B. M. Bass and M. J. Avolio, "Transformational Leadership and Organizational Culture," *International Journal of Public Administration* 17 (1994): 541–554; also see F. J. Yammarino and A. J. Dubinsky, "Transformational Leadership Theory: Using Levels of Analysis to Determine Boundary Conditions," *Personnel Psychology* 47 (1994): 787–809; J. Cha, Y, Kim, J. Y. Lee and D. G. Bachrach, "Transformational Leadership and Inter-Team Collaboration: Exploring the Mediating Role of Teamwork Quality and Moderating Role of Team Size," *Group & Organizational Management* 40 (2015): 715-743.

75 For additional research about the efficacy of transformational leadership, see J. McCann, P. Langford, and R. M. Rawlings, "Testing Behling and McFillen's Syncretical Model of Charismatic Transformational Leadership," *Group & Organization Management* 31 (2006): 237–263; R. F. Piccolo and J. Colquitt, "Transformational Leadership and Job Behaviors: The Mediating Role of Core Job Characteristics," *Academy of Management Journal* 49 (2006): 327–340; R. S. Rubin, D. C. Muniz, and W. H. Bommer, "Leading from Within: The Effects of Emotion Recognition and Personality on Transformational Leadership Behavior," *Academy of Management Journal* 48 (2005): 845–858; A. Ergeneli, R. Gohar, and Z. Temirbekova, "Transformational Leadership: Its Relationship to Culture Value Dimensions," *International Journal of Intercultural Relations* 31 (2007): 703–724; B. J. Hoffman, B. H. Bynum, R. F. Piccolo, and A. W. Sutton, "Person-Organization Value Congruence: How Transformational Leaders Influence Work Group Effectiveness," *Academy of Management Journal* 54 (2011): 779–796; J.-W. Huang, "The Effects of Transformational Leadership on the Distinct Aspects Development of Social Identity," *Group Processes & Intergroup Relations* 16 (2013): 87–104; P. Wang, J. C. Rode, K. Shi, Z. Luo, and W. Chen, "A Workgroup Climate Perspective on the Relationships Among Transformational Leadership, Workgroup Diversity, and Employee Creativity," *Group & Organizational Management* 38 (2013): 334–360; P. Wang, J. C. Rode, K. Shi, Z. Luo, and W. Chen, "A Workgroup Climate Perspective on the Relationships Among Transformational Leadership, Workgroup Diversity, and Employee Creativity," *Group & Organizational Management* 38 (2013): 334–360.

76 P. M. Senge, "The Leader's New Role: Building Learning Organizations," *Sloan Management Review* 32 (1990).

77 M. Zellmer-Bruhn and C. Gibson, "Multinational Organization Context: Implications for Team Learning and Performance," *Academy of Management Journal* 49 (2006): 501–518.

78 D. I. Jung and J. J. Sosik, "Transformational Leadership in Work Groups: The Role of Empowerment, Cohesiveness, and Collective Efficacy on Perceived Group Performance," *Small Group Research* 33 (2002): 313–336; also see T. Dvir, D. Eden, B. J. Avolio, and B. Shamir, "Impact of Transformational Leadership on Follower Development and Performance: A Field Experiment," *Academy of Management Journal* 45 (2002): 735–744; C. L. Hoyt and J. Blascovich, "Transformational and Transactional Leadership in Virtual and Physical Environments," *Small Group Research* 34 (2003): 678–715; S. S. Kahai, R. Huang, and R. J. Jestice, "Interaction Effect of Leadership and Communication Media on Feedback Positivity in Virtual Teams," *Group & Organizational Management* 37 (2012): 716–751; J. Cha, Y. Kim, J.-Y. Lee, and D. G. Bachrach, "Transformational Leadership and Inter-Team Collaboration: Exploring the Mediating Role of Teamwork Quality and Moderating Role of Team Size," *Group and Organization Management* 40 (2015): 715–743.

79 V. U. Druskar and J. V. Wheeler, "Managing from the Boundary: The Effective Leadership of Self-Managing Work Teams," *Academy of Management Journal* 46 (2003): 435–457.

80 J. A. Raelin, "Don't Bother Putting Leadership into People," *Academy of Management Executive* 18 (2004): 131–135; M. W. McCall, "Leadership Development through Experience," *Academy of Management Executive* 18 (2004): 127–130; J. Conger, "Developing Leadership Capability: What's Inside the Black Box?" *Academy of Management Executive* 18 (2004): 136–139; D. Vera and M. Crossan, "Strategic Leadership and Organizational Learning," *Academy of Management Review* 29 (2004): 222–239.

81 D. Barry, *Dave Barry Turns 50* (New York: Ballantine, 1998), 182.

82 T. A. O'Neill and N. J. Allen, "Team Meeting Attitudes: Conceptualization and Investigation of a New Construct," *Small Group Research* 43 (2012): 186–210.

83 S. Kauffeld and N. Lehmann-Willenbrock, "Meetings Matter: Effects of Team Meetings on Team and Organizational Success," *Small Group Research* 43 (2012): 130–158; S. Boerner, M. Schaffner, and D. Gebert, "The Complementarity of Team Meetings and Cross-Functional Communication: Empirical Evidence from New Services Development Teams," *Journal of Leadership & Organizational Studies* 19 (2012): 256–266.

84 R. K. Mosvick and R. B. Nelson, *We've Got to Start Meeting Like This!* (Glenview, IL: Scott, Foresman, 1987).

85 Suggestions about organizing meeting agendas are based on M. Doyle and D. Straus, *How to Make Meetings Work* (New York: Playboy Press, 1976); Mosvick and Nelson, *We've Got to Start Meeting Like This!*; G. Lumsden and D. Lumsden, *Communicating in Groups and Teams: Sharing Leadership* (Belmont, CA: Wadsworth, 1993); D. B. Curtis, J. J. Floyd, and J. L. Winsor, *Business and Professional Communication* (New York: Harper-Collins, 1992); Romig, *Breakthrough Teamwork*; T. A. Kayser, *Mining Group Gold* (El Segundo, CA: Serif, 1990); J. E. Tropman and G. Clark Morningstar, *Meetings: How to Make Them Work for You* (New York: Van Nostrand Reinhold, 1985), 56; Beebe and Masterson, *Communicating in Small Groups*.

86 J. E. Tropman, *Making Meetings Work* (Thousand Oaks, CA: Sage, 1996).

87 J. B. Walther and U. Bunz, "The Rules of Virtual Groups: Trust, Liking, and Performance in Computer-Mediated Communication," *Journal of Communication* (December 2005): 828–846.

88 Several suggestions adapted from Harvard University Business School, *Leading Virtual Teams* (Boston: Harvard Business Press, 2010).

89 *Leading Virtual Teams.*

90 D. S. Staples and J. Webster, "Exploring Traditional and Virtual Team Members' 'Best Practices': A Social Cognitive Theory Perspective," *Small Group Research* 38 (2007): 60–97.

91 P. L. McLeod, "Distributed People and Distributed Information: Vigilant Decision-Making in Virtual Teams," *Small Group Research* 44 (2013): 627–657; B. Behring, "Extending the Functional Theory of Communication and Decision-Making in Groups to the Virtual World: A Study of the Relationship of Modality and Cultural Background to Satisfaction, Creativity, and Decision Quality in Virtual Team Interaction," Unpublished doctoral dissertation, The Pennsylvania State University, Department of Communication Arts and Sciences (2016).

92 S. Wright, "Examining the Impact of Collaboration Technology Training Support on Virtual Team Collaboration Effectiveness," Unpublished doctoral dissertation, Nova Southeastern University, Graduate School of Computer and Information Sciences (2013).

93 J. R. Mesmer-Magnus, L. A. DeChurch, M. Jimenez-Rodriguez, and J. Wildman, "A Meta-Analytic Investigation of Virtuality and Information Sharing in Teams," *Organizational Behavior and Human Decision Processes* 115 (2011): 214–225.

94 See J. A. Bonito, "A Longitudinal Social Relations Analysis of Participation in Small Groups," *Human Communication Research* 32 (2006): 302–321; M. W. Kramer, P. J. Benoit, M. A. Dixon, and J. Benoit-Bryan, "Group Processes in a Teaching Renewal Retreat: Communication Function and Dialectal Tensions," *Southern Communication Journal* 72 (2007): 145–168; J. A. Bonito, M. H. DeCamp, and E. K. Ruppel, "The Process of Information Sharing in Small Groups: Application of a Local Model," *Communication Monographs* 75 (2008): 136–157.

95 See D. S. Gouran, "Variables Related to Consensus in Group Discussions of Questions of Policy," *Speech Monographs* 36 (1969): 385–391; T. J. Knutsun, "An Experimental Study of the Effects of Orientation Behavior on Small Group Consensus," *Speech Monographs* 39 (1972): 159–165; A. Kline, "Orientation and Group Consensus," *Central States Speech Journal* 23 (1972): 44–47.

96 J. Wildman and W. L. Bedwell, "Practicing What We Preach: Teaching Teams Using Validated Team Science," *Small Group Research* 44 (2013): 381–394.

97 S. A. Beebe and J. K. Barge, "Evaluating Group Discussion," in *Small Group Communication: Theory & Practice*, edited by R. Y. Hirokawa, R. S. Cathcart, L. A. Samovar, and L. D. Henman (Los Angeles: Roxbury, 2003).

Chapter 11

1 G. Bodie, "A Racing Heart, Rattling Knees, and Ruminative Thoughts: Defining, Explaining, and Treating Public Speaking Anxiety," *Communication Education* 59 (2010): 70–105.

2 S. Booth-Butterfield, "Instructional Interventions for Reducing Situational Anxiety and Avoidance," *Communication Education* 37 (1988): 214–223.

3 K. Dwyer and M. Davidson, "Is Public Speaking Really More Feared Than Death?" *Communication Research Reports* 29 (April–June 2012): 99–107; survey conducted by R. H. Bruskin and Associates, *Spectra* 9 (December 1973), 4.

4 S. Campbell and J. Larson, "Public Speaking Anxiety: Comparing Face-to-Face and Web-Based Speeches," *Journal of Instructional Pedagogies* 10 (April 2013), 1–12.

5 A. Bippus and J. Daly, "What Do People Think Causes Stage Fright? Naïve Attributions About the Reasons for Public-Speaking Anxiety," *Communication Education* 48 (1999): 63–72; G. D. Bodie, "A Racing Heart, Rattling Knees, and Ruminative Thoughts: Defining and Explaining Public Speaking Anxiety," *Communication Education* 59 (2010): 70–105; J. Pearson, L. DeWitt, J. Child, D. Kahl, and V. Dandamudi, "Facing the Fear: An Analysis of Speech-Anxiety Content in Public-Speaking Textbooks," *Communication Research Reports* 24 (2007): 159–168; M. Beatty, J. McCroskey, and A. D. Heisel, "Communication Apprehension as Temperamental Expression: A Communibiological Paradigm," *Communication Monographs* 65 (1998): 197–219; Y. Lin and A. Rancer, "Sex Differences in Intercultural Communication Apprehension, Ethnocentrism, and Intercultural

Willingness to Communicate," *Psychological Reports* 92 (2003): 195–200; S. Shimotsu and T. P. Mottet, "The Relationships Among Perfectionism, Communication Apprehension, and Temperament," *Communication Research Reports* 26, 3 (2009): 188–197.

6 The sample speech referenced in this chapter is adapted from D. Reyes, "The Health Risks of Soft Drinks," prepared for Public Speaking at Texas State University, Fall 2016.

7 Pearson et al., "Facing the Fear: An Analysis of Speech-Anxiety Content in Public-Speaking Textbooks"; Bodie, "A Racing Heart, Rattling Knees, and Ruminative Thoughts: Defining and Explaining Public Speaking Anxiety"; see also: K. H. White, M. C. Howard, B. Zhong, J. A. Soto, C. R. Perez, E. A. Lee, N. A. Dawson-Andoh and M. R. Minnick, "The Communication Anxiety Regulation Scale: Development and Initial Validation," *Communication Quarterly* 63 (2015): 23–43.

8 A. Finn, C. Sawyer, and P. Schrodt, "Examining the Effect of Exposure Therapy on Public Speaking State Anxiety," *Communication Education* 58 (2009): 92–109.

9 A. Goberman, S. Hughes, and T. Haydock, "Acoustic Characteristics of Public Speaking: Anxiety and Practice Effects," *Speech Communication* 53 (2011), 875; K. Savitsky and T. Gilovich, "The Illusion of Transparency and the Alleviation of Speech Anxiety," *Journal of Experimental Social Psychology* 39 (2003): 618–625.

10 K. Dwyer and D. Fus, "Perceptions of Communication Competence, Self-Efficacy, and Trait Communication Apprehension: Is There an Impact on Basic Course Success?" *Communication Research Reports* 19 (2002): 29–37.

11 C. Berger, "Speechlessness: Causal Attributions, Emotional Features, and Social Consequences," *Journal of Language and Social Psychology* 23 (2004): 147–179; M. Booth-Butterfield, "Stifle or Stimulate? The Effects of Communication Task Structure on Apprehensive and Non-Apprehensive Students," *Communication Education* 35 (1986): 337–348.

12 J. Ayres, "Speech Preparation Processes and Speech Apprehension," *Communication Education* 45 (July 1996): 228–235.

13 N. Greengold and E. Grodziak, "Making Smart Use of Smart Phones to Improve Public Speaking," *Journal of Technology Integration in the Classroom* 5 (Spring 2013), 14.

14 A. Brooks, "Get Excited: Reappraising Pre-performance Anxiety as Excitement," *Journal of Experimental Psychology* 143 (June 2014): 1144–1158.

15 S. McCullough, S. Russell, R. Behnke, C. Sawyer, and P. Witt, "Anticipatory Public Speaking State Anxiety as a Function of Body Sensations and State of Mind," *Communication Quarterly* 54 (2006): 101–109; P. Witt, K. Brown, J. Roberts, J. Weisel, C. Sawyer, and R. Behnke, "Somatic Anxiety Patterns Before, During, and After Giving a Public Speech," *Southern Communication Journal* 71 (2006): 87–100.

16 K. Macklin, "Speak Easier," *Yoga Journal* 245 (March 2012), 28.

17 P. Addison, E. Clay, S. Xie, C. Sawyer, and R. Behnke, "Worry as a Function of Public Speaking State Anxiety Type," *Communication Research Reports* 16 (2003): 125–131; D. Duff, T. Levine, M. Beatty, J. Woolbright, and H. Park, "Testing Public Anxiety Treatments Against a Credible Placebo Control," *Communication Education* 56 (2007): 72–88.

18 Addison et al., "Worry as a Function of Public Speaking State Anxiety Type."

19 K. Hunter, J. Westwick, and L. Haleta, "Assessing Success: The Impacts of a Fundamentals of Speech Course on Decreasing Public Speaking Anxiety," *Communication Education* 63 (April 2014): 124–135.

20 L. Tracy, "Taming Hostile Audiences," *Vital Speeches of the Day* 71.10 (2005).

21 L. Zanteson, "Building a Career Through Public Speaking," *Today's Dietician* (August 2014), 39.

22 Adapted from J. Boyle, "Spyware Stalking: Time to Take Back the Technology," *Winning Orations 2015* (Mankato, MN: Interstate Oratorical Association, 2015), 32–34.

23 J. Humphrey, "Taking the Stage: How Women Can Achieve a Leadership Presence," *Vital Speeches of the Day* 67.14 (2001).

24 "African 'Fairy Circles' May Be by Termites," *Austin American-Statesman* (January 19, 2017), A2.

25 Adapted from Samantha Begley, "Libraries Without Borders," *Winning Orations 2015* (Mankato, MN: Interstate Oratorical Association, 2015), 67–69.

26 "Refugee Population by Country or Territory of Origin," *World Bank*, 2016, worldbank.org. *24/7 Wall Street*, September 21, 2015, *247wallst.com*.

27 R. Setoodeh, "My Favorite Mistake" (Interview with Ann Curry), *Newsweek* (June 5, 2011).

28 J. Gottfried, M. Barthel, and A. Mitchell, "Trump, Clinton Voters Divided in Their Main Source for Election News," *PewResearchCenter Journalism & Media*, January 18, 2017, pewresearch.org.

29 G. W. Bush, State of the Union address, January 28, 2008, *Vital Speeches of the Day* 74.3 (March 2008).

30 M. Sanchez, "Diplomatic Immunity Unjustified," *Winning Orations 1996* (Mankato, MN: Interstate Oratorical Association, 1996), 66.

31 M. Limon and D. Kazoleas, "A Comparison of Exemplar and Statistical Evidence in Reducing Counter-Arguments and Responses to a Message," *Communication Research Reports* 21 (2004): 291–298.

32 D. Lessing, "On Not Winning the Nobel Prize," *Vital Speeches of the Day* 74.2 (2008).

33 B. Lindsay, "Exposing the Truth Behind the Walls of Solitary Confinement: A Tribute to Kalief Browder," *Winning Orations 2016* (Mankato, MN: Interstate Oratorical Association, 2016), 99.

34 V. Scott, "When We Fight the Wrong Enemy," *Winning Orations 2016* (Mankato, MN: Interstate Oratorical Association, 2016), 60.

35 B. Obama, "The Last of the Founding Generation Is Gone," *Vital Speeches of the Day* 82.12 (2016).

36 S. Sandberg, "You Will Be Defined by Not Just What you Achieve, But by How You Survive," *Vital Speeches of the Day* 82.8 (2016).

37 E. Holcomb, "Domestic Abuse: No Shelter from the Storm," *Winning Orations 2016* (Mankato, MN: Interstate Oratorical Association, 2016), 51.

38 J. Sweeney, "Fairness and Economic Equality," *Vital Speeches of the Day* 74.5 (2008).

39 K. Huber, "Things Don't Happen for a Reason. But They Do Often Happen Because Nobody Has Yet Found a Better Way," *Vital Speeches of the Day* 82.8 (2016).

40 I. Ruiz, "Indonesian Palm Oil: A Persuasive Speech," *Winning Orations 2016* (Mankato, MN: Interstate Oratorical Association, 2016), 14.

41 J. Pruitt, "College Credit Card Crisis," *Winning Orations 1996* (Mankato, MN: Interstate Oratorical Association, 1996), 26.

42 R. Brown, "Seven Ways of Looking at a Crisis," *Vital Speeches of the Day* 76.6 (2010).

43 See D. A. Lieberman, *Public Speaking in the Multicultural Environment* 2e (Boston: Allyn & Bacon, 1997).

44 J. T. Masterson and N. Watson, "The Effects of Culture on Preferred Speaking Style," paper presented at the meeting of the Speech Communication Association, November 1979.

45 N. Norton, "Beyond Flint: The Poison in Our Pipes," *Winning Orations 2016* (Mankato, MN: Interstate Oratorical Association, 2016), 77.

Chapter 12

1 J. Pearson, J. Child, and D. Kahl Jr., "Preparation Meeting Opportunity: How Do College Students Prepare for Public Speeches?" *Communication Quarterly* 54 (August 2006): 351–366.

2 A. Rynne, "How to Build a Perfectly Published Content Sandwich [Infographic]," *LinkedIn Marketing Solutions Blog*, February 7, 2017, https://business.linkedin.com/marketing-solutions/blog/publishing-on-linkedin/2017/

how-to-build-a-perfectly-published-content-sandwich–infographic.

3 Adapted from P. Steiger, "A Closer Look: Three Golden Ages of Journalism?" *Vital Speeches of the Day* 80.4 (2014).

4 Adapted from A. Zerull, "Resident Evil: How America's Teaching Hospitals Neglect the Care of Our Caregivers," *Winning Orations 2016* (Mankato, MN: Interstate Oratorical Association, 2016), 161–166.

5 Adapted from R. Tabor, "Open Secret in Southeast Asia's Waters," *Winning Orations 2016* (Mankato, MN: Interstate Oratorical Association, 2016), 112–116.

6 D. A. Lieberman, *Public Speaking in the Multicultural Environment* 2e (Boston: Allyn & Bacon, 1997), 23.

7 Lieberman, *Public Speaking in the Multicultural Environment.*

8 C. Flaherty, "Demanding 10 Percent," *Inside Higher Ed*, November 30, 2015, www.insidehighered.com.

9 K. Huber, "Things Don't Happen For a Reason. But They Do Often Happen Because Nobody Has Yet Found a Better Way," *Vital Speeches of the Day* 82.8 (2016).

10 A. Kolousek, "Hidden Home School Abuse: Denying Children a Safe Place to Call Home," *Winning Orations 2016* (Mankato, MN: Interstate Oratorical Association, 2016), 35–36.

11 C. Kay, "The U.S. Chamber of Commerce: Commerce or Coerce?" *Winning Orations 2016* (Mankato, MN: Interstate Oratorical Association, 2016), 32.

12 G. Hildebrand, "Cinderella," Texas State University student speech, 2013.

13 K. Kane, "Prescription Drug Pricing: America's Sanctioned Drug Problem," *Winning Orations 2016* (Mankato, MN: Interstate Oratorical Association, 2016), 182.

14 P. Manning, "You Don't Have to Wonder if I'll Miss It," *Vital Speeches of the Day* 82.5 (2016).

15 Z. Smith, "Being with People, Doing for People, It Will Bring You Joy," *Vital Speeches of the Day* 82.8 (2016).

16 C. Ghosn, "Rather Than Fear the Disruption, the Auto Industry Must Embrace It," *Vital Speeches of the Day* 82.5 (2016).

17 R. Brown, "Mental Illness Is Not a Learning Disability," *Winning Orations 2015* (Mankato, MN: Interstate Oratorical Association, 2015), 41.

18 A. Watson, "Post-Traumatic Stress Disorder: Our Soldiers' Next War," *Winning Orations 2007* (Mankato, MN: Interstate Oratorical Association, 2007), 81.

19 Watson, "Post-Traumatic Stress Disorder."

20 A. Lincoln, "Gettysburg Address," delivered at Gettysburg, PA, November 19, 1863, *Douglass Archives of American Public Address,* August 19, 1998, douglass.speech.nwu.edu/linc_b33.htm.

21 D. MacArthur, "Farewell to the Cadets," address delivered at West Point, May 12, 1962, in *Contemporary American Speeches* 7e, edited by R. L. Johannesen, R. R. Allen, and W. A. Linkugel (Dubuque, IA: Kendall/Hunt, 1992), 393.

22 P. Sterman, "The New World Champion of Public Speaking," *Toastmasters* November 2016.

23 K. King, "Bystander Intervention: Addressing the Epidemic of Sexual Assault," *Winning Orations 2016* (Mankato, MN: Interstate Oratorical Association, 2016), 213.

24 S. Acevedo, "The Future for Girl Scouts in America and Abroad," *Vital Speeches of the Day* 82.10 (2016).

25 The preparation outline and speaking notes in this chapter are adapted from a speech by D. Reyes, "The Health Risks of Soft Drinks," prepared for Public Speaking at Texas State University, Fall 2016.

Chapter 13

1 P. Heinbert, "Relationship of Content and Delivery to General Effectiveness," *Speech Monographs* 30 (1963): 105–107.

2 A. Mehrabian, *Nonverbal Communication* (Hawthorne, NY: Aldine, 1972).

3 J. Detz, "Delivery Plus Content Equals Successful Presentation," *Communication World* 15 (1998): 34.

4 P. Begala, "Flying Solo," PBS, *The Clinton Years: Anecdotes*, 2000, www.pbs.org.

5 L. White and L. Messer, "An Analysis of Interstate Speeches: Are They Structurally Different?" *National Forensic Journal* 21.2 (2003): 15.

6 G. Orwell, "Politics and the English Language," in *About Language*, edited by W. H. Roberts and G. Turgeson (Boston: Houghton Mifflin, 1986), 282.

7 D. Hersman, "I Saw a Woman Today," *Vital Speeches of the Day* 80.5 (2014): 151.

8 M. Klepper, *I'd Rather Die Than Give a Speech* (New York: Carol Publishing Group, 1994), 45.

9 J. Lewis, "This Is a Great Achievement," *Vital Speeches of the Day* 82.11 (2016): 348; S. Acevedo, "The Future for Girl Scouts in America and Abroad," *Vital Speeches of the Day* 82.10 (2016): 312; K. Burns, "You Are, Whether You Are Yet Aware of It or Not, Charged with Saving Our Union," *Vital Speeches of the Day* 82.8 (2016): 223.

10 B. Moyers, "What Adam Said to Eve," prepared remarks for the annual conference of the Association for Education in Journalism and Mass Communication, Washington, DC, *PBS*, August 8, 2007, www.pbs.org.

11 D. Trump, inaugural address, January 20, 2017, www .whitehouse.gov

12 D. Trump, "Time to Restore the Bonds Between Citizens," *Vital Speeches of the Day* 83.1 (2017): 8.

13 B. Obama, farewell address to the American people, delivered in Chicago, IL, *The New York Times*, January 10, 2017, http://nyti .ms/2jsJlmM

14 J. Biden, remarks commemorating the fiftieth anniversary of Kennedy's "Moon Shot" Speech, delivered at the John F. Kennedy Library and Museum, Boston, MA, *White House*, May 25, 2011, www.whitehouse.gov

15 J. Huber, "Things Don't Happen for a Reason. But They Do Often Happen Because Nobody Has Yet Found a Better Way," *Vital Speeches of the Day* 82.8 (2016): 227.

16 M. Kent, "The Role of Global Companies in Bridging Wealth Disparity," *Vital Speeches of the Day* 82.10 (2016): 315.

17 S. A. Beebe, "Eye Contact: A Nonverbal Determinant of Speaker Credibility," *Speech Teacher* 23 (1974): 21–25; S. A. Beebe, "Effects of Eye Contact, Posture and Vocal Inflection upon Credibility and Comprehension," *Australian Scan Journal of Nonverbal Communication* 7–8 (1979–1980): 57–70; M. Cobin, "Response to Eye Contact," *Quarterly Journal of Speech* 48 (1963): 415–419.

18 Beebe, "Eye Contact."

19 S. Campbell and J. Larson, "Public Speaking Anxiety: Comparing Face-to-Face and Web-Based Speeches," *Journal of Instructional Pedagogies* 10 (April 2013): 4.

20 E. Adler, "Gestures May Give You a Hand with Speaking," *Austin American-Statesman* (November 25, 1998): E6.

21 J. C. McCroskey, V. P. Richmond, A. Sallinen, J. M. Fayer, and R. A. Barraclough, "A Cross-Cultural and Multi-Behavioral Analysis of the Relationship between Nonverbal Immediacy and Teacher Evaluation," *Communication Education* 44 (1995): 281–290.

22 M. J. Beatty, "Some Effects of Posture on Speaker Credibility," library paper, Central Missouri State University, Warrensburg, MO, 1973.

23 P. Ekman, W. V. Friesen, and S. S. Tomkins, "Facial Affect Scoring Technique: A First Validity Study," *Semiotica* 3 (1971): 37–58.

24 P. Ekman and W. Friesen, *Unmasking the Face* (Englewood Cliffs, NJ: Prentice Hall, 1975).

25 M. M. Gill, "Accents and Stereotypes: Their Effect on Perceptions of Teachers and Lecture Comprehension," *Journal of Applied Communication Research* 22 (1994): 348–361.

26 E. Bohn and D. Jabusch, "The Effect of Four Methods of Instruction on the Use of Visual Aids in Speeches," *Western Journal of Speech Communication* 46 (1982): 253–265.

27 S. Greenwood, A. Perrin, and M. Duggan, *Social Media Update 2016*, November 11, 2016, www.pewresearch.org

28 Greenwood et al., *Social Media Update 2016*.

29 N. Norton, "Beyond Flint: The Poison in Our Pipes," *Winning Orations 2016* (Mankato, MN: Interstate Oratorical Association, 2016), 79.

30 A. Wilson, "In Defense of Rhetoric," *The Toastmaster* 70.2 (2004): 11.

31 Detz, "Delivery plus Content Equals Successful Presentation."

32 S. Cain, "10 Public Speaking Tips for Introverts: Introverts Can Seize the Microphone—and Bring the House Down," *Psychology Today*, 25 July 2011, www.psychologytoday.com

33 T. Smith and A. B. Frymier, "Get 'Real': Does Practicing Speeches before an Audience Improve Performance?" *Communication Quarterly* 54 (2006): 111–125.

34 "Presidential Seal Falls Off Podium as Obama Speaks," *Washington Times*, October 6, 2010, www.washingtontimes.com

35 J. Masterson, S. Beebe, and N. Watson, *Invitation to Effective Speech Communication* (Glenview, IL: Scott, Foresman, 1989), 4.

Chapter 14

1 J. R. Johnson and N. Szczupakiewicz, "The Public Speaking Course: Is It Preparing Students with Work-Related Public Speaking Skills?" *Communication Education* 36 (1987): 131–137.

2 L. Lefever, *The Art of Explanation* (New Jersey: John Wiley & Sons, 2013), 10.

3 For an excellent discussion of teaching someone to perform a skill, especially a social skill, see M. Argyle, *The Psychology of Interpersonal Behavior* (London: Penguin, 1990).

4 G. K. Chesterton, "On Mr. Rudyard Kipling and Making the World Small," *Heretics*, 1905, *Project Gutenberg*, http://www.gutenberg.org/files/470/470-h/470-h.htm#chap03.

5 A. Slagell, "Why Should You Use a Clear Pattern of Organization? Because It Works," *Communication Teacher* 27.4 (October 2013): 200.

6 For an excellent discussion of strategies for informing others, see K. E. Rowan, "A New Pedagogy for Explanatory Public Speaking: Why Arrangement Should Not Substitute for Invention," *Communication Education* 44 (1995): 236–250.

7 J. Chesebro, "Effects of Teacher Clarity and Nonverbal Immediacy on Student Learning, Receiver Apprehension, and Affect," *Communication Education* 52 (Apr. 2003): 135–147.

8 J. Zimmer, "Phrases to Avoid on Stage," *Toastmaster* (May 2016): 9.

9 E. Holt, "Gone but Not Forgotten: Desegregation and the Demise of Black-Owned Businesses in San Marcos," lecture delivered at the San Marcos, Texas, Public Library, February 16, 2017.

10 This suggestion is based on an excellent review of the literature found in Rowan, "A New Pedagogy for Explanatory Public Speaking."

11 M. Groover, "Learning to Communicate: The Importance of Speech Education in Public Schools," in *Winning Orations 1984* (Mankato, MN: Interstate Oratorical Association, 1984), 7.

12 R. Radice, "How to Put Together a Killer Social Media Presentation," *Sprout Social*, November 2, 2016, https://medium.com/sprout-social/.

13 See, for example, L. Rehling, "Teaching in a High-Tech Conference Room: Academic Adaptations and Workplace Simulations," *Journal of Business and Technical Communication* 19 (2005): 98–113; M. Patterson et al., "Effects of Communication Aids and Strategies on Cooperative Teaching," *Journal of Educational Psychology* 84 (1992): 453–461.

14 M. Klepper and R. Gunther, *I'd Rather Die Than Give a Speech* (New York: Carol Publishing Group, 1995).

15 Our discussion of using humor is adapted from Klepper and Gunther, *I'd Rather Die Than Give a Speech*.

16 J. Meyer, "Humor as a Double-Edged Sword: Four Functions of Humor in Communication," *Communication Theory* 10 (2000): 311.

17 Klepper and Gunther, *I'd Rather Die Than Give a Speech*.

18 J. Macks, *How to Be Funny* (New York: Simon & Schuster, 2003).

19 S. Beebe, T. Mottet, and K. D. Roach, *Training and Development: Communicating for Success* (Boston: Pearson, 2013); M. Knowles, *The Adult Learner: A Neglected Species* 3e (Houston: Gulf Publishing, 1990).

20 A. Armijo, "Elvis," Texas State University student speech, 2013.

Chapter 15

1 S. McLaughlin, "The Dirty Truth about Your Kitchen: Using Common Sense to Prevent Food Poisoning," in *Winning Orations 1996* (Mankato, MN: Interstate Oratorical Association, 1996), 73.

2 A. Maslow, "A Theory of Human Motivation," in *Motivation and Personality* (New York: Harper & Row, 1954), Chapter 5.

3 See K. L. Higbee, "Fifteen Years of Fear Arousal: Research on Threat Appeals, 1953–1968," *Psychological Bulletin* 72 (1969): 426–444; I. L. Janis and S. Feshback, "Effects of Fear Arousing Communications," *Journal of Abnormal and Social Psychology* 48 (1953): 78–92; P. A. Mongeau, "Another Look at Fear-Arousing Persuasive Appeals," in *Persuasion: Advances through Meta-Analysis*, edited by M. Allen and R. W. Preiss (Cresskill, NJ: Hampton Press, 1998), 65; F. A. Powell and G. R. Miller, "Social Approval and Disapproval Cues in Anxiety Arousing Situations," *Speech Monographs* 34 (1967): 152–159.

4 R. Petty and D. Wegener, "The Elaboration Likelihood Model: Current Status and Controversies," in *Dual Process Theories in Social Psychology*, edited by S. Chaiken and Y. Trope (New York: Guilford, 1999), 41–72; see also R. Petty and J. T. Cacioppo, *Communication and Persuasion: Central and Peripheral Routes to Attitude Change* (New York: Springer-Verlag, 1986).

5 E. McQuarrie and B. Phillips, "Indirect Persuasion in Advertising: How Consumers Process Metaphors Presented in Pictures and Words," *Journal of Advertising* 34.2 (Summer 2005): 7–20.

6 T. Chmielewski, "Applying the Elaboration Likelihood Model to Voting," *International Journal of Interdisciplinary Social Sciences* 6.10 (2012): 33–47.

7 Aristotle, *Rhetoric*, translated by L. Cooper (New York: Appleton-Century-Crofts, 1960).

8 For a discussion of the effects of both verbal and nonverbal messages on the persuasiveness of a speech, see N. Jackob et al., "The Effects of Verbal and Nonverbal Elements in Persuasive Communication: Findings from Two Multi-Method Experiments," *Communications: The European Journal of Communication Research* 36 (2011): 245–271.

9 A. Bogeajis, "The Danger of Child Safety Seats: Why Aren't They Safe?" in Winning Orations 1996 (Mankato, MN: Interstate Oratorical Association, 1996), 10.

10 N. Barton, "The Death of Reading," in *Winning Orations 2004* (Mankato, MN: Interstate Oratorical Association, 2004), 33–35.

11 S. Groom, "Hope for Foster Care," in *Winning Orations 2004*, 60–62.

12 Adapted from L. Ford and S. Smith, "Memorability and Persuasiveness of Organ Donation Message Strategies," *American Behavioral Scientist* 34 (1991): 695.

13 D. Ehninger, B. Gronbeck, R. McKerrow, and A. Monroe, *Principles and Types of Speech Communication* (Glenview, IL: Scott, Foresman, 1986), 15.

14 The illustrations for the steps of the motivated sequence are adapted from S. Agha, "The International Landmine Crisis," prepared for the Interstate Oratorical Association competition, Texas State University, Spring 2011.

15 A. Quagliata, "Move Your Audience to Action: Using YouTube to Teach Persuasion," *Communication Teacher* 28 (April 2014): 183–187.

16 D. C. Bryant, "Rhetoric: Its Functions and Its Scope," *Quarterly Journal of Speech* 39 (1953): 26.

17 B. Sosnowchick, "The Cries of American Ailments," in *Winning Orations 2000* (Mankato, MN: Interstate Oratorical Association, 2000), 114.

18 G. Ficca, et al., "Effects of Different Types of Hand Gestures in Persuasive Speech on Receivers' Evaluations," *Language and Cognitive Processes* 24 (2009): 239–266.

19 B. Bergeron, "Private Ambulances," prepared for Individual Events/Persuasive Speaking competition, The University of Texas, Spring 2017.

Appendix A

1 Examples from *CareerBuilder*, as cited by *Reader's Digest* (May 2008): 34.

2 Our discussion of interview questions is based on J. T. Masterson, S. A. Beebe, and N. Watson, *An Invitation to Effective Speech Communication* (Glenview, IL: Scott, Foresman, 1989). We especially acknowledge the contributions of Norm Watson to this discussion.

3 *CareerBuilder*, accessed March 21, 2008, www.CareerBuilder.com.

4 N. St. Anthony, "For Job Seekers, In-Person Networking Tops Online Path," *Austin-American Statesman*, (January 16, 2017): B5

5 This résumé and our suggestions for developing a résumé are based on the 2017 *Texas State University Career Services Manual* (San Marcos, TX: Office of Career Services, 2017).

6 These tips and suggestions are adapted from K. Hansen, "Top 10 Things Job-Seekers Need to Know about Submitting and Posting Your Resume Online," *Quintessential Careers*, accessed September 10, 2014, www.quintcareers.com/e-resumes.html. Also see K. Hansen, "Your E-Resume's File Format Aligns with Its Delivery Method," *Quintessential Careers*, accessed March 30, 2011, www.quintcareers.com/e-resume_format.html.

7 "What Everyone Should Know about Electronic Resumes (E-Resumes)," *CareerPerfect*, accessed September 11, 2014, www.careerperfect.com/tips/archives/electronic-e-resumes.

8 J. L. Winsor, D. B. Curtis, and R. D. Stephens, "National Preferences in Business and Communication Education: A Survey Update," *Journal of the Association for Communication Administration* 3 (1997): 174.

9 D. Dean, "How to Get an On-Site Interview," *Black Collegian*, Second Semester Super Issue (2010): 54.

10 *CareerBuilder*, retrieved March 21, 2008, www.CareerBuilder.com. Suggestions for managing your online persona were taken from A. Simmons, "How to Click and Clean," *Reader's Digest* (April 2008): 154–159.

11 G. Yilmaz and J. M. Q. Johnson, "Tweeting Facts, Facebooking Lives: The Influence of Language Use and Modality on Online Source Credibility," *Communication Research Reports* 33,2 (2016): 137–144.

12 C. Purdy, "The Biggest Lies Job Seekers Tell on Their Resumes—and How They Get Caught," *Monster*, accessed March 31, 2013, career-advice.monster.com/resumes-cover-letters/resume-writing-tips/the-truth-about-resume-lies-hot-jobs/article.aspx.

13 Purdy, "The Biggest Lies Job Seekers Tell on Their Resumes."

14 A. Klein, "How to Clean Up Your Facebook Before You Apply for a Job or Internship," *Job Advice @Hercampus*, accessed February 17, 2017, www.hercampus.com/career/job-advice/how-clean-your-facebook-you-apply-job-or-internship.

15 K. Kasper, "Jobvite Social Recruiting Survey Finds Over 90% of Employers Will Use Social Recruiting," *Jobvite*, accessed February 17, 2017, www.jobvite.com/press-releases/2012/jobvite-social-recruiting-survey-finds-90-employers-will-use-social-recruiting-2012.

16 L. Herman, "How to Clean Up Your Social Media During the Job Search," *The Muse*, accessed February 17, 2017, https://www.themuse.com/advice/how-to-clean-up-your-social-media-during-the-job-search.

17 These tips were compiled from: L. Herman, "How to Clean Up Your Social Media During the Job Search," *The Muse*. www.themuse.com/advice/how-to-clean-up-your-social-media-during-the-job-search; The Glassdoor Team, "How to Clean Up Your Social Media Presence and Get a Job," *Glassdoor*, accessed February 17, 2017, www.glassdoor.com/blog/clean-social-media-presence-job; A. Klein, "How to Clean Up Your Facebook Before You Apply for a Job or Internship," *Job Advice @Hercampus*, accessed February 17, 2017, www.hercampus.com/career/job-advice/how-clean-your-facebook-you-apply-job-or-internship; K. Kasper, "Jobvite Social Recruiting Survey Finds Over 90% of Employers Will Use Social Recruiting," *Jobvite*, accessed February 17, 2017, www.jobvite.com/press-releases/2012/jobvite-social-recruiting-survey-finds-90-employers-will-use-social-recruiting-2012.

18 M. Minto, "The Relative Effects of Content and Vocal Delivery during a Simulated Employment Interview," *Communication Research Reports* 13 (1996): 225–238.

19 Adapted from M. S. Hanna and G. Wilson, *Communicating in Business and Professional Settings* (New York: McGraw-Hill, 1991), 263–265.

20 *Texas State University Career Services Manual*.

Appendix B

1 C. Alvarez, "Audism," prepared for Individual Events/Informative Speaking competition, The University of Texas, Spring 2017.

2 C. Hanzlicek, "Doctors and Sex Abuse," prepared for Individual Events/Persuasive Speaking competition, The University of Texas, Spring 2017.

Credits

Chapter 1 Page 1: Michel de Montaigne, "Of Vanity," in *The Essays of Michel de Montaigne*, translated by Charles Cotton, edited by William Carew Hazlitt, 1877, www.gutenberg.org/files/3600/3600-h/3600-h.htm.; **p. 3:** J. C. Humes, *The Sir Winston Method: The Five Secrets of Speaking the Language of Leadership* (New York: William Morrow, 1991).; **p. 3:** J. H. McConnell, *Are You Communicating? You Can't Manage Without It* (New York: McGraw-Hill, 1995).; **p. 3:** Hart Research Associates, "Falling Short? College Learning and Career Success," *Association of American Colleges and Universities*, January 20, 2015, accessed February 12, 2017, www.aacu.org; Hart Research Associates, "Employer Priorities for Most Important College Learning Outcomes," *Association of American Colleges and Universities*, January 20, 2015, accessed February 12, 2017, www.aacu.org; "Staffing in Special Markets," *Society for Human Resources Management*, September 3, 2016, accessed February 12, 2017, www.shrm.org. Also see: J. L. Winsor, D. Curtis, and R. D. Stephens, "National Preferences in Business and Communication Education: A Survey Update," *Journal of the Association of Communication Administration* 3 (1997): 170–179. For a summary of the values and virtues of studying communication, see S. P. Morreale and J. C. Pearson, "Why Communication Education Is Important: The Centrality of the Discipline in the 21st Century," *Communication Education* 57.2 (2008): 224–240; also see S. P. Morreale, D. W. Worley, and B. Hugenberg, "The Basic Communication Course at Two- and Four-Year U.S. Colleges and Universities: Study VIII—The 40th Anniversary," Communication Education 59.4 (2010): 405–430; Hart Research Associates, "Raising the Bar: Employers' Views on College Learning in the Wake of the Economic Downturn," Washington, DC, Association of American Colleges and Universities (January 10, 2010); D. Sellnow, "Integrated Composition and Communication: Addressing the Needs of the 21st Century," paper presented at the Rhetoric Society of America annual conference, Minneapolis, Minnesota (May 2010).; **p. 3:** Value Investors Portal, "Warren Buffet on Communication Skills," YouTube, December 6, 2010, accessed May 14, 2013, www.youtube.com/watch?v=tpgcEYpLzP0.; **p. 4:** Virginia Satir, *Peoplemaking*, Science and Behavior Books, 1972: 30.; **p. 7:** D. Barnlund, *Interpersonal Communication: Survey and Studies* (Boston: Houghton Mifflin, 1968).; **p. 7:** O. Wiio, *Wiio's Laws—and Some Others* (Espoo, Finland: Welin-Goos, 1978).; **p. 8:** S. B. Shimanoff, *Communication Rules: Theory and Research* (Beverly Hills, CA: Sage, 1980).; **p. 9:** H. Lasswell, "The Structure and Function of Communication in Society," in *The Communication of Ideas*, edited by L. Bryson (New York: Institute for Religious and Social Studies, 1948): 37.; **p. 12:** See V. E. Cronen, W. B. Pearce, and L. M. Harris, "The Coordinated Management of Meaning: A Theory of Communication," in *Human Communication Theory: Comparative Essays*, edited by F. E. X. Dance (New York: Harper & Row, 1982): 61–89.; **p. 12:** This section is based on Masterson, Beebe, and Watson, *Invitation to Effective Speech Communication*. We are especially indebted to J. T. Masterson for this discussion.; **p. 13:** Clifford G. Christians and Michael

Traber, *Communication Ethics and Universal Values*, Sage Publications, 1997.; **p. 14:** "NCA Credo for Communication Ethics," National Communication Association, 1999, accessed June 27, 2001, www.natcom.org/conferences/Ethicslethicsconfcred099.htm.; **p. 15:** Anderson, "6 facts about Americans and their smartphones," Pew Research Center (April 5, 2015), www.pewresearch.org/fact-tank/2015/04/01/6-facts-about-americans-and-their-smartphones.; **p. 17:** S. Turkle, *Alone Together: Why We Expect More from Technology and Less from Each Other*, Readhowyouwant.com, 2011.; **p. 21:** Daniel Quinn, *My Ishmael*, (New York: Bantam Books, 1996).; **p. 22:** Robert Fulghum, *All I Really Need to Know I Learned in Kindergarten* (New York: Ballantine Books, 1988).

Chapter 2 Page 27: L. W. Clark, *Women, women, women* (1977), Drake Publishers: 160.; **p. 28:** D. W. Johnson, *Reaching Out: Interpersonal Effectiveness and Self-Actualization* 11e (Boston: Pearson, 2012): 51.; **p. 28:** S. R. Covey, *The Seven Habits of Highly Effective People*, Anniversary Edition (New York: Simon & Schuster, 2013): 74.; **p. 29:** Benjamin Franklin, *Poor Richard's Almanac 1850–52*, J. Doggett Jr., 1849.; **p. 29:** S. E. Wood, E. Green Wood, and D. Boyd, *Mastering the World of Psychology* 6e (Boston: Pearson, 2017): 115.; **p. 30:** P. C. McGraw, *Life Strategies Self-Discovery Journal: Finding What Matters Most for You*, Hyperion Books, 2001.; **p. 30:** Karen Horney, *Neurosis and Human Growth: The Struggle Toward Self-Realization*, Norton, 1991: 17.; **p. 31:** G. Bukobza, "The Epistemological Basis of Selfhood," *New Ideas in Psychology* 25 (2007): 39.; **p. 34:** G. Steinem, *Revolution from Within: A Book of Self-Esteem* (Boston: Little, Brown, 1993): 26.; **p. 44:** D. T. Kenrick, S. L. Neuberg, and R. B. Cialdini, *Social Psychology: Goals in Interaction* 6e (Boston: Pearson, 2014): 360.; **pp. 46–47:** M. Rosenberg, *Society and the Adolescent Self-Image*, rev. ed. (Middletown, CT: Wesleyan University Press, 1989), reprinted with permission, retrieved from www.bsos.umd.edu.

Chapter 3 Page 49: *The Atlantic Monthly* (Atlantic Monthly Company 1866), 18: 690.; **p. 53:** *Oxford Desk Dictionary and Thesaurus, American Edition* (New York: Oxford University Press, 2007).; **p. 54:** D. K. Ivy, *GenderSpeak: Communicating in a Gendered World* 6e (Dubuque, IA: Kendall Hunt, 2017).; **p. 55:** E. Sher, *The Emotionary: A Dictionary of Words That Don't Exist for Feelings That Do* (New York: Razor-bill/Penguin Random House, 2016), 57.; **p. 57:** Table based on information from M. Anderson and S. Feinberg, 2000, "Race and Ethnicity and the Controversy over the U.S. Census," *Current Sociology* 48.3: 87–110; National Research Council, *Measuring Racial Discrimination* (Washington, DC: National Academies Press, 2004); U.S. Census Bureau, 2001, "Population by Race and Hispanic or Latino Origin for All Ages and for 18 Years and Over for the United States: 2000," www.census.gov/PressRelease/www/2001/tables/st00_1.pdf; U.S. Census Bureau, 2010, *Questionnaire Reference Book* (Washington, DC: U.S. Department of Commerce, Bureau of the Census, Washington DC), retrieved from 2010census.gov. **p. 63:** L. H. Turner, "Message from the

President," *Spectra* (November 2011), accessed February 25, 2017, www.natcom.org.; **p. 65:** Dane Cook tweet on Twitter.

Chapter 4   Page 69: E. Sapir, Selected Writings of Edward Sapir in *Language, Culture and Personality*, University of California Press, 1985, pp. 556/617.; **p. 82:** John F. Kennedy Inaugural Address, January 20, 1961.; **p. 82:** Franklin D. Roosevelt.; **p. 82:** Dr. Martin Luther King Jr.; **p. 82:** Richard M. Nixon.; **p. 82:** Ronald Reagan.; **p. 85:** P. A. Andersen, *Nonverbal Communication: Forms and Functions* 2e (Long Grove, IL: Waveland, 2008): 168.

Chapter 5   Page 91: Dr. Joyce Brothers as quoted in *Wisdom for the Soul: Five Millennia of Prescriptions for Spiritual Healing* (2006) by Larry Chang.; **p. 94:** D. Mount and A. Mattila, "Last Chance to Listen: Listening Behaviors and Their Effect on Call Center Satisfaction," *Journal of Hospitality & Tourism Research* 26.2 (2002).; **p. 98:** W. Kelly, *Pogo: We Have Met the Enemy and He Is Us* (Simon and Schuster, 1972).; **p. 99:** J. L. Gonzalez-Balado, ed., *Mother Teresa: In My Own Words* (New York: Gramercy Books, 1997).; **p. 111:** Antoine de Saint-Exupéry/Penguin Random House.; **p. 111:** H. J. M. Nouwen, "Listening as Spiritual Hospitality," in *Bread for the Journey*.; **p. 114:** Dr. Nanette Johnson-Curiskis/ Listen, International Listening Association.

Chapter 6   Page 117: C. S. Lewis, *The Abolition of Man* (New York: Macmillan, 1947).; **p. 119:** C. S. Lewis, *The Weight of Glory*, 1949.; **p. 120:** A. C. Selbe, *Are You from Another Planet or What?* Workshop presented at the Joint Service Family Readiness Matters Conference, Phoenix, AZ (July 1999).; **p. 123–124:** Information summarized from N. Howe and W. Strauss, *Millennials Rising: The Next Great Generation* (New York: Vintage Books, 2000).; **p. 126:** U.S. Census Bureau; **p. 126:** "One in Three US Residents Member of a Minority Group," *Marketing Charts*, May 21, 2007, accessed September 25, 2014, www.marketingcharts.com/traditional/one-in-three-us-residents-a-member-of-a-minority-group-418.; **p. 126:** G. Hofstede, *Culture's Consequences: International Differences in Work Related Values* (Beverly Hills, CA: Sage, 1980); G. Hofstede and G. J. Hofstede, *Cultures and Organizations: Software of the Mind* 3e (New York: McGraw-Hill, 2010).; **p. 127:** C. H. Dodd, *Dynamics of Intercultural Communication* (New York: McGraw-Hill, 1998).; **p. 127:** Levine et al., "Some Conceptual and Theoretical Challenges for Cross-Cultural Communication Research in the 21st Century.; **p. 130:** G. Hofstede and G. J. Hofstede, *Cultures and Organizations: Software of the Mind* 2e (New York: McGraw-Hill, 2005).; **p. 130:** W. B. Gudykunst, *Bridging Differences: Effective Intergroup Communication* (Newbury Park, CA: Sage, 1998).; **p. 132:** Table adapted with permission from Geert Hofstede, Gert Jan Hofstede, and Michael Minkov, *Cultures and Organizations, Software of the Mind*, Third Revised Edition (New York: McGraw Hill, 2010). ISBN 0-07-166418-1 © Geert Hofstede BV.; **p. 132:** The Declaration of Independence, www.ushistory.org/declaration/document, accessed January 23, 2017.; **p. 137:** Mark Twain; **p. 137:** E. Roosevelt, as cited by Lustig and Koester, *Intercultural Competence*.; **p. 139:** André Gide.; **p. 142:** H. J. M. Nouwen, *Bread for the Journey* (New York: HarperCollins, 1997).; **pp. 142–143:** R. H. Farrell, ed., *Off the Record: The Private Papers of Harry S. Truman* (New York: Harper & Row, 1980): 310.

Chapter 7   Page 148: Ralph Waldo Emerson, *The Conduct of Life* (J. R. Osgood, 1873).; **p. 152:** A. Cooper, I. P. McLoughlin,

and K. M. Campbell, "Sexuality in Cyberspace: Update for the 21st Century," *Cyberpsychology & Behavior* 32 (2000): 521–536.; **p. 152:** L. K. Guerrero, P. A. Andersen, and W. A. Afifi, *Close Encounters: Communicating in Relationships* 5e (Los Angeles: Sage, 2017), 54.; **p. 155:** "Netflix and chill," Wikipedia, accessed March 11, 2017, en.wikipedia.org.; **p. 155:** Figure 7.1: © Pearson Education, Inc.; **p. 159:** J. Holmes, "Complimenting—A Positive Politeness Strategy," in *Language and Gender: A Reader*, edited by J. Coates (Malden, MA: Blackwell, 1998): 100–120.; **p. 159:** J. H. Harvey and A. L. Weber, *Odyssey of the Heart: Close Relationships in the 21st Century* 2e (Mahwah, NJ: Erlbaum, 2002): 105–106.; **p. 163:** Paul D. Bolls, "Understanding Emotion from a Superordinate Dimensional Perspective: A Productive Way Forward for Communication Processes and Effects Studies," *Communication Monographs* 77 (2010): 146–152.; **p. 163:** D. Hample, A. S. Richards, and C. Skubisz, "Blurting," *Communication Monographs* 80 (2013): 507.

Chapter 8   Page 168: Franklin D. Roosevelt, undelivered address prepared for Jefferson Day, April 13, 1945.; **p. 169:** H. G. Bohn.; **p. 171:** *Miami Herald* (July 9, 1982): 12A.; **p. 174:** Figure 8.1, from Steven A. Beebe, Susan J. Beebe, and Mark V. Redmond, *Interpersonal Communication: Relating to Others*, 8e, reprinted and electronically reproduced by permission of Pearson Education, Inc., Hoboken, NJ. Copyright © 2017.; **p. 176:** M. Rabbitt, "Is Infidelity Obsolete?" *Women's Health* (July/August 2010): 144.; **p. 182:** S. Morrison and P. Schrodt, "The Perceived Threat and Resolvability of Serial Arguments as Correlates of Relational Uncertainty in Romantic Relationships," *Communication Studies* 68 (2017): 56–71; A. J. Johnson and I. A. Cionea, "Serial Arguments in Interpersonal Relationships: Relational Dynamics and Interdependence," in *Communicating Interpersonal Conflict in Close Relationships*, edited by J. A. Samp (New York: Routledge, 2016), 111–127; J. L. Bevan, M. Cummings, M. L. Engert, and L. Sparks, "Romantic Serial Argument Perceived Resolvability, Goals, Rumination, and Conflict Strategy Usage: A Preliminary Longitudinal Study," *Communicating Interpersonal Conflict in Close Relationships*, 128–143; M. E. Roloff, R. M. Reznik, C. Waite Miller, and K. L. Johnson, "'I Thought We Settled This?!' Antecedents and Consequences of Resolution of an Initial Episode in a Serial Argument," *Argumentation & Advocacy* 52 (2015): 8–31; M. R. Roloff and K. L. Johnson, "Serial Arguing over the Relational Life Course: Antecedents and Consequences," in *Stability and Change in Relationships* (Cambridge, UK: Cambridge University Press, 2002), 107–128, as cited in M. R. Roloff and R. M. Reznik, "Communication During Serial Arguments," in *Studies in Applied Interpersonal Communication*, edited by M. T. Motley (Thousand Oaks, CA: Sage, 2008), 97; M. R. Roloff, "Conflict and Communication: A Roadmap through the Literature," *Managing Interpersonal Conflict*, 42–58.

Chapter 9   Page 193: Andrew Carnegie; **p. 197:** Margaret Mead quoted in Frank G. Sommers and Tana Dineen (1984) *Curing Nuclear Madness*: 158.; **p. 208:** Walter Lippmann quoted in Roger Lajoie, *Greatest. Day. Ever.: How to Make Every Day Your Greatest* (Balboa Press, 2014).

Chapter 10   Page 215: Margaret Mead quoted in Frank G. Sommers and Tana Dineen (1984) *Curing Nuclear Madness*, 158.; **p. 224:** Adapted from Julius E. Etington, *The Winning Trainer* (Houston: Gulf Publishing, 1989).; **p. 235:** Lao Tsu, from the *Tao Te Ching*, 1963: 77.; **p. 235:** D. Barry, *Dave Barry Turns 50* (New York: Ballantine, 1998), 182.

Chapter 11   Page 246: Franklin D. Roosevelt, "Campaign Address at Cleveland, Ohio," November 2, 1940, online by Gerhard Peters and John T. Woolley, The American Presidency Project, www.presidency.ucsb.edu/ws/?pid=15893.; **p. 250:** A. Brooks, "Get Excited: Reappraising Pre-performance Anxiety as Excitement," *Journal of Experimental Psychology* 143 (June 2014): 1144–1158.; **p. 254:** L. Zanteson, "Building a Career Through Public Speaking," *Today's Dietician* (August 2014), 39.; **p. 255:** Adapted from J. Boyle, "Spyware Stalking: Time to Take Back the Technology," *Winning Orations* 2015 (Mankato, MN: Interstate Oratorical Association, 2015), 32–34.; **p. 257:** J. Humphrey, "Taking the Stage: How Women Can Achieve a Leadership Presence," *Vital Speeches of the Day* 67.14 (2001).; **p. 262:** Steven Beebe et. al, "Six Criteria for Evaluating Internet Resources," Pearson Education, Inc.; **p. 263:** J. Gottfried, M. Barthel, and A. Mitchell, "Trump, Clinton Voters Divided in Their Main Source for Election News," *PewResearchCenter Journalism & Media*, January 18, 2017, pewresearch.org.; **p. 264:** G. W. Bush, State of the Union address, January 28, 2008, *Vital Speeches of the Day* 74.3 (March 2008).; **p. 265:** M. Sanchez, "Diplomatic Immunity Unjustified," in *Winning Orations* 1996 (Mankato, MN: Interstate Oratorical Association, 1996), 66.; **p. 265:** D. Lessing, "On Not Winning the Nobel Prize," *Vital Speeches of the Day* 74.2 (2008).; **p. 265:** B. Lindsay, "Exposing the Truth Behind the Walls of Solitary Confinement: A Tribute to Kalief Browder," *Winning Orations* 2016 (Mankato, MN: Interstate Oratorical Association, 2016), 99.; **p. 266:** V. Scott, "When We Fight the Wrong Enemy," *Winning Orations* 2016 (Mankato, MN: Interstate Oratorical Association, 2016), 60.; **p. 266:** J. Sweeney, "Fairness and Economic Equality," *Vital Speeches of the Day* 74.5 (2008).; **p. 266:** E. Holcomb, "Domestic Abuse: No Shelter from the Storm," *Winning Orations 2016* (Mankato, MN: Interstate Oratorical Association, 2016), 51.; **p. 266:** S. Sandberg, "You Will Be Defined by Not Just What You Achieve, But by How You Survive," *Vital Speeches of the Day* 82.8 (2016).; **p. 266:** B. Obama, "The Last of the Founding Generation Is Gone," *Vital Speeches of the Day* 82.12 (2016).; **p. 267:** G. Bradt, "Lessons In Storytelling From Lin-Manuel Miranda's University of Pennsylvania Commencement Address," *Forbes Digital,* May 24, 2016, accessed September 9, 2017, www.forbes.com.; **p. 267:** J. Pruitt, "College Credit Card Crisis," *Winning Orations 1996* (Mankato, MN: Interstate Oratorical Association, 1996), 26.; **p. 267:** I. Ruiz, "Indonesian Palm Oil: A Persuasive Speech," *Winning Orations 2016* (Mankato, MN: Interstate Oratorical Association, 2016), 14.; **p. 267:** K. Huber, "Things Don't Happen for a Reason. But They Do Often Happen Because Nobody Has Yet Found a Better Way," *Vital Speeches of the Day* 82.8 (2016).; **p. 268:** R. Brown, "Seven Ways of Looking at a Crisis," *Vital Speeches of the Day* 76.6 (2010).; **p. 270:** N. Norton, "Beyond Flint: The Poison in Our Pipes," *Winning Orations* 2016 (Mankato, MN: Interstate Oratorical Association, 2016), 77.

Chapter 12   Page 274: F. R. Kennedy, "The Verbal Karate of Florynce R. Kennedy, Esq.," quoted by Gloria Steinem in *Ms. Magazine* (New York, March 1973); **p. 278:** D. Lieberman, *Public Speaking in the Multicultural Environment,* 2nd Ed., 1997, reprinted and electronically reproduced by permission of Pearson Education, Inc., Hoboken, New Jersey.; **p. 279:** C. Flaherty, "Demanding 10 Percent," *Inside Higher Ed*, November 30, 2015, www.insidehighered.com.; **p. 279:** K. Huber, "Things Don't Happen For a Reason. But They Do Often Happen Because Nobody Has Yet Found a Better

Way," *Vital Speeches of the Day* 82.8 (2016).; **p. 280:** A. Kolousek, "Hidden Home School Abuse: Denying Children a Safe Place to Call Home," *Winning Orations 2016* (Mankato, MN: Interstate Oratorical Association, 2016), 35–36.; **p. 280:** C. Kay, "The U.S. Chamber of Commerce: Commerce or Coerce?" *Winning Orations 2016* (Mankato, MN: Interstate Oratorical Association, 2016), 32.; **p. 281:** G. Hildebrand, "Cinderella," Texas State University student speech, 2013.; **p. 281:** K. Kane, "Prescription Drug Pricing: America's Sanctioned Drug Problem," *Winning Orations 2016* (Mankato, MN: Interstate Oratorical Association, 2016), 182.; **p. 282:** C. Ghosn, "Rather Than Fear the Disruption, the Auto Industry Must Embrace It," *Vital Speeches of the Day* 82.5 (2016).; **p. 282:** P. Manning, "You Don't Have to Wonder if I'll Miss It," *Vital Speeches of the Day* 82.5 (2016).; **p. 282:** Z. Smith, "Being with People, Doing for People, It Will Bring You Joy," *Vital Speeches of the Day* 82.8 (2016).; **p. 283:** R. Brown, "Mental Illness Is Not a Learning Disability," *Winning Orations 2015* (Mankato, MN: Interstate Oratorical Association, 2015), 41.; **p. 283:** A. Watson, "Post-Traumatic Stress Disorder: Our Soldiers' Next War," *Winning Orations 2007* (Mankato, MN: Interstate Oratorical Association, 2007), 81.; **p. 283:** A. Lincoln, "Gettysburg Address," delivered at Gettysburg, PA, November 19, 1863, *Douglass Archives of American Public Address*, August 19, 1998, douglass.speech.nwu.edu/linc_b33.htm.; **p. 283:** D. MacArthur, "Farewell to the Cadets," address delivered at West Point, May 12, 1962, in *Contemporary American Speeches* 7e, edited by R. L. Johannesen, R. R. Allen, and W. A. Linkugel (Dubuque, IA: Kendall/Hunt, 1992), 393.; **p. 284:** P. Sterman, "The New World Champion of Public Speaking," *Toastmaster November 2016.*; **p. 284:** K. King, "Bystander Intervention: Addressing the Epidemic of Sexual Assault," *Winning Orations 2016* (Mankato, MN: Interstate Oratorical Association, 2016), 213.; **p. 284:** S. Acevedo, "The Future for Girl Scouts in America and Abroad," *Vital Speeches of the Day* 82.10 (2016).

Chapter 13   Page 293: W. Whitman, "Calamus: A Song of Joys," *Leaves of Grass* (1855).; **p. 294:** J. Detz, "Delivery Plus Content Equals Successful Presentation," *Communication World* 15 (1998): 34.; **p. 296:** P. Begala, "Flying Solo," PBS, *The Clinton Years: Anecdotes,* 2000, www.pbs.org.; **p. 297:** L. White and L. Messer, "An Analysis of Interstate Speeches: Are They Structurally Different?" *National Forensic Journal* 21.2 (2003): 15.; **p. 297:** G. Orwell, "Politics and the English Language," in *About Language,* edited by W. H. Roberts and G. Turgeson (Boston: Houghton Mifflin, 1986), 282.; **p. 298:** D. Hersman, "I Saw a Woman Today," *Vital Speeches of the Day* 80.5 (2014): 151.; **p. 298:** M. Klepper, *I'd Rather Die Than Give a Speech* (New York: Carol Publishing Group, 1994), 45.; **p. 299:** B. Moyers, "What Adam Said to Eve," prepared remarks for the annual conference of the Association for Education in Journalism and Mass Communication, Washington, DC, PBS, August 8, 2007, www.pbs.org.; **p. 299:** D. Trump, inaugural address, January 20, 2017, www.whitehouse.gov; **p. 299:** D. Trump, "Time to Restore the Bonds Between Citizens," *Vital Speeches of the Day* 83.1 (2017): 8.; **p. 299:** B. Obama, farewell address to the American people, delivered in Chicago, IL, *The New York Times,* January 10, 2017, nyti.ms/2jsJlmM; **p. 300:** J. Biden, remarks commemorating the fiftieth anniversary of Kennedy's "Moon Shot" speech, delivered at the John F. Kennedy Library and Museum, Boston, MA, White House, May 25, 2011, www.whitehouse.gov; **p. 300:** J. Huber, "Things Don't Happen for a Reason. But They Do Often Happen Because Nobody Has Yet

Found a Better Way," *Vital Speeches of the Day* 82.8 (2016): 227.; **p. 300:** M. Kent, "The Role of Global Companies in Bridging Wealth Disparity," *Vital Speeches of the Day* 82.10 (2016): 315.; **p. 307:** © Pearson Education, Inc.; **p. 308:** S. Greenwood, A. Perrin, and M. Duggan, *Social Media Update 2016*, November 11, 2016, www.pewresearch.org.; **p. 309:** A. Wilson, "In Defense of Rhetoric," *The Toastmaster* 70.2 (2004): 11.; **p. 311:** J. Detz, "Delivery Plus Content Equals Successful Presentation," *Communication World* 15 (1998): 34.; **p. 312:** Susan Cain, "10 Public Speaking Tips for Introverts: Introverts Can Seize the Microphone—and Bring the House Down," *Psychology Today*, 25 July 2011, www.psychologytoday.com; **p. 313:** "Presidential Seal Falls Off Podium as Obama Speaks," *Washington Times*, October 6, 2010, www.washingtontimes.com.

Chapter 14   Page 318: "From Thomas Jefferson to Uriah Forrest, with Enclosure," 31 December 1787, https://founders.archives.gov/documents/Jefferson/01-12-02-0490; **p. 319:** L. Lefever, *The Art of Explanation* (New Jersey: John Wiley & Sons, 2013), 10.; **p. 322:** G. K. Chesterton, "On Mr. Rudyard Kipling and Making the World Small," *Heretics*, 1905, Project Gutenberg, www.gutenberg.org/files/470/470-h/470-h.htm#chap03.; **p. 326:** J. Zimmer, "Phrases to Avoid on Stage," *Toastmaster* (May 2016): 9.; **p. 328:** M. Groover, "Learning to Communicate: The Importance of Speech Education in Public Schools," in *Winning Orations 1984* (Mankato, MN: Interstate Oratorical Association, 1984), 7.; **p. 329:** M. Klepper and R. Gunther, *I'd Rather Die Than Give a Speech* (New York: Carol Publishing Group, 1995).; **p. 329:** J. Meyer, "Humor as a Double-Edged Sword: Four Functions of Humor in Communication," *Communication Theory* 10 (2000): 311.; **p. 333–334:** A. Armijo, "Elvis," Texas State University student speech, 2013.

Chapter 15   Page 337: Joseph Conrad, *A Personal Record*, 1912; **p. 339** S. McLaughlin, "The Dirty Truth About Your Kitchen: Using Common Sense to Prevent Food Poisoning," in *Winning Orations 1996* (Mankato, MN: Interstate Oratorical Association, 1996), 73.; **p. 340:** Based on A. Maslow, *Motivation and Personality* (New York: HarperCollins, 1954).; **p. 341:** See K. L. Higbee, "Fifteen Years of Fear Arousal: Research on Threat Appeals, 1953–1968," *Psychological Bulletin* 72 (1969): 426–444; I. L. Janis and S. Feshback, "Effects of Fear Arousing Communications," *Journal of Abnormal and Social Psychology* 48 (1953): 78–92; P. A. Mongeau, "Another Look at Fear-Arousing Persuasive Appeals," in *Persuasion: Advances Through MetaAnalysis*, edited by M. Allen and R. W. Preiss (Cresskill, NJ: Hampton Press, 1998), 65; F. A. Powell and G. R. Miller, "Social Approval and Disapproval Cues in Anxiety Arousing Situations," *Speech Monographs* 34 (1967): 152–159.; **p. 341:** E. McQuarrie and

B. Phillips, "Indirect Persuasion in Advertising: How Consumers Process Metaphors Presented in Pictures and Words," *Journal of Advertising* 34.2 (Summer 2005): 7–20.; **p. 344:** Pearson Education; **p. 344:** Aristotle, *Rhetoric*, translated by L. Cooper (New York: Appleton-Century-Crofts, 1960).; **p. 345:** Pearson Education; **p. 349:** Bogeajis, "The Danger of Child Safety Seats: Why Aren't They Safe?" in *Winning Orations* 1996 Mankato, MN: Interstate Oratorical Association, 1996), 10.; **p. 351:** The illustrations for the steps of the motivated sequence are adapted from S. Agha, "The International Landmine Crisis," prepared for the Interstate Oratorical Association competition, Texas State University, Spring 2011.; **p. 352:** Pearson Education; **p. 354:** B. Sosnowchick, "The Cries of American Ailments," in *Winning Orations 2000* (Mankato, MN: Interstate Oratorical Association, 2000), 114.; **p. 356–358:** B. Bergeron, "Private Ambulances," prepared for Individual Events/Persuasive Speaking competition, The University of Texas, Spring 2017.

Appendix A   Page 364: Examples from *CareerBuilder*, as cited by *Reader's Digest* (May 2008): 34.; **p. 375:** C. Purdy, "The Biggest Lies Job Seekers Tell on Their Resumes—and How They Get Caught," Monster, accessed March 31, 2013, career-advice.monster.com/resumes-cover-letters/resume-writing-tips/the-truth-about-resume-lies-hot-jobs/article.aspx.; **p. 375:** CareerBuilder, retrieved March 21, 2008, www.CareerBuilder.com. Suggestions for managing your online persona taken from A. Simmons, "How to Click and Clean," *Reader's Digest* (April 2008): 154–159.; **p. 375:** D. Dean, "How to Get an On-Site Interview," *Black Collegian*, Second Semester Super Issue (2010): 54.; **p. 370:** Woody Allen, as quoted in William Safire's "On Language; The Elision Fields," *The New York Times*, August 13, 1989.; **p. 378:** Zig Ziglar, as quoted in Jennifer Beckham's *Get Over Yourself! 7 Principles to Get Over Your Self and On With Your Destiny* (Destiny Image Publishers, 2011).

Appendix B   Page 387: C. Alvarez, "Audism," prepared for Individual Events/Informative Speaking competition, The University of Texas, Spring 2017.; **p. 387:** Thomas Holcomb, *Introduction to American Deaf Culture*, OUP USA.; **p. 388:** ADA Amendments Act of 2008, Sec. 4, (1a); **p. 389:** C. Hanzlicek, "Doctors and Sex Abuse," prepared for Individual Events/Persuasive Speaking competition, The University of Texas, Spring 2017.; **p. 389:** Alan Judd, "System Shields Doctors' Abuse Nationwide, Leaves Patients in the Dark," *The Atlanta-Journal Constitution.*; **p. 390:** Susan Scutti, "Report on Physician Sexual Abuse Stirs Alarm," CNN International Edition, www.cnn.com/2016/07/11/health/doctor-sexual-abuse/index.html.

Index